SHADOWS
FROM A
VEILED
CREATION

SHADOWS
FROM A
VEILED
CREATION

CLASSIC TALES OF SUPERNATURAL FICTION
IN THE CHRISTIAN TRADITION

Edited by
Chad Arment

Coachwhip Publications
Landisville, Pennsylvania

CONTENTS

INTRODUCTION

It is no surprise when Christian writers pen supernatural stories. A Christian worldview incorporates both physical and spiritual worlds, while the literary imagination opens our eyes to otherwise invisible landscapes. Angels and demons, heaven and hell, souls lost and saved—all share domain within the spiritual realm.

These classic tales range from light fantasy to the darkly weird. A Christian perspective permeates all, and even those tinted with the horrific follow a path recommended by the late Russell Kirk:

> Literary naturalism is not the only path to apprehension of reality. All important literature has some ethical end; and the tale of the preternatural—as written by George Macdonald, C. S. Lewis, Charles Williams, and other masters—can be an instrument for the recovery of moral order. ("A Cautionary Note on the Ghostly Tale.")

These stories do not merely moralize, of course. C. S. Lewis noted that story-telling for that purpose is poor writing and poor theology:

> The truth is, it is very bad to reach the stage of thinking deeply and frequently about duty unless you are prepared to go a stage further. The Law, as St. Paul first clearly explained, only takes you to the school gates. Morality exists to be transcended. We act from duty in the hope that someday we shall do the same acts freely and delightfully. ("The Novels of Charles Williams.")

Even the darkest stories serve to edify the church. Susan Wise Bauer suggests to Christian writers that,

> Their evildoers should reenact the great and true story of the Fall, showing a willingness to yield to the transcendent evil that

9

ultimately overcomes them. And their portrayals of evil should point, without apology, toward the reality of a transcendent realm where evil exists—along with the good that will ultimately defeat it. ("Three Faces of Evil: Christian Writers and the Portrayal of Moral Evil," in *The Christian Imagination*.)

Just as certainly, Madeleine L'Engle notes that writers should not step away from their duty to present evil:

It was adults who thought that children would be afraid of the Dark Thing in [*A Wrinkle in Time*], not children, who understand the need to see thingness, non-ness, and to fight it.

We should note, as it is often misunderstood, that horror is not fear. It is, rather, a divine gift to the human soul—the ability to sense imbalance in God's creation. This allows us to see and correct moral depravity, injustice, and misuse of God's creation. It is to this sense God appealed when He gave Old Testament prophets warning of the shocking consequences of Israel's idolatry. Horror can be misused or misplaced, as can any emotion, but it is not intrinsically evil.

While the stories presented are within the tradition of Christianity, no judgment is made concerning any author's relationship to Jesus Christ. Each does have a verifiable history of hearing the Word of God; beyond that, God only knows. Doctrinal beliefs vary among the authors, and acceptance of key tenets of the Christian faith may not have been immediate in their lives. Coleridge, for example, was Unitarian for a period, before coming to recognize the Trinity as "the one truth which is the form, manner and involvement of all truths."

These stories motivate Christian writers to embrace the supernatural as they use their gifts for God's glory. For readers, these tales beckon us to thoughtful consideration of a created universe, visible and invisible.

Kirk, Russell. 2004. *Ancestral Shadows*. Grand Rapids, MI: W. B. Eerdmans.

L'Engle, M. 2001. *Madeleine L'Engle Herself*. Colorado Springs, CO: Shaw.

Lewis, C. S. 1982. *On Stories*. San Diego: Harcourt.

Ryken, L., ed. 2002. *The Christian Imagination*. Colorado Springs, CO: Shaw.

A TRUE RELATION OF THE
APPARITION OF ONE MRS. VEAL...

Daniel Defoe (1660-1731)

Preface

This relation is matter of fact, and attended with such circumstances, as may induce any reasonable man to believe it. It was sent by a gentleman, a justice of peace, at Maidstone in Kent, and a very intelligent person, to his friend in London, as it is here worded; which discourse is attested by a very sober and understanding gentlewoman, a kinswoman of the said gentleman's, who lives in Canterbury, within a few doors of the house in which the within-named Mrs. Bargrave lives; who believes his kinswoman to be of so discerning a spirit, as not to be put upon by any fallacy; and who positively assured him that the whole matter, as it is related and laid down, is really true; and what she herself had in the same words, as near as may be, from Mrs. Bargrave's own mouth, who, she knows, had no reason to invent and publish such a story, or any design to forge and tell a lie, being a woman of much honesty and virtue, and her whole life a course, as it were, of piety. The use which we ought to make of it, is to consider that there is a life to come after this, and a just God, who will retribute to every one according to the deeds done in the body; and therefore to reflect upon our past course of life we have led in the world; that our time is short and uncertain; and that if we would escape the punishment of the ungodly, and receive the reward of the righteous, which is the laying hold of eternal life, we ought, for the time to come, to return to God by a speedy repentance, ceasing to do evil, and learning to do well: to seek after God early, if haply he may be found of us, and lead such lives for the future, as may be well pleasing in his sight.

This thing is so rare in all its circumstances, and on so good authority, that my reading and conversation has not given me anything like it. It is fit to gratify the most ingenious and serious inquirer.

Mrs. Bargrave is the person to whom Mrs. Veal appeared after her death; she is my intimate friend, and I can avouch for her reputation, for these last fifteen or sixteen years, on my own knowledge; and I can confirm the good character she had from her youth, to the time of my acquaintance. Though, since this relation, she is calumniated by some people that are friends to the brother of this Mrs. Veal, who appeared, who think the relation of this appearance to be a reflection, and endeavour what they can to blast Mrs. Bargrave's reputation, and to laugh the story out of countenance. But by the circumstances thereof, and the cheerful disposition of Mrs. Bargrave, notwithstanding the unheard-of ill usage of a very wicked husband, there is not yet the least sign of dejection in her face; nor did I ever hear her let fall a desponding or murmuring expression; nay, not when actually under her husband's barbarity; which I have been witness to, and several other persons of undoubted reputation.

Now you must know, Mrs. Veal was a maiden gentlewoman of about thirty years of age, and for some years last past had been troubled with fits, which were perceived coming on her, by her going off from her discourse very abruptly to some impertinence. She was maintained by an only brother, and kept his house in Dover. She was a very pious woman, and her brother a very sober man to all appearance; but now he does all he can to null or quash the story.

Mrs. Veal was intimately acquainted with Mrs. Bargrave from her childhood. Mrs. Veal's circumstances were then mean; her father did not take care of his children as he ought, so that they were exposed to hardships, and Mrs. Bargrave, in those days, had as unkind a father, though she wanted neither for food nor clothing, whilst Mrs. Veal wanted for both; insomuch that she would often say, "Mrs. Bargrave, you are not only the best, but the only friend I have in the world, and no circumstance of life shall ever dissolve my friendship." They would often condole each other's adverse fortunes, and read together *Drelincourt upon Death*, and other good books. And so, like two Christian friends, they comforted each other under their sorrow.

Some time after, Mr. Veal's friends got him a place in the custom-house at Dover, which occasioned Mrs. Veal, by little and little, to fall off from her intimacy with Mrs. Bargrave, though there was never any such thing as a quarrel; but an indifference came on by degrees, till at last Mrs. Bargrave had not seen her in two years and a half; though above a twelve-month of the time Mrs. Bargrave hath been absent from Dover, and this last half year has been in Canterbury about two months of the time, dwelling in a house of her own.

In this house, on the 8th of September, 1705, she was sitting alone in the forenoon, thinking over her unfortunate life, and arguing herself into a due resignation to Providence, though her condition seemed hard. "And," said she, "I have been provided for hitherto, and doubt not but I shall be still; and am well satisfied that my afflictions shall end when it is most fit for me" and then took up her sewing-work, which she had no sooner done, but she hears a knocking at the door. She went to see who was there, and this proved to be Mrs. Veal, her old friend, who was in a riding-habit. At that moment of time the clock struck twelve at noon.

"Madam," says Mrs. Bargrave, "I am surprised to see you, you have been so long a stranger!" but told her, she was glad to see her, and offered to salute her; which Mrs. Veal complied with, till their lips almost touched; and then Mrs. Veal drew her hand across her own eyes, and said, "I am not very well," and so waived it. She told Mrs. Bargrave, she was going a journey, and had a great mind to see her first.

"But," says Mrs. Bargrave, "how came you to take a journey alone? I am amazed at it, because I know you have a fond brother."

"Oh!" says Mrs. Veal, "I gave my brother the slip, and came away because I had so great a desire to see you before I took my journey."

So Mrs. Bargrave went in with her, into another room within the first, and Mrs. Veal sat her down in an elbow-chair, in which Mrs. Bargrave was sitting when she heard Mrs. Veal knock. Then says Mrs. Veal, "My dear friend, I am come to renew our old friendship again, and beg your pardon for my breach of it; and if you can forgive me, you are the best of women."

"Oh," says Mrs. Bargrave, "do not mention such a thing; I have not had an uneasy thought about it; I can easily forgive it."

"What did you think of me?" said Mrs. Veal.

Says Mrs. Bargrave, "I thought you were like the rest of the world, and that prosperity had made you forget yourself and me."

Then Mrs. Veal reminded Mrs. Bargrave of the many friendly offices she did her in former days, and much of the conversation they had with each other in the times of their adversity; what books they read, and what comfort, in particular, they received from Drelincourt's *Book of Death*, which was the best, she said, on that subject ever written. She also mentioned Dr. Sherlock, the two Dutch books which were translated, written upon death, and several others. But Drelincourt, she said, had the clearest notions of death, and of the future state, of any who had handled that subject. Then she asked Mrs. Bargrave, whether she had Drelincourt.

She said, "Yes."

Says Mrs. Veal, "Fetch it."

And so Mrs. Bargrave goes up stairs and brings it down.

Says Mrs. Veal, "Dear Mrs. Bargrave, if the eyes of our faith were as open as the eyes of our body, we should see numbers of angels about us for our guard. The notions we have of heaven now, are nothing like what it is, as Drelincourt says; therefore be comforted under your afflictions, and believe that the Almighty has a particular regard to you; and that your afflictions are marks of God's favour; and when they have done the business they are sent for, they shall be removed from you. And, believe me, my dear friend, believe what I say to you, one minute of future happiness will infinitely reward you for all your sufferings. For, I can never believe," (and claps her hand upon her knee with great earnestness, which indeed ran through most of her discourse,) "that ever God will suffer you to spend all your days in this afflicted state; but be assured, that your afflictions shall leave you, or you them, in a short time." She spake in that pathetical and heavenly manner, that Mrs. Bargrave wept several times, she was so deeply affected with it.

Then Mrs. Veal mentioned Dr. Kenrick's *Ascetic*, at the end of which he gives an account of the lives of the primitive Christians. Their pattern she recommended to our imitation, and said, their conversation was not like this of our age.

"For now," says she, "there is nothing but frothy, vain discourse, which is far different from theirs. Theirs was to edification, and to build one another up in faith; so that they were not as we are, nor are we as they were: but, says she, we ought to do as they did. There was an hearty friendship among them; but where is it now to be found?"

Says Mrs. Bargrave, " 'T is hard indeed to find a true friend in these days."

Says Mrs. Veal, "Mr. Norris has a fine copy of verses, called *Friendship in Perfection*, which I wonderfully admire. Have you seen the book?" says Mrs. Veal.

"No," says Mrs. Bargrave, "but I have the verses of my own writing out."

"Have you?" says Mrs. Veal, "then fetch them."

Which she did from above stairs, and offered them to Mrs. Veal to read, who refused, and waived the thing, saying, holding down her head would make it ache; and then desired Mrs. Bargrave to read them to her, which she did.

As they were admiring friendship, Mrs. Veal said, "Dear Mrs. Bargrave, I shall love you for ever." In these verses there is twice used the word *Elysian*. "Ah!" says Mrs. Veal, "these poets have such names for heaven." She would often draw her hand across her own eyes, and say, "Mrs. Bargrave, do not you think I am mightily impaired by my fits?"

"No," says Mrs. Bargrave, "I think you look as well as ever I knew you."

After all this discourse, which the apparition put in much finer words than Mrs. Bargrave said she could pretend to, and as much more than she can remember, (for it cannot be thought, that an hour and three quarters' conversation could all be retained, though the main of it she thinks she does,) she said to Mrs. Bargrave, she would have her write a letter to her brother, and tell him, she would have him give rings to such and such; and that there was a purse of gold in her cabinet, and that she would have two broad pieces given to her cousin Watson.

Talking at this rate, Mrs. Bargrave thought that a fit was coming upon her, and so placed herself in a chair just before her knees, to keep her from falling to the ground, if her fits should occasion it. For the elbow-chair, she thought, would keep her from falling on either side. And to divert Mrs. Veal, as she thought, took hold of her gown-sleeve several times, and commended it. Mrs. Veal told her it was a scowered silk, and newly made up.

But for all this, Mrs. Veal persisted in her request, and told Mrs. Bargrave she must not deny her: and she would have her tell her brother all their conversation, when she had opportunity. "Dear Mrs. Veal," says Mrs. Bargrave, "this seems so impertinent, that I cannot tell how to comply with it; and what a mortifying story will our conversation be to a young gentleman?"

"Well," says Mrs. Veal, "I must not be denied."

"Why," says Mrs. Bargrave, "'t is much better, methinks to do it yourself."

"No," says Mrs. Veal, "though it seems impertinent to you now, you will see more reason for it hereafter."

Mrs. Bargrave then, to satisfy her importunity, was going to fetch a pen and ink; but Mrs. Veal said, "Let it alone now, but do it when I am gone; but you must be sure to do it," which was one of the last things she enjoined her at parting; and so she promised her.

Then Mrs. Veal asked for Mrs. Bargrave's daughter; she said, she was not at home: "But if you have a mind to see her," says Mrs. Bargrave, "I'll send for her."

"Do," says Mrs. Veal.

On which she left her, and went to a neighbour's to see for her; and by the time Mrs. Bargrave was returning, Mrs. Veal was got without the door in the street, in the face of the beast-market, on a Saturday, which is market-day, and stood ready to part, as soon as Mrs. Bargrave came to her.

She asked her, why she was in such haste.

She said she must be going, though perhaps she might not go her journey till Monday; and told Mrs. Bargrave, she hoped she should see her again at her cousin Watson's, before she went whither she was a-going. Then she said she would take her leave of her, and walked from

Mrs. Bargrave in her view, till a turning interrupted the sight of her, which was three quarters after one in the afternoon.

Mrs. Veal died the 7th of September, at twelve o'clock at noon, of her fits, and had not above four hours' senses before her death, in which time she received the sacrament. The next day after Mrs. Veal's appearing, being Sunday, Mrs. Bargrave was mightily indisposed with a cold, and a sore throat, that she could not go out that day; but on Monday morning she sent a person to Captain Watson's, to know if Mrs. Veal was there.

They wondered at Mrs. Bargrave's inquiry, and sent her word, that she was not there, nor was expected. At this answer Mrs. Bargrave told the maid she had certainly mistook the name, or made some blunder.

And though she was ill, she put on her hood, and went herself to Captain Watson's, though she knew none of the family, to see if Mrs. Veal was there or not. They said they wondered at her asking, for that she had not been in town; they were sure, if she had, she would have been there.

Says Mrs. Bargrave, "I am sure she was with me on Saturday almost two hours." They said it was impossible; for they must have seen her if she had.

In comes Captain Watson, while they were in dispute, and said that Mrs. Veal was certainly dead, and her escutcheons were making. This strangely surprised Mrs. Bargrave, when she sent to the person immediately who had the care of them, and found it true.

Then she related the whole story to Captain Watson's family, and what gown she had on, and how striped; and that Mrs. Veal told her, it was scowered. Then Mrs. Watson cried out, "You have seen her indeed, for none knew but Mrs. Veal and myself, that the gown was scowered." And Mrs. Watson owned that she described the gown exactly: "For," said she, "I helped her to make it up."

This Mrs. Watson blazed all about the town, and avouched the demonstration of the truth of Mrs. Bargrave's seeing Mrs. Veal's apparition. And Captain Watson carried two gentlemen immediately to Mrs. Bargrave's house, to hear the relation of her own mouth.

And then it spread so fast, that gentlemen and persons of quality, the judicious and sceptical part of the world, flocked in upon her, it at last became such a task, that she was forced to go out of the way. For they were, in general, extremely satisfied of the truth of the thing, and plainly saw that Mrs. Bargrave was no hypochondriac; for she always appears with such a cheerful air, and pleasing mien, that she has gained the favour and esteem of all the gentry; and it is thought a great favour, if they can but get the relation from her own mouth.

I should have told you before that Mrs. Veal told Mrs. Bargrave that her sister and brother-in-law were just come down from London to see her.

Says Mrs. Bargrave, "How came you to order matters so strangely?" "It could not be helped," says Mrs. Veal.

And her brother and sister did come to see her, and entered the town of Dover just as Mrs. Veal was expiring.

Mrs. Bargrave asked her whether she would drink some tea. Says Mrs. Veal, "I do not care if I do; but I'll warrant you, this mad fellow," (meaning Mrs. Bargrave's husband,) "has broke all your trinkets."

"But," says Mrs. Bargrave, "I'll get something to drink in for all that." But Mrs. Veal waived it, and said, "It is no matter, let it alone." And so it passed.

All the time I sat with Mrs. Bargrave, which was some hours, she recollected fresh sayings of Mrs. Veal. And one material thing more she told Mrs. Bargrave, that old Mr. Breton allowed Mrs. Veal ten pounds a year; which was a secret, and unknown to Mrs. Bargrave, till Mrs. Veal told it her.

Mrs. Bargrave never varies in her story; which puzzles those who doubt of the truth, or are unwilling to believe it. A servant in the neighbour's yard, adjoining to Mrs. Bargrave's house, heard her talking to somebody an hour of the time Mrs. Veal was with her. Mrs. Bargrave went out to her next neighbour's the very moment she parted with Mrs. Veal, and told her what ravishing conversation she had with an old friend, and told the whole of it. Drelincourt's *Book of Death* is, since this happened, bought up strangely. And it is to be observed, that notwithstanding all the trouble and fatigue Mrs. Bargrave has undergone upon this account, she never took the value of a farthing, nor suffered her daughter to take anything of anybody, and therefore can have no interest in telling the story.

But Mr. Veal does what he can to stifle the matter, and said he would see Mrs. Bargrave; but yet it is certain matter of fact that he has been at Captain Watson's since the death of his sister, and yet never went near Mrs. Bargrave; and some of his friends report her to be a liar, and that she knew of Mr. Breton's ten pounds a year. But the person who pretends to say so, has the reputation of a notorious liar, among persons whom I know to be of undoubted credit. Now Mr. Veal is more of a gentleman than to say she lies, but says a bad husband has crazed her. But she needs only present herself, and it will effectually confute that pretense. Mr. Veal says he asked his sister on her death-bed, whether she had a mind to dispose of anything? And she said no.

Now, the things which Mrs. Veal's apparition would have disposed of were so trifling, and nothing of justice aimed at in their disposal, that the design of it appears to me to be only in order to make Mrs. Bargrave so to demonstrate the truth of her appearance, as to satisfy the world of the reality thereof, as to what she had seen and heard; and to secure her reputation among the reasonable and understanding part of mankind. And then again, Mr. Veal owns that there was a purse of gold; but it was not found in her cabinet, but in a comb-box. This looks improbable; for that Mrs. Watson owned that Mrs. Veal was so very careful of the key of the cabinet that she would trust nobody with it. And if so, no doubt she would not trust her gold out of it. And Mrs. Veal's often drawing her hand over her eyes, and asking Mrs. Bargrave whether her fits had not impaired her, looks to me as if she did it on purpose to remind Mrs. Bargrave of her fits, to prepare her not to think it strange that she should put her upon writing to her brother to dispose of rings and gold, which looked so much like a dying person's request; and it took accordingly with Mrs. Bargrave, as the effects of her fits coming upon her; and was one of the many instances of her wonderful love to her, and care of her, that she should not be affrighted; which indeed appears in her whole management, particularly in her coming to her in the day-time, waiving the salutation, and when she was alone; and then the manner of her parting, to prevent a second attempt to salute her.

Now, why Mr. Veal should think this relation a reflection, as it is plain he does, by his endeavouring to stifle it, I cannot imagine; because the generality believe her to be a good spirit, her discourse was so heavenly. Her two great errands were to comfort Mrs. Bargrave in her affliction, and to ask her forgiveness for the breach of friendship, and with a pious discourse to encourage her. So that, after all, to suppose that Mrs. Bargrave could hatch such an invention as this from Friday noon till Saturday noon, supposing that she knew of Mrs. Veal's death the very first moment, without jumbling circumstances, and without any interest too; she must be more witty, fortunate, and wicked too, than any indifferent person, I dare say, will allow.

I asked Mrs. Bargrave several times, if she was sure she felt the gown? She answered modestly, "If my senses be to be relied on, I am sure of it."

I asked her if she heard a sound when she clapped her hand upon her knee? She said she did not remember she did; but said, "She appeared to be as much a substance as I did, who talked with her. And I may," said she, "be as soon persuaded, that your apparition is talking to me now, as that I did not really see her: for I was under no manner of fear, and received her as a friend, and parted with her as such. I would not," says she, "give one farthing to make any one believe it: I have no interest in it; nothing but trouble is entailed upon me for a long time, for aught I know; and had it not come to light by accident, it would never have been made public."

But now she says she will make her own private use of it, and keep herself out of the way as much as she can; and so she has done since. She says she had a gentleman who came thirty miles to her to hear the relation; and that she had told it to a room full of people at a time. Several particular gentlemen have had the story from Mrs. Bargrave's own mouth.

This thing has very much affected me, and I am as well satisfied, as I am of the best-grounded matter of fact. And why we should dispute matter of fact, because we cannot solve things of which we can have no certain or demonstrative notions, seems strange to me. Mrs. Bargrave's authority and sincerity alone would have been undoubted in any other case.

O see ye not yon narrow road,
 So thick beset wi' thorns and briers?
That is the Path of Righteousness,
 Though after it but few inquires.

And see ye not yon braid, braid road,
 That lies across the lily leven?
That is the Path of Wickedness,
 Though some call it the Road to
Heaven.

And see ye not yon bonny road
 That winds about the fernie brae?
That is the Road to fair Elfland,
 Where thou and I this night maun gae.

     —from *Thomas the Rhymer*,
     Scottish ballad

THE BROWNIE OF THE BLACK HAGGS

James Hogg (1770-1835)

When the Sprots were Lairds of Wheelhope, which is now a long time ago, there was one of the ladies who was very badly spoken of in the country. People did not just openly assert that Lady Wheelhope (for every landward laird's wife was then styled Lady) was a witch, but every one had an aversion even at hearing her named; and when by chance she happened to be mentioned, old men would shake their heads and say, "Ah! let us alane o' her! The less ye meddle wi' her the better." Old wives would give over spinning, and, as a pretence for hearing what might be said about her, poke in the fire with the tongs, cocking up their ears all the while; and then, after some meaning coughs, hems, and haws, would haply say, "Hech-wow, sirs! An a' be true that's said!" or something equally wise and decisive.

In short, Lady Wheelhope was accounted a very bad woman. She was an inexorable tyrant in her family, quarrelled with her servants, often cursing them, striking them, and turning them away, especially if they were religious, for she could not endure people of that character, but charged them with everything bad. Whenever she found out that any of the servant men of the laird's establishment were religious, she gave them up to the military and got them shot, and several girls that were regular in their devotions, she was supposed to have got rid of by poison. She was certainly a tricked woman, else many good people were mistaken in her character; and the poor persecuted Covenanters were obliged to unite in their prayers against her.

As for the laird, he was a big, dun-faced, pluffy body, that cared neither for good nor evil, and did not well know the one from the other. He laughed at his lady's tantrums and barley-hoods; and the greater the rage that she got into, the laird thought it the better sport. One day, when two maid-servants came running to him, in great agitation, and told him that his lady had felled one of their competitions, the laird laughed heartily, and said he did not doubt it.

"Why, sir, how can you laugh?" said they; "the poor girl is killed."

"Very likely, very likely," said the laird. "Well, it will teach her to take care who she angers again."

"And, sir, your lady will be hanged."

"Very likely; well, it will teach her how to strike so rashly again—Ha, ha, ha! Will it not, Jessy?"

But when this same Jessy died suddenly one morning, the laird was greatly confounded, and seemed dimly to comprehend that there had been unfair play going on. There was little doubt that she was taken off by poison, but whether the lady did it through jealousy or not was never divulged; but it greatly bamboozled and astonished the poor laird, for his nerves failed him, and his whole frame became paralytic. He seems to have been exactly in the came state of mind with a collie that I once had. He was extremely fond of the gun as long as I did not kill anything with it (there being no game laws in Ettrick Forest in those days), and he got a grand chase after the hares when I missed them. But there was one day that I chanced for a marvel to shoot one dead a few paces before his nose. I'll never forget the astonishment that the poor beast manifested. He stared one while at the gun, and another while at the dead hare, and seemed to be drawing the conclusion, that if the case stood thus, there was no creature sure of its life. Finally, he took his tail between his legs and ran away home, and never would face a gun all his life again.

So was it precisely with Laird Sprot of Wheelhope. As long as his lady's wrath produced only noise and uproar among the servants, he thought it fine sport; but when he saw what he believed the dreadful effects of it, he became like a barrel organ out of tune, and could only discourse one note, which he did to every one he met. "I wish she mayna hae gotten something she had been the waur of." This note he repeated early and late, night and day, sleeping and waking, alone and in company, from the moment that Jessy died till she was buried; and on going to the churchyard as chief mourner, he whispered it to her relatives by the way. When they came to the grave, he took his stand at the head, nor would he give place to the girl's father; but there he stood, like a huge post, as though he neither saw nor heard; and when he had lowered her head into the grave and dropped the cord, he slowly lifted his hat with one hand, wiped his dim eyes with the back of the other, and said, in a deep tremulous tone, "Poor lassie! I wish she didna get something she had been the waur of."

This death made a great noise among the common people; but there was little protection for the life of the subject in those days; and provided a man or woman was a real anti-Covenanter, they might kill a good many without being quarrelled for it. So there was no one to take cognizance of the circumstances relating to the death of poor Jessy.

After this the lady walked softly for the space of two or three years. She saw that she had rendered herself odious, and had entirely lost her husband's countenance, which she liked worst of all. But the evil propensity could not be overcome; and a poor boy, whom the laird out of sheer compassion had taken into his service, being found dead one morning, the country people could no longer be restrained; so they went in a body to the sheriff, and insisted on an investigation. It was proved that she detested the boy, had often threatened him, and had given him brose and butter the afternoon before he died; but notwithstanding of all this, the cause was ultimately dismissed, and the pursuers fined.

No one can tell to what height of wickedness she might now have proceeded, had not a check of a very singular kind been laid upon her. Among the servants that came home at the next term, was one who called himself Merodach, and a strange person he was. He had the form of a boy, but the features of one a hundred years old, save that his eyes had a brilliancy and restlessness which were very extraordinary, bearing a strong resemblance to the eyes of a well-known species of monkey. He was froward and perverse, and disregarded the pleasure or displeasure of any person; but he performed his work well, and with apparent ease. From the moment he entered the house, the lady conceived a mortal antipathy against him, and besought the laird to turn him away. But the laird would not consent; he never turned away any servant, and moreover he had hired this fellow for a trivial wage, and he neither wanted activity nor perseverance. The natural consequence of this refusal was, that the lady instantly set herself to embitter Merodach's life as much as possible, in order to get early quit of a domestic every way so disagreeable. Her hatred of him was not like a common antipathy entertained by one human being against another—she hated him as one might hate a toad or an adder, and his occupation of jotteryman (as the laird termed his servant of all work) keeping him always about her hand, it must have proved highly annoying.

She scolded him, she raged at him, but he only mocked her wrath, and giggled and laughed at her, with the most provoking derision. She tried to fell him again and again, but never, with all her address, could she hit him, and never did she make a blow at him that she did not repent it. She was heavy and unwieldy, and he as quick in his motions as a monkey; besides, he generally contrived that she should be in such an ungovernable rage, that when she flew at him, she hardly knew what she was doing. At one time she guided her blow towards him, and he at the same instant avoided it with such dexterity, that she knocked down the chief hind, or fore-man, and then Merodach giggled so heartily, that, lifting the kitchen poker, she threw it at him with a full design of knocking out his brains, but the missile only broke every article of crockery on the kitchen dresser.

She then hasted to the laird, crying bitterly, and telling him she would not suffer that wretch Merodach, as she called him, to stay another night in the family.

"Why, then, put him away, and trouble me no more about him," said the laird.

"Put him away!" exclaimed she; "I have already ordered him away a hundred times, and charged him never to let me see his horrible face again, but he only grins, and answers with some intolerable piece of impertinence."

The pertinacity of the fellow amused the laird: his dim eyes turned upwards into his head with delight; he then looked two ways at once, turned round his back, and laughed till the tears ran down his dun cheeks, but he could only articulate, "You're fitted now."

The lady's agony of rage still increasing from this derision, she up-braided the laird bitterly, and said he was not worthy the name of man, if he did not turn away that pestilence, after the way he had abused her.

"Why, Shusy, my dear, what has he done to you?"

"What done to me! has he not caused me to knock down John Thomson? and I do not know if ever he will come to life again!"

"Have you felled your favourite, John Thomson?" said the laird, laughing more heartily than before; "You might have done a worse deed than that."

"And has he not broke every plate and dish on the whole dresser!" continued the lady, "and for all this devastation, he only mocks at my displeasure—absolutely mocks me; and if you do not have him turned away, and hanged or shot for his deeds, you are not worthy the name of man."

"Oh alack! What a devastation among the cheena metal!" said the laird, and calling on Merodach, he said, "Tell me, thou evil Merodach of Babylon, how thou darest knock down thy lady's favourite servant, John Thomson?"

"Not I, your honour. It was my lady herself, who got into such a furious rage at me, that she mistook her man, and felled Mr. Thomson, and the good man's skull is fractured."

"That was very odd," said the laird, chuckling, "I do not comprehend it. But then, what set you on smashing all my lady's delft and cheena ware? That was a most infamous and provoking action."

"It was she herself, your honour. Sorry would I be to break one dish belonging to the house. I take all the house servants to witness, that my lady smashed all the dishes with a poker, and now lays the blame on me!"

The laird turned his dim eyes on his lady, who was crying with vexation and rage, and seemed meditating another personal attack on the culprit, which he did not at all appear to shun, but rather to court. She, however, vented her wrath in threatenings of the most deep and desperate revenge, the creature all the while assuring her that she would be foiled, and that in all her encounters and contests with him, she would uniformly come to the worst: he was resolved to do his duty, and there before his master he defied her.

The laird thought more than he considered it prudent to reveal; he had little doubt that his wife would find some means of wreaking her vengeance on the object of her displeasure, and he shuddered when he recollected one who had taken "something that she had been the waur of."

In a word, the Lady of Wheelhope's inveterate malignity against this one object was like the rod of Moses, that swallowed up the rest of the serpents. All her wicked and evil propensities seemed to be superseded if not utterly absorbed by it. The rest of the family now lived in comparative peace and quietness, for early and late her malevolence was venting itself against the jotteryman, and against him alone. It was a delirium of hatred and vengeance, on which the whole bent and bias of her inclination was set. She could not stay from the creature's presence, or, in the intervals when absent from him, she spent her breath in curses and execrations, and then, not able to rest, she ran again to seek him, her eyes gleaming with the anticipated delights of vengeance, while, ever and anon, all the ridicule and the harm redounded on herself.

Was it not strange that she could not get quit of this sole annoyance of her life? One would have thought she easily might. But by this time there was nothing further from her wishes; she wanted vengeance, full, adequate, and delicious vengeance, on her audacious opponent. But he was a strange and terrible creature, and the means of retaliation constantly came, as it were, to his hand.

Bread and sweet milk was the only fare that Merodach cared for, and having bargained for that, he would not want it, though he often got it with a curse and with ill will. The lady having, upon one occasion, intentionally kept back his wonted allowance for some days, on the Sabbath morning following, she set him down a bowl of rich sweet milk, well drugged with a deadly poison, and then she lingered in a little ante-room to watch the success of her grand plot, and prevent any other creature from tasting of the potion. Merodach came in, and the housemaid said to him, "There is your breakfast, creature."

"Oho! my lady has been liberal this morning," said he, "but I am beforehand with her. Here, little Missie, you seem very hungry to-day; take you my breakfast." And with that he set the beverage down to the lady's little favourite spaniel. It so happened that the lady's only son came at that instant into the ante-room seeking her, and teasing his mamma about something, which withdrew her attention from the hall-table for a space. When she looked again, and saw Missie lapping up the sweet milk, she burst from her biding-place like a fury, screaming as if her head had been on fire, kicked the remainder of its contents against the wall, and lifting Missie in her bosom, retreated hastily, crying all the way.

"Ha, ha, ha; I have you now!" cried Merodach, as she vanished from the hall.

Poor Missie died immediately, and very privately; indeed, she would have died and been buried, and never one have seen her, save her mistress, had not Merodach, by a luck that never failed him, looked over the wall of the flower garden, just as his lady was laying her favourite in a grave of her own digging. She, not perceiving her tormentor, plied on at her task, apostrophizing the insensate little carcass. "Ah! poor dear little creature, thou hast had a hard fortune, and hast drank of the bitter potion that was not intended for thee; but he shall drink it three times double for thy sake."

"Is that little Missie?" said the eldritch voice of the jotteryman, close at the lady's ear. She uttered a loud scream, and sank down on the bank. "Alack for poor Missie," continued the creature, in a tone of mockery. "My dear heart is sorry for Missie. What has befallen her, whose breakfast cup did she drink?"

"Hence with thee, fiend!" cried the lady; "what right hast thou to intrude on thy mistress's privacy! Thy turn is coming yet, or may the nature of woman change within me!"

"It is changed already," said the creature, grinning with delight; "I have thee now, I have thee now! And were it not to show my superiority over thee, which I do every hour, I should soon see thee strapped like a mad cat or a worrying bratch. What wilt thou try next?"

"I will cut thy throat, and if I die for it, will rejoice in the deed—a deed of charity to all that dwell on the face of the earth."

"I have warned thee before, dame, and I now warn thee again, that all thy mischief meditated against me will fall double on thine own head."

"I want none of your warning, fiendish cur. Hence with your elvish face, and take care of yourself."

It would be too disgusting and horrible to relate or read all the incidents that fell out between this unaccountable couple. Their enmity against each other had no end and no mitigation, and scarcely a single day passed over on which the lady's acts of malevolent ingenuity did not terminate fatally for some favourite article of her own. Scarcely was there a thing, animate or inanimate, on which she set a value, left to her, that was not destroyed; and yet scarcely one hour or minute could she remain absent from her tormentor, and all the while, it seems, solely for the purpose of tormenting him. While all the rest of the establishment enjoyed peace and quietness from the fury of their termagant dame, matters still grew worse and worse between the fascinated pair. The lady haunted the menial, in the same manner as the raven haunts the eagle—for a perpetual quarrel, though the former knows that in every encounter she is to come off the loser. Noises were heard on the stairs by night, and it was whispered among the servants, that the lady had been seeking Merodach's chamber, on some horrible intent. Several of them would have sworn that they had seen her passing and repassing on the stair after midnight, when all was quiet; but then, it was likewise well known that Merodach slept with well-fastened doors, and a companion in another bed in the same room, whose bed, too, was nearest the door. Nobody cared much what became of the jotteryman, for he was an unsocial and disagreeable person; but some one told him what they had seen, and hinted a suspicion of the lady's intent. But the creature only bit his upper lip, winked with his eyes, and said, "She had better let that alone; she will be the first to rue that."

Not long after this, to the horror of the family and the whole country side, the laird's only son was found murdered in his bed one morning, under circumstances that manifested the most fiendish cruelty and inveteracy on the part of his destroyer. As soon as the atrocious act was divulged, the lady fell into convulsions, and lost her reason; and happy had it been for her had she never recovered the use of it, for there was blood upon her hand, which she took no care to conceal, and there was little doubt that it was the blood of her own innocent and beloved boy, the sole heir and hope of the family.

This blow deprived the laird of all power of action; but the lady had a brother, a man of the law, who came and instantly proceeded to an investigation of this unaccountable murder. Before the sheriff arrived, the housekeeper took the lady's brother aside, and told him he had better not go on with the scrutiny, for she was sure the crime would be brought home to her unfortunate mistress; and after examining into several corroborative circumstances, and viewing the state of the raving maniac, with the blood on her hand and arm, he made the investigation a very short one, declaring the domestics all exculpated.

The laird attended his boy's funeral, and laid his head in the grave, but appeared exactly like a man walking in a trance, an automaton, without feelings or sensations, often times gazing at the funeral procession, as on something he could not comprehend. And when the death-bell of the parish church fell a-tolling, as the corpse approached the kirk-stile, he cast a dim eye up towards the belfry, and said hastily, "What, what's that? Och ay, we're just in time, just in time." And often was he hammering over the name of "Evil Merodach, king of Babylon," to him-self. He seemed to have some far-fetched conception that his unaccount-able jotteryman was in some way connected with the death of his only son and other lesser calamities, although the evidence in favour of Merodach's innocence was as usual quite decisive.

This grievous mistake of Lady Wheelhope can only be accounted for, by supposing her in a state of derangement, or rather under some evil influence over which she had no control, and to a person in such a state the mistake was not so very unnatural. The mansion-house of Wheelhope was old and irregular. The stair had four acute turns, and four landing-places, all the same. In the uppermost chamber slept the two domestics, Merodach in the bed farthest in, and in the chamber immediately below that, which was exactly similar, slept the young laird and his tutor, the former in the bed farthest in, and thus, in the turmoil of her wild and raging passions, her own hand made herself childless.

Merodach was expelled the family forthwith, but refused to accept of his wages, which the man of law pressed upon him, for fear of further mischief; but he went away in apparent sullenness and discontent, no one knowing whither.

When his dismissal was announced to the lady, who was watched day and night in her chamber, the news had such an effect on her, that her whole frame seemed electrified; the horrors of remorse vanished, and another passion, which I neither can comprehend nor define, took the sole possession of her distempered spirit. "He *must* not go! He *shall* not go!" she exclaimed. "No, no, no; he shall not, he shall not, he shall not!" and then she instantly set herself about making ready to follow him, uttering all the while the most diabolical expressions, indicative of antici-pated vengeance. "Oh, could I but snap his nerves one by one, and birl among his vitals! Could I but slice his heart off piecemeal in small messes, and see his blood lopper, and bubble, and spin away in purple slays, and then to see him grin, and grin, and grin, and grin! Oh-oh-oh! How beau-tiful and grand a sight it would be to see him grin, and grin, and grin!" And in such a style would she run on for hours together.

She thought of nothing, she spake of nothing, but the discarded jotteryman, whom most people now began to regard as a creature that was "not canny." They had seen him eat, and drink, and work, like other people; still he had that about him that was not like other men. He was a boy in form, and an antediluvian in feature. Some thought he was a mongrel, between a Jew and an ape, some a wizard, some a kelpie, or a fairy, but most of all, that he was really and truly a brownie. What he was I do not know, and therefore will not pretend to say; but be that as it may, in spite of locks and keys, watching and waking, the Lady of Wheelhope soon made her escape, and eloped after him. The attendants, indeed, would have made oath that she was carried away by some invisible hand, for it was impossible, they said, that she could have escaped on foot like other people; and this edition of the story took in the country, but sensible people viewed the matter in another light.

As for instance, when Wattie Blythe, the laird's old shepherd, came in from the hill one morning, his wife Bessie thus accosted him: "His presence be about us, Wattie Blythe! have you heard what has happened at the ha'? Things are aye turning waur and waur there, and it looks like as if Providence had gi'en up our laird's house to destruction. This grand estate maun now gang frae the Sprots, for it has finished them."

"Na, na, Bessie, it isna the estate that has finished the Sprots, but the Sprots that hae finished the estate, and themsels into the boot. They hae been a wicked and degenerate race, and aye the langer the waur, till they hae reached the utmost bounds o' earthly wickedness; and it's time the deil were looking after his ain."

"Ah, Wattie Blythe, ye never said a truer say. And that's just the very point where your story ends and mine begins; for hasna the deil, or the fairies, or the brownies ta'en away our leddy bodily! and the haill country is running and riding in search o' her, and there is twenty hunder merks offered to the first that can find her and bring her safe back. They hae ta'en her away skin and bane, body and soul and a', Wattie!"

"Hech-wow, but that is awesome! And where is it thought they have ta'en her to, Bessie?"

"Oh, they hae some guess at that frae her ain hints afore. It is thought they hae carried her after that Satan of a creature wha wrought sae muckle wae about the house. It is for him they are a' looking, for they ken weel that where they get the tane they will get the tither."

"Whew! is that the gate o't, Bessie? Why, then, the awfu' story is nouther mair nor less than this, that the leddy has made a 'lopement, as they ca't, and run away after a blackguard jotteryman. Hech-wow! wae's me for human frailty! But that's just the gate. When aince the deil gets in the point o' his finger he will soon have in his haill hand. Ay, he wants but a hair to make a tether of ony day! I hae seen her a braw sonsy lass; but even then I feared she was devoted to destruction, for she aye mockit at religion, Bessie, and that's no a good mark of a young body. And she made a' its servants her enemies; and think you these good men's prayers were a' to blaw away i' the wind, and be nae mair regarded? Na, na, Bessie, my woman, take ye this mark baith o' our ain bairns and other folk's:—If ever ye see a young body that disregards the Sabbath, and makes a mock at the ordinances o' religion, ye will never see that body come to muckle good. A braw hand our leddy has made o' her gibes and jeers at religion, and her mockeries o' the poor persecuted hill-folk!—sunk down by degrees into the very dregs o' sin and misery! run away after a scullion!"

"Fy, fy, Wattie; how can ye say sae? It was weel kenn'd that she hatit him wi' a perfect and mortal hatred, and tried to make away wi' him mae ways nor ane."

"Aha, Bessie, but nipping and scarting is Scots folk's wooing; and though it is but right that we suspend our judgments, there will naebody persuade me, if she be found alang wi' the creature, but that she has run away after him in the natural way, on her twa shanks, without help either frae fairy or brownie."

"I'll never believe sic a thing of ony woman born, let be a leddy weel up in years."

"'Od help ye, Bessie! ye dinna ken the stretch o' corrupt nature. The best o' us, when left to oursels, are nae better than strayed sheep that will never find the way back to their ain pastures; and of a' things made o' mortal flesh a wicked woman is the warst."

"Alack-a-day! we get the blame o' muckle that we little deserve. But, Wattie, keep ye a geyan sharp look-out about the cleuchs and the caves o' our Hope, for the leddy kens them a' geyan weel; and gin the twenty hunder marks wad come our way, it might gang a waur gate. It wad tocher a' our bonny lasses."

"Ay, weel I wat, Bessie, that's nae lee. And now when ye bring me amind o't, I'm sair mistaen if I didna hear a creature up in the Brockholes this morning skirling as if something were cutting its throat. It gars a' the hairs stand on my head when I think it may hae been our leddy, and the droich of a creature murdering her. I took it for a battle of wulcats, and wished they might pu' out ane anither's thrapples; but when I think on it again, they were unco like some o' our leddy's unearthly screams."

"His presence be about us, Wattie! Haste ye; pit on your bonnet, tak' your star in your hand, and gang and see what it is."

"Shame fa' me if I daur gang, Bessie."

"Hout, Wattie, trust in the Lord."

"Aweel, sae I do. But ane's no to throw himsel ower a linn, and trust that the Lord will kep him in a blanket. And its nae muckle safer for an auld stiff man like me to gang away out to a wild remote place, where there is ae body murdering another.—What is that I hear, Bessie? Haud the lang tongue o' you, and rin to the door and see what noise that is."

Bessie ran to the door, but soon returned with her mouth wide open, and her eyes set in her head.

"It is them, Wattie! it is them! His presence be about us! What will we do?"

"Them! Whaten them!"

"Why, that blackguard creature coming here leading our leddy by the hair o' the head, and yerking her wi' a stick. I am terrified out o' my wits. What will we do?"

"We'll *see* what they *say*," said Wattie, manifestly in as great terror as his wife; and by a natural impulse or as a last resource he opened the Bible, not knowing what he did, and then hurried on his spectacles; but before he got two leaves turned over, the two entered—a frightful-looking couple indeed. Merodach, with his old withered face and ferret eyes, leading the Lady of Wheelhope by the long hair, which was mixed with gray, and whose face was all bloated with wounds and bruises, and having stripes of blood on her garments.

"How's this! how's this, sirs!" said Wattie Blythe.

"Close that book and I will tell you, goodman," said Merodach.

"I can hear what you hae' to say wi' the beuk open, sir," said Wattie, turning over the leaves, pretending to look for some particular passage, but apparently not knowing what he was doing. "It is a shamefu' business this, but some will hae to answer for't. My leddy, I am unco grieved to see you in sic a plight. Ye hae surely been dooms sair left to yoursel."

The lady shook her head, uttered a feeble hollow laugh, and fixed her eyes on Merodach. But such a look! It almost frightened the simple aged couple out of their senses. It was not a look of love nor of hatred exclusively, neither was it of desire or disgust, but it was a combination of them all. It was such a look as one fiend would cast on another in whose everlasting destruction he rejoiced. Wattie was glad to take his eyes from such countenances, and look into the Bible, that firm foundation of all his hopes and all his joy.

"I request that you will shut that book sir," said the horrible creature, "or if you do not, I will shut it for you with a vengeance," and with that he seized it, and flung it against the wall. Bessie uttered a scream, and Wattie was quite paralyzed; and although he seemed disposed to run after his best friend, as he called it, the hellish looks of the brownie interposed, and glued him to his seat.

"Hear what I have to say first," said the creature, "and then pore your fill on that precious book of yours. One concern at a time is enough. I came to do you a service. Here, take this cursed, wretched woman, whom you style your lady, and deliver her up to the lawful authorities, to be restored to her husband and her place in society. She has followed one that hates her, and never said one kind word to her in his life; and though I have beat her like a dog, still she clings to me, and will not depart, so enchanted is she with the laudable purpose of cutting my throat. Tell your master and her brother that I am not to be burdened with their maniac. I have scourged, I have spurned and kicked her, afflicting her night and day, and yet from my side she will not depart. Take her, claim the reward in full, and your fortune is made; and so farewell!"

The creature went away, and the moment his back was turned, the lady fell a-screaming and struggling, like one in an agony, and, in spite of all the couple's exertions, she forced herself out of their hands, and ran after the retreating Merodach. When he saw better would not be, he turned upon her, and, by one blow with his stick, struck her down; and, not content with that, continued to maltreat her in such a manner, as to all appearance would have killed twenty ordinary persons. The poor devoted dame could do nothing but now and then utter a squeak like a half-worried cat, and writhe and grovel on the sward, till Wattie and his wife came up, and withheld her tormentor from further violence. He then bound her hands behind her back with a strong cord, and delivered her once more to the charge of the old couple, who contrived to hold her by that means, and take her home.

Wattie was ashamed to take her into the hall, but led her into one of the out-houses, whither he brought her brother to receive her. The man of the law was manifestly vexed at her reappearance, and scrupled not to testify his dissatisfaction; for when Wattie told him how the wretch had abused his sister, and that, had it not been for Bessie's inter-ference and his own, the lady would have been killed outright, he said, "Why, Walter, it is a great pity that he did not kill her outright. What good can her life now do to her, or of what value is her life to any creature living? After one has lived to disgrace all connected with them, the sooner they are taken off the better."

The man, however, paid old Walter down his two thousand merks, a great fortune for one like him in those days; and not to dwell longer on this unnatural story I shall only add, very shortly, that the Lady of Wheelhope soon made her escape once more, and flew, as if drawn by an irresistible charm, to her tormentor. Her friends looked no more after her; and the last time she was seen alive, it was following the uncouth creature up the water of Daur, weary, wounded, and lame, while he was all the way beating her, as a piece of excellent amusement. A few days after that, her body was found among some wild haggs, in a place called Crook-burn, by a party of the persecuted Covenanters that were in hiding there, some of the very men whom she had exerted herself to de-stroy, and who had been driven, like David of old, to pray for a curse and earthly punishment upon her. They buried her like a dog at the Yetts of Keppel, and rolled three huge stones upon her grave, which are lying there to this day. When they found her corpse, it was mangled and wounded in a most shocking manner, the fiendish creature having manifestly tor-mented her to death. He was never more seen or heard of in this king-dom, though all that country side was kept in terror for him many years afterwards; and to this day, they will tell you of *The Brownie of the Black Haggs*, which title he seems to have acquired after his disappearance.

This story was told to me by an old man named Adam Halliday, whose great-grandfather, Thomas Halliday, was one of those that found the body and buried it. It is many years since I heard it; but, however ridiculous it may appear, I remember it made a dreadful impression on my young mind. I never heard any story like it, save one of an old foxhound that pursued a fox through the Grampians for a fortnight, and when at last discovered by the Duke of Athole's people, neither of them could run, but the hound was still continuing to walk after the fox, and when the latter lay down, the other lay down beside him, and looked at him steadily all the while, though unable to do him the least harm. The passion of inveterate malice seems to have influenced these two exactly alike. But, upon the whole, I can scarcely believe the tale can be true.

"You write as if a fairytale were a thing of importance: must it have a meaning?"

It cannot help having some meaning; if it have proportion and harmony it has vitality, and vitality is truth. The beauty may be plainer in it than the truth, but without the truth the beauty could not be, and the fairytale would give no delight. Everyone, however, who feels the story, will read its meaning after his own nature and development: one man will read one meaning in it, another will read another.

"If so, how am I to assure myself that I am not reading my own meaning into it, but yours out of it?"

Why should you be so assured? It may be better that you should read your meaning into it. That may be a higher operation of your intellect than the mere reading of mine out of it: your meaning may be superior to mine.

"Suppose my child ask me what the fairytale means, what am I to say?"

If you do not know what it means, what is easier than to say so? If you do see a meaning in it, there it is for you to give him. A genuine work of art must mean many things; the truer its art, the more things it will mean. If my drawing, on the other hand, is so far from being a work of art that it needs This Is A Horse written under it, what can it matter that neither you nor your child should know what it means? It is there not so much to convey a meaning as to wake a meaning. If it do not even wake an interest, throw it aside. A meaning may be there, but it is not for you. If, again, you do not know a horse when you see it, the name written under it will not serve you much. At all events, the business of the painter is not to teach zoology.

—George MacDonald, "The Fantastic Imagination."

THE RIME OF THE ANCIENT MARINER
IN SEVEN PARTS

Samuel Taylor Coleridge (1772-1834)

Facile credo, plures esse Naturas invisibles, quam visibiles in verum universitate. Sed horum omnium familiam quis nobis enarrabit? et gradus et cognotiones et discrimina et singulorum munera? Quid agunt? quae loca habitant? Horum rerum notitiam semper ambivit ingenium humanum, numquam attigit. Juvat, interea, non diffiteor, quandoque in anima, tanquam in tabula, majoris et melioris mundi imaginem contemplari: ne mens assuefacta hodiernae vitae minutiis te contrahat nimis, et tota subsidat in pusillas cogitationes. Sed veritati interea invigilandum est, modusque servandus, ut cera ab incertis, diem a nocte, distinguamus. (T. Burnet, *Archaeol. Phil.*)

Part I.

It is an ancient Mariner,
And he stoppeth one of three.
"By thy long grey beard and glittering eye,
Now wherefore stopp'st thou me?

"The Bridegroom's doors are opened wide,
And I am next of kin;
The guests are met, the feast is set:
May'st hear the merry din."

An ancient Mariner meeteth three Gallants bidden to a wedding feast, and detaineth one.

He holds him with his skinny hand,
"There was a ship," quoth he.
"Hold off! unhand me, grey-beard loon!"
Eftsoons his hand dropt he.

He holds him with his glittering eye—
The Wedding-Guest stood still,
And listens like a three years child:
The Mariner hath his will.

The Wedding-Guest sat on a stone:
He cannot chuse but hear;
And thus spake on that ancient man,
The bright-eyed Mariner.

*The Wedding Guest is
spell bound by the eye
of the old seafaring
man, and constrained
to hear his tale.*

The ship was cheered, the harbour cleared,
Merrily did we drop
Below the kirk, below the hill,
Below the light-house top.

The Sun came up upon the left,
Out of the sea came he!
And he shone bright, and on the right
Went down into the sea.

*The mariner tells how
the ship sailed south-
ward with a good wind
and fair weather, till it
reached the line.*

Higher and higher every day,
Till over the mast at noon—
The Wedding-Guest here beat his breast,
For he heard the loud bassoon.

The bride hath paced into the hall,
Red as a rose is she;
Nodding their heads before her goes
The merry minstrelsy.

*The Wedding Guest
heareth the bridal
music; but the Mariner
continueth his tale.*

The Wedding-Guest he beat his breast,
Yet he cannot chuse but hear;
And thus spake on that ancient man,
The bright-eyed Mariner.

And now the *Storm-blast* came, and he
Was tyrannous and strong:
He struck with his o'ertaking wings,
And chased south along.

The ship driven by a storm toward the South Pole

With sloping masts and dipping prow,
As who pursued with yell and blow
Still treads the shadow of his foe
And forward bends his head,
The ship drove fast, loud roared the blast,
And southward aye we fled.

And now there came both mist and snow,
And it grew wondrous cold:
And ice, mast-high, came floating by,
As green as emerald.

And through the drifts the snowy clifts
Did send a dismal sheen:
Nor shapes of men nor beasts we ken—
The ice was all between.

The land of ice, and of fearful sounds where no living thing was to be seen.

The ice was here, the ice was there,
The ice was all around:
It cracked and growled, and roared and howled,
Like noises in a swound!

At length did cross an Albatross:
Thorough the fog it came;
As if it had been a Christian soul,
We hailed it in God's name.

Till a great sea bird, called the Albatross, came through the snow-fog, and was received with great joy and hospitality.

It ate the food it ne'er had eat,
And round and round it flew.
The ice did split with a thunder-fit;
The helmsman steered us through!

And a good south wind sprung up behind;
The Albatross did follow,
And every day, for food or play,
Came to the mariners' hollo!

And lo! the Albatross proveth a bird of good omen, and followeth the ship as it returned northward through fog and floating ice.

In mist or cloud, on mast or shroud,
It perched for vespers nine;
Whiles all the night, through fog-smoke white,
Glimmered the white Moon-shine.

"God save thee, ancient Mariner!
From the fiends, that plague thee thus!—
Why look'st thou so?"—With my cross-bow
I shot the *Albatross*.

The ancient Mariner inhospitably killeth the pious bird of good omen.

Part II.

The Sun now rose upon the right:
Out of the sea came he,
Still hid in mist, and on the left
Went down into the sea.

And the good south wind still blew behind
But no sweet bird did follow,
Nor any day for food or play
Came to the mariners' hollo!

And I had done an hellish thing,
And it would work 'em woe:
For all averred, I had killed the bird
That made the breeze to blow.
Ah wretch! said they, the bird to slay
That made the breeze to blow!

His shipmates cry out against the ancient Mariner for killing the bird of good omen.

Nor dim nor red, like God's own head,
The glorious Sun uprist:
Then all averred, I had killed the bird
That brought the fog and mist.
'Twas right, said they, such birds to slay,
That bring the fog and mist.

But when the fog cleared off, they justify the same, and thus make themselves accomplices in the crime.

The fair breeze blew, the white foam flew,
The furrow followed free:
We were the first that ever burst
Into that silent sea.

The fair breeze continues; the ship enters the Pacific Ocean, and sails northward even till it reaches the Line.

Down dropt the breeze, the sails dropt down,
'Twas sad as sad could be;
And we did speak only to break
The silence of the sea!

The ship hath been sud-denly becalmed.

All in a hot and copper sky,
The bloody Sun, at noon,
Right up above the mast did stand,
No bigger than the Moon.

Day after day, day after day,
We stuck, nor breath nor motion;
As idle as a painted ship
Upon a painted ocean.

Water, water, every where,
And all the boards did shrink;
Water, water, every where,
Nor any drop to drink.

And the Albatross be-gins to be avenged.

The very deep did rot: O Christ!
That ever this should be!
Yea, slimy things did crawl with legs
Upon the slimy sea.

About, about, in reel and rout
The death-fires danced at night;
The water, like a witch's oils,
Burnt green, and blue and white.

A Spirit had followed them; one of the invis-ible inhabitants of this planet, neither departed souls nor angels; con-cerning whom the learned Jew, Josephus, and the Platonic Constantinopolitan, Michael Pselius, may be consulted. They are very numerous, and there is no climate or element without one of them.

And some in dreams assured were
Of the spirit that plagued us so:
Nine fathom deep he had followed us
From the land of mist and snow.

And every tongue, through utter drought,
Was withered at the root;
We could not speak, no more than if
We had been choked with soot.

Ah! well a-day! what evil looks
Had I from old and young!
Instead of the cross, the Albatross
About my neck was hung.

*The shipmates, in their
sore distress, would
fain throw the whole
guilt on the ancient
Mariner: in sign where-
of they hang the dead
sea bird around his
neck.*

Part III.

There passed a weary time. Each throat
Was parched, and glazed each eye.
A weary time! a weary time!
How glazed each weary eye,
When looking westward, I beheld
A something in the sky.

*The ancient Mariner
beholdeth a sign in the
element afar off.*

At first it seemed a little speck,
And then it seemed a mist:
It moved and moved, and took at last
A certain shape, I wist.

A speck, a mist, a shape, I wist!
And still it neared and neared:
As if it dodged a water-sprite,
It plunged and tacked and veered.

With throats unslaked, with black lips baked,
We could not laugh nor wail;
Through utter drought all dumb we stood!
I bit my arm, I sucked the blood,
And cried, A sail! a sail!

*At its nearer appear-
ance, it seemeth him to
be a ship; and at a dear
ransom he freeth his
speech from the bonds
of thirst.*

With throats unslaked, with black lips baked,
Agape they heard me call:
Gramercy! they for joy did grin,
And all at once their breath drew in,
As they were drinking all.

A flash of joy;

See! see! (I cried) she tacks no more!
Hither to work us weal;
Without a breeze, without a tide,
She steadies with upright keel!

*And horror follows.
For can it be a ship that
comes onward without
wind or tide?*

The western wave was all a-flame
The day was well nigh done!
Almost upon the western wave
Rested the broad bright Sun;
When that strange shape drove suddenly
Betwixt us and the Sun.

And straight the Sun was flecked with bars,   *It seemeth him but the*
(Heaven's Mother send us grace!)   *skeleton of a ship.*
As if through a dungeon-grate he peered,
With broad and burning face.

Alas! (thought I, and my heart beat loud)   *And its ribs are seen as*
How fast she nears and nears!   *bars on the face of the*
Are those her sails that glance in the Sun,   *setting Sun.*
Like restless gossameres!

Are those her ribs through which the Sun   *The Specter-Woman*
Did peer, as through a grate?   *and her Deathmate,*
And is that Woman all her crew?   *and no other on board*
Is that a *Death*? and are there two?   *the skeleton ship.*
Is *Death* that woman's mate?

Her lips were red, her looks were free,   *Like vessel, like crew!*
Her locks were yellow as gold:
Her skin was as white as leprosy,
The Night-Mare *Life-in-Death* was she,
Who thicks man's blood with cold.

The naked hulk alongside came,   *Death and Life-in-*
And the twain were casting dice;   *Death have diced for*
"The game is done! I've won! I've won!"   *the ship's crew, and she*
Quoth she, and whistles thrice.   *(the latter) winneth the*
     ancient Mariner.

The Sun's rim dips; the stars rush out: *No twilight within the*
At one stride comes the dark;   *courts of the Sun*
With far-heard whisper, o'er the sea.
Off shot the spectre-bark.

We listened and looked sideways up!   *At the rising of the*
Fear at my heart, as at a cup,   *Moon.*
My life-blood seemed to sip!
The stars were dim, and thick the night,

The steersman's face by his lamp gleamed white;
From the sails the dew did drip—
Till clombe above the eastern bar
The horned Moon, with one bright star
Within the nether tip.

One after one, by the star-dogged Moon   *One after another.*
Too quick for groan or sigh,
Each turned his face with a ghastly pang,
And cursed me with his eye.

Four times fifty living men,   *His shipmates drop*
(And I heard nor sigh nor groan)   *down dead.*
With heavy thump, a lifeless lump,
They dropped down one by one.

The souls did from their bodies fly,—   *But Life-in-Death be-*
They fled to bliss or woe!   *gins her work on the*
And every soul, it passed me by,   *ancient Mariner.*
Like the whizz of my *Cross-Bow*!

Part IV.

"I fear thee, ancient Mariner!   *The Wedding Guest*
I fear thy skinny hand!   *feareth that a Spirit is*
And thou art long, and lank, and brown,   *talking to him;*
As is the ribbed sea-sand.

"I fear thee and thy glittering eye,   *But the ancient Mari-*
And thy skinny hand, so brown."—   *ner assureth him of his*
Fear not, fear not, thou Wedding-Guest!   *bodily life, and pro-*
This body dropt not down.   *ceedeth to relate his*
                                                 horrible penance.

Alone, alone, all, all alone,
Alone on a wide wide sea!
And never a saint took pity on
My soul in agony.

The many men, so beautiful!   *He despiseth the crea-*
And they all dead did lie: *tures of the calm,*
And a thousand thousand slimy things
Lived on; and so did I.

I looked upon the rotting sea,
And drew my eyes away;
I looked upon the rotting deck,
And there the dead men lay.

And envieth that they
should live, and so
many lie dead.

I looked to Heaven, and tried to pray:
But or ever a prayer had gusht,
A wicked whisper came, and made
my heart as dry as dust.

I closed my lids, and kept them close,
And the balls like pulses beat;
For the sky and the sea, and the sea and the sky
Lay like a load on my weary eye,
And the dead were at my feet.

The cold sweat melted from their limbs,
Nor rot nor reek did they:
The look with which they looked on me
Had never passed away.

But the curse liveth for
him in the eye of the
dead men.

An orphan's curse would drag to Hell
A spirit from on high;
But oh! more horrible than that
Is a curse in a dead man's eye!
Seven days, seven nights, I saw that curse,
And yet I could not die.

In his loneliness and
fixedness he yearneth
towards the journey-
ing Moon, and the
stars that still sojourn,
yet still move onward;
and everywhere the
blue sky belongs to
them, and is their ap-
pointed rest, and their
native country and
their own natural
homes, which they en-
ter unannounced, as
lords that are certainly
expected and yet there
is a silent joy at their
arrival.

The moving Moon went up the sky,
And no where did abide:
Softly she was going up,
And a star or two beside.

Her beams bemocked the sultry main,
Like April hoar-frost spread;
But where the ship's huge shadow lay,
The charmed water burnt alway
A still and awful red.

Beyond the shadow of the ship,
I watched the water-snakes:
They moved in tracks of shining white,
And when they reared, the elfish light
Fell off in hoary flakes.

By the light of the
Moon he beholdeth
God's creatures of the
great calm.

Within the shadow of the ship
I watched their rich attire:
Blue, glossy green, and velvet black,
They coiled and swam; and every track
Was a flash of golden fire.

O happy living things! no tongue
Their beauty might declare:
A spring of love gushed from my heart,
And I blessed them unaware:
Sure my kind saint took pity on me,
And I blessed them unaware.

Their beauty and their happiness. He blesseth them in his heart.

The self same moment I could pray;
And from my neck so free
The Albatross fell off, and sank
Like lead into the sea.

The spell begins to break.

Part V.

Oh sleep! it is a gentle thing,
Beloved from pole to pole!
To Mary Queen the praise be given!
She sent the gentle sleep from Heaven,
That slid into my soul.

The silly buckets on the deck,
That had so long remained,
I dreamt that they were filled with dew;
And when I awoke, it rained.

By grace of the holy Mother, the ancient Mariner is refreshed with rain

My lips were wet, my throat was cold,
My garments all were dank;
Sure I had drunken in my dreams,
And still my body drank.

I moved, and could not feel my limbs:
I was so light—almost
I thought that I had died in sleep,
And was a bless'ed ghost.

And soon I heard a roaring wind:
It did not come anear;
But with its sound it shook the sails,
That were so thin and sere.

He heareth sounds and seeth strange sights and commotions in the sky and the element.

The upper air burst into life!
And a hundred fire-flags sheen,
To and fro they were hurried about!
And to and fro, and in and out,
The wan stars danced between.

And the coming wind did roar more loud,
And the sails did sigh like sedge;
And the rain poured down from one black cloud;
The Moon was at its edge.

The thick black cloud was cleft, and still
The Moon was at its side:
Like waters shot from some high crag,
The lightning fell with never a jag,
A river steep and wide.

The loud wind never reached the ship,
Yet now the ship moved on!
Beneath the lightning and the Moon
The dead men gave a groan.

The bodies of the ship's crew are inspirited, and the ship moves on;

They groaned, they stirred, they all uprose,
Nor spake, nor moved their eyes;
It had been strange, even in a dream,
To have seen those dead men rise.

The helmsman steered, the ship moved on;
Yet never a breeze up blew;
The mariners all 'gan work the ropes,
Were they were wont to do:
They raised their limbs like lifeless tools—
We were a ghastly crew.

The body of my brother's son,
Stood by me, knee to knee:
The body and I pulled at one rope,
But he said nought to me.

"I fear thee, ancient Mariner!"
Be calm, thou Wedding-Guest!
'Twas not those souls that fled in pain,
Which to their corses came again,
But a troop of spirits blest:

But not by the souls of the men, nor by demons of earth or middle air, but by a blessed troop of angelic spirits, sent down by the invocation of the guardian saint.

For when it dawned—they dropped their arms,
And clustered round the mast;
Sweet sounds rose slowly through their mouths,
And from their bodies passed.

Around, around, flew each sweet sound,
Then darted to the Sun;
Slowly the sounds came back again,
Now mixed, now one by one.

Sometimes a-dropping from the sky
I heard the sky-lark sing;
Sometimes all little birds that are,
How they seemed to fill the sea and air
With their sweet jargoning!

And now 'twas like all instruments,
Now like a lonely flute;
And now it is an angel's song,
That makes the Heavens be mute.

It ceased; yet still the sails made on
A pleasant noise till noon,
A noise like of a hidden brook
In the leafy month of June,
That to the sleeping woods all night
Singeth a quiet tune.

Till noon we quietly sailed on,
Yet never a breeze did breathe:
Slowly and smoothly went the ship,
Moved onward from beneath.

Under the keel nine fathom deep,
From the land of mist and snow,
The spirit slid: and it was he
That made the ship to go.

The lonesome Spirit from the South Pole carries on the ship as far as the Line, in obedience to the angelic troop, but still requireth vengeance.

The sails at noon left off their tune,
And the ship stood still also.

The Sun, right up above the mast,
Had fixed her to the ocean:
But in a minute she 'gan stir,
With a short uneasy motion—
Backwards and forwards half her length
With a short uneasy motion.

Then like a pawing horse let go,
She made a sudden bound:
It flung the blood into my head,
And I fell down in a swound.

The Polar Spirit's fellow demons, the invisible inhabitants of the element, take part in his wrong; and two of them relate, one to the other, that penance long and heavy for the ancient Mariner hath been accorded to the Polar Spirit, who returneth southward.

How long in that same fit I lay,
I have not to declare;
But ere my living life returned,
I heard and in my soul discerned
Two *Voices* in the air.

"Is it he?" quoth one, "Is this the man?
By him who died on cross,
With his cruel bow he laid full low,
The harmless Albatross.

"The spirit who bideth by himself
In the land of mist and snow,
He loved the bird that loved the man
Who shot him with his bow."

The other was a softer voice,
As soft as honey-dew:
Quoth he, "The man hath penance done,
And penance more will do."

Part VI.

First Voice.

But tell me, tell me! speak again,
Thy soft response renewing—

What makes that ship drive on so fast?
What is the *Ocean* doing?

Second Voice.

Still as a slave before his lord,
The *Ocean* hath no blast;
His great bright eye most silently
Up to the Moon is cast—

If he may know which way to go;
For she guides him smooth or grim
See, brother, see! how graciously
She looketh down on him.

First Voice.

But why drives on that ship so fast,   *The Mariner hath been*
Without or wave or wind?   *cast into a trance; for*
                                             the angelic power
                                             causeth the vessel to
                                             drive northward faster
Second Voice.   *than human life could*
                                             endure.
The air is cut away before,
And closes from behind.

Fly, brother, fly! more high, more high
Or we shall be belated:
For slow and slow that ship will go,
When the Mariner's trance is abated.

I woke, and we were sailing on   *The supernatural mo-*
As in a gentle weather: *tion is retarded; the*
'Twas night, calm night, the Moon was high; *Mariner awakens, and*
The dead men stood together.   *his penance begins*
                                             anew.
All stood together on the deck,
For a charnel-dungeon fitter:
All fixed on me their stony eyes,
That in the Moon did glitter.

The pang, the curse, with which they died,
Had never passed away:
I could not draw my eyes from theirs,
Nor turn them up to pray.

And now this spell was snapt: once more
I viewed the ocean green.
And looked far forth, yet little saw
Of what had else been seen—

*The curse is finally ex-
piated.*

Like one that on a lonesome road
Doth walk in fear and dread,
And having once turned round walks on,
And turns no more his head;
Because he knows, a frightful fiend
Doth close behind him tread.

But soon there breathed a wind on me,
Nor sound nor motion made:
Its path was not upon the sea,
In ripple or in shade.

It raised my hair, it fanned my cheek
Like a meadow-gale of spring—
It mingled strangely with my fears,
Yet it felt like a welcoming.

Swiftly, swiftly flew the ship,
Yet she sailed softly too:
Sweetly, sweetly blew the breeze—
On me alone it blew.

Oh! dream of joy! is this indeed
The light-house top I see?
Is this the hill? is this the kirk?
Is this mine own countree!

*And the ancient Mariner
beholdeth his native country.*

We drifted o'er the harbour-bar,
And I with sobs did pray—
O let me be awake, my God!
Or let me sleep alway.

The harbour-bay was clear as glass,
So smoothly it was strewn!
And on the bay the moonlight lay,
And the shadow of the moon.

The rock shone bright, the kirk no less,
That stands above the rock:
The moonlight steeped in silentness
The steady weathercock.

And the bay was white with silent light,
Till rising from the same,
Full many shapes, that shadows were,
In crimson colours came.

A little distance from the prow
Those crimson shadows were:
I turned my eyes upon the deck—
Oh, Christ! what saw I there!

*The angelic spirits leave the
dead bodies, And appear in
their own forms of light.*

Each corse lay flat, lifeless and flat,
And, by the holy rood!
A man all light, a seraph-man,
On every corse there stood.

This seraph band, each waved his hand:
It was a heavenly sight!
They stood as signals to the land,
Each one a lovely light:

This seraph-band, each waved his hand,
No voice did they impart—
No voice; but oh! the silence sank
Like music on my heart.

But soon I heard the dash of oars;
I heard the Pilot's cheer;
My head was turned perforce away,
And I saw a boat appear.

The Pilot, and the Pilot's boy,
I heard them coming fast:

Dear Lord in Heaven! it was a joy
The dead men could not blast.

I saw a third—I heard his voice:
It is the Hermit good!
He singeth loud his godly hymns
That he makes in the wood.
He'll shrieve my soul, he'll wash away
The Albatross's blood.

Part VII.

This Hermit good lives in that wood   *The Hermit of the*
Which slopes down to the sea.   *Wood*
How loudly his sweet voice he rears!
He loves to talk with marineres
That come from a far countree.

He kneels at morn and noon and eve—
He hath a cushion plump:
It is the moss that wholly hides
The rotted old oak-stump.

The skiff-boat neared: I heard them talk,
"Why this is strange, I trow!
Where are those lights so many and fair,
That signal made but now?"

"Strange, by my faith!" the Hermit said—   *Approacheth the ship*
"And they answered not our cheer!   *with wonder*
The planks looked warped! and see those sails,
How thin they are and sere!
I never saw aught like to them,
Unless perchance it were

"Brown skeletons of leaves that lag
My forest-brook along;
When the ivy-tod is heavy with snow,
And the owlet whoops to the wolf below,
That eats the she-wolf's young."

"Dear Lord! it hath a fiendish look—
(The Pilot made reply)
I am a-feared"—"Push on, push on!"
Said the Hermit cheerily.

The boat came closer to the ship,
But I nor spake nor stirred;
The boat came close beneath the ship,
And straight a sound was heard.

Under the water it rumbled on,
Still louder and more dread:
It reached the ship, it split the bay;
The ship went down like lead.

The ship suddenly sinketh

Stunned by that loud and dreadful sound,
Which sky and ocean smote,
Like one that hath been seven days drowned
My body lay afloat;
But swift as dreams, myself I found
Within the Pilot's boat.

The ancient Mariner is saved in the Pilot's boat.

Upon the whirl, where sank the ship,
The boat spun round and round;
And all was still, save that the hill
Was telling of the sound.

I moved my lips—the Pilot shrieked
And fell down in a fit;
The holy Hermit raised his eyes,
And prayed where he did sit.

I took the oars: the Pilot's boy,
Who now doth crazy go,
Laughed loud and long, and all the while
His eyes went to and fro.
"Ha! ha!" quoth he, "full plain I see,
The Devil knows how to row."

And now, all in my own countree,
I stood on the firm land!
The Hermit stepped forth from the boat,
And scarcely he could stand.

"O shrieve me, shrieve me, holy man!"
The Hermit crossed his brow.
"Say quick," quoth he, "I bid thee say—
What manner of man art thou?"

The ancient Mariner earnestly entreateth the Hermit to shrieve him, and the penance of life falls on him.

Forthwith this frame of mine was wrenched
With a woeful agony,
Which forced me to begin my tale;
And then it left me free.

Since then, at an uncertain hour,
That agony returns;
And till my ghastly tale is told,
This heart within me burns.

And ever and anon throughout his future life an agony constraineth him to travel from land to land;

I pass, like night, from land to land;
I have strange power of speech;
That moment that his face I see,
I know the man that must hear me:
To him my tale I teach.

What loud uproar bursts from that door!
The wedding-guests are there:
But in the garden-bower the bride
And bride-maids singing are:
And hark the little vesper bell,
Which biddeth me to prayer!

O Wedding-Guest! this soul hath been
Alone on a wide wide sea:
So lonely 'twas, that God himself
Scarce seemed there to be.

O sweeter than the marriage-feast,
'Tis sweeter far to me,
To walk together to the kirk
With a goodly company!—

To walk together to the kirk,
And all together pray,
While each to his great Father bends,
Old men, and babes, and loving friends,
And youths and maidens gay!

Farewell, farewell! but this I tell
To thee, thou Wedding-Guest!
He prayeth well, who loveth well
Both man and bird and beast.

*And to teach, by his
own example, love and
reverence to all things
that God made and
loveth.*

He prayeth best, who loveth best
All things both great and small;
For the dear God who loveth us
He made and loveth all.

The Mariner, whose eye is bright,
Whose beard with age is hoar,
Is gone: and now the Wedding-Guest
Turned from the bridegroom's door.

He went like one that hath been stunned,
And is of sense forlorn:
A sadder and a wiser man,
He rose the morrow morn.

THE TAPEJTRIED CHAMBER

Sir Walter Scott (1771-1832)

Introduction.

This is another little story from The Keepsake of 1828. It was told to me many years ago by the late Miss Anna Seward, who, among other accomplishments that rendered her an amusing inmate in a country house, had that of recounting narratives of this sort with very considerable effect—much greater, indeed, than any one would be apt to guess from the style of her written performances. There are hours and moods when most people are not displeased to listen to such things; and I have heard some of the greatest and wisest of my contemporaries take their share in telling them.

August 1831

*

The Tapestried Chamber;

Or,

The Lady in the Sacque.

The following narrative is given from the pen, so far as memory permits, in the same character in which it was presented to the author's ear; nor has he claim to further praise, or to be more deeply censured, than in proportion to the good or bad judgment which he has employed in selecting his materials, as he has studiously avoided any attempt at ornament which might interfere with the simplicity of the tale.

At the same time, it must be admitted that the particular class of stories which turns on the marvellous possesses a stronger influence when told than when committed to print. The volume taken up at noonday, though rehearsing the same incidents, conveys a much more feeble impression than is achieved by the voice of the speaker on a circle of fireside auditors, who hang upon the narrative as the narrator details the minute incidents which serve to give it authenticity, and lowers his voice with an affectation of mystery while he approaches the fearful and wonderful part. It was with such advantages that the present writer heard the following events related, more than twenty years since, by the celebrated Miss Seward of Litchfield, who, to her numerous accomplishments, added, in a remarkable degree, the power of narrative in private conversation. In its present form the tale must necessarily lose all the interest which was attached to it by the flexible voice and intelligent features of the gifted narrator. Yet still, read aloud to an undoubting audience by the doubtful light of the closing evening, or in silence by a decaying taper, and amidst the solitude of a half- lighted apartment, it may redeem its character as a good ghost story. Miss Seward always affirmed that she had derived her information from an authentic source, although she suppressed the names of the two persons chiefly concerned. I will not avail myself of any particulars I may have since received concerning the localities of the detail, but suffer them to rest under the same general description in which they were first related to me; and for the same reason I will not add to or diminish the narrative by any circumstance, whether more or less material, but simply rehearse, as I heard it, a story of supernatural terror.

About the end of the American war, when the officers of Lord Cornwallis's army, which surrendered at Yorktown, and others, who had been made prisoners during the impolitic and ill-fated controversy, were returning to their own country, to relate their adventures, and repose themselves after their fatigues, there was amongst them a general officer, to whom Miss S. gave the name of Browne, but merely, as I understood, to save the inconvenience of introducing a nameless agent in the narrative. He was an officer of merit, as well as a gentleman of high consideration for family and attainments.

Some business had carried General Browne upon a tour through the western counties, when, in the conclusion of a morning stage, he found himself in the vicinity of a small country town, which presented a scene of uncommon beauty, and of a character peculiarly English.

The little town, with its stately old church, whose tower bore testimony to the devotion of ages long past, lay amidst pastures and cornfields of small extent, but bounded and divided with hedgerow timber of great age and size. There were few marks of modern improvement. The environs of the place intimated neither the solitude of decay nor the bustle of novelty; the houses were old, but in good repair; and the beautiful little river murmured freely on its way to the left of the town, neither restrained by a dam nor bordered by a towing-path.

Upon a gentle eminence, nearly a mile to the southward of the town, were seen, amongst many venerable oaks and tangled thickets, the turrets of a castle as old as the walls of York and Lancaster, but which seemed to have received important alterations during the age of Elizabeth and her successor, it had not been a place of great size; but whatever accommodation it formerly afforded was, it must be supposed, still to be obtained within its walls. At least, such was the inference which General Browne drew from observing the smoke arise merrily from several of the ancient wreathed and carved chimney-stalks. The wall of the park ran alongside of the highway for two or three hundred yards; and through the different points by which the eye found glimpses into the woodland scenery, it seemed to be well stocked. Other points of view opened in succession—now a full one of the front of the old castle, and now a side glimpse at its particular towers, the former rich in all the bizarrerie of the Elizabethan school, while the simple and solid strength of other parts of the building seemed to show that they had been raised more for defence than ostentation.

Delighted with the partial glimpses which he obtained of the castle through the woods and glades by which this ancient feudal fortress was surrounded, our military traveller was determined to inquire whether it might not deserve a nearer view, and whether it contained family pictures or other objects of curiosity worthy of a stranger's visit, when, leaving the vicinity of the park, he rolled through a clean and well-paved street, and stopped at the door of a well-frequented inn.

Before ordering horses, to proceed on his journey, General Browne made inquiries concerning the proprietor of the chateau which had so attracted his admiration, and was equally surprised and pleased at hearing in reply a nobleman named, whom we shall call Lord Woodville. How fortunate! Much of Browne's early recollections, both at school and at college, had been connected with young Woodville, whom, by a few questions, he now ascertained to be the same with the owner of this fair domain. He had been raised to the peerage by the decease of his father a few months before, and, as the General learned from the landlord, the term of mourning being ended, was now taking possession of his paternal estate in the jovial season of merry, autumn, accompanied by a select party of friends, to enjoy the sports of a country famous for game.

This was delightful news to our traveller. Frank Woodville had been Richard Browne's fag at Eton, and his chosen intimate at Christ Church; their pleasures and their tasks had been the same; and the honest soldier's

heart warmed to find his early friend in possession of so delightful a residence, and of an estate, as the landlord assured him with a nod and a
wink, fully adequate to maintain and add to his dignity. Nothing was more
natural than that the traveller should suspend a journey, which there was
nothing to render hurried, to pay a visit to an old friend under such agreeable circumstances.

The fresh horses, therefore, had only the brief task of conveying the
General's travelling carriage to Woodville Castle. A porter admitted them
at a modern Gothic lodge, built in that style to correspond with the castle
itself, and at the same time rang a bell to give warning of the approach of
visitors. Apparently the sound of the bell had suspended the separation
of the company, bent on the various amusements of the morning; for, on
entering the court of the chateau, several young men were lounging about
in their sporting dresses, looking at and criticizing the dogs which the
keepers held in readiness to attend their pastime. As General Browne
alighted, the young lord came to the gate of the hall, and for an instant
gazed, as at a stranger, upon the countenance of his friend, on which
war, with its fatigues and its wounds, had made a great alteration. But
the uncertainty lasted no longer than till the visitor had spoken, and the
hearty greeting which followed was such as can only be exchanged
betwixt those who have passed together the merry days of careless boyhood or early youth.

"If I could have formed a wish, my dear Browne," said Lord Woodville,
"it would have been to have you here, of all men, upon this occasion,
which my friends are good enough to hold as a sort of holiday. Do not
think you have been unwatched during the years you have been absent
from us. I have traced you through your dangers, your triumphs, your
misfortunes, and was delighted to see that, whether in victory or defeat,
the name of my old friend was always distinguished with applause."

The General made a suitable reply, and congratulated his friend on
his new dignities, and the possession of a place and domain so beautiful.

"Nay, you have seen nothing of it as yet," said Lord Woodville, "and I
trust you do not mean to leave us till you are better acquainted with it. It
is true, I confess, that my present party is pretty large, and the old house,
like other places of the kind, does not possess so much accommodation
as the extent of the outward walls appears to promise. But we can give
you a comfortable old-fashioned room, and I venture to suppose that your
campaigns have taught you to be glad of worse quarters."

The General shrugged his shoulders, and laughed. "I presume," he
said, "the worst apartment in your chateau is considerably superior to
the old tobacco-cask in which I was fain to take up my night's lodging
when I was in the Bush, as the Virginians call it, with the light corps.
There I lay, like Diogenes himself, so delighted with my covering from

the elements, that I made a vain attempt to have it rolled on to my next quarters; but my commander for the time would give way to no such luxurious provision, and I took farewell of my beloved cask with tears in my eyes."

"Well, then, since you do not fear your quarters," said Lord Woodville, "you will stay with me a week at least. Of guns, dogs, fishing-rods, flies, and means of sport by sea and land, we have enough and to spare—you cannot pitch on an amusement but we will find the means of pursuing it. But if you prefer the gun and pointers, I will go with you myself, and see whether you have mended your shooting since you have been amongst the Indians of the back settlements."

The General gladly accepted his friendly host's proposal in all its points. After a morning of manly exercise, the company met at dinner, where it was the delight of Lord Woodville to conduce to the display of the high properties of his recovered friend, so as to recommend him to his guests, most of whom were persons of distinction. He led General Browne to speak of the scenes he had witnessed; and as every word marked alike the brave officer and the sensible man, who retained possession of his cool judgment under the most imminent dangers, the company looked upon the soldier with general respect, as on one who had proved himself possessed of an uncommon portion of personal courage—that attribute of all others of which everybody desires to be thought possessed.

The day at Woodville Castle ended as usual in such mansions. The hospitality stopped within the limits of good order. Music, in which the young lord was a proficient, succeeded to the circulation of the bottle; cards and billiards, for those who preferred such amusements, were in readiness; but the exercise of the morning required early hours, and not long after eleven o'clock the guests began to retire to their several apartments.

The young lord himself conducted his friend, General Browne, to the chamber destined for him, which answered the description he had given of it, being comfortable, but old-fashioned. The bed was of the massive form used in the end of the seventeenth century, and the curtains of faded silk, heavily trimmed with tarnished gold. But then the sheets, pillows, and blankets looked delightful to the campaigner, when he thought of his "mansion, the cask." There was an air of gloom in the tapestry hangings, which, with their worn-out graces, curtained the walls of the little chamber, and gently undulated as the autumnal breeze found its way through the ancient lattice window, which pattered and whistled as the air gained entrance. The toilet, too, with its mirror, turbaned after the manner of the beginning of the century, with a coiffure of murrey-coloured silk, and its hundred strange-shaped boxes, providing for arrangements which had been obsolete for more than fifty years, had an antique, and in so far a melancholy, aspect. But nothing could blaze more brightly and cheerfully than the two large wax candles; or if aught could rival them, it was the flaming, bickering fagots in the chimney, that sent at once their gleam and their warmth through the snug apartment, which, notwithstanding the general antiquity of its appearance, was not wanting in the least convenience that modern habits rendered either necessary or desirable.

"This is an old-fashioned sleeping apartment, General," said the young lord; "but I hope you find nothing that makes you envy your old tobacco-cask."

"I am not particular respecting my lodgings," replied the General; "yet were I to make any choice, I would prefer this chamber by many degrees to the gayer and more modern rooms of your family mansion. Believe me that, when I unite its modern air of comfort with its venerable antiquity, and recollect that it is your lordship's property, I shall feel in better quarters here than if I were in the best hotel London could afford."

"I trust—I have no doubt—that you will find yourself as comfortable as I wish you, my dear General," said the young nobleman; and once more bidding his guest good-night, he shook him by the hand, and withdrew.

The General once more looked round him, and internally congratulating himself on his return to peaceful life, the comforts of which were endeared by the recollection of the hardships and dangers he had lately sustained, undressed himself, and prepared for a luxurious night's rest.

Here, contrary to the custom of this species of tale, we leave the General in possession of his apartment until the next morning.

The company assembled for breakfast at an early hour, but without the appearance of General Browne, who seemed the guest that Lord Woodville was desirous of honouring above all whom his hospitality had assembled around him. He more than once expressed surprise at the General's absence, and at length sent a servant to make inquiry after him. The man brought back information that General Browne had been walking abroad since an early hour of the morning, in defiance of the weather, which was misty and ungenial.

"The custom of a soldier," said the young nobleman to his friends. "Many of them acquire habitual vigilance, and cannot sleep after the early hour at which their duty usually commands them to be alert."

Yet the explanation which Lord Woodville thus offered to the company seemed hardly satisfactory to his own mind, and it was in a fit of silence and abstraction that he waited the return of the General. It took place near an hour after the breakfast bell had rung. He looked fatigued and feverish. His hair, the powdering and arrangement of which was at this time one of the most important occupations of a man's whole day, and marked his fashion as much as in the present time the tying of a cravat, or the want of one, was dishevelled, uncurled, void of powder, and dank with dew. His clothes were huddled on with a careless negligence, remarkable in a military man, whose real or supposed duties are usually held to include some attention to the toilet; and his looks were haggard and ghastly in a peculiar degree.

"So you have stolen a march upon us this morning, my dear General," said Lord Woodville; "or you have not found your bed so much to your mind as I had hoped and you seemed to expect. How did you rest last night?"

"Oh, excellently well! remarkably well! never better in my life," said General Browne rapidly, and yet with an air of embarrassment which was obvious to his friend. He then hastily swallowed a cup of tea, and neglecting or refusing whatever else was offered, seemed to fall into a fit of abstraction.

"You will take the gun to-day, General?" said his friend and host, but had to repeat the question twice ere he received the abrupt answer, "No, my lord; I am sorry I cannot have the opportunity of spending another day with your lordship; my post horses are ordered, and will be here directly."

All who were present showed surprise, and Lord Woodville immediately replied, "Post horses, my good friend! What can you possibly want with them when you promised to stay with me quietly for at least a week?"

"I believe," said the General, obviously much embarrassed, "that I might, in the pleasure of my first meeting with your lordship, have said something about stopping here a few days; but I have since found it altogether impossible."

"That is very extraordinary," answered the young nobleman. "You seemed quite disengaged yesterday, and you cannot have had a summons to-day, for our post has not come up from the town, and therefore you cannot have received any letters."

General Browne, without giving any further explanation, muttered something about indispensable business, and insisted on the absolute necessity of his departure in a manner which silenced all opposition on the part of his host, who saw that his resolution was taken, and forbore all further importunity.

"At least, however," he said, "permit me, my dear Browne, since go you will or must, to show you the view from the terrace, which the mist, that is now rising, will soon display."

He threw open a sash-window, and stepped down upon the terrace as he spoke. The General followed him mechanically, but seemed little to attend to what his host was saying, as, looking across an extended and rich prospect, he pointed out the different objects worthy of observation.

Thus they moved on till Lord Woodville had attained his purpose of drawing his guest entirely apart from the rest of the company, when, turning round upon him with an air of great solemnity, he addressed him thus:—

"Richard Browne, my old and very dear friend, we are now alone. Let me conjure you to answer me upon the word of a friend, and the honour of a soldier. How did you in reality rest during last night?"

"Most wretchedly indeed, my lord," answered the General, in the same tone of solemnity—"so miserably, that I would not run the risk of such a second night, not only for all the lands belonging to this castle, but for all the country which I see from this elevated point of view."

"This is most extraordinary," said the young lord, as if speaking to himself; "then there must be something in the reports concerning that apartment." Again turning to the General, he said, "For God's sake, my dear friend, be candid with me, and let me know the disagreeable particulars which have befallen you under a roof, where, with consent of the owner, you should have met nothing save comfort."

The General seemed distressed by this appeal, and paused a moment before he replied. "My dear lord," he at length said, "what happened to me last night is of a nature so peculiar and so unpleasant, that I could hardly bring myself to detail it even to your lordship, were it not that, independent of my wish to gratify any request of yours, I think that sincerity on my part may lead to some explanation about a circumstance equally painful and mysterious. To others, the communication I am about to make, might place me in the light of a weak-minded, superstitious fool, who suffered his own imagination to delude and bewilder him; but you have known me in childhood and youth, and will not suspect me of having adopted in manhood the feelings and frailties from which my early years were free." Here he paused, and his friend replied,—

"Do not doubt my perfect confidence in the truth of your communication, however strange it may be," replied Lord Woodville. "I know your firmness of disposition too well, to suspect you could be made the object of imposition, and am aware that your honour and your friendship will equally deter you from exaggerating whatever you may have witnessed."

"Well, then," said the General, "I will proceed with my story as well as I can, relying upon your candour, and yet distinctly feeling that I would rather face a battery than recall to my mind the odious recollections of last night."

He paused a second time, and then perceiving that Lord Woodville remained silent and in an attitude of attention, he commenced, though not without obvious reluctance, the history of his night's adventures in the Tapestried Chamber.

"I undressed and went to bed so soon as your lordship left me yesterday evening; but the wood in the chimney, which nearly fronted my bed, blazed brightly and cheerfully, and, aided by a hundred exciting recollections of my childhood and youth, which had been recalled by the unexpected pleasure of meeting your lordship, prevented me from falling immediately asleep. I ought, however, to say that these reflections were all of a pleasant and agreeable kind, grounded on a sense of having for a time exchanged the labour, fatigues, and dangers of my profession for the enjoyments of a peaceful life, and the reunion of those friendly and affectionate ties which I had torn asunder at the rude summons of war.

"While such pleasing reflections were stealing over my mind, and gradually lulling me to slumber, I was suddenly aroused by a sound like that of the rustling of a silken gown, and the tapping of a pair of high-heeled shoes, as if a woman were walking in the apartment. Ere I could draw the curtain to see what the matter was, the figure of a little woman passed between the bed and the fire. The back of this form was turned to me, and I could observe, from the shoulders and neck, it was that of an old woman, whose dress was an old-fashioned gown, which I think ladies call a sacque—that is, a sort of robe completely loose in the body, but gathered into broad plaits upon the neck and shoulders, which fall down to the ground, and terminate in a species of train.

"I thought the intrusion singular enough, but never harboured for a moment the idea that what I saw was anything more than the mortal form of some old woman about the establishment, who had a fancy to dress like her grandmother, and who, having perhaps (as your lordship mentioned that you were rather straitened for room) been dislodged from her chamber for my accommodation, had forgotten the circumstance, and returned by twelve to her old haunt. Under this persuasion I moved myself in bed and coughed a little, to make the intruder sensible of my being in possession of the premises. She turned slowly round, but, gracious Heaven! my lord, what a countenance did she display to me! There was no longer any question what she was, or any thought of her being a living being. Upon a face which wore the fixed features of a corpse were imprinted the traces of the vilest and most hideous passions which had animated her while she lived. The body of some atrocious criminal seemed to have been given up from the grave, and the soul restored from the penal fire, in order to form for a space a union with the ancient accomplice of its guilt. I started up in bed, and sat upright, supporting myself on my palms, as I gazed on this horrible spectre. The hag made, as it seemed, a single and swift stride to the bed where I lay, and squatted herself down upon it, in precisely the same attitude which I had assumed in the extremity of horror, advancing her diabolical countenance within half a yard of mine, with a grin which seemed to intimate the malice and the derision of an incarnate fiend."

Here General Browne stopped, and wiped from his brow the cold perspiration with which the recollection of his horrible vision had covered it.

"My lord," he said, "I am no coward, I have been in all the mortal dangers incidental to my profession, and I may truly boast that no man ever knew Richard Browne dishonour the sword he wears; but in these horrible circumstances, under the eyes, and, as it seemed, almost in the grasp of an incarnation of an evil spirit, all firmness forsook me, all manhood melted from me like wax in the furnace, and I felt my hair individually bristle. The current of my life-blood ceased to flow, and I sank back in a swoon, as very a victim to panic terror as ever was a village girl, or a child of ten years old. How long I lay in this condition I cannot pretend to guess.

"But I was roused by the castle clock striking one, so loud that it seemed as if it were in the very room. It was some time before I dared open my eyes, lest they should again encounter the horrible spectacle. When, however, I summoned courage to look up, she was no longer visible. My first idea was to pull my bell, wake the servants, and remove to a garret or a hay-loft, to be ensured against a second visitation. Nay, I will confess the truth that my resolution was altered, not by the shame of exposing myself, but by the fear that, as the bell-cord hung by the chimney, I might, in making my way to it, be again crossed by the fiendish hag, who, I figured to myself, might be still lurking about some corner of the apartment.

"I will not pretend to describe what hot and cold fever-fits tormented me for the rest of the night, through broken sleep, weary vigils, and that dubious state which forms the neutral ground between them. A hundred terrible objects appeared to haunt me; but there was the great difference betwixt the vision which I have described, and those which followed, that I knew the last to be deceptions of my own fancy and over-excited nerves.

"Day at last appeared, and I rose from my bed ill in health and humiliated in mind. I was ashamed of myself as a man and a soldier, and still more so at feeling my own extreme desire to escape from the haunted apartment, which, however, conquered all other considerations; so that, huddling on my clothes with the most careless haste, I made my escape from your lordship's mansion, to seek in the open air some relief to my nervous system, shaken as it was by this horrible rencounter with a visitant, for such I must believe her, from the other world. Your lordship has now heard the cause of my discomposure, and of my sudden desire to leave your hospitable castle. In other places I trust we may often meet, but God protect me from ever spending a second night under that roof!"

Strange as the General's tale was, he spoke with such a deep air of conviction that it cut short all the usual commentaries which are made on such stories. Lord Woodville never once asked him if he was sure he did not dream of the apparition, or suggested any of the possibilities by which it is fashionable to explain supernatural appearances as wild vagaries of the fancy, or deceptions of the optic nerves. On the contrary, he seemed deeply impressed with the truth and reality of what he had heard; and, after a considerable pause regretted, with much appearance of sincerity, that his early friend should in his house have suffered so severely.

"I am the more sorry for your pain, my dear Browne," he continued, "that it is the unhappy, though most unexpected, result of an experiment of my own. You must know that, for my father and grandfather's time, at least, the apartment which was assigned to you last night had been shut on account of reports that it was disturbed by supernatural sights and noises. When I came, a few weeks since, into possession of the estate, I thought the accommodation which the castle afforded for my friends was not extensive enough to permit the inhabitants of the invisible world to retain possession of a comfortable sleeping apartment. I therefore caused the Tapestried Chamber, as we call it, to be opened, and, without destroying its air of antiquity, I had such new articles of furniture placed in it as became the modern times. Yet, as the opinion that the room was haunted very strongly prevailed among the domestics, and was also known in the neighbourhood and to many of my friends, I feared some prejudice might be entertained by the first occupant of the Tapestried Chamber, which might tend to revive the evil report which it had laboured under, and so disappoint my purpose of rendering it a useful part or the house. I must confess, my dear Browne, that your arrival yesterday, agreeable to me for a thousand reasons besides, seemed the most favourable opportunity of removing the unpleasant rumours which attached to the room, since your courage was indubitable, and your mind free of any preoccupation on the subject. I could not, therefore, have chosen a more fitting subject for my experiment."

"Upon my life," said General Browne, somewhat hastily, "I am infinitely obliged to your lordship—very particularly indebted indeed. I am likely to remember for some time the consequences of the experiment, as your lordship is pleased to call it."

"Nay, now you are unjust, my dear friend," said Lord Woodville. "You have only to reflect for a single moment, in order to be convinced that I could not augur the possibility of the pain to which you have been so unhappily exposed. I was yesterday morning a complete sceptic on the subject of supernatural appearances. Nay, I am sure that, had I told you what was said about that room, those very reports would have induced you, by your own choice, to select it for your accommodation. It was my misfortune, perhaps my error, but really cannot be termed my fault, that you have been afflicted so strangely."

"Strangely indeed!" said the General, resuming his good temper; "and I acknowledge that I have no right to be offended with your lordship for treating me like what I used to think myself—a man of some firmness and courage. But I see my post horses are arrived, and I must not detain your lordship from your amusement."

"Nay, my old friend," said Lord Woodville, "since you cannot stay with us another day—which, indeed, I can no longer urge—give me at least half an hour more. You used to love pictures, and I have a gallery of portraits, some of them by Vandyke, representing ancestry to whom this property and castle formerly belonged. I think that several of them will strike you as possessing merit."

General Browne accepted the invitation, though somewhat unwillingly. It was evident he was not to breathe freely or at ease till he left Woodville Castle far behind him. He could not refuse his friend's invitation, however; and the less so, that he was a little ashamed of the peevishness which he had displayed towards his well-meaning entertainer.

The General, therefore, followed Lord Woodville through several rooms into a long gallery hung with pictures, which the latter pointed out to his guest, telling the names, and giving some account of the personages whose portraits presented themselves in progression. General Browne was but little interested in the details which these accounts conveyed to him. They were, indeed, of the kind which are usually found in an old family gallery. Here was a Cavalier who had ruined the estate in the royal cause; there a fine lady who had reinstated it by contracting a match with a wealthy Roundhead. There hung a gallant who had been in danger for corresponding with the exiled Court at Saint Germain's; here one who had taken arms for William at the Revolution; and there a third that had thrown his weight alternately into the scale of Whig and Tory.

While lord Woodville was cramming these words into his guest's ear, "against the stomach of his sense," they gained the middle of the gallery, when he beheld General Browne suddenly start, and assume an attitude of the utmost surprise, not unmixed with fear, as his eyes were suddenly caught and riveted by a portrait of an old lady in a sacque, the fashionable dress of the end of the seventeenth century.

"There she is!" he exclaimed—"there she is, in form and features, though Inferior in demoniac expression to the accursed hag who visited me last night!"

"If that be the case," said the young nobleman, "there can remain no longer any doubt of the horrible reality of your apparition. That is the picture of a wretched ancestress of mine, of whose crimes a black and fearful catalogue is recorded in a family history in my charter-chest. The recital of them would be too horrible; it is enough to say, that in yon fatal apartment incest and unnatural murder were committed. I will restore it to the solitude to which the better judgment of those who preceded me had consigned it; and never shall any one, so long as I can prevent it, be exposed to a repetition of the supernatural horrors which could shake such courage as yours."

Thus the friends, who had met with such glee, parted in a very different mood—Lord Woodville to command the Tapestried Chamber to be unmantled, and the door built up; and General Browne to seek in some less beautiful country, and with some less dignified friend, forgetfulness of the painful night which he had passed in Woodville Castle.

And the sixth angel trumpeted, and I heard a voice from the four horns of the golden altar before God,

Saying to the sixth angel which had the trumpet, "Loose the four angels which are bound at the great river Euphrates."

And the four angels were loosed, which were prepared for this hour, and day, and month, and year, to slay a third of men.

And the number of the army of horsemen was two hundred million: I heard their number.

And thus I saw the horses in the vision, and those sitting on them, having breastplates of fiery-red, and of dusky-red, and sulfur-yellow: and the heads of the horses were as the heads of lions; and out of their mouths came fire and smoke and sulfur.

By these three plagues was a third of men killed, by the fire, and by the smoke, and by the sulfur, which came out of their mouths.

For the power of the horses is in their mouths and in their tails: for their tails were like serpents, having heads, and with them they do harm.

Revelation 9: 13-19.

THE DEVIL AND TOM WALKER

Washington Irving (1783-1859)

A few miles from Boston, in Massachusetts, there is a deep inlet winding several miles into the interior of the country from Charles Bay, and terminating in a thickly wooded swamp, or morass. On one side of this inlet is a beautiful dark grove; on the opposite side the land rises abruptly from the water's edge, into a high ridge on which grow a few scattered oaks of great age and immense size. Under one of these gigantic trees, according to old stories, there was a great amount of treasure buried by Kidd the pirate. The inlet allowed a facility to bring the money in a boat secretly and at night to the very foot of the hill. The elevation of the place permitted a good look out to be kept that no one was at hand, while the remarkable trees formed good landmarks by which the place might easily be found again. The old stories add, moreover, that the devil presided at the hiding of the money, and took it under his guardianship; but this, it is well known, he always does with buried treasure, particularly when it has been ill gotten. Be that as it may, Kidd never returned to recover his wealth; being shortly after seized at Boston, sent out to England, and there hanged for a pirate.

About the year 1727, just at the time when earthquakes were prevalent in New England, and shook many tall sinners down upon their knees, there lived near this place a meagre miserly fellow of the name of Tom Walker. He had a wife as miserly as himself; they were so miserly that they even conspired to cheat each other. Whatever the woman could lay hands on she hid away: a hen could not cackle but she was on the alert to secure the new-laid egg. Her husband was continually prying about to detect her secret hoards, and many and fierce were the conflicts that took place about what ought to have been common property. They lived in a forlorn looking house, that stood alone and had an air of starvation. A few straggling savin trees, emblems of sterility, grew near it; no smoke ever curled from its chimney; no traveller stopped at its door. A miserable horse, whose ribs were as articulate as the bars of a gridiron, stalked about a field where a thin carpet of moss, scarcely covering the ragged beds of pudding stone, tantalized and balked his hunger; and sometimes he would lean his head over the fence, look piteously at the passer by, and seem to petition deliverance from this land of famine. The house and its inmates had altogether a bad name. Tom's wife was a tall termagant, fierce of temper, loud of tongue, and strong of arm. Her voice was often heard in wordy warfare with her husband; and his face sometimes showed signs that their conflicts were not confined to words. No one ventured, however, to interfere between them; the lonely wayfarer shrunk within himself at the horrid clamour and clapper clawing; eyed the den of discord askance, and hurried on his way, rejoicing, if a bachelor, in his celibacy.

One day that Tom Walker had been to a distant part of the neighbourhood, he took what he considered a short cut homewards through the swamp. Like most short cuts, it was an ill chosen route. The swamp was thickly grown with great gloomy pines and hemlocks, some of them ninety feet high; which made it dark at noonday, and a retreat for all the owls of the neighbourhood. It was full of pits and quagmires, partly covered with weeds and mosses; where the green surface often betrayed the traveller into a gulf of black smothering mud; there were also dark and stagnant pools, the abodes of the tadpole, the bull-frog, and the water snake, and where trunks of pines and hemlocks lay half drowned, half rotting, looking like alligators, sleeping in the mire.

Tom had long been picking his way cautiously through this treacherous forest; stepping from tuft to tuft of rushes and roots which afforded precarious footholds among deep sloughs; or pacing carefully, like a cat, along the prostrate trunks of trees; startled now and then by the sudden screaming of the bittern, or the quacking of a wild duck, rising on the wing from some solitary pool. At length he arrived at a piece of firm ground, which ran out like a peninsula into the deep bosom of the swamp. It had been one of the strong holds of the Indians during their wars with the first colonists. Here they had thrown up a kind of fort which they had looked upon as almost impregnable, and had used as a place of refuge for their squaws and children. Nothing remained of the Indian fort but a few embankments gradually sinking to the level of the surrounding earth, and already overgrown in part by oaks and other forest trees, the foliage of which formed a contrast to the dark pines and hemlocks of the swamp.

It was late in the dusk of evening that Tom Walker reached the old fort, and he paused there for a while to rest himself. Any one but he would have felt unwilling to linger in this lonely melancholy place, for the common people had a bad opinion of it from the stories handed down from the time of the Indian wars; when it was asserted that the savages held incantations here and made sacrifices to the evil spirit. Tom Walker, however, was not a man to be troubled with any fears of the kind.

He reposed himself for some time on the trunk of a fallen hemlock, listening to the boding cry of the tree toad, and delving with his walking staff into a mound of black mould at his feet. As he turned up the soil unconsciously, his staff struck against something hard. He raked it out of the vegetable mould, and lo! a cloven skull with an Indian tomahawk buried deep in it, lay before him. The rust on the weapon showed the time that had elapsed since this death blow had been given. It was a dreary memento of the fierce struggle that had taken place in this last foothold of the Indian warriors.

"Humph!" said Tom Walker, as he gave the skull a kick to shake the dirt from it.

"Let that skull alone!" said a gruff voice.

Tom lifted up his eyes and beheld a great black man, seated directly opposite him on the stump of a tree. He was exceedingly surprised, having neither seen nor heard any one approach, and he was still more perplexed on observing, as well as the gathering gloom would permit, that the stranger was neither negro nor Indian. It is true, he was dressed in a rude, half Indian garb, and had a red belt or sash swathed round his body, but his face was neither black nor copper colour, but swarthy and dingy and begrimed with soot, as if he had been accustomed to toil among fires and forges. He had a shock of coarse black hair, that stood out from his head in all directions; and bore an axe on his shoulder.

He scowled for a moment at Tom with a pair of great red eyes.

"What are you doing in my grounds?" said the black man, with a hoarse growling voice.

"Your grounds?" said Tom, with a sneer; "no more your grounds than mine: they belong to Deacon Peabody."

"Deacon Peabody be d—d," said the stranger, "as I flatter myself he will be, if he does not look more to his own sins and less to his neighbour's. Look yonder, and see how Deacon Peabody is faring."

Tom looked in the direction that the stranger pointed, and beheld one of the great trees, fair and flourishing without, but rotten at the core, and saw that it had been nearly hewn through, so that the first high wind was likely to below it down. On the bark of the tree was scored the name of Deacon Peabody. He now looked round and found most of the tall trees marked with the name of some great men of the colony, and all more or less scored by the axe. The one on which he had been seated, and which had evidently just been hewn down, bore the name of Crowninshield; and he recollected a mighty rich man of that name, who made a vulgar display of wealth, which it was whispered he had acquired by buccaneering.

"He's just ready for burning!" said the black man, with a growl of triumph. "You see I am likely to have a good stock of firewood for winter."

"But what right have you," said Tom, "to cut down Deacon Peabody's timber?"

"The right of prior claim," said the other. "This woodland belonged to me long before one of your white faced race put foot upon the soil."

"And pray, who are you, if I may be so bold?" said Tom.

"Oh, I go by various names. I am the Wild Huntsman in some countries; the Black Miner in others. In this neighbourhood I am known by the name of the Black Woodsman. I am he to whom the red men devoted this spot, and now and then roasted a white man by way of sweet smelling sacrifice. Since the red men have been exterminated by you white savages, I amuse myself by presiding at the persecutions of quakers and anabaptists; I am the great patron and prompter of slave dealers, and the grand master of the Salem witches."

"The upshot of all which is, that, if I mistake not," said Tom, sturdily, "you are he commonly called Old Scratch."

"The same at your service!" replied the black man, with a half civil nod.

Such was the opening of this interview, according to the old story, though it has almost too familiar an air to be credited. One would think that to meet with such a singular personage in this wild lonely place, would have shaken any man's nerves: but Tom was a hard-minded fellow, not easily daunted, and he had lived so long with a termagant wife, that he did not even fear the devil.

It is said that after this commencement, they had a long and earnest conversation together, as Tom returned homewards. The black man told him of great sums of money which had been buried by Kidd the pirate, under the oak trees on the high ridge not far from the morass. All these were under his command and protected by his power, so that none could find them but such as propitiated his favour. These he offered to place within Tom Walker's reach, having conceived an especial kindness for him: but they were to be had only on certain conditions. What these conditions were, may easily be surmised, though Tom never disclosed them publicly. They must have been very hard, for he required time to think of them, and he was not a man to stick at trifles where money was in view. When they had reached the edge of the swamp the stranger paused.

"What proof have I that all you have been telling me is true?" said Tom.

"There is my signature," said the black man, pressing his finger on Tom's forehead. So saying, he turned off among the thickets of the swamp, and seemed, as Tom said, to go down, down, down, into the earth, until nothing but his head and shoulders could be seen, and so on until he totally disappeared.

When Tom reached home he found the black print of a finger burnt, as it were, into his forehead, which nothing could obliterate.

The first news his wife had to tell him was the sudden death of Absalom Crowninshield the rich buccaneer. It was announced in the papers with the usual flourish, that "a great man had fallen in Israel."

Tom recollected the tree which his black friend had just hewn down, and which was ready for burning. "Let the freebooter roast," said Tom, "who cares!" He now felt convinced that all he had heard and seen was no illusion.

He was not prone to let his wife into his confidence; but as this was an uneasy secret, he willingly shared it with her. All her avarice was awakened at the mention of hidden gold, and she urged her husband to comply with the black man's terms and secure what would make them wealthy for life. However Tom might have felt disposed to sell himself to the devil, he was determined not to do so to oblige his wife; so he flatly refused out of the mere spirit of contradiction. Many and bitter were the quarrels they had on the subject, but the more she talked the more resolute was Tom not to be damned to please her. At length she determined to drive the bargain on her own account, and if she succeeded, to keep all the gain to herself.

Being of the same fearless temper as her husband, she set off for the old Indian fort towards the close of a summer's day. She was many hours absent. When she came back she was reserved and sullen in her replies. She spoke something of a black man whom she had met about twilight, hewing at the root of a tall tree. He was sulky, however, and would not come to terms; she was to go again with a propitiatory offering, but what it was she forebore to say.

The next evening she set off again for the swamp, with her apron heavily laden. Tom waited and waited for her, but in vain: midnight came, but she did not make her appearance; morning, noon, night returned, but still she did not come. Tom now grew uneasy for her safety; especially as he found she had carried off in her apron the silver teapot and spoons and every portable article of value. Another night elapsed, another morning came; but no wife. In a word, she was never heard of more.

What was her real fate nobody knows, in consequence of so many pretending to know. It is one of those facts that have become confounded by a variety of historians. Some asserted that she lost her way among the tangled mazes of the swamp and sunk into some pit or slough; others, more uncharitable, hinted that she had eloped with the household booty, and made off to some other province; while others assert that the tempter had decoyed her into a dismal quagmire on top of which her hat was found lying. In confirmation of this, it was said a great black man with an axe on his shoulder was seen late that very evening coming out of the swamp, carrying a bundle tied in a check apron, with an air of surly triumph.

The most current and probable story, however, observes that Tom Walker grew so anxious about the fate of his wife and his property that he sat out at length to seek them both at the Indian fort. During a long summer's afternoon he searched about the gloomy place, but no wife was to be seen. He called her name repeatedly, but she was no where to be heard. The bittern alone responded to his voice, as he flew screaming by; or the bull frog croaked dolefully from a neighbouring pool. At length, it is said, just in the brown hour of twilight, when the owls began to hoot and the bats to flit about, his attention was attracted by the clamour of carrion crows that were hovering about a cypress tree. He looked and beheld a bundle tied in a check apron and hanging in the branches of the tree; with a great vulture perched hard by, as if keeping watch upon it. He leaped with joy, for he recognized his wife's apron, and supposed it to contain the household valuables.

"Let us get hold of the property," said he, consolingly to himself, "and we will endeavour to do without the woman."

As he scrambled up the tree the vulture spread its wide wings, and sailed off screaming into the deep shadows of the forest. Tom seized the check apron, but, woful sight! found nothing but a heart and liver tied up in it.

Such, according to the most authentic old story, was all that was to be found of Tom's wife. She had probably attempted to deal with the black man as she had been accustomed to deal with her husband; but though a female scold is generally considered a match for the devil, yet in this instance she appears to have had the worst of it. She must have died game however; for it is said Tom noticed many prints of cloven feet deeply stamped about the tree, and several handsful of hair, that looked as if they had been plucked from the coarse black shock of the woodsman. Tom knew his wife's prowess by experience. He shrugged his shoulders as he looked at the signs of a fierce clapper clawing. "Egad," said he to himself, "Old Scratch must have had a tough time of it!"

Tom consoled himself for the loss of his property with the loss of his wife; for he was a man of fortitude. He even felt something like gratitude towards the black woodsman, who he considered had done him a kindness. He sought, therefore, to cultivate a farther acquaintance with him, but for some time without success; the old black legs played shy, for whatever people may think, he is not always to be had for calling for; he knows how to play his cards when pretty sure of his game.

At length, it is said, when delay had whetted Tom's eagerness to the quick, and prepared him to agree to any thing rather than not gain the promised treasure, he met the black man one evening in his usual woodman dress, with his axe on his shoulder, sauntering along the edge of the swamp, and humming a tune. He affected to receive Tom's advance with great indifference, made brief replies, and went on humming his tune.

By degrees, however, Tom brought him to business, and they began to haggle about the terms on which the former was to have the pirate's treasure. There was one condition which need not be mentioned, being generally understood in all cases where the devil grants favours; but there were others about which, though of less importance, he was inflexibly obstinate. He insisted that the money found through his means should be employed in his service. He proposed, therefore, that Tom should employ it in the black traffick; that is to say, that he should fit out a slave ship. This, however, Tom resolutely refused; he was bad enough in all conscience; but the devil himself could not tempt him to turn slave dealer.

Finding Tom so squeamish on this point, he did not insist upon it, but proposed instead that he should turn usurer; the devil being extremely anxious for the increase of usurers, looking upon them as his peculiar people.

To this no objections were made, for it was just to Tom's taste.

"You shall open a broker's shop in Boston next month," said the black man.

"I'll do it to-morrow, if you wish," said Tom Walker.

"You shall lend money at two per cent. a month."

"Egad, I'll charge four!" replied Tom Walker.

"You shall extort bonds, foreclose mortgages, drive the merchant to bankruptcy—"

"I'll drive him to the d—l," cried Tom Walker, eagerly.

"You are the usurer for my money!" said the black legs, with delight. "When will you want the rhino?"

"This very night."

"Done!" said the devil.

"Done!" said Tom Walker. —So they shook hands, and struck a bargain.

A few days' time saw Tom Walker seated behind his desk in a counting house in Boston. His reputation for a ready moneyed man, who would lend money out for a good consideration, soon spread abroad. Every body remembers the days of Governor Belcher, when money was particularly scarce. It was a time of paper credit. The country had been deluged with government bills; the famous Land Bank had been established; there had been a rage for speculating; the people had run mad with schemes for new settlements; for building cities in the wilderness; land jobbers went about with maps of grants, and townships, and Eldorados, lying nobody knew where, but which every body was ready to purchase. In a word, the great speculating fever which breaks out every now and then in the country, had raged to an alarming degree, and every body was dreaming of making sudden fortunes from nothing. As usual the fever had subsided; the dream had gone off, and the imaginary fortunes with it; the patients were left in doleful plight, and the whole country resounded with the consequent cry of "hard times."

At this propitious time of public distress did Tom Walker set up as a usurer in Boston. His door was soon thronged by customers. The needy and the adventurous; the gambling speculator; the dreaming land jobber; the thriftless tradesman; the merchant with cracked credit; in short, every one driven to raise money by desperate means and desperate sacrifices, hurried to Tom Walker.

Thus Tom was the universal friend of the needy, and he acted like a "friend in need;" that is to say, he always exacted good pay and good security. In proportion to the distress of the applicant was the hardness of his terms. He accumulated bonds and mortgages; gradually squeezed his customers closer and closer; and sent them at length, dry as a sponge from his door.

In this way he made money hand over hand; became a rich and mighty man, and exalted his cocked hat upon change. He built himself, as usual, a vast house, out of ostentation; but left the greater part of it unfinished and unfurnished out of parsimony. He even set up a carriage in the fullness of his vain glory, though he nearly starved the horses which drew it; and as the ungreased wheels groaned and screeched on the axle trees, you would have thought you heard the souls of the poor debtors he was squeezing.

As Tom waxed old, however, he grew thoughtful. Having secured the good things of this world, he began to feel anxious about those of the next. He thought with regret on the bargain he had made with his black friend, and set his wits to work to cheat him out of the conditions. He became, therefore, all of a sudden, a violent church goer. He prayed loudly and strenuously as if heaven were to be taken by force of lungs. Indeed, one might always tell when he had sinned most during the week, by the clamour of his Sunday devotion. The quiet christians who had been modestly and steadfastly travelling Zionward, were struck with self reproach at seeing themselves so suddenly outstripped in their career by this new-made convert. Tom was as rigid in religious, as in money matters; he was a stern supervisor and censurer of his neighbours, and seemed to think every sin entered up to their account became a credit on his own side of the page. He even talked of the expediency of reviving the persecution of quakers and anabaptists. In a word, Tom's zeal became as notorious as his riches.

Still, in spite of all this strenuous attention to forms, Tom had a lurking dread that the devil, after all, would have his due. That he might not be taken unawares, therefore, it is said he always carried a small bible in his coat pocket. He had also a great folio bible on his counting house desk, and would frequently be found reading it when people called on business; on such occasions he would lay his green spectacles on the book, to mark the place, while he turned round to drive some usurious bargain.

Some say that Tom grew a little crack brained in his old days, and that fancying his end approaching, he had his horse new shod, saddled and bridled, and buried with his feet uppermost; because he supposed that at the last day the world would be turned upside down; in which case he should find his horse standing ready for mounting, and he was determined at the worst to give his old friend a run for it. This, however, is probably a mere old wives fable. If he really did take such a precaution it was totally superfluous; at least so says the authentic old legend which closes his story in the following manner.

On one hot afternoon in the dog days, just as a terrible black thundergust was coming up, Tom sat in his counting house in his white linen cap and India silk morning gown. He was on the point of foreclosing a mortgage, by which he would complete the ruin of an unlucky land speculator for whom he had professed the greatest friendship. The poor land jobber begged him to grant a few months indulgence. Tom had grown testy and irritated and refused another day.

"My family will be ruined and brought upon the parish," said the land jobber.

"Charity begins at home," replied Tom, "I must take care of myself in these hard times."

"You have made so much money out of me," said the speculator.

Tom lost his patience and his piety—"The devil take me," said he, "if I have made a farthing!"

Just then there were three loud knocks at the street door. He stepped out to see who was there. A black man was holding a black horse which neighed and stamped with impatience.

"Tom, you're come for!" said the black fellow, gruffly. Tom shrunk back, but too late. He had left his little bible at the bottom of his coat pocket, and his big bible on the desk buried under the mortgage he was about to foreclose: never was sinner taken more unawares. The black man whisked him like a child astride the horse and away he galloped in the midst of a thunder storm. The clerks stuck their pens behind their ears and stared after him from the windows. Away went Tom Walker, dashing down the streets; his white cap bobbing up and down; his morning gown fluttering in the wind, and his steed striking fire out of the pavement at every bound. When the clerks turned to look for the black man he had disappeared.

Tom Walker never returned to foreclose the mortgage. A country-man who lived on the borders of the swamp, reported that in the height of the thunder gust he had heard a great clattering of hoofs and a howling along the road, and that when he ran to the window he just caught sight of a figure, such as I have described, on a horse that galloped like mad across the fields, over the hills and down into the black hemlock swamp towards the old Indian fort; and that shortly after a thunderbolt fell in that direction which seemed to set the whole forest in a blaze.

The good people of Boston shook their heads and shrugged their shoulders, but had been so much accustomed to witches and goblins and tricks of the devil in all kinds of shapes from the first settlement of the colony, that they were not so much horror struck as might have been expected. Trustees were appointed to take charge of Tom's effects. There was nothing, however, to administer upon. On searching his coffers all his bonds and mortgages were found reduced to cinders. In place of gold and silver his iron chest was filled with chips and shavings; two skeletons lay in his stable instead of his half starved horses, and the very next day his great house took fire and was burnt to the ground.

Such was the end of Tom Walker and his ill gotten wealth. Let all griping money brokers lay this story to heart. The truth of it is not to be doubted. The very hole under the oak trees, from whence he dug Kidd's money is to be seen to this day; and the neighbouring swamp and old Indian fort is often haunted in stormy nights by a figure on horseback, in a morning gown and white cap, which is doubtless the troubled spirit of the usurer. In fact, the story has resolved itself into a proverb, and is the origin of that popular saying, prevalent throughout New-England, of "The Devil and Tom Walker."

UNCLE CORNELIUS, HIS STORY

George MacDonald (1824-1905)

It was a dull evening in November. A drizzling mist had been falling all day about the old farm. Harry Heywood and his two sisters sat in the house-place, expecting a visit from their uncle, Cornelius Heywood. This uncle lived alone, occupying the first floor above a chemist's shop in the town, and had just enough of money over to buy books that nobody seemed ever to have heard of but himself; for he was a student in all those regions of speculation in which anything to be called knowledge is impossible.

"What a dreary night!" said Kate. "I wish uncle would come and tell us a story."

"A cheerful wish," said Harry. "Uncle Cornie is a lively companion—isn't he? He can't even blunder through a Joe Miller without tacking a moral to it, and then trying to persuade you that the joke of it depends on the moral."

"Here he comes!" said Kate, as three distinct blows with the knob of his walking-stick announced the arrival of Uncle Cornelius. She ran to the door to open it.

The air had been very still all day, but as he entered he seemed to have brought the wind with him, for the first moan of it pressed against rather than shook the casement of the low-ceiled room.

Uncle Cornelius was very tall, and very thin, and very pale, with large gray eyes that looked greatly larger because he wore spectacles of the most delicate hair-steel, with the largest pebble-eyes that ever were seen. He gave them a kindly greeting, but too much in earnest even in shaking hands to smile over it. He sat down in the arm-chair by the chimney corner.

I have been particular in my description of him, in order that my reader may give due weight to his words. I am such a believer in words,

79

that I believe everything depends on who says them. Uncle Cornelius Heywood's story told word for word by Uncle Timothy Warren, would not have been the same story at all. Not one of the listeners would have believed a syllable of it from the lips of round-bodied, red-faced, small-eyed, little Uncle Tim; whereas from Uncle Cornie—disbelieve one of his stories if you could!

One word more concerning him. His interest in everything conjectured or believed relative to the awful borderland of this world and the next, was only equalled by his disgust at the vulgar, unimaginative forms which curiosity about such subjects has assumed in the present day. With a yearning after the unseen like that of a child for the lifting of the curtain of a theatre, he declared that, rather than accept such a spirit-world as the would-be seers of the nineteenth century thought or pretended to reveal,—the prophets of a pauperised, workhouse immortality, invented by a poverty-stricken soul, and a sense so greedy that it would gorge on carrion,—he would rejoice to believe that a man had just as much of a soul as the cabbage of Iamblichus, namely, an aerial double of his body.

"I'm so glad you're come, uncle!" said Kate. "Why wouldn't you come to dinner? We have been so gloomy!"

"Well, Katey, you know I don't admire eating. I never could bear to see a cow tearing up the grass with her long tongue." As he spoke he looked very much like a cow. He had a way of opening his jaws while he kept his lips closely pressed together, that made his cheeks fall in, and his face look awfully long and dismal. "I consider eating," he went on, "such an animal exercise that it ought always to be performed in private. You never saw me dine, Kate."

"Never, uncle; but I have seen you drink;—nothing but water, I must confess."

"Yes, that is another affair. According to one eyewitness that is no more than the disembodied can do. I must confess, however, that, although well attested, the story is to me scarcely credible. Fancy a glass of Bavarian beer lifted into the air without a visible hand, turned upside down, and set empty on the table!—and no splash on the floor or anywhere else!"

A solitary gleam of humour shone through the great eyes of the spectacles as he spoke.

"Oh, uncle! how can you believe such nonsense!" said Janet.

"I did not say I believed it—did I? But why not? The story has at least a touch of imagination in it."

"That is a strange reason for believing a thing, uncle," said Harry.

"You might have a worse, Harry. I grant it is not sufficient; but it is better than that commonplace aspect which is the ground of most faith. I believe I did say that the story puzzled me."

"But how can you give it any quarter at all, uncle?"

"It does me no harm. There it is—between the boards of an old German book. There let it remain."

"Well, you will never persuade me to believe such things," said Janet.

"Wait till I ask you, Janet," returned her uncle, gravely. "I have not the slightest desire to convince you. How did we get into this unprofitable current of talk? We will change it at once. How are consols, Harry?"

"Oh, uncle!" said Kate, "we were longing for a story, and just as I thought you were coming to one, off you go to consols!"

"I thought a ghost story at least was coming," said Janet.

"You did your best to stop it, Janet," said Harry.

Janet began an angry retort, but Cornelius interrupted her. "You never heard me tell a ghost story, Janet."

"You have just told one about a drinking ghost, uncle," said Janet—in such a tone that Cornelius replied—

"Well, take that for your story, and let us talk of something else."

Janet apparently saw that she had been rude, and said as sweetly as she might—"Ah! but you didn't make that one, uncle. You got it out of a German book."

"Make it!—Make a ghost story!" repeated Cornelius. "No; that I never did."

"Such things are not to be trifled with, are they?" said Janet.

"I at least have no inclination to trifle with them."

"But, really and truly, uncle," persisted Janet, "you don't believe in such things?"

"Why should I either believe or disbelieve in them? They are not essential to salvation, I presume."

"You must do the one or the other, I suppose."

"I beg your pardon. You suppose wrong. It would take twice the proof I have ever had to make me believe in them; and exactly your prejudice, and allow me to say ignorance, to make me disbelieve in them. Neither is within my reach. I postpone judgment. But you, young people, of course, are wiser, and know all about the question."

"Oh, uncle! I'm so sorry!" said Kate. "I'm sure I did not mean to vex you."

"Not at all, not at all, my dear.—It wasn't you."

"Do you know," Kate went on, anxious to prevent anything unpleasant, for there was something very black perched on Janet's forehead, "I have taken to reading about that kind of thing."

"I beg you will give it up at once. You will bewilder your brains till you are ready to believe anything, if only it be absurd enough. Nay, you may come to find the element of vulgarity essential to belief. I should be sorry to the heart to believe concerning a horse or dog what they tell you nowadays about Shakespeare and Burns. What have you been reading, my girl?"

"Don't be alarmed, uncle. Only some Highland legends, which are too absurd either for my belief or for your theories."

"I don't know that, Kate."

"Why, what could you do with such shapeless creatures as haunt their fords and pools for instance? They are as featureless as the faces of the mountains."

"And so much the more terrible."

"But that does not make it easier to believe in them," said Harry.

"I only said," returned his uncle, "that their shapelessness adds to their horror."

"But you allowed—almost, at least, uncle," said Kate, "that you could find a place in your theories even for those shapeless creatures."

Cornelius sat silent for a moment; then, having first doubled the length of his face, and restored it to its natural condition, said thoughtfully, "I suspect, Katey, if you were to come upon an ichthyosaurus or a pterodactyl asleep in the shubbery, you would hardly expect your report of it to be believed all at once either by Harry or Janet."

"I suppose not, uncle. But I can't see what—"

"Of course such a thing could not happen here and now. But there was a time when and a place where such a thing may have happened. Indeed, in my time, a traveller or two have got pretty soundly disbelieved for reporting what they saw,—the last of an expiring race, which had strayed over the natural verge of its history, coming to life in some neglected swamp, itself a remnant of the slime of Chaos."

"I never heard you talk like that before, uncle," said Harry. "If you go on like that, you'll land me in a swamp, I'm afraid."

"I wasn't talking to you at all, Harry. Kate challenged me to find a place for kelpies, and such like, in the theories she does me the honour of supposing I cultivate."

"Then you think, uncle, that all these stories are only legends which, if you could follow them up, would lead you back to some one of the awful monsters that have since quite disappeared from the earth."

"It is possible those stories may be such legends; but that was not what I intended to lead you to. I gave you that only as something like what I am going to say now. What if,—mind, I only suggest it,—what if the direful creatures, whose report lingers in these tales, should have an origin far older still? What if they were the remnants of a vanishing period of the earth's history long antecedent to the birth of mastodon and iguanodon; a stage, namely, when the world, as we call it, had not yet become quite visible, was not yet so far finished as to part from the invisible world that was its mother, and which, on its part, had not then become quite invisible—was only almost such; and when, as a credible consequence, strange shapes of those now invisible regions, Gorgons and Chimæras dire, might be expected to gloom out occasionally from the awful Fauna of an ever-generating world upon that one which was being born of it. Hence, the life-periods of a world being long and slow, some of these huge, unformed bulks of half-created matter might, somehow, like the megatherium of later times,—a baby creation to them,—roll at age—long intervals, clothed in a mighty terror of shapelessness into the half-recognition of human beings, whose consternation at the uncertain vision were barrier enough to prevent all further knowledge of its substance."

"I begin to have some notion of your meaning, uncle," said Kate.

"But then," said Janet, "all that must be over by this time. That world has been invisible now for many years."

"Ever since you were born, I suppose, Janet. The changes of a world are not to be measured by the changes of its generations."

"Oh, but, uncle, there can't be any such things. You know that as well as I do."

"Yes, just as well, and no better."

"There can't be any ghosts now. Nobody believes such things."

"Oh, as to ghosts, that is quite another thing. I did not know you were talking with reference to them. It is no wonder if one can get nothing sensible out of you, Janet, when your discrimination is no greater than to lump everything marvellous, kelpies, ghosts, vampires, doubles, witches, fairies, nightmares, and I don't know what all, under the one head of ghosts; and we haven't been saying a word about them. If one were to disprove to you the existence of the afreets of Eastern tales, you would consider the whole argument concerning the reappearance of the departed upset. I congratulate you on your powers of analysis and induction, Miss Janet. But it matters very little whether we believe in ghosts, as you say, or not, provided we believe that we are ghosts—that within this body, which so many people are ready to consider their own very selves, their lies a ghostly embryo, at least, which has an inner side to it God only can see, which says I concerning itself, and which will soon have to know whether or not it can appear to those whom it has left behind, and thus solve the question of ghosts for itself, at least."

"Then you do believe in ghosts, uncle?" said Janet, in a tone that certainly was not respectful.

"Surely I said nothing of the sort, Janet. The man most convinced that he had himself had such an interview as you hint at, would find— ought to find it impossible to convince any one else of it."

"You are quite out of my depth, uncle," said Harry. "Surely any honest man ought to be believed?"

"Honesty is not all, by any means, that is necessary to being believed. It is impossible to convey a conviction of anything. All you can do is to convey a conviction that you are convinced. Of course, what satisfied you might satisfy another; but, till you can present him with the sources of your conviction, you cannot present him with the conviction—and perhaps not even then."

"You can tell him all about, it, can't you?"

"Is telling a man about a ghost, affording him the source of your conviction? Is it the same as a ghost appearing to him? Really, Harry!— You cannot even convey the impression a dream has made upon you."

"But isn't that just because it is only a dream?"

"Not at all. The impression may be deeper and clearer on your mind than any fact of the next morning will make. You will forget the next day altogether, but the impression of the dream will remain through all the following whirl and storm of what you call facts. Now a conviction may be likened to a deep impression on the judgment or the reason, or both. No one can feel it but the person who is convinced. It cannot be conveyed."

"I fancy that is just what those who believe in spirit-rapping would say."

"There are the true and false of convictions, as of everything else. I mean that a man may take that for a conviction in his own mind which is not a conviction, but only resembles one. But those to whom you refer profess to appeal to facts. It is on the ground of those facts, and with the more earnestness the more reason they can give for receiving them as facts, that I refuse all their deductions with abhorrence. I mean that, if what they say is true, the thinker must reject with contempt the claim to anything like revelation therein."

"Then you do not believe in ghosts, after all?" said Kate, in a tone of surprise.

"I did not say so, my dear. Will you be reasonable, or will you not?"

"Dear uncle, do tell us what you really think."

"I have been telling you what I think ever since I came, Katey; and you won't take in a word I say."

"I have been taking in every word, uncle, and trying hard to understand it as well.—Did you ever see a ghost, uncle?"

Cornelius Heywood was silent. He shut his lips and opened his jaws till his cheeks almost met in the vacuum. A strange expression crossed the strange countenance, and the great eyes of his spectacles looked as if, at the very moment, they were seeing something no other spectacles could see. Then his jaws closed with a snap, his countenance brightened, a flash of humour came through the goggle eyes of pebble, and, at length, he actually smiled as he said—"Really, Katey, you must take me for a simpleton!"

"How, uncle?"

"To think, if I had ever seen a ghost, I would confess the fact before a set of creatures like you—all spinning your webs like so many spiders to catch and devour old Daddy Longlegs."

By this time Harry had grown quite grave. "Indeed, I am very sorry, uncle," he said, "if I have deserved such a rebuke."

"No, no, my boy," said Cornelius; "I did not mean it more than half. If I had meant it, I would not have said it. If you really would like—" Here he paused.

"Indeed we should, uncle," said Kate, earnestly. "You should have heard what we were saying just before you came in."

"All you were saying, Katey?"

"Yes," answered Kate, thoughtfully. "The worst we said was that you could not tell a story without—well, we did say tacking a moral to it."

"Well, well! I mustn't push it. A man has no right to know what people say about him. It unfits him for occupying his real position amongst them. He, least of all, has anything to do with it. If his friends won't defend him, he can't defend himself. Besides, what people say is so often un-true!—I don't mean to others, but to themselves. Their hearts are more honest than their mouths. But Janet doesn't want a strange story, I am sure."

Janet certainly was not one to have chosen for a listener to such a tale. Her eyes were so small that no satisfaction could possibly come of it. "Oh! I don't mind, uncle," she said, with half-affected indifference, as she searched in her box for silk to mend her gloves.

"You are not very encouraging, I must say," returned her uncle, making another cow-face.

"I will go away, if you like," said Janet, pretending to rise.

"No, never mind," said her uncle hastily. "If you don't want me to tell it, I want you to hear it; and, before I have done, that may have come to the same thing perhaps."

"Then you really are going to tell us a ghost story!" said Kate, draw-ing her chair nearer to her uncle's; and then, finding this did not satisfy her sense of propinquity to the source of the expected pleasure, drawing a stool from the corner, and seating herself almost on the hearth-rug at his knee.

"I did not say so," returned Cornelius, once more. "I said I would tell you a strange story. You may call it a ghost story if you like; I do not pretend to determine what it is. I confess it will look like one, though."

After so many delays, Uncle Cornelius now plunged almost hurriedly into his narration.

"In the year 1820," he said, "in the month of August, I fell in love." Here the girls glanced at each other. The idea of Uncle Cornie in love, and in the very same century in which they were now listening to the confession, was too astonishing to pass without ocular remark; but, if he observed it, he took no notice of it; he did not even pause. "In the month of September, I was refused. Consequently, in the month of October, I was ready to fall in love again. Take particular care of yourself, Harry, for a whole month, at least, after your first disappointment; for you will never be more likely to do a foolish thing. Please yourself after the second. If you are silly then, you may take what you get, for you will deserve it—except it be good fortune."

"Did you do a foolish thing then, uncle?" asked Harry, demurely.

"I did, as you will see; for I fell in love again."

"I don't see anything so very foolish in that."

"I have repented it since, though. Don't interrupt me again, please. In the middle of October, then, in the year 1820, in the evening, I was walking across Russell Square, on my way home from the British Museum, where I had been reading all day. You see I have a full intention of being precise, Janet."

"I'm sure I don't know why you make the remark to me, uncle," said Janet, with an involuntary toss of her head. Her uncle only went on with his narrative.

"I begin at the very beginning of my story," he said; "for I want to be particular as to everything that can appear to have had anything to do with what came afterwards. I had been reading, I say, all the morning in the British Museum; and, as I walked, I took off my spectacles to ease my eyes. I need not tell you that I am short-sighted now, for that you know well enough. But I must tell you that I was short-sighted then, and helpless enough without my spectacles, although I was not quite so much so as I am now;—for I find it all nonsense about short-sighted eyes improving with age. Well, I was walking along the south side of Russell Square, with my spectacles in my hand, and feeling a little bewildered in consequence—for it was quite the dusk of the evening, and short-sighted people require more light than others. I was feeling, in fact, almost blind. I had got more than half-way to the other side, when, from the crossing that cuts off the corner in the direction of Montagu Place, just as I was about to turn towards it, an old lady stepped upon the kerbstone of the pavement, looked at me for a moment, and passed—an occurrence not very remarkable, certainly. But the lady was remarkable, and so was her dress. I am not good at observing, and I am still worse at describing dress, therefore I can only say that hers reminded me of an old picture—that is, I had never seen anything like it, except in old pictures. She had no bonnet, and looked as if she had walked straight out of an ancient drawing-room in her evening attire. Of her face I shall say nothing now. The next instant I met a man on the crossing, who stopped and addressed me.

So short-sighted was I that, although I recognised his voice as one I ought to know, I could not identify him until I had put on my spectacles, which I did instinctively in the act of returning his greeting. At the same moment I glanced over my shoulder after the old lady. She was nowhere to be seen.

"'What are you looking at?' asked James Hetheridge.

"'I was looking after that old lady,' I answered, 'but I can't see her.'

"'What old lady?' said Hetheridge, with just a touch of impatience.

"'You must have seen her,' I returned. 'You were not more than three yards behind her.'

"'Where is she then?'

"'She must have gone down one of the areas, I think. But she looked a lady, though an old-fashioned one.'

"'Have you been dining?' asked James, in a tone of doubtful inquiry.

"'No,' I replied, not suspecting the insinuation; 'I have only just come from the Museum.'

"'Then I advise you to call on your medical man before you go home.'

"'Medical man!' I returned; 'I have no medical man. What do you mean? I never was better in my life.'

"'I mean that there was no old lady. It was an illusion, and that indicates something wrong. Besides, you did not know me when I spoke to you.'

"'That is nothing" I returned. 'I had just taken off my spectacles, and without them I shouldn't know my own father.'

"'How was it you saw the old lady, then?'

"The affair was growing serious under my friend's cross-questioning. I did not at all like the idea of his supposing me subject to hallucinations. So I answered, with a laugh, 'Ah! to be sure, that explains it. I am so blind without my spectacles, that I shouldn't know an old lady from a big dog.'

"'There was no big dog,' said Hetheridge, shaking his head, as the fact for the first time dawned upon me that, although I had seen the old lady clearly enough to make a sketch of her, even to the features of her care-worn, eager old face, I had not been able to recognise the well-known countenance of James Hetheridge.

"'That's what comes of reading till the optic nerve is weakened,' he went on. 'You will cause yourself serious injury if you do not pull up in time. I'll tell you what; I'm going home next week—will you go with me?'

"'You are very kind,' I answered, not altogether rejecting the proposal, for I felt that a little change to the country would be pleasant, and I was quite my own master. For I had unfortunately means equal to my wants, and had no occasion to follow any profession—not a very desirable thing for a young man, I can tell you, Master Harry. I need not keep you over the commonplaces of pressing and yielding. It is enough to say that he pressed and that I yielded. The day was fixed for our departure together; but something or other, I forget what, occurred, to make him advance the date, and it was resolved that I should follow later in the month.

"It was a drizzly afternoon in the beginning of the last week of October when I left the town of Bradford in a post-chaise to drive to Lewton Grange, the property of my friend's father. I had hardly left the town, and the twilight had only begun to deepen, when, glancing from one of the windows of the chaise, I fancied I saw, between me and the hedge, the dim figure of a horse keeping pace with us. I thought, in the first interval of unreason, that it was a shadow from my own horse, but reminded myself the next moment that there could be no shadow where there was no light. When I looked again, I was at the first glance convinced that my eyes had deceived me. At the second, I believed once more that a shadowy something, with the movements of a horse in harness, was keeping pace with us. I turned away again with some discomfort, and not till we had reached an open moorland road, whence a little watery light was visible on the horizon, could I summon up courage enough to look out once more. Certainly then there was nothing to be seen, and I persuaded myself that it had been all a fancy, and lighted a cigar. With my feet on the cushions before me, I had soon lifted myself on the clouds of tobacco far above all the terrors of the night, and believed them banished for ever. But, my cigar coming to an end just as we turned into the avenue that led up to the Grange, I found myself once more glancing nervously out of the window. The moment the trees were about me, there was, if not a shadowy horse out there by the side of the chaise, yet certainly more than half that conviction in here in my consciousness. When I saw my friend, however, standing on the doorstep, dark against the glow of the hall fire, I forgot all about it; and I need not add that I did not make it a subject of conversation when I entered, for I was well aware that it was essential to a man's reputation that his senses should be accurate, though his heart might without prejudice swarm with shadows, and his judgment be a very stable of hobbies.

"I was kindly received. Mrs. Hetheridge had been dead for some years, and Lætitia, the eldest of the family, was at the head of the household. She had two sisters, little more than girls. The father was a burly, yet gentlemanlike Yorkshire squire, who ate well, drank well, looked radiant, and hunted twice a week. In this pastime his son joined him when in the humour, which happened scarcely so often. I, who had never crossed a horse in my life, took his apology for not being able to mount me very coolly, assuring him that I would rather loiter about with a book than be in at the death of the best-hunted fox in Yorkshire.

"I very soon found myself at home with the Hetheridges; and very soon again I began to find myself not so much at home; for Miss Hetheridge-Lætitia as I soon ventured to call her—was fascinating. I have told you, Katey, that there was an empty place in my heart. Look to the door then, Katey. That was what made me so ready to fall in love with Lætitia. Her figure was graceful, and I think, even now, her face would have been beautiful but for a certain contraction of the skin over the nostrils, suggesting an invisible thumb and forefinger pinching them, which repelled me, although I did not then know what it indicated. I had not been with her one evening before the impression it made on me had vanished, and that so entirely that I could hardly recall the perception of the peculiarity which had occasioned it. Her observation was remarkably keen, and her judgment generally correct. She had great confidence in it herself; nor was she devoid of sympathy with some of the forms of human imagination, only they never seemed to possess for her any relation to practical life. That was to be ordered by the judgment alone. I do not mean she ever said so. I am only giving the conclusions I came to afterwards. It is not necessary that you should have any more thorough acquaintance with her mental character. One point in her moral nature, of special consequence to my narrative, will show itself by and by.

"I did all I could to make myself agreeable to her, and the more I succeeded the more delightful she became in my eyes. We walked in the garden and grounds together; we read, or rather I read and she listened;—read poetry, Katey—sometimes till we could not read any more for certain haziness and huskiness which look now, I am afraid, considerably more absurd than they really were, or even ought to look. In short, I considered myself thoroughly in love with her."

"And wasn't she in love with you, uncle?"

"Don't interrupt me, child. I don't know. I hoped so then. I hope the contrary now. She liked me I am sure. That is not much to say. Liking is very pleasant and very cheap. Love is as rare as a star."

"I thought the stars were anything but rare, uncle."

"That's because you never went out to find one for yourself, Katey. They would prove a few miles apart then."

"But it would be big enough when I did find it."

"Right, my dear. That is the way with love.—Lætitia was a good housekeeper. Everything was punctual as clockwork. I use the word advisedly. If her father, who was punctual to one date,—the dinner-hour,—made any remark to the contrary as he took up the carving-knife, Lætitia would instantly send one of her sisters to question the old clock in the hall, and report the time to half a minute. It was sure to be found that, if there was a mistake, the mistake was in the clock. But although it was certainly a virtue to have her household in such perfect order, it was not a virtue to be impatient with every infringement of its rules on the part of others. She was very severe, for instance, upon her two younger sisters if, the moment after the second bell had rung, they were not seated at the dinner-table, washed and aproned. Order was a very idol with her. Hence the house was too tidy for any sense of comfort. If you left an open book on the table, you would, on returning to the room a moment after, find it put aside. What the furniture of the drawing-room was like, I never saw; for not even on Christmas Day, which was the last day I spent there, was it uncovered. Everything in it was kept in bibs and pinafores. Even the carpet was covered with a cold and slippery sheet of brown holland. Mr. Hetheridge never entered that room, and therein was wise. James remonstrated once. She answered him quite kindly, even playfully, but no change followed. What was worse, she made very wretched tea. Her father never took tea; neither did James. I was rather fond of it, but I soon gave it up. Everything her father partook of was first-rate. Everything else was somewhat poverty-stricken. My pleasure in Lætitia's society prevented me from making practical deductions from such trifles."

"I shouldn't have thought you knew anything about eating, uncle," said Janet.

"The less a man eats, the more he likes to have it good, Janet. In short,—there can be no harm in saying it now,—Lætitia was so far from being like the name of her baptism,—and most names are so good that they are worth thinking about; no children are named after bad ideas,— Lætitia was so far unlike hers as to be stingy—an abominable fault. But, I repeat, the notion of such a fact was far from me then. And now for my story.

"The first of November was a very lovely day, quite one of the 'halcyon days' of 'St. Martin's summer.' I was sitting in a little arbour I had just discovered, with a book in my hand,—not reading, however, but daydreaming,—when, lifting my eyes from the ground, I was startled to see, through a thin shrub in front of the arbour, what seemed the form of an old lady seated, apparently reading from a book on her knee. The sight instantly recalled the old lady of Russell Square. I started to my feet, and then, clear of the intervening bush, saw only a great stone such as abounded on the moors in the neighbourhood, with a lump of quartz set on the top of it. Some childish taste had put it there for an ornament. Smiling at my own folly, I sat down again, and reopened my book. After reading for a while, I glanced up again, and once more started to my feet, overcome by the fancy that there verily sat the old lady reading. You will say it indicated an excited condition of the brain. Possibly; but I was, as far as I can recall, quite collected and reasonable. I was almost vexed this second time, and sat down once more to my book. Still, every time I looked up, I was startled afresh. I doubt, however, if the trifle is worth mentioning, or has any significance even in relation to what followed.

"After dinner I strolled out by myself, leaving father and son over their claret. I did not drink wine; and from the lawn I could see the windows of the library, whither Lætitia commonly retired from the dinner-table. It was a very lovely soft night. There was no moon, but the stars looked wider awake than usual. Dew was falling, but the grass was not yet wet, and I wandered about on it for half an hour. The stillness was somehow strange. It had a wonderful feeling in it as if something were expected—as if the quietness were the mould in which some event or other was about to be cast.

"Even then I was a reader of certain sorts of recondite lore. Suddenly I remembered that this was the eve of All Souls. This was the night on which the dead came out of their graves to visit their old homes. 'Poor dead!' I thought with myself; 'have you any place to call a home now? If you have, surely you will not wander back here, where all that you called home has either vanished or given itself to others, to be their home now and yours no more! What an awful doom the old fancy has allotted you! To dwell in your graves all the year, and creep out, this one night, to enter at the midnight door, left open for welcome! A poor welcome truly!—just an open door, a clean-swept floor, and a fire to warm your rain-sodden limbs! The household asleep, and the house-place swarming with the ghosts of ancient times,—the miser, the spend-thrift, the profligate, the coquette,—for the good ghosts sleep, and are troubled with no waking like yours! Not one man, sleepless like your-selves, to question you, and be answered after the fashion of the old nursery rhyme—

"'What makes your eyes so holed?'
'I've lain so long among the mould.'
'What makes your feet so broad?'
'I've walked more than ever I rode!'

"'Yet who can tell?' I went on to myself. 'It may be your hell to return thus. It may be that only on this one night of all the year you can show yourselves to him who can see you, but that the place where you were wicked is the Hades to which you are doomed for ages.' I thought and thought till I began to feel the air alive about me, and was enveloped in the vapours that dim the eyes of those who strain them for one peep through the dull mica windows that will not open on the world of ghosts. At length I cast my fancies away, and fled from them to the library, where the bodily presence of Lætitia made the world of ghosts appear shadowy indeed.

"'What a reality there is about a bodily presence!' I said to myself, as I took my chamber-candle in my hand. 'But what is there more real in a body?' I said again, as I crossed the hall. 'Surely nothing,' I went on, as I ascended the broad staircase to my room. 'The body must vanish. If there be a spirit, that will remain. A body can but vanish. A ghost can appear.'

"I woke in the morning with a sense of such discomfort as made me spring out of bed at once. My foot lighted upon my spectacles. How they came to be on the floor I could not tell, for I never took them off when I went to bed. When I lifted them I found they were in two pieces; the bridge was broken. This was awkward. I was so utterly helpless without them! Indeed, before I could lay my hand on my hair-brush I had to peer through one eye of the parted pair. When I looked at my watch after I was dressed, I found I had risen an hour earlier than usual. I groped my way downstairs to spend the hour before breakfast in the library.

"No sooner was I seated with a book than I heard the voice of Lætitia scolding the butler, in no very gentle tones, for leaving the garden door open all night. The moment I heard this, the strange occurrences I am about to relate began to dawn upon my memory. The door had been open the night long between All Saints and All Souls. In the middle of that night I awoke suddenly. I knew it was not the morning by the sensations I had, for the night feels altogether different from the morning. It was quite dark. My heart was beating violently, and I either hardly could or hardly dared breathe. A nameless terror was upon me, and my sense of hearing was, apparently by the force of its expectation, unnaturally roused and keen. There it was—a slight noise in the room!—slight, but clear, and with an unknown significance about it! It was awful to think it would come again. I do believe it was only one of those creaks in the timbers which announce the torpid, age-long, sinking flow of every house back to the dust—a motion to which the flow of the glacier is as a torrent, but which is no less inevitable and sure. Day and night it ceases not; but only in the night, when house and heart are still, do we hear it. No wonder it should sound fearful! for are we not the immortal dwellers in ever-crumbling clay? The clay is so near us, and yet not of us, that its every movement starts a fresh dismay. For what will its final ruin disclose? When it falls from about us, where shall we find that we have existed all the time?

"My skin tingled with the bursting of the moisture from its pores. Something was in the room beside me. A confused, indescribable sense of utter loneliness, and yet awful presence, was upon me, mingled with a dreary, hopeless desolation, as of burnt-out love and aimless life. All at once I found myself sitting up. The terror that a cold hand might be laid upon me, or a cold breath blow on me, or a corpse-like face bend down

through the darkness over me, had broken my bonds!—I would meet half-
way whatever might be approaching. The moment that my will burst into
action the terror began to ebb.

"The room in which I slept was a large one, perfectly dreary with
tidiness. I did not know till afterwards that it was Lætitia's room, which
she had given up to me rather than prepare another. The furniture, all
but one article, was modern and commonplace. I could not help remark-
ing to myself afterwards how utterly void the room was of the nameless
charm of feminine occupancy. I had seen nothing to wake a suspicion of
its being a lady's room. The article I have excepted was an ancient
bureau, elaborate and ornate, which stood on one side of the large bow
window. The very morning before, I had seen a bunch of keys hanging
from the upper part of it, and had peeped in. Finding however, that the
pigeon-holes were full of papers, I closed it at once. I should have been
glad to use it, but clearly it was not for me. At that bureau the figure of a
woman was now seated in the posture of one writing. A strange dim light
was around her, but whence it proceeded I never thought of inquiring.
As if I, too, had stepped over the bourne, and was a ghost myself, all fear
was now gone. I got out of bed, and softly crossed the room to where she
was seated. 'If she should be beautiful!' I thought—for I had often dreamed
of a beautiful ghost that made love to me. The figure did not move. She
was looking at a faded brown paper. 'Some old love-letter,' I thought,
and stepped nearer. So cool was I now, that I actually peeped over her
shoulder. With mingled surprise and dismay I found that the dim page
over which she bent was that of an old account-book. Ancient household
records, in rusty ink, held up to the glimpses of the waning moon, which
shone through the parting in the curtains, their entries of shillings and
pence!—Of pounds there was not one. No doubt pounds and farthings
are much the same in the world of thought—the true spirit-world; but in
the ghost-world this eagerness over shillings and pence must mean something awful! I To think that coins which had since been worn smooth in
other pockets and purses, which had gone back to the Mint, and been
melted down, to come out again and yet again with the heads of new kings
and queens,—that dinners, eaten by men and women and children whose
bodies had since been eaten by the worms,—that polish for the floors,
inches of whose thickness had since been worn away,—that the hundred
nameless trifles of a life utterly vanished, should be perplexing, annoying, and worst of all, interesting the soul of a ghost who had been in
Hades for centuries! The writing was very old-fashioned, and the words
were contracted. I could read nothing but the moneys and one single
entry—'Corinths, Vs.'

"Currants for a Christmas pudding, most likely!—Ah, poor lady!
the pudding and not the Christmas was her care; not the delight of the

children over it, but the beggarly pence which it cost. And she cannot get it out of her head, although her brain was 'powdered all as thin as flour' ages ago in the mortar of Death. 'Alas, poor ghost!' It needs no treasured hoard left behind, no floor stained with the blood of the murdered child, no wickedly hidden parchment of landed rights! An old account-book is enough for the hell of the house-keeping gentlewoman!

"She never lifted her face, or seemed to know that I stood behind her. I left her, and went into the bow window, where I could see her face. I was right. It was the same old lady I had met in Russell Square, walking in front of James Hetheridge. Her withered lips went moving as if they would have uttered words had the breath been commissioned thither; her brow was contracted over her thin nose; and once and again her shining forefinger went up to her temple as if she were pondering some deep problem of humanity. How long I stood gazing at her I do not know, but at last I withdrew to my bed, and left her struggling to solve that which she could never solve thus. It was the symbolic problem of her own life, and she had failed to read it. I remember nothing more. She may be sitting there still, solving at the insolvable.

"I should have felt no inclination, with the broad sun of the squire's face, the keen eyes of James, and the beauty of Lætitia before me at the breakfast table, to say a word about what I had seen, even if I had not been afraid of the doubt concerning my sanity which the story would certainly awaken. What with the memories of the night and the want of my spectacles, I passed a very dreary day, dreading the return of the night, for, cool as I had been in her presence, I could not regard the possible reappearance of the ghost with equanimity. But when the night did come, I slept soundly till the morning.

"The next day, not being able to read with comfort, I went wandering about the place, and at length began to fit the outside and inside of the house together. It was a large and rambling edifice, parts of it very old, parts comparatively modern. I first found my own window, which looked out of the back. Below this window, on one side, there was a door. I wondered whither it led, but found it locked. At the moment James approached from the stables. 'Where does this door lead?' I asked him. 'I will get the key,' he answered. 'It is rather a queer old place. We used to like it when we were children.' 'There's a stair, you see,' he said, as he threw the door open. 'It leads up over the kitchen.' I followed him up the stair. 'There's a door into your room,' he said, 'but it's always locked now.—And here's Grannie's room, as they call it, though why, I have not the least idea,' he added, as he pushed open the door of an old-fashioned parlour, smelling very musty. A few old books lay on a side table. A china bowl stood beside them, with some shrivelled, scentless rose-leaves in the bottom of it. The cloth that covered the table was riddled by moths, and the spider-legged chairs were covered with dust.

"A conviction seized me that the old bureau must have belonged to this room, and I soon found the place where I judged it must have stood. But the same moment I caught sight of a portrait on the wall above the spot I had fixed upon. 'By Jove!' I cried, involuntarily, 'that's the very old lady I met in Russell Square!'

"'Nonsense!' said James. 'Old-fashioned ladies are like babies—they all look the same. That's a very old portrait.'

"'So I see,' I answered. 'It is like a Zucchero.'

"'I don't know whose it is," he answered hurriedly, and I thought he looked a little queer.

"'Is she one of the family?' I asked.

"'They say so; but who or what she was, I don't know. You must ask Letty," he answered.

"'The more I look at it,' I said, 'the more I am convinced it is the same old lady.'

"'Well,' he returned with a laugh, 'my old nurse used to say she was rather restless. But it's all nonsense.'

"'That bureau in my room looks about the same date as this furniture,' I remarked.

"'It used to stand just there,' he answered, pointing to the space under the picture. 'Well I remember with what awe we used to regard it; for they said the old lady kept her accounts at it still. We never dared touch the bundles of yellow papers in the pigeon-holes. I remember thinking Letty a very heroine once when she touched one of them with the tip of her forefinger. She had got yet more courageous by the time she had it moved into her own room.'

"'Then that is your sister's room I am occupying?' I said.

"'Yes.'

"'I am ashamed of keeping her out of it.'

"'Oh! she'll do well enough.'

"'If I were she though,' I added, 'I would send that bureau back to its own place.'

"'What do you mean, Heywood? Do you believe every old wife's tale that ever was told?'

"'She may get a fright some day—that's all!' I replied.

"He smiled with such an evident mixture of pity and contempt that for the moment I almost disliked him; and feeling certain that Lætitia would receive any such hint in a somewhat similar manner, I did not feel inclined to offer her any advice with regard to the bureau.

"Little occurred during the rest of my visit worthy of remark. Somehow or other I did not make much progress with Lætitia. I believe I had

begun to see into her character a little, and therefore did not get deeper
in love as the days went on. I know I became less absorbed in her society,
although I was still anxious to make myself agreeable to her—or perhaps,
more properly, to give her a favourable impression of me. I do not know
whether she perceived any difference in my behaviour, but I remember
that I began again to remark the pinched look of her nose, and to be a
little annoyed with her for always putting aside my book. At the same
time, I daresay I was provoking, for I never was given to tidiness myself.

"At length Christmas Day arrived. After breakfast, the squire, James,
and the two girls arranged to walk to church. Lætitia was not in the room
at the moment. I excused myself on the ground of a headache, for I had
had a bad night. When they left, I went up to my room, threw myself on
the bed, and was soon fast asleep.

"How long I slept I do not know, but I woke again with that indescribable yet well-known sense of not being alone. The feeling was scarcely
less terrible in the daylight than it had been in the darkness. With the same
sudden effort as before, I sat up in the bed. There was the figure at the
open bureau, in precisely the same position as on the former occasion. But I
could not see it so distinctly. I rose as gently as I could, and approached it,
after the first physical terror. I am not a coward. Just as I got near enough
to see the account book open on the folding cover of the bureau, she started
up, and, turning, revealed the face of Lætitia. She blushed crimson.

"'I beg your pardon, Mr. Heywood,' she said in great confusion; 'I
thought you had gone to church with the rest.'

"'I had lain down with a headache, and gone to sleep,' I replied. 'But,—
forgive me, Miss Hetheridge,' I added, for my mind was full of the dreadful coincidence,—'don't you think you would have been better at church
than balancing your accounts on Christmas Day?'

"'The better day the better deed,' she said, with a somewhat offended
air, and turned to walk from the room.

"'Excuse me, Lætitia,' I resumed, very seriously, 'but I want to tell
you something.'

"She looked conscious. It never crossed me, that perhaps she fancied
I was going to make a confession. Far other things were then in my mind.
For I thought how awful it was, if she too, like the ancestral ghost, should
have to do an age-long penance of haunting that bureau and those horrid
figures, and I had suddenly resolved to tell her the whole story. She
listened with varying complexion and face half turned aside. When I had
ended, which I fear I did with something of a personal appeal, she lifted
her head and looked me in the face, with just a slight curl on her thin lip,
and answered me. 'If I had wanted a sermon, Mr. Heywood, I should have
gone to church for it. As for the ghost, I am sorry for you.' So saying she
walked out of the room.

"The rest of the day I did not find very merry. I pleaded my headache as an excuse for going to bed early. How I hated the room now! Next morning, immediately after breakfast, I took my leave of Lewton Grange."

"And lost a good wife, perhaps, for the sake of a ghost, uncle!" said Janet.

"If I lost a wife at all, it was a stingy one. I should have been ashamed of her all my life long."

"Better than a spendthrift," said Janet.

"How do you know that?" returned her uncle. "All the difference I see is, that the extravagant ruins the rich, and the stingy robs the poor."

"But perhaps she repented, uncle," said Kate.

"I don't think she did, Katey. Look here."

Uncle Cornelius drew from the breast pocket of his coat a black-edged letter.

"I have kept up my friendship with her brother," he said. "All he knows about the matter is, that either we had a quarrel, or she refused me;—he is not sure which. I must say for Lætitia, that she was no tattler. Well, here's a letter I had from James this very morning. I will read it to you.

"'My Dear Mr. Heywood,—We have had a terrible shock this morning. Letty did not come down to breakfast, and Lizzie went to see if she was ill. We heard her scream, and, rushing up, there was poor Letty, sitting at the old bureau, quite dead. She had fallen forward on the desk, and her housekeeping-book was crumpled up under her. She had been so all night long, we suppose, for she was not undressed, and was quite cold. The doctors say it was disease of the heart.'

"There!" said Uncle Cornie, folding up the letter.

"Do you think the ghost had anything to do with it, uncle?" asked Kate, almost under her breath.

"How should I know, my dear? Possibly."

"It's very sad," said Janet; "but I don't see the good of it all. If the ghost had come to tell that she had hidden away money in some secret place in the old bureau, one would see why she had been permitted to come back. But what was the good of those accounts after they were over and done with? I don't believe in the ghost."

"Ah, Janet, Janet! but those wretched accounts were not over and done with, you see. That is the misery of it."

Uncle Cornelius rose without another word, bade them good-night, and walked out into the wind.

By those who consider a balanced repose the end of culture, the imagination must necessarily be regarded as the one faculty before all others to be suppressed. "Are there not facts?" say they. "Why forsake them for fancies? Is there not that which, may be *known*? Why forsake it for inventions? What God hath made, into that let man inquire."

We answer: To inquire into what God has made is the main function of the imagination. It is aroused by facts, is nourished by facts; seeks for higher and yet higher laws in those facts; but refuses to regard science as the sole interpreter of nature, or the laws of science as the only region of discovery.

—George MacDonald, "The Imagination: Its Functions and Its Culture."

THE CRUEL PAINTER

George MacDonald

Among the young men assembled at the University of Prague, in the year 159-, was one called Karl von Wolkenlicht. A somewhat careless student, he yet held a fair position in the estimation of both professors and men, because he could hardly look at a proposition without understanding it. Where such proposition, however, had to do with anything relating to the deeper insights of the nature, he was quite content that, for him, it should remain a proposition; which, however, he laid up in one of his mental cabinets, and was ready to reproduce at a moment's notice. This mental agility was more than matched by the corresponding corporeal excellence, and both aided in producing results in which his remarkable strength was equally apparent. In all games depending upon the combination of muscle and skill, he had scarce rivalry enough to keep him in practice. His strength, however, was embodied in such a softness of muscular outline, such a rare Greek-like style of beauty, and associated with such a gentleness of manner and behaviour, that, partly from the truth of the resemblance, partly from the absurdity of the contrast, he was known throughout the university by the diminutive of the feminine form of his name, and was always called Lottchen.

"I say, Lottchen," said one of his fellow-students, called Richter, across the table in a wine-cellar they were in the habit of frequenting, "do you know, Heinrich Höllenrachen here says that he saw this morning, with mortal eyes, whom do you think?—Lilith."

"Adam's first wife?" asked Lottchen, with an attempt at carelessness, while his face flushed like a maiden's.

"None of your chaff!" said Richter. "Your face is honester than your tongue, and confesses what you cannot deny, that you would give your chance of salvation—a small one to be sure, but all you've got—for one peep at Lilith. Wouldn't you now, Lottchen?"

99

"Go to the devil!" was all Lottchen's answer to his tormentor; but he turned to Heinrich, to whom the students had given the surname above mentioned, because of the enormous width of his jaws, and said with eagerness and envy, disguising them as well as he could, under the appearance of curiosity—

"You don't mean it, Heinrich? You've been taking the beggar in! Confess now."

"Not I. I saw her with my two eyes."

"Notwithstanding the different planes of their orbits," suggested Richter.

"Yes, notwithstanding the fact that I can get a parallax to any of the fixed stars in a moment, with only the breadth of my nose for the base," answered Heinrich, responding at once to the fun, and careless of the personal defect insinuated. "She was near enough for even me to see her perfectly."

"When? Where? How?" asked Lottchen.

"Two hours ago. In the churchyard of St. Stephen's. By a lucky chance. Any more little questions, my child?" answered Höllenrachen.

"What could have taken her there, who is seen nowhere?" said Richter.

"She was seated on a grave. After she left, I went to the place; but it was a new-made grave. There was no stone up. I asked the sexton about her. He said he supposed she was the daughter of the woman buried there last Thursday week. I knew it was Lilith."

"Her mother dead!" said Lottchen, musingly. Then he thought with himself—"She will be going there again, then!" But he took care that this ghost-thought should wander unembodied. "But how did you know her, Heinrich? You never saw her before."

"How do you come to be over head and ears in love with her, Lottchen, and you haven't seen her at all?" interposed Richter.

"Will you or will you not go to the devil?" rejoined Lottchen, with a comic crescendo; to which the other replied with a laugh.

"No one could miss knowing her," said Heinrich.

"Is she so very like, then?"

"It is always herself, her very self."

A fresh flask of wine, turning out to be not up to the mark, brought the current of conversation against itself; not much to the dissatisfaction of Lottchen, who had already resolved to be in the churchyard of St. Stephen's at sun-down the following day, in the hope that he too might be favoured with a vision of Lilith.

This resolution he carried out. Seated in a porch of the church, not knowing in what direction to look for the apparition he hoped to see, and desirous as well of not seeming to be on the watch for one, he was gazing at the fallen rose-leaves of the sunset, withering away upon the sky; when, glancing aside by an involuntary movement, he saw a woman seated upon a new-made grave, not many yards from where he sat, with her face buried in her hands, and apparently weeping bitterly. Karl was in the shadow of the porch, and could see her perfectly, without much danger of being discovered by her; so he sat and watched her. She raised her head for a moment, and the rose-flush of the west fell over it, shining on the tears with which it was wet, and giving the whole a bloom which did not belong to it, for it was always pale, and now pale as death. It was indeed the face of Lilith, the most celebrated beauty of Prague.

Again she buried her face in her hands; and Karl sat with a strange feeling of helplessness, which grew as he sat; and the longing to help her whom he could not help, drew his heart towards her with a trembling reverence which was quite new to him. She wept on. The western roses withered slowly away, and the clouds blended with the sky, and the stars gathered like drops of glory sinking through the vault of night, and the trees about the churchyard grew black, and Lilith almost vanished in the wide darkness. At length she lifted her head, and seeing the night around her, gave a little broken cry of dismay. The minutes had swept over her head, not through her mind, and she did not know that the dark had come.

Hearing her cry, Karl rose and approached her. She heard his foot-steps, and started to her feet. Karl spoke—

"Do not be frightened," he said. "Let me see you home. I will walk behind you."

"Who are you?" she rejoined.

"Karl Wolkenlicht."

"I have heard of you. Thank you. I can go home alone."

Yet, as if in a half-dreamy, half-unconscious mood, she accepted his offered hand to lead her through the graves, and allowed him to walk beside her, till, reaching the corner of a narrow street, she suddenly bade him good-night and vanished. He thought it better not to follow her, so he returned her good-night and went home.

How to see her again was his first thought the next day; as, in fact, how to see her at all had been his first thought for many days. She went nowhere that ever he heard of; she knew nobody that he knew; she was never seen at church, or at market; never seen in the street. Her home had a dreary, desolate aspect. It looked as if no one ever went out or in. It was like a place on which decay had fallen because there was no in-dwelling spirit. The mud of years was baked upon its door, and no faces looked out of its dusty windows.

How then could she be the most celebrated beauty of Prague? How then was it that Heinrich Höllenrachen knew her the moment he saw her? Above all, how was it that Karl Wolkenlicht had, in fact, fallen in love with her before ever he saw her? It was thus—

Her father was a painter. Belonging thus to the public, it had taken the liberty of re-naming him. Every one called him Teufelsbürst, or Devilsbrush. It was a name with which, to judge from the nature of his representations, he could hardly fail to be pleased. For, not as a nightmare dream, which may alternate with the loveliest visions, but as his ordinary everyday work, he delighted to represent human suffering.

Not an aspect of human woe or torture, as expressed in countenance or limb, came before his willing imagination, but he bore it straightway to his easel. In the moments that precede sleep, when the black space before the eyes of the poet teems with lovely faces, or dawns into a spirit-landscape, face after face of suffering, in all varieties of expression, would crowd, as if compelled by the accompanying fiends, to present themselves, in awful levée, before the inner eye of the expectant master. Then he would rise, light his lamp, and, with rapid hand, make notes of his visions; recording, with swift successive sweeps of his pencil, every individual face which had rejoiced his evil fancy. Then he would return to his couch, and, well satisfied, fall asleep to dream yet further embodiments of human ill.

What wrong could man or mankind have done him, to be thus fearfully pursued by the vengeance of the artist's hate?

Another characteristic of the faces and form which he drew was, that they were all beautiful in the original idea. The lines of each face, however distorted by pain, would have been, in rest, absolutely beautiful; and the whole of the execution bore witness to the fact that upon this original beauty the painter had directed the artillery of anguish to bring down the sky-soaring heights of its divinity to the level of a hated existence. To do this, he worked in perfect accordance with artistic law, falsifying no line of the original forms. It was the suffering, rather than his pencil, that wrought the change. The latter was the willing instrument to record what the imagination conceived with a cruelty composed enough to be correct.

To enhance the beauty he had thus distorted, and so to enhance yet further the suffering that produced the distortion, he would often represent attendant demons, whom he made as ugly as his imagination could compass; avoiding, however, all grotesqueness beyond what was sufficient to indicate that they were demons, and not men. Their ugliness rose from hate, envy, and all evil passions; amongst which he especially delighted to represent a gloating exultation over human distress. And often in the midst of his clouds of demon faces, would some one who knew him recognise the painter's own likeness, such as the mirror might have presented it to him when he was busiest over the incarnation of some exquisite torture.

But apparently with the wish to avoid being supposed to choose such representations for their own sakes, he always found a story, often in the histories of the church, whose name he gave to the painting, and which he pretended to have inspired the pictorial conception. No one, however, who looked upon his suffering martyrs, could suppose for a moment that he honoured their martyrdom. They were but the vehicles for his hate of humanity. He was the torturer, and not Diocletian or Nero.

But, stranger yet to tell, there was no picture, whatever its subject, into which he did not introduce one form of placid and harmonious loveliness. In this, however, his fierceness was only more fully displayed. For in no case did this form manifest any relation either to the actors or the endurers in the picture. Hence its very loveliness became almost hateful to those who beheld it. Not a shade crossed the still sky of that brow, not a ripple disturbed the still sea of that cheek. She did not hate, she did not love the sufferers: the painter would not have her hate, for that would be to the injury of her loveliness: would not have her love, for he hated. Sometimes she floated above, as a still, unobservant angel, her gaze turned upward, dreaming along, careless as a white summer cloud, across the blue. If she looked down on the scene below, it was only that the beholder might see that she saw and did not care—that not a feather of her out-spread pinions would quiver at the sight. Sometimes she would stand in the crowd, as if she had been copied there from another picture, and had nothing to do with this one, nor any right to be in it at all. Or when the red blood was trickling drop by drop from the crushed limb, she might be seen standing nearest, smiling over a primrose or the bloom on a peach. Some had said that she was the painter's wife; that she had been false to him; that he had killed her; and, finding that that was no sufficing revenge, thus half in love, and half in deepest hate, immortalised his vengeance. But it was now universally understood that it was his daughter, of whose loveliness extravagant reports went abroad; though all said, doubtless reading this from her father's pictures, that she was a beauty without a heart. Strange theories of something else supplying its place were rife among the anatomical students. With the girl in the pictures, the wild imagination of Lottchen, probably in part from her apparently absolute unattainableness and her undisputed heartlessness, had fallen in love, as far as the mere imagination can fall in love.

But again, how was he to see her? He haunted the house night after night. Those blue eyes never met his. No step responsive to his came from that door. It seemed to have been so long unopened that it had grown as fixed and hard as the stones that held its bolts in their passive clasp. He dared not watch in the daytime, and with all his watching at night, he never saw father or daughter or domestic cross the threshold. Little he thought that, from a shot-window near the door, a pair of blue eyes, like

Lilith's, but paler and colder, were watching him just as a spider watches the fly that is likely ere long to fall into his toils. And into those toils Karl soon fell. For her form darkened the page; her form stood on the threshold of sleep; and when, overcome with watching, he did enter its precincts, her form entered with him, and walked by his side. He must find her; or the world might go to the bottomless pit for him. But how?

Yes. He would be a painter. Teufelsbürst would receive him as a humble apprentice. He would grind his colours, and Teufelsbürst would teach him the mysteries of the science which is the handmaiden of art. Then he might see her, and that was all his ambition.

In the clear morning light of a day in autumn, when the leaves were beginning to fall seared from the hand of that Death which has his dance in the chapels of nature as well as in the cathedral aisles of men—he walked up and knocked at the dingy door. The spider painter opened it himself. He was a little man, meagre and pallid, with those faded blue eyes, a low nose in three distinct divisions, and thin, curveless, cruel lips. He wore no hair on his face; but long grey locks, long as a woman's, were scattered over his shoulders, and hung down on his breast. When Wolkenlicht had explained his errand, he smiled a smile in which hypocrisy could not hide the cunning, and, after many difficulties, consented to receive him as a pupil, on condition that he would become an inmate of his house. Wolkenlicht's heart bounded with delight, which he tried to hide: the second smile of Teufelsbürst might have shown him that he had ill succeeded. The fact that he was not a native of Prague, but coming from a distant part of the country, was entirely his own master in the city, rendered this condition perfectly easy to fulfil; and that very afternoon he entered the studio of Teufelsbürst as his scholar and servant.

It was a great room, filled with the appliances and results of art. Many pictures, festooned with cobwebs, were hung carelessly on the dirty walls. Others, half finished, leaned against them, on the floor. Several, in different stages of progress, stood upon easels. But all spoke the cruel bent of the artist's genius. In one corner a lay figure was extended on a couch, covered with a pall of black velvet. Through its folds, the form beneath was easily discernible; and one hand and forearm protruded from beneath it, at right angles to the rest of the frame. Lottchen could not help shuddering when he saw it. Although he overcame the feeling in a moment, he felt a great repugnance to seating himself with his back towards it, as the arrangement of an easel, at which Teufelsbürst wished him to draw, rendered necessary. He contrived to edge himself round, so that when he lifted his eyes he should see the figure, and be sure that it could not rise without his being aware of it. But his master saw and understood his altered position; and under some pretence about the light, compelled him to resume the position in which he had placed him at first;

after which he sat watching, over the top of his picture, the expression of his countenance as he tried to draw; reading in it the horrid fancy that the figure under the pall had risen, and was stealthily approaching to look over his shoulder. But Lottchen resisted the feeling, and, being already no contemptible draughtsman, was soon interested enough to forget it. And then, any moment she might enter.

Now began a system of slow torture, for the chance of which the painter had been long on the watch— especially since he had first seen Karl lingering about the house. His opportunities of seeing physical suffering were nearly enough even for the diseased necessities of his art; but now he had one in his power, on whom, his own will fettering him, he could try any experiments he pleased for the production of a kind of suffering, in the observation of which he did not consider that he had yet sufficient experience. He would hold the very heart of the youth in his hand, and wring it and torture it to his own content. And lest Karl should be strong enough to prevent those expressions of pain for which he lay on the watch, he would make use of further means, known to himself, and known to few besides.

All that day Karl saw nothing of Lilith; but he heard her voice once— and that was enough for one day. The next, she was sitting to her father the greater part of the day, and he could see her as often as he dared glance up from his drawing. She had looked at him when she entered, but had shown no sign of recognition; and all day long she took no further notice of him. He hoped, at first, that this came of the intelligence of love; but he soon began to doubt it. For he saw that, with the holy shadow of sorrow, all that distinguished the expression of her countenance from that which the painter so constantly reproduced, had vanished likewise. It was the very face of the unheeding angel whom, as often as he lifted his eyes higher than hers, he saw on the wall above her, playing on a psaltery in the smoke of the torment ascending for ever from burning Babylon.— The power of the painter had not merely wrought for the representation of the woman of his imagination; it had had scope as well in realising her.

Karl soon began to see that communication, other than of the eyes, was all but hopeless; and to any attempt in that way she seemed altogether indisposed to respond. Nor if she had wished it, would it have been safe; for as often as he glanced towards her, instead of hers, he met the blue eyes of the painter gleaming upon him like winter lightning. His tones, his gestures, his words, seemed kind: his glance and his smile refused to be disguised.

The first day he dined alone in the studio, waited upon by an old woman; the next he was admitted to the family table, with Teufelsbürst and Lilith. The room offered a strange contrast to the study. As far as handicraft, directed by a sumptuous taste, could construct a house-paradise, this was one. But it seemed rather a paradise of demons; for the walls were covered with Teufelsbürst's paintings. During the dinner, Lilith's gaze scarcely met that of Wolkenlicht; and once or twice, when their eyes did meet, her glance was so perfectly unconcerned, that Karl wished he might look at her for ever without the fear of her looking at him again. She seemed like one whose love had rushed out glowing with seraphic fire, to be frozen to death in a more than wintry cold: she now walked lonely without her love. In the evenings, he was expected to continue his drawing by lamplight; and at night he was conducted by Teufelsbürst to his chamber. Not once did he allow him to proceed thither alone, and not once did he leave him there without locking and bolting the door on the outside. But he felt nothing except the coldness of Lilith.

Day after day she sat to her father, in every variety of costume that could best show the variety of her beauty. How much greater that beauty might be, if it ever blossomed into a beauty of soul, Wolkenlicht never imagined; for he soon loved her enough to attribute to her all the possibilities of her face as actual possessions of her being. To account for everything that seemed to contradict this perfection, his brain was prolific in inventions; till he was compelled at last to see that she was in the condition of a rose-bud, which, on the point of blossoming, had been chilled into a changeless bud by the cold of an untimely frost. For one day, after the father and daughter had become a little more accustomed to his silent presence, a conversation began between them, which went on until he saw that Teufelsbürst believed in nothing except his art. How much of his feeling for that could be dignified by the name of belief, seeing its objects were such as they were, might have been questioned. It seemed to Wolkenlicht to amount only to this: that, amidst a thousand distastes, it was a pleasant thing to reproduce on the canvas the forms he beheld around him, modifying them to express the prevailing feelings of his own mind.

A more desolate communication between souls than that which then passed between father and daughter could hardly be imagined. The father spoke of humanity and all its experiences in a tone of the bitterest scorn. He despised men, and himself amongst them; and rejoiced to think that the generations rose and vanished, brood after brood, as the crops of corn grew and disappeared. Lilith, who listened to it all unmoved, taking only an intellectual interest in the question, remarked that even the corn had more life than that; for, after its death, it rose again in the new crop. Whether she meant that the corn was therefore superior to man, forgetting that the superior can produce being without losing its own, or only advanced an objection to her father's argument, Wolkenlicht could not tell. But Teufelsbürst laughed like the sound of a saw, and said:

"Follow out the analogy, my Lilith, and you will see that man is like the corn that springs again after it is buried; but unfortunately the only result we know of is a vampire."

Wolkenlicht looked up, and saw a shudder pass through the frame, and over the pale thin face of the painter. This he could not account for. But Teufelsbürst could have explained it, for there were strange whispers abroad, and they had reached his ear; and his philosophy was not quite enough for them. But the laugh with which Lilith met this frightful attempt at wit, grated dreadfully on Wolkenlicht's feeling. With her, too, however, a reaction seemed to follow. For, turning round a moment after, and looking at the picture on which her father was working, the tears rose in her eyes, and she said: "Oh! father, how like my mother you have made me this time!" "Child!" retorted the painter with a cold fierceness, "you have no mother. That which is gone out is gone out. Put no name in my hearing on that which is not. Where no substance is, how can there be a name?"

Lilith rose and left the room. Wolkenlicht now understood that Lilith was a frozen bud, and could not blossom into a rose. But pure love lives by faith. It loves the vaguely beheld and unrealised ideal. It dares believe that the loved is not all that she ever seemed. It is in virtue of this that love loves on. And it was in virtue of this, that Wolkenlicht loved Lilith yet more after he discovered what a grave of misery her unbelief was digging for her within her own soul. For her sake he would bear anything—bear even with calmness the torments of his own love; he would stay on, hoping and hoping.—The text, that we know not what a day may bring forth, is just as true of good things as of evil things; and out of Time's womb the facts must come.

But with the birth of this resolution to endure, his suffering abated; his face grew more calm; his love, no less earnest, was less imperious; and he did not look up so often from his work when Lilith was present. The master could see that his pupil was more at ease, and that he was making rapid progress in his art. This did not suit his designs, and he would betake himself to his further schemes.

For this purpose he proceeded first to simulate a friendship for Wolkenlicht, the manifestations of which he gradually increased, until, after a day or two, he asked him to drink wine with him in the evening. Karl readily agreed. The painter produced some of his best; but took care not to allow Lilith to taste it; for he had cunningly prepared and mingled with it a decoction of certain herbs and other ingredients, exercising specific actions upon the brain, and tending to the inordinate excitement of those portions of it which are principally under the rule of the imagination. By the reaction of the brain during the operation of these stimulants, the imagination is filled with suggestions and images. The nature of these is determined by the prevailing mood of the time. They are such as the imagination would produce of itself, but increased in number and intensity. Teufelsbürst, without philosophising about it, called his preparation simply a love-philtre, a concoction well known by name, but the composition of which was the secret of only a few. Wolkenlicht had, of course, not the least suspicion of the treatment to which he was subjected.

Teufelsbürst was, however, doomed to fresh disappointment. Not that his potion failed in the anticipated effect, for now Karl's real sufferings began; but that such was the strength of Karl's will, and his fear of doing anything that might give a pretext for banishing him from the presence of Lilith, that he was able to conceal his feelings far too successfully for the satisfaction of Teufelsbürst's art. Yet he had to fetter himself with all the restraints that self-exhortation could load him with, to refrain from falling at the feet of Lilith and kissing the hem of her garment. For that, as the lowliest part of all that surrounded her, itself kissing the earth, seemed to come nearest within the reach of his ambition, and therefore to draw him the most.

No doubt the painter had experience and penetration enough to perceive that he was suffering intensely; but he wanted to see the suffering embodied in outward signs, bringing it within the region over which his pencil held sway. He kept on, therefore, trying one thing after another, and rousing the poor youth to agony; till to his other sufferings were added, at length, those of failing health; a fact which notified itself evidently enough even for Teufelsbürst, though its signs were not of the sort he chiefly desired. But Karl endured all bravely.

Meantime, for various reasons, he scarcely ever left the house.

I must now interrupt the course of my story to introduce another element.

A few years before the period of my tale, a certain shoemaker of the city had died under circumstances more than suggestive of suicide. He was buried, however, with such precautions, that six weeks elapsed before the rumour of the facts broke out; upon which rumour, not before, the most fearful reports began to be circulated, supported by what seemed to the people of Prague incontestable evidence.—A spectrum of the deceased appeared to multitudes of persons, playing horrible pranks, and occasioning indescribable consternation throughout the whole town. This went on till at last, about eight months after his burial, the magistrates caused his body to be dug up; when it was found in just the condition of the bodies of those who in the eastern countries of Europe are called vampires. They buried the corpse under the gallows; but neither the digging up nor the reburying were of avail to banish the spectre. Again the spade and pick-axe were set to work, and the dead man being found considerably improved in condition since his last interment, was, with various horrible indignities, burnt to ashes, "after which the spectrum was never seen more."

And a second epidemic of the same nature had broken out a little before the period to which I have brought my story.

About midnight, after a calm frosty day, for it was now winter, a terrible storm of wind and snow came on. The tempest howled frightfully about the house of the painter, and Wolkenlicht found some solace in listening to the uproar, for his troubled thoughts would not allow him to sleep. It raged on all the next three days, till about noon on the fourth day, when it suddenly fell, and all was calm. The following night, Wolkenlicht, lying awake, heard unaccountable noises in the next house, as of things thrown about, of kicking and fighting horses, and of opening and shutting gates. Flinging wide his lattice and looking out, the noise of howling dogs came to him from every quarter of the town. The moon was bright and the air was still. In a little while he heard the sounds of a horse going at full gallop round the house, so that it shook as if it would fall; and flashes of light shone into his room. How much of this may have been owing to the effect of the drugs on poor Lottchen's brain, I leave my readers to determine. But when the family met at breakfast in the morning, Teufelsbürst, who had been already out of doors, reported that he had found the marks of strange feet in the snow, all about the house and through the garden at the back; stating, as his belief, that the tracks must be continued over the roofs, for there was no passage otherwise. There was a wicked gleam in his eye as he spoke; and Lilith believed that he was only trying an experiment on Karl's nerves. He persisted that he had never seen any footprints of the sort before. Karl informed him of his experiences during the night; upon which Teufelsbürst looked a little graver still, and proceeded to tell them that the storm, whose snow was still covering the ground, had arisen the very moment that their next door neighbour died, and had ceased as suddenly the moment he was buried, though it had raved furiously all the time of the funeral, so that "it made men's bodies quake and their teeth chatter in their heads." Karl had heard that the man, whose name was John Kuntz, was dead and buried. He knew that he had been a very wealthy, and therefore most respectable, alderman of the town; that he had been very fond of horses; and that he had died in consequence of a kick received from one of his own, as he was looking at his hoof. But he had not heard that, just before he died, a black cat "opened the casement with her nails, ran to his bed, and violently scratched his face and the bolster, as if she endeavoured by force to remove him out of the place where he lay. But the cat afterwards was suddenly gone, and she was no sooner gone, but he breathed his last."

So said Teufelsbürst, as the reporter of the town talk. Lilith looked very pale and terrified; and it was perhaps owing to this that the painter brought no more tales home with him. There were plenty to bring, but he heard them all and said nothing. The fact was that the philosopher himself could not resist the infection of the fear that was literally raging in the city; and perhaps the reports that he himself had sold himself to the devil had sufficient response from his own evil conscience to add to the influence of the epidemic upon him. The whole place was infested with the presence of the dead Kuntz, till scarce a man or woman would dare to be alone. He strangled old men; insulted women; squeezed children to death; knocked out the brains of dogs against the ground; pulled up posts; turned milk into blood; nearly killed a worthy clergyman by breathing upon him the intolerable airs of the grave, cold and malignant and noisome; and, in short, filled the city with a perfect madness of fear, so that every report was believed without the smallest doubt or investigation.

Though Teufelsbürst brought home no more of the town talk, the old servant was a faithful purveyor, and frequented the news-mart assiduously. Indeed she had some nightmare experiences of her own that she was proud to add to the stock of horrors which the city enjoyed with such a hearty community of goods. For those regions were not far removed from the birthplace and home of the vampire. The belief in vampires is the quintessential concentration and embodiment of all the passion of fear in Hungary and the adjacent regions. Nor, of all the other inventions of the human imagination, has there ever been one so perfect in crawling terror as this. Lilith and Karl were quite familiar with the popular ideas on the subject. It did not require to be explained to them, that a vampire was a body retaining a kind of animal life after the soul had departed. If any relation existed between it and the vanished ghost, it was only sufficient to make it restless in its grave. Possessed of vitality enough to keep it uncorrupted and pliant, its only instinct was a blind hunger for the sole food which could keep its awful life persistent—living human blood. Hence it, or, if not it, a sort of semi-material exhalation or essence of it, retaining its form and material relations, crept from its tomb, and went roaming about till it found some one asleep, towards whom it had an attraction, founded on old affection. It sucked the blood of this unhappy being, transferring so much of its life to itself as a vampire could assimilate. Death was the certain consequence. If suspicion conjectured aright, and they opened the proper grave, the body of the vampire would be found perfectly fresh and plump, sometimes indeed of rather florid complexion;—with grown hair, eyes half open, and the stains of recent blood about its greedy, leech-like lips. Nothing remained but to consume the corpse to ashes, upon which the vampire would show itself no more. But what added infinitely to the horror was the certainty that whoever died from the mouth of the vampire, wrinkled grandsire or delicate maiden, must in turn rise from the grave, and go forth a vampire, to suck the blood of the dearest left behind. This was the generation of the vampire brood. Lilith trembled at the very name of the creature. Karl was too much in love to be afraid of anything. Yet the evident fear of the unbelieving painter took a hold of his imagination; and, under the influence of the potions of which he still partook unwittingly, when he was not thinking about Lilith, he was thinking about the vampire.

Meantime, the condition of things in the painter's household continued much the same for Wolkenlicht— work all day; no communication between the young people; the dinner and the wine; silent reading when work was done, with stolen glances many over the top of the book, glances that were never returned; the cold good-night; the locking of the door; the wakeful night and the drowsy morning. But at length a change came, and sooner than any of the party had expected. For, whether it was that the impatience of Teufelsbürst had urged him to yet more dangerous experiments, or that the continuance of those he had been so long employing had overcome at length the vitality of Wolkenlicht—one afternoon, as he was sitting at his work, he suddenly dropped from his chair, and his master hurrying to him in some alarm, found him rigid and apparently lifeless. Lilith was not in the study when this took place. In justice to Teufelsbürst, it must be confessed that he employed all the skill he was master of, which for beneficent purposes was not very great, to restore the youth; but without avail. At last, hearing the footsteps of Lilith, he desisted in some consternation; and that she might escape being shocked by the sight of a dead body where she had been accustomed to see a living one, he removed the lay figure from the couch, and laid Karl in its place, covering him with a black velvet pall. He was just in time. She started at seeing no one in Karl's place and said—

"Where is your pupil, father?"

"Gone home," he answered, with a kind of convulsive grin.

She glanced round the room, caught sight of the lay figure where it had not been before, looked at the couch, and saw the pall yet heaved up from beneath, opened her eyes till the entire white sweep around the iris suggested a new expression of consternation to Teufelsbürst, though from a quarter whence he did not desire or look for it; and then, without a word, sat down to a drawing she had been busy upon the day before. But her father, glancing at her now, as Wolkenlicht had used to do, could not help seeing that she was frightfully pale. She showed no other sign of uneasiness. As soon as he released her, she withdrew, with one more glance, as she passed, at the couch and the figure blocked out in black upon it. She hastened to her chamber, shut and locked the door, sat down on the side of the couch, and fell, not a-weeping, but a-thinking. Was he dead? What did it matter? They would all be dead soon. Her mother was dead already. It was only that the earth could not bear more children, except she devoured those to whom she had already given birth. But what if they had to come back in another form, and live another sad, hopeless, loveless life over again?—And so she went on questioning, and receiving no replies; while through all her thoughts passed and repassed the eyes of Wolkenlicht, which she had often felt to be upon her when she did not see them, wild with repressed longing, the light of their love shining through the veil of diffused tears, ever gathering and never overflowing. Then came the pale face, so worshipping, so distant in its self-withdrawn devotion, slowly dawning out of the vapours of her reverie. When it vanished, she tried to see it again. It would not come when she called it; but when her thoughts left knocking at the door of the lost, and wandered away, out came the pale, troubled, silent face again, gathering itself up from some unknown nook in her world of phantasy, and once more, when she tried to steady it by the fixedness of her own regard, fading back into the mist. So the phantasm of the dead drew near and wooed, as the living had never dared.—What if there were any good in loving? What if men and women did not die all out, but some dim shade of each, like that pale, mind-ghost of Wolkenlicht, floated through the eternal vapours of chaos? And what if they might sometimes cross each other's path, meet, know that they met, love on? Would not that revive the withered memory, fix the fleeting ghost, give a new habitation, a body even, to the poor, unhoused wanderers, frozen by the eternal frosts, no longer thinking beings, but thoughts wandering through the brain of the "Melancholy Mass?" Back with the thought came the face of the dead Karl, and the maiden threw herself on her bed in a flood of bitter tears. She could have loved him if he had only lived: she did love him, for he was dead. But even in the midst of the remorse that followed—for had she not killed him?—life seemed a less hard and hopeless thing than before. For it is love itself and not its responses or results that is the soul of life and its pleasures.

Two hours passed ere she could again show herself to her father, from whom she seemed in some new way divided by the new feeling in which he did not, and could not share. But at last, lest he should seek her, and finding her, should suspect her thoughts, she descended and sought him.— For there is a maidenliness in sorrow, that wraps her garments close around her.—But he was not to be seen; the door of the study was locked. A shudder passed through her as she thought of what her father, who lost no opportunity of furthering his all but perfect acquaintance with the human form and structure, might be about with the figure which she knew lay dead beneath that velvet pall, but which had arisen to haunt the hollow caves and cells of her living brain. She rushed away, and up once more to her silent room, through the darkness which had now settled down in the house; threw herself again on her bed, and lay almost paralysed with horror and distress.

But Teufelsbürst was not about anything so frightful as she supposed, though something frightful enough. I have already implied that Wolkenlicht was, in form, as fine an embodiment of youthful manhood as any old Greek republic could have provided one of its sculptors with as model for an Apollo. It is true, that to the eye of a Greek artist he would not have been more acceptable in consequence of the regimen he had been going through for the last few weeks; but the emaciation of Wolkenlicht's frame, and the consequent prominence of the muscles, indicating the pain he had gone through, were peculiarly attractive to Teufelsbürst.—He was busy preparing to take a cast of the body of his dead pupil, that it might aid to the perfection of his future labours.

He was deep in the artistic enjoyment of a form, at the same time so beautiful and strong, yet with the lines of suffering in every limb and feature, when his daughter's hand was laid on the latch. He started, flung the velvet drapery over the body, and went to the door. But Lilith had vanished. He returned to his labours. The operation took a long time, for he performed it very carefully. Towards midnight, he had finished encasing the body in a close-clinging shell of plaster, which, when broken off, and fitted together, would be the matrix to the form of the dead Wolkenlicht. Before leaving it to harden till the morning, he was just proceeding to strengthen it with an additional layer all over, when a flash of lightning, reflected in all its dazzle from the snow without, almost blinded him. A peal of long-drawn thunder followed; the wind rose; and just such a storm came on as had risen some time before at the death of Kuntz, whose spectre was still tormenting the city. The gnomes of terror, deep hidden in the caverns of Teufelsbürst's nature, broke out jubilant. With trembling hands he tried to cast the pall over the awful white chrysalis,— failed, and fled to his chamber. And there lay the studio naked to the eyes of the lightning, with its tortured forms throbbing out of the dark, and quivering, as with life, in the almost continuous palpitations of the light; while on the couch lay the motionless mass of whiteness, gleaming blue in the lightning, almost more terrible in its crude indications of the human form, than that which it enclosed. It lay there as if dropped from some tree of chaos, haggard with the snows of eternity—a huge misshapen nut, with a corpse for its kernel.

But the lightning would soon have revealed a more terrible sight still, had there been any eyes to behold it. At midnight, while a peal of thunder was just dying away in the distance, the crust of death flew asunder, rending in all directions; and, pale as his investiture, staring with ghastly eyes, the form of Karl started up sitting on the couch. Had he not been far beyond ordinary men in strength, he could not thus have rent his sepulchre. Indeed, had Teufelsbürst been able to finish his task by the additional layer of gypsum which he contemplated, he must have died the moment life revived; although, so long as the trance lasted, neither the exclusion from the air, nor the practical solidification of the walls of his chest, could do him any injury. He had lain unconscious throughout the operations of Teufelsbürst, but now the catalepsy had passed away, possibly under the influence of the electric condition of the atmosphere. Very likely the strength he now put forth was intensified by a convulsive reaction of all the powers of life, as is not infrequently the case in sudden awakenings from similar interruptions of vital activity. The coming to himself and the bursting of his case were simultaneous. He sat staring about him, with, of all his mental faculties, only his imagination awake, from which the thoughts that occupied it when he fell senseless had not yet faded. These thoughts had been compounded of feelings about Lilith, and speculations about the vampire that haunted the neighbourhood; and the fumes of the last drug of which he had partaken, still hovering in his brain, combined with these thoughts and fancies to generate the delu-sion that he had just broken from the embrace of his coffin, and risen, the last-born of the vampire race. The sense of unavoidable obligation to fulfil his doom, was yet mingled with a faint flutter of joy, for he knew that he must go to Lilith. With a deep sigh, he rose, gathered up the pall of black velvet, flung it around him, stepped from the couch, and left the study to find her.

Meantime, Teufelsbürst had sufficiently recovered to remember that he had left the door of the studio unfastened, and that any one entering would discover in what he had been engaged, which, in the case of his getting into any difficulty about the death of Karl, would tell power-fully against him. He was at the farther end of a long passage, leading from the house to the studio, on his way to make all secure, when Karl appeared at the door, and advanced towards him. The painter, seized with invincible terror, turned and fled. He reached his room, and fell sense-less on the floor. The phantom held on its way, heedless.

Lilith, on gaining her room the second time, had thrown herself on her bed as before, and had wept herself into a troubled slumber. She lay dreaming—and dreadful dreams. Suddenly she awoke in one of those peals of thunder which tormented the high regions of the air, as a storm billows the surface of the ocean. She lay awake and listened. As it died away, she thought she heard, mingling with its last muffled murmurs, the sound of moaning. She turned her face towards the room in keen terror. But she saw nothing. Another light, long-drawn sigh reached her ear, and at the same moment a flash of lightning illumined the room. In the corner farthest from her bed, she spied a white face, nothing more. She was dumb and motionless with fear. Utter darkness followed, a darkness that seemed to enter into her very brain. Yet she felt that the face was slowly crossing the black gulf of the room, and drawing near to where she lay. The next flash revealed, as it bended over her, the ghastly face of Karl, down which flowed fresh tears. The rest of his form was lost in blackness. Lilith did not faint, but it was the very force of her fear that seemed to keep her alive. It became for the moment the atmosphere of her life. She lay trembling and staring at the spot in the darkness where she supposed the face of Karl still to be. But the next flash showed her the face far off, looking at her through the panes of her lattice-window.

For Lottchen, as soon as he saw Lilith, seemed to himself to go through a second stage of awaking. Her face made him doubt whether he could be a vampire after all; for instead of wanting to bite her arm and suck the blood, he all but fell down at her feet in a passion of speechless love. The next moment he became aware that his presence must be at least very undesirable to her; and in an instant he had reached her window, which he knew looked upon a lower roof that extended between two different parts of the house, and before the next flash came, he had stepped through the lattice and closed it behind him.

Believing his own room to be attainable from this quarter, he proceeded along the roof in the direction he judged best. The cold winter air by degrees restored him entirely to his right mind, and he soon comprehended the whole of the circumstances in which he found himself. Peeping through a window he was passing, to see whether it belonged to his room, he spied Teufelsbürst, who, at the very moment, was lifting his head from the faint into which he had fallen at the first sight of Lottchen. The moon was shining clear, and in its light the painter saw, to his horror, the pale face staring in at his window. He thought it had been there ever since he had fainted, and dropped again in a deeper swoon than before. Karl saw him fall, and the truth flashed upon him that the wicked artist took him for what he had believed himself to be when first he recovered from his trance—namely, the vampire of the former Karl Wolkenlicht. The moment he comprehended it, he resolved to keep up the delusion if possible. Meantime he was innocently preparing a new ingredient for the popular dish of horrors to be served at the ordinary of the city the next day. For the old servant's were not the only eyes that had seen him besides those of Teufelsbürst. What could be more like a vampire, dragging his pall after him, than this apparition of poor, half-frozen Lottchen, crawling across the roof? Karl remembered afterwards that he had heard the dogs howling awfully in every direction, as he crept along; but this was hardly necessary to make those who saw him conclude that it was the same phantasm of John Kuntz, which had been infesting the whole city, and especially the house next door to the painter's, which had been the dwelling of the respectable alderman who had degenerated into this most disreputable of moneyless vagabonds. What added to the consternation of all who heard of it, was the sickening conviction that the extreme measures which they had resorted to in order to free the city from the ghoul, beyond which nothing could be done, had been utterly unavailing, successful as they had proved in every other known case of the kind. For, urged as well by various horrid signs about his grave, which not even its close proximity to the altar could render a place of repose, they had opened it, had found in the body every peculiarity belonging to a vampire, had pulled it out with the greatest difficulty on account of a quite supernatural ponderosity; which rendered the horse which had killed him—a strong animal—all but unable to drag it along, and had at last, after cutting it in pieces, and expending on the fire two hundred and sixteen great billets, succeeded in conquering its incombustibleness, and reducing it to ashes. Such, at least, was the story which had reached the painter's household, and was believed by many; and if all this did not compel the perturbed corpse to rest, what more could be done?

When Karl had reached his room, and was dressing himself, the thought struck him that something might be made of the report of the extreme weight of the body of old Kuntz, to favour the continuance of the delusion of Teufelsbürst, although he hardly knew yet to what use he could turn this delusion. He was convinced that he would have made no progress however long he might have remained in his house; and that he would have more chance of favour with Lilith if he were to meet her in any other circumstances whatever than those in which he invariably saw her—namely, surrounded by her father's influences, and watched by her father's cold blue eyes.

As soon as he was dressed, he crept down to the studio, which was now quiet enough, the storm being over, and the moon filling it with her steady shine. In the corner lay in all directions the fragments of the mould which his own body had formed and filled. The bag of plaster and the bucket of water which the painter had been using stood beside. Lottchen gathered all the pieces together, and then making his way to an outhouse where he had seen various odds and ends of rubbish lying, chose from the heap as many pieces of old iron and other metal as he could find. To these he added a few large stones from the garden. When he had got all into the studio, he locked the door, and proceeded to fit together the parts of the mould, filling up the hollow as he went on with the heaviest things he could get into it, and solidifying the whole by pouring in plaster; till, having at length completed it, and obliterated, as much as possible, the marks of joining, he left it to harden, with the conviction that now it would make a considerable impression on Teufelsbürst's imagination, as well as on his muscular sense. He then left everything else as nearly undisturbed as he could; and, knowing all the ways of the house, was soon in the street, without leaving any signs of his exit.

Karl soon found himself before the house in which his friend Höllenrachen resided. Knowing his studious habits, he had hoped to see his light still burning, nor was he disappointed. He contrived to bring him to his window, and a moment after, the door was cautiously opened.

"Why, Lottchen, where do you come from?"

"From the grave, Heinrich, or next door to it."

"Come in, and tell me all about it. We thought the old painter had made a model of you, and tortured you to death."

"Perhaps you were not far wrong. But get me a horn of ale, for even a vampire is thirsty, you know."

"A vampire!" exclaimed Heinrich, retreating a pace, and involuntarily putting himself upon his guard.

Karl laughed.

"My hand was warm, was it not, old fellow?" he said. "Vampires are cold, all but the blood."

"What a fool I am!" rejoined Heinrich. "But you know we have been hearing such horrors lately that a fellow may be excused for shuddering a little when a pale-faced apparition tells him at two o'clock in the morning that he is a vampire, and thirsty, too."

Karl told him the whole story; and the mental process of regarding it for the sake of telling it, revealed to him pretty clearly some of the treatment of which he had been unconscious at the time. Heinrich was quite sure that his suspicions were correct. And now the question was, what was to be done next?

"At all events," said Heinrich, "we must keep you out of the way for some time. I will represent to my landlady that you are in hiding from enemies, and her heart will rule her tongue. She can let you have a garret-room, I know; and I will do as well as I can to bear you company. We shall have time then to invent some plan of operation."

To this proposal Karl agreed with hearty thanks, and soon all was arranged. The only conclusion they could yet arrive at was, that somehow or other the old demon-painter must be tamed.

Meantime, how fared it with Lilith? She too had no doubt that she had seen the body-ghost of poor Karl, and that the vampire had, according to rule, paid her the first visit because he loved her best. This was horrible enough if the vampire were not really the person he represented; but if in any sense it were Karl himself, at least it gave some expectation of a more prolonged existence than her father had taught her to look for; and if love anything like her mother's still lasted, even along with the habits of a vampire, there was something to hope for in the future. And then, though he had visited her, he had not, as far as she was aware, deprived her of a drop of blood. She could not be certain that he had not bitten her, for she had been in such a strange condition of mind that she might not have felt it, but she believed that he had restrained the impulses of his vampire nature, and had left her, lest he should yet yield to them. She fell fast asleep; and, when morning came, there was not, as far as she could judge, one of those triangular leech-like perforations to be found upon her whole body. Will it be believed that the moment she was satisfied of this, she was seized by a terrible jealousy, lest Karl should have gone and bitten some one else? Most people will wonder that she should not have gone out of her senses at once; but there was all the difference between a visit from a real vampire and a visit from a man she had begun to love, even although she took him for a vampire. All the difference does not lie in a name. They were very different causes, and the effects must be very different.

When Teufelsbürst came down in the morning, he crept into the studio like a murderer. There lay the awful white block, seeming to his eyes just the same as he had left it. What was to be done with it? He dared not open it. Mould and model must go together. But whither? If inquiry should be made after Wolkenlicht, and this were discovered anywhere on his premises, would it not be enough to bring him at once to the gallows? Therefore it would be dangerous to bury it in the garden, or in the cellar.

"Besides," thought he, with a shudder, "that would be to fix the vampire as a guest for ever."—And the horrors of the past night rushed back upon his imagination with renewed intensity. What would it be to have the dead Karl crawling about his house for ever, now inside, now out, now sitting on the stairs, now staring in at the windows?

He would have dragged it to the bottom of his garden, past which the Moldau flowed, and plunged it into the stream; but then, should the spectre continue to prove troublesome, it would be almost impossible to reach the body so as to destroy it by fire; besides which, he could not do it without assistance, and the probability of discovery. If, however, the apparition should turn out to be no vampire, but only a respectable ghost, they might manage to endure its presence, till it should be weary of haunting them.

He resolved at last to convey the body for the meantime into a concealed cellar in the house, seeing something must be done before his daughter came down. Proceeding to remove it, his consternation as greatly increased when he discovered how the body had grown in weight since he had thus disposed of it, leaving on his mind scarcely a hope that it could turn out not to be a vampire after all. He could scarcely stir it, and there was but one whom he could call to his assistance—the old woman who acted as his housekeeper and servant.

He went to her room, roused her, and told her the whole story. Devoted to her master for many years, and not quite so sensitive to fearful influences as when less experienced in horrors, she showed immediate readiness to render him assistance. Utterly unable, however, to lift the mass between them, they could only drag and push it along; and such a slow toil was it that there was no time to remove the traces of its track, before Lilith came down and saw a broad white line leading from the door of the studio down the cellar-stairs. She knew in a moment what it meant; but not a word was uttered about the matter, and the name of Karl Wolkenlicht seemed to be entirely forgotten.

But how could the affairs of a house go on all the same when every one of the household knew that a dead body lay in the cellar?—nay more, that, although it lay still and dead enough all day, it would come half alive at nightfall, and, turning the whole house into a sepulchre by its presence, go creeping about like a cat all over it in the dark—perhaps with phosphorescent eyes? So it was not surprising that the painter abandoned his studio early, and that the three found themselves together in the gorgeous room formerly described, as soon as twilight began to fall.

Already Teufelsbürst had begun to experience a kind of shrinking from the horrid faces in his own pictures, and to feel disgusted at the abortions of his own mind. But all that he and the old woman now felt was an increasing fear as the night drew on, a kind of sickening and paralysing terror. The thing down there would not lie quiet—at least its phantom in the cellars of their imagination would not. As much as possible, however, they avoided alarming Lilith, who, knowing all they knew, was as silent as they. But her mind was in a strange state of excitement, partly from the presence of a new sense of love, the pleasure of which all the atmosphere of grief into which it grew could not totally quench. It comforted her somehow, as a child may comfort when his father is away.

Bedtime came, and no one made a move to go. Without a word spoken on the subject, the three remained together all night; the elders nodding and slumbering occasionally, and Lilith getting some share of repose on a couch. All night the shape of death might be somewhere about the house; but it did not disturb them. They heard no sound, saw no sight; and when the morning dawned, they separated, chilled and stupid, and for the time beyond fear, to seek repose in their private chambers. There they remained equally undisturbed.

But when the painter approached his easel a few hours after, looking more pale and haggard still than he was wont, from the fears of the night, a new bewilderment took possession of him. He had been busy with a fresh embodiment of his favourite subject, into which he had sketched the form of the student as the sufferer. He had represented poor

Wolkenlicht as just beginning to recover from a trance, while a group of surgeons, unaware of the signs of returning life, were absorbed in a minute dissection of one of the limbs. At an open door he had painted Lilith passing, with her face buried in a bunch of sweet peas. But when he came to the picture, he found, to his astonishment and terror, that the face of one of the group was now turned towards that of the victim, regarding his revival with demoniac satisfaction, and taking pains to prevent the others from discovering it. The face of this prince of torturers was that of Teufelsbürst himself. Lilith had altogether vanished, and in her place stood the dim vampire reiteration of the body that lay extended on the table, staring greedily at the assembled company. With trembling hands the painter removed the picture from the easel, and turned its face to the wall.

Of course this was the work of Lottchen. When he left the house, he took with him the key of a small private door, which was so seldom used that, while it remained closed, the key would not be missed, perhaps for many months. Watching the windows, he had chosen a safe time to enter, and had been hard at work all night on these alterations. Teufelsbürst attributed them to the vampire, and left the picture as he found it, not daring to put brush to it again.

The next night was passed much after the same fashion. But the fear had begun to die away a little in the hearts of the women, who did not know what had taken place in the studio on the previous night. It burrowed, however, with gathered force in the vitals of Teufelsbürst. But this night likewise passed in peace; and before it was over, the old woman had taken to speculating in her own mind as to the best way of disposing of the body, seeing it was not at all likely to be troublesome. But when the painter entered his studio in trepidation the next morning, he found that the form of the lovely Lilith was painted out of every picture in the room. This could not be concealed; and Lilith and the servant became aware that the studio was the portion of the house in haunting which the vampire left the rest in peace.

Karl recounted all the tricks he had played to his friend Heinrich, who begged to be allowed to bear him company the following night. To this Karl consented, thinking it would be considerably more agreeable to have a companion. So they took a couple of bottles of wine and some provisions with them, and before midnight found themselves snug in the studio. They sat very quiet for some time, for they knew that if they were seen, two vampires would not be so terrible as one, and might occasion discovery. But at length Heinrich could bear it no longer.

"I say, Lottchen, let's go and look; for your dead body. What has the old beggar done with it?"

"I think I know. Stop; let me peep out. All right! Come along."

With a lamp in his hand, he led the way to the cellars, and after searching about a little they discovered it.

"It looks horrid enough," said Heinrich, "but think a drop or two of wine would brighten it up a little."

So he took a bottle from his pocket, and after they had had a glass apiece, he dropped a third in blots all over the plaster. Being red wine, it had the effect Höllenrachen desired.

"When they visit it next, they will know that the vampire can find the food he prefers," said he.

In a corner close by the plaster, they found the clothes Karl had worn.

"Hillo!" said Heinrich, "we'll make something of this find."

So he carried them with him to the studio. There he got hold of the lay-figure.

"What are you about, Heinrich?"

"Going to make a scarecrow to keep the ravens off old Teufel's pictures," answered Heinrich, as he went on dressing the lay-figure in Karl's clothes. He next seated the creature at an easel with its back to the door, so that it should be the first thing the painter should see when he entered. Karl meant to remove this before he went, for it was too comical to fall in with the rest of his proceedings. But the two sat down to their supper, and by the time they had finished the wine, they thought they should like to go to bed. So they got up and went home, and Karl forgot the lay-figure, leaving it in busy motionlessness all night before the easel.

When Teufelsbürst saw it, he turned and fled with a cry that brought his daughter to his help. He rushed past her, able only to articulate:

"The vampire! The vampire! Painting!"

Far more courageous than he, because her conscience was more peaceful, Lilith passed on to the studio. She too recoiled a step or two when she saw the figure; but with the sight of the back of Karl, as she supposed it to be, came the longing to see the face that was on the other side. So she crept round and round by the wall, as far off as she could. The figure remained motionless, It was a strange kind of shock that she experienced when she saw the face, disgusting from its inanity. The absurdity next struck her; and with the absurdity flashed into her mind the conviction that this was not the doing of a vampire; for of all creatures under the moon, he could not be expected to be a humorist. A wild hope sprang up in her mind that Karl was not dead. Of this she soon resolved to make herself sure.

She closed the door of the studio; in the strength of her new hope undressed the figure, put it in its place, concealed the garments—all the work of a few minutes; and then, finding her father just recovering from the worst of his fear, told him there was nothing in the studio but what ought to be there, and persuaded him to go and see. He not only saw no one, but found that no further liberties had been taken with his pictures. Reassured, he soon persuaded himself that the spectre in this case had been the offspring of his own terror-haunted brain. But he had no spirit for painting now. He wandered about the house, himself haunting it like a restless ghost.

When night came, Lilith retired to her own room. The waters of fear had begun to subside in the house; but the painter and his old attendant did not yet follow her example.

As soon, however, as the house was quite still, Lilith glided noise-lessly down the stairs, went into the studio, where as yet there assuredly was no vampire, and concealed herself in a corner.

As it would not do for an earnest student like Heinrich to be away from his work very often, he had not asked to accompany Lottchen this time. And indeed Karl himself, a little anxious about the result of the scarecrow, greatly preferred going alone.

While she was waiting for what might happen, the conviction grew upon Lilith, as she reviewed all the past of the story, that these phenom-ena were the work of the real Karl, and of no vampire. In a few moments she was still more sure of this. Behind the screen where she had taken refuge, hung one of the pictures out of which her portrait had been painted the night before last. She had taken a lamp with her into the studio, with the intention of extinguishing it the moment she heard any sign of ap-proach; but as the vampire lingered, she began to occupy herself with examining the picture beside her. She had not looked at it long, before she wetted the tip of her forefinger, and began to rub away at the oblit-eration. Her suspicions were instantly confirmed: the substance employed was only a gummy wash over the paint. The delight she experienced at the discovery threw her into a mischievous humour.

"I will see," she said to herself, "whether I cannot match Karl Wolkenlicht at this game."

In a closet in the room hung a number of costumes, which Lilith had at different times worn for her father. Among them was a large white drapery, which she easily disposed as a shroud. With the help of some chalk, she soon made herself ghastly enough, and then placing her lamp on the floor behind the screen, and setting a chair over it, so that it should throw no light in any direction, she waited once more for the vampire. Nor had she much longer to wait. She soon heard a door move, the sound of which she hardly knew, and then the studio door opened. Her heart beat dreadfully, not with fear lest it should be a vampire after all, but with hope that it was Karl. To see him once more was too great joy. Would she not make up to him for all her coldness! But would he care for her now? Perhaps he had been quite cured of his longing for a hard heart like hers. She peeped. It was he sure enough, looking as handsome as ever.

He was holding his light to look at her last work, and the expression of his face, even in regarding her handiwork, was enough to let her know that he loved her still. If she had not seen this, she dared not have shown herself from her hiding-place. Taking the lamp in her hand, she got upon the chair, and looked over the screen, letting the light shine from below upon her face. She then made a slight noise to attract Karl's attention. He looked up, evidently rather startled, and saw the face of Lilith in the air. He gave a stifled cry threw himself on his knees with his arms stretched towards her, and moaned—

"I have killed her! I have killed her!"

Lilith descended, and approached him noiselessly. He did not move. She came close to him and said—

"Are you Karl Wolkenlicht?"

His lips moved, but no sound came.

"If you are a vampire, and I am a ghost," she said—but a low happy laugh alone concluded the sentence.

Karl sprang to his feet. Lilith's laugh changed into a burst of sobbing and weeping, and in another moment the ghost was in the arms of the vampire.

Lilith had no idea how far her father had wronged Karl, and though, from thinking over the past, he had no doubt that the painter had drugged him, he did not wish to pain her by imparting this conviction. But Lilith was afraid of a reaction of rage and hatred in her father after the terror was removed; and Karl saw that he might thus be deprived of all further intercourse with Lilith, and all chance of softening the old man's heart towards him; while Lilith would not hear of forsaking him who had banished all the human race but herself. They managed at length to agree upon a plan of operation.

The first thing they did was to go to the cellar where the plaster mass lay, Karl carrying with him a great axe used for cleaving wood. Lilith shuddered when she saw it, stained as it was with the wine Heinrich had spilt over it, and almost believed herself the midnight companion of a vampire after all, visiting with him the terrible corpse in which he lived all day. But Karl soon reassured her; and a few good blows of the axe revealed a very different core to that which Teufelsbürst supposed to be in it. Karl broke it into pieces, and with Lilith's help, who insisted on carrying her share, the whole was soon at the bottom of the Moldau and every trace of its ever having existed removed. Before morning, too, the form of Lilith had dawned anew in every picture. There was no time to restore to its former condition the one Karl had first altered; for in it the changes were all that they seemed; nor indeed was he capable of restoring it in the master's style; but they put it quite out of the way, and hoped that sufficient time might elapse before the painter thought of it again.

When they had done, and Lilith, for all his entreaties, would remain with him no longer, Karl took his former clothes with him, and having spent the rest of the night in his old room, dressed in them in the morning. When Teufelsbürst entered his studio next day, there sat Karl, as if nothing had happened, finishing the drawing on which he had been at work when the fit of insensibility came upon him. The painter started, stared, rubbed his eyes, thought it was another spectral illusion, and was on the point of yielding to his terror, when Karl rose, and approached him with a smile. The healthy, sunshiny countenance of Karl, let him be ghost or goblin, could not fail to produce somewhat of a tranquillising effect on Teufelsbürst. He took his offered hand mechanically, his countenance utterly vacant with idiotic bewilderment. Karl said—

"I was not well, and thought it better to pay a visit to a friend for a few days; but I shall soon make up for lost time, for I am all right now."

He sat down at once, taking no notice of his master's behaviour, and went on with his drawing. Teufelsbürst stood staring at him for some minutes without moving, then suddenly turned and left the room. Karl heard him hurrying down the cellar stairs. In a few moments he came up again. Karl stole a glance at him. There he stood in the same spot, no doubt more full of bewilderment than ever, but it was not possible that his face should express more. At last he went to his easel, and sat down with a long-drawn sigh as if of relief. But though he sat at his easel, he painted none that day; and as often as Karl ventured a glance, he saw him still staring at him. The discovery that his pictures were restored to their former condition aided, no doubt, in leading him to the same conclusion as the other facts, whatever that conclusion might be—probably that he had been the sport of some evil power, and had been for the greater part of a week utterly bewitched. Lilith had taken care to instruct the old woman, with whom she was all-powerful; and as neither of them showed the smallest traces of the astonishment which seemed to be slowly vitrifying his own brain, he was at last perfectly satisfied that things had been going on all right everywhere but in his inner man; and in this conclusion he certainly was not far wrong, in more senses than one. But when all was restored again to the old routine, it became evident that the peculiar direction of his art in which he had hitherto indulged had ceased to interest him. The shock had acted chiefly upon that part of his mental being which had been so absorbed. He would sit for hours without doing anything, apparently plunged in meditation.—Several weeks elapsed without any change, and both Lilith and Karl were getting dreadfully anxious about him. Karl paid him every attention; and the old man, for he now looked much older than before, submitted to receive his services as well as those of Lilith. At length, one morning, he said in a slow thoughtful tone—

"Karl Wolkenlicht, I should like to paint you."

"Certainly, sir," answered Karl, jumping up, "where would you like me to sit?"

So the ice of silence and inactivity was broken, and the painter drew and painted; and the spring of his art flowed once more; and he made a beautiful portrait of Karl—a portrait without evil or suffering. And as soon as he had finished Karl, he began once more to paint Lilith; and when he had painted her, he composed a picture for the very purpose of introducing them together; and in this picture there was neither ugliness nor torture, but human feeling and human hope instead. Then Karl knew that he might speak to him of Lilith; and he spoke, and was heard with a smile. But he did not dare to tell him the truth of the vampire story till one day that Teufelsbürst was lying on the floor of a room in Karl's ancestral castle, half smothered in grandchildren; when the only answer it drew from the old man was a kind of shuddering laugh and the words "Don't speak of it, Karl, my boy!"

And Elisha died, and they buried him. Now Moabite raiders invaded the land in the spring of the year.

Once, as they were burying a man, behold, some men
spied a band of raiders; so they threw the man into the tomb
of Elisha: when the man's body touched the bones of Elisha,
he came to life and stood up on his feet.

II Kings 13: 20-21

A DEAD FINGER

Sabine Baring-Gould (1834-1924)

I

Why the National Gallery should not attract so many visitors as, say, the British Museum, I cannot explain. The latter does not contain much that, one would suppose, appeals to the interest of the ordinary sight-seer. What knows such of prehistoric flints and scratched bones? Of Assyrian sculpture? Of Egyptian hieroglyphics? The Greek and Roman statuary is cold and dead.

The paintings in the National Gallery glow with colour, and are instinct with life. Yet, somehow, a few listless wanderers saunter yawning through the National Gallery, whereas swarms pour through the halls of the British Museum, and talk and pass remarks about the objects there exposed, of the date and meaning of which they have not the faintest conception.

I was thinking of this problem, and endeavouring to unravel it, one morning whilst sitting in the room for English masters at the great collection in Trafalgar Square. At the same time another thought forced itself upon me. I had been through the rooms devoted to foreign schools, and had then come into that given over to Reynolds, Morland, Gainsborough, Constable, and Hogarth. The morning had been for a while propitious, but towards noon a dense umber-tinted fog had come on, making it all but impossible to see the pictures, and quite impossible to do them justice. I was tired, and so seated myself on one of the chairs, and fell into the consideration first of all of—why the National Gallery is not as popular as it should be; and secondly, how it was that the British School had no beginnings, like those of Italy and the Netherlands. We can see the art of the painter from its first initiation in the Italian peninsula, and among the Flemings.

It starts on its progress like a child, and we can trace every stage of its growth. Not so with English art. It springs to life in full and splendid maturity. Who were there before Reynolds and Gainsborough and Hogarth? The great names of those portrait and subject painters who have left their canvases upon the walls of our country houses were those of foreigners—Holbein, Kneller, Van Dyck, and Lely for portraits, and Monnoyer for flower and fruit pieces. Landscapes, figure subjects were all importations, none home-grown. How came that about? Was there no limner that was native? Was it that fashion trampled on homegrown pictorial beginnings as it flouted and spurned native music?

Here was food for contemplation. Dreaming in the brown fog, looking through it without seeing its beauties, at Hogarth's painting of Lavinia Fenton as Polly Peachum, without wondering how so indifferent a beauty could have captivated the Duke of Bolton and held him for thirty years, I was recalled to myself and my surroundings by the strange conduct of a lady who had seated herself on a chair near me, also discouraged by the fog, and awaiting its dispersion.

I had not noticed her particularly. At the present moment I do not remember particularly what she was like. So far as I can recollect she was middle-aged, and was quietly yet well dressed. It was not her face nor her dress that attracted my attention and disturbed the current of my thoughts; the effect I speak of was produced by her strange movements and behaviour.

She had been sitting listless, probably thinking of nothing at all, or nothing in particular, when, in turning her eyes round, and finding that she could see nothing of the paintings, she began to study me. This did concern me greatly. A cat may look at the king; but to be contemplated by a lady is a compliment sufficient to please any gentleman. It was not gratified vanity that troubled my thoughts, but the consciousness that my appearance produced—first of all a startled surprise, then undisguised alarm, and, finally, indescribable horror.

Now a man can sit quietly leaning on the head of his umbrella, and glow internally, warmed and illumined by the consciousness that he is being surveyed with admiration by a lovely woman, even when he is middle-aged and not fashionably dressed; but no man can maintain his composure when he discovers himself to be an object of aversion and terror.

What was it? I passed my hand over my chin and upper lip, thinking it not impossible that I might have forgotten to shave that morning, and in my confusion not considering that the fog would prevent the lady from discovering neglect in this particular, had it occurred, which it had not. I am a little careless, perhaps, about shaving when in the country; but when in town, never.

The next idea that occurred to me was—a smut. Had a London black, curdled in that dense pea-soup atmosphere, descended on my nose and blackened it? I hastily drew my silk handkerchief from my pocket, moistened it, and passed to my nose, and then each cheek. I then turned my eyes into the corners and looked at the lady, to see whether by this means I had got rid of what was objectionable in my personal appearance.

Then I saw that her eyes, dilated with horror, were riveted, not on my face, but on my leg.

My leg! What on earth could that harmless member have in it so terrifying? The morning had been dull; there had been rain in the night, and I admit that on leaving my hotel I had turned up the bottoms of my trousers. That is a proceeding not so uncommon, not so outrageous as to account for the stony stare of this woman's eyes.

If that were all I would turn my trousers down.

Then I saw her shrink from the chair on which she sat to one further removed from me, but still with her eyes fixed on my leg—about the level of my knee. She had let fall her umbrella, and was grasping the seat of her chair with both hands, as she backed from me.

I need hardly say that I was greatly disturbed in mind and feelings, and forgot all about the origin of the English schools of painters, and the question why the British Museum is more popular than the National Gallery.

Thinking that I might have been spattered by a hansom whilst crossing Oxford Street, I passed my hand down my side hastily, with a sense of annoyance, and all at once touched something, cold, clammy, that sent a thrill to my heart, and made me start and take a step forward. At the same moment, the lady, with a cry of horror, sprang to her feet, and with raised hands fled from the room, leaving her umbrella where it had fallen.

There were other visitors to the Picture Gallery besides ourselves, who had been passing through the saloon, and they turned at her cry, and looked in surprise after her.

The policeman stationed in the room came to me and asked what had happened. I was in such agitation that I hardly knew what to answer. I told him that I could explain what had occurred little better than himself. I had noticed that the lady had worn an odd expression, and had behaved in most extraordinary fashion, and that he had best take charge of her umbrella, and wait for her return to claim it.

This questioning by the official was vexing, as it prevented me from at once and on the spot investigating the cause of her alarm and mine—hers at something she must have seen on my leg, and mine at something I had distinctly felt creeping up my leg.

The numbing and sickening effect on me of the touch of the object I had not seen was not to be shaken off at once. Indeed, I felt as though my hand were contaminated, and that I could have no.rest till I had thoroughly washed the hand, and, if possible, washed away the feeling that had been produced.

I looked on the floor, I examined my leg, but saw nothing. As I wore my overcoat, it was probable that in rising from my seat the skirt had fallen over my trousers and hidden the thing, whatever it was: I therefore hastily removed my overcoat and shook it, then I looked at my trousers. There was nothing whatever on my leg, and nothing fell from my overcoat when shaken.

Accordingly I reinvested myself, and hastily left the Gallery; then took my way as speedily as I could, without actually running, to Charing Cross Station and down the narrow way leading to the Metropolitan, where I went into Faulkner's bath and hairdressing establishment, and asked for hot water to thoroughly wash my hand and well soap it. I bathed my hand in water as hot as I could endure it, employed carbolic soap, and then, after having a good brush down, especially on my left side where my hand had encountered the object that had so affected me, I left. I had entertained the intention of going to the Princess's Theatre that evening, and of securing a ticket in the morning; but all thought of theatre-going was gone from me. I could not free my heart from the sense of nausea and cold that had been produced by the touch. I went into Gatti's to have lunch, and ordered something, I forget what, but, when served, I found that my appetite was gone. I could eat nothing; the food inspired me with disgust. I thrust it from me untasted, and, after drinking a couple of glasses of claret, left the restaurant, and returned to my hotel.

Feeling sick and faint, I threw my overcoat over the sofa-back, and cast myself on my bed.

I do not know that there was any particular reason for my doing so, but as I lay my eyes were on my great-coat.

The density of the fog had passed away, and there was light again, not of first quality, but sufficient for a Londoner to swear by, so that I could see everything in my room, though through a veil, darkly.

I do not think my mind was occupied in any way. About the only occasions on which, to my knowledge, my mind is actually passive or inert is when crossing the Channel in The Foam from Dover to Calais, when I am always, in every weather, abjectly seasick—and thoughtless. But as I now lay on my bed, uncomfortable, squeamish, without knowing why—I was in the same inactive mental condition. But not for long.

I saw something that startled me.

First, it appeared to me as if the lappet of my overcoat pocket were in movement, being raised.

I did not pay much attention to this, as I supposed that the garment was sliding down on to the seat of the sofa, from the back, and that this displacement of gravity caused the movement I observed. But this I soon saw was not the case. That which moved the lappet was something in the pocket that was struggling to get out. I could see now that it was working its way up the inside, and that when it reached the opening it lost balance and fell down again. I could make this out by the projections and indentations in the cloth; these moved as the creature, or whatever it was, worked its way up the lining.

"A mouse," I said, and forgot my seediness; I was interested. "The little rascal! However did he contrive to seat himself in my pocket? and I have worn that overcoat all the morning!" But no—it was not a mouse. I saw something white poke its way out from under the lappet; and in another moment an object was revealed that, though revealed, I could not understand, nor could I distinguish what it was.

Now roused by curiosity, I raised myself on my elbow. In doing this I made some noise, the bed creaked. Instantly the something dropped on the floor, lay outstretched for a moment, to recover itself, and then began, with the motions of a maggot, to run along the floor.

There is a caterpillar called "The Measurer," because, when it advances, it draws its tail up to where its head is and then throws forward its full length, and again draws up its extremity, forming at each time a loop, and with each step measuring its total length. The object I now saw on the floor was advancing precisely like the measuring caterpillar. It had the colour of a cheese-maggot, and in length was about three and a half inches. It was not, however, like a caterpillar, which is flexible throughout its entire length, but this was, as it seemed to me, jointed in two places, one joint being more conspicuous than the other. For some moments I was so completely paralysed by astonishment that I remained motionless, looking at the thing as it crawled along the carpet—a dull green carpet with darker green, almost black, flowers in it.

It had, as it seemed to me, a glossy head, distinctly marked; but, as the light was not brilliant, I could not make out very clearly, and, moreover, the rapid movements prevented close scrutiny.

Presently, with a shock still more startling than that produced by its apparition at the opening of the pocket of my great-coat, I became convinced that what I saw was a finger, a human forefinger, and that the glossy head was no other than the nail.

The finger did not seem to have been amputated. There was no sign of blood or laceration where the knuckle should be, but the extremity of the finger, or root rather, faded away to indistinctness, and I was unable to make out the root of the finger.

I could see no hand, no body behind this finger, nothing whatever except a finger that had little token of warm life in it, no coloration as though blood circulated in it; and this finger was in active motion creeping along the carpet towards a wardrobe that stood against the wall by the fireplace.

I sprang off the bed and pursued it.

Evidently the finger was alarmed, for it redoubled its pace, reached the wardrobe, and went under it. By the time I had arrived at the article of furniture it had disappeared. I lit a vesta match and held it beneath the wardrobe, that was raised above the carpet by about two inches, on turned feet, but I could see nothing more of the finger.

I got my umbrella and thrust it beneath, and raked forwards and backwards, right and left, and raked out flue, and nothing more solid.

II

I packed my portmanteau next day and returned to my home in the country. All desire for amusement in town was gone, and the faculty to transact business had departed as well.

A languor and qualms had come over me, and my head was in a maze. I was unable to fix my thoughts on anything. At times I was disposed to believe that my wits were deserting me, at others that I was on the verge of a severe illness. Anyhow, whether likely to go off my head or not, or take to my bed, home was the only place for me, and homeward I sped, accordingly. On reaching my country habitation, my servant, as usual, took my portmaneau to my bedroom, unstrapped it, but did not unpack it. I object to his throwing out the contents of my Gladstone bag; not that there is anything in it he may not see, but that he puts my things where I cannot find them again. My clothes—he is welcome to place them where he likes and where they belong, and this latter he knows better than I do; but, then, I carry about with me other things than a dress suit, and changes of linen and flannel. There are letters, papers, books—and the proper.destinations of these are known only to myself. A servant has a singular and evil knack of putting away literary matter and odd volumes in such places that it takes the owner half a day to find them again. Although I was uncomfortable, and my head in a whirl, I opened and unpacked my own portmanteau. As I was thus engaged I saw something curled up in my collar-box, the lid of which had got broken in by a boot-heel impinging on it. I had pulled off the damaged cover to see if my collars had been spoiled, when something curled up inside suddenly rose on end and leapt, just like a cheese-jumper, out of the box, over the edge of the Gladstone bag, and scurried away across the floor in a manner already familiar to me.

I could not doubt for a moment what it was—here was the finger again. It had come with me from London to the country.

Whither it went in its run over the floor I do not know, I was too bewildered to observe.

Somewhat later, towards evening, I seated myself in my easy-chair, took up a book, and tried to read. I was tired with the journey, with the knocking about in town, and the discomfort and alarm produced by the apparition of the finger. I felt worn out. I was unable to give my attention to what I read, and before I was aware was asleep. Roused for an instant by the fall of the book from my hands, I speedily relapsed into unconsciousness. I am not sure that a doze in an armchair ever does good. It usually leaves me in a semi-stupid condition and with a headache.

Five minutes in a horizontal position on my bed is worth thirty in a chair. That is my experience.

In sleeping in a sedentary position the head is a difficulty; it drops forward or lolls on one side or the other, and has to be brought back into a position in which the line to the centre of gravity runs through the trunk, otherwise the head carries the body over in a sort of general capsize out of the chair on to the floor.

I slept, on the occasion of which I am speaking, pretty healthily, because deadly weary; but I was brought to waking, not by my head falling over the arm of the chair, and my trunk tumbling after it, but by a feeling of cold extending from my throat to my heart. When I awoke I was in a diagonal position, with my right ear resting on my right shoulder, and exposing the left side of my throat, and it was here— where the jugular vein throbs—that I felt the greatest intensity of cold. At once I shrugged my left shoulder, rubbing my neck with the collar of my coat in so doing. Immediately something fell off, upon the floor, and I again saw the finger.

My disgust—horror, were intensified when I perceived that it was dragging something after it, which might have been an old stocking, and which I took at first glance for something of the sort.

The evening sun shone in through my window, in a brilliant golden ray that lighted the object as it scrambled along. With this illumination I was able to distinguish what the object was. It is not easy to describe it, but I will make the attempt.

The finger I saw was solid and material; what it drew after it was neither, or was in a nebulous, protoplasmic condition. The finger was attached to a hand that was curdling into matter and in process of acquiring solidity; attached to the hand was an arm in a very filmy condition, and this arm belonged to a human body in a still more vaporous, immaterial condition. This was being dragged along the floor by the finger, just as a silkworm might pull after it the tangle of its web. I could see legs and arms, and head, and coat-tail tumbling about and interlacing and disentangling again in a promiscuous manner. There were no bone, no muscle, no substance in the figure; the members were attached to the trunk, which was spineless, but they had evidently no functions, and were wholly dependent on the finger which pulled them along in a jumble of parts as it advanced.

In such confusion did the whole vaporous matter seem, that I think—I cannot say for certain it was so, but the impression left on my mind was—that one of the eyeballs was looking out at a nostril, and the tongue lolling out of one of the ears.

It was, however, only for a moment that I saw this germ-body; I cannot call by another name that which had not more substance than smoke. I saw it only so long as it was being dragged athwart the ray of sunlight. The moment it was pulled jerkily out of the beam into the shadow beyond, I could see nothing of it, only the crawling finger.

I had not sufficient moral energy or physical force in me to rise, pursue, and stamp on the finger, and grind it with my heel into the floor. Both seemed drained out of me. What became of the finger, whither it went, how it managed to secrete itself, I do not know. I had lost the power to inquire. I sat in my chair, chilled, staring before me into space.

"Please, sir," a voice said, "there's Mr. Square below, electrical engineer."

"Eh?" I looked dreamily round.

My valet was at the door.

"Please, sir, the gentleman would be glad to be allowed to go over the house and see that all the electrical apparatus is in order."

"Oh, indeed! Yes—show him up."

III

I had recently placed the lighting of my house in the hands of an electrical engineer, a very intelligent man, Mr. Square, for whom I had contracted a sincere friendship.

He had built a shed with a dynamo out of sight, and had entrusted the laying of the wires to subordinates, as he had been busy with other orders and could not personally watch every detail.

But he was not the man to let anything pass unobserved, and he knew that electricity was not a force to be played with. Bad or careless workmen will often insufficiently protect the wires, or neglect the insertion of the lead which serves as a safety-valve in the event of the current being too strong. Houses may be set on fire, human beings fatally shocked, by the neglect of a bad or slovenly workman.

The apparatus for my mansion was but just completed, and Mr Square had come to inspect it and make sure that all was right.

He was an enthusiast in the matter of electricity, and saw for it a vast perspective, the limits of which could not be predicted.

"All forces," said he, "are correlated. When you have force in one form, you may just turn it into this or that, as you like. In one form it is motive power, in another it is light, in another heat. Now we have electricity for illumination. We employ it, but not as freely as in the States, for propelling vehicles. Why should we have horses drawing our buses? We should use only electric trains. Why do we burn coal to warm our shins? There is electricity, which throws out no filthy smoke as does coal. Why should we let the tides waste their energies in the Thames? in other estuaries? There we have Nature supplying us—free, gratis, and for nothing—with all the force we want for propelling, for heating, for lighting. I will tell you something more, my dear sir," said Mr Square. "I have mentioned but three modes of force, and have instanced but a limited number of uses to which electricity may be turned. How is it with photography? Is not electric light becoming an artistic agent? I bet you", said he, "before long it will become a therapeutic agent as well."

"Oh, yes; I have heard of certain impostors with their life-belts."

Mr. Square did not relish this little dig I gave him. He winced, but returned to the charge. "We don't know how to direct it aright, that is all," said he. "I haven't taken the matter up, but others will, I bet; and we shall have electricity used as freely as now we use powders and pills. I don't believe in doctors' stuffs myself. I hold that disease lays hold of a man because he lacks physical force to resist it. Now, is it not obvious that you are beginning at the wrong end when you attack the disease? What you want is to supply force, make up for the lack of physical power, and force is force wherever you find it—here motive, there illuminating, and so on. I don't see why a physician should not utilize the tide rushing out under London Bridge for restoring the feeble vigour of all who are languid and a prey to disorder in the Metropolis. It will come to that, I bet, and that is not all. Force is force, everywhere. Political, moral force, physical force, dynamic force, heat, light, tidal waves, and so on—all are one, all is one. In time we shall know how to galvanize into aptitude and moral energy all the limp and crooked consciences and wills that need taking in hand, and such there always will be in modem civilisation. I don't know how to do it. I don't know how it will be done, but in the future the priest as well as the doctor will turn electricity on as his principal, nay, his only agent. And he can get his force anywhere, out of the running stream, out of the wind, out of the tidal wave.

"I'll give you an instance," continued Mr. Square, chuckling and rubbing his hands, "to show you the great possibilities in electricity, used in a crude fashion. In a certain great city away far west in the States, a go-ahead place, too, more so than New York, they had electric trains all up and down and along the roads to everywhere. The union men working for the company demanded that the non-unionists should be turned off. But the company didn't see it. Instead, it turned off the union men. It had up its sleeve a sufficiency of the others, and filled all places at once. Union men didn't like it, and passed word that at a given hour on a certain day every wire was to be cut. The company knew this by means of its spies, and turned on, ready for them, three times the power into all the wires. At the fixed moment, up the poles went the strikers to cut the cables, and down they came a dozen times quicker than they went up, I bet. Then there came wires to the hospitals from all quarters for stretchers to carry off the disabled men, some with broken legs, arms, ribs; two or three had their necks broken. I reckon the company was wonderfully merciful—it didn't put on sufficient force to make cinders of them then and there; possibly opinion might not have liked it. Stopped the strike, did that. Great moral effect—all done by electricity." In this manner Mr. Square was wont to rattle on. He interested me, and I came to think that there might be something in what he said—that his suggestions were not mere nonsense. I was glad to see Mr. Square enter my room, shown in by my man. I did not rise from my chair to shake his hand, for I had not sufficient energy to do so. In a languid tone I welcomed him and signed to him to take a seat. Mr. Square looked at me with some surprise.

"Why, what's the matter?" he said. "You seem unwell. Not got the 'flu, have you?"

"I beg your pardon?"

"The influenza. Every third person is crying out that he has it, and the sale of eucalyptus is enormous, not that eucalyptus is any good. Influenza microbes indeed! What care they for eucalyptus? You've gone down some steps of the ladder of life since I saw you last, squire. How do you account for that?"

I hesitated about mentioning the extraordinary circumstances that had occurred; but Square was a man who would not allow any beating about the bush. He was downright and straight, and in ten minutes had got the entire story out of me.

"Rather boisterous for your nerves that—a crawling finger," said he. "It's a queer story taken on end."

Then he was silent, considering.

After a few minutes he rose, and said: "I'll go and look at the fittings, and then I'll turn this little matter of yours over again, and see if I can't knock the bottom out of it, I'm kinder fond of these sort of things."

Mr. Square was not a Yankee, but he had lived for some time in America, and affected to speak like an American. He used expressions, terms of speech common in the States, but had none of the Transatlantic twang. He was a man absolutely without affectation in every other particular; this was his sole weakness, and it was harmless.

The man was so thorough in all he did that I did not expect his return immediately. He was certain to examine every portion of the dynamo engine, and all the connections and burners. This would necessarily engage him for some hours. As the day was nearly done, I knew he could not accomplish what he wanted that evening, and accordingly gave orders that a room should be prepared for him. Then, as my head was full of pain, and my skin was burning, I told my servant to apologize for my absence from dinner, and tell Mr. Square that I was really forced to return to my bed by sickness, and that I believed I was about to be prostrated by an attack of influenza.

The valet—a worthy fellow, who has been with me for six years—was concerned at my appearance, and urged me to allow him to send for a doctor. I had no confidence in the local practitioner, and if I sent for another from the nearest town I should offend him, and a row would perhaps ensue, so I declined. If I were really in for an influenza attack, I knew about as much as any doctor how to deal with it. Quinine, quinine—that was all. I bade my man light a small lamp, lower it, so as to give sufficient illumination to enable me to find some lime-juice at my bed head, and my pocket-handkerchief, and to be able to read my watch. When he had done this, I bade him leave me.

I lay in bed, burning, racked with pain in my head, and with my eye-balls on fire.

Whether I fell asleep or went off my head for a while I cannot tell. I may have fainted. I have no recollection of anything after having gone to bed and taken a sip of lime-juice that tasted to me like soap—till I was roused by a sense of pain in my ribs—a slow, gnawing, torturing pain, waxing momentarily more intense. In half-consciousness I was partly dreaming and partly aware of actual suffering. The pain was real; but in my fancy I thought that a great maggot was working its way into my side between my ribs. I seemed to see it. It twisted itself half round, then reverted to its former position, and again twisted itself, moving like a bradawl, not like a gimlet, which latter forms a complete revolution.

This, obviously, must have been a dream, hallucination only, as I was lying on my back and my eyes were directed towards the bottom of the bed, and the coverlet and blankets and sheet intervened between my eyes and my side. But in fever one sees without eyes, and in every direction, and through all obstructions.

Roused thoroughly by an excruciating twinge, I tried to cry out, and succeeded in throwing myself over on my right side, that which was in pain. At once I felt the thing withdrawn that was awling—if I may use the word—in between my ribs.

And now I saw, standing beside the bed, a figure that had its arm under the bedclothes, and was slowly removing it. The hand was leisurely drawn from under the coverings and rested on the eiderdown coverlet, with the forefinger extended.

The figure was that of a man, in shabby clothes, with a sallow, mean face, a retreating forehead, with hair cut after the French fashion, and a moustache, dark. The jaws and chin were covered with a bristly growth, as if shaving had been neglected for a fortnight. The figure did not appear to be thoroughly solid, but to be of the consistency of curd, and the face was of the complexion of curd. As I looked at this object it withdrew, sliding backward in an odd sort of manner, and as though overweighted by the hand, which was the most substantial, indeed the only substantial portion of it. Though the figure retreated stooping, yet it was no longer huddled along by the finger, as if it had no material existence. If the same, it had acquired a consistency and a solidity which it did not possess before.

How it vanished I do not know, nor whither it went. The door opened, and Square came in.

"What!" he exclaimed with cheery voice; "influenza is it?"

"I don't know—I think it's that finger again."

IV

"Now, look here," said Square, "I'm not going to have that cuss at its pranks anymore. Tell me all about it."

I was now so exhausted, so feeble, that I was not able to give a connected account of what had taken place, but Square put to me just a few pointed questions and elicited the main facts. He pieced them together in his own orderly mind, so as to form a connected whole. "There is a feature in the case," said he, "that strikes me as remarkable and important. At first—a finger only, then a hand, then a nebulous figure attached to the hand, without backbone, without consistency.

Lastly, a complete form, with consistency and with backbone, but the latter in a gelatinous condition, and the entire figure overweighted by the hand, just as hand and figure were previously overweighted by the finger. Simultaneously with this compacting and consolidating of the figure, came your degeneration and loss of vital force and, in a word, of health. What you lose, that object acquires, and what it acquires, it gains by contact with you. That's clear enough, is it not?"

"I dare say. I don't know. I can't think."

"I suppose not; the faculty of thought is drained out of you. Very well, I must think for you, and I will. Force is force, and see if I can't deal with your visitant in such a way as will prove just as truly a moral dissuasive as that employed on the union men on strike in—never mind where it was. That's not to the point."

"Will you kindly give me some lime-juice?" I entreated.

I sipped the acid draught, but without relief. I listened to Square, but without hope. I wanted to be left alone. I was weary of my pain, weary of everything, even of life. It was a matter of indifference to me whether I recovered or slipped out of existence.

"It will be here again shortly," said the engineer. "As the French say, *l'appetit vient en mangeant*. It has been at you thrice, it won't be content without another peck. And if it does get another, I guess it will pretty well about finish you."

Mr. Square rubbed his chin, and then put his hands into his trouser pockets. That also was a trick acquired in the States, an inelegant one. His hands, when not actively occupied, went into his pockets, inevitably they gravitated thither. Ladies did not like Square; they said he was not a gentleman. But it was not that he said or did anything "off colour," only he spoke to them, looked at them, walked with them, always with his hands in his pockets. I have seen a lady turn her back on him deliberately because of this trick.

Standing now with his hands in his pockets, he studied my bed, and said contemptuously:

"Old-fashioned and bad, fourposter. Oughtn't to be allowed, I guess; unwholesome all the way round."

I was not in a condition to dispute this. I like a fourposter with curtains at head and feet; not that I ever draw them, but it gives a sense of privacy that is wanting in one of your half-tester beds.

If there is a window at one's feet, one can lie in bed without the glare in one's eyes, and yet without darkening the room by drawing the blinds. There is much to be said for a fourposter, but this is not the place in which to say it.

Mr. Square pulled his hands out of his pockets and began fiddling with the electric point near the head of my bed, attached a wire, swept it in a semicircle along the floor, and then thrust the knob at the end into my hand in the bed.

"Keep your eye open," said he, "and your hand shut and covered. If that finger comes again tickling your ribs, try it with the point. I'll manage the switch, from behind the curtain."

Then he disappeared.

I was too indifferent in my misery to turn my head and observe where he was. I remained inert, with the knob in my hand, and my eyes closed, suffering and thinking of nothing but the shooting pains through my head and the aches in my loins and back and legs.

Some time probably elapsed before I felt the finger again at work at my ribs; it groped, but no longer bored. I now felt the entire hand, not a single finger, and the hand was substantial, cold, and clammy. I was aware, how, I know not, that if the finger-point reached the region of my heart, on the left side, the hand would, so to speak, sit down on it, with the cold palm over it, and that then immediately my heart would cease to beat, and it would be, as Square might express it, "gone coon" with me.

In self-preservation I brought up the knob of the electric wire against the hand—against one of the fingers, I think—and at once was aware of a rapping, squealing noise. I turned my head languidly, and saw the form, now more substantial than before, capering in an ecstasy of pain, endeavouring fruitlessly to withdraw its arm from under the bedclothes, and the hand from the electric point.

At the same moment Square stepped from behind the curtain, with a dry laugh, and said: "I thought we should fix him. He has the coil about him, and can't escape. Now let us drop to particulars. But I shan't let you off till I know all about you."

The last sentence was addressed, not to me, but to the apparition.

Thereupon he bade me take the point away from the hand of the figure—being—whatever it was, but to be ready with it at a moment's notice. He then proceeded to catechize my visitor, who moved restlessly within the circle of wire, but could not escape from it. It replied in a thin, squealing voice that sounded as if it came from a distance, and had a querulous tone in it. I do not pretend to give all that was said. I cannot recollect everything that passed. My memory was affected by my illness, as well as my body. Yet I prefer giving the scraps that I recollect to what Square told me he had heard.

"Yes—I was unsuccessful, always was. Nothing answered with me. The world was against me. Society was. I hate Society. I don't like work neither, never did. But I like agitating against what is established. I hate the Royal Family, the landed interest, the parsons, everything that is, except the people—that is, the unemployed. I always did. I couldn't get work as suited me. When I died they buried me in a cheap coffin, dirt cheap, and gave me a nasty grave, cheap, and a service rattled away cheap, and no monument. Didn't want none. Oh! there are lots of us. All discontented. Discontent! That's a passion, it is—it gets into the veins, it fills the brain, it occupies the heart; it's a sort of divine cancer that takes possession of the entire man, and makes him dissatisfied with everything, and hate everybody. But we must have our share of happiness at some time. We all crave for it in one way or other. Some think there's a future state of blessedness and so have hope, and look to attain to it, for hope is a cable and anchor that attaches to what is real, But when you have no hope of that sort, don't believe in any future state, you must look for happiness in life here. We didn't get it when we were alive, so we seek to procure it after we are dead. We can do it, if we can get out of our cheap and nasty coffins. But not till the greater part of us is mouldered away. If a finger or two remains, that can work its way up to the surface, those cheap deal coffins go to pieces quick enough. Then the only solid part of us left can pull the rest of us that has gone to nothing after it. Then we grope about after the living. The well-to-do if we can get at them—the honest working poor if we can't—we hate them too, because they are content and happy. If we reach any of these, and can touch them, then we can draw their vital force out of them into ourselves, and recuperate at their expense. That was about what I was going to do with you. Getting on famous. Nearly solidified into a new man; and given another chance in life. But I've missed it this time. Just like my luck. Miss everything. Always have, except misery and disappointment. Get plenty of that."

"What are you all?" asked Square. "Anarchists out of employ?"

"Some of us go by that name, some by other designations, but we are all one, and own allegiance to but one monarch—Sovereign discontent. We are bred to have a distaste for manual work; and we grow up loafers, grumbling at everything and quarrelling with Society that is around us and the Providence that is above us."

"And what do you call yourselves now?"

"Call ourselves? Nothing; we are the same, in another condition, that is all. Folk once called us Anarchists, Nihilists, Socialists, Levelers, now they call us the Influenza. The learned talk of microbes, and bacilli, and bacteria. Microbes, bacilli, and bacteria be blowed! We are the Influenza; we the social failures, the generally discontented, coming up out of our cheap and nasty graves in the form of physical disease—We are the Influenza."

"There you are, I guess!" exclaimed Square triumphantly. "Did I not say that all forces were correlated? If so, then all negations, deficiencies of force are one in their several manifestations. Talk of Divine discontent as a force impelling to progress! Rubbish, it is a paralysis of energy. It turns all it absorbs to acid, to envy, spite, gall. It inspires nothing, but rots the whole moral system. Here you have it—moral, social, political discontent in another form, nay aspect—that is all. What Anarchism is in the body Politic, that Influenza is in the body Physical. Do you see that?"

"Ye-e-e-e-s," I believe I answered, and dropped away into the land of dreams.

I recovered. What Square did with the Thing I know not, but believe that he reduced it again to its former negative and self-decomposing condition.

Let fairytale of mine go for a firefly that now flashes, now is dark, but may flash again. Caught in a hand which does not love its kind, it will turn to an insignificant, ugly thing, that can neither flash nor fly.

—George MacDonald, "The Fantastic Imagination."

AUNT JOANNA

Sabine Baring-Gould

In the Land's End district is the little church-town of Zennor. There is no village to speak of—a few scattered farms, and here and there a cluster of cottages. The district is bleak, the soil does not lie deep over granite that peers through the surface on exposed spots, where the furious gales from the ocean sweep the land. If trees ever existed there, they have been swept away by the blast, but the golden furze or gorse defies all winds, and clothes the moorland with a robe of splendour, and the heather flushes the slopes with crimson towards the decline of summer, and mantles them in soft, warm brown in winter, like the fur of an animal.

In Zennor is a little church, built of granite, rude and simple of construction, crouching low, to avoid the gales, but with a tower that has defied the winds and the lashing rains, because wholly devoid of sculptured detail, which would have afforded the blasts something to lay hold of and eat away. In Zennor parish is one of the finest cromlechs in Cornwall, a huge slab of unwrought stone like a table, poised on the points of standing upright blocks as rude as the mass they sustain.

Near this monument of a hoar and indeed unknown antiquity lived an old woman by herself, in a small cottage of one story in height, built of moor stones set in earth, and pointed only with lime. It was thatched with heather, and possessed but a single chimney that rose but little above the apex of the roof, and had two slates set on the top to protect the rising smoke from being blown down the chimney into the cottage when the wind was from the west or from the east. When, however, it drove from north or south, then the smoke must take care of itself. On such occasions it was wont to find its way out of the door, and little or none went up the chimney.

The only fuel burnt in this cottage was peat—not the solid black peat from deep, bogs, but turf of only a spade graft, taken from the surface, and composed of undissolved roots. Such fuel gives flame, which the other does not; but, on the other hand, it does not throw out the same amount of heat, nor does it last one half the time.

The woman who lived in the cottage was called by the people of the neighbourhood Aunt Joanna. What her family name was but few remembered, nor did it concern herself much. She had no relations at all, with the exception of a grand-niece, who was married to a small tradesman, a wheelwright near the church. But Joanna and her great-niece were not on speaking terms. The girl had mortally offended the old woman by going to a dance at St. Ives, against her express orders. It was at this dance that she had met the wheelwright, and this meeting, and the treatment the girl had met with from her aunt for having gone to it, had led to the marriage. For Aunt Joanna was very strict in her Wesleyanism, and bitterly hostile to all such carnal amusements as dancing and play-acting. Of the latter there was none in that wild west Cornish district, and no temptation ever afforded by a strolling company setting up its booth within reach of Zennor. But dancing, though denounced, still drew the more independent spirits together. Rose Penaluna had been with her great-aunt after her mother's death. She was a lively girl, and when she heard of a dance at St. Ives, and had been asked to go to it, although forbidden by Aunt Joanna, she stole from the cottage at night, and found her way to St. Ives.

Her conduct was reprehensible certainly. But that of Aunt Joanna was even more so, for when she discovered that the girl had left the house she barred her door, and refused to allow Rose to re-enter it. The poor girl had been obliged to take refuge the same night at the nearest farm and sleep in an outhouse, and next morning to go into St. Ives and entreat an acquaintance to take her in till she could enter into service. Into service she did not go, for when Abraham Hext, the carpenter, heard how she had been treated, he at once proposed, and in three weeks married her. Since then no communication had taken place between the old woman and her grand-niece. As Rose knew, Joanna was implacable in her resentments, and considered that she had been acting aright in what she had done.

The nearest farm to Aunt Joanna's cottage was occupied by the Hockins. One day Elizabeth, the farmer's wife, saw the old woman outside the cottage as she was herself returning from market; and, noticing how bent and feeble Joanna was, she halted, and talked to her, and gave her good advice.

"See you now, auntie, you'm gettin' old and crimmed wi' rheumatics. How can you get about? An' there's no knowin' but you might be took bad in the night. You ought to have some little lass wi' you to mind you."

"I don't want nobody, thank the Lord."

"Not just now, auntie, but suppose any chance ill-luck were to come on you. And then, in the bad weather, you'm not fit to go abroad after the turves, and you can't get all you want—tay and sugar and milk for yourself now. It would be handy to have a little maid by you."

"Who should I have?" asked Joanna.

"Well, now, you couldn't do better than take little Mary, Rose Hext's eldest girl. She's a handy maid, and bright and pleasant to speak to."

"No," answered the old woman, "I'll have none o' they Hexts, not I. The Lord is agin Rose and all her family, I know it. I'll have none of them."

"But, auntie, you must be nigh on ninety."

"I be ower that. But what o' that? Didn't Sarah, the wife of Abraham, live to an hundred and seven and twenty years, and that in spite of him worritin' of her wi' that owdacious maid of hem, Hagar? If it hadn't been for their goings on, of Abraham and Hagar, it's my belief that she'd ha' held on to a hundred and fifty-seven. I thank the Lord I've never had no man to worrit me. So why I shouldn't equal Sarah's life I don't see."

Then she went indoors and shut the door.

After that a week elapsed without Mrs. Hockin seeing the old woman. She passed the cottage, but no Joanna was about. The door was not open, and usually it was. Elizabeth spoke about this to her husband. "Jabez," said she, "I don't like the looks o' this; I've kept my eye open, and there be no Auntie Joanna hoppin' about. Whativer can be up? It's my opinion us ought to go and see."

"Well, I've naught on my hands now," said the farmer, "so I reckon we will go." The two walked together to the cottage. No smoke issued from the chimney, and the door was shut. Jabez knocked, but there came no answer; so he entered, followed by his wife.

There was in the cottage but the kitchen, with one bedroom at the side. The hearth was cold. "There's some'ut up," said Mrs. Hockin.

"I reckon it's the old lady be down," replied her husband, and, throwing open the bedroom door, he said: "Sure enough, and no mistake—there her be, dead as a dried pilchard."

And in fact Auntie Joanna had died in the night, after having so confidently affirmed her conviction that she would live to the age of a hundred and twenty-seven.

"Whativer shall we do?" asked Mrs. Hockin. "I reckon," said her husband, "us had better take an inventory of what is here, lest wicked rascals come in and steal anything and everything."

"Folks bain't so bad as that, and a corpse in the house," observed Mrs. Hockin.

"Don't be sure o' that—these be terrible wicked times," said the husband. "And I sez, sez I, no harm is done in seein' what the old creetur had got."

"Well, surely," acquiesced Elizabeth, "there is no harm in that." In the bedroom was an old oak chest, and this the farmer and his wife opened. To their surprise they found in it a silver teapot, and half a dozen silver spoons.

"Well, now," exclaimed Elizabeth Hockin, "fancy her havin' these— and me only Britannia metal."

"I reckon she came of a good family," said Jabez. "Leastwise, I've heard as how she were once well off"

"And look here!" exclaimed Elizabeth, "there's fine and beautiful linen underneath—sheets and pillow-cases."

"But look here!" cried Jabez, "blessed if the taypot bain't chock-full o' money! Whereiver did she get it from?"

"Her's been in the way of showing folk the Zennor Quoit, visitors from St. Ives and Penzance, and she's had scores o' shillings that way."

"Lord!" exclaimed Jabez. "I wish she'd left it to me, and I could buy a cow; I want another cruel bad."

"Ay, we do, terrible," said Elizabeth. "But just look to her bed, what torn and wretched linen be on that—and here these fine bedclothes all in the chest."

"Who'll get the silver taypot and spoons, and the money?" inquired Jabez.

"Her had no kin—none but Rose Hext, and her couldn't abide her. Last words her said to me was that she'd 'have never naught to do wi' the Hexts, they and all their belongings.'"

"That was her last words?"

"The very last words her spoke to me—or to anyone."

"Then," said Jabez, "I'll tell ye what, Elizabeth, it's our moral dooty to abide by the wishes of Aunt Joanna. It never does to go agin what is might. And as hem expressed herself that strong, why us, as honest folks, must carry out her wishes, and see that none of all her savings go to them darned and dratted Hexts."

"But who be they to go to, then?"

"Well—we'll see. Fust us will have her removed, and provide that her be daycent buried. Them Hexts be in a poor way, and couldn't afford the expense, and it do seem to me, Elizabeth, as it would be a liberal and a kindly act in us to take all the charges on ourselves. Us is the closest neighbours."

"Ay—and her have had milk of me these ten or twelve years, and I've never charged her a penny, thinking her couldn't afford it. But her could, her were a-hoardin' of hem money—and not paying me. That were not honest, and what I say is, that I have a right to some of her savin's, to pay the milk bill—and it's butter I've let her have now and then in a liberal way."

"Very well, Elizabeth. Fust of all, we'll take the silver taypot and the spoons wi' us, to get 'em out of harm's way."

"And I'll carry the linen sheets and pillow-cases. My word I—why didn't she use 'em, instead of them rags?"

All Zennor declared that the Hockins were a most neighbourly and generous couple, when it was known that they took upon themselves to defray the funeral expenses.

Mrs. Hext came to the farm, and said that she was willing to do what she could, but Mrs. Hockin replied:

"My good Rose, it's no good. I seed your aunt when her was ailin', and nigh on death, and her laid it on me solemn as could be that we was to bury her, and that she'd have nothin' to do wi' the Hexts at no price."

Rose sighed, and went away.

Rose had not expected to receive anything from her aunt. She had never been allowed to look at the treasures in the oak chest. As far as she had been aware, Aunt Joanna had been extremely poor. But she remembered that the old woman had at one time befriended her, and she was ready to forgive the harsh treatment to which she had finally been subjected. In fact, she had repeatedly made overtures to her great-aunt to be reconciled, but these overtures had been always rejected. She was, accordingly, not surprised to learn from Mrs. Hockin that the old woman's last words had been as reported.

But, although disowned and disinherited, Rose, her husband, and children dressed in black, and were chief mourners at the funeral. Now it had so happened that when it came to the laying out of Aunt Joanna, Mrs. Hockin had looked at the beautiful linen sheets she had found in the oak chest, with the object of furnishing the corpse with one as a winding-sheet. But—she said to herself—it would really be a shame to spoil a pair, and where else could she get such fine and beautiful old linen as was this? So she put the sheets away, and furnished for the purpose a clean but coarse and ragged sheet such as Aunt Joanna had in common use. That was good enough to moulder in the grave. It would be positively sinful, because wasteful, to give up to corruption and the worm such fine white linen as Aunt Joanna had hoarded. The funeral was conducted, otherwise, liberally. Aunt Joanna was given an elm, and not a mean deal board coffin, such as is provided for paupers; and a handsome escutcheon of white metal was put on the lid.

Moreover, plenty of gin was drunk, and cake and cheese eaten at the house, all at the expense of the Hockins. And the conversation among those who attended, and ate and drank, and wiped their eyes, was rather anent the generosity of the Hockins than of the virtues of the departed.

Mr. and Mrs. Hockin heard this, and their hearts swelled within them. Nothing so swells the heart as the consciousness of virtue being recognised. Jabez in an undertone informed a neighbour that he were'nt goin' to stick at the funeral expenses, not he; he'd have a neat stone erected above the grave with work on it, at twopence a letter. The name and the date of departure of Aunt Joanna, and her age, and two lines of a favourite hymn of his, all about earth being no dwelling-place, heaven being properly her home.

It was not often that Elizabeth Hockin cried, but she did this day; she wept tears of sympathy with the deceased, and happiness at the ovation accorded to herself and her husband. At length, as the short winter day closed in, the last of those who had attended the funeral, and had returned to the farm to recruit and regale after it, departed, and the Hockins were left to themselves.

"It were a beautiful day," said Jabez.

"Ay," responded Elizabeth, "and what a sight o' people came here."

"This here buryin' of Aunt Joanna have set us up tremendous in the estimation of the neighbours."

"I'd like to know who else would ha' done it for a poor old creetur as is no relation; ay—and one as owed a purty long bill to me for milk and butter through ten or twelve years."

"Well," said Jabez, "I've allus heard say that a good deed brings its own reward wi' it—and it's a fine proverb. I feels it in my insides."

"P'raps it's the gin, Jabez."

"No—it's virtue. It's warmer nor gin a long sight. Gin gives a smouldering spark, but a good conscience is a blaze of furze."

The farm of the Hockins was small, and Hockin looked after his cattle himself. One maid was kept, but no man in the house. All were wont to retire early to bed; neither Hockin nor his wife had literary tastes, and were not disposed to consume much oil, so as to read at night.

During the night, at what time she did not know, Mrs. Hockin awoke with a start, and found that her husband was sitting up in bed listening. There was a moon that night, and no clouds in the sky. The room was full of silver light. Elizabeth Hockin heard a sound of feet in the kitchen, which was immediately under the bedroom of the couple.

"There's someone about," she whispered; "go down, Jabez."

"I wonder, now, who it be. P'raps its Sally."

"It can't be Sally—how can it, when she can't get out o' hem room wi'out passin' through ours?"

"Run down, Elizabeth, and see."

"It's your place to go, Jabez."

"But if it was a woman—and me in my night-shirt?"

"And, Jabez, if it was a man, a robber—and me in my night-shirt? It 'ud be shameful."

"I reckon us had best go down together."

"We'll do so—but I hope it's not—"

"What?"

Mrs. Hockin did not answer. She and her husband crept from bed, and, treading on tiptoe across the room, descended the stair.

There was no door at the bottom, but the staircase was boarded up at the side; it opened into the kitchen.

They descended very softly and cautiously, holding each other, and when they reached the bottom, peered timorously into the apartment that served many purposes—kitchen, sitting-room, and dining-place. The moonlight poured in through the broad, low window.

By it they saw a figure. There could be no mistaking it—it was that of Aunt Joanna, clothed in the tattered sheet that Elizabeth Hockin had allowed for her grave-clothes. The old woman had taken one of the fine linen sheets out of the cupboard in which it had been placed, and had spread it over the long table, and was smoothing it down with her bony hands.

The Hockins trembled, not with cold, though it was mid-winter, but with terror. They dared not advance, and they felt powerless to retreat.

Then they saw Aunt Joanna go to the cupboard, open it, and return with the silver spoons; she placed all six on the sheet, and with a lean finger counted them.

She turned her face towards those who were watching her proceedings, but it was in shadow, and they could not distinguish the features nor note the expression with which she regarded them.

Presently she went back to the cupboard, and returned with the silver teapot. She stood at one end of the table, and now the reflection of the moon on the linen sheet was cast upon her face, and they saw that she was moving her lips—but no sound issued from them.

She thrust her hand into the teapot and drew forth the coins, one by one, and rolled them along the table. The Hockins saw the glint of the metal, and the shadow cast by each piece of money as it rolled. The first coin lodged at the further left-hand corner and the second rested near it; and so on, the pieces were rolled, and ranged themselves in order, ten in a row. Then the next ten were run across the white cloth in the same manner, and dropped over on their sides below the first row; thus also the third ten. And all the time the dead woman was mouthing, as though counting, but still inaudibly.

The couple stood motionless observing proceedings, till suddenly a cloud passed before the face of the moon, so dense as to eclipse the light.

Then in a paroxysm of terror both turned and fled up the stairs, bolted their bedroom door, and jumped into bed.

There was no sleep for them that night. In the gloom when the moon was concealed, in the glare when it shone forth, it was the same, they could hear the light rolling of the coins along the table, and the click as they fell over. Was the supply inexhaustible? It was not so, but apparently the dead woman did not weary of counting the coins. When all had been ranged, she could be heard moving to the further end of the table, and there re-commencing the same proceeding of coin-rolling.

Not till near daybreak did this sound cease, and not till the maid, Sally, had begun to stir in the inner bedchamber did Hockin and his wife venture to rise. Neither would suffer the servant girl to descend till they had been down to see in what condition the kitchen was. They found that the table had been cleared, the coins were all back in the teapot, and that and the spoons were where they had themselves placed them. The sheet, moreover, was neatly folded, and replaced where it had been before.

The Hockins did not speak to one another of their experiences during the past night, so long as they were in the house, but when Jabez was in the field, Elizabeth went to him and said: "Husband, what about Aunt Joanna?"

"I don't know—maybe it were a dream."

"Curious us should ha' dreamed alike."

"I don't know that; 'twere the gin made us dream, and us both had gin, so us dreamed the same thing."

"'Twere more like real truth than dream," observed Elizabeth.

"We'll take it as dream," said Jabez.

"Mebbe it won't happen again."

But precisely the same sounds were heard on the following night. The moon was obscured by thick clouds, and neither of the two had the courage to descend to the kitchen. But they could hear the patter of feet, and then the roll and click of the coins. Again sleep was impossible.

"Whatever shall we do?" asked Elizabeth Hockin next morning of her husband. "Us can't go on like this wi' the dead woman about our house nightly. There's no tellin' she might take it into her head to come upstairs and pull the sheets off us. As we took hers, she may think it fair to carry off ours."

"I think," said Jabez sorrowfully, "we'll have to return 'em."

"But how?"

After some consultation the couple resolved on conveying all the deceased woman's goods to the churchyard, by night, and placing them on her grave.

"I reckon," said Hockin, "we'll bide in the porch and watch what happens. If they be left there till mornin', why we may carry 'em back wi' an easy conscience. We've spent some pounds over her buryin'."

"What have it come to?"

"Three pounds five and fourpence, as I make it out."

"Well," said Elizabeth, "we must risk it."

When night had fallen murk, the farmer and his wife crept from their house, carrying the linen sheets, the teapot, and the silver spoons. They did not start till late, for fear of encountering any villagers on the way, and not till after the maid, Sally, had gone to bed.

They fastened the farm door behind them. The night was dark and stormy, with scudding clouds, so dense as to make deep night, when they did not part and allow the moon to peer forth.

They walked timorously, and side by side, looking about them as they proceeded, and on reaching the churchyard gate they halted to pluck up courage before opening and venturing within. Jabez had furnished himself with a bottle of gin, to give courage to himself and his wife.

Together they heaped the articles that had belonged to Aunt Joanna upon the fresh grave, but as they did so the wind caught the linen and unfurled and flapped it, and they were forced to place stones upon it to hold it down. Then, quaking with fear, they retreated to the church porch, and Jabez, uncorking the bottle, first took a long pull himself, and then presented it to his wife.

And now down came a tearing rain, driven by a blast from the Atlantic, howling among the gravestones, and screaming in the battlements of the tower and its bell-chamber windows. The night was so dark, and the rain fell so heavily, that they could see nothing for full half an hour. But then the clouds were rent asunder, and the moon glared white and ghastly over the churchyard.

Elizabeth caught her husband by the arm and pointed. There was, however, no need for her to indicate that on which his eyes were fixed already.

Both saw a lean hand come up out of the grave, and lay hold of one of the fine linen sheets and drag at it. They saw it drag the sheet by one corner, and then it went down underground, and the sheet followed, as though sucked down in a vortex; fold on fold it descended, till the entire sheet had disappeared.

"Her have taken it for her windin' sheet," whispered Elizabeth. "Whativer will her do wi' the rest?"

"Have a drop o' gin; this be terrible tryin'," said Jabez in an undertone; and again the couple put their lips to the bottle, which came away considerably lighter after the draughts.

"Look!" gasped Elizabeth.

Again the lean hand with long fingers appeared above the soil, and this was seen groping about the grass till it laid hold of the teapot. Then it groped again, and gathered up the spoons, that flashed in the moonbeams. Next, up came the second hand, and a long arm that stretched along the grave till it reached the other sheets. At once, on being raised, these sheets were caught by the wind, and flapped and fluttered like half-hoisted sails. The hands retained them for a while till they bellied with the wind, and then let them go, and they were swept away by the blast across the churchyard, over the wall, and lodged in the carpenter's yard that adjoined, among his timber.

"She have sent 'em to the Hexts," whispered Elizabeth. Next the hands began to trifle with the teapot, and to shake out some of the coins.

In a minute some silver pieces were flung with so true an aim that they fell clinking down on the floor of the porch.

How many coins, how much money was cast, the couple were in no mood to estimate. Then they saw the hands collect the pillow-cases, and proceed to roll up the teapot and silver spoons in them, and, that done, the white bundle was cast into the air, and caught by the wind and carried over the churchyard wall into the wheelwright's yard.

At once a curtain of vapour rushed across the face of the moon, and again the graveyard was buried in darkness. Half an hour elapsed before the moon shone out again. Then the Hockins saw that nothing was stirring in the cemetery.

"I reckon us may go now," said Jabez.

"Let us gather up what she chucked to us," advised Elizabeth. So the couple felt about the floor, and collected a number of coins. What they were they could not tell till they reached their home, and had lighted a candle.

"How much be it?" asked Elizabeth.

"Three pound five and fourpence, exact," answered Jabez.

THE GRAY MAN

Sarah Orne Jewett (1849-1909)

High on the southern slope of Agamenticus there may still be seen the remnant of an old farm. Frost-shaken stone walls surround a fast-narrowing expanse of smooth turf which the forest is overgrowing on every side. The cellar is nearly filled up, never having been either wide or deep, and the fruit of a few mossy apple-trees drops ungathered to the ground. Along one side of the forsaken garden is a thicket of seedling cherry-trees to which the shouting robins come year after year in busy flights; the caterpillars' nests are unassailed and populous in this untended hedge. At night, perhaps, when summer twilights are late in drawing their brown curtain of dusk over the great rural scene,—at night an owl may sit in the hemlocks near by and hoot and shriek until the far echoes answer back again. As for the few men and women who pass this deserted spot, most will be repulsed by such loneliness, will even grow impatient with those mistaken fellow-beings who choose to live in solitude, away from neighbors and from schools,—yes, even from gossip and petty care of self or knowledge of the trivial fashions of a narrow life.

Now and then one looks out from this eyrie, across the wide-spread country, who turns to look at the sea or toward the shining foreheads of the mountains that guard the inland horizon, who will remember the place long afterward. A peaceful vision will come, full of rest and benediction into busy and troubled hours, to those who understand why some one came to live in this place so near the sky, so silent, so full of sweet air and woodland fragrance; so beaten and buffeted by winter storms and garlanded with summer greenery; where the birds are nearest neighbors and a clear spring the only wine-cellar, and trees of the forest a choir of singers who rejoice and sing aloud by day and night as the winds sweep over. Under the cherry thicket or at the edge of the woods you may find a stray-away blossom, some half-savage, slender grandchild of the old

153

flower-plots, that you gather gladly to take away, and every year in June a red rose blooms toward which the wild pink roses and the pale sweet briars turn wondering faces as if a queen had shown her noble face suddenly at a peasant's festival.

There is everywhere a token of remembrance, of silence and secrecy. Some stronger nature once ruled these neglected trees and this fallow ground. They will wait the return of their master as long as roots can creep through mould, and the mould make way for them. The stories of strange lives have been whispered to the earth, their thoughts have burned themselves into the cold rocks. As one looks from the lower country toward the long slope of the great hillside, this old abiding-place marks the dark covering of trees like a scar. There is nothing to hide either the sunrise or the sunset. The low lands reach out of sight into the west and the sea fills all the east.

The first owner of the farm was a seafaring man who had through freak or fancy come ashore and cast himself upon the bounty of nature for support in his later years, though tradition keeps a suspicion of buried treasure and of a dark history. He cleared his land and built his house, but save the fact that he was a Scotsman no one knew to whom he belonged, and when he died the state inherited the unclaimed property. The only piece of woodland that was worth anything was sold and added to another farm, and the dwelling-place was left to the sunshine and the rain, to the birds that built their nests in the chimney or under the eaves. Sometimes a strolling company of country boys would find themselves near the house on a holiday afternoon, but the more dilapidated the small structure became, the more they believed that some uncanny existence possessed the lonely place, and the path that led toward the clearing at last became almost impassable.

Once a number of officers and men in the employ of the Coast Survey were encamped at the top of the mountain, and they smoothed the rough track that led down to the spring that bubbled from under a sheltering edge. One day a laughing fellow, not content with peering in at the small windows of the house, put his shoulder against the rain-blackened door and broke the simple fastening. He hardly knew that he was afraid as he first stood within the single spacious room, so complete a curiosity took possession of him. The place was clean and bare, the empty cupboard doors stood open, and yet the sound of his companions' voices outside seemed far away, and an awful sense that some unseen inhabitant followed his footsteps made him hurry out again pale and breathless to the fresh air and sunshine. Was this really a dwelling-place of spirits, as had been already hinted? The story grew more fearful, and spread quickly like a mist of terror among the lowland farms. For years the tale of the coast-surveyor's adventure in the haunted house was slowly magnified and told to strangers or to wide-eyed children by the dim firelight. The former owner was supposed to linger still about his old home, and was held accountable for deep offense in choosing for the scene of his unsuccessful husbandry a place that escaped the properties and restraints of life upon lower levels. His grave was concealed by the new growth of oaks and beeches, and many a lad and full-grown man beside has taken to his heels at the flicker of light from across a swamp or under a decaying tree in that neighborhood. As the world in some respects grew wiser, the good people near the mountain understood less and less the causes of these simple effects, and as they became familiar with the visible world, grew more shy of the unseen and more sensitive to unexplained foreboding.

One day a stranger was noticed in the town, as a stranger is sure to be who goes his way with quick, furtive steps straight through a small village or along a country road. This man was tall and had just passed middle age. He was well made and vigorous, but there was an unusual pallor in his face, a grayish look, as if he had been startled by bad news. His clothes were somewhat peculiar, as if they had been made in another country, yet they suited the chilly weather, being homespun of undyed wools, just the color of his hair, and only a little darker than his face or hands. Some one observed in one brief glance as he and this gray man met and passed each other, that his eyes had a strange faded look; they might, however, flash and be coal-black in a moment of rage. Two or three persons stepped forward to watch the wayfarer as he went along the road with long, even strides, like one taking a journey on foot, but he quickly reached a turn of the way and was out of sight. They wondered who he was; one recalled some recent advertisement of an escaped criminal, and another the appearance of a native of the town who was supposed to be long ago lost at sea, but one surmiser knew as little as the next. If they had followed fast enough they might have tracked the mysterious man straight across the country, threading the by-ways, the shorter paths that led across the fields where the road was roundabout and hindering. At last he disappeared in the leafless, trackless woods that skirted the mountain.

That night there was for the first time in many years a twinkling light in the window of the haunted house, high on the hill's great shoulder; one farmer's wife and another looked up curiously, while they wondered what daring human being had chosen that awesome spot of all others for his home or for even a transient shelter. The sky was already heavy with snow; he might be a fugitive from justice, and the startled people looked to the fastening of their doors unwontedly that night, and waked often from a troubled sleep.

An instinctive curiosity and alarm possessed the country men and women for a while, but soon faded out and disappeared. The newcomer was by no means a hermit; he tried to be friendly, and inclined toward a certain kindliness and familiarity. He bought a comfortable store of winter provisions from his new acquaintances, giving every one his price, and spoke more at length, as time went on, of current events, of politics and the weather, and the town's own news and concerns. There was a sober cheerfulness about the man, as if he had known trouble and perplexity, and was fulfilling some mission that gave him pain; yet he saw some gain and reward beyond; therefore he could be contented with his life and such strange surroundings. He was more and more eager to form brotherly relations with the farmers near his home. There was almost a pleading look in his kind face at times, as if he feared the later prejudice of his associates. Surely this was no common or uneducated person, for in every way he left the stamp of his character and influence upon men and things. His reasonable words of advice and warning are current as sterling coins in that region yet; to one man he taught a new rotation of crops, to another he gave some priceless cures for devastating diseases of cattle. The lonely women of those remote country homes learned of him how to achieve their household toil with less labor and drudgery, and here and there he singled out promising children and kept watch of their growth, giving freely a most affectionate companionship, and a fair start in the journey of life. He taught those who were guardians of such children to recognize and further the true directions and purposes of existence; and the easily warped natures grew strong and well-established under his thoughtful care. No wonder that some people were filled with amazement, and thought his wisdom supernatural, from so many proofs that his horizon was wider than their own.

Perhaps some envious soul, or one aggrieved by being caught in treachery or deception, was the first to find fault with the stranger. The prejudice against his dwelling-place, and the superstition which had become linked to him in consequence, may have led back to the first suspicious attitude of the community. The whisper of distrust soon started on an evil way. If he were not a criminal, his past was surely a hidden one, and shocking to his remembrance, but the true foundation of all dislike was the fact that the gray man who went to and fro, living his simple, harmless life among them, never was seen to smile. Persons who remember him speak of this with a shudder, for nothing is more evident than that his peculiarity became at length intolerable to those whose minds lent themselves readily to suspicion. At first, blinded by the gentle good fellowship of the stranger, the changeless expression of his face was scarcely observed, but as the winter wore away he was watched with renewed disbelief and dismay.

After the first few attempts at gayety nobody tried to tell a merry story in his presence. The most conspicuous of a joker's audience does a deep-rankling injustice if he sits with unconscious, unamused face at the receipt of raillery. What a chilling moment when the gray man softly opened the door of a farmhouse kitchen, and seated himself like a skeleton at the feast of walnuts and roasted apples beside the glowing fire! The children whom he treated so lovingly, to whom he ever gave his best, though they were won at first by his gentleness, when they began to prattle and play with him would raise their innocent eyes to his face and hush their voices and creep away out of his sight. Once only he was bidden to a wedding, but never afterward, for a gloom was quickly spread through the boisterous company; the man who never smiled had no place at such a festival. The wedding guests looked over their shoulders again and again in strange foreboding, while he was in the house, and were burdened with a sense of coming woe for the newly-married pair. As one caught sight of his, among the faces of the rural folk, the gray man was like a sombre mask, and at last the bridegroom flung open the door with a meaning gesture, and the stranger went out like a hunted creature, into the bitter coldness and silence of the winter night.

Through the long days of the next summer the outcast of the wedding, forbidden, at length, all the once-proffered hospitality, was hardly seen from one week's end to another's. He cultivated his poor estate with patient care, and the successive crops of his small garden, the fruits and berries of the wilderness, were food enough. He seemed unchangeable, and was always ready when he even guessed at a chance to be of use. If he were repulsed, he only turned away and went back to his solitary home. Those persons who by chance visited him there tell wonderful tales of the wild birds which had been tamed to come at his call and cluster about him, of the orderliness and delicacy of his simple life. The once-neglected house was covered with vines that he had brought from the woods, and planted about the splintering, decaying walls. There were three or four books in worn bindings on a shelf above the fire-place; one longs to know what volumes this mysterious exile had chosen to keep him company!

There may have been a deeper reason for the withdrawal of friendliness; there are vague rumors of the gray man's possession of strange powers. Some say that he was gifted with amazing strength, and once when some belated hunters found shelter at his fireside, they told eager listeners afterward that he did not sleep but sat by the fire reading gravely while they slumbered uneasily on his own bed of boughs. And in the dead of night an empty chair glided silently toward him across the floor as he softly turned his pages in the flickering light.

But such stories are too vague, and in that neighborhood too common to weigh against the true dignity and bravery of the man. At the beginning of the war of the rebellion he seemed strangely troubled and

disturbed, and presently disappeared, leaving his house key with a neigh-
bor as if for a few days' absence. He was last seen striding rapidly through
the village a few miles away, going back along the road by which he had
come a year or two before. No, not last seen either; for in one of the first
battles of the war, as the smoke suddenly lifted, a farmer's boy, reared in
the shadow of the mountain, opened his languid pain-dulled eyes as he
lay among the wounded, and saw the gray man riding by on a tall horse.
At that moment the poor lad thought in his faintness and fear that Death
himself rode by in the gray man's likeness; unsmiling Death who tries to
teach and serve mankind so that he may at the last win welcome as a
faithful friend!

A SOMEWHAT IMPROBABLE STORY

G. K. Chesterton (1874-1936)

I cannot remember whether this tale is true or not. If I read it through very carefully I have a suspicion that I should come to the conclusion that it is not. But, unfortunately, I cannot read it through very carefully, because, you see, it is not written yet. The image and the idea of it clung to me through a great part of my boyhood; I may have dreamt it before I could talk; or told it to myself before I could read; or read it before I could remember. On the whole, however, I am certain that I did not read it, for children have very clear memories about things like that; and of the books which I was really fond I can still remember, not only the shape and bulk and binding, but even the position of the printed words on many of the pages. On the whole, I incline to the opinion that it happened to me before I was born.

At any rate, let us tell the story now with all the advantages of the atmosphere that has clung to it. You may suppose me, for the sake of argument, sitting at lunch in one of those quick-lunch restaurants in the City where men take their food so fast that it has none of the quality of food, and take their half-hour's vacation so fast that it has none of the qualities of leisure; to hurry through one's leisure is the most unbusiness-like of actions. They all wore tall shiny hats as if they could not lose an instant even to hang them on a peg, and they all had one eye a little off, hypnotised by the huge eye of the clock. In short, they were the slaves of the modern bondage, you could hear their fetters clanking. Each was, in fact, bound by a chain; the heaviest chain ever tied to a man—it is called a watch-chain.

Now, among these there entered and sat down opposite to me a man who almost immediately opened an uninterrupted monologue. He was like all the other men in dress, yet he was startlingly opposite to them in all manner. He wore a high shiny hat and a long frock coat, but he wore them as such solemn things were meant to be worn; he wore the silk hat as if it were a mitre, and the frock coat as if it were the ephod of a high priest. He not only hung his hat up on the peg, but he seemed (such was his stateliness) almost to ask permission of the hat for doing so, and to apologise to the peg for making use of it. When he had sat down on a wooden chair with the air of one considering its feelings and given a sort of slight stoop or bow to the wooden table itself, as if it were an altar, I could not help some comment springing to my lips. For the man was a big, sanguine-faced, prosperous-looking man, and yet he treated everything with a care that almost amounted to nervousness.

For the sake of saying something to express my interest I said, "This furniture is fairly solid; but, of course, people do treat it much too carelessly."

As I looked up doubtfully my eye caught his, and was fixed as his was fixed in an apocalyptic stare. I had thought him ordinary as he entered, save for his strange, cautious manner; but if the other people had seen him then they would have screamed and emptied the room. They did not see him, and they went on making a clatter with their forks, and a murmur with their conversation. But the man's face was the face of a maniac.

"Did you mean anything particular by that remark?" he asked at last, and the blood crawled back slowly into his face.

"Nothing whatever," I answered. "One does not mean anything here; it spoils people's digestions."

He limped back and wiped his broad forehead with a big handkerchief; and yet there seemed to be a sort of regret in his relief.

"I thought perhaps," he said in a low voice, "that another of them had gone wrong."

"If you mean another digestion gone wrong," I said, "I never heard of one here that went right. This is the heart of the Empire, and the other organs are in an equally bad way."

"No, I mean another street gone wrong," and he said heavily and quietly, "but as I suppose that doesn't explain much to you, I think I shall have to tell you the story. I do so with all the less responsibility, because I know you won't believe it. For forty years of my life I invariably left my office, which is in Leadenhall Street, at half-past five in the afternoon, taking with me an umbrella in the right hand and a bag in the left hand. For forty years two months and four days I passed out of the side office door, walked down the street on the left-hand side, took the first turning to the left and the third to the right, from where I bought an evening paper, followed the road on the right-hand side round two obtuse angles, and came out just outside a Metropolitan station, where I took a train home. For forty years two months and four days I fulfilled this course by accumulated habit: it was not a long street that I traversed, and it took me about four and a half minutes to do it. After forty years two months and four days, on the fifth day I went out in the same manner, with my umbrella in the right hand and my bag in the left, and I began to notice that walking along the familiar street tired me somewhat more than usual; and when I turned it I was convinced that I had turned down the wrong one. For now the street shot up quite a steep slant, such as one only sees in the hilly parts of London, and in this part there were no hills at all. Yet it was not the wrong street; the name written on it was the same; the shuttered shops were the same; the lamp-posts and the whole look of the perspective was the same; only it was tilted upwards like a lid. Forgetting any trouble about breathlessness or fatigue I ran furiously forward, and reached the second of my accustomed turnings, which ought to bring me almost within sight of the station. And as I turned that corner I nearly fell on the pavement. For now the street went up straight in front of my face like a steep staircase or the side of a pyramid. There was not for miles round that place so much as a slope like that of Ludgate Hill. And this was a slope like that of the Matterhorn. The whole street had lifted itself like a single wave, and yet every speck and detail of it was the same, and I saw in the high distance, as at the top of an Alpine pass, picked out in pink letters the name over my paper shop.

"I ran on and on blindly now, passing all the shops and coming to a part of the road where there was a long grey row of private houses. I had, I know not why, an irrational feeling that I was a long iron bridge in empty space. An impulse seized me, and I pulled up the iron trap of a coal-hole. Looking down through it I saw empty space and the stars.

"When I looked up again a man was standing in his front garden, having apparently come out of his house; he was leaning over the railings and gazing at me. We were all alone on that nightmare road; his face was in shadow; his dress was dark and ordinary; but when I saw him standing so perfectly still I knew somehow that he was not of this world. And the stars behind his head were larger and fiercer than ought to be endured by the eyes of men.

"'If you are a kind angel,' I said, 'or a wise devil, or have anything in common with mankind, tell me what is this street possessed of devils.'

"After a long silence he said, 'What do you say that it is?'

"'It is Bumpton Street, of course,' I snapped. 'It goes to Oldgate Station.'

"'Yes,' he admitted gravely; 'it goes there sometimes. Just now, however, it is going to heaven.'

"'To heaven?' I said. 'Why?'

"'It is going to heaven for justice,' he replied. 'You must have treated it badly. Remember always that there is one thing that cannot be endured by anybody or anything. That one unendurable thing is to be overworked and also neglected.For instance, you can overwork women—everybody does. But you can't neglect women—I defy you to. At the same time, you can neglect tramps and gypsies and all the apparent refuse of the State so long as you do not overwork it. But no beast of the field, no horse, no dog can endure long to be asked to do more than his work and yet have less than his honour. It is the same with streets. You have worked this street to death, and yet you have never remembered its existence. If you had a healthy democracy, even of pagans, they would have hung this street with garlands and given it the name of a god. Then it would have gone quietly. But at last the street has grown tired of your tireless insolence; and it is bucking and rearing its head to heaven. Have you never sat on a bucking horse?'

"I looked at the long grey street, and for a moment it seemed to me to be exactly like the long grey neck of a horse flung up to heaven. But in a moment my sanity returned, and I said, 'But this is all nonsense. Streets go to the place they have to go. A street must always go to its end.'

"'Why do you think so of a street?' he asked, standing very still.

"'Because I have always seen it do the same thing,' I replied, in reasonable anger. 'Day after day, year after year, it has always gone to Oldgate Station; day after ...'

"I stopped, for he had flung up his head with the fury of the road in revolt.

"'And you?' he cried terribly. 'What do you think the road thinks of you? Does the road think you are alive? Are you alive? Day after day, year after year, you have gone to Oldgate Station ...' Since then I have respected the things called inanimate."

And bowing slightly to the mustard-pot, the man in the restaurant withdrew.

THE PERFECT GAME

G. K. Chesterton

We have all met the man who says that some odd things have happened to him, but that he does not really believe that they were supernatural. My own position is the opposite of this. I believe in the supernatural as a matter of intellect and reason, not as a matter of personal experience. I do not see ghosts; I only see their inherent probability. But it is entirely a matter of the mere intelligence, not even of the motions; my nerves and body are altogether of this earth, very earthy. But upon people of this temperament one weird incident will often leave a peculiar impression. And the weirdest circumstance that ever occurred to me occurred a little while ago. It consisted in nothing less than my playing a game, and playing it quite well for some seventeen consecutive minutes. The ghost of my grandfather would have astonished me less.

On one of these blue and burning afternoons I found myself, to my inexpressible astonishment, playing a game called croquet. I had imagined that it belonged to the epoch of Leach and Anthony Trollope, and I had neglected to provide myself with those very long and luxuriant side whiskers which are really essential to such a scene. I played it with a man whom we will call Parkinson, and with whom I had a semi-philosophical argument which lasted through the entire contest. It is deeply implanted in my mind that I had the best of the argument; but it is certain and beyond dispute that I had the worst of the game.

"Oh, Parkinson, Parkinson!" I cried, patting him affectionately on the head with a mallet, "how far you really are from the pure love of the sport—you who can play. It is only we who play badly who love the Game itself. You love glory; you love applause; you love the earthquake voice of victory; you do not love croquet. You do not love croquet until you love being beaten at croquet. It is we the bunglers who adore the occupation in the abstract. It is we to whom it is art for art's sake. If we may see the

163

face of Croquet herself (if I may so express myself) we are content to see her face turned upon us in anger. Our play is called amateurish; and we wear proudly the name of amateur, for amateurs is but the French for Lovers. We accept all adventures from our Lady, the most disastrous or the most dreary. We wait outside her iron gates (I allude to the hoops), vainly essaying to enter. Our devoted balls, impetuous and full of chivalry, will not be confined within the pedantic boundaries of the mere croquet ground. Our balls seek honour in the ends of the earth; they turn up in the flower-beds and the conservatory; they are to be found in the front garden and the next street. No, Parkinson! The good painter has skill. It is the bad painter who loves his art. The good musician loves being a musician, the bad musician loves music. With such a pure and hopeless passion do I worship croquet. I love the game itself. I love the parallelogram of grass marked out with chalk or tape, as if its limits were the frontiers of my sacred Fatherland, the four seas of Britain. I love the mere swing of the mallets, and the click of the balls is music. The four colours are to me sacramental and symbolic, like the red of martyrdom, or the white of Easter Day. You lose all this, my poor Parkinson. You have to solace yourself for the absence of this vision by the paltry consolation of being able to go through hoops and to hit the stick."

And I waved my mallet in the air with a graceful gaiety.

"Don't be too sorry for me," said Parkinson, with his simple sarcasm. "I shall get over it in time. But it seems to me that the more a man likes a game the better he would want to play it. Granted that the pleasure in the thing itself comes first, does not the pleasure of success come naturally and inevitably afterwards? Or, take your own simile of the Knight and his Lady-love. I admit the gentleman does first and foremost want to be in the lady's presence. But I never yet heard of a gentleman who wanted to look an utter ass when he was there."

"Perhaps not; though he generally looks it," I replied. "But the truth is that there is a fallacy in the simile, although it was my own. The happiness at which the lover is aiming is an infinite happiness, which can be extended without limit. The more he is loved, normally speaking, the jollier he will be. It is definitely true that the stronger the love of both lovers, the stronger will be the happiness. But it is not true that the stronger the play of both croquet players the stronger will be the game. It is logically possible—(follow me closely here, Parkinson!)—it is logically possible, to play croquet too well to enjoy it at all. If you could put this blue ball through that distant hoop as easily as you could pick it up with your hand, then you would not put it through that hoop any more than you pick it up with your hand; it would not be worth doing. If you could play unerringly you would not play at all. The moment the game is perfect the game disappears."

"I do not think, however," said Parkinson, "that you are in any immediate danger of effecting that sort of destruction. I do not think your croquet will vanish through its own faultless excellence. You are safe for the present."

I again caressed him with the mallet, knocked a ball about, wired myself, and resumed the thread of my discourse.

The long, warm evening had been gradually closing in, and by this time it was almost twilight. By the time I had delivered four more fundamental principles, and my companion had gone through five more hoops, the dusk was verging upon dark.

"We shall have to give this up," said Parkinson, as he missed a ball almost for the first time, "I can't see a thing."

"Nor can I," I answered, "and it is a comfort to reflect that I could not hit anything if I saw it."

With that I struck a ball smartly, and sent it away into the darkness towards where the shadowy figure of Parkinson moved in the hot haze. Parkinson immediately uttered a loud and dramatic cry. The situation, indeed, called for it. I had hit the right ball.

Stunned with astonishment, I crossed the gloomy ground, and hit my ball again. It went through a hoop. I could not see the hoop; but it was the right hoop. I shuddered from head to foot.

Words were wholly inadequate, so I slouched heavily after that impossible ball. Again I hit it away into the night, in what I supposed was the vague direction of the quite invisible stick. And in the dead silence I heard the stick rattle as the ball struck it heavily.

I threw down my mallet. "I can't stand this," I said. "My ball has gone right three times. These things are not of this world."

"Pick your mallet up," said Parkinson, "have another go."

"I tell you I daren't. If I made another hoop like that I should see all the devils dancing there on the blessed grass."

"Why devils?" asked Parkinson; "they may be only fairies making fun of you. They are sending you the 'Perfect Game,' which is no game."

I looked about me. The garden was full of a burning darkness, in which the faint glimmers had the look of fire. I stepped across the grass as if it burnt me, picked up the mallet, and hit the ball somewhere—somewhere where another ball might be. I heard the dull click of the balls touching, and ran into the house like one pursued.

"Can you not see," I said, "that fairy tales in their essence are quite solid and straightforward; but that this everlasting fiction about modern life is in its nature essentially incredible? Folk-lore means that the soul is sane, but that the universe is wild and full of marvels. Realism means that the world is dull and full of routine, but that the soul is sick and screaming. The problem of the fairy tale is—what will a healthy man do with a fantastic world? The problem of the modern novel is—what will a madman do with a dull world? In the fairy tales the cosmos goes mad; but the hero does not go mad. In the modern novels the hero is mad before the book begins, and suffers from the harsh steadiness and cruel sanity of the cosmos. In the excellent tale of 'The Dragon's Grandmother,' in all the other tales of Grimm, it is assumed that the young man setting out on his travels will have all substantial truths in him; that he will be brave, full of faith, reasonable, that he will respect his parents, keep his word, rescue one kind of people, defy another kind, *parcere subjectis et debellare*, etc. Then, having assumed this centre of sanity, the writer entertains himself by fancying what would happen if the whole world went mad all round it, if the sun turned green and the moon blue, if horses had six legs and giants had two heads. But your modern literature takes insanity as its centre. Therefore, it loses the interest even of insanity. A lunatic is not startling to himself, because he is quite serious; that is what makes him a lunatic. A man who thinks he is a piece of glass is to himself as dull as a piece of glass. A man who thinks he is a chicken is to himself as common as a chicken. It is only sanity that can see even a wild poetry in insanity. Therefore, these wise old tales made the hero ordinary and the tale extraordinary. But you have made the hero extraordinary and the tale ordinary—so ordinary—oh, so very ordinary."

—G. K. Chesterton, "The Dragon's Grandmother."

THE SHOP OF GHOSTS

G. K. Chesterton

Nearly all the best and most precious things in the universe you can get for a halfpenny. I make an exception, of course, of the sun, the moon, the earth, people, stars, thunderstorms, and such trifles. You can get them for nothing. Also I make an exception of another thing, which I am not allowed to mention in this paper, and of which the lowest price is a penny halfpenny. But the general principle will be at once apparent. In the street behind me, for instance, you can now get a ride on an electric tram for a halfpenny. To be on an electric tram is to be on a flying castle in a fairy tale. You can get quite a large number of brightly coloured sweets for a halfpenny. Also you can get the chance of reading this article for a halfpenny; along, of course, with other and irrelevant matter.

But if you want to see what a vast and bewildering array of valuable things you can get at a halfpenny each you should do as I was doing last night. I was gluing my nose against the glass of a very small and dimly lit toy shop in one of the greyest and leanest of the streets of Battersea. But dim as was that square of light, it was filled (as a child once said to me) with all the colours God ever made. Those toys of the poor were like the children who buy them; they were all dirty; but they were all bright. For my part, I think brightness more important than cleanliness; since the first is of the soul, and the second of the body. You must excuse me; I am a democrat; I know I am out of fashion in the modern world.

As I looked at that palace of pigmy wonders, at small green omnibuses, at small blue elephants, at small black dolls, and small red Noah's arks, I must have fallen into some sort of unnatural trance. That lit shop-window became like the brilliantly lit stage when one is watching some highly coloured comedy. I forgot the grey houses and the grimy people behind me as one forgets the dark galleries and the dim crowds at a theatre. It seemed as if the little objects behind the glass were small, not because they were toys, but because they were objects far away. The green omnibus was really a green omnibus, a green Bayswater omnibus, passing across some huge desert on its ordinary way to Bayswater. The blue elephant was no longer blue with paint; he was blue with distance. The black doll was really a negro relieved against passionate tropic foliage in the land where every weed is flaming and only man is black. The red Noah's ark was really the enormous ship of earthly salvation riding on the rain-swollen sea, red in the first morning of hope.

Every one, I suppose, knows such stunning instants of abstraction, such brilliant blanks in the mind. In such moments one can see the face of one's own best friend as an unmeaning pattern of spectacles or moustaches. They are commonly marked by the two signs of the slowness of their growth and the suddenness of their termination. The return to real thinking is often as abrupt as bumping into a man. Very often indeed (in my case) it is bumping into a man. But in any case the awakening is always emphatic and, generally speaking, it is always complete. Now, in this case, I did come back with a shock of sanity to the consciousness that I was, after all, only staring into a dingy little toy-shop; but in some strange way the mental cure did not seem to be final. There was still in my mind an unmanageable something that told me that I had strayed into some odd atmosphere, or that I had already done some odd thing. I felt as if I had worked a miracle or committed a sin. It was as if I had at any rate, stepped across some border in the soul.

To shake off this dangerous and dreamy sense I went into the shop and tried to buy wooden soldiers. The man in the shop was very old and broken, with confused white hair covering his head and half his face, hair so startlingly white that it looked almost artificial. Yet though he was senile and even sick, there was nothing of suffering in his eyes; he looked rather as if he were gradually falling asleep in a not unkindly decay. He gave me the wooden soldiers, but when I put down the money he did not at first seem to see it; then he blinked at it feebly, and then he pushed it feebly away.

"No, no," he said vaguely. "I never have. I never have. We are rather old-fashioned here."

"Not taking money," I replied, "seems to me more like an uncommonly new fashion than an old one."

"I never have," said the old man, blinking and blowing his nose; "I've always given presents. I'm too old to stop."

"Good heavens!" I said. "What can you mean? Why, you might be Father Christmas."

"I am Father Christmas," he said apologetically, and blew his nose again.

The lamps could not have been lighted yet in the street outside. At any rate, I could see nothing against the darkness but the shining shop-window. There were no sounds of steps or voices in the street; I might have strayed into some new and sunless world. But something had cut the chords of common sense, and I could not feel even surprise except sleepily. Something made me say, "You look ill, Father Christmas."

"I am dying," he said.

I did not speak, and it was he who spoke again.

"All the new people have left my shop. I cannot understand it. They seem to object to me on such curious and inconsistent sort of grounds, these scientific men, and these innovators. They say that I give people superstitions and make them too visionary; they say I give people sausages and make them too coarse. They say my heavenly parts are too heavenly; they say my earthly parts are too earthly; I don't know what they want, I'm sure. How can heavenly things be too heavenly, or earthly things too earthly? How can one be too good, or too jolly? I don't understand. But I understand one thing well enough. These modern people are living and I am dead."

"You may be dead," I replied. "You ought to know. But as for what they are doing, do not call it living."

A silence fell suddenly between us which I somehow expected to be unbroken. But it had not fallen for more than a few seconds when, in the utter stillness, I distinctly heard a very rapid step coming nearer and nearer along the street. The next moment a figure flung itself into the shop and stood framed in the doorway. He wore a large white hat tilted back as if in impatience; he had tight black old-fashioned pantaloons, a gaudy old-fashioned stock and waistcoat, and an old fantastic coat. He had large, wide-open, luminous eyes like those of an arresting actor; he had a pale, nervous face, and a fringe of beard. He took in the shop and the old man in a look that seemed literally a flash and uttered the exclamation of a man utterly staggered.

"Good lord!" he cried out; "it can't be you! It isn't you! I came to ask where your grave was."

"I'm not dead yet, Mr. Dickens," said the old gentleman, with a feeble smile; "but I'm dying," he hastened to add reassuringly.

"But, dash it all, you were dying in my time," said Mr. Charles Dickens with animation; "and you don't look a day older."

"I've felt like this for a long time," said Father Christmas.

Mr. Dickens turned his back and put his head out of the door into the darkness.

"Dick," he roared at the top of his voice; "he's still alive."

Another shadow darkened the doorway, and a much larger and more full-blooded gentleman in an enormous periwig came in, fanning his flushed face with a military hat of the cut of Queen Anne. He carried his head well back like a soldier, and his hot face had even a look of arrogance, which was suddenly contradicted by his eyes, which were literally as humble as a dog's. His sword made a great clatter, as if the shop were too small for it.

"Indeed," said Sir Richard Steele, "'tis a most prodigious matter, for the man was dying when I wrote about Sir Roger de Coverley and his Christmas Day."

My senses were growing dimmer and the room darker. It seemed to be filled with newcomers.

"It hath ever been understood," said a burly man, who carried his head humorously and obstinately a little on one side—I think he was Ben Jonson—"It hath ever been understood, consule Jacobo, under our King James and her late Majesty, that such good and hearty customs were fallen sick, and like to pass from the world. This grey beard most surely was no lustier when I knew him than now."

And I also thought I heard a green-clad man, like Robin Hood, say in some mixed Norman French, "But I saw the man dying."

"I have felt like this a long time," said Father Christmas, in his feeble way again.

Mr. Charles Dickens suddenly leant across to him.

"Since when?" he asked. "Since you were born?"

"Yes," said the old man, and sank shaking into a chair. "I have been always dying."

Mr. Dickens took off his hat with a flourish like a man calling a mob to rise.

"I understand it now," he cried, "you will never die."

A PICTURE OF TUESDAY

G. K. Chesterton

Oscar Plumtree was a rising artist, who painted his general impressions of his intimate friends, and belonged to a sketching club which met every Tuesday. He was a small square man with masses of black hair, and stood with his hands in his pockets, a little too conscious that his head was against a green curtain.

"How decorative Plumtree is," said Noel Starwood, symbolist, to Patrick Staunton, realist. "I never noticed that his colour was so arbitrary. But, like all the works of God, you have to see him twenty times before you see him for the first time."

"If you can suggest any course likely to result in seeing him for the last time," said Staunton, lighting a pipe, "I shall be more gratified. So he looks decorative, does he?"

"So flat," murmured Starwood, dreamily. "So admirably flat. He looks as if he had just come out of a panel by Albert Moor."

"Yes," said Staunton; "I wish he'd go back again."

Patrick Staunton was a large young man with a handsome passive face, that looked blase but was only sleepy. He was very young, it is true, but not quite young enough to have grown weary of the world. He was, in fact, the average young man, with the average young man's two admirable qualities, a sense of humour and an aversion to egoists. This was why he disliked Plumtree. Noel Starwood, a slight, fiery-haired, fiery-tinted type, like a high-spirited girl, was a visionary, the painter of a series of *Seven Dreams of Adam before the Creation of Eve*. He did not dislike Plumtree. He said it was the great test and trial of true Christian philosophy not to dislike Plumtree.

He moved off, and another member came up to Staunton.

"Do you know it is Plumtree's turn to give out a subject for the sketches?" he said. "These subject days are generally rather a lark. Do

171

you remember the first time Starwood was asked for one? There was a silence, and then such a gentle, plaintive little voice said, *The Resurrection of Cain*. But then he's a mystic, don't you know, and pities the Devil."

"Well, well," said Staunton charitably. "I heard Plumtree was going to the devil the other day and since then I rather pitied the devil myself."

"But the joke of the thing is," continued the other, "that Plumtree is for ever telling us that the artistic mind cares no more for the subject of a picture, than for its weight in avoirdupois. He was immensely proud of his last picture, because three eminent art-critics looked at it the wrong way up."

A small crowd had already gathered round Plumtree, and were pressing him for a subject.

"What do you want with a subject?" he said, contemptuously. "I don't want a subject, I want a picture. Won't anything do?"

"The primal enigma, Anything," said Starwood thoughtfully. "A fine conception. Something bizarre, hasty, fantastic. Some wild, low shape of life, to symbolise the germ-fact, the indestructible minimum, the everlasting Yea. After all, it is but a superficial philosophy which is founded on the existence of everything. The deeper philosophy is founded on the existence of anything.

"Well, we won't have that," said Plumtree, abruptly. "You fellows don't seem to understand that art—"

Staunton cut him short hastily. "I say, Plumtree, I asked for bread and you gave me a piece of india-rubber. Thanks. You were saying that the subject—"

"Oh, take anything you like: what does the subject matter? What's the day of the week? Tuesday; very well." He turned to the throng and said in a clear voice, "The subject for the sketches will be Tuesday."

"I beg your pardon," said Staunton politely.

"Tuesday," repeated Plumtree. "A picture of Tuesday."

Patrick Staunton lifted his full six feet two from the bench, and formally announced that he was relegated to a state of spiritual reprobation.

Only four members of the club exhibited sketches on this singular subject. The group consisted of Plumtree, Staunton and Starwood, and one Middleton, who had before him a lucrative career in virtue of an inexhaustible output of corpulent and comic monks.

The uncovering of his picture was received with loud cheers and laughter. It represented six monastic gentlemen of revolting joviality tossing pancakes. Thus it suggested Shrove Tuesday. Plumtree's was an admirable little suggestion of gaslight in early morning. It might just as well be Tuesday morning as any other morning.

Staunton annoyed him very much by elaborately describing the noble thoughts that the picture suggested to him. His own was a study of his mother's at-home day, which occurred on Tuesday, in which he introduced all the uncles who had told him things for his own good.

Starwood's picture was the largest. When it was unveiled it seemed to fill the room. It was a dark picture, dark with an intricate density of profound colours, a complex scheme of sombre and subtle harmonies, a kind of gorgeous twilight. Plumtree, who was far too good an artist to let cynicism rob him of the gift of wonder, followed the labyrinth of colour keenly and slowly.

Suddenly he gave a little cry and stepped back.

The whole was a huge human figure. Grey and gigantic, it rose with its back to the spectator. As far as the vast outline could be traced, he had one hand heaved above his head, driving up a load of waters, while below, his feet moved upon a solemn, infinite sea. It was a dark picture, but when grasped, it blinded like a sun.

Above it was written 'Tuesday,' and below, 'And God divided the waters that were under the firmament from the waters that were above the firmament: and the evening and the morning were the second day.' There was a long silence, and Staunton was heard damning himself softly.

"It is certainly very good," he said, "like creation. But why did you reckon Tuesday the second instead of the third day of the Jewish week?"

"I had to reckon from my own seventh day: the day of praise, the day of saying 'It is good,' or I could not have felt it a reality."

"Do you seriously mean that you, yourself, look at the days of the week in that way?"

"The week is the colossal epic of creation," cried Starwood excitedly. "Why are there not rituals for every day? The Day of the Creation of Light, why is it not honoured with mystic illuminations? The Day of the Waters, why is it not the day of awful cleansings and sacred immersions—"

"Do you Transcendentalists only wash once a week?" asked Staunton.

"The Day of the Earth—what a fire of flowers and fruit; the Day of Birds, what a blaze of decorative plumage; the Day of Beasts, what a—"

"What a deed lot of nonsense," said Middleton, who was getting a trifle tired of all this. "If it comes to religion, and quotations from the Bible, what is there for us, Staunton? Can you think of a text for an at-home day?"

Staunton suggested, "And Job lifted up his voice and cursed his day."

But Plumtree was staring at the picture of Tuesday.

The best thing you can do for your fellow, next to rousing his conscience, is—not to give him things to think about, but to wake things up that are in him; or say, to make him think things for himself. The best Nature does for us is to work in us such moods in which thoughts of high import arise. Does any aspect of Nature wake but one thought? Does she ever suggest only one definite thing? Does she make any two men in the same place at the same moment think the same thing? Is she therefore a failure, because she is not definite? Is it nothing that she rouses the something deeper than the understanding—the power that underlies thoughts? Does she not set feeling, and so thinking at work? Would it be better that she did this after one fashion and not after many fashions? Nature is mood-engendering, thought-provoking: such ought the sonata, such ought the fairytale to be.

—George MacDonald, "The Fantastic Imagination."

THE GREEN ROBE

Robert H. Benson (1871-1914)

"To see a world in a grain of sand,
   And a heaven in a wild flower;
Hold infinity in the palm of your hand,
   And eternity in an hour."
      Blake.

The old priest was silent for a moment. The song of a great bee boomed up out of the distance and ceased as the white bell of a flower beside me drooped suddenly under his weight.

"I have not made myself clear," said the priest again. "Let me think a minute." And he leaned back.

We were sitting on a little red-tiled platform in his garden, in a sheltered angle of the wall. On one side of us rose the old irregular house, with its latticed windows, and its lichened roofs culminating in a bell-turret; on the other I looked across the pleasant garden where great scarlet poppies hung like motionless flames in the hot June sunshine, to the tall living wall of yew, beyond which rose the heavy green masses of an elm in which a pigeon lamented, and above all a tender blue sky. The priest was looking out steadily before him with great childlike eyes that shone strangely in his thin face under his white hair. He was dressed in an old cassock that showed worn and green in the high lights.

"No," he said presently, "it is not faith that I mean; it is only an intense form of the gift of spiritual perception that God has given me; which gift indeed is common to us all in our measure. It is the faculty by which we verify for ourselves what we have received on authority and hold by faith. Spiritual life consists partly in exercising this faculty. Well, then, this form of that faculty God has been pleased to bestow upon me, just as He has been pleased to bestow on you a keen power of seeing and

175

enjoying beauty where others perhaps see none; this is called artistic perception. It is no sort of credit to you or to me, any more than is the colour of our eyes, or a faculty for mathematics, or an athletic body.

"Now in my case, in which you are pleased to be interested, the perception occasionally is so keen that the spiritual world appears to me as visible as what we call the natural world. In such moments, although I generally know the difference between the spiritual and the natural, yet they appear to me simultaneously, as if on the same plane. It depends on my choice as to which of the two I see the more clearly.

"Let me explain a little. It is a question of focus. A few minutes ago you were staring at the sky, but you did not see the sky. Your own thought lay before you instead. Then I spoke to you, and you started a little and looked at me; and you saw me, and your thought vanished. Now can you understand me if I say that these sudden glimpses that God has granted me, were as though when you looked at the sky, you saw both the sky and your thought at once, on the same plane, as I have said? Or think of it in another way. You know the sheet of plate-glass that is across the upper part of the fireplace in my study. Well, it depends on the focus of your eyes, and your intention, whether you see the glass and the fire-plate behind, or the room reflected in the glass. Now can you imagine what it would be to see them all at once? It is like that." And he made an outward gesture with his hands.

"Well," I said, "I scarcely understand. But please tell me, if you will, your first vision of that kind."

"I believe," he began, "that when I was a child the first clear vision came to me, but I only suppose it from my mother's diary. I have not the diary with me now but there is an entry in it describing how I said I had seen a face look out of a wall and had run indoors from the garden; half frightened, but not terrified. But I remember nothing of it myself, and my mother seems to have thought it must have been a waking dream; and if it were not for what has happened to me since perhaps I should have thought it a dream too. But now the other explanation seems to me more likely. But the first clear vision that I remember for myself was as follows:

"When I was about fourteen years old I came home at the end of one July for my summer holidays. The pony-cart was at the station to meet me when I arrived about four o'clock in the afternoon; but as there was a short cut through the woods, I put my luggage into the cart, and started to walk the mile and a half by myself. The field path presently plunged into a pine wood, and I came over the slippery needles under the high arches of the pines with that intense ecstatic happiness of home-coming that some natures know so well, I hope sometimes that the first steps on the other side of death may be like that. The air was full of mellow sounds that seemed to emphasise the deep stillness of the woods, and of mellow lights that stirred among the shadowed greenness. I know this now, though I did not know it then. Until that day although the beauty and the colour and sound of the world certainly affected me, yet I was not conscious of them, any more than of the air I breathed, because I did not then know what they meant. Well, I went on in this glowing dimness, noticing only the trees that might be climbed, the squirrels and moths that might be caught, and the sticks that might be shaped into arrows or bows.

"I must tell you, too, something of my religion at that time. It was the religion of most well-taught boys. In the fore-ground, if I may put it so, was morality—I must not do certain things; I must do certain other things. In the middle distance was a perception of God. Let me say that I realised that I was present to Him, but not that He was present to me. Our Saviour dwelt in this middle distance, one whom I fancied ordinarily tender, sometimes stern. In the background there lay certain mysteries, sacramental and otherwise. These were chiefly the affairs of grown-up people. And infinitely far away, like clouds piled upon the horizon of a sea, was the invisible world of heaven whence God looked at me, golden gates and streets, now towering in their exclusiveness, now on Sunday evenings bright with a light of hope, now on wet mornings unutterably dreary. But all this was uninteresting to me. Here about me lay the tangible enjoyable world—this was reality: there in a misty picture lay religion, claiming, as I knew, my homage, but not my heart. Well; so I walked through these woods, a tiny human creature, yet, greater, if I had only known it, than these giants of ruddy bodies and arms, and garlanded heads that stirred above me.

"My path presently came over a rise in the ground; and on my left lay a long glade, bordered by pines, fringed with bracken, but itself a folded carpet of smooth rabbit-cropped grass, with a quiet oblong pool in the centre, some fifty yards below me.

"Now I cannot tell you how the vision began; but I found myself, without experiencing any conscious shock, standing perfectly still, my lips dry, my eyes smarting with the intensity with which I had been staring down the glade, and one foot aching with the pressure with which I had rested upon it. It must have come upon me and enthralled me so swiftly that my brain had no time to reflect. It was no work, therefore, of the imagination, but a clear and sudden vision. This is what I remember to have seen.

"I stood on the border of a vast robe; its material was green. A great fold of it lay full in view, but I was conscious that it stretched for almost unlimited miles. This great green robe blazed with embroidery. There were straight lines of tawny work on either side which melted again into a darker green in high relief. Right in the centre lay a pate agate stitched delicately into the robe with fine dark stitches; overhead the blue lining of this silken robe arched out. I was conscious that this robe was vast beyond conception, and that I stood as it were in a fold of it, as it lay stretched out on some unseen floor. But, clearer than any other thought, stood out in my mind the certainty that this robe had not been flung down and left, but that it clothed a Person. And even as this thought showed itself a ripple ran along the high relief in dark green, as if the wearer of the robe had just stirred. And I felt on my face the breeze of His motion. And it was this I suppose that brought me to myself.

"And then I looked again, and all was as it had been the last time I had passed this way. There was the glade and the pool and the pines and the sky overhead, and the Presence was gone. I was a boy walking home from the station, with dear delights of the pony and the air-gun, and the wakings morning by morning in my own carpeted bedroom, before me.

"I tried, however, to see it again as I had seen it. No, it was not in the least like a robe; and above all where was the Person that wore it? There was no life about me, except my own, and the insect life that sang in the air, and the quiet meditative life of the growing things. But who was this Person I had suddenly perceived? And then it came upon me with a shock, and yet I was incredulous. It could not be the God of sermons and long prayers who demanded my presence Sunday by Sunday in His little church, that God Who watched me like a stern father. Why religion, I thought, told me that all was vanity and unreality, and that rabbits and pools and glades were nothing compared to Him who sits on the great white throne.

"I need not tell you that I never spoke of this at home. It seemed to me that I had stumbled upon a scene that was almost dreadful, that might be thought over in bed, or during an idle lonely morning in the garden, but must never be spoken of, and I can scarcely tell you when the time came that I understood that there was but one God after all."

The old man stopped talking. And I looked out again at the garden without answering him, and tried myself to see how the poppies were embroidered into a robe, and to hear how the chatter of the starlings was but the rustic of its movement, the clink of jewel against jewel, and the moan of the pigeon the creaking of the heavy silk, but I could not. The poppies flamed and the birds talked and sobbed, but that was all.

THE BRIDGE OVER THE STREAM

Robert H. Benson

"Lo, I am free! I choose the pain thou bearest;
   Thou art the messenger of one who waits;
Thou wilt reveal the hidden face thou wearest
   When my feet falter at the Eternal Gates."
   Old Foes.

We were at tea one afternoon on the little low, tiled platform that marked the site of an old summer-house. Tall hurdles covered with briar-roses on the further side of the path fenced off the rest of the garden from us, and the sun had just sunk below the level of the house, throwing both ourselves and the garden into cool shadow. The servant had brought out the tea-things, but he presently returned with something of horror on his face. The old man looked up and saw him.

"What is it, Parker?" he asked.

"There's been an accident, sir. Tom Awcock at the home farm has been drawn into some machine, and they say he must lose both arms, and maybe his life."

The old man turned quite white, and his eyes grew larger and brighter.

"Is the doctor with him?" he asked, in a perfectly steady voice.

"Yes, sir, and they've sent a message, Would you be good enough to step down? The rector's away, and Tom's mother's crying terrible. But not yet, sir. About seven o'clock, they say. It won't be over till then, and there's no immediate danger."

"Tell them I will be there at seven," said the clergyman.

Parker went back to the house, and presently we heard the footsteps of a child running down the drive towards the farm.

"How shocking it is!" I said in a moment or two.

"Ah!" said the old man, smiling, "I have learnt my lesson. It is not really so shocking as you think. Does that sound very hard?"

I said nothing, for it seemed to me that all the consolations of religion could not soften the horror of such things. If such agonies are necessary as remedies or atonements, at least they are terrible.

"I learnt my lesson," the old man went on, "down the road there outside the hedge—down by the bridge. Would you like to hear it? Or are you tired of an old dreamer's stories?" and he smiled at me.

"Now I know you think that I am hard—that I am a little apart maybe from human life—that I cannot understand the blind misery of those who suffer in ignorance; yet you would be the first, I believe, to think that Mrs. Awcock's consolations are unreal, and that when she tells me that she knows there is a wise purpose behind, she is only repeating what is proper to say to a clergyman. But that is not so; that old threadbare sentence is intensely real to these people, and, I hope, to myself too. For there is nothing that I desire more than to be a child like them. It is the apparent purposelessness that distresses you: it is the certainty of a deliberate purpose that comforts me. Well, shall I tell you what I saw?"

I was a little distressed at what looked like callousness, but I told him I would like to hear the story.

"I was standing one evening-it would be about five years ago—in the field down there near the stream. You remember the bridge there, over which the road goes, just outside the hedge. I love running water, and I went slowly up and down by the side of the beck. There were children on the road, coming back from school, and they stopped on the bridge to look at the water, as children and old men will. They did not see me, as the field is a little below the road, and besides their backs were turned to me. I could see a pink frock or two, and a pair of stout bare legs. Two girls were taking their brother home—he was between them, a hand clasped by each of the sisters. I suppose the eldest girl would be about nine, and the boy five. They were talking solemnly, and I could hear every word.

"Why are children always supposed to be gay? There is no solemnity in the world to be compared to the solemnity of a little boy, or of his sister who has charge of him.

"One of the girls said, 'Look, Johnny, there are little fishes down there.'

"'When I am a man'—Johnny began, very slowly.

"'Look, Johnny,' said the other girl, 'there's a blue flower.'

"Up to this I remember every word. But then I began to watch Johnny.

"The girls went on talking, but they leaned over more, and I could not hear them plainly. Johnny stealthily withdrew a hand from each of his sisters, and began to look for a stone to throw at the fishes or the blue flower, I suppose; for man is lord of Creation. I could see him presently through the hedge digging patiently with his fingers and loosening a stone that was firm in the road. And at that moment I heard a far-away shout and the distant bark of a dog.

"The evening was wonderfully still, every leaf hung quiet: and there were far-off clouds heaping themselves up in the west, tower over tower. We had a thunderstorm that night, I remember. The brook was quiet, just slipping noiselessly from pool to pool.

"Still Johnny was digging and the girls were talking. Then out of the village above us came again far-off noises. I could hear a rumble and the clatter of hoofs, then a cry or two more, and the nearer terrified yelp of a dog. But the girls were intent on the brook—and Johnny on the stone.

"Even now I did not understand what was happening: but I grew uneasy—and with great difficulty, for I was an old man even then, tried to scramble up the high bank by the bridge. As I reached the top I saw that one of the girls had gone. She had run, I suppose, off the bridge down by the side of the road. The other girl was still standing—but looking in a frightened way up the hill. Down the hill came the loud rumble of a cart and the clatter of hoofs, terribly near.

"The girl by the side of the road began to scream to her sister, who darted off, and then remembered Johnny and turned. Johnny got up too and ran to the parapet and stood against it.

"I was shouting too by now, through the hedge: but I could do nothing more, nothing more, because the hedge was high and thick, and I was an old man. Then in a moment I remembered that shouting would only distract them, and I stopped. It was useless. I could do absolutely nothing. But it was very hard.

"Then I saw the galloping body of a horse through the branches, with a butcher's cart that rocked behind him. There was no one on the cart.

"Now there was room for the cart to pass the boy safely. By the wheelmarks, which I looked at afterwards, there were three clear feet—if only the boy had stood still.

"The girls seemed petrified as they stood, one in act to run, the other crouching and hiding her face against the hedge. The cart was now within ten yards, as I could see, though I was still staring at Johnny. Then this is what I saw.

"Somewhere behind him over the parapet of the bridge there was a figure. I remember nothing about it except the face and the hands. The face was, I think, the tenderest I have ever seen. The eyes were downcast, looking upon the boy's head with indescribable love, the lips were smiling. One hand was over the boy's eyes, the other against his shoulder behind. In a moment the memory of other stories I had heard came to mind—and I gave a sob of relief that the boy was safe in such care.

"But as the iron hoofs and rocking wheels came up, the hand on the boy's shoulder suddenly pushed him to meet them; and yet those tender eyes and mouth never flinched, and the child took a step forward in front of the horse, and was beaten down without a cry: and the cart lurched heavily, righted itself, and dashed on out of sight.

"When the cloud of dust had passed, the little body lay quiet on the road, and the two girls were clinging to one another, screaming and sobbing, but there was nothing else.

"I was as angry at first as an old man could be. I nearly (may He forgive me for it now!) cursed God and died. But the memory of that tender face did its work. It was as the face of a mother who nurses her first-born child, as the face of a child who kisses a wounded creature, it was as I think the Father's Face itself must have been, which those angels always behold, as He looked down upon the Sacrifice of His only Son.

"Will you forgive me now if I seemed hard a few minutes ago? Perhaps you still think it was hardness that made me speak as I did. But, for myself, I hope I may call it by a better name than that."

UNDER WHICH KING?

Robert H. Benson

"All such knowledge as this, whether it comes from God or not, can be but of little profit to the soul in the way of perfection, if it trusts to it: yea, rather, if it is not careful to reject it, ... it will bring upon it great evil; ... for all the dangers and inconveniences of the supernatural apprehensions, and many more, are to be found here."

The Ascent of Mount Carmel.

Within a day or two of our conversation on St. Teresa, I asked the old priest about what is called "Quietism." A friend had given me an old copy of Molinos' *Spiritual Guide*, and I knew that the writer had been condemned and imprisoned for life, and yet I could not understand in what lay his crime.

"It is difficult to put into words," said the priest, "or even to understand, why certain sentences are condemned, since it is probably possible to parallel them from other Catholic mystics whose names are honoured. Yet the fact remains that the result of Molinos' teaching was neglect of the Sacraments and of external means of grace, which was not so in the case of the schools of other mystics."

"But I will tell you a story," he went on, "to illustrate the effect of certain kinds of mysticism; and I must leave you to judge whether my friend was right or wrong in what he decided, for I must tell you first that the incident did not happen to me. On the whole I may say that I have my own opinion on the subject, but I will not tell you what it is, as sometimes I am strongly inclined to change it. However, you shall hear the story. Shall we take a stroll on the terrace?"

And when we had reached it, he began

My friend was a priest of about thirty years of age (this happened some forty years ago). He was working in the country at the time, and

had a great deal of leisure for reading, and this he chiefly occupied in
the study of various mystics, and most of them of the Quietistic school.
You know, too, that one of their characteristic lines of thought lies in the
abandonment of all effort save that of adhering to God, and even that is
to be a passive rather than an active effort. The soul must lie still, says
one of them, and be drawn as if by a rope up the Mount of Perfection. The
slightest movement will check or divert that swift and steady approach
towards God.

"But my friend not only studied writers of this school intellectually,
but he put himself more or less under their spiritual direction. He told
me afterwards that it seemed to him that if he used the Sacraments
faithfully, and if he found that his devotion towards them did not cool,
he would be sufficiently protected against possible extravagances or
heresies in his spiritual reading. His daily meditation, too, he told me,
began to mean more to him than ever in his lifetime: the presence of God
seemed more real and accessible, and, above all, the guidance of God in
his daily life more apparent. The time that really matters, as he said to
me once, is the time between our religious exercises; and in this time,
too, God manifested Himself. In fact from all that he said to me, I have
very little doubt that his character and spiritual life were both deepened
and purified, at any rate at first, by his devotional study of these mystics.

"One word more before I begin the actual story.

"I said just now that the guidance of God began to be more apparent
in his daily life. There are two main ways of settling questions that come
up for decision, and both ways are possible to a religious man. One way
is to lay stress on the intellectual side, to weigh the arguments carefully,
and decide, as it were, by reasoning alone: the other is to lay comparatively little stress on the arguments and the intellectual side generally,
and to make the main effort lie in the aspiration of the will towards God
for guidance. We may call them, roughly, the intellectual and the intui-
tive. Now of course my friend's mystical studies inclined him more and
more towards the latter. He told me, in fact, that in the most ordinary
questions—in his visiting his people—in his preaching—in his dealings
with souls—he began more and more to refuse intellectual light, and to trust
instead to the immediate interior guidance of the Holy Ghost. More than
once, for example, he laid aside the sermon he had prepared, as he entered
the pulpit, and preached from a text that had seemed to be suggested to
him. Of course it was not so good from the literary point of view; but that, as
he very justly said, is not the most important question in judging of a
sermon. He seemed to find, he told me, that his spiritual power in every
way developed, both in his interior life and in his dealings with others.

"In his conversations, too, he would allow long silences to come, if it
did not seem to him that God moved him to speak; at other times he

would drop conventional modes of speech and say things that, humanly judged, were calculated to do the very opposite of what he personally desired. Sometimes in such a case his wish was attained, and sometimes not; but in both cases he forced himself to regard it as if he had succeeded. In short, he acted and spoke in obedience to this interior drawing, and disregarded consequences entirely. And this, I need hardly say, is one road to interior peace.

"And then at last a startling thing happened.

"There had been some crime committed: I have not an idea what it was. Two men were involved in the consequences. One, whom we will call A., had committed the crime: but he could only be prosecuted if B., whom he had seriously injured, consented to take action. Now my friend was deeply interested in A., and he thought he knew that the one chance of A.'s salvation lay in his being allowed to go unpunished. But Lord B., who, by the way, was an Irish peer, of no importance himself, though his father had been well known, was a hard, vindictive man, and had publicly announced his intention of ruining A. In this state of affairs my friend was asked to intercede by A. and his friends.

"Lord B. lived in a large country-house some four or five miles from my friend's house. He was an unmarried man, but generally had his house fairly full of his friends, who did not bear the best possible reputation.

"My friend arrived at the house by appointment with B., whom he did not personally know, towards the close of a rainy autumn afternoon. In spite of his anxiety he had resolved to be guided as usual by the interior monitor whom he had learnt to trust, and he had hardly thought of a single argument which he could use. Yet he felt confident that he was right in coming, and equally confident that he would know what to say when the time came. As he got near the house this confident sense of guidance increased to an extent that almost terrified him. It seemed to him, as he walked under the dripping yellow branches, that a strong, almost physical, oppression carried him forward. As if in a dream he saw the manservant appear in answer to his ring, and heard, as from a great distance, the man tell him that Lord B. had come in a little while before, and was now expecting him in the smoking-room.

"On entering the house these curious sensations, which he hardly attempted to describe to me, seemed to diminish a little, and he felt cool and confident. He told me that the sense of oppression resting on him was dispelled, as if by a breeze, as he passed along the corridor on the ground floor on his way to the smoking-room in the west wing of the house.

"The servant threw open the door and announced him, and my friend went through, and the door closed behind him: but the moment he had crossed the threshold he felt that something was wrong.

"There was a circle of men, some in shooting costume, and some as if they had not been out all day, sitting in easy chairs round the fire, which was to the right of the door. My friend could see most of their faces, and Lord B.'s face among them, as he paused at the door; but not one offered to move, though all looked curiously at him.

"There was silence for a moment, and then Lord B. said suddenly and loudly:

"'Well, here's the parson at last, sermon and all.'

"And then two or three of the men laughed.

"My friend saw of course that Lord B. had arranged the interview in this way simply in order to insult him, and that he would not be able to speak to him in private at all, as he had hoped. There was, he told me, just one great heave of anger in his heart at this offensive behaviour; but he did his best to crush it down, and still stood without speaking. He had not, he said, an idea what to say or do, so he stood and waited.

"Lord B. got up in a moment and lit a cigarette with his back to my friend; and then turned and faced him, leaning against the mantelpiece.

"'Well,' he said, 'we're all waiting.'

"Still there was silence. One of the men beyond the fire suddenly laughed.

"'Now then,' said Lord B. impatiently, 'for God's sake say what you came to say, and go.'

"As this sentence ended my friend felt a curious sensation run over him, like those he had experienced in the park, but far stronger. He could never give me any description of it, except by saying that it seemed as if a force were laying hold of him in every remote fibre of his bodily and spiritual being. His own will seemed to give up the control into some stronger hand, and he felt a sense of being steadied and quieted.

"Then he was aware that his own voice said a single sentence of some half-dozen words; but though he heard each word, it was instantly obliterated from his mind. In his description of it all to me afterwards, he said it was like words that we hear immediately before we fall asleep in a lecture-room or a railway carriage: each word is English and intelligible, but the sentence conveys no impression.

"While his voice spoke for perhaps two or three seconds, his eyes were fixed on Lord B.'s face, and in that momentary interval he saw a terrible fear and astonishment suddenly stamped upon it. The mouth opened in loose lines and the cigarette fell out, and B.'s hands rose instinctively as if to keep my friend off. One of the men, too, at the further end of the circle suddenly sprang, erect, with the same kind of imploring horror on his face.

"That was all that my friend had time to see; for the same power that had laid hold of him turned him immediately to the door, and he opened it and went out and down the corridor. As he went the strange sensation passed, but he felt the sweat prick to his skin and then pour down his face. He heard, too, as he reached the end of the corridor, a bell peal violently somewhere. He passed out into the hall, and even as he opened the front door a servant dashed past him through the hall and down the corridor, up which he had just come.

"He went straight home, feeling terribly tired and overwrought, and had to go to bed on reaching his house, tortured by neuralgia.

"Two hours later a note was brought by a groom from Lord B., written in a shaking hand, with an abject apology for his reception in the afternoon; an entreaty to him not to mention the subject again which he had spoken of in the sitting-room, with a scarcely veiled offer of a bribe, and an emphatic promise to withdraw all proceedings against A.

"On the following day he was told that Lord B. was supposed to be unwell, and that the house-party had been hurriedly broken up the night before.

"From that day to this he has never had an idea of what the sentence was that his voice spoke that worked such a miracle."

"That is a most curious story," I said. "What do you make of it?"

The priest smiled.

"I will tell you what my friend made of it. He gave up his study of mysticism, yet without in any sense condemning that line of thought of which I have spoken. His reasons, which he explained to me after coming to a decision, were that such a visitation might or might not be from God. If it were not from God, then that proved that he had been meddling with high things, and had somehow slipped under some other control. If it were from God, it might be that it was just for that very purpose that he had been brought so far, but that he dared not pursue that path without some distinct further sign. 'In any case,' he said, 'no soul can be lost by following the simple and well-beaten path of ordinary devotion and prayer.' And so he returned to intellectual forms of meditation, such as most Christians use. He died a few years ago, full of holiness and good works.

"But for you there are several opinions open. Either that it was an intensely strong case of hypnotic thought-transference from Lord B. to my friend, and that the latter only spoke mechanically of something that lay in the former's mind; or you may decide that the whole affair was of the Evil One, and that A. would have been all the better for prosecution, and that an evil being somehow found entrance into the strained nature of my friend, and used it for his own purposes; or that the prophetic gift was bestowed on him, but that the ordeal was too fierce and he too cowardly to claim it. And there are other solutions as well, no doubt possible.

"For myself I think I have formed my opinion; but I would prefer, as Herodotus says, to keep it to myself."

UNTO BABEſ

Robert H. Benson

Saint Bernard speaks of the words of Job that he says: '*Abscondit lucem in manibus*' (that is to say, 'God has light hid in His hands');—'Thou wot well, he that has a candle a-light between his hands, he may hide it and shew it at his own will. So does our Lord to His chosen.'"

The Abbey of the Holy Ghost

A few days after the conversation I have described my visit to the old man came to an end, and my work drew me back to London; but I left behind me a promise to return and spend Christmas at his house. He in the meantime would, he promised me, try to put together some other stories for me against the time that I should return. There were many others, he said, that he had come across in his life which he hoped would interest me, besides a few more personal experiences of his own.

And so I left him smiling and waving to me from his bedroom window that overlooked the drive (for I had to go by an early train), with the clean-shaven face of his old servant looking at me discreetly and gravely from the clear-glass chapel window next to the priest's room, where he had been setting things ready before his master was dressed.

It was a dark winter afternoon when I returned, a week or so before Christmas.

The coachman told me on my inquiry that his master seemed very much aged during the autumn and winter, that he had scarcely left the house since the leaves had fallen, except to sit for an hour or two in sun-shiny weather in the sheltered angle of the wall where was the tiled plat-form that I have spoken of; and that he was afraid he had been suffering from depression. There had been days of almost complete silence, at least

189

so Parker had told him, when the master had sat all day turning over letters and books and old drawers.

I reproached myself with having troubled the old man with demands for more stories; and feared that it had been in the attempt to please me that he had fallen brooding over the past, perhaps dwelling too much on sorrows of which I knew nothing.

As we passed under the pines that tossed their sombre plumes in the wind, the sun, breaking through clouds in an angry glory on my right, blazed on the little square-paned windows of the house on my left. The chapel-window on the top story seemed especially full of red light streaming from within, but the flame swept across the upper story as we drove past, and left the windows blank and colourless just before we turned the corner at the back of the house.

The old man met me in the hall, and I was startled to see the change that had come to him. His eyes seemed larger than ever, and there was a sorrow in them that I had not seen before. They had been the eyes of a stainless child, wide and smiling; now they were the eyes of one who was under some burden almost too heavy to be borne. In the stronger light of the sitting-room as the candles shone on his face, I saw that my impression had only been caused by a drooping of the eyelids, that now hung down a little further. But it looked a tired face.

He welcomed me, and said several charming things to me that I should be ashamed to quote, but he made me feel that he was glad that I had come; and so I was glad too. But he said among other things this:

"I am glad you have come now, because I think I shall have something further to tell you. I have had indications during this autumn that the end is coming, and I think that if I have to pass through a dark valley,—and I feel that I am at its entrance even now,—I think that He will give me His staff as well as His rod. But I am an old man and fall of fancies, so please do not question me. But I am very glad," and he took my hand and stroked it for a moment, "very glad that you are here, because I do not think that you will be afraid."

During the following days he told me many stories, bringing out the old books and letters of which the coachman had spoken, and spelling out notes through his tortoiseshell glass, as he sat by the open fireplace in the central sitting-room, with the logs crackling and overrun with swift sparks as they rested on their bed of ashes. The door into the garden where the old drive had once been was now kept closed, and a heavy curtain hung over it.

We did not go out very much together—only in the early afternoons we would walk for an hour or so, he leaning on my arm and on a stick, up and down the terraced walk that lay next the drive under the pities, as the sunset burned across the hills like a far-away judgment. Someday perhaps I will write out some of the stories that he told me, although not all. I have the notes by me.

Here is one of them.

We were walking on one of these dark winter afternoons very slowly uphill towards the village that the priest might get a change from the garden. The morning had been gusty and wet, with sleet showers and even a sprinkle of pure snow as the sky cleared after lunch-time; and now the weather was settling down for a frost, and the snow lay thinly here and there on the rapidly hardening ground.

"It is remarkable," the old man was saving to me, "how in spite of our Lord's words people still think that faith is a matter more or less of intellect. Such a phrase as 'intelligent faith' is, of course, strictly most incorrect."

He stopped and looked at me as he said this, as if prepared for dispute. I did not disappoint him.

"You are very puzzling;" I said. "I cannot believe that you do not value intellect. Surely it is a gift of God, and therefore may adorn faith, as any other gift may do."

"Yes," he said, walking on, "it may adorn it; but it has nothing more to do with it really than jewels have to do with a beautiful woman. In fact, sometimes faith is far more beautiful unadorned, and it is quite possible to crush a delicate and growing faith with a weight of learned arguments intended to adorn and perfect it. Christian apologetics, it seems to me, are only really useful in the mouth of one who realises their entire inadequacy. You can demonstrate nothing of God. You can, by arguments, draw a number of lines that converge towards God, and render His existence and His attributes probable; but you cannot reach Him along those lines. Faith depends not on intellectual but on moral conditions. 'Blessed are the pure in heart,' said our Saviour, not 'Blessed are the profound or acute of intellect'— 'for they shall see God.' It is certainly true of intellectual as of all other riches that they who possess them shall find difficulty in entering into the kingdom of God."

"And so," I said, "you think that intellectual powers are not things to covet, and that education is not a very important question after all?"

"No more than wealth," he answered, "at least so far as you mean by education instruction in demonstrable facts or exact sciences. The point of our existence here is to know God. Well, you know for yourself how the race for wealth is ruining millions of souls to-day. No less surely is keen intellectual competition ruining souls. Mr. —, for instance," he said, naming a well-known critic and poet; "was there ever a man of keener and finer intellect, or of more unerring instinct in matters of literary taste? Well, once I talked with that man most of a day on all his own subjects; in fact, he did nearly all the talking, and I was astonished, I must confess, at the perfection of the training of his already brilliant powers. So much I could perceive, though of course I could not follow him. And of course there were many delicate shades of beauty, if not much more, invisible to me in his talk and criticism. His scale of intellectual beauty ran up out of my sight altogether. But what astonished me more was the coarseness and dullness of his spiritual instinct. I will not call him a child in matters of faith, because that would be high praise; but he was just an ill-bred boor. I have known many a Sussex villager of far purer and finer spiritual fibre. No, no; faith can and does exist quite apart from intellect; and to increase or develop the one often means the decrease and incoherence of the other. *Seigneur, donnez-moi la foi du charbonnier!*"

I must confess that this was a new point of view for me; and I am not sure now whether I do not still think it exaggerated and dangerous; but I said nothing, because it did seem to open up difficult questions, and also to throw light on other difficult questions. The priest turned to me again as he walked.

"Why, it must be so," he said; "if it were not, clever people would have a better hope of salvation than stupid people; and that is absurd—as absurd as if rich people should be nearer God than poor people. No, no; talents are distributed unevenly, it is true: to one ten and to another five but each has one pound, all alike."

We had reached the top of the slope, and the towering hedges had gradually fallen away, so that we could now see far and wide over the country. Away behind us, as we paused for breath, we could see the misty Brighton downs, while in the middle distance lay tumbled wooded hills, with smoke beginning to curl up here and there from the evening fires of hidden villages. The sky was clear overhead, but in the west, where the sunset was beginning to smoulder, a few heavy clouds still lingered.

"And God sees all:" said the priest. "Can you put up with another story as we walk home again? I think I ought to be turning now."

We turned and began to retrace our steps downhill.

"This is not an experience of my own," he said. "It was told me by a friend of mine in Cornwall. He was the squire of a little village a few miles out of Truro, and lived there most of the year except a few weeks in the spring, when he would go abroad. He was a man of great learning and taste, but had the faith of a little child. It was like a spring of clear water to hear him speak of God and heavenly things.

"There was a boy in the village who was an idiot. His parents were dead, and he lived alone with his old grandmother, who was a strict Calvinist, and who regarded her grandson as hopelessly damned because his faith and his expression of it were not as hers. There were evident signs, she said, that God's inscrutable decrees were against him. The local preachers there would have nothing to do with the boy; and the clergyman of the parish, after an attempt or two, had given the child up as hopeless. I think my friend told me that the clergyman had tried to teach him Old Testament history.

"Well, the boy was a terrible and disgusting case. I will not go into details beyond saying that the boy's head had the look of a mule about it; his mother, I think, had had a fright shortly before his birth, and the boy used to think sometimes that he was a horse or mule, and the village children used to encourage him in it, and ride and drive him on the green, for he was quite harmless. And so he grew up, neglected and untaught, spending much of his time out of doors, and creeping home on all fours in the evening, snorting and stamping and neighing when he was much excited; and he would stable himself in a corner of the wide dark kitchen, and munch grass; while his grandmother sat in her high chair by the fire reading in her Bible, or looking over her spectacles at the poor misshapen body in the corner that held a damned soul.

"Now my friend hated to see this child. It was the one thing that troubled his faith. Those who have the faith of children have also the troubles of children; and this living example before his eyes of what looked like the carelessness of God, or worse, was a greater offence to my friend's faith than all infidel arguments, or the mere knowledge that such things happened.

"On a certain Christmas Eve my friend had been a long tramp over the hills with a guest who was staying with him for the shooting. They were returning through his own property towards evening, and were just dropping down from the hill. Their path lay along the upper edge of an old disused stone-quarry, whose entrance lay perhaps a hundred yards away from the valley-road that led into the village—so it was a lonely and unfrequented place. The evening was closing in; and my friend, as he led the way along the path, was trying to make out the outlines of stones and bushes on the floor of the quarry, which lay perhaps seventy feet below them. All at once his eye was caught by the steady glimmer of light somewhere in the dimness beneath, and the sound of a voice. He guessed at once that there were tramps below, and was angry at the thought that they must have wilfully disregarded the notice he had put up about making a fire so close to the wood: and he determined to turn them out, and, if need be, to give them shelter for the night in one of his own outhouses. So he stopped and explained to his friend which path would take him home, while that he himself intended to make his way along the lip of the quarry to the entrance, and then to go on into its interior where the tramps had made their camp; and he promised to be at the house five minutes after his friend.

"So they separated, and he himself soon found his way down a narrow overgrown path that brought him to the opening of the quarry.

"It was a good deal darker here, as the hill shadowed it from the west, and high trees rose on one side; but he was able to stumble along the stony path which led to the interior, though it grew darker still as he went. Presently he turned the corner of a tall boulder, and emerged into the kind of semi-circus that formed the heart of the quarry: before him, about a third way up the slope, burned the glimmer of light he had noticed from above, but even as he saw it it went out: my friend stood in the path and called out, explaining who he was, not threatening at all, but offering, if it was any one who wanted shelter, to provide it for the night. There was no answer, only the sound of scuffling in the dimness in front, and then the confused sound of footsteps scrambling: my friend ran forward, calling, and made out presently an oddly shaped thing scrambling over the silt and stone towards a shoulder of rock that stood out against the sky on his left (I think he said). He tried to follow, but it was too dark, and after he had stumbled once or twice, he gave up the pursuit. In a moment more the climbing figure stood out clear against the sky for an instant, and then disappeared: and the squire saw with a shock of disgust the mule-like head and tangled hair rising from the high shoulders of the village idiot, and his hands dangling on each side of him; and he heard a high-screaming neighing. But at least, he thought, to himself, he would go and see what the boy had been doing.

"He made his way up the slope of silted gravel and mud that lay against the face of the rock, and at last reached a little platform apparently stamped and cut out at the top of the skree just where it touched the quarry-side. It was too dark for him to distinguish anything clearly, so he struck a match and held it in the still sheltered air while he looked about him. This is what he saw.

There was a short halter, with a kind of rude head-stall, fastened to a rusty iron staple driven into the rock. There was a little pile of cut grass below it. There was a kind of mud trough constructed against the stone, with a little straw sprinkled in it and holly berries and leaves in front of it; but this showed signs of having been hastily trampled down, though parts of it survived: there were marks of hobnailed boots in it here and there. So much my friend had noticed when the match burned his fingers but just before he dropped it he noticed something else which made him open his box and light another match: and then he saw the end of a farthing taper sticking out of the ground into which it had been pushed, and another crushed into a ball. He drew out the first and lighted it, and then noticed this last thing. Quite plainly marked on the soft edge of the mud-trough, in a place which the hobnailed boots had not touched, was the mark of a tiny child's naked foot, as if a baby had stood in the trough or manger, with one foot on the floor and another on the edge.

"Now I do not know what you think of this, but I know what my friend thought of it, and what I myself think of it. But before he went home he went first to the Cottage where the boy lived and found him as usual tethered in the corner, with his grandmother nodding before the fire. The boy would do nothing but snort and stamp: and the grandmother could only say that ten minutes ago the boy had run in and gone straight to his corner as usual. The squire asked whether the boy had been trusted with a child by any one; but the grandmother said it was impossible. Nor indeed did he ever after hear a word of a child having been missed on that afternoon.

"Then, before he went home, he went to the little church, already decorated for the festival, and there with the fragrance of the holly and yew in the air about him, and the glimmer of a candle near the altar where the church-cleaner was sweeping, he praised the Holy Child whose Birthnight it was, and who had not disdained to lie in a manger and be adored by the beasts of the stall.

"The following morning on his way back from church he went to the quarry again with his friend to show him what he had seen; but the manger and the holly-berries and crumpled taper were all gone, and there was nothing to see but the iron staple and the platform beaten hard and flat."

We had reached the avenue of pines by now that led to the house, and turned in by the little garden-gate.

"The story seems to show," the priest added, "that intellect has not much to do with the knowledge of God; and that the things which He hides from the wise and prudent He reveals to babes."

I have now arrived, by a devious path, at the conclusion of
this letter, the object of which is to show from what attributes
of our nature, whether mental or corporeal, arises that pre-
disposition to believe in supernatural occurrences. It is, I
think, conclusive that mankind, from a very early period, have
their minds prepared for such events by the consciousness
of the existence of a spiritual world, inferring in the general
proposition the undeniable truth that each man, from the
monarch to the beggar, who has once acted his part on the
stage, continues to exist, and may again, even in a disembodied state, if such is the pleasure of Heaven, for aught that we
know to the contrary, be permitted or ordained to mingle
amongst those who yet remain in the body. The abstract possibility of apparitions must be admitted by every one who
believes in a Deity, and His superintending omnipotence. But
imagination is apt to intrude its explanations and inferences
founded on inadequate evidence. Sometimes our violent and
inordinate passions, originating in sorrow for our friends,
remorse for our crimes, our eagerness of patriotism, or our deep
sense of devotion—these or other violent excitements of a
moral character, in the visions of night, or the rapt ecstasy
of the day, persuade us that we witness, with our eyes and
ears, an actual instance of that supernatural communication,
the possibility of which cannot be denied. At other times the
corporeal organs impose upon the mind, while the eye and
the ear, diseased, deranged, or misled, convey false impressions to the patient. Very often both the mental delusion and the
physical deception exist at the same time, and men's belief
of the phenomena presented to them, however erroneously,
by the senses, is the firmer and more readily granted, that the
physical impression corresponded with the mental excitement.

—Sir Walter Scott, *Letters on*
Demonology and Witchcraft

THE TRAVELLER

Robert H. Benson

On one of these evenings as we sat together after dinner in front of the wide open fireplace in the central room of the house, we began to talk on that old subject—the relation of Science to Faith.

"It is no wonder," said the priest, "if their conclusions appear to differ, to shallow minds who think that the last words are being said on both sides; because their standpoints are so different. The scientific view is that you are not justified in committing yourself one inch ahead of your intellectual evidence: the religious view is that in order to find out anything worth knowing your faith must always be a little in advance of your evidence; you must advance *en échelon*. There is the principle of our Lord's promises. 'Act as if it were true, and light will be given.' The scientist on the other hand says, 'Do not presume to commit yourself until light is given.' The difference between the methods lies, of course, in the fact that Religion admits the heart and the whole man to the witness-box, while Science only admits the head—scarcely even the senses. Yet surely the evidence of experience is on the side of Religion. Every really great achievement is inspired by motives of the heart, and not of the head; by feeling and passion, not by a calculation of probabilities. And so are the mysteries of God unveiled by those who carry them first by assault; 'The Kingdom of Heaven suffereth violence; and the violent take it by force.'

"For example," he continued after a moment, " the scientific view of haunted houses is that there is no evidence for them beyond that which may be accounted for by telepathy, a kind of thought-reading. Yet if you can penetrate that veneer of scientific thought that is so common now, you find that by far the larger part of mankind still believes in them. Practically not one of us really accepts the scientific view as an adequate one."

"Have you ever had an experience of that kind yourself? " I asked.

197

"Well," said the priest, smiling, "you are sure you will not laugh at it? There is nothing commoner than to think such things a subject for humour; and that I cannot bear. Each such story is sacred to one person at the very least, and therefore should be to all reverent people."

I assured him that I would not treat his story with disrespect.

"Well," he answered, "I do not think you will, and I will tell you. It only happened a very few years ago. This was how it began:

"A friend of mine was, and is still, in charge of a church in Kent, which I will not name; but it is within twenty miles of Canterbury. The district fell into Catholic hands a good many years ago. I received a telegram, in this house, a day or two before Christmas, from my friend, saying that he had been suddenly seized with a very bad attack of influenza, which was devastating Kent at that time; and asking me to come down, if possible at once, and take his place over Christmas. I had only lately given up active work, owing to growing infirmity, but it was impossible to resist this appeal; so Parker packed my things and we went together by the next train.

"I found my friend really ill, and quite incapable of doing anything; so I assured him that I could manage perfectly, and that he need not be anxious.

"On the next day, a Wednesday, and Christmas Eve, I went down to the little church to hear confessions. It was a beautiful old church, though tiny, and full of interesting things: the old altar had been set up again; there was a rood-loft with a staircase leading on to it; and an awmbry on the north of the sanctuary had been fitted up as a receptacle for the Most Holy Sacrament, instead of the old hanging pyx. One of the most interesting discoveries made in the church was that of the old confessional. In the lower half of the rood-screen, on the south side, a square hole had been found, filled up with an insertion of oak; but an antiquarian of the Alcuin Club, whom my friend had asked to examine the church, declared that this without doubt was the place where in the pre-Reformation times confessions were heard. So it had been restored, and put to its ancient use; and now on this Christmas Eve I sat within the chancel in the dim fragrant light, while penitents came and knelt outside the screen on the single step, and made their confessions through the old opening.

"I know this is a great platitude, but I never can look at a piece of old furniture without a curious thrill at a thing that has been so much saturated with human emotion; but, above all that I have ever seen, I think that this old confessional moved me. Through that little opening had come so many thousands of sins, great and little, weighted with sorrow; and back again, in Divine exchange for those burdens, had returned the balm of the Saviour's blood. 'Behold! a door opened in heaven,' through which that strange commerce of sin and grace may be carried on—grace pressed down and running over, given into the bosom in exchange for sin! *O bonum commercium!*"

The priest was silent for a moment, his eyes glowing. Then he went on.

"Well, Christmas Day and the three following festivals passed away very happily. On the Sunday night after service, as I came out of the vestry, I saw a child waiting. She told me, when I asked her if she wanted me, that her father and others of her family wished to make their confessions on the following evening about six o'clock. They had had influenza in the house, and had not been able to come out before; but the father was going to work next day, as he was so much better, and would come, if it pleased me, and some of his children to make their confessions in the evening and their communions the following morning.

"Monday dawned, and I offered the Holy Sacrifice as usual, and spent the morning chiefly with my friend, who was now able to sit up and talk a good deal, though he was not yet allowed to leave his bed.

"In the afternoon I went for a walk.

"All the morning there had rested a depression on my soul such as I have not often felt; it was of a peculiar quality. Every soul that tries, however poorly, to serve God, knows by experience those heavinesses by which our Lord tests and confirms His own: but it was not like that. An element of terror mingled with it, as of impending evil.

"As I started for my walk along the high road this depression deepened. There seemed no physical reason for it that I could perceive. I was well myself, and the weather was fair; yet air and exercise did not affect it. I turned at last, about half-past three o'clock, at a milestone that marked sixteen miles to Canterbury.

"I rested there for a moment, looking to the south-east, and saw that far on the horizon heavy clouds were gathering; and then I started homewards. As I went I heard a far-away boom, as of distant guns, and I thought at first that there was some sea-fort to the south where artillery practice was being held; but presently I noticed that it was too irregular and prolonged for the report of a gun; and then it was with a sense of relief that I came to the conclusion it was a far-away thunderstorm, for I felt that the state of the atmosphere might explain away this depression that so troubled me. The thunder seemed to come nearer, pealed more loudly three or four times and ceased.

"But I felt no relief. When I reached home a little after four Parker brought me in some tea, and I fell asleep. Afterwards in a chair before the fire. I was wakened after a troubled and unhappy dream by Parker bringing in my coat and telling me it was time to keep my appointment at the church. I could not remember what my dream was, but it was sinister and suggestive of evil, and, with the shreds of it still clinging to me, I looked at Parker with something of fear as he stood silently by my chair holding the coat. The church stood only a few steps away, for the garden and churchyard adjoined one another. As I went down carrying the lantern that Parker had lighted for me, I remember hearing far away to the south, beyond the village, the beat of a horse's hoofs. The horse seemed to be in a gallop, but presently the noise died away behind a ridge.

"When I entered the church I found that the sacristan had lighted a candle or two as I had asked him, and I could just make out the kneeling figures of three or four people in the north aisle.

"When I was ready I took my seat in the chair set beyond the screen, at the place I have described; and then, one by one, the labourer and his children came up and made their confessions. I remember feeling again, as on Christmas Eve, the strange charm of this old place of penitence, so redolent of God and man, each in his tenderest character of Saviour and penitent; with the red light burning like a luminous flower in the dark before me, to remind me how God was indeed tabernacling with men, and was their God.

"Now I do not know how long I had been there, when again I heard the beat of a horse's hoofs, but this time in the village just below the churchyard; then again there fell a sudden silence. Then presently a gust of wind flung the door wide, and the candles began to gutter and flare in the draught. One of the girls went and closed the door.

"Presently the boy who was kneeling by me at that time finished his confession, received absolution and went down the church, and I waited for the next, not knowing how many there were.

"After waiting a minute or two I turned in my seat, and was about to get up, thinking there was no one else, when a voice whispered sharply through the hole a single sentence. I could not catch the words, but I supposed they were the usual formula for asking a blessing, so I gave the blessing and waited, a little astonished at not having heard the penitent come up.

"Then the voice began again."

The priest stopped a moment and looked round, and I could see that he was trembling a little.

"Would you rather not go on?" I said. "I think it disturbs you to tell me."

"No, no," he said; "it is all right, but it was very dreadful—very dreadful.

"Well, the voice began again in a loud quick whisper, but the odd thing was that I could hardly understand a word; there were just phrases here and there, like the name of God and of our Lady, that I could catch. Then there were a few old French words that I knew; '*le roy*' came over and over again, just at first I thought it must be some extreme form of dialect unknown to me; then I thought it must be a very old man who was deaf, because when I tried, after a few sentences, to explain that I could not understand, the penitent paid no attention, but whispered on quickly without a pause. Presently I could perceive that he was in a terrible state of mind; the voice broke and sobbed, and then almost cried out but still in this loud whisper; then on the other side of the screen I could hear fingers working and moving uneasily, as if entreating admittance at some barred door. Then at last there was silence for a moment, and then plainly some closing formula was repeated, which gradually grew lower and ceased. Then, as I rose, meaning to come round and explain that I had not been able to hear, a loud moan or two came from the penitent. I stood up quickly and looked through the upper part of the screen, and there was no one there.

"I can give you no idea of what a shock that was to me. I stood there glaring, I suppose, through the screen down at the empty step for a moment or two, and perhaps I said something aloud, for I heard a voice from the end of the church.

"'Did you call, sir?' And there stood the sacristan, with his keys and lantern, ready to lock up.

"I still stood without answering for a moment, and then I spoke; my voice sounded oddly in my ears.

"'Is there any one else, Williams? Are they all gone?' or something like that.

"Williams lifted his lantern and looked round the dusky church.

"'No, sir; there is no one.'

"I crossed the chancel to go to the vestry, but as I was half-way, suddenly again in the quiet village there broke out the desperate gallop of a horse.

"'There! there!' I cried, I do you hear that?'

"Williams came up the church towards me.

"'Are you ill, sir?' he said. 'Shall I fetch your servant?'

"I made an effort and told him it was nothing; but he insisted on seeing me home: I did not like to ask him whether he had heard the gallop of the horse; for, after all, I thought, perhaps there was no connection between that and the voice that whispered.

"I felt very much shaken and disturbed, and after dinner, which I took alone of course, I thought I would go to bed very soon. On my way up, however, I looked into my friend's room for a few minutes. He seemed very bright and eager to talk, and I stayed very much longer than I had intended. I said nothing of what had happened in the church; but listened to him while he talked about the village and the neighbourhood. Finally, as I was on the point of bidding him good-night, he said something like this:

"'Well, I mustn't keep you, but I've been thinking while you've been in church of an old story that is told by antiquarians about this place. They say that one of St. Thomas à Becket's murderers came here on the very evening of the murder. It is his day, to-day, you know, and that is what put me in mind of it, I suppose.'

"While my friend said this, my old heart began to beat furiously; but, with a strong effort of self-control, I told him I should like to hear the story.

"'Oh! there's nothing much to tell,' said my friend; 'and they don't know who it's supposed to have been; but it is said to have been either one of the four knights, or one of the men-at-arms.'

"'But how did he come here?' I asked, 'and what for?'

"'Oh! he's supposed to have been in terror for his soul, and that he rushed here to get absolution, which, of course, was impossible.'

"'But tell me,' I said. 'Did he come here alone, or how?'

"'Well, you know, after the murder they ransacked the Archbishop's house and stables: and it is said that this man got one of the fastest horses and rode like a madman, not knowing where he was going: and that he dashed into the village, and into the church where the priest was: and then afterwards, mounted again and rode off. The priest, too, is buried in the chancel, somewhere, I believe. You see it's a very vague and improbable story. At the Gatehouse at Malling, too, you know, they say that one of the knights slept there the night after the murder.'

"I said nothing more; but I suppose I looked strange, because my friend began to look at me with some anxiety, and then ordered me off to bed: so I took my candle and went.

"Now," said the priest, turning to me, "that is the story. I need not say that I have thought about it a great deal ever since: and there are only two theories which appear to me credible, and two others, which would no doubt be suggested, which appear to me incredible.

"First, you may say that I was obviously unwell: my previous depression and dreaming showed that, and therefore that I dreamt the whole thing. If you wish to think that—well, you must think it.

"Secondly, you may say, with the Psychical Research Society, that the whole thing was transmitted from my friend's brain to mine; that his was in an energetic, and mine in a passive state, or something of the kind.

"These two theories would be called 'scientific,' which term means that they are not a hairsbreadth in advance of the facts with which the intellect, a poor instrument at the best, is capable of dealing. And these two 'scientific' theories create in their turn a new brood of insoluble difficulties.

"Or you may take your stand upon the spiritual world, and use the faculties which God has given you for dealing with it, and then you will no longer be helplessly puzzled, and your intellect will no longer overstrain itself at a task for which it was never made. And you may say, I think, that you prefer one of two theories.

"First, that human emotion has a power of influencing or saturating inanimate nature. Of course this is only the old familiar sacramental principle of all creation. The expressions of your face, for instance, caused by the shifting of the chemical particles of which it is composed vary with your varying emotions. Thus we might say that the violent passions of hatred, anger, terror, remorse, of this poor murderer, seven hundred years ago, combined to make a potent spiritual fluid that bit so deep into the very place where it was all poured out, that under certain circumstances it is reproduced. A phonograph for example, is a very coarse parallel, in which the vibrations of sound translate themselves first into terms of wax, and then re-emerge again as vibrations when certain conditions are fulfilled.

"Or, secondly, you may be old-fashioned and simple, and say that by some law, vast and inexorable, beyond our perception, the personal spirit of the very man is chained to the place, and forced to expiate his sin again and again, year by year, by attempting to express his grief and to seek forgiveness, without the possibility of receiving it. Of course we do not know who he was; whether one of the knights who afterwards did receive absolution, which possibly was not ratified by God; or one of the men-at-arms who assisted, and who, as an anonymous chronicle says, '*sine confessione et viatico subito rapti sunt.*'

"There is nothing materialistic, I think, in believing that spiritual beings may be bound to express themselves within limits of time and space; and that inanimate nature, as well as animate, may be the vehicles of the unseen. Arguments against such possibilities have surely, once for all, been silenced, for Christians at any rate, by the Incarnation and the Sacramental system, of which the whole principle is that the Infinite and Eternal did once, and does still, express Itself under forms of inanimate nature, in terms of time and space.

"With regard to another point, perhaps I need not remind you that a thunderstorm broke over Canterbury on the day and hour of the actual murder of the Archbishop."

"It was to no imagination such as you have been setting forth that we were opposed, but to those wild fancies and vague reveries in which young people indulge, to the damage and loss of the real in the world around them."

"And," we insist, "you would rectify the matter by smothering the young monster at once—because he has wings, and, young to their use, flutters them about in a way discomposing to your nerves, and destructive to those notions of propriety of which this creature—you stop not to inquire whether angel or pterodactyle—has not yet learned even the existence. Or, if it is only the creature's vagaries of which you disapprove, why speak of them as *the* exercise of the imagination? As well speak of religion as the mother of cruelty because religion has given more occasion of cruelty, as of all dishonesty and devilry, than any other object of human interest. Are we not to worship, because our forefathers burned and stabbed for religion? It is more religion we want. It is more imagination we need. Be assured that these are but the first vital motions of that whose results, at least in the region of science, you are more than willing to accept." That evil may spring from the imagination, as from everything except the perfect love of God, cannot be denied. But infinitely worse evils would be the result of its absence. Selfishness, avarice, sensuality, cruelty, would flourish tenfold; and the power of Satan would be well established ere some children had begun to choose. Those who would quell the apparently lawless tossing of the spirit, called the youthful imagination, would suppress all that is to grow out of it. They fear the enthusiasm they never felt; and instead of cherishing this divine thing, instead of giving it room and air for healthful growth, they would crush and confine it—with but one result of their victorious endeavours—imposthume, fever, and corruption. And the disastrous consequences would soon appear in the intellect likewise which they worship. Kill that whence spring the crude fancies and wild daydreams of the young, and you will never lead them beyond dull facts—dull because their relations to each other, and the one life that works in them all, must remain undiscovered. Whoever would have his children avoid this arid region will do well to allow no teacher to approach them—not even of mathematics—who has no imagination.

—George MacDonald, "The Imagination: Its
Functions and Its Culture."

THE MAN WITH THE ROLLER

E. G. Swain (1861-1938)

On the edge of that vast tract of East Anglia, which retains its ancient name of the Fens, there may be found, by those who know where to seek it, a certain village called Stoneground. It was once a picturesque village. To-day it is not to be called either a village, or picturesque. Man dwells not in one "house of clay," but in two, and the material of the second is drawn from the earth upon which this and the neighbouring villages stood. The unlovely signs of the industry have changed the place alike in aspect and in population. Many who have seen the fossil skeletons of great saurians brought out of the clay in which they have lain from pre-historic times, have thought that the inhabitants of the place have not since changed for the better. The chief habitations, however, have their foundations not upon clay, but upon a bed of gravel which anciently gave to the place its name, and upon the highest part of this gravel stands, and has stood for many centuries, the Parish Church, dominating the landscape for miles around.

Stoneground, however, is no longer the inaccessible village, which in the middle ages stood out above a waste of waters. Occasional floods serve to indicate what was once its ordinary outlook, but in more recent times the construction of roads and railways, and the drainage of the Fens, have given it freedom of communication with the world from which it was formerly isolated.

The Vicarage of Stoneground stands hard by the Church, and is renowned for its spacious garden, part of which, and that (as might be expected) the part nearest the house, is of ancient date. To the original plot successive Vicars have added adjacent lands, so that the garden has gradually acquired the state in which it now appears.

The Vicars have been many in member. Since Henry de Greville was instituted in the year 1140 there have been 30, all of whom have lived,

205

and most of whom have died, in successive vicarage houses upon the present site.

The present incumbent, Mr. Batchel, is a solitary man of somewhat studious habits, but is not too much enamoured of his solitude to receive visits, from time to time, from schoolboys and such. In the summer of the year 1906 he entertained two, who are the occasion of this narrative, though still unconscious of their part in it, for one of the two, celebrating his 15th birthday during his visit to Stoneground, was presented by Mr. Batchel with a new camera, with which he proceeded to photograph, with considerable skill, the surroundings of the house.

One of these photographs Mr. Batchel thought particularly pleasing. It was a view of the house with the lawn in the foreground. A few small copies, such as the boy's camera was capable of producing, were sent to him by his young friend, some weeks after the visit, and again Mr. Batchel was so much pleased with the picture, that he begged for the negative, with the intention of having the view enlarged.

The boy met the request with what seemed a needlessly modest plea. There were two negatives, he replied, but each of them had, in the same part of the picture, a small blur for which there was no accounting otherwise than by carelessness. His desire, therefore, was to discard these films, and to produce something more worthy of enlargement, upon a subsequent visit.

Mr. Batchel, however, persisted in his request, and upon receipt of the negative, examined it with a lens. He was just able to detect the blur alluded to; an examination under a powerful glass, in fact revealed something more than he had at first detected. The blur was like the nucleus of a comet as one sees it represented in pictures, and seemed to be connected with a faint streak which extended across the negative. It was, however, so inconsiderable a defect that Mr. Batchel resolved to disregard it. He had a neighbour whose favourite pastime was photography, one who was notably skilled in everything that pertained to the art, and to him he sent the negative, with the request for an enlargement, reminding him of a longstanding promise to do any such service, when as had now happened, his friend might see fit to ask it.

This neighbour who had acquired such skill in photography, was one Mr. Groves, a young clergyman, residing in the Precincts of the Minster near at hand, which was visible from Mr. Batchel's garden. He lodged with a Mrs. Rumney, a superannuated servant of the Palace, and a strong-minded vigorous woman still, exactly such a one as Mr. Groves needed to have about him. For he was a constant trial to Mrs. Rumney, and but for the wholesome fear she begot in him, would have converted his rooms into a mere den. Her carpets and tablecloths were continually bespattered with chemicals; her chimney-piece ornaments had been unceremoniously stowed away and replaced by labelled bottles; even the bed of Mr. Groves was, by day, strewn with drying film and mounts, and her old and favourite cat had a bald patch on his flank, the result of a mishap with the pyrogallic acid.

Mrs. Rumney's lodger, however, was a great favourite with her, as such helpless men are apt to be with motherly women, and she took no small pride in his work. A life-size portrait of herself, originally a, peace-offering, hung in her parlour, and had long excited the envy of every friend who took tea with her.

"Mr. Groves," she was wont to say, "is a nice gentleman, *and* a gentle-man; and chemical though he may be, I'd rather wait on him for nothing than what I would on anyone else for twice the money."

Every new piece of photographic work was of interest to Mrs. Rumney, and she expected to be allowed both to admire and to criticism. The view of Stoneground Vicarage, therefore, was shown to her upon its arrival. "Well may it want enlarging," she remarked, "and it no bigger than a post-age stamp; it looks more like a doll's house than a vicarage," and with this she went about her work, whilst Mr. Groves retired to his dark room with the film, to see what he could make of the task assigned to him.

Two days later, after repeated visits to his dark room, he had made something considerable; and when Mrs. Rumney brought him his chop for luncheon, she was lost in admiration. A large but unfinished print stood upon his easel, and such a picture of Stoneground Vicarage was in the making as was calculated to delight both the young photographer and the Vicar.

Mr. Groves spent only his mornings, as a rule, in photography. His afternoons he gave to pastoral work, and the work upon this enlarge-ment was over for the day. It required little more than "touching up," but it was this "touching up" which made the difference between the enlarge-ments of Mr. Groves and those of other men. The print, therefore, was to be left upon the easel until the morrow, when it was to be finished. Mrs. Rumney and he, together, gave it an admiring inspection as she was carrying away the tray, and what they agreed in admiring most particu-larly was the smooth and open stretch of lawn, which made so excellent a foreground for the picture. "It looks," said Mrs. Rumney, who had once been young, "as if it was waiting for someone to come and dance on it."

Mr. Groves left his lodgings—we must now be particular about the hours—at half-past two, with the intention of returning, as usual, at five. "As reg'lar as a clock," Mrs. Rumney was wont to say, "and a sight more reg'lar than some clocks I knows of."

Upon this day he was, nevertheless, somewhat late, some visit had detained him unexpectedly, and it was a quarter-past five when he inserted his latch-key in Mrs. Rumney's door.

Hardly had he entered, when his landlady, obviously awaiting him, appeared in the passage: her face, usually florid, was of the colour of parchment, and, breathing hurriedly and shortly, she pointed at the door of Mr. Groves' room.

In some alarm at her condition, Mr. Groves hastily questioned her; all she could say was: "The photograph! the photograph!" Mr. Groves could only suppose that his enlargement had met with some mishap for which Mrs. Rumney was responsible. Perhaps she had allowed it to flutter into the fire. He turned towards his room in order to discover the worst, but at this Mrs. Rumney laid a trembling hand upon his arm, and held him back. "Don't go in," she said, "have your tea in the parlour."

"Nonsense," said Mr. Groves, "if that is gone we can easily do another."

"Gone," said his landlady, "I wish to Heaven it was."

The ensuing conversation shall not detain us. It will suffice to say that after a considerable time Mr. Groves succeeded in quieting his land-lady, so much so that she consented, still trembling violently, to enter the room with him. To speak truth, she was as much concerned for him as for herself, and she was not by nature a timid woman.

The room, so far from disclosing to Mr. Groves any cause for excitement, appeared wholly unchanged. In its usual place stood every article of his stained and ill-used furniture, on the easel stood the photograph, precisely where he had left it; and except that his tea was not upon the table, everything was in its usual state and place.

But Mrs. Rumney again became excited and tremulous, "It's there," she cried. "Look at the lawn."

Mr. Groves stopped quickly forward and looked at the photograph. Then he turned as pale as Mrs. Rumney herself.

There was a man, a man with an indescribably horrible suffering face, rolling the lawn with a large roller.

Mr. Groves retreated in amazement to where Mrs. Rumney had remained standing. "Has anyone been in here?" he asked.

"Not a soul," was the reply, "I came in to make up the fire, and turned to have another look at the picture, when I saw that dead-alive face at the edge. It gave me the creeps," she said, "particularly from not having noticed it before. If that's anyone in Stoneground, I said to myself, I wonder the Vicar has him in the garden with that awful face. It took that hold of me I thought I must come and look at it again, and at five o'clock I brought your tea in. And then I saw him moved along right in front, with a roller dragging behind him, like you see."

Mr. Groves was greatly puzzled. Mrs. Rumney's story, of course, was incredible, but this strange evil-faced man had appeared in the photograph somehow. That he had not been there when the print was made was quite certain.

The problem soon ceased to alarm Mr. Groves; in his mind it was investing itself with a scientific interest. He began to think of suspended chemical action, and other possible avenues of investigation. At Mrs. Rumney's urgent entreaty, however, he turned the photograph upon the easel, and with only its white back presented to the room, he sat down and ordered tea to be brought in.

He did not look again at the picture. The face of the man had about it something unnaturally painful: he could remember, and still see, as it were, the drawn features, and the look of the man had unaccountably distressed him.

He finished his slight meal, and having lit a pipe, began to brood over the scientific possibilities of the problem. Had any other photograph upon the original film become involved in the one he had enlarged? Had the image of any other face, distorted by the enlarging lens, become a part of this picture? For the space of two hours he debated this possibility, and that, only to reject them all. His optical knowledge told him that no conceivable accident could have brought into his picture a man with a roller. No negative of his had ever contained such a man; if it had, no natural causes would suffice to leave him, as it were, hovering about the apparatus.

His repugnance to the actual thing had by this time lost its freshness, and he determined to end his scientific musings with another inspection of the object. So he approached the easel and turned the photograph round again. His horror returned, and with good cause. The man with the roller had now advanced to the middle of the lawn. The face was stricken still with the same indescribable look of suffering. The man seemed to be appealing to the spectator for some kind of help. Almost, he spoke.

Mr. Groves was naturally reduced to a condition of extreme nervous excitement. Although not by nature what is called a nervous man, he trembled from head to foot. With a sudden effort, he turned away his head, took hold of the picture with his outstretched hand, and opening a drawer in his sideboard thrust the thing underneath a folded tablecloth which was lying there. Then he closed the drawer and took up an entertaining book to distract his thoughts from the whole matter.

In this he succeeded very ill. Yet somehow the rest of the evening passed, and as it wore away, be lost something of his alarm. At ten o'clock, Mrs. Rumney, knocking and receiving answer twice, lest by any chance she should find herself alone in the room, brought in the cocoa usually taken by her lodger at that hour. A hasty glance at the easel showed her that it stood empty, and her face betrayed her relief. She made no comment, and Mr. Groves invited none.

The latter, however, could not make up his mind to go to bed. The face he had seen was taking firm hold upon his imagination, and seemed to fascinate him and repel him at the same time. Before long, he found himself wholly unable to resist the impulse to look at it once more. He took it again, with some indecision, from the drawer and laid it under the lamp.

The man with the roller had now passed completely over the lawn, and was near the left of the picture.

The shock to Mr. Groves was again considerable. He stood facing the fire, trembling with excitement which refused to be suppressed. In this state his eye lighted upon the calendar hanging before him, and it furnished him with some distraction. The next day was his mother's birth-day. Never did he omit to write a letter which should lie upon her break-fast-table, and the pre-occupation of this evening had made him wholly forgetful of the matter. There was a collection of letters, however, from the pillar-box near at hand, at a quarter before midnight, so he turned to his desk, wrote a letter which would at least serve to convey his affectionate greetings, and having written it, went out into the night and posted it.

The clocks were striking midnight as he returned to his room. We may be sure that he did not resist the desire to glance at the photograph he had left on his table. But the results of that glance, he, at any rate, had not anticipated. The man with the roller had disappeared.

The lawn lay as smooth and clear as at first, "looking," as Mrs. Rumney had said, "as if it was waiting for someone to come and dance on it."

The photograph, after this, remained a photograph and nothing more. Mr. Groves would have liked to persuade himself that it had never undergone these changes which he had witnessed, and which we have endeavoured to describe, but his sense of their reality was too insistent. He kept the print lying for a week upon his easel. Mrs. Rumney, although she had ceased to dread it, was obviously relieved at its disappearance, when it was carried to Stoneground to be delivered to Mr. Batchel. Mr. Groves said nothing of the man with the roller, but gave the enlarge-ment, without comment, into his friend's hands. The work of enlarge-ment had been skilfully done, and was deservedly praised.

Mr. Groves, making some modest disclaimer, observed that the view, with its spacious foreground of lawn, was such as could not have failed to enlarge well. And this lawn, he added, as they sat looking out of the Vicar's study, looks as well from within your house as from without. It must give you a sense of responsibility, he added, reflectively, to be sitting where your predecessors have sat for so many centuries and to be continuing their peaceful work. The mere presence before your window, of the turf upon which good men have walked, is an inspiration.

The Vicar made no reply to these somewhat sententious remarks. For a moment he seemed as if he would speak some words of conventional assent. Then he abruptly left the room, to return in a few minutes with a parchment book. "Your remark, Groves," he said as he seated himself again, "recalled to me a curious bit of history: I went up to the old library to get the book. This is the journal of William Longue who was Vicar here up to the year 1602. What you said about the lawn will give you an interest in a certain portion of the journal. I will read it."

Aug. 1, 1600.—I am now returned in haste from a journey to Brightelmstone whither I had gone with full intention to remain about the space of two months. Master Josiah Wilburton, of my dear College of Emmanuel, having consented to assume the charge of my parish of Stoneground in the meantime. But I had intelligence, after 12 days' absence, by a messenger from the Churchwardens, that Master Wilburton had disappeared last Monday sennight, and had been no more seen. So here I am again in my study to the entire frustration of my plans, and can do nothing in my perplexity but sit and look out from my window, before which Andrew Birch rolleth the grass with much persistence. Andrew passeth so many times over the same place with his roller that I have just now stepped without to demand why he so wasteth his labour, and upon this he hath pointed out a place which is not levelled, and hath continued his rolling.

Aug. 2.—There is a change in Andrew Birch since my absence, who hath indeed the aspect of one in great depression, which is noteworthy of so chearful a man. He haply shares our common trouble in respect of Master Wilburton, of whom we remain without tidings. Having made part of a sermon upon the seventh Chapter of the former Epistle of St. Paul to the Corinthians and the 27th verse, I found Andrew again at his task, and bade him desist and saddle my horse, being minded to ride forth and take counsel with my good friend John Palmer at the Deanery, who bore Master Wilburton great affection.

Aug. 2 continued.—Dire news awaiteth me upon my return. The Sheriff's men have disinterred the body of poor Master W. from beneath the grass Andrew was rolling, and have arrested him on the charge of being his cause of death.

Aug. 10.—Alas! Andrew Birch hath been hanged, the Justice having mercifully ordered that he should hang by the neck until he should be dead, and not sooner molested. May the Lord have mercy on his soul. He made full confession before me, that he had slain Master Wilburton in heat upon his threatening to make me privy to certain peculation of which I should not have suspected so old a servant. The poor man bemoaned his evil temper in great contrition, and beat his breast, saying that he knew himself doomed for ever to roll the grass in the place where he had tried to conceal his wicked fact.

"Thank you," said Mr. Groves. "Has that little negative got the date upon it?" Yes, replied Mr. Batchel, as he examined it with his glass. The boy has marked it August 10. The Vicar seemed not to remark the coincidence with the date of Birch's execution. Needless to say that it did not escape Mr. Groves. But he kept silence about the man with the roller, who has been no more seen to this day.

Doubtless there is more in our photography than we yet know of. The camera sees more than the eye, and chemicals in a freshly prepared and active state, have a power which they afterwards lose. Our units of time, adopted for the convenience of persons dealing with the ordinary movements of material objects, are of course conventional. Those who turn the instruments of science upon nature will always be in danger of seeing more than they looked for. There is such a disaster as that of knowing too much, and at some time or another it may overtake each of us. May we then be as wise as Mr. Groves in our reticence, if our turn should come.

BONE TO HIS BONE

E. G. Swain

William Whitehead, Fellow of Emmanuel College, in the University of Cambridge, became Vicar of Stoneground in the year 1731. The annals of his incumbency were doubtless short and simple: they have not survived. In his day were no newspapers to collect gossip, no Parish Magazines to record the simple events of parochial life. One event, however, of greater moment then than now, is recorded in two places. Vicar Whitehead failed in health after 23 years of work, and journeyed to Bath in what his monument calls "the vain hope of being restored." The duration of his visit is unknown; it is reasonable to suppose that he made his journey in the summer, it is certain that by the month of November his physician told him to lay aside all hope of recovery.

Then it was that the thoughts of the patient turned to the comfortable straggling vicarage he had left at Stoneground, in which he had hoped to end his days. He prayed that his successor might be as happy there as he had been himself. Setting his affairs in order, as became one who had but a short time to live, he executed a will, bequeathing to the Vicars of Stoneground, for ever, the close of ground he had recently purchased because it lay next the vicarage garden. And by a codicil, he added to the bequest his library of books. Within a few days, William Whitehead was gathered to his fathers.

A mural tablet in the north aisle of the church, records, in Latin, his services and his bequests, his two marriages, and his fruitless journey to Bath. The house he loved, but never again saw, was taken down 40 years later, and re-built by Vicar James Devie. The garden, with Vicar Whitehead's "close of ground" and other adjacent lands, was opened out and planted, somewhat before 1850, by Vicar Robert Towerson. The aspect of everything has changed But in a convenient chamber on the first floor of the present vicarage the library of Vicar Whitehead stands

213

very much as he used it and loved it, and as he bequeathed it to his successors "for ever."

The hooks there are arranged as he arranged and ticketed them. Little slips of paper, sometimes bearing interesting fragments of writing, still mark his places. His marginal comments still give life to pages from which all other interest has faded, and he would have but a dull imagination who could sit in the chamber amidst these books without ever being carried back 180 years into the past, to the time when the newest of them left the printer's hands.

Of those into whose possession the books have come, some have doubtless loved them more, and some less; some, perhaps, have left them severely alone. But neither those who loved them, nor those who loved them not, have lost them, and they passed, some century and a half after William Whitehead's death, into the hands of Mr. Batchel, who loved them as a father loves his children. He lived alone, and had few domestic cares to distract his mind. He was able, therefore, to enjoy to the full what Vicar Whitehead had enjoyed so long before him. During many a long summer evening would he sit poring over long-forgotten books; and since the chamber, otherwise called the library, faced the south, he could also spend sunny winter mornings there without discomfort. Writing at a small table, or reading as he stood at a tall desk, he would browse amongst the books like an ox in a pleasant pasture.

There were other times also, at which Mr. Batchel would use the books. Not being a sound sleeper (for book-loving men seldom are), he elected to use as a bedroom one of the two chambers which opened at either side into the library. The arrangement enabled him to beguile many a sleepless hour amongst the books, and in view of these nocturnal visits he kept a candle standing in a sconce above the desk, and matches always ready to his hand.

There was one disadvantage in this close proximity of his bed to the library. Owing, apparently, to some defect in the fittings of the room, which, having no mechanical tastes, Mr. Batchel had never investigated, there could be heard, in the stillness of the night, exactly such sounds as might arise from a person moving about amongst the books. Visitors using the other adjacent room would often remark at breakfast, that they had heard their host in the library at one or two o'clock in the morning, when, in fact, he had not left his bed. Invariably Mr. Batchel allowed them to suppose that he had been where they thought him. He disliked idle controversy, and was unwilling to afford an opening for supernatural talk. Knowing well enough the sounds by which his guests had been deceived, he wanted no other explanation of them than his own, though it was of too vague a character to count as an explanation. He conjectured that the window-sashes, or the doors, or "something," were defective, and was too phlegmatic and too un-practical to make any investigation. The matter gave him no concern.

Persons whose sleep is uncertain are apt to have their worst nights when they would like their best. The consciousness of a special need for rest seems to bring enough mental disturbance to forbid it. So on Christmas Eve, in the year 1907, Mr. Batchel, who would have liked to sleep well, in view of the labours of Christmas Day, lay hopelessly wide awake. He exhausted all the known devices for courting sleep, and, at the end, found himself wider awake than ever. A brilliant moon shone into his room, for he hated window-blinds. There was a light wind blowing, and the sounds in the library were more than usually suggestive of a person moving about. He almost determined to have the sashes "seen to," although he could seldom be induced to have anything "seen to." He disliked changes, even for the better, and would submit to great inconvenience rather than have things altered with which he had become familiar.

As he revolved these matters in his mind, he heard the clocks strike the hour of midnight, and having now lost all hope of falling asleep, he rose from his bed, got into a large dressing gown which hung in readiness for such occasions, and passed into the library, with the intention of reading himself sleepy, if he could.

The moon, by this time, had passed out of the south, and the library seemed all the darker by contrast with the moonlit chamber he had left. He could see nothing but two blue-grey rectangles formed by the windows against the sky, the furniture of the room being altogether invisible. Groping along to where the table stood, Mr. Batchel felt over its surface for the matches which usually lay there; he found, however, that the table was cleared of everything. He raised his right hand, therefore, in order to feel his way to a shelf where the matches were sometimes mislaid, and at that moment, whilst his hand was in mid-air, the matchbox was gently put into it!

Such an incident could hardly fail to disturb even a phlegmatic person, and Mr. Batchel cried "Who's this?" somewhat nervously. There was no answer. He struck a match, looked hastily round the room, and found it empty, as usual. There was everything, that is to say, that he was accustomed to see, but no other person than himself.

It is not quite accurate, however, to say that everything was in its usual state. Upon the tall desk lay a quarto volume that he had certainly not placed there. It was his quite invariable practice to replace his books upon the shelves after using them, and what we may call his library habits were precise and methodical. A book out of place like this, was not only an offence against good order, but a sign that his privacy had been intruded upon. With some surprise, therefore, he lit the candle standing ready in the sconce, and proceeded to examine the book, not sorry, in the disturbed condition in which he was, to have an occupation found for him.

The book proved to be one with which he was unfamiliar, and this made it certain that some other hand than his had removed it from its place. Its title was "The Compleat Gard'ner" of M. de la Quintinye made English by John Evelyn Esquire. It was not a work in which Mr. Batchel felt any great interest. It consisted of divers reflections on various parts of husbandry, doubtless entertaining enough, but too deliberate and discursive for practical purposes. He had certainly never used the book, and growing restless now in mind, said to himself that some boy having the freedom of the house, had taken it down from its place in the hope of finding pictures.

But even whilst he made this explanation he felt its weakness. To begin with, the desk was too high for a boy. The improbability that any boy would place a book there was equalled by the improbability that he would leave it there. To discover its uninviting character would be the work only of a moment, and no boy would have brought it so far from its shelf.

Mr. Batchel had, however, come to read, and habit was too strong with him to be wholly set aside. Leaving "The Compleat Gard'ner" on the desk, he turned round to the shelves to find some more congenial reading.

Hardly had he done this when he was startled by a sharp rap upon the desk behind him, followed by a rustling of paper. He turned quickly about and saw the quarto lying open. In obedience to the instinct of the moment, he at once sought a natural cause for what he saw. Only a wind, and that of the strongest, could have opened the book, and laid back its heavy cover; and though he accepted, for a brief moment, that explanation, he was too candid to retain it longer. The wind out of doors was very light. The window sash was closed and latched, and, to decide the matter finally, the book had its back, and not its edges, turned towards the only quarter from which a wind could strike.

Mr. Batchel approached the desk again and stood over the book. With increasing perturbation of mind (for he still thought of the matchbox) he looked upon the open page. Without much reason beyond that he felt constrained to do something, he read the words of the half completed sentence at the turn of the page— "at dead of night he left the house and passed into the solitude of the garden."

But he read no more, nor did he give himself the trouble of discovering whose midnight wandering was being described, although the habit was singularly like one of his own. He was in no condition for reading, and turning his back upon the volume he slowly paced the length of the chamber, "wondering at that which had come to pass."

He reached the opposite end of the chamber and was in the act of turning, when again he heard the rustling of paper, and by the time he had faced round, saw the leaves of the book again turning over. In a moment the volume lay at rest, open in another place, and there was no further movement as he approached it. To make sure that he had not been deceived, he read again the words as they entered the page. The author was following a not uncommon practice of the time, and throwing common speech into forms suggested by Holy Writ: "So dig," it said, "that ye may obtain."

This passage, which to Mr. Batchel seemed reprehensible in its levity, excited at once his interest and his disapproval. He was prepared to read more, but this time was not allowed. Before his eye could pass beyond the passage already cited, the leaves of the book slowly turned again, and presented but a termination of five words and a colophon.

The words were, "to the North, an Ilex." These three passages, in which he saw no meaning and no connection, began to entangle themselves together in Mr. Batchel's mind. He found himself repeating them in different orders, now beginning with one, and now with another. Any further attempt at reading he felt to be impossible, and he was in no mind for any more experiences of the unaccountable. Sleep was, of course, further from him than ever, if that were conceivable. What he did, therefore, was to blow out the candle, to return to his moonlit bedroom, and put on more clothing, and then to pass downstairs with the object of going out of doors.

It was not unusual with Mr. Batchel to walk about his garden at night-time. This form of exercise had often, after a wakeful hour, sent him back to his bed refreshed and ready for sleep.

The convenient access to the garden at such times lay through his study, whose French windows opened on to a short flight of steps, and upon these he now paused for a moment to admire the snow-like appearance of the lawns, bathed as they were in the moonlight. As he paused, he heard the city clocks strike the half-hour after midnight, and he could not forbear repeating aloud

"At dead of night he left the house, and passed into the solitude of the garden."

It was solitary enough. At intervals the screech of an owl, and now and then the noise of a train, seemed to emphasise the solitude by drawing attention to it and then leaving it in possession of the night. Mr. Batchel found himself wondering and conjecturing what Vicar Whitehead, who had acquired the close of land to secure quiet and privacy for a garden, would have thought of the railways to the west and north. He turned his face northwards, whence a whistle had just sounded, and saw a tree beautifully outlined against the sky. His breath caught at the sight. Not because the tree was unfamiliar. Mr. Batchel knew all his trees. But what he had seen was "to the north, an Ilex."

Mr. Batchel knew not what to make of it all. He had walked into the garden hundreds of times and as often seen the Ilex, but the words out of "The Compleat Gard'ner" seemed to be pursuing him in a way that made him almost afraid. His temperament, however, as has been said already, was phlegmatic. It was commonly said, and Mr. Batchel approved the verdict, whilst he condemned its inexactness, that "his nerves were made of fiddle-string," so he braced himself afresh and set upon his walk round the silent garden, which he was accustomed to begin in a northerly direction, and was now too proud to change. He usually passed the Ilex at the beginning of his perambulation, and so would pass it now.

He did not pass it. A small discovery, as he reached it, annoyed and disturbed him. His gardener, as careful and punctilious as himself, never failed to house all his tools at the end of a day's work. Yet there, under the Ilex, standing upright in moonlight brilliant enough to cast a shadow of it, was a spade.

Mr. Batchel's second thought was one of relief. After his extraordinary experiences in the library (he hardly knew now whether they had been real or not) something quite commonplace would act sedatively, and he determined to carry the spade to the tool-house.

The soil was quite dry, and the surface even a little frozen, so Mr. Batchel left the path, walked up to the spade, and would have drawn it towards him. But it was as if he had made the attempt upon the trunk of the Ilex itself. The spade would not be moved. Then, first with one hand, and then with both, he tried to raise it, and still it stood firm. Mr. Batchel, of course, attributed this to the frost, slight as it was. Wondering at the spade's being there, and annoyed at its being frozen, he was about to leave it and continue his walk, when the remaining works of "The Compleat Gard'ner" seemed rather to utter themselves, than to await his will— "So dig, that ye may obtain."

Mr. Batchel's power of independent action now deserted him. He took the spade, which no longer resisted, and began to dig. "Five spadefuls and no more," he said aloud. "This is all foolishness."

Four spadefuls of earth he then raised and spread out before him in the moonlight. There was nothing unusual to be seen. Nor did Mr. Batchel decide what he would look for, whether coins, jewels, documents in canisters, or weapons. In point of fact, he dug against what he deemed his better judgement, and expected nothing. He spread before him the fifth and last spadeful of earth, not quite without result, but with no result that was at all sensational. The earth contained a bone. Mr. Batchel's knowledge of anatomy was sufficient to show him that it was a human bone. He identified it, even by moonlight, as the radius, a bone of the forearm, as he removed the earth from it, with his thumb.

Such a discovery might be thought worthy of more than the very ordinary interest Mr. Batchel showed. As a matter of fact, the presence of a human bone was easily to be accounted for. Recent excavations within the church had caused the upturning of numberless bones, which had been collected and reverently buried. But an earth-stained bone is also easily overlooked, and this radius had obviously found its way into the garden with some of the earth brought out of the church.

Mr. Batchel was glad, rather than regretful at this termination to his adventure. He was once more provided with something to do. The reinterment of such bones as this had been his constant care, and he decided at once to restore the bone to consecrated earth. The time seemed opportune. The eyes of the curious were closed in sleep, he himself was still alert and wakeful. The spade remained by his side and the bone in his hand. So he betook himself, there and then, to the churchyard. By the still generous light of the moon, he found a place where the earth yielded to his spade, and within a few minutes the bone was laid decently to earth, some 18 inches deep.

The city clocks struck one as he finished. The whole world seemed asleep, and Mr. Batchel slowly returned to the garden with his spade. As he hung it in its accustomed place he felt stealing over him the welcome desire to sleep. He walked quietly on to the house and ascended to his room. It was now dark: the moon had passed on and left the room in shadow. He lit a candle, and before undressing passed into the library. He had an irresistible curiosity to see the passages in John Evelyn's book which had so strangely adapted themselves to the events of the past hour.

In the library a last surprise awaited him. The desk upon which the book had lain was empty. "The Compleat Gard'ner" stood in its place on the shelf. And then Mr. Batchel knew that he had handled a bone of William Whitehead, and that in response to his own entreaty.

The timidity of the child or the savage is entirely reasonable; they are alarmed at this world, because this world is a very alarming place. They dislike being alone because it is verily and indeed an awful idea to be alone. Barbarians fear the unknown for the same reason that Agnostics worship it—because it is a fact. Fairy tales, then, are not responsible for producing in children fear, or any of the shapes of fear; fairy tales do not give the child the idea of the evil or the ugly; that is in the child already, because it is in the world already. Fairy tales do not give the child his first idea of bogey. What fairy tales give the child is his first clear idea of the possible defeat of bogey. The baby has known the dragon intimately ever since he had an imagination. What the fairy tale provides for him is a St. George to kill the dragon.

Exactly what the fairy tale does is this: it accustoms him for a series of clear pictures to the idea that these limitless terrors had a limit, that these shapeless enemies have enemies in the knights of God, that there is something in the universe more mystical than darkness, and stronger than strong fear.

—G. K. Chesterton, "The Red Angel."

THE RICHPINS

E. G. Swain

Something of the general character of Stoneground and its people has been indicated by stray allusions in the preceding narratives. We must here add that of its present population only a small part is native, the remainder having been attracted during the recent prosperous days of brickmaking, from the nearer parts of East Anglia and the Midlands. The visitor to Stoneground now finds little more than the signs of an unlovely industry, and of the hasty and inadequate housing of the people it has drawn together. Nothing in the place pleases him more than the excellent train-service which makes it easy to get away. He seldom desires a long acquaintance either with Stoneground or its people.

The impression so made upon the average visitor is, however, unjust, as first impressions often are. The few who have made further acquaintance with Stoneground have soon learned to distinguish between the permanent and the accidental features of the place, and have been astonished by nothing so much as by the unexpected evidence of French influence. Amongst the household treasures of the old Inhabitants are invariably found French knickknacks: there are pieces of French furniture in what is called "the room" of many houses. A certain ten-acre field is called the "Frenchman's meadow." Upon the voters' lists hanging at the church door are to be found French names, often corrupted; and boys who run about the streets can be heard shrieking to each other such names as Bunnum, Dangibow, Planchey, and so on.

Mr. Batchel himself is possessed of many curious little articles of French handiwork—boxes deftly covered with split straws, arranged ingeniously in patterns; models of the guillotine, built of carved meat-bones, and various other pieces of handiwork, amongst them an accurate road-map of the country between Stoneground and Yarmouth, drawn upon a flyleaf torn from some book, and bearing upon the other side the name of

221

Jules Richepin. The latter had been picked up, according to a pencilled-note written across one corner, by a shepherd, in the year 1811.

The explanation of this French influence is simple enough. Within five miles of Stoneground a large barracks had been erected for the custody of French prisoners during the war with Bonaparte. Many thousands were confined there during the years 1808-14. The prisoners were allowed to sell what articles they could make in the barracks; and many of them, upon their release, settled in the neighbourhood, where their descendants remain. There is little curiosity amongst these descendants about their origin. The events of a century ago seem to them as remote as the Deluge, and as immaterial. To Thomas Richpin, a weakly man who blew the organ in church, Mr. Batchel shewed the map. Richpin, with a broad, black-haired skull and a narrow chin which grew a little pointed beard, had always a foreign look about him: Mr. Batchel thought it more than possible that he might be descended from the owner of the book, and told him as much upon showing him the fly-leaf. Thomas, however, was content to observe that "his name hadn't got no E," and shewed no further interest in the matter. His interest in it, before we have done with him, will have become very large.

For the growing boys of Stoneground, with whom he was on generally friendly terms, Mr. Batchel formed certain clubs to provide them with occupation on winter evenings; and in these clubs, in the interests of peace and good-order, he spent a great deal of time. Sitting one December evening, in a large circle of boys who preferred the warmth of the fire to the more temperate atmosphere of the tables, he found Thomas Richpin the sole topic of conversation.

"We seen Mr. Richpin in Frenchman's Meadow last night," said one.

"What time?" said Mr. Batchel, whose function it was to act as a sort of fly-wheel, and to carry the conversation over dead points. He had received the information with some little surprise, because Frenchman's Meadow was an unusual place for Richpin to have been in, but his question had no further object than to encourage talk.

"Half-past nine," was the reply.

This made the question much more interesting. Mr. Batchel, on the preceding evening, had taken advantage of a warmed church to practise upon the organ. He had played it from nine o'clock until ten, and Richpin had been all that time at the bellows.

"Are you sure it was half-past nine?" he asked.

"Yes," (we reproduce the answer exactly), "we come out o' night-school at quarter-past, and we was all goin' to the Wash to look if it was friz."

"And you saw Mr. Richpin in Frenchman's Meadow?" said Mr. Batchel.

"Yes. He was looking for something on the ground," added another boy.

"And his trousers was tore," said a third.

The story was clearly destined to stand in no need of corroboration.
"Did Mr. Richpin speak to you?" enquired Mr. Batchel.
"No, we run away afore he come to us," was the answer.
"Why?"
"Because we was frit."
"What frightened you?"
"Jim Lallement hauled a flint at him and hit him in the face, and he didn't take no notice, so we run away."
"Why?" repeated Mr. Batchel.
"Because he never hollered nor looked at us, and it made us feel so funny."
"Did you go straight down to the Wash?"
They had all done so.
"What time was it when you reached home?"
They had all been at home by ten, before Richpin had left the church.
"Why do they call it Frenchman's Meadow?" asked another boy, evidently anxious to change the subject.
Mr. Batchel replied that the meadow had probably belonged to a Frenchman whose name was not easy to say, and the conversation after this was soon in another channel. But, furnished as he was with an unmistakeable alibi, the story about Richpin and the torn trousers, and the flint, greatly puzzled him.
"Go straight home," he said, as the boys at last bade him good-night, "and let us have no more stone-throwing." They were reckless boys, and Richpin, who used little discretion in reporting their misdemeanours about the church, seemed to Mr. Batchel to stand in real danger.
Frenchman's Meadow provided ten acres of excellent pasture, and the owners of two or three hard-worked horses were glad to pay three shillings a week for the privilege of turning them into it. One of these men came to Mr. Batchel on the morning which followed the conversation at the club.
"I'm in a bit of a quandary about Tom Richpin," he began.
This was an opening that did not fail to command Mr. Batchel's attention. "What is it?" he said.
"I had my mare in Frenchman's Meadow," replied the man, "and Sam Bower come and told me last night as he heard her gallopin' about when he was walking this side the hedge."
"But what about Richpin?" said Mr. Batchel.
"Let me come to it," said the other. "My mare hasn't got no wind to gallop, so I up and went to see to her, and there she was sure enough, like a wild thing, and Tom Richpin walking across the meadow."
"Was he chasing her?" asked Mr. Batchel, who felt the absurdity of the question as he put it.

"He was not," said the man, "but what he could have been doin' to put the mare into that state, I can't think."

"What was he doing when you saw him?" asked Mr. Batchel.

"He was walking along looking for something he'd dropped, with his trousers all tore to ribbons, and while I was catchin' the mare, he made off."

"He was easy enough to find, I suppose?" said Mr. Batchel.

"That's the quandary I was put in," said the man. "I took the mare home and gave her to my lad, and straight I went to Richpin's, and found Tom havin' his supper, with his trousers as good as new."

"You'd made a mistake," said Mr. Batchel.

"But how come the mare to make it too?" said the other.

"What did you say to Richpin?" asked Mr. Batchel.

"'Tom,' I says, 'when did you come in?' 'Six o'clock,' he says, 'I bin mendin' my boots'; and there, sure enough, was the bobbin' iron by his chair, and him in his stockin'-feet. I don't know what to do."

"Give the mare a rest," said Mr. Batchel, "and say no more about it."

"I don't want to harm a pore creature like Richpin," said the man, "but a mare's a mare, especially where there's a family to bring up." The man consented, however, to abide by Mr. Batchel's advice, and the interview ended. The evenings just then were light, and both the man and his mare had seen something for which Mr. Batchel could not, at present, account. The worst way, however, of arriving at an explanation is to guess it. He was far too wise to let himself wander into the pleasant fields of conjecture, and had determined, even before the story of the mare had finished, upon the more prosaic path of investigation.

Mr. Batchel, either from strength or indolence of mind, as the reader may be pleased to determine, did not allow matters even of this exciting kind, to disturb his daily round of duty. He was beginning to fear, after what he had heard of the Frenchman's Meadow, that he might find it necessary to preach a plain sermon upon the Witch of Endor, for he foresaw that there would soon be some ghostly talk in circulation. In small communities, like that of Stoneground, such talk arises upon very slight provocation, and here was nothing at all to check it. Richpin was a weak and timid man, whom no one would suspect, whilst an alternative remained open, of wandering about in the dark; and Mr. Batchel knew that the alternative of an apparition, if once suggested, would meet with general acceptance, and this he wished, at all costs, to avoid. His own view of the matter he held in reserve, for the reasons already stated, but he could not help suspecting that there might be a better explanation of the name "Frenchman's Meadow" than he had given to the boys at their club.

Afternoons, with Mr. Batchel, were always spent in making pastoral visits, and upon the day our story has reached he determined to include amongst them a call upon Richpin, and to submit him to a cautious cross-examination. It was evident that at least four persons, all perfectly familiar with his appearance, were under the impression that they had seen him in the meadow, and his own statement upon the matter would be at least worth hearing.

Richpin's home, however, was not the first one visited by Mr. Batchel on that afternoon. His friendly relations with the boys has already been mentioned, and it may now be added that this friendship was but part of a generally keen sympathy with young people of all ages, and of both sexes. Parents knew much less than he did of the love affairs of their young people; and if he was not actually guilty of matchmaking, he was at least a very sympathetic observer of the process. When lovers had their little differences, or even their greater ones, it was Mr. Batchel, in most cases, who adjusted them, and who suffered, if he failed, hardly less than the lovers themselves.

It was a negotiation of this kind which, on this particular day, had given precedence to another visit, and left Richpin until the later part of the afternoon. But the matter of the Frenchman's Meadow had, after all, not to wait for Richpin. Mr. Batchel was calculating how long he should be in reaching it, when he found himself unexpectedly there. Selina Broughton had been a favourite of his from her childhood; she had been sufficiently good to please him, and naughty enough to attract and challenge him; and when at length she began to walk out with Bob Rockfort, who was another favourite, Mr. Batchel rubbed his hands in satisfaction. Their present difference, which now brought him to the Broughtons' cottage, gave him but little anxiety. He had brought Bob half-way towards reconciliation, and had no doubt of his ability to lead Selina to the same place. They would finish the journey, happily enough, together.

But what has this to do with the Frenchman's Meadow? Much every way. The meadow was apt to be the rendezvous of such young people as desired a higher degree of privacy than that afforded by the public paths; and these two had gone there separately the night before, each to nurse a grievance against the other. They had been at opposite ends, as it chanced, of the field; and Bob, who believed himself to be alone there, had been awakened from his reverie by a sudden scream. He had at once run across the field, and found Selina sorely in need of him. Mr. Batchel's work of reconciliation had been there and then anticipated, and Bob had taken the girl home in a condition of great excitement to her mother. All this was explained, in breathless sentences, by Mrs. Broughton, by way of accounting for the fact that Selina was then lying down in "the room."

There was no reason why Mr. Batchel should not see her, of course, and he went in. His original errand had lapsed, but it was now replaced by one of greater interest. Evidently there was Selina's testimony to add to that of the other four; she was not a girl who would scream without good cause, and Mr. Batchel felt that he knew how his question about the cause would be answered, when he came to the point of asking it.

He was not quite prepared for the form of her answer, which she gave without any hesitation. She had seen Mr. Richpin "looking for his eyes." Mr. Batchel saved for another occasion the amusement to be derived from the curiously illogical answer. He saw at once what had suggested it. Richpin had until recently had an atrocious squint, which an operation in London had completely cured. This operation, of which, of course, he knew nothing, he had described, in his own way, to anyone who would listen, and it was commonly believed that his eyes had ceased to be fixtures. It was plain, however, that Selina had seen very much what had been seen by the other four. Her information was precise, and her story perfectly coherent. She preserved a maidenly reticence about his trousers, if she had noticed them; but added a new fact, and a terrible one, in her description of the eyeless sockets. No wonder she had screamed. It will be observed that Mr. Richpin was still searching, if not looking, for something upon the ground.

Mr. Batchel now proceeded to make his remaining visit. Richpin lived in a little cottage by the church, of which cottage the Vicar was the indulgent landlord. Richpin's creditors were obliged to shew some indulgence, because his income was never regular and seldom sufficient. He got on in life by what is called "rubbing along," and appeared to do it with surprisingly little friction. The small duties about the church, assigned to him out of charity, were overpaid. He succeeded in attracting to himself all the available gifts of masculine clothing, of which he probably received enough and to sell, and he had somehow wooed and won a capable, if not very comely, wife, who supplemented his income by her own labour, and managed her house and husband to admiration.

Richpin, however, was not by any means a more dependent upon charity. He was, in his way, a man of parts. All plants, for instance, were his friends, and he had inherited, or acquired, great skill with fruit-trees, which never failed to reward his treatment with abundant crops. The two or three vines, too, of the neighbourhood, he kept in fine order by methods of his own, whose merit was proved by their success. He had other skill, though of a less remunerative kind, in fashioning toys out of wood, cardboard, or paper; and every correctly-behaving child in the parish had some such product of his handiwork. And besides all this, Richpin had a remarkable aptitude for making music. He could do something upon every musical instrument that came in his way, and, but for his voice, which was like that of the pea-hen, would have been a singer. It was his voice that had secured him the situation of organ-blower, as one remote from all incitement to join in the singing in church.

Like all men who have not wit enough to defend themselves by argument, Richpin had a plaintive manner. His way of resenting injury was to complain of it to the next person he met, and such complaints as he found no other means of discharging, he carried home to his wife, who treated his conversation just as she treated the singing of the canary, and other domestic sounds, being hardly conscious of it until it ceased.

The entrance of Mr. Batchel, soon after his interview with Selina, found Richpin engaged in a loud and fluent oration. The fluency was achieved mainly by repetition, for the man had but small command of words, but it served none the less to shew the depth of his indignation.

"I aren't bin in Frenchman's Meadow, am I?" he was saying in appeal to his wife—this is the Stoneground way with auxiliary verbs—"What am I got to go there for?" He acknowledged Mr. Batchel's entrance in no other way than by changing to the third person in his discourse, and he continued without pause—"if she'd let me out o' nights, I'm got better places to go to than Frenchman's Meadow. Let policeman stick to where I am bin, or else keep his mouth shut. What call is he got to say I'm bin where I aren't bin?"

From this, and much more to the same effect, it was clear that the matter of the meadow was being noised abroad, and even receiving official attention. Mr. Batchel was well aware that no question he could put to Richpin, in his present state, would change the flow of his eloquence, and that he had already learned as much as he was likely to learn. He was content, therefore, to ascertain from Mrs. Richpin that her husband had indeed spent all his evenings at home, with the single exception of the one hour during which Mr. Batchel had employed him at the organ. Having ascertained this, he retired, and left Richpin to talk himself out.

No further doubt about the story was now possible. It was not twenty-four hours since Mr. Batchel had heard it from the boys at the club, and it had already been confirmed by at least two unimpeachable witnesses. He thought the matter over, as he took his tea, and was chiefly concerned in Richpin's curious connexion with it. On his account, more than on any other, it had become necessary to make whatever investigation might be feasible, and Mr. Batchel determined, of course, to make the next stage of it in the meadow itself.

The situation of "Frenchman's Meadow" made it more conspicuous than any other enclosure in the neighbourhood. It was upon the edge of what is locally known as "high land"; and though its elevation was not great, one could stand in the meadow and look sea-wards over many miles of flat country, once a waste of brackish water, now a great chess-board of fertile fields bounded by straight dykes of glistening water. The point of view derived another interest from looking down upon a long straight bank which disappeared into the horizon many miles away, and might have been taken for a great railway embankment of which no use had been made. It was, in fact, one of the great works of the Dutch Engineers in the time of Charles I., and it separated the river basin from a large drained area called the "Middle Level," some six feet below it. In this embankment, not two hundred yards below "Frenchman's Meadow," was one of the huge water gates which admitted traffic through a sluice, into the lower level, and the picturesque thatched cottage of the sluice-keeper formed a pleasing addition to the landscape. It was a view with which Mr. Batchel was naturally very familiar. Few of his surroundings were pleasant to the eye, and this was about the only place to which he could take a visitor whom he desired to impress favourably. The way to the meadow lay through a short lane, and he could reach it in five minutes: he was frequently there.

It was, of course, his intention to be there again that evening: to spend the night there, if need be, rather than let anything escape him. He only hoped he should not find half the parish there also. His best hope of privacy lay in the inclemency of the weather; the day was growing colder, and there was a north-east wind, of which Frenchman's Meadow would receive the fine edge.

Mr. Batchel spent the next three hours in dealing with some arrears of correspondence, and at nine o'clock put on his thickest coat and boots, and made his way to the meadow. It became evident, as he walked up the lane, that he was to have company. He heard many voices, and soon recognised the loudest amongst them. Jim Lallement was boasting of the accuracy of his aim: the others were not disputing it, but were asserting their own merits in discordant chorus. This was a nuisance, and to make matters worse, Mr. Batchel heard steps behind him.

A voice soon bade him "Good evening." To Mr. Batchel's great relief it proved to be the policeman, who soon overtook him. The conversation began on his side.

"Curious tricks, sir, these of Richpin's."

"What tricks?" asked Mr. Batchel, with an air of innocence.

"Why, he's been walking about Frenchman's Meadow these three nights, frightening folk and what all."

"Richpin has been at home every night, and all night long," said Mr. Batchel.

"I'm talking about where he was, not where he says he was," said the policeman. "You can't go behind the evidence."

"But Richpin has evidence too. I asked his wife."

"You know, sir, and none better, that wives have got to obey. Richpin wants to be took for a ghost, and we know that sort of ghost. Whenever we hear there's a ghost, we always know there's going to be turkeys missing."

"But there are real ghosts sometimes, surely?" said Mr. Batchel.

"No," said the policeman, "me and my wife have both looked, and there's no such thing."

"Looked where?" enquired Mr. Batchel.

"In the 'Police Duty' Catechism. There's lunatics, and deserters, and dead bodies, but no ghosts."

Mr. Batchel accepted this as final. He had devised a way of ridding himself of all his company, and proceeded at once to carry it into effect. The two had by this time reached the group of boys.

"These are all stone-throwers," said he, loudly.

There was a clatter of stones as they dropped from the hands of the boys.

"These boys ought all to be in the club instead of roaming about here damaging property. Will you take them there, and see them safely in? If Richpin comes here, I will bring him to the station."

The policeman seemed well pleased with the suggestion. No doubt he had overstated his confidence in the definition of the "Police Duty." Mr. Batchel, on his part, knew the boys well enough to be assured that they would keep the policeman occupied for the next half-hour, and as the party moved slowly away, felt proud of his diplomacy.

There was no sign of any other person about the field gate, which he climbed readily enough, and he was soon standing in the highest part of the meadow and peering into the darkness on every side.

It was possible to see a distance of about thirty yards; beyond that it was too dark to distinguish anything. Mr. Batchel designed a zigzag course about the meadow, which would allow of his examining it systematically and as rapidly as possible, and along this course he began to walk briskly, looking straight before him as he went, and pausing to look well about him when he came to a turn. There were no beasts in the meadow—their owners had taken the precaution of removing them; their absence was, of course, of great advantage to Mr. Batchel.

In about ten minutes he had finished his zig-zag path and arrived at the other corner of the meadow; he had seen nothing resembling a man. He then retraced his steps, and examined the field again, but arrived at his starting point, knowing no more than when he had left it. He began to fear the return of the policeman as he faced the wind and set upon a third journey.

The third journey, however, rewarded him. He had reached the end of his second traverse, and was looking about him at the angle between that and the next, when he distinctly saw what looked like Richpin crossing his circle of vision, and making straight for the sluice. There was no gate on that side of the field; the hedge, which seemed to present no obstacle to the other, delayed Mr. Batchel considerably, and still retains some of his clothing, but he was not long through before he had again marked his man. It had every appearance of being Richpin. It went down the slope, crossed the plank that bridged the lock, and disappeared round the corner of the cottage, where the entrance lay.

Mr. Batchel had had no opportunity of confirming the gruesome observation of Selina Broughton, but had seen enough to prove that the others had not been romancing. He was not a half-minute behind the figure as it crossed the plank over the lock—it was slow going in the darkness—and he followed it immediately round the corner of the house. As he expected, it had then disappeared.

Mr. Batchel knocked at the door, and admitted himself, as his custom was. The sluicekeeper was in his kitchen, charring a gate post. He was surprised to see Mr. Batchel at that hour, and his greeting took the form of a remark to that effect.

"I have been talking an evening walk," said Mr. Batchel. "Have you seen Richpin lately?"

"I see him last Saturday week," replied the sluice-keeper, "not since."

"Do you feel lonely here at night?"

"No," replied the sluice-keeper, "people drop in at times. There was a man in on Monday, and another yesterday."

"Have you had no one to-day?" said Mr. Batchel, coming to the point.

The answer showed that Mr. Batchel had been the first to enter the door that day, and after a little general conversation he brought his visit to an end.

It was now ten o'clock. He looked in at Richpin's cottage, where he saw a light burning, as he passed. Richpin had tired himself early, and had been in bed since half-past eight. His wife was visibly annoyed at the rumours which had upset him, and Mr. Batchel said such soothing words as he could command, before he left for home.

He congratulated himself, prematurely, as he sat before the fire in his study, that the day was at an end. It had been cold out of doors, and it was pleasant to think things over in the warmth of the cheerful fire his housekeeper never failed to leave for him. The reader will have no more difficulty than Mr. Batchel had in accounting for the resemblance between Richpin and the man in the meadow. It was a mere question of family likeness. That the ancestor had been seen in the meadow at some former time might perhaps be inferred from its traditional name. The reason for his return, then and now, was a matter of more conjecture, and Mr. Batchel let it alone.

The next incident has, to some, appeared incredible, which only means, after all, that it has made demands upon their powers of imagination and found them bankrupt.

Critics of story-telling have used severe language about authors who avail themselves of the short-cut of coincidence. "That must be reserved,

I suppose," said Mr. Batchel, when he came to tell of Richpin, "for what really happens; and that fiction is a game which must be played according to the rules."

"I know," he went on to say, "that the chances were some millions to one against what happened that night, but if that makes it incredible, what is there left to believe?"

It was thereupon remarked by someone in the company, that the credible material would not be exhausted.

"I doubt whether anything happens," replied Mr. Batchel in his dogmatic way, "without the chances being a million to one against it. Why did they choose such a word? What does 'happen' mean?"

There was no reply: it was clearly a rhetorical question.

"Is it incredible," he went on, "that I put into the plate last Sunday the very half-crown my uncle tipped me with in 1881, and that I spent next day?"

"Was that the one you put in?" was asked by several.

"How do I know?" replied Mr. Batchel, "but if I knew the history of the half-crown I did put in, I know it would furnish still more remarkable coincidences."

All this talk arose out of the fact that at midnight on the eventful day, whilst Mr. Batchel was still sitting by his study fire, he had news that the cottage at the sluice had been burnt down. The thatch had been dry; there was, as we know, a stiff east-wind, and an hour had sufficed to destroy all that was inflammable. The fire is still spoken of in Stoneground with great regret. There remains only one building in the place of sufficient merit to find its way on to a postcard.

It was just at midnight that the sluice-keeper rung at Mr. Batchel's door. His errand required no apology. The man had found a night-fisherman to help him as soon as the fire began, and with two long sprits from a lighter they had made haste to tear down the thatch, and upon this had brought down, from under the ridge at the South end, the bones and some of the clothing of a man. Would Mr. Batchel come down and see?

Mr. Batchel put on his coat and returned to the place. The people whom the fire had collected had been kept on the further side of the water, and the space about the cottage was vacant. Near to the smouldering heap of ruin were the remains found under the thatch. The fingers of the right hand still firmly clutched a sheep bone which had been gnawed as a dog would gnaw it.

"Starved to death," said the sluice-keeper, "I see a tramp like that ten years ago."

They laid the bones decently in an out-house, and turned the key, Mr. Batchel carried home in his hand a metal cross, threaded upon a cord. He found an engraved figure of Our Lord on the face of it, and the name of Pierre Richepin upon the back. He went next day to make the matter known to the nearest Priest of the Roman Faith, with whom he left the cross. The remains, after a brief inquest, were interred in the cemetery, with the rites of the Church to which the man had evidently belonged.

Mr. Batchel's deductions from the whole circumstances were curious, and left a great deal to be explained. It seemed as if Pierre Richepin had been disturbed by some premonition of the fire, but had not foreseen that his mortal remains would escape; that he could not return to his own people without the aid of his map, but had no perception of the interval that had elapsed since he had lost it. This map Mr. Batchel put into his pocket-book next day when he went to Thomas Richpin for certain other information about his surviving relatives.

Richpin had a father, it appeared, living a few miles away in Jakesley Fen, and Mr. Batchel concluded that he was worth a visit. He mounted his bicycle, therefore, and made his way to Jakesley that same afternoon.

Mr. Richpin was working not far from home, and was soon brought in. He and his wife shewed great courtesy to their visitor, whom they knew well by repute. They had a well-ordered house, and with a natural and dignified hospitality, asked him to take tea with them. It was evident to Mr. Batchel that there was a great gulf between the elder Richpin and his son; the former was the last of an old race, and the latter the first of a new. In spite of the Board of Education, the latter was vastly the worse.

The cottage contained some French kickshaws which greatly facilitated the enquiries Mr. Batchel had come to make. They proved to be family relies.

"My grandfather," said Mr. Richpin, as they sat at tea, "was a prisoner—he and his brother."

"Your grandfather was Pierre Richepin?" asked Mr. Batchel.

"No! Jules," was the reply. "Pierre got away."

"Shew Mr. Batchel the book," said his wife.

The book was produced. It was a Book of Meditations, with the name of Jules Richepin upon the title-page. The fly-leaf was missing. Mr. Batchel produced the map from his pocketbook. It fitted exactly. The slight indentures along the torn edge fell into their place, and Mr. Batchel left the leaf in the book, to the great delight of the old couple, to whom he told no more of the story than he thought fit.

THE ROCKERY

E. G. Swain

The Vicar's garden at Stoneground has certainly been enclosed for more than seven centuries, and during the whole of that time its almost sacred privacy has been regarded as permanent and unchangeable. It has remained for the innovators of later and more audacious days to hint that it might be given into other hands, and still carry with it no curse that should make a new possessor hasten to undo his irreverence. Whether there can be warrant for such confidence, time will show. The experiences already related will show that the privacy of the garden has been counted upon both by good men and worse. And here is a story, in its way, more strange than any.

By way of beginning, it may be well to describe a part of the garden not hitherto brought into notice. That part lies on the western boundary, where the garden slopes down to a sluggish stream, hardly a stream at all, locally known as the Lode. The Lode bounds the garden on the west along its whole length, and there the moor-hen builds her nest, and the kingfisher is sometimes, but in these days too rarely, seen. But the centre of vision, as it were, of this western edge lies in a cluster of tall elms. Towards these all the garden paths converge, and about their base is raised a bank of earth, upon which is heaped a rockery of large stones lately overgrown with ferns.

Mr. Batchel's somewhat prim taste in gardening had long resented this disorderly bank. In more than one place in his garden had wild confusion given place to a park-like trimness, and there were not a few who would say that the change was not for the better. Mr. Batchel, however, went his own way, and in due time determined to remove the rockery. He was puzzled by its presence; he could see no reason why a bank should have been raised about the feet of the elms, and surmounted with stones; not a ray of sunshine ever found its way there, and none but

233

coarse and uninteresting plants had established themselves. Whoever had raised the bank had done it ignorantly, or with some purpose not easy for Mr. Batchel to conjecture.

Upon a certain day, therefore, in the early part of December, when the garden had been made comfortable for its winter rest, he began, with the assistance of his gardener, to remove the stones into another place.

We do but speak according to custom in this matter, and there are few readers who will not suspect the truth, which is that the gardener began to remove the stones, whilst Mr. Batchel stood by and delivered criticisms of very slight value. Such strength, in fact, as Mr. Batchel possessed had concentrated itself upon the mind, and somewhat neglected his body, and what he called help, during his presence in the garden, was called by another name when the gardener and his boy were left to themselves, with full freedom of speech.

There were few of the stones rolled down by the gardener that Mr. Batchel could even have moved, but his astonishment at their size soon gave place to excitement at their appearance. His antiquarian tastes were strong, and were soon busily engaged. For, as the stones rolled down, his eyes were feasted, in a rapid succession, by capitals of columns, fragments of moulded arches and mullions, and other relics of ecclesiastical building.

Repeatedly did he call the gardener down from his work to put these fragments together, and before long there were several complete lengths of arcading laid upon the path. Stones which, perhaps, had been separated for centuries, once more came together, and Mr. Batchel, rubbing his hands in excited satisfaction, declared that he might recover the best parts of a Church by the time the rockery had been demolished.

The interest of the gardener in such matters was of a milder kind. "We must go careful," he merely observed, "when we come to the organ." They went on removing more and more stones, until at length the whole bank was laid bare, and Mr. Batchel's chief purpose achieved. How the stones were carefully arranged, and set up in other parts of the garden, is well known, and need not concern us now.

One detail, however, must not be omitted. A large and stout stake of yew, evidently of considerable age, but nevertheless quite sound, stood exposed after the clearing of the bank. There was no obvious reason for its presence, but it had been well driven in, so well that the strength of the gardener, or, if it made any difference, of the gardener and Mr. Batchel together, failed even to shake it. It was not unsightly, and might have remained where it was, had not the gardener exclaimed, "This is the very thing we want for the pump." It was so obviously "the very thing" that its removal was then and there decided upon.

The pump referred to was a small iron pump used to draw water from the lode. It had been affixed to many posts in turn, and defied them all to hold it. Not that the pump was at fault. It was a trifling affair enough. But the pumpers were usually garden-boys, whose impatient energy had never failed, before many days, to wriggle the pump away from its supports. When the gardener had, upon one occasion, spent half a day in attaching it firmly to a post, they had at once shaken out the post itself. Since, therefore, the matter was causing daily inconvenience, and the gardener becoming daily more concerned for his reputation as a rough carpenter, it was natural for him to exclaim, "This is the very thing." It was a better stake than he had ever used, and as had just been made evident, a stake that the ground would hold.

"Yes!" said Mr. Batchel, "it is the very thing; but can we get it up?" The gardener always accepted this kind of query as a challenge, and replied only by taking up a pick and setting to work, Mr. Batchel, as usual, looking on, and making, every now and then, a fruitless suggestion. After a few minutes, however, he made somewhat more than a suggestion. He darted forward and laid his hand upon the pick. "Don't you see some copper?" he asked quickly.

Every man who digs knows what a hiding place there is in the earth. The monotony of spade work is always relieved by a hope of turning up something unexpected. Treasure lies dimly behind all these hopes, so that the gardener, having seen Mr. Batchel excited over so much that was precious from his own point of view, was quite ready to look for something of value to an ordinary reasonable man. Copper might lead to silver, and that, in turn, to gold. At Mr. Batchel's eager question, therefore, he peered into the hole he had made, and examined everything there that might suggest the rounded form of a coin.

He soon saw what had arrested Mr. Batchel. There was a lustrous scratch on the side of the stake, evidently made by the pick, and though the metal was copper, plainly enough, the gardener felt that he had been deceived, and would have gone on with his work. Copper of that sort gave him no sort of excitement, and only a feeble interest.

Mr. Batchel, however, was on his hands and knees. There was a small irregular plate of copper nailed to the stake; without any difficulty he tore it away from the nails, and soon scraped it clean with a shaving of wood; then, rising to his feet, he examined his find.

There was an inscription upon it, so legible as to need no deciphering. It had been roughly and effectually made with a hammer and nail, the letters being formed by series of holes punched deeply into the metal, and what he read was—*Move Not This Stake*, Nov. 1, 1702.

But to move the stake was what Mr. Batchel had determined upon, and the metal plate he held in his hand interested him chiefly as showing how long the post had been there. He had happened, as he supposed, upon an ancient landmark. The discovery, recorded elsewhere, of a well, near to the edge of his present lawn, had shown him that his premises had once been differently arranged. One of the minor antiquarian tasks he had set himself was to discover and record the old arrangement, and he felt that the position of this stake would help him. He felt no doubt of its being a point upon the western limit of the garden; not improbably marked in this way to show where the garden began, and where ended the ancient hauling-way, which had been secured to the public for purposes of navigation.

The gardener, meanwhile, was proceeding with his work. With no small difficulty he removed the rubble and clay which accounted for the firmness of the stake. It grew dark as the work went on, and a distant clock struck five before it was completed. Five was the hour at which the gardener usually went home; his day began early. He was not, however, a man to leave a small job unfinished, and he went on loosening the earth with his pick, and trying the effect, at intervals, upon the firmness of the stake. It naturally began to give, and could be moved from side to side through a space of some few inches. He lifted out the loosened stones, and loosened more. His pick struck iron, which, after loosening, proved to be links of a rusted chain. "They've buried a lot of rubbish in this hole," he remarked, as he went on loosening the chain, which, in the growing darkness, could hardly be seen. Mr. Batchel, meanwhile, occupied himself in a simpler task of working the stake to and fro, by way of loosening its hold. Ultimately it began to move with greater freedom. The gardener laid down his tool and grasped the stake, which his master was still holding; their combined efforts succeeded at once; the stake was lifted out.

It turned out to be furnished with an unusually long and sharp point, which explained the firmness of its hold upon the ground. The gardener carried it to the neighbourhood of the pump, in readiness for its next purpose, and made ready to go home. He would drive the stake to-morrow, he said, in the new place, and make the pump so secure that not even the boys could shake it. He also spoke of some designs he had upon the chain, should it prove to be of any considerable length. He was an ingenious man, and his skill in converting discarded articles to now uses was embarrassing to his master. Mr. Batchel, as has been said, was a prim gardener, and he had no liking for makeshift devices. He had that day seen his runner beans trained upon a length of old gas-piping, and had no intention of leaving the gardener in possession of such a treasure as a rusty chain. What he said, however, and said with truth, was that he wanted the chain for himself. He had no practical use for it, and hardly expected it to yield him any interest. But a chain buried in 1702 must be examined—nothing ancient comes amiss to a man of antiquarian tastes.

Mr. Batchel had noticed, whilst the gardener had been carrying away the stake, that the chain lay very loosely in the earth. The pick had worked well round it. He said, therefore, that the chain must be lifted out and brought to him upon the morrow, bade his gardener good night, and went in to his fireside.

This will appear to the reader to be a record of the merest trifles, but all readers will accept the reminder that there is no such thing as a trifle, and that what appears to be trivial has that appearance only so long as it stands alone.

Regarded in the light of their consequences, those matters which have seemed to be least in importance, turn out, often enough, to be the greatest. And these trifling occupations, as we may call them for the last time, of Mr. Batchel and the gardener, had consequences which shall now be set down as Mr. Batchel himself narrated them. But we must take events in their order. At present Mr. Batchel is at his fireside, and his gardener at home with his family. The stake is removed, and the hole, in which lies some sort of an iron chain, is exposed.

Upon this particular evening Mr. Batchel was dining out. He was a good natured man, with certain mild powers of entertainment, and his presence as an occasional guest was not unacceptable at some of the more considerable houses of the neighbourhood. And let us hasten to observe that he was not a guest who made any great impression upon the larders or the cellars of his hosts. He liked port, but he liked it only of good quality, and in small quantity. When he returned from a dinner party, therefore, he was never either in a surfeited condition of body, or in any confusion of mind. Not uncommonly after his return upon such occasions did he perform accurate work. Unfinished contributions to sundry local journals were seldom absent from his desk. They were his means of recreation. There they awaited convenient intervals of leisure, and Mr. Batchel was accustomed to say that of these intervals he found none so productive as a late hour, or hour and a half, after a dinner party.

Upon the evening in question he returned, about an hour before midnight, from dining at the house of a retired officer residing in the neighbourhood, and the evening had been somewhat less enjoyable than usual. He had taken in to dinner a young lady who had too persistently assailed him with antiquarian questions. Now Mr. Batchel did not like talking what he regarded as "shop," and was not much at home with young ladies, to whom he knew that, in the nature of things, he could be but imperfectly acceptable. With infinite good will towards them, and a genuine liking for their presence, he felt that he had but little to offer them in exchange. There was so little in common between his life and theirs, he felt distinctly at his worst when he found himself treated as a mere scrapbook of information. It made him seem, as he would express it, dehumanised.

Upon this particular evening the young lady allotted to him, perhaps at her own request, had made a scrap-book of him, and he had returned home somewhat discontented, if also somewhat amused. His discontent arose from having been deprived of the general conversation he so greatly, but so rarely, enjoyed. His amusement was caused by the incongruity between a very light-hearted young lady and the subject upon which she had made him talk, for she had talked of nothing else but modes of burial.

He began to recall the conversation as he lit his pipe and dropped into his armchair. She had either been reflecting deeply upon the matter, or, as seemed to Mr. Batchel, more probable, had read something and half forgotten it. He recalled her questions, and the answers by which he had vainly tried to lead her to a more attractive topic. For example:

She: Will you tell me why people were buried at cross roads?

He: Well, consecrated ground was so jealously guarded that a criminal would be held to have forfeited the right to be buried amongst Christian folk. His friends would therefore choose cross roads where there was set a wayside cross, and make his grave at the foot of it. In some of my journeys in Scotland I have seen crosses...

But the young lady had refused to be led into Scotland. She had stuck to her subject.

She: Why have coffins come back into use? There is nothing in our Civil Service about a coffin.

He: True, and the use of the coffin is due, in part, to an ignorant notion of confining the corpse, lest, like Hamlet's father, he should walk the earth. You will have noticed that the corpse is always carried out of the house feet foremost, to suggest a final exit, and that the grave is often covered with a heavy slab. Very curious epitaphs are to be found on these slabs...

But she was not to be drawn into the subject of epitaphs. She had made him tell of other devices for confining spirits to their prison, and securing the peace of the living, especially of those adopted in the case of violent and mischievous men. Altogether an unusual sort of young lady.

The conversation, however, had revived his memories of what was, after all, a matter of some interest, and he determined to look through his parish registers for records of exceptional burials. He was surprised at himself for never having done it. He dismissed the matter from his mind for the time being, and as it was a bright moonlight night he thought he would finish his pipe in the garden.

Therefore, although midnight was close at hand, he strolled compla-cently round his garden, enjoying the light of the moon no less than in the daytime he would have enjoyed the sun; and thus it was that he arrived at the scene of his labours upon the old rockery. There was more light than there had been at the end of the afternoon, and when he had walked up the bank, and stood over the hole we have already described, he could distinctly see the few exposed links of the iron chain. Should he remove it at once to a place of safety, out of the way of the gardener? It was about time for bed. The city clocks were then striking midnight. He would let the chain decide. If it came out easily he would remove it; otherwise, it should remain until morning.

The chain came out more than easily. It seemed to have a force within itself. He gave but a slight tug at the free end with a view of ascertaining what resistance he had to encounter, and immediately found himself lying upon his back with the chain in his hand. His back had fortunately turned towards an elm three feet away which broke his fall, but there had been violence enough to cause him no little surprise.

The effort he had made was so shift that he could not account for having lost his feet; and being a careful man, he was a little anxious about his evening coat, which he was still wearing. The chain, however, was in his hand, and he made haste to coil it into a portable shape, and to return to the house.

Some fifty yards from the spot was the northern boundary of the garden, a long wall with a narrow lane beyond. It was not unusual, even at this hour of the night, to hear footsteps there. The lane was used by rail-way men, who passed to and from their work at all hours, as also by some who returned late from entertainments in the neighbouring city.

But Mr. Batchel, as he turned back to the house, with his chain over one arm, heard more than footsteps. He heard for a few moments the unmistakable sound of a scuffle, and then a piercing cry, loud and sharp, and a noise of running. It was such a cry as could only have come from one in urgent need of help.

Mr. Batchel dropped his chain. The garden wall was some ten feet high and he had no means of scaling it. But he ran quickly into the house, passed out by the hall door into the street, and so towards the lane with-out a moment's loss of time.

Before he has gone many yards he sees a man running from the lane with his clothing in great disorder, and this man, at the sight of Mr. Batchel, darts across the road, runs along in the shadow of an opposite wall and attempts to escape.

The man is known well enough to Mr. Batchel. It is one Stephen Medd, a respectable and sensible man, by occupation a shunter, and Mr. Batchel at once calls out to ask what has happened. Stephen, however, makes no reply but continues to run along the shadow of the wall, whereupon Mr. Batchel crosses over and intercepts him, and again asks what is amiss. Stephen answers wildly and breathlessly, "I'm not going to stop here, let me go home."

As Mr. Batchel lays his hand upon the man's arm and draws him into the light of the moon, it is seen that his face is streaming with blood from a wound near the eye.

He is somewhat calmed by the familiar voice of Mr. Batchel, and is about to speak, when another scream is heard from the lane. The voice is that of a boy or woman, and no sooner does Stephen bear it than he frees himself violently from Mr. Batchel and makes away towards his home. With no less speed does Mr. Batchel make for the lane, and finds about half way down a boy lying on the ground wounded and terrified.

At first the boy clings to the ground, but he, too, is soon reassured by Mr. Batchel's voice, and allows himself to be lifted on to his feet. His wound is also in the face, and Mr. Batchel takes the boy into his house, bathes and plasters his wound, and soon restores him to something like calm. He is what is termed a call-boy, employed by the Railway Company to awaken drivers at all hours, and give them their instructions.

Mr. Batchel is naturally impatient for the moment he can question the boy about his assailant, who is presumably also the assailant of Stephen Medd. No one had been visible in the lane, though the moon shone upon it from end to end. At the first available moment, therefore, he asks the boy, "Who did this?"

The answer came, without any hesitation, "Nobody."

"There was nobody there," he said, "and all of a sudden somebody hit me with an iron thing."

Then Mr. Batchel asked, "Did you see Stephen Medd?" He was becoming greatly puzzled.

The boy replied that he had seen Mr. Medd "a good bit in front," with nobody near him, and that all of a sudden someone knocked him down.

Further questioning seemed useless. Mr. Batchel saw the boy to his home, left him at the door, and returned to bed, but not to sleep. He could not cease from thinking, and he could think of nothing but assaults from invisible hands. Morning seemed long in coming, but came at last.

Mr. Batchel was up betimes and made a very poor breakfast. Dallying with the morning paper, rather than reading it, his eye was arrested by a headline about "Mysterious assaults in Elmham." He felt that he had mysteries of his own to occupy him and was in no mood to be interested in more assaults. But he had some knowledge of Elmham, a small town ten miles distant from Stoneground, and he read the brief paragraph, which contained no more than the substance of a telegram. It said, however, that three persons had been victims of unaccountable assaults.

Two of them had escaped with slight injuries, but the third, a young woman, was dangerously wounded, though still alive and conscious. She declared that she was quite alone in her house and had been suddenly struck with great violence by what felt like a piece of iron, and that she must have bled to death but for a neighbour who heard her cries. The neighbour had at once looked out and seen nobody, but had bravely gone to her friend's assistance.

Mr. Batchel laid down his newspaper considerably impressed, as was natural, by the resemblance of these tragedies to what he had witnessed himself. He was in no condition, after his excitement and his sleepless night, to do his usual work. His mind reverted to the conversation at the dinner party and the trifle of antiquarian research it had suggested. Such occupation had often served him when he found himself suffering from a cold, or otherwise indisposed for more serious work. He would get the registers and collect what entries there might be of irregular burial.

He found only one such entry, but that one was enough. There was a note dated All Hallows, 1702, to this effect:

"This day did a vagrant from Elmham beat cruelly to death two poor men who had refused him alms, and upon a hue and cry being raised, took his own life. He was buried in one Parson's Close with a stake through his body and his arms confined in chains, and stoutly covered in."

No further news came from Elmham. Either the effort had been exhausted, or its purpose achieved. But what could have led the young lady, a stranger to Mr. Batchel and to his garden, to hit upon so appropriate a topic? Mr. Batchel could not answer the question as he put it to himself again and again during the day. He only knew that she had given him a warning, by which, to his shame and regret, he had been too obtuse to profit.

The instances tell us, 1. That the state, converse, policy, laws of the aerial world, or regions, are much (though not wholly) unknown to us here. 2. And so is the natural state of the departed souls of wicked men, as to their having bodies, or no bodies, their power, their wits, their motions, and passions. 3. And also whether they be proper devils when joyned with them, or of another species. 4. And 'tis hard to know by their words or signs, when it is a devil, and when it is a humane soul that appeareth. 5. Yea, it is oft hard to know whether it be the soul of a good person or a bad. 6. And consequently, what distance there is in their habitations. 7. Yeah, and oft whether it be a good angel, or a bad, seeing bad ones may do good deceitfully, or by constraint. 8. And 'tis unsearchable to us, how far God leaveth invisible, intellectual powers to free will about inferior things, suspending his predetermining motion, though not his general motion and concourse. 9. Yea, we are not fully certain whether these aerial regions have not a third sort of wights, that are neither angels, (good or fallen,) nor souls of men, but such as have been there placed as fishes in the sea, and men on earth: and whether those called fairies and goblins are not such.

—Richard Baxter, *The Certainty of
the World of Spirits...* (1691)

THE KIRK ſPOOK

E. G. Swain

Before many years have passed it will be hard to find a person who has ever seen a Parish Clerk. The Parish Clerk is all but extinct. Our grandfathers knew him well—an oldish, clean-shaven man, who looked as if he had never been young, who dressed in rusty black, bestowed upon him, as often as not, by the Rector, and who usually wore a white tie on Sundays, out of respect for the seriousness of his office. He it was who laid out the Rector's robes, and helped him to put them on; who found the places in the large Bible and Prayer Book, and indicated them by means of decorous silken book-markers; who lighted and snuffed the candles in the pulpit and desk, and attended to the little stove in the squire's pew; who ran busily about, in short, during the quarter-hour which preceded Divine Service, doing a hundred little things, with all the activity, and much of the appearance, of a beetle.

Just such a one was Caleb Dean, who was clerk of Stoneground in the days of William IV. Small in stature, he possessed a voice which Nature seemed to have meant for a giant, and in the discharge of his duties he had a dignity of manner disproportionate even to his voice. No one was afraid to sing when he led the Psalm, so certain was it that no other voice could be noticed, and the gracious condescension with which he received his meagre fees would have been ample acknowledgement of double their amount.

Man, however, cannot live by dignity alone, and Caleb was glad enough to be sexton as well as clerk, and to undertake any other duties by which he might add to his modest income. He kept the churchyard tidy, trimmed the lamps, chimed the bells, taught the choir their simple tunes, turned the barrel of the organ, and managed the stoves.

It was this last duty in particular, which took him into church "last thing," as he used to call it, on Saturday night. There were people in those

243

days, and may be some in these, whom nothing would induce to enter a church at midnight; Caleb, however, was so much at home there that all hours were alike to him. He was never an early man on Saturdays. His wife, who insisted upon sitting up for him, would often knit her way into Sunday before he appeared, and even then would find it hard to get him to bed. Caleb, in fact, when off duty, was a genial little fellow; he had many friends, and on Saturday evenings he knew where to find them.

It was not, therefore, until the evening was spent that he went to make up his fires; and his voice, which served for other singing than that of Psalms, could usually be heard, within a little of midnight, beguiling the way to church with snatches of convivial songs. Many a belated traveller, homeward bound, would envy him his spirits, but no one envied him his duties. Even such as walked with him to the neighbourhood of the church-yard would bid him "Good-night" whilst still a long way from the gate. They would see him disappear into the gloom amongst the graves, and shudder as they turned homewards.

Caleb, meanwhile, was perfectly content. He knew every stone in the path; long practice enabled him, even on the darkest night, to thrust his huge key into the lock at the first attempt, and on the night we are about to describe—it had come to Mr. Batchel from an old man who heard it from Caleb's lips—he did it with a feeling of unusual cheerfulness and contentment.

Caleb always locked himself in. A prank had once been played upon him, which had greatly wounded his dignity; and though it had been no midnight prank, he had taken care, ever since, to have the church to him-self. He locked the door, therefore, as usual, on the night we speak of, and made his way to the stove. He used no candle. He opened the little iron door of the stove, and obtained sufficient light to show him the fuel he had laid in readiness; then, when he had made up his fire, he closed this door again, and left the church in darkness. He never could say what induced him upon this occasion to remain there after his task was done. He knew that his wife was sitting up, as usual, and that, as usual, he would have to hear what she had to say. Yet, instead of making his way home, he sat down in the corner of the nearest seat. He supposed that he must have felt tired, but had no distinct recollection of it.

The church was not absolutely dark. Caleb remembered that he could make out the outlines of the windows, and that through the window near-est to him he saw a few stars. After his eyes had grown accustomed to the gloom he could see the lines of the seats taking shape in the darkness, and he had not long sat there before he could dimly see everything there was. At last he began to distinguish where books lay upon the shelf in front of him. And then he closed his eyes. He does not admit having fallen asleep, even for a moment. But the seat was restful, the neighbouring stove was growing warm, he had been through a long and joyous evening, and it was natural that he should at least close his eyes.

He insisted that it was only for a moment. Something, he could not say what, caused him to open his eyes again immediately. The closing of them seemed to have improved what may be called his dark sight. He saw everything in the church quite distinctly, in a sort of grey light. The pulpit stood out, large and bulky, in front. Beyond that, he passed his eyes along the four windows on the north side of the church. He looked again at the stars, still visible through the nearest window on his left hand as he was sitting. From that, his eyes fell to the further end of the seat in front of him, where he could even see a faint gleam of polished wood. He traced this gleam to the middle of the seat, until it disappeared in black shadow, and upon that his eye passed on to the seat he was in, and there he saw a man sitting beside him.

Caleb described the man very clearly. He was, he said, a pale, old-fashioned looking man, with something very churchy about him. Reasoning also with great clearness, he said that the stranger had not come into the church either with him or after him, and that therefore he must have been there before him. And in that case, seeing that the church had been locked since two in the afternoon, the stranger must have been there for a considerable time.

Caleb was puzzled; turning therefore, to the stranger, he asked "How long have you been here?"

The stranger answered at once "Six hundred years."

"Oh! come!" said Caleb.

"Come where?" said the stranger.

"Well, if you come to that, come out," said Caleb.

"I wish I could," said the stranger, and heaved a great sigh.

"What's to prevent you?" said Caleb. "There's the door, and here's the key."

"That's it," said the other.

"Of course it is," said Caleb. "Come along."

With that he proceeded to take the stranger by the sleeve, and then it was that he says you might have knocked him down with a feather. His hand went right into the place where the sleeve seemed to be, and Caleb distinctly saw two of the stranger's buttons on the top of his own knuckles.

He hastily withdrew his hand, which began to feel icy cold, and sat still, not knowing what to say next. He found that the stranger was gently chuckling with laughter, and this annoyed him.

"What are you laughing at?" he enquired peevishly.

"It's not funny enough for two," answered the other.

"Who are you, anyhow?" said Caleb.

"I am the kirk spook," was the reply.

Now Caleb had not the least notion what a "kirk spook" was. He was not willing to admit his ignorance, but his curiosity was too much for his pride, and he asked for information.

"Every church has a spook," said the stranger, "and I am the spook of this one."

"Oh," said Caleb, "I've been about this church a many years, but I've never seen you before."

"That," said the spook, "is because you've always been moving about. I'm flimsy—very flimsy indeed—and I can only keep myself together when everything is quite still."

"Well," said Caleb, "you've got your chance now. What are you going to do with it?"

"I want to go out," said the spook, "I'm tired of this church, and I've been alone for six hundred years. It's a long time."

"It does seem rather a long time," said Caleb, "but why don't you go if you want to? There's three doors."

"That's just it," said the spook, "They keep me in."

"What?" said Caleb, "when they're open."

"Open or shut," said the spook, "it's all one."

"Well, then," said Caleb, "what about the windows?"

"Every bit as bad," said the spook, "They're all pointed." Caleb felt out of his depth. Open doors and windows that kept a person in—if it was a person—seemed to want a little understanding. And the flimsier the person, too, the easier it ought to be for him to go where he wanted. Also, what could it matter whether they were pointed to not?

The latter question was the one which Caleb asked first.

"Six hundred years ago," said the Spook, "all arches were made round, and when these pointed things came in I cursed them. I hate new-fangled things."

"That wouldn't hurt them much," said Caleb.

"I said I would never go under one of them," said the spook.

"That would matter more to you than to them," said Caleb.

"It does," said the spook, with another great sigh.

"But you could easily change your mind," said Caleb.

"I was tied to it," said the spook, "I was told that I never more should go under one of them, whether I would or not."

"Some people will tell you anything," answered Caleb.

"It was a Bishop," explained the spook.

"Ah!" said Caleb, "that's different, of course."

The spook told Caleb how often he had tried to go under the pointed arches, sometimes of the doors, sometimes of the windows, and how a stream of wind always struck him from the point of the arch, and drifted him back into the church. He had long given up trying.

"You should have been outside," said Caleb, "before they built the last door."

"It was my church," said the spook, "and I was too proud to leave."

Caleb began to sympathize with the spook. He had a pride in the church himself, and disliked even to hear another person say *Amen* before him. He also began to be a little jealous of this stranger who had been six hundred years in possession of the church in which Caleb had believed himself, under the Vicar, to be master. And he began to plot.

"Why do you want to get out?" he asked.

"I'm no use here," was the reply, "I don't get enough to do to keep myself warm. And I know there are scores of churches now without any kirk-spooks at all. I can hear their cheap little bells dinging every Sunday."

"There's very few bells hereabouts," said Caleb.

"There's no hereabouts for spooks," said the other. "We can hear any distance you like."

"But what good are you at all?" said Caleb.

"Good!" said the spook. "Don't we secure proper respect for churches, especially after dark? A church would be like any other place if it wasn't for us. You must know that."

"Well, then," said Caleb, "you're no good here. This church is all right. What will you give me to let you out?"

"Can you do it?" asked the spook.

"What will you give me?" said Caleb.

"I'll say a good word for you amongst the spooks," said the other.

"What good will that do me?" said Caleb.

"A good word never did anybody any harm yet," answered the spook.

"Very well then, come along," said Caleb.

"Gently then," said the spook; "don't make a draught."

"Not yet," said Caleb, and he drew the spook very carefully (as one takes a vessel quite full of water) from the seat.

"I can't go under pointed arches," cried the spook, as Caleb moved off.

"Nobody wants you to," said Caleb. "Keep close to me."

He led the spook down the aisle to the angle of the wall where a small iron shutter covered an opening into the flue. It was used by the chimney sweep alone, but Caleb had another use for it now. Calling to the spook to keep close, he suddenly removed the shutter.

The fires were by this time burning briskly. There was a strong up-draught as the shutter was removed. Caleb felt something rush across his face, and heard a cheerful laugh away up in the chimney. Then he knew that he was alone. He replaced the shutter, gave another look at his stoves, took the keys, and made his way home.

He found his wife asleep in her chair, sat down and took off his boots, and awakened her by throwing them across the kitchen.

"I've been wondering when you'd wake," he said.

"What?" she said, "Have you been in long?"

"Look at the clock," said Caleb. "Half after twelve."

"My gracious," said his wife. "Let's be off to bed."

"Did you tell her about the spook?" he was naturally asked.

"Not I," said Caleb. "You knew what she'd say. Same as she always does of a Saturday night."

This fable Mr. Batchel related with reluctance. His attitude towards it was wholly deprecatory.

Psychic phenomena, he said, lay outside the province of the mere humourist, and the levity with which they had been treated was largely responsible for the presumptuous materialism of the age.

He said more, as he warmed to the subject, than can here be repeated. The reader of the foregoing tales, however, will be interested to know that Mr. Batchel's own attitude was one of humble curiosity. He refused even to guess why the *revenant* was sometimes invisible, and at other times partly or wholly visible; sometimes capable of using physical force, and at other times powerless. He knew that they had their periods, and that was all.

There is room, he said, for the romancer in these matters; but for the humourist, none. Romance was the play of intelligence about the confines of truth. The invisible world, like the visible, must have its romancers, its explorers, and its interpreters; but the time of the last was not yet come.

Criticism, he observed in conclusion, was wholesome and necessary. But of the idle and mischievous remarks which were wont to pose as criticism, he held none in so much contempt as the cheap and irrational *pooh-pooh*.

AN EPIJODE OF CATHEDRAL HIJTORY

M. R. James (1862-1936)

There was once a learned gentleman who was deputed to examine and report upon the archives of the Cathedral of Southminster. The examination of these records demanded a very considerable expenditure of time: hence it became advisable for him to engage lodgings in the city: for though the Cathedral body were profuse in their offers of hospitality, Mr. Lake felt that he would prefer to be master of his day. This was recognized as reasonable. The Dean eventually wrote advising Mr. Lake, if he were not already suited, to communicate with Mr. Worby, the principal Verger, who occupied a house convenient to the church and was prepared to take in a quiet lodger for three or four weeks. Such an arrangement was precisely what Mr. Lake desired. Terms were easily agreed upon, and early in December, like another Mr. Datchery (as he remarked to himself), the investigator found himself in the occupation of a very comfortable room in an ancient and "cathedraly" house.

One so familiar with the customs of Cathedral churches, and treated with such obvious consideration by the Dean and Chapter of this Cathedral in particular, could not fail to command the respect of the Head Verger. Mr. Worby even acquiesced in certain modifications of statements he had been accustomed to offer for years to parties of visitors. Mr. Lake, on his part, found the Verger a very cheery companion, and took advantage of any occasion that presented itself for enjoying his conversation when the day's work was over.

One evening, about nine o'clock, Mr. Worby knocked at his lodger's door. "I've occasion," he said, "to go across to the Cathedral, Mr. Lake, and I think I made you a promise when I did so next I would give you the opportunity to see what it looks like at night time. It's quite fine and dry outside, if you care to come."

"To be sure I will; very much obliged to you, Mr. Worby, for thinking of it, but let me get my coat."

"Here it is, Sir, and I've another lantern here that you'll find advisable for the steps, as there's no moon."

"Anyone might think we were Jasper and Durdles, over again, mightn't they?" said Lake, as they crossed the close, for he had ascertained that the Verger had read *Edwin Drood*.

"Well, so they might," said Mr. Worby, with a short laugh, "though I don t know whether we ought to take it as a compliment. Odd ways, I often think, they had at that Cathedral, don't it seem so to you, sit? Full choral matins at seven o'clock in the morning all the year round. Wouldn't suit our boys' voices nowadays, and I think there's one of two of the men would be applying for a rise if the Chapter was to bring it in—particular the alltoes."

They were now at the south-west door. As Mr. Worby was unlocking it, Lake said, "Did you ever find anybody locked in here by accident?"

"Twice I did. One was a drunk sailor; however he got in I don't know. I s'pose he went to sleep in the service, but by the time I got to him he was praying fit to bring the roof in. Lor'! what a noise that man did make! said it was the first time he'd been inside a church for ten years, and blest if ever he'd try it again. The other was an old sheep: them boys it was, up to their games. That was the last time they tried it on, though. There, sit, now you see what we look like; our late Dean used now and again to bring parties in, but he preferred a moonlight night, and there was a piece of verse he'd coat to 'em, relating to a Scotch cathedral, I understand; but I don't know; I almost think the effect's better when it's all dark-like. Seems to add to the size and heighth. Now if you won't mind stopping somewhere in the nave while I go up into the choir where my business lays, you'll see what I mean."

Accordingly Lake waited, leaning against a pillar, and watched the light wavering along the length of the church, and up the steps into the choir, until it was intercepted by some screen or other furniture, which only allowed the reflection to be seen on the piers and roof. Not many minutes had passed before Worby reappeared at the door of the choir and by waving his lantern signalled to Lake to rejoin him.

"I suppose it *is* Worby, and not a substitute," thought Lake to himself, as he walked up the nave. There was, in fact, nothing untoward. Worby showed him the papers which he had come to fetch out of the Dean's stall, and asked him what he thought of the spectacle: Lake agreed that it was well worth seeing. "I suppose," he said, as they walked towards the altar-steps together, "that you're too much used to going about here at night to feel nervous—but you must get a start every now and then, don't you, when a book falls down or a door swings to?"

"No, Mr. Lake, I can't say I think much about noises, not nowadays: I'm much more afraid of finding an escape of gas or a burst in the stove pipes than anything else. Still there have been times, years ago. Did you notice that plain altar-tomb there—fifteenth century we say it is, I don't know if you agree to that? Well, if you didn't look at it, just come back and give it a glance, if you'd be so good." It was on the north side of the choir, and rather awkwardly placed: only about three feet from the enclosing stone screen. Quite plain, as the Verger had said, but for some ordinary stone panelling. A metal cross of some size on the northern side (that next to the screen) was the solitary feature of any interest.

Lake agreed that it was not earlier than the Perpendicular period: "but," he said, "unless it's the tomb of some remarkable person, you'll forgive me for saying that. I don't think it's particularly noteworthy."

"Well, I can't say as it is the tomb of anybody noted in 'istory," said Worby, who had a dry smile on his face, "for we don't own any record whatsoever of who it was put up to. For all that, if you've half in hour to spare, Sir, when we get back to the house, Mr. Lake, I could tell you a tale about that tomb. I won't begin on it now; it strikes cold here, and we don't want to be dawdling about all night."

"Of course I should like to hear it immensely."

"Very well, Sir, you shall. Now if I might put a question to you," he went on, as they passed down the choir aisle, "in our little local guide— and not only there, but in the little book on our Cathedral in the series— you'll find it stated that this portion of the building was erected previous to the twelfth century. Now of course I should be glad enough to take that view, but—mind the step, sir—but, I put it to you—does the lay of the stone 'ere in this portion of the wall (which he tapped with his key), does it to your eye carry the flavour of what you might call Saxon masonry? No, I thought not; no more it does to me: now, if you'll believe me, I've said as much to those men—one's the librarian of our Free Libry here, and the other came down from London on purpose—fifty times, if I have once, but I might just as well have talked to that bit of stonework. But there it is, I suppose every one's got their opinions."

The discussion of this peculiar trait of human nature occupied Mr. Worby almost up to the moment when he and Lake re-entered the former's house. The condition of the fire in Lake's sitting-room led to a suggestion from Mr. Worby that they should finish the evening in his own parlour. We find them accordingly settled there some short time afterwards.

Mr. Worby made his story a long one, and I will not undertake to tell it wholly in his own words, or in his own order. Lake committed the substance of it to paper immediately after hearing it, together with some few passages of the narrative which had fixed themselves *verbatim* in his mind; I shall probably find it expedient to condense Lake's record to some extent.

Mr. Worby was born, it appeared, about the year 1929. His father before him had been connected with the Cathedral, and likewise his grandfather. One or both had been choristers, and in later life both had done work as mason and carpenter respectively about the fabric. Worby himself, though possessed, as he frankly acknowledged, of an indifferent voice, had been drafted into the choir at about ten years of age.

It was in 1840 that the wave of the Gothic revival smote the Cathedral of Southtminster. "There was a lot of lovely stuff went then, Sir," said Worby, with a sigh. "My father couldn't hardly believe it when he got his orders to clear out the choir. There was a new dean just come in— Dean Burscough it was—and my father had been 'prenticed to a good firm of joiners in the city, and knew what good work was when he saw it. Crool it was, he used to say: all that beautiful wainscot oak, as good as the day it was put up, and garlands-like of foliage and fruit, and lovely old gilding work on the coats of arms and the organ pipes. All went to the timber yard—every bit except some little pieces worked up in the Lady Chapel, and 'ere in this overmantel. Well ... I may be mistook, but I say our choir never looked as well since. Still there was a lot found out about the history of the church, and no doubt but what it did stand in need of repair. There was very few winters passed but what we'd lose a pinnicle." Mr. Lake expressed his concurrence with Worby's views of restoration, but owns to a fear about this point lest the story proper should never be reached. Possibly this was perceptible in his manner.

Worby hastened to reassure him, "Not but what I could carry on about that topic for hours at a time, and do do when I see my opportunity. But Dean Burscough he was very set on the Gothic period, and nothing would serve him but everything must be made agreeable to that. And one morning after service he appointed for my father to meet him in the choir, and he came back after he'd taken off his robes in the vestry, and he'd got a roll of paper with him, and the verger that was then brought in a table, and they begun spreading it out on the table with prayer books to keep it down, and my father helped em, and he saw it was a picture of the inside of a choir in a Cathedral; and the Dean—he was a quick-spoken gentleman—he says, 'Well, Worby, what do you think of that?' 'Why,' says my father, 'I don't think I 'ave the pleasure of knowing that view. Would that be Hereford Cathedral, Mr. Dean?' 'No, Worby,' says the Dean, 'that's Southminster Cathedral as we hope to see it before many years.' 'In-deed, Sir,' says my father' and that was all he did say—leastways to the Dean— but he used to tell me he felt really faint in himself when he looked round our choir as I can remember it, comfortable, and furnished-like, and then see this nasty little dry picter, as he called it, drawn out by some London architect. Well there I am again. But you'll see what I mean if you look at this old view."

Worby reached down a framed print from the wall. "Well, the long and the short of it was that the Dean he handed over to my father a copy of an order of the Chapter that he was to clear out every bit of the choir—make a clean sweep—ready for the new work that was being designed up in town, and he was to put it in hand as soon as ever he could get the breakers together. Now then, Sir, if you look at that view, You'll see where the pulpit used to stand—that's what I want you to notice, if you please." It was, indeed, easily seen; an unusually large structure of timber with a domed sounding-board, standing at the east end of the stalls on the north side of the choir, facing the bishop's throne. Worby proceeded to explain that during the alterations, services were held in the nave, the member of the choir being thereby disappointed of an anticipated holiday, and the organist in particular incurring the suspicion of having wilfully damaged the mechanism of the temporary organ that was hired at considerable expense from London.

The work of demolition began with the choir screen and organ loft, and proceeded gradually east-wards, disclosing, as Worby said, many interesting features of older work. While this was going on, the members of the Chapter were, naturally, in and about the choir a great deal, and it soon became apparent to the elder Worby—who could not help overhearing some of their talk—that, on the part of the senior Canons especially, there must have been a good deal of disagreement before the policy now being carried out had been adopted. Some were of opinion that they should catch their deaths of cold in the return-stalls, unprotected by a screen from the draughts in the nave: others objected to being exposed to the view of persons in the choir aisles, especially, they said, during the sermons, when they found it helpful to listen in a posture which was liable to misconstruction. The strongest opposition, however, came from the oldest of the body, who up to the last moment objected to the removal of the pulpit. "You ought not to touch it, Mr. Dean," he said with great emphasis one morning, when the two were standing before it: "you don't know what mischief you may do." "Mischief? it's not a work of any particular merit, Canon." "Don't call me Canon," said the old man with great asperity, that is, for thirty years I've been known as Dr. Ayloff, and I shall be obliged, Mr. Dean, if you would kindly humour me in that matter. And as to the pulpit (which I've preached from for thirty years, though I don't insist on that), all I'll say is, I *know* you're doing wrong in moving it." "But what sense could there be, my dear Doctor, in leaving it where it is, when we're fitting up the rest of the choir in a totally different *style*? What reason could be given—apart from the look of the thing?" "Reason! Reason!" said old Dr. Ayloff; "if you young men— if I may say so without any disrespect, Mr. Dean—if you'd only listen to reason a little, and not be always asking for it, we should get on better. But there, I've said my say." The old gentleman hobbled off, and as it proved, never entered the Cathedral again. The season—it was a hot summer—turned sickly on a sudden, Dr. Ayloff was one of the first to go, with some affection of the muscles of the thorax, which took him painfully at night. And at many services the number of choir-men and boys was very thin.

Meanwhile the pulpit had been done away with. In fact, the sounding-board (part of which still exists as a table in a summer-house in the palace garden) was taken down within an hour or two of Dr. Ayloff's protest. The removal of the base—not effected without considerable trouble—disclosed to view, greatly to the exultation of the restoring party, an altar-tomb—the tomb, of course, to which Worby had attracted Lake's attention that same evening. Much fruitless research was expended in attempts to identify the occupant; from that day to this he has never had a name put to him. The structure had been most carefully boxed in under the pulpit-base, so that such slight ornament as it possessed was not defaced; only on the north side of it there was what looked like an injury; a gap between two of the slabs composing the side. It might be two or three inches across. Palmer, the mason, was directed to fill it up in a week's time, when he came to do some other small jobs near that part of the choir.

The season was undoubtedly a very trying one. Whether the church was built on a site that had once been a marsh, as was suggested, or for whatever reason, the residents in its immediate neighbourhood had, many of them, but little enjoyment of the exquisite sunny days and the calm nights of August and September. To several of the older people— Dr. Ayloff, among others, as we have seen—the summer proved down-right fatal, but even among the younger, few escaped either a sojourn in bed for a matter of weeks, or at the least, a brooding sense of oppression, accompanied by hateful nightmares. Gradually there formulated itself a suspicion—which grew into a conviction—that the alterations in the Cathedral had something to say in the matter. The widow of a former old verger, a pensioner of the Chapter of Southminster, was visited by dreams, which she retailed to her friends, of a shape that slipped out of the little door of the south transept as the dark fell in, and flitted—taking a fresh direction every night—about the Close, disappearing for a while in house after house, and finally emerging again when the night sky was paling. She could see nothing of it, she said, but that it was a moving form: only she had an impression that when it returned to the church, as it seemed to do in the end of the dream, it turned its head: and then, she could not tell why, but she thought it had red eyes. Worby remembered hearing the old lady tell this dream at a tea-party in the house of the chapter clerk. Its recurrence might, perhaps, he said, be taken as a symptom of approaching illness; at any rate before the end of September the old lady was in her grave.

The interest excited by the restoration of this great church was not confined to its own county. One day that summer an F.S.A., of some celebrity, visited the place. His business was to write an account of the discoveries that had been made, for the Society of Antiquaries, and his wife, who accompanied him, was to make a series of illustrative draw-ings for his report. In the morning she employed herself in making a general sketch of the choir; in the afternoon she devoted herself to details. She first drew the newly-exposed altar-tomb, and when that was finished, she called her husband's attention to a beautiful piece of diaper-ornament on the screen just behind it, which had, like the tomb itself, been completely concealed by the pulpit. Of course, he said, an illustration of that must be made; so she seated herself on the tomb and began a careful drawing which occupied her till dusk.

Her husband had by this time finished his work of measuring and description, and they agreed that it was time to be getting back to their hotel. "You may as well brush my skirt, Frank," said the, lady, "it must have got covered with dust, I'm sure." He obeyed dutifully; but, after a moment, he said, "I don't know whether you value this dress particu-larly, my dear, but I'm inclined to think it's seen its best days. There's a great bit of it gone." "Gone? Where? "said she. "I don't know where it's gone, but it's off at the bottom edge behind here." She pulled it hastily into sight, and was horrified to find a jagged tear extending some way into the substance of the stuff; very much, she said, as if a dog had rent it away. The dress was, in any case, hopelessly spoilt, to her great vexation, and though they looked everywhere, the missing piece could not be found. There were in which injury might have come about, for the choir was full of old bits of woodwork with nails sticking out of them. Finally, they could only the any ways, they concluded, in suppose that one of these had caused the mischief, and that the workmen, who had been about all day, had carried off the particular piece with the fragment of dress still attached to it.

It was about this time, Worby thought, that his little dog began to wear in anxious expression when the hour for it to be put into the shed in the back yard approached. (For his mother had ordained that it must not sleep in the house.) One evening, he said, when he was just going to pick it up and carry it out, it looked at him "like a Christian, and waved its 'and, I was going to say—well, you know 'ow they do carry on sometimes, and the end of it was I put it under my coat, and 'uddled it upstairs—and I'm afraid I as good as deceived my poor mother on the subject. After that the dog acted very artful with 'iding itself under the bed for half an hour or more before bed-time came, and we worked it so as my mother never found out what we'd done." Of course Worby was glad of its company anyhow, but more particularly when the nuisance that is still remembered in Southminster as "the crying" set in.

"Night after night," said Worby, "that dog seemed to know it was coming; he'd creep out, he would, and snuggle into the bed and cuddle right up to me shivering, and when the crying come he'd be like a wild thing, shoving his head under my arm, and I was fully near as bad. Six or seven times we'd hear it, not more, and when he'd dror out his 'ed again I'd know it was over for that night. What was it like, sir? Well, I never heard but one thing that seemed to hit it off. I happened to be playing about in the Close, and there was two of the Canons met and said 'Good morning' one to another. 'Sleep well last night?' says one—it was Mr. Henslow that one, and Mr. Lyall was the other. 'Can't say I did,' says Mr. Lyall, 'rather too much of Isaiah xxxiv. 14 for me.' 'xxxiv. 14,' says Mr. Henslow, 'what's that?' 'You call yourself a Bible reader!' says Mr. Lyall. (Mr. Henslow, you must know, he was one of what used to be termed Simeon's lot—pretty much what we should call the Evangelical party.) 'You go and look it up.' I wanted to know what he was getting at myself, and so off I ran home and got out my own Bible, and there it was: 'the satyr shall cry to his fellow.' Well, I thought, is that what we've been listening to these past nights? and I tell you it made me look over my shoulder a time or two. Of course I'd asked my father and mother about what it could be before that, but they both said it was most likely cats: but they spoke very short, and I could see they was troubled. My word I that was a noise—'ungry-like, as if it was calling after someone that wouldn't come. If ever you felt you wanted company, it would be when you was waiting for it to begin again. I believe two or three nights there was men put on to watch in different parts of the Close; but they all used to get together in one comer, the nearest they could to the High Street, and nothing came of it.

"Well, the next thing was this. Me and another of the boys—he's in business in the city now as a grocer, like his father before him—we'd gone up in the choir after morning service was over, and we heard old Palmer the mason bellowing to some of his men. So we went up nearer, because we knew he was a rusty old chap and there might be some fun going. It appears Palmer 'd told this man to stop up the chink in that old tomb. Well, there was this man keeping on saying he'd done it the best he could, and there was Palmer carrying on like all possessed about it. 'Call that making a job of it?' he says. 'If you had your rights you'd get the sack for

this. What do you suppose I pay you your wages for? What do you suppose I'm going to say to the Dean and Chapter when they come round, as
come they may do any time, and see where you've been bungling about
covering the 'ole place with mess and plaster and Lord knows what?' 'Well,
master, I done the best I could,' says the man; 'I don't know no more
than what you do 'ow it come to fall out this, way. I tamped it right in the
'ole,' he says, 'and now it's fell out,' he says, 'I never see.'

"'Fell out?' says old Palmer, 'why it's nowhere near the place. Blowed
out, you mean'; and he picked up a bit of plaster, and so did I, that was
laying up against the screen, three or four feet off, and not dry yet; and
old Palmer he looked at it curious-like, and then he turned round on me
and he says, 'Now then, you boys, have you been up to some of your games
here?' 'No,' I says, 'I haven't, Mr. Palmer; there's none of us been about
here till just this minute'; and while I was talking the other boy, Evans,
he got looking in through the chink, and I heard him draw in his breath,
and he came away sharp and up to us, and says he, 'I believe there's something in there. I saw something shiny.' 'What! I dare say!' says old Palmer;
'well, I ain't got time to stop about there. You, William, you go off and get
some more stuff and make a job of it this time; if not, there'll be trouble
in my yard,' he says.

"So the man he went off, and Palmer too, and us boys stopped behind, and I says to Evans, 'Did you really see, anything in there?' 'Yes,' he
says, 'I did indeed.' So then I says, 'Let's shove something in and stir it
up.' And we tried several of the bits of wood that was laying about, but
they were all too big. Then Evans he had a sheet of music he'd brought
with him, an anthem or a service, I forget which it was now, and he rolled
it up small and shoved it in the chink; two or three times he did it, and
nothing happened. 'Give it me, boy,' I said, and I had a try. No, nothing
happened. Then, I don't know why I thought of it, I'm sure, but I stooped
down just opposite the chink and put my two fingers in my mouth and
whistled—you know the way—and at that I seemed to think I heard something stirring, and I says to Evans, 'Come away,' I says; 'I don't like this.'
'Oh, rot,' he says, 'give me that roll,' and he took it and shoved it in. And
I don't think ever I see anyone go so pale as he did. 'I say, Worby,' he
says, 'it's caught, or else someone's got hold of it.' 'Pull it out or leave it,'
I says. 'Come and let's get off.' So he gave a good pull, and it came away.
Leastways most of it did, but the end was gone. Torn off it was, and Evans
looked at it for a second and then he gave a sort of a croak and let it drop,
and we both made off out of there as quick as ever we could. When we got
outside Evans says to me, 'Did you see the end of that paper?' 'No,' I says,
'only it was torn.' 'Yes, it was,' he says, 'but it was wet too, and black!'
Well, partly because of the fright we had, and partly because that music
was wanted in a day or two, and we knew there'd be a set-out about it

with the organist, we didn't say nothing to anyone else, and I suppose the workmen they swept up the bit that was left along with the rest of the rubbish. But Evans, if you were to ask him this very day about it, he'd stick to it he saw that paper wet and black at the end where it was torn."

After that the boys gave the choir a wide berth, so that Worby was not sure what was the result of the mason's renewed mending of the tomb. Only he made out from fragments of conversation dropped by the workmen passing through the choir that some difficulty had been—met with, and that the governor—Mr. Palmer to wit—had tried his own hand at the job. A little later, he happened to see Mr. Palmer himself knocking at the door of the Deanery and being admitted by the butler. A day or so after that, he gathered from a remark his father let fall at breakfast that something a little out of the common was to be done in the Cathedral after morning service on the morrow. "And I'd just as soon it was to-day," his father added; "I don't see the use of running risks."

"'Father,' I says, 'what are you going to do in the Cathedral to-morrow?' And he turned on me as savage as I ever see him—he was a wonderful good-tempered man as a general thing, my poor father was. 'My lad,' he says, 'I'll trouble you not to go picking up your elders' and betters' talk: it's not manners and it's not straight. What I'm going to do or not going to do in the Cathedral to-morrow is none of your business: and if I catch sight of you hanging about the place to-morrow after your work's done, I'll send you home with a flea in your ear. Now you mind that.' Of course I said I was very sorry and that, and equally of course I went off and laid my plans with Evans. We knew there was a stair up in the corner of the transept which you can get up to the triforium, and in them days the door to it was pretty well always open, and even if it wasn't we knew the key usually laid under a bit of matting hard by. So we made up our minds we'd be putting away music and that, next morning while the rest of the boys was clearing off, and then slip up the stairs and watch from the triforium if there was any signs of work going on.

"Well, that same night I dropped off asleep as sound as a boy does, and all of a sudden the dog woke me up, coming into the bed, and thought I, now we're going to get it sharp, for he seemed more frightened than usual. After about five minutes sure enough came this cry. I can't give you no idea what it was like; and so near too—nearer than I'd heard it yet—and a funny thing, Mr. Lake, you know what a place this Close is for in echo, and particular if you stand this side of it. Well, this crying never made no sign of an echo at all. But, as I said, it was dreadful near this night; and on the top of the start I got with hearing it, I got another fright; for I heard something rustling outside in the passage. Now to be sure I thought I was done; but I noticed the dog seemed to perk up a bit, and next there was someone whispered outside the door, and I very near laughed out loud, for I knew it was my father and mother that had got out of bed with the noise. 'Whatever is it?' says my mother. 'Hush! I don't know,' says my father, excited-like, 'don't disturb the boy. I hope he didn't hear nothing.'

"So, me knowing they were just outside, it made me bolder, and I slipped out of bed across to my little window—giving on the Close—but the dog he bored right down to the bottom of the bed—and I looked out. First go off I couldn't see anything. Then right down in the shadow under a buttress I made out what I shall always say was two spots of red—a dull red it was—nothing like a lamp or a fire, but just so as you could pick 'em out of the black shadow. I hadn't but just sighted 'em when it seemed we wasn't the only people that had been disturbed, because I see a window in a house on the left-hand side become lighted up, and the light moving. I just turned my head to make sure of it, and then looked back into the shadow for those two red things, and they were gone, and for all I peered about and stared, there was not a sign more of them. Then come my last fright that night—something come against my bare leg—but that was all right: that was my little dog had come out of bed, and prancing about making a great to-do, only holding his tongue, and me seeing he was quite in spirits again, I took him back to bed and we slept the night out!

"Next morning I made out to tell my mother I'd had the dog in my room, and I was surprised, after all she'd said about it before, how quiet she took it. 'Did you?' she says. 'Well, by good rights you ought to go without your breakfast for doing such a thing behind my back: but I don't know as there's any great harm done, only another time you ask my permission, do you hear?' A bit after that I said something to my father about having heard the cats again. 'Cats?' he says; and he looked over at my poor mother, and she coughed and he says, 'Oh! ah! yes, cats. I believe I heard 'em myself.'

"That was a funny morning altogether: nothing seemed to go right. The organist he stopped in bed, and the minor Canon he forgot it was the 19th day and waited for the *Venite*; and after a bit the deputy he set off playing the chant for evensong, which was a minor; and then the Decani boys were laughing so much they couldn't sing, and when it came to the anthem the solo boy he got took with the giggles, and made out his nose was bleeding, and shoved the book at me what hadn't practised the verse and wasn't much of a singer if I had known it. Well, things was rougher, you see, fifty years ago, and I got a nip from the counter-tenor behind me that I remembered.

"So we got through somehow, and neither the men nor the boys weren't by way of waiting to see whether the Canon in residence—Mr. Henslow it was—would come to the vestries and fine 'em, but I don't believe he did: for one thing I fancy he'd read the wrong lesson for the first time in his life, and knew it. Anyhow, Evans and me didn't find no difficulty in slipping up the stairs as I told you, and when we got up we laid ourselves down flat on our stomachs where we could just stretch our heads out over the old tomb, and we hadn't but just done so when we heard the verger that was then, first shutting the iron porch-gates and locking the south-west door, and then the transept door, so we knew there was something up, and they meant to keep the public out for a bit.

"Next thing was, the Dean and the Canon come in by their door on the north, and then I see my father, and old Palmer, and a couple of their best men, and Palmer stood a talking for a bit with the Dean in the middle of the choir. He had a coil of rope and the men had crows. All of 'em looked a bit nervous. So there they stood talking, and at last I heard the Dean say, 'Well, I've no time to waste, Palmer. If you think this'll satisfy Southminster people, I'll permit it to be done; but I must say this, that never in the whole course of my life have I heard such arrant nonsense from a practical man as I have from you. Don't you agree with me, Henslow?' As far as I could hear Mr. Henslow said something like 'Oh well! we're told, aren't we, Mr. Dean, not to judge others?' And the Dean he gave a kind of sniff, and walked straight up to the tomb, and took his stand behind it with his back to the screen, and the others they come edging up rather gingerly. Henslow, he stopped on the south side and scratched on his chin, he did. Then the Dean spoke up: 'Palmer,' he says, 'which can you do easiest, get the slab off the top, or shift one of the side slabs?'

"Old Palmer and his men they pottered about a bit looking round the edge of the top slab and sounding the sides on the south and east and west and everywhere but the north. Henslow said something about it being better to have a try at the south side, because there was more light and more room to move about in. Then my father who'd been watching of them, went round to the north side, and knelt down and felt of the slab by the chink, and he got up and dusted his knees and says to the Dean: 'Beg pardon, Mr. Dean, but I think if Mr. Palmer'll try this here slab he'll find it'll come out easy enough. Seems to me one of the men could prise it out with his crow by means of this chink.' 'Ah! thank you, Worby,' says the Dean; 'that's a good suggestion. Palmer, let one of your men do that, will you?'

"So the man come round, and put his bar in and bore on it, and just that minute when they were all bending over, and we boys got our heads well over the edge of the triforium, there come a most fearful crash down at the west end of the choir, as if a whole stick of big timber had fallen down a flight of stairs. Well, you can't expect me to tell you everything that happened all in a minute. Of course there was a terrible commotion. I heard the slab fall out, and the crowbar on the floor, and I heard the Dean say, 'Good God!'

"When I looked down again I saw the Dean tumbled over on the floor, the men was making off down the choir, Henslow was just going to help the Dean up, Palmer was going to stop the men (as he said afterwards) and my father was sitting on the altar step with his face in his hands. The Dean he was very cross. 'I wish to goodness you'd look where you're coming to, Henslow,' he says. 'Why you should all take to your heels when a stick of wood tumbles down I cannot imagine'; and all Henslow could do, explaining he was right away on the other side of the tomb, would not satisfy him.

"Then Palmer came back and reported there was nothing to account for this noise and nothing seemingly fallen down, and when the Dean finished feeling of himself they gathered round—except my father, he sat where he was—and someone lighted up a bit of candle and they looked into the tomb. 'Nothing there,' says the Dean, 'what did I tell you? Stay! here's something. What's this? a bit of music paper, and a piece of torn stuff—part of a dress it looks like. Both quite modern—no interest whatever. Another time perhaps you'll take the advice of an educated man'— or something like that, and off he went, limping a bit, and out through the north door, only as he went he called back angry to Palmer for leaving the door standing open. Palmer called out 'Very sorry, Sir,' but he shrugged his shoulders, and Henslow says, 'I fancy Mr. Dean's mistaken. I closed the door behind me, but he's a little upset.' Then Palmer says, 'Why, where's Worby?' and they saw him sitting on the step and went up to him. He was recovering himself, it seemed, and wiping his forehead, and Palmer helped him up on to his legs, as I was glad to see.

"They were too far off for me to hear what they said, but my father pointed to the north door in the aisle, and Palmer and Henslow both of them looked very surprised and scared. After a bit, my father and Henslow went out of the church, and the others made what haste they could to put the slab back and plaster it in. And about as the clock struck twelve the Cathedral was opened again and us boys made the best of our way home.

"I was in a great taking to know what it was had given my poor father such a turn, and when I got in and found him sitting in his chair taking a glass of spirits, and my mother standing looking anxious at him, I couldn't keep from bursting out and making confession where I'd been. But he didn't seem to take on, not in the way of losing his temper. 'You was there, was you? Well, did you see it?' 'I see everything, father,' I said, 'except when the noise came.' 'Did you see what it was knocked the Dean over?' he says, 'that what come out of the monument? You didn't? Well, that's a mercy.' 'Why, what was it, father?' I said. 'Come, you must have seen it,' he says. '*Didn't* you see? A thing like a man, all over hair, and two great eyes to it?'

"Well, that was all I could get out of him that time, and later on he seemed as if he was ashamed of being so frightened, and he used to put me off when I asked him about it. But years after, when I was got to be a grown man, we had more talk now and again on the matter, and he always said the same thing. 'Black it was,' he'd say, 'and a mass of hair, and two legs, and the light caught on its eyes.'

"Well, that's the tale of that tomb, Mr. Lake; it's one we don't tell to our visitors, and I should be obliged to you not to make any use of it till I'm out of the way. I doubt Mr. Evans'll feel the same as I do, if you ask him."

This proved to be the case. But over twenty years have passed by, and the grass is growing over both Worby and Evans; so Mr. Lake felt no difficulty about communicating his notes—taken in 1890—to me. He accompanied them with a sketch of the tomb and a copy of the short inscription on the metal cross which was affixed at the expense of Dr. Lyall to the centre of the northern side. It was from the Vulgate of Isaiah xxxiv., and consisted merely of the three words—

IBI CUBAVIT LAMIA.

CANON ALBERIC'S SCRAP-BOOK

M. R. James

St Bertrand de Comminges is a decayed town on the spurs of the
Pyrenees, not very far from Toulouse, and still nearer to Bagnères-de-
Luchon. It was the site of a bishopric until the Revolution, and has a
cathedral which is visited by a certain number of tourists. In the spring
of 1883 an Englishman arrived at this old-world place—I can hardly dignify
it with the name of city, for there are not a thousand inhabitants. He was
a Cambridge man, who had come specially from Toulouse to see St
Bertrand's Church, and had left two friends, who were less keen archae-
ologists than himself, in their hotel at Toulouse, under promise to join
him on the following morning. Half an hour at the church would satisfy
them, and all three could then pursue their journey in the direction of
Auch. But our Englishman had come early on the day in question, and
proposed to himself to fill a notebook and to use several dozens of plates
in the process of describing and photographing every corner of the wonderful church that dominates the little hill of Comminges. In order to
carry out this design satisfactorily, it was necessary to monopolize the
verger of the church for the day. The verger or sacristan (I prefer the
latter appellation, inaccurate as it may be) was accordingly sent for by
the somewhat brusque lady who keeps the inn of the *Chapeau Rouge*;
and when he came, the Englishman found him an unexpectedly interesting object of study. It was not in the personal appearance of the little,
dry, wizened old man that the interest lay, for he was precisely like
dozens of other church-guardians in France, but in a curious furtive, or
rather hunted and oppressed, air which he had. He was perpetually half
glancing behind him; the muscles of his back and shoulders seemed
to be hunched in a continual nervous contraction, as if he were expecting
every moment to find himself in the clutch of an enemy. The Englishman hardly knew whether to put him down as a man haunted by a fixed

263

delusion, or as one oppressed by a guilty conscience, or as an unbearably henpecked husband. The probabilities, when reckoned up, certainly pointed to the last idea; but, still, the impression conveyed was that of a more formidable persecutor even than a termagant wife.

However, the Englishman (let us call him Dennistoun) was soon too deep in his notebook and too busy with his camera to give more than an occasional glance to the sacristan. Whenever he did look at him, he found him at no great distance, either huddling himself back against the wall or crouching in one of the gorgeous stalls. Dennistoun became rather fidgety after a time. Mingled suspicions that he was keeping the old man from his *déjeuner*—that he was regarded as likely to make away with St Bertrand's ivory crozier, or with the dusty stuffed crocodile that hangs over the font—began to torment him. "Won't you go home?" he said at last; "I'm quite well able to finish my notes alone; you can lock me in if you like. I shall want at least two hours more here, and it must be cold for you, isn't it?"

"Good Heavens!" said the little man, whom the suggestion seemed to throw into a state of unaccountable terror, "such a thing cannot be thought of for a moment. Leave monsieur alone in the church? No, no; two hours, three hours, all will be the same to me. I have breakfasted, I am not at all cold, with many thanks to monsieur."

"Very well, my little man," quoth Dennistoun to himself: "you have been warned, and you must take the consequences."

Before the expiration of the two hours, the stalls, the enormous dilapidated organ, the choir-screen of Bishop John de Mauléon, the remnants of glass and tapestry, and the objects in the treasure-chamber, had been well and truly examined; the sacristan still keeping at Dennistoun's heels, and every now and then whipping round as if he had been stung, when one or other of the strange noises that trouble a large empty building fell on his ear. Curious noises they were sometimes. "Once," Dennistoun said to me, I could have sworn I heard a thin metallic voice laughing high up in the tower. I darted an inquiring glance at my sacristan. He was white to the lips. "It is he—that is—it is no one; the door is locked," was all he said, and we looked at each other for a full minute."

Another little incident puzzled Dennistoun a good deal. He was examining a large dark picture that hangs behind the altar, one of a series illustrating the miracles of St Bertrand. The composition of the picture is well-nigh indecipherable, but there is a Latin legend below, which runs thus: *Qualiter S. Bertrandus liberavit hominem quem diabolus diu volebat strangulare.**

Dennistoun was turning to the sacristan with a smile and a jocular remark of some sort on his lips, but he was confounded to see the old man on his knees, gazing at the picture with the eye of a suppliant in agony, his hands tightly clasped, and a rain of tears on his cheeks. Dennistoun naturally pretended to have noticed nothing, but the question would not away from him, "Why should a daub of this kind affect anyone so strongly?" He seemed to himself to be getting some sort of clue to the reason of the strange look that had been puzzling him all the day: the man must be a monomaniac; but what was his monomania?

It was nearly five o'clock; the short day was drawing in, and the church began to fill with shadows, while the curious noises—the muffled footfalls and distant talking voices that had been perceptible all day—seemed, no doubt because of the fading light and the consequently quickened sense of hearing, to become more frequent and insistent. The sacristan began for the first time to show signs of hurry and impatience. He heaved a sigh of relief when camera and notebook were finally packed up and stowed away, and hurriedly beckoned Dennistoun to the western door of the church, under the tower. It was time to ring the *Angelus*. A few pulls at the reluctant rope, and the great bell Bertrande, high in the tower, began to speak, and swung her voice up among the pines and down to the valleys, loud with mountain-streams, calling the dwellers on those lonely hills to remember and repeat the salutation of the angel to her whom he called Blessed among women. With that a profound quiet seemed to fall for the first time that day upon the little town, and Dennistoun and the sacristan went out of the church. On the doorstep they fell into conversation. "Monsieur seemed to interest himself in the old choir-books in the sacristy."

"Undoubtedly. I was going to ask you if there were a library in the town."

"No, monsieur; perhaps there used to be one belonging to the Chapter, but it is now such a small place—" Here came a strange pause of irresolution, as it seemed; then, with a sort of plunge, he went on: "But if monsieur is *amateur des vieux livres*, I have at home something that might interest him. It is not a hundred yards." At once all Dennistoun's cherished dreams of finding priceless manuscripts in untrodden corners of France flashed up, to die down again the next moment. It was probably a stupid missal of Plantin's printing, about 1580. Where was the likelihood that a place so near Toulouse would not have been ransacked long ago by collectors? However, it would be foolish not to go; he would reproach himself for ever after if he refused. So they set off.

On the way the curious irresolution and sudden determination of the sacristan recurred to Dennistoun, and he wondered in a shamefaced way whether he was being decoyed into some purlieu to be made away with as a supposed rich Englishman. He contrived, therefore, to begin talking with his guide, and to drag in, in a rather clumsy fashion, the fact that he expected two friends to join him early the next morning. To his surprise, the announcement seemed to relieve the sacristan at once of some of the anxiety that oppressed him. "That is well," he said quite brightly—"that is very well. Monsieur will travel in company with his friends; they will be always near him. It is a good thing to travel thus in company—sometimes." The last word appeared to be added as an afterthought, and to bring with it a relapse into gloom for the poor little man.

They were soon at the house, which was one rather larger than its neighbours, stone-built, with a shield carved over the door, the shield of Alberic de Mauléon, a collateral descendant, Dennistoun tells me, of Bishop John de Mauléon. This Alberic was a Canon of Comminges from 1680 to 1701. The upper windows of the mansion were boarded up, and the whole place bore, as does the rest of Comminges, the aspect of decaying age. Arrived on his doorstep, the sacristan paused a moment.

"Perhaps," he said, "perhaps, after all, monsieur has not the time?"

"Not at all—lots of time—nothing to do till tomorrow. Let us see what it is you have got."

The door was opened at this point, and a face looked out, a face far younger than the sacristan's, but bearing something of the same distressing look: only here it seemed to be the mark, not so much of fear for personal safety as of acute anxiety on behalf of another. Plainly, the owner of the face was the sacristan's daughter; and, but for the expression I have described, she was a handsome girl enough. She brightened up considerably seeing her father accompanied by an able-bodied stranger. A few remarks passed between father and daughter, of which Dennistoun only caught these words, said by the sacristan, "He was laughing in the church," words which were answered only by a look of terror from the girl.

But in another minute they were in the sitting-room of the house, a small, high chamber with a stone floor, full of moving shadows cast by a wood-fire that flickered on a great hearth. Something of the character of an oratory was imparted to it by a tall crucifix, which reached almost to the ceiling on one side; the figure was painted of the natural colours, the cross was black. Under this stood a chest of some age and solidity, and when a lamp had been brought, and chairs set, the sacristan went to this chest, and produced therefrom, with growing excitement and nervousness, as Dennistoun thought, a large book, wrapped in a white cloth, on which cloth a cross was rudely embroidered in red thread. Even before the wrapping had been removed, Dennistoun began to be interested by the size and shape of the volume. "Too large for a missal," he thought, "and not the shape of an antiphoner; perhaps it may be something good, after all." The next moment the book was open, and Dennistoun felt that he had at last lit upon something better than good. Before him lay a large folio, bound, perhaps, late in the seventeenth century, with the arms of Canon Alberic de Mauléon stamped in gold on the sides. There may have been a hundred and fifty leaves of paper in the book, and on almost every one of them was fastened a leaf from an illuminated manuscript. Such a collection Dennistoun had hardly dreamed of in his wildest moments. Here were ten leaves from a copy of Genesis, illustrated with pictures, which could not be later than a d 700. Further on was a complete set of pictures from a Psalter, of English execution, of the very finest kind that the thirteenth century could produce; and, perhaps best of all, there were twenty leaves of uncial writing in Latin, which, as a few words seen here and there told him at once, must belong to some very early unknown patristic treatise. Could it possibly be a fragment of the copy of Papias *On the Words of Our Lord*, which was known to have existed as late as the twelfth century at Nîmes?[1] In any case, his mind was made up; that book must return to Cambridge with him, even if he had to draw the whole of his balance from the bank and stay at St Bertrand till the money came. He glanced up at the sacristan to see if his face yielded any hint that the book was for sale. The sacristan was pale, and his lips were working.

"If monsieur will turn on to the end," he said.

So monsieur turned on, meeting new treasures at every rise of a leaf; and at the end of the book he came upon two sheets of paper, of much more recent date than anything he had yet seen, which puzzled him considerably. They must be contemporary, he decided, with the unprincipled Canon Alberic, who had doubtless plundered the Chapter library of St Bertrand to form this priceless scrap-book. On the first of the paper sheets was a plan, carefully drawn and instantly recognizable by a person who knew the ground, of the south aisle and cloisters of St Bertrand's. There were curious signs looking like planetary symbols, and a few Hebrew words, in the corners; and in the north-west angle of the cloister was a cross drawn in gold paint. Below the plan were some lines of writing in Latin, which ran thus: *Responsa 12mi Dec. 1694. Interrogatum est: Inveniamne? Responsum est: Invenies. Fiamne dives? Fies. Vivamne invidendus? Vives. Moriarne in lecto meo? Ita.**

"A good specimen of the treasure-hunter's record—quite reminds one of Mr Minor-Canon Quatremain in Old St Paul's," was Dennistoun's comment, and he turned the leaf.

What he then saw impressed him, as he has often told me, more than he could have conceived any drawing or picture capable of impressing him. And, though the drawing he saw is no longer in existence, there is a photograph of it (which I possess) which fully bears out that statement. The

---

[1] We now know that these leaves did contain a considerable fragment of that work, if not of that actual copy of it.

picture in question was a sepia drawing at the end of the seventeenth century, representing, one would say at first sight, a Biblical scene; for the architecture (the picture represented an interior) and the figures had that semi-classical flavour about them which the artists of two hundred years ago thought appropriate to illustrations of the Bible. On the right was a King on his throne, the throne elevated on twelve steps, a canopy overhead, lions on either side—evidently King Solomon. He was bending forward with outstretched sceptre, in attitude of command; his face expressed horror and disgust, yet there was in it also the mark of imperious will and confident power. The left half of the picture was the strangest, however. The interest plainly centred there. On the pavement before the throne were grouped four soldiers, surrounding a crouching figure which must be described in a moment. A fifth soldier lay dead on the pavement, his neck distorted, and his eyeballs starting from his head. The four surrounding guards were looking at the King. In their faces the sentiment of horror was intensified; they seemed, in fact, only restrained from flight by their implicit trust in their master. All this terror was plainly excited by the being that crouched in their midst. I entirely despair of conveying by any words the impression which this figure makes upon anyone who looks at it. I recollect once showing the photograph of the drawing to a lecturer on morphology— a person of, I was going to say, abnormally sane and unimaginative habits of mind. He absolutely refused to be alone for the rest of that evening, and he told me afterwards that for many nights he had not dared to put out his light before going to sleep. However, the main traits of the figure I can at least indicate. At first you saw only a mass of coarse, matted black hair; presently it was seen that this covered a body of fearful thinness, almost a skeleton, but with the muscles standing out like wires. The hands were of a dusky pallor, covered, like the body, with long, coarse hairs, and hideously taloned. The eyes, touched in with a burning yellow, had intensely black pupils, and were fixed upon the throned King with a look of beast-like hate. Imagine one of the awful bird-catching spiders of South America translated into human form, and endowed with intelligence just less than human, and you will have some faint conception of the terror inspired by this appalling effigy. One remark is universally made by those to whom I have shown the picture: "It was drawn from the life."

As soon as the first shock of his irresistible fright had subsided, Dennistoun stole a look at his hosts. The sacristan's hands were pressed upon his eyes; his daughter, looking up at the cross on the wall, was telling her beads feverishly.

At last the question was asked, "Is this book for sale?"

There was the same hesitation, the same plunge of determination that he had noticed before, and then came the welcome answer. "If monsieur pleases."

"How much do you ask for it?"

"I will take two hundred and fifty francs."

This was confounding. Even a collector's conscience is sometimes stirred, and Dennistoun's conscience was tenderer than a collector's.

"My good man!" he said again and again, "your book is worth far more than two hundred and fifty francs, I assure you—far more."

But the answer did not vary: "I will take two hundred and fifty francs, not more."

There was really no possibility of refusing such a chance. The money was paid, the receipt signed, a glass of wine drunk over the transaction, and then the sacristan seemed to become a new man. He stood upright, he ceased to throw those suspicious glances behind him, he actually laughed or tried to laugh. Dennistoun rose to go.

"I shall have the honour of accompanying monsieur to his hotel?" said the sacristan.

"Oh no, thanks! it isn't a hundred yards. I know the way perfectly, and there is a moon."

The offer was pressed three or four times, and refused as often.

"Then, monsieur will summon me if—if he finds occasion; he will keep the middle of the road, the sides are so rough."

"Certainly, certainly," said Dennistoun, who was impatient to examine his prize by himself; and he stepped out into the passage with his book under his arm.

Here he was met by the daughter; she, it appeared, was anxious to do a little business on her own account; perhaps, like Gehazi, to "take somewhat" from the foreigner whom her father had spared.

"A silver crucifix and chain for the neck; monsieur would perhaps be good enough to accept it?"

Well, really, Dennistoun hadn't much use for these things. What did mademoiselle want for it?

"Nothing—nothing in the world. Monsieur is more than welcome to it."

The tone in which this and much more was said was unmistakably genuine, so that Dennistoun was reduced to profuse thanks, and submitted to have the chain put round his neck. It really seemed as if he had rendered the father and daughter some service which they hardly knew how to repay. As he set off with his book they stood at the door looking after him, and they were still looking when he waved them a last good night from the steps of the *Chapeau Rouge*.[2]

---

[2] He died that summer; his daughter married, and settled at St Papoul. She never understood the circumstances of her father's "obsession".

Dinner was over, and Dennistoun was in his bedroom, shut up alone with his acquisition. The landlady had manifested a particular interest in him since he had told her that he had paid a visit to the sacristan and bought an old book from him. He thought, too, that he had heard a hurried dialogue between her and the said sacristan in the passage outside the salle à manger, some words to the effect that "Pierre and Bertrand would be sleeping in the house" had closed the conversation.

All this time a growing feeling of discomfort had been creeping over him—nervous reaction, perhaps, after the delight of his discovery. Whatever it was, it resulted in a conviction that there was someone behind him, and that he was far more comfortable with his back to the wall. All this, of course, weighed light in the balance as against the obvious value of the collection he had acquired. And now, as I said, he was alone in his bedroom, taking stock of Canon Alberic's treasures, in which every moment revealed something more charming.

"Bless Canon Alberic!" said Dennistoun, who had an inveterate habit of talking to himself. "I wonder where he is now? Dear me! I wish that landlady would learn to laugh in a more cheering manner; it makes one feel as if there was someone dead in the house. Half a pipe more, did you say? I think perhaps you are right. I wonder what that crucifix is that the young woman insisted on giving me? Last century, I suppose. Yes, probably. It is rather a nuisance of a thing to have round one's neck—just too heavy. Most likely her father had been wearing it for years. I think I might give it a clean up before I put it away."

He had taken the crucifix off, and laid it on the table, when his attention was caught by an object lying on the red cloth just by his left elbow. Two or three ideas of what it might be flitted through his brain with their own incalculable quickness.

"A penwiper? No, no such thing in the house. A rat? No, too black. A large spider? I trust to goodness not—no. Good God! a hand like the hand in that picture!"

In another infinitesimal flash he had taken it in. Pale, dusky skin, covering nothing but bones and tendons of appalling strength; coarse black hairs, longer than ever grew on a human hand; nails rising from the ends of the fingers and curving sharply down and forward, grey, horny and wrinkled.

He flew out of his chair with deadly, inconceivable terror clutching at his heart. The shape, whose left hand rested on the table, was rising to a standing posture behind his seat, its right hand crooked above his scalp. There was black and tattered drapery about it; the coarse hair covered it as in the drawing. The lower jaw was thin—what can I call it? —shallow, like a beast's; teeth showed behind the black lips; there was no nose; the eyes, of a fiery yellow, against which the pupils showed black and intense, and the exulting hate and thirst to destroy life which shone there, were the most horrifying features in the whole vision. There was intelligence of a kind in them—intelligence beyond that of a beast, below that of a man.

The feelings which this horror stirred in Dennistoun were the intensest physical fear and the most profound mental loathing. What did he do? What could he do? He has never been quite certain what words he said, but he knows that he spoke, that he grasped blindly at the silver crucifix, that he was conscious of a movement towards him on the part of the demon, and that he screamed with the voice of an animal in hideous pain.

Pierre and Bertrand, the two sturdy little serving-men, who rushed in, saw nothing, but felt themselves thrust aside by something that passed out between them, and found Dennistoun in a swoon. They sat up with him that night, and his two friends were at St Bertrand by nine o'clock next morning. He himself, though still shaken and nervous, was almost himself by that time, and his story found credence with them, though not until they had seen the drawing and talked with the sacristan.

Almost at dawn the little man had come to the inn on some pretence, and had listened with the deepest interest to the story retailed by the landlady. He showed no surprise.

"It is he—it is he! I have seen him myself," was his only comment; and to all questionings but one reply was vouchsafed: "*Deux fois je l'ai vu; mille fois je l'ai senti.*" He would tell them nothing of the provenance of the book, nor any details of his experiences. "I shall soon sleep, and my rest will be sweet. Why should you trouble me?" he said.

We shall never know what he or Canon Alberic de Mauléon suffered. At the back of that fateful drawing were some lines of writing which may be supposed to throw light on the situation:

Contradictio Salomonis cum demonio nocturno.
Albericus de Mauleone delineavit.
V. Deus in adiutorium. Ps. Qui habitat.
Sancte Bertrande, demoniorum effugator,
intercede pro me miserrimo.
Primum uidi nocte 12mi Dec. 1694: uidebo mox ultimum.
Peccaui et passus sum, plura adhuc passurus. Dec. 29,1701. [3]

---

[3] *i.e.* The Dispute of Solomon with a demon of the night. Drawn by Alberic de Mauléon. Versicle. O Lord, make haste to help me. Psalm. Whoso dwelleth (xci). (cont.)

I have never quite understood what was Dennistoun's view of the events I have narrated. He quoted to me once a text from Ecclesiasticus: "Some spirits there be that are created for vengeance, and in their fury lay on sore strokes." On another occasion he said: "Isaiah was a very sensible man; doesn't he say something about night monsters living in the ruins of Babylon? These things are rather beyond us at present."

Another confidence of his impressed me rather, and I sympathized with it. We had been, last year, to Comminges, to see Canon Alberic's tomb. It is a great marble erection with an effigy of the Canon in a large wig and soutane, and an elaborate eulogy of his learning below. I saw Dennistoun talking for some time with the Vicar of St Bertrand's, and as we drove away he said to me: "I hope it isn't wrong: you know I am a Presbyterian—but I—I believe there will be 'saying of Mass and singing of dirges' for Alberic de Mauléon's rest." Then he added, with a touch of the Northern British in his tone, "I had no notion they came so dear."

The book is in the Wentworth Collection at Cambridge. The drawing was photographed and then burnt by Dennistoun on the day when he left Comminges on the occasion of his first visit.

[3] (cont.) Saint Bertrand, who puttest devils to flight, pray for me most unhappy. I saw it first on the night of Dec. 12, 1694: soon I shall see it for the last time. I have sinned and suffered, and have more to suffer yet. Dec. 29, 1701.
The "Gallia Christiana" gives the date of the Canon's death as December 31, 1701, "in bed, of a sudden seizure." Details of this kind are not common in the great work of the Sammarthani.

CAJTING THE RUNEJ

M. R. James

April 15th, 190-

Dear Sir,—I am requested by the Council of the __ Association to return to you the draft of a paper on The Truth of Alchemy,
which you have been good enough to offer to read at our forth-
coming meeting, and to inform you that the Council do not see
their way to including it in the programme.

I am,
Yours faithfully,
—Secretary

April 18th

Dear Sir,—I am sorry to say that my engagements do not
permit of my affording you an interview on the subject of your
proposed paper. Nor do our laws allow of your discussing the
matter with a Committee of our Council, as you suggest. Please
allow me to assure you that the fullest consideration was given to
the draft which you submitted, and that it was not declined without having been referred to the judgement of a most competent
authority. No personal question (it can hardly be necessary for
me to add) can have had the slightest influence on the decision of
the Council.

Believe me (*ut supra*).

April 20th

The Secretary of the ____ Association begs respectfully to inform Mr. Karswell that it is impossible for him to communicate

the name of any person or persons to whom the draft of Mr. Karswell's paper may have been submitted; and further desires to intimate that he cannot undertake to reply to any further letters on this subject.

"And who *is* Mr. Karswell?" inquired the Secretary's wife. She had called at his office, and (perhaps unwarrantably) had picked up the last of these three letters, which the typist had just brought in.

"Why, my dear, just at present Mr. Karswell is a very angry man. But I don't know much about him otherwise, except that he is a person of wealth, his address is Lufford Abbey, Warwickshire, and he's an alchemist, apparently, and wants to tell us all about it; and that's about all—except that I don't want to meet him for the next week or two. Now, if you're ready to leave this place, I am."

"What have you been doing to make him angry?" asked Mrs. Secretary.

"The usual thing, my dear, the usual thing: he sent in a draft of a paper he wanted to read at the next meeting, and we referred it to Edward Dunning—almost the only man in England who knows about these things—and he said it was perfectly hopeless, so we declined it. So Karswell has been pelting me with letters ever since. The last thing he wanted was the name of the man we referred his nonsense to; you saw my answer to that. But don't you say anything about it, for goodness' sake."

"I should think not, indeed. Did I ever do such a thing? I do hope, though, he won't get to know that it was poor Mr. Dunning."

"Poor Mr. Dunning? I don't know why you call him that; he's a very happy man, is Dunning. Lots of hobbies and a comfortable home, and all his time to himself."

"I only meant I should be sorry for him if this man got hold of his name, and came and bothered him."

"Oh, ah! yes. I dare say he would be poor Mr. Dunning then."

The Secretary and his wife were lunching out, and the friends to whose house they were bound were Warwickshire people. So Mrs. Secretary had already settled it in her own mind that she would question them judiciously about Mr. Karswell. But she was saved the trouble of leading up to the subject, for the hostess said to the host, before many minutes had passed, "I saw the Abbot of Lufford this morning." The host whistled. "*Did* you? What in the world brings him up to town?" "Goodness knows; he was coming out of the British Museum gate as I drove past." It was not unnatural that Mrs. Secretary should inquire whether this was a real Abbot who was being spoken of. "Oh no, my dear: only a neighbour of ours in the country who bought Lufford Abbey a few years ago. His real name is Karswell." "Is he a friend of yours?" asked Mr. Secretary, with a private wink to his wife. The question let loose a torrent of declamation. There was really nothing to be said for Mr. Karswell. Nobody knew what he did with himself: his servants were a horrible set of people; he had invented a new religion for himself, and practised no one could tell what appalling rites; he was very easily offended, and never forgave anybody: he had a dreadful face (so the lady insisted, her husband somewhat demurring); he never did a kind action, and whatever influence he did exert was mischievous. "Do the poor man justice, dear," the husband interrupted. "You forgot the treat he gave the school children." "Forget it, indeed! But I'm glad you mentioned it, because it gives an idea of the man. Now, Florence, listen to this. The first winter he was at Lufford this delightful neighbour of ours wrote to the clergyman of his parish (he's not ours, but we know him very well) and offered to show the school children some magic-lantern slides. He said he had some new kinds, which he thought would interest them. Well, the clergyman was rather surprised, because Mr. Karswell had shown himself inclined to be unpleasant to the children—complaining of their trespassing, or something of the sort; but of course he accepted, and the evening was fixed, and our friend went himself to see that everything went right. He said he never had been so thankful for anything as that his own children were all prevented from being there: they were at a children's party at our house, as a matter of fact. Because this Mr. Karswell had evidently set out with the intention of frightening these poor village children out of their wits, and I do believe, if he had been allowed to go on, he would actually have done so. He began with some comparatively mild things. Red Riding Hood was one, and even then, Mr. Farrer said, the wolf was so dreadful that several of the smaller children had to be taken out: and he said Mr. Karswell began the story by producing a noise like a wolf howling in the distance, which was the most gruesome thing he had ever heard. All the slides he showed, Mr. Farrer said, were most clever; they were absolutely realistic, and where he had got them or how he worked them he could not imagine. Well, the show went on, and the stories kept on becoming a little more terrifying each time, and the children were mesmerized into complete silence. At last he produced a series which represented a little boy passing through his own park—Lufford, I mean—in the evening. Every child in the room could recognize the place from the pictures. And this poor boy was followed, and at last pursued and overtaken, and either torn in pieces or somehow made away with, by a horrible hopping creature in white, which you saw first dodging about among the trees, and gradually it appeared more and more plainly. Mr. Farrer said it gave him one of the worst nightmares he ever remembered, and what it must have meant to the children doesn't bear thinking of. Of course this was too much, and he spoke very sharply indeed to Mr. Karswell, and said it couldn't go on. All he said was: "Oh, you think it's time to bring our little show to an end and send them home to their beds? *Very* well!" And then, if you please, he switched on another slide, which showed a great mass of snakes, centipedes, and disgusting creatures with wings, and somehow or other made it seem as if they were climbing out of the picture and getting in amongst the audience; and this was accompanied by a sort of dry rustling noise which sent the children nearly mad, and of course they stampeded. A good many of them were rather hurt in getting out of the room, and I don't suppose one of them closed an eye that night. There was the most dreadful trouble in the village afterwards. Of course the mothers threw a good part of the blame on poor Mr. Farrer, and, if they could have got past the gates, I believe the fathers would have broken every window in the Abbey. Well, now, that's Mr. Karswell: that's the Abbot of Lufford, my dear, and you can imagine how we covet *his* society."

"Yes, I think he has *all* the possibilities of a distinguished criminal, has Karswell," said the host. "I should be sorry for anyone who got into his bad books."

"Is he the man, or am I mixing him up with someone else?" asked the Secretary (who for some minutes had been wearing the frown of the man who is trying to recollect something). "Is he the man who brought out a *History of Witchcraft* some time back—ten years or more?"

"That's the man; do you remember the reviews of it?"

"Certainly I do; and what's equally to the point, I knew the author of the most incisive of the lot. So did you: you must remember John Harrington; he was at John's in our time."

"Oh, very well indeed, though I don't think I saw or heard anything of him between the time I went down and the day I read the account of the inquest on him."

"Inquest?" said one of the ladies. "What has happened to him?"

"Why, what happened was that he fell out of a tree and broke his neck. But the puzzle was, what could have induced him to get up there. It was a mysterious business, I must say. Here was this man—not an athletic fellow, was he? and with no eccentric twist about him that was ever noticed—walking home along a country road late in the evening— no tramps about—well known and liked in the place—and he suddenly begins to run like mad, loses his hat and stick, and finally shins up a tree—quite a difficult tree—growing in the hedgerow: a dead branch gives way, and he comes down with it and breaks his neck, and there he's found next morning with the most dreadful face of fear on him that could be imagined. It was pretty evident, of course, that he had been chased by something, and people talked of savage dogs, and beasts escaped out of menageries; but there was nothing to be made of that. That was in '89, and I believe his brother Henry (whom I remember as well at Cambridge, but *you* probably don't) has been trying to get on the track of an explanation ever since. He, of course, insists there was malice in it, but I don't know. It's difficult to see how it could have come in."

After a time the talk reverted to the *History of Witchcraft*. "Did you ever look into it?" asked the host.

"Yes, I did," said the Secretary. "I went so far as to read it."

"Was it as bad as it was made out to be?"

"Oh, in point of style and form, quite hopeless. It deserved all the pulverizing it got. But, besides that, it was an evil book. The man believed every word of what he was saying, and I'm very much mistaken if he hadn't tried the greater part of his receipts."

"Well, I only remember Harrington's review of it, and I must say if I'd been the author it would have quenched my literary ambition for good. I should never have held up my head again."

"It hasn't had that effect in the present case. But come, it's half-past three; I must be off."

On the way home the Secretary's wife said, "I do hope that horrible man won't find out that Mr. Dunning had anything to do with the rejection of his paper." "I don't think there's much chance of that," said the Secretary. "Dunning won't mention it himself, for these matters are confidential, and none of us will for the same reason. Karswell won't know his name, for Dunning hasn't published anything on the same subject yet. The only danger is that Karswell might find out, if he was to ask the British Museum people who was in the habit of consulting alchemical manuscripts: I can't very well tell them not to mention Dunning, can I? It would set them talking at once. Let's hope it won't occur to him."

However, Mr. Karswell was an astute man.

This much is in the way of prologue. On an evening rather later in the same week, Mr. Edward Dunning was returning from the British Museum, where he had been engaged in research, to the comfortable house in a suburb where he lived alone, tended by two excellent women who had been long with him. There is nothing to be added by way of description of him to what we have heard already. Let us follow him as he takes his sober course homewards.

A train took him to within a mile or two of his house, and an electric tram a stage farther. The line ended at a point some three hundred yards from his front door. He had had enough of reading when he got into the car, and indeed the light was not such as to allow him to do more than study the advertisements on the panes of glass that faced him as he sat. As was not unnatural, the advertisements in this particular line of cars

were objects of his frequent contemplation, and, with the possible exception of the brilliant and convincing dialogue between Mr. Lamplough and
an eminent KC on the subject of Pyretic Saline, none of them afforded
much scope to his imagination. I am wrong: there was one at the corner
of the car farthest from him which did not seem familiar. It was in blue
letters on a yellow ground, and all that he could read of it was a name—
John Harrington—and something like a date. It could be of no interest to
him to know more; but for all that, as the car emptied, he was just curious enough to move along the seat until he could read it well. He felt to a
slight extent repaid for his trouble; the advertisement was not of the usual
type. It ran thus: "In memory of John Harrington, FSA, of The Laurels,
Ashbrooke. Died Sept. 18th, 1889. Three months were allowed."

The car stopped. Mr. Dunning, still contemplating the blue letters on
the yellow ground, had to be stimulated to rise by a word from the conductor. "I beg your pardon," he said, "I was looking at that advertisement; it's a very odd one, isn't it?" The conductor read it slowly. "Well,
my word," he said, "I never see that one before. Well, that is a cure, ain't
it? Someone bin up to their jokes 'ere, I should think." He got out a duster
and applied it, not without saliva, to the pane and then to the outside.
"No," he said, returning, "that ain't no transfer; seems to me as if it was
reg'lar in the glass, what I mean in the substance, as you may say. Don't
you think so, sir?" Mr. Dunning examined it and rubbed it with his glove,
and agreed. "Who looks after these advertisements, and gives leave for
them to be put up? I wish you would inquire. I will just take a note of the
words." At this moment there came a call from the driver: "Look alive,
George, time's up." "All right, all right; there's somethink else what's
up at this end. You come and look at this 'ere glass." "What's gorn with
the glass?" said the driver, approaching. "Well, and oo's 'Arrington?
What's it all about?" "I was just asking who was responsible for putting
the advertisements up in your cars, and saying it would be as well to make
some inquiry about this one." "Well, sir, that's all done at the Company's
orfice, that work is: it's our Mr. Timms, I believe, looks into that. When
we put up tonight I'll leave word, and per'aps I'll be able to tell you
tomorrer if you 'appen to be coming this way."

This was all that passed that evening. Mr. Dunning did just go to the
trouble of looking up Ashbrooke, and found that it was in Warwickshire.

Next day he went to town again. The car (it was the same car) was too
full in the morning to allow of his getting a word with the conductor: he
could only be sure that the curious advertisement had been made away
with. The close of the day brought a further element of mystery into the
transaction. He had missed the tram, or else preferred walking home,
but at a rather late hour, while he was at work in his study, one of the
maids came to say that two men from the tramways was very anxious to

speak to him. This was a reminder of the advertisement, which he had, he says, nearly forgotten. He had the men in—they were the conductor and driver of the car—and when the matter of refreshment had been attended to, asked what Mr. Timms had had to say about the advertisement. "Well, sir, that's what we took the liberty to step round about," said the conductor. "Mr. Timms 'e give William 'ere the rough side of his tongue about that: 'cordin' to 'im there warn't no advertisement of that description sent in, nor ordered, nor paid for, nor put up, nor nothink, let alone not bein' there, and we was playing the fool takin' up his time. 'Well,' I says, 'if that's the case, all I ask of you, Mr. Timms,' I says, 'is to take and look at it for yourself,' I says. 'Of course if it ain't there,' I says, 'you may take and call me what you like.' 'Right,' he says, 'I will': and we went straight off. Now, I leave it to you, sir, if that ad., as we term 'em, with 'Arrington on it warn't as plain as ever you see anythink—blue letters on yeller glass, and as I says at the time, and you borne me out, reg'lar in the glass, because, if you remember, you recollect of me swabbing it with my duster." "To be sure I do, quite clearly—well?" "You may say well, I don't think. Mr. Timms he gets in that car with a light—no, he telled William to 'old the light outside. 'Now,' he says, 'where's your precious ad. what we've 'eard so much about?' "Ere it is,' I says, 'Mr. Timms,' and I laid my 'and on it." The conductor paused.

"Well," said Mr. Dunning, "it was gone, I suppose. Broken?"

"Broke!—not it. There warn't, if you'll believe me, no more trace of them letters—blue letters they was—on that piece o' glass, than—well, it's no good me talkin'. I never see such a thing. I leave it to William here if—but there, as I says, where's the benefit in me going on about it?"

"And what did Mr. Timms say?"

"Why 'e did what I give 'im leave to—called us pretty much anythink he liked, and I don't know as I blame him so much neither. But what we thought, William and me did, was as we seen you take down a bit of a note about that well, that letterin"—,

"I certainly did that, and I have it now. Did you wish me to speak to Mr. Timms myself, and show it to him? Was that what you came in about?"

"There, didn't I say as much?" said William. "Deal with a gent if you can get on the track of one, that's my word. Now perhaps, George, you'll allow as I ain't took you very far wrong tonight."

"Very well, William, very well; no need for you to go on as if you'd 'ad to frog's-march me 'ere. I come quiet, didn't I! All the same for that, we 'adn't ought to take up your time this way, sir; but if it so 'appened you could find time to step round to the Company's orfice in the morning and tell Mr. Timms what you seen for yourself, we should lay under a very 'igh obligation to you for the trouble. You see it ain't bein' called—well, one thing and another, as we mind, but if they got it into their 'ead at the orfice as we seen things as warn't there, why, one thing leads to another, and where we should be a twelvemunce 'ence—well, you can understand what I mean."

Amid further elucidations of the proposition, George, conducted by William, left the room.

The incredulity of Mr. Timms (who had a nodding acquaintance with Mr. Dunning) was greatly modified on the following day by what the latter could tell and show him; and any bad mark that might have been attached to the names of William and George was not suffered to remain on the Company's books; but explanation there was none.

Mr. Dunning's interest in the matter was kept alive by an incident of the following afternoon. He was walking from his club to the train, and he noticed some way ahead a man with a handful of leaflets such as are distributed to passers-by by agents of enterprising firms. This agent had not chosen a very crowded street for his operations: in fact, Mr. Dunning did not see him get rid of a single leaflet before he himself reached the spot. One was thrust into his hand as he passed: the hand that gave it touched his, and he experienced a sort of little shock as it did so. It seemed unnaturally rough and hot. He looked in passing at the giver, but the impression he got was so unclear that, however much he tried to reckon it up subsequently, nothing would come. He was walking quickly, and as he went on glanced at the paper. It was a blue one. The name of Harrington in large capitals caught his eye. He stopped, startled, and felt for his glasses. The next instant the leaflet was twitched out of his hand by a man who hurried past, and was irrecoverably gone. He ran back a few paces, but where was the passer-by? and where the distributor?

It was in a somewhat pensive frame of mind that Mr. Dunning passed on the following day into the Select Manuscript Room of the British Museum, and filled up tickets for Harley 3586, and some other volumes. After a few minutes they were brought to him, and he was settling the one he wanted first upon the desk, when he thought he heard his own name whispered behind him. He turned round hastily, and in doing so, brushed his little portfolio of loose papers on to the floor. He saw no one he recognized except one of the staff in charge of the room, who nodded to him, and he proceeded to pick up his papers. He thought he had them all, and was turning to begin work, when a stout gentleman at the table behind him, who was just rising to leave, and had collected his own belongings, touched him on the shoulder, saying, "May I give you this? I think it should be yours," and handed him a missing quire. "It is mine, thank you," said Mr. Dunning. In another moment the man had left the room. Upon finishing his work for the afternoon, Mr. Dunning had some conversation with the assistant in charge, and took occasion to ask who the stout gentleman was. "Oh, he's a man named Karswell," said the assistant; "he was asking me a week ago who were the great authorities on alchemy, and of course I told him you were the only one in the country. I'll see if I can't catch him: he'd like to meet you, I'm sure."

"For heaven's sake don't dream of it!" said Mr. Dunning, "I'm particularly anxious to avoid him."

"Oh! very well," said the assistant, "he doesn't come here often: I dare say you won't meet him."

More than once on the way home that day Mr. Dunning confessed to himself that he did not look forward with his usual cheerfulness to a solitary evening. It seemed to him that something ill-defined and impalpable had stepped in between him and his fellow-men—had taken him in charge, as it were. He wanted to sit close up to his neighbours in the train and in the tram, but as luck would have it both train and car were markedly empty. The conductor George was thoughtful, and appeared to be absorbed in calculations as to the number of passengers. On arriving at his house he found Dr Watson, his medical man, on his doorstep. "I've had to upset your household arrangements, I'm sorry to say, Dunning. Both your servants hors de combat. In fact, I've had to send them to the Nursing Home."

"Good heavens! what's the matter?"

"It's something like ptomaine poisoning, I should think: you've not suffered yourself, I can see, or you wouldn't be walking about. I think they'll pull through all right."

"Dear, dear! Have you any idea what brought it on?"

"Well, they tell me they bought some shell-fish from a hawker at their dinner-time. It's odd. I've made inquiries, but I can't find that any hawker has been to other houses in the street. I couldn't send word to you; they won't be back for a bit yet. You come and dine with me tonight, anyhow, and we can make arrangements for going on. Eight o'clock. Don't be too anxious."

The solitary evening was thus obviated; at the expense of some distress and inconvenience, it is true. Mr. Dunning spent the time pleasantly enough with the doctor (a rather recent settler), and returned to his lonely home at about 11.30. The night he passed is not one on which he looks back with any satisfaction. He was in bed and the light was out. He was wondering if the charwoman would come early enough to get him hot water next morning, when he heard the unmistakable sound of his study door opening. No step followed it on the passage floor, but the sound must mean mischief, for he knew that he had shut the door that evening after putting his papers away in his desk. It was rather shame than courage that induced him to slip out into the passage and lean over the banister in his nightgown, listening. No light was visible; no further sound came: only a gust of warm, or even hot air played for an instant round his shins. He went back and decided to lock himself into his room. There was more unpleasantness, however. Either an economical suburban company had decided that their light would not be required in the small hours, and had stopped working, or else something was wrong with the meter; the effect was in any case that the electric light was off. The obvious course was to find a match, and also to consult his watch: he might as well know how many hours of discomfort awaited him. So he put his hand into the well-known nook under the pillow: only, it did not get so far. What he touched was, according to his account, a mouth, with teeth, and with hair about it, and, he declares, not the mouth of a human being. I do not think it is any use to guess what he said or did; but he was in a spare room with the door locked and his ear to it before he was clearly conscious again. And there he spent the rest of a most miserable night, looking every moment for some fumbling at the door: but nothing came.

The venturing back to his own room in the morning was attended with many listenings and quiverings. The door stood open, fortunately, and the blinds were up (the servants had been out of the house before the hour of drawing them down); there was, to be short, no trace of an inhabitant. The watch, too, was in its usual place; nothing was disturbed, only the wardrobe door had swung open, in accordance with its confirmed habit. A ring at the back door now announced the charwoman, who had been ordered the night before, and nerved Mr. Dunning, after letting her in, to continue his search in other parts of the house. It was equally fruitless.

The day thus begun went on dismally enough. He dared not go to the Museum: in spite of what the assistant had said, Karswell might turn up there, and Dunning felt he could not cope with a probably hostile stranger. His own house was odious; he hated sponging on the doctor. He spent some little time in a call at the Nursing Home, where he was slightly cheered by a good report of his housekeeper and maid. Towards lunchtime he betook himself to his club, again experiencing a gleam of satisfaction at seeing the Secretary of the Association. At luncheon Dunning told his friend the more material of his woes, but could not bring himself to speak to those that weighed most heavily on his spirits. "My poor dear man," said the Secretary, "what an upset! Look here: we're alone at home, absolutely. You must put up with us. Yes! no excuse: send your things in this afternoon." Dunning was unable to stand out: he was, in truth, becoming acutely anxious, as the hours went on, as to what that night might have waiting for him. He was almost happy as he hurried home to pack up.

His friends, when they had time to take stock of him, were rather shocked at his lorn appearance, and did their best to keep him up to the mark. Not altogether without success: but, when the two men were smoking alone later, Dunning became dull again. Suddenly he said, "Gayton, I believe that alchemist man knows it was I who got his paper rejected." Gayton whistled. "What makes you think that?" he said. Dunning told of his conversation with the Museum assistant, and Gayton could only agree that the guess seemed likely to be correct. "Not that I care much," Dunning went on, "only it might be a nuisance if we were to meet. He's a bad-tempered party, I imagine." Conversation dropped again; Gayton became more and more strongly impressed with the desolateness that came over Dunning's face and bearing, and finally—though with a considerable effort—he asked him point-blank whether something serious was not bothering him. Dunning gave an exclamation of relief. "I was perishing to get it off my mind," he said. "Do you know anything about a man named John Harrington?" Gayton was thoroughly startled, and at the moment could only ask why. Then the complete story of Dunning's experiences came out—what had happened in the tramcar, in his own house, and in the street, the troubling of spirit that had crept over him, and still held him; and he ended with the question he had begun with. Gayton was at a loss how to answer him. To tell the story of Harrington's end would perhaps be right; only, Dunning was in a nervous state, the story was a grim one, and he could not help asking himself whether there were not a connecting link between these two cases, in the person of Karswell. It was a difficult concession for a scientific man, but it could be eased by the phrase "hypnotic suggestion." In the end he decided that his answer tonight should be guarded; he would talk the situation over with his wife. So he said that he had known Harrington at Cambridge, and believed he had died suddenly in 1889, adding a few details about the man and his published work. He did talk over the matter with Mrs. Gayton, and, as he had anticipated, she leapt at once to the conclusion which had been hovering before him. It was she who reminded him of the surviving brother, Henry Harrington, and she also who suggested that he might be got hold of by means of their hosts of the day before. "He might be a hopeless crank," objected Gayton. "That could be ascertained from the Bennetts, who knew him," Mrs. Gayton retorted; and she undertook to see the Bennetts the very next day.

It is not necessary to tell in further detail the steps by which Henry Harrington and Dunning were brought together.

The next scene that does require to be narrated is a conversation that took place between the two. Dunning had told Harrington of the strange ways in which the dead man's name had been brought before him, and had said something, besides, of his own subsequent experiences. Then he had asked if Harrington was disposed, in return, to recall any of the circumstances connected with his brother's death. Harrington's surprise at what he heard can be imagined: but his reply was readily given.

"John," he said, "was in a very odd state, undeniably, from time to time, during some weeks before, though not immediately before, the catastrophe. There were several things; the principal notion he had was that he thought he was being followed. No doubt he was an impressionable man, but he never had had such fancies as this before. I cannot get it out of my mind that there was ill-will at work, and what you tell me about yourself reminds me very much of my brother. Can you think of any possible connecting link?"

"There is just one that has been taking shape vaguely in my mind. I've been told that your brother reviewed a book very severely not long before he died, and just lately I have happened to cross the path of the man who wrote that book in a way he would resent."

"Don't tell me the man was called Karswell."

"Why not? that is exactly his name."

Henry Harrington leant back. "That is final to my mind. Now I must explain further. From something he said, I feel sure that my brother John was beginning to believe—very much against his will—that Karswell was at the bottom of his trouble. I want to tell you what seems to me to have a bearing on the situation. My brother was a great musician, and used to run up to concerts in town. He came back, three months before he died, from one of these, and gave me his programme to look at—an analytical programme: he always kept them. "I nearly missed this one," he said. "I suppose I must have dropped it: anyhow, I was looking for it under my seat and in my pockets and so on, and my neighbour offered me his: said 'might he give it me, he had no further use for it,' and he went away just afterwards. I don't know who he was—a stout, clean-shaven man. I should have been sorry to miss it; of course I could have bought another, but this cost me nothing." At another time he told me that he had been very uncomfortable both on the way to his hotel and during the night. I piece things together now in thinking it over. Then, not very long after, he was going over these programmes, putting them in order to have them bound up, and in this particular one (which by the way I had hardly glanced at), he found quite near the beginning a strip of paper with some very odd writing on it in red and black—most carefully done—it looked to me more like Runic letters than anything else. "Why," he said, "this must belong to my fat neighbour. It looks as if it might be worth returning to him; it may be a copy of something; evidently someone has taken trouble over it. How can I find his address?" We talked it over for a little and agreed that it wasn't worth advertising about, and that my brother had better look out for the man at the next concert, to which he was going very soon. The paper was lying on the book and we were both by the fire; it was a cold, windy summer evening. I suppose the door blew open, though I didn't notice it: at any rate a gust—a warm gust it was—came quite suddenly between us, took the paper and blew it straight into the fire: it was light, thin paper, and flared and went up the chimney in a single ash. "Well," I said, "you can't give it back now." He said nothing for a minute: then rather crossly, "No, I can't; but why you should keep on saying so I don't know." I remarked that I didn't say it more than once. "Not more than four times, you mean," was all he said. I remember all that very clearly, without any good reason; and now to come to the point. I don't know if you looked at that book of Karswell's which my unfortunate brother reviewed. It's not likely that you should: but I did, both before his death and after it. The first time we made game of it together. It was written in no style at all—split infinitives, and every sort of thing that makes an Oxford gorge rise. Then there was nothing that the man didn't swallow: mixing up classical myths, and stories out of the *Golden Legend* with reports of savage customs of today—all very proper, no doubt, if you know how to use them, but he didn't: he seemed to put the *Golden Legend* and the *Golden Bough* exactly on a par, and to believe both: a pitiable exhibition, in short. Well, after the misfortune, I looked over the book again. It was no better than before, but the impression which it left this time on my mind was different. I suspected—as I told you—that Karswell had borne ill-will to my brother, even that he was in some way responsible for what had happened; and now his book seemed to me to be a very sinister performance indeed. One chapter in particular struck me, in which he spoke of "casting the Runes" on people, either for the purpose of gaining their affection or of getting them out of the way— perhaps more especially the latter: he spoke of all this in a way that really seemed to me to imply actual knowledge. I've got no time to go into details, but the upshot is that I am pretty sure from information received that the civil man at the concert was Karswell: I suspect—I more than suspect—that the paper was of importance: and I do believe that if my brother had been able to give it back, he might have been alive now. Therefore, it occurs to me to ask you whether you have anything to put beside what I have told you."

By way of answer, Dunning had the episode in the Manuscript Room at the British Museum to relate. "Then he did actually hand you some papers; have you examined them? No? because we must, if you'll allow it, look at them at once, and very carefully."

They went to the still empty house—empty, for the two servants were not yet able to return to work. Dunning's portfolio of papers was gathering dust on the writing-table. In it were the quires of small-sized scribbling paper which he used for his transcripts: and from one of these, as he took it up, there slipped and fluttered out into the room with uncanny quickness, a strip of thin light paper. The window was open, but Harrington slammed it to, just in time to intercept the paper, which he caught. "I thought so," he said; "it might be the identical thing that was given to my brother. You'll have to look out, Dunning; this may mean something quite serious for you."

A long consultation took place. The paper was narrowly examined. As Harrington had said, the characters on it were more like Runes than anything else, but not decipherable by either man, and both hesitated to copy them, for fear, as they confessed, of perpetuating whatever evil purpose they might conceal. So it has remained impossible (if I may anticipate a little) to ascertain what was conveyed in this curious message or commission. Both Dunning and Harrington are firmly convinced that it had the effect of bringing its possessors into very undesirable company. That it must be returned to the source whence it came they were agreed, and further, that the only safe and certain way was that of personal service; and here contrivance would be necessary, for Dunning was known by sight to Karswell. He must, for one thing, alter his appearance by shaving his beard. But then might not the blow fall first? Harrington thought they could time it. He knew the date of the concert at which the "black spot" had been put on his brother: it was June 18th. The death had followed on Sept. 18th. Dunning reminded him that three months had been mentioned on the inscription on the car-window. "Perhaps," he added, with a cheerless laugh, "mine may be a bill at three months too. I believe I can fix it by my diary. Yes, April 23rd was the day at the Museum; that brings us to July 23rd. Now, you know, it becomes extremely important to me to know anything you will tell me about the progress of your brother's trouble, if it is possible for you to speak of it." "Of course. Well, the sense of being watched whenever he was alone was the most distressing thing to him. After a time I took to sleeping in his room, and he was the better for that: still, he talked a great deal in his sleep. What about? Is it wise to dwell on that, at least before things are straightened out? I think not, but I can tell you this: two things came for him by post during those weeks, both with a London postmark, and addressed in a commercial hand. One was a woodcut of Bewick's, roughly torn out of the page: one which shows a moonlit road and a man walking along it, followed by an awful demon creature. Under it were written the lines out of the "Ancient Mariner" (which I suppose the cut illustrates) about one who, having once looked round—

> walks on,
> And turns no more his head,
> Because he knows a frightful fiend
> Doth close behind him tread.

The other was a calendar, such as tradesmen often send. My brother paid no attention to this, but I looked at it after his death, and found that everything after Sept. 18 had been torn out. You may be surprised at his having gone out alone the evening he was killed, but the fact is that during the last ten days or so of his life he had been quite free from the sense of being followed or watched."

The end of the consultation was this. Harrington, who knew a neighbour of Karswell's, thought he saw a way of keeping a watch on his movements. It would be Dunning's part to be in readiness to try to cross Karswell's path at any moment, to keep the paper safe and in a place of ready access.

They parted. The next weeks were no doubt a severe strain upon Dunning's nerves: the intangible barrier which had seemed to rise about him on the day when he received the paper, gradually developed into a brooding blackness that cut him off from the means of escape to which one might have thought he might resort. No one was at hand who was likely to suggest them to him, and he seemed robbed of all initiative. He waited with inexpressible anxiety as May, June, and early July passed on, for a mandate from Harrington. But all this time Karswell remained immovable at Lufford.

At last, in less than a week before the date he had come to look upon as the end of his earthly activities, came a telegram: "Leaves Victoria by boat train Thursday night. Do not miss. I come to you tonight. Harrington."

He arrived accordingly, and they concocted plans. The train left Victoria at nine and its last stop before Dover was Croydon West. Harrington would mark down Karswell at Victoria, and look out for Dunning at Croydon, calling to him if need were by a name agreed upon. Dunning, disguised as far as might be, was to have no label or initials on any hand luggage, and must at all costs have the paper with him.

Dunning's suspense as he waited on the Croydon platform I need not attempt to describe. His sense of danger during the last days had only been sharpened by the fact that the cloud about him had perceptibly been lighter; but relief was an ominous symptom, and, if Karswell eluded him now, hope was gone: and there were so many chances of that. The rumour of the journey might be itself a device. The twenty minutes in which he paced the platform and persecuted every porter with inquiries as to the boat train were as bitter as any he had spent. Still, the train came, and Harrington was at the window. It was important, of course, that there should be no recognition: so Dunning got in at the farther end of the corridor carriage, and only gradually made his way to the compartment where Harrington and Karswell were. He was pleased, on the whole, to see that the train was far from full.

Karswell was on the alert, but gave no sign of recognition. Dunning took the seat not immediately facing him, and attempted, vainly at first, then with increasing command of his faculties, to reckon the possibilities of making the desired transfer. Opposite to Karswell, and next to Dunning, was a heap of Karswell's coats on the seat. It would be of no use to slip the paper into these—he would not be safe, or would not feel so, unless in some way it could be proffered by him and accepted by the other. There was a handbag, open, and with papers in it. Could he manage to conceal this (so that perhaps Karswell might leave the carriage without it), and then find and give it to him? This was the plan that suggested itself. If he could only have counselled with Harrington! but that could not be. The minutes went on. More than once Karswell rose and went out into the corridor. The second time Dunning was on the point of attempting to make the bag fall off the seat, but he caught Harrington's eye, and read in it a warning. Karswell, from the corridor, was watching: probably to see if the two men recognized each other. He returned, but was evidently restless: and, when he rose the third time, hope dawned, for something did slip off his seat and fall with hardly a sound to the floor. Karswell went out once more, and passed out of range of the corridor window. Dunning picked up what had fallen, and saw that the key was in his hands in the form of one of Cook's ticket-cases, with tickets in it. These cases have a pocket in the cover, and within very few seconds the paper of which we have heard was in the pocket of this one. To make the operation more secure, Harrington stood in the doorway of the compartment and fiddled with the blind. It was done, and done at the right time, for the train was now slowing down towards Dover.

In a moment more Karswell re-entered the compartment. As he did so, Dunning, managing, he knew not how, to suppress the tremble in his voice, handed him the ticket-case, saying, "May I give you this, sir? I believe it is yours." After a brief glance at the ticket inside, Karswell uttered the hoped-for response, "Yes, it is; much obliged to you, sir," and he placed it in his breast pocket.

Even in the few moments that remained—moments of tense anxiety, for they knew not to what a premature finding of the paper might lead—both men noticed that the carriage seemed to darken about them and to grow warmer; that Karswell was fidgety and oppressed; that he drew the heap of loose coats near to him and cast it back as if it repelled him; and that he then sat upright and glanced anxiously at both. They, with sickening anxiety, busied themselves in collecting their belongings; but they both thought that Karswell was on the point of speaking when the train stopped at Dover Town. It was natural that in the short space between town and pier they should both go into the corridor.

At the pier they got out, but so empty was the train that they were forced to linger on the platform until Karswell should have passed ahead of them with his porter on the way to the boat, and only then was it safe for them to exchange a pressure of the hand and a word of concentrated congratulation. The effect upon Dunning was to make him almost faint. Harrington made him lean up against the wall, while he himself went forward a few yards within sight of the gangway to the boat, at which Karswell had now arrived. The man at the head of it examined his ticket, and, laden with coats, he passed down into the boat. Suddenly the official called after him, "You, sir, beg pardon, did the other gentleman show his ticket?" "What the devil do you mean by the other gentleman?" Karswell's snarling voice called back from the deck. The man bent over and looked at him. "The devil? Well, I don't know, I'm sure," Harrington heard him say to himself, and then aloud, "My mistake, sir; must have been your rugs! ask your pardon." And then, to a subordinate near him, "'Ad he got a dog with him, or what? Funny thing: I could 'a' swore 'e wasn't alone. Well, whatever it was, they'll 'ave to see to it aboard. She's off now. Another week and we shall be gettin' the 'oliday customers." In five minutes more there was nothing but the lessening lights of the boat, the long line of the Dover lamps, the night breeze, and the moon.

Long and long the two sat in their room at the "Lord Warden." In spite of the removal of their greatest anxiety, they were oppressed with a doubt, not of the lightest. Had they been justified in sending a man to his death, as they believed they had? Ought they not to warn him, at least? "No," said Harrington; "if he is the murderer I think him, we have done no more than is just. Still, if you think it better—but how and where can you warn him?" "He was booked to Abbéville only," said Dunning. "I saw that. If I wired to the hotels there in Joanne's Guide, "Examine your ticket-case, Dunning," I should feel happier. This is the 21st: he will have a day. But I am afraid he has gone into the dark." So telegrams were left at the hotel office.

It is not clear whether these reached their destination, or whether, if they did, they were understood. All that is known is that, on the afternoon of the 23rd, an English traveller, examining the front of St Wulfram's Church at Abbéville, then under extensive repair, was struck on the head and instantly killed by a stone falling from the scaffold erected round the north-western tower, there being, as was clearly proved, no workman on the scaffold at that moment: and the traveller's papers identified him as Mr. Karswell.

Only one detail shall be added. At Karswell's sale a set of Bewick, sold with all faults, was acquired by Harrington. The page with the wood-cut of the traveller and the demon was, as he had expected, mutilated.

Also, after a judicious interval, Harrington repeated to Dunning something of what he had heard his brother say in his sleep: but it was not long before Dunning stopped him.

THE MEZZOTINT

M. R. James

Some time ago I believe I had the pleasure of telling you the story of an adventure which happened to a friend of mine by the name of Dennistoun, during his pursuit of objects of art for the museum at Cambridge.

He did not publish his experiences very widely upon his return to England; but they could not fail to become known to a good many of his friends, and among others to the gentleman who at that time presided over an art museum at another University. It was to be expected that the story should make a considerable impression on the mind of a man whose vocation lay in lines similar to Dennistoun's, and that he should be eager to catch at any explanation of the matter which tended to make it seem improbable that he should ever be called upon to deal with so agitating an emergency. It was, indeed, somewhat consoling to him to reflect that he was not expected to acquire ancient MSS for his institution; that was the business of the Shelburnian Library. The author-ities of that might, if they pleased, ransack obscure corners of the Continent for such matters. He was glad to be obliged at the moment to confine his attention to enlarging the already unsurpassed collection of English topographical drawings and engravings possessed by his museum. Yet, as it turned out, even a department so homely and familiar as this may have its dark corners, and to one of these Mr. Williams was unexpectedly introduced.

Those who have taken even the most limited interest in the acquisition of topographical pictures are aware that there is one London dealer whose aid is indispensable to their researches. Mr. J. W. Britnell publishes at short intervals very admirable catalogues of a large and constantly changing stock of engravings, plans, and old sketches of mansions, churches, and towns in England and Wales. These catalogues were, of course, the ABC of his subject to Mr. Williams: but as his museum

291

already contained an enormous accumulation of topographical pictures, he was a regular, rather than a copious, buyer; and he rather looked to Mr. Britnell to fill up gaps in the rank and file of his collection than to supply him with rarities.

Now, in February of last year there appeared upon Mr. Williams's desk at the museum a catalogue from Mr. Britnell's emporium, and accompanying it was a typewritten communication from the dealer himself. This latter ran as follows:

> Dear Sir,
> We beg to call your attention to No. 978 in our accompanying catalogue, which we shall be glad to send on approval.
> Yours faithfully,
> J. W. Britnell

To turn to No. 978 in the accompanying catalogue was with Mr. Williams (as he observed to himself) the work of a moment, and in the place indicated he found the following entry:

> 978.—*Unknown*. Interesting mezzotint: View of a manor-house, early part of the century, 15 by 10 inches; black frame. £2 2s.

It was not specially exciting, and the price seemed high. However, as Mr. Britnell, who knew his business and his customer, seemed to set store by it, Mr. Williams wrote a postcard asking for the article to be sent on approval, along with some other engravings and sketches which appeared in the same catalogue. And so he passed without much excitement of anticipation to the ordinary labours of the day.

A parcel of any kind always arrives a day later than you expect it, and that of Mr. Britnell proved, as I believe the right phrase goes, no exception to the rule. It was delivered at the museum by the afternoon post of Saturday, after Mr. Williams had left his work, and it was accordingly brought round to his rooms in college by the attendant, in order that he might not have to wait over Sunday before looking through it and returning such of the contents as he did not propose to keep. And here he found it when he came in to tea, with a friend.

The only item with which I am concerned was the rather large, black-framed mezzotint of which I have already quoted the short description given in Mr. Britnell's catalogue. Some more details of it will have to be given, though I cannot hope to put before you the look of the picture as clearly as it is present to my own eye. Very nearly the exact duplicate of it may be seen in a good many old inn parlours, or in the passages of undisturbed country mansions at the present moment. It was a rather indifferent mezzotint, and an indifferent mezzotint is, perhaps, the worst form of engraving known. It presented a full-face view of a not very large manor-house of the last century, with three rows of plain sashed windows with rusticated masonry about them, a parapet with balls or vases at the angles, and a small portico in the centre. On either side were trees, and in front a considerable expanse of lawn. The legend "A. W. F. sculpsit" was engraved on the narrow margin; and there was no further inscription. The whole thing gave the impression that it was the work of an amateur. What in the world Mr. Britnell could mean by affixing the price of £2 2s. to such an object was more than Mr. Williams could imagine. He turned it over with a good deal of contempt; upon the back was a paper label, the left-hand half of which had been torn off. All that remained were the ends of two lines of writing: the first had the letters —*ngley Hall*; the second, —*ssex*.

It would, perhaps, be just worth while to identify the place represented, which he could easily do with the help of a gazetteer, and then he would send it back to Mr. Britnell, with some remarks reflecting upon the judgement of that gentleman.

He lighted the candles, for it was now dark, made the tea, and supplied the friend with whom he had been playing golf (for I believe the authorities of the University I write of indulge in that pursuit by way of relaxation); and tea was taken to the accompaniment of a discussion which golfing persons can imagine for themselves, but which the conscientious writer has no right to inflict upon any non-golfing persons.

The conclusion arrived at was that certain strokes might have been better, and that in certain emergencies neither player had experienced that amount of luck which a human being has a right to expect. It was now that the friend—let us call him Professor Binks—took up the framed engraving, and said:

"What's this place, Williams?"

"Just what I am going to try to find out," said Williams, going to the shelf for a gazetteer. "Look at the back. Somethingley Hall, either in Sussex or Essex. Half the name's gone, you see. You don't happen to know it, I suppose?"

"It's from that man Britnell, I suppose, isn't it?" said Binks. "Is it for the museum?"

"Well, I think I should buy it if the price was five shillings," said Williams; "but for some unearthly reason he wants two guineas for it. I can't conceive why. It's a wretched engraving, and there aren't even any figures to give it life."

"It's not worth two guineas, I should think," said Binks; "but I don't think it's so badly done. The moonlight seems rather good to me; and I should have thought there were figures, or at least a figure, just on the edge in front."

"Let's look," said Williams. "Well, it's true the light is rather cleverly given. Where's your figure? Oh yes! Just the head, in the very front of the picture."

And indeed there was—hardly more than a black blot on the extreme edge of the engraving—the head of a man or woman, a good deal muffled up, the back turned to the spectator, and looking towards the house.

Williams had not noticed it before.

"Still," he said, "though it's a cleverer thing than I thought, I can't spend two guineas of museum money on a picture of a place I don't know."

Professor Binks had his work to do, and soon went; and very nearly up to Hall time Williams was engaged in a vain attempt to identify the subject of his picture. "If the vowel before the ng had only been left, it would have been easy enough," he thought; "but as it is, the name may be anything from Guestingley to Langley, and there are many more names ending like this than I thought; and this rotten book has no index of terminations."

Hall in Mr. Williams's college was at seven. It need not be dwelt upon; the less so as he met there colleagues who had been playing golf during the afternoon, and words with which we have no concern were freely bandied across the table—merely golfing words, I would hasten to explain.

I suppose an hour or more to have been spent in what is called common-room after dinner. Later in the evening some few retired to Williams's rooms, and I have little doubt that whist was played and tobacco smoked. During a lull in these operations Williams picked up the mezzotint from the table without looking at it, and handed it to a person mildly interested in art, telling him where it had come from, and the other particulars which we already know.

The gentleman took it carelessly, looked at it, then said, in a tone of some interest:

"It's really a very good piece of work, Williams; it has quite a feeling of the romantic period. The light is admirably managed, it seems to me, and the figure, though it's rather too grotesque, is somehow very impressive."

"Yes, isn't it?" said Williams, who was just then busy giving whisky-and-soda to others of the company, and was unable to come across the room to look at the view again.

It was by this time rather late in the evening, and the visitors were on the move. After they went Williams was obliged to write a letter or two and clear up some odd bits of work. At last, some time past midnight, he was disposed to turn in, and he put out his lamp after lighting his bedroom candle. The picture lay face upwards on the table where the last man who looked at it had put it, and it caught his eye as he turned the lamp down. What he saw made him very nearly drop the candle on the floor, and he declares now that if he had been left in the dark at that moment he would have had a fit. But, as that did not happen, he was able to put down the light on the table and take a good look at the picture. It was indubitable—rankly impossible, no doubt, but absolutely certain. In the middle of the lawn in front of the unknown house there was a figure where no figure had been at five o'clock that afternoon. It was crawling on all-fours towards the house, and it was muffled in a strange black garment with a white cross on the back.

I do not know what is the ideal course to pursue in a situation of this kind. I can only tell you what Mr. Williams did. He took the picture by one corner and carried it across the passage to a second set of rooms which he possessed. There he locked it up in a drawer, sported the doors of both sets of rooms, and retired to bed; but first he wrote out and signed an account of the extraordinary change which the picture had undergone since it had come into his possession.

Sleep visited him rather late; but it was consoling to reflect that the behaviour of the picture did not depend upon his own unsupported testimony. Evidently the man who had looked at it the night before had seen something of the same kind as he had, otherwise he might have been tempted to think that something gravely wrong was happening either to his eyes or his mind. This possibility being fortunately precluded, two matters awaited him on the morrow. He must take stock of the picture very carefully, and call in a witness for the purpose, and he must make a determined effort to ascertain what house it was that was represented. He would therefore ask his neighbour Nisbet to breakfast with him, and he would subsequently spend a morning over the gazetteer.

Nisbet was disengaged, and arrived about 9.30. His host was not quite dressed, I am sorry to say, even at this late hour. During breakfast nothing was said about the mezzotint by Williams, save that he had a picture on which he wished for Nisbet's opinion. But those who are familiar with University life can picture for themselves the wide and delightful range of subjects over which the conversation of two Fellows of Canterbury College is likely to extend during a Sunday morning breakfast. Hardly a topic was left unchallenged, from golf to lawn-tennis. Yet I am bound to say that Williams was rather distraught; for his interest naturally centred in that very strange picture which was now reposing, face downwards, in the drawer in the room opposite.

The morning pipe was at last lighted, and the moment had arrived for which he looked. With very considerable—almost tremulous—excitement, he ran across, unlocked the drawer, and, extracting the picture—still face downwards—ran back, and put it into Nisbet's hands.

"Now," he said, "Nisbet, I want you to tell me exactly what you see in that picture. Describe it, if you don't mind, rather minutely. I'll tell you why afterwards."

"Well," said Nisbet, "I have here a view of a country-house—English, I presume—by moonlight."

"Moonlight? You're sure of that?"

"Certainly. The moon appears to be on the wane, if you wish for details, and there are clouds in the sky."

"All right. Go on. I'll swear," added Williams in an aside, "there was no moon when I saw it first."

"Well, there's not much more to be said," Nisbet continued. "The house has one—two—three rows of windows, five in each row, except at the bottom, where there's a porch instead of the middle one, and—"

"But what about figures?" said Williams, with marked interest.

"There aren't any," said Nisbet; "but—"

"What! No figure on the grass in front?"

"Not a thing."

"You'll swear to that?"

"Certainly I will. But there's just one other thing."

"What?"

"Why, one of the windows on the ground floor—left of the door—is open."

"Is it really? My goodness! he must have got in," said Williams, with great excitement; and he hurried to the back of the sofa on which Nisbet was sitting, and, catching the picture from him, verified the matter for himself.

It was quite true. There was no figure, and there was the open window. Williams, after a moment of speechless surprise, went to the writing-table and scribbled for a short time. Then he brought two papers to Nisbet, and asked him first to sign one—it was his own description of the picture, which you have just heard—and then to read the other which was Williams's statement written the night before.

"What can it all mean?" said Nisbet.

"Exactly," said Williams. "Well, one thing I must do—or three things, now I think of it. I must find out from Garwood"—this was his last night's visitor— "what he saw, and then I must get the thing photographed before it goes further, and then I must find out what the place is."

"I can do the photographing myself," said Nisbet, "and I will. But, you know, it looks very much as if we were assisting at the working out of a tragedy somewhere. The question is, Has it happened already, or is it going to come off? You must find out what the place is. Yes," he said, looking at the picture again, "I expect you're right: he has got in. And if I don't mistake there'll be the devil to pay in one of the rooms upstairs."

"I'll tell you what," said Williams: "I'll take the picture across to old Green" (this was the senior Fellow of the College, who had been Bursar for many years). "It's quite likely he'll know it. We have property in Essex and Sussex, and he must have been over the two counties a lot in his time."

"Quite likely he will," said Nisbet; "but just let me take my photograph first. But look here, I rather think Green isn't up today. He wasn't in Hall last night, and I think I heard him say he was going down for the Sunday."

"That's true, too," said Williams; "I know he's gone to Brighton. Well, if you'll photograph it now, I'll go across to Garwood and get his statement, and you keep an eye on it while I'm gone. I'm beginning to think two guineas is not a very exorbitant price for it now."

In a short time he had returned, and brought Mr. Garwood with him. Garwood's statement was to the effect that the figure, when he had seen it, was clear of the edge of the picture, but had not got far across the lawn. He remembered a white mark on the back of its drapery, but could not have been sure it was a cross. A document to this effect was then drawn up and signed, and Nisbet proceeded to photograph the picture.

"Now what do you mean to do?" he said. "Are you going to sit and watch it all day?"

"Well, no, I think not," said Williams. "I rather imagine we're meant to see the whole thing. You see, between the time I saw it last night and this morning there was time for lots of things to happen, but the creature only got into the house. It could easily have got through its business in the time and gone to its own place again; but the fact of the window being open, I think, must mean that it's in there now. So I feel quite easy about leaving it. And, besides, I have a kind of idea that it wouldn't change much, if at all, in the daytime. We might go out for a walk this afternoon, and come in to tea, or whenever it gets dark. I shall leave it out on the table here) and sport the door. My skip can get in, but no one else."

The three agreed that this would be a good plan; and, further, that if they spent the afternoon together they would be less likely to talk about the business to other people; for any rumour of such a transaction as was going on would bring the whole of the Phasmatological Society about their ears.

We may give them a respite until five o'clock.

At or near that hour the three were entering Williams's staircase. They were at first slightly annoyed to see that the door of his rooms was unsported; but in a moment it was remembered that on Sunday the skips came for orders an hour or so earlier than on week-days. However, a surprise was awaiting them. The first thing they saw was the picture leaning up against a pile of books on the table, as it had been left, and the next thing was Williams's skip, seated on a chair opposite, gazing at it with undisguised horror. How was this? Mr. Filcher (the name is not my own invention) was a servant of considerable standing, and set the standard of etiquette to all his own college and to several neighbouring ones, and nothing could be more alien to his practice than to be found sitting on his master's chair, or appearing to take any particular notice of his master's furniture or pictures. Indeed, he seemed to feel this himself. He started violently when the three men came into the room, and got up with a marked effort. Then he said: "I ask your pardon, sir, for taking such a freedom as to set down."

"Not at all, Robert," interposed Mr. Williams. "I was meaning to ask you some time what you thought of that picture."

"Well, sir, of course I don't set up my opinion again yours, but it ain't the pictur I should 'ang where my little girl could see it, sir."

"Wouldn't you, Robert? Why not?"

"No, sir. Why, the pore child, I recollect once she see a Door Bible, with pictures not 'alf what that is, and we 'ad to set up with her three or four nights afterwards, if you'll believe me; and if she was to ketch a sight of this skelinton here, or whatever it is, carrying off the pore baby, she would be in a taking. You know 'ow it is with children; 'ow nervish they git with a little thing and all. But what I should say, it don't seem a right pictur to be laying about, sir, not where anyone that's liable to be startled could come on it. Should you be wanting anything this evening, sir? Thank you, sir."

With these words the excellent man went to continue the round of his masters, and you may be sure the gentlemen whom he left lost no time in gathering round the engraving. There was the house, as before under the waning moon and the drifting clouds. The window that had been open was shut, and the figure was once more on the lawn: but not this time crawling cautiously on hands and knees. Now it was erect and stepping swiftly, with long strides, towards the front of the picture. The moon was behind it, and the black drapery hung down over its face so that only hints of that could be seen, and what was visible made the spectators profoundly thankful that they could see no more than a white dome-like forehead and a few straggling hairs. The head was bent down, and the arms were tightly clasped over an object which could be dimly seen and identified as a child, whether dead or living it was not possible to say. The legs of the appearance alone could be plainly discerned, and they were horribly thin.

From five to seven the three companions sat and watched the picture by turns. But it never changed. They agreed at last that it would be safe to leave it, and that they would return after Hall and await further developments.

When they assembled again, at the earliest possible moment, the engraving was there, but the figure was gone, and the house was quiet under the moonbeams. There was nothing for it but to spend the evening over gazetteers and guide-books. Williams was the lucky one at last, and perhaps he deserved it. At 11.30 p.m. he read from Murray's *Guide to Essex* the following lines:

16½ miles, *Anningley*. The church has been an interesting building of Norman date, but was extensively classicized in the last century. It contains the tombs of the family of Francis, whose mansion, Anningley Hall, a solid Queen Anne house, stands immediately beyond the churchyard in a park of about 80 acres. The family is now extinct, the last heir having disappeared mysteriously in infancy in the year 1802. The father, Mr. Arthur Francis, was locally known as a talented amateur engraver in mezzotint. After his son's disappearance he lived in complete retirement at the Hall, and was found dead in his studio on the third anniversary of the disaster, having just completed an engraving of the house, impressions of which are of considerable rarity.

This looked like business, and, indeed, Mr. Green on his return at once identified the house as Anningley Hall.

"Is there any kind of explanation of the figure, Green?" was the question which Williams naturally asked.

"I don't know, I'm sure, Williams. What used to be said in the place when I first knew it, which was before I came up here, was just this: old Francis was always very much down on these poaching fellows, and whenever he got a chance he used to get a man whom he suspected of it turned off the estate, and by degrees he got rid of them all but one. Squires could do a lot of things then that they daren't think of now. Well, this man that was left was what you find pretty often in that country—the last remains of a very old family. I believe they were Lords of the Manor at one time. I recollect just the same thing in my own parish."

"What, like the man in *Tess of the D'Urbervilles*?" Williams put in.

"Yes, I dare say; it's not a book I could ever read myself. But this fellow could show a row of tombs in the church there that belonged to his ancestors, and all that went to sour him a bit; but Francis, they said, could never get at him—he always kept just on the right side of the law—until one night the keepers found him at it in a wood right at the end of the estate. I could show you the place now; it marches with some land that used to belong to an uncle of mine. And you can imagine there was a row; and this man Gawdy (that was the name, to be sure—Gawdy; I thought I should get it—Gawdy), he was unlucky enough, poor chap! to shoot a keeper. Well, that was what Francis wanted, and grand juries—you know what they would have been then—and poor Gawdy was strung up in double-quick time; and I've been shown the place he was buried in, on the north side of the church—you know the way in that part of the world: anyone that's been hanged or made away with themselves, they bury them that side. And the idea was that some friend of Gawdy's—not a relation, because he had none, poor devil! he was the last of his line: kind of spes ultima gentis—must have planned to get hold of Francis's boy and put an end to his line, too. I don't know—it's rather an out-of-the-way thing for an Essex poacher to think of—but, you know, I should say now it looks, more as if old Gawdy had managed the job himself. Booh! I hate to think of it! Have some whisky, Williams!"

The facts were communicated by Williams to Dennistoun, and by him to a mixed company, of which I was one, and the Sadducean Professor of Ophiology another. I am sorry to say that the latter, when asked what he thought of it, only remarked: "Oh, those Bridgeford people will say any-thing"—a sentiment which met with the reception it deserved.

I have only to add that the picture is now in the Ashleian Museum; that it has been treated with a view to discovering whether sympathetic ink has been used in it, but without effect; that Mr. Britnell knew noth-ing of it save that he was sure it was uncommon; and that, though care-fully watched, it has never been known to change again.

THE STALLS OF BARCHESTER CATHEDRAL

M. R. James

This matter began, as far as I am concerned, with the reading of a notice in the obituary section of the *Gentleman's Magazine* for an early year in the nineteenth century:

"On February 26th, at his residence in the Cathedral Close of Barchester, the Venerable John Benwell Haynes, D.D., aged 57, Archdeacon of Sowerbridge and Rector of Pickhill and Candley. He was of — College, Cambridge, and where, by talent and assiduity, he commanded the esteem of his seniors; when, at the usual time, he took his first degree, his name stood high in the list of wranglers. These academical honours procured for him within a short time a Fellowship of his College. In the year 1783 he received Holy Orders, and was shortly afterwards presented to the perpetual Curacy of Ranxton-sub-Ashe by his friend and patron the late truly venerable Bishop of Lichfield ... His speedy preferments, first to a Prebend, and subsequently to the dignity of Precentor in the Cathedral of Barchester, form an eloquent testimony to the respect in which he was held and to his eminent qualifications. He succeeded to the Archdeaconry upon the sudden decease of Archdeacon Pulteney in 1810. His sermons, ever conformable to the principles of the religion and Church which he adorned, displayed in no ordinary degree, without the least trace of enthusiasm, the refinement of the scholar united with the graces of the Christian. Free from sectarian violence, and informed by the spirit of the truest charity, they will long dwell in the memories of his hearers. (Here a further omission.) The productions of his pen include an able defence of Episcopacy, which, though often perused by the author of this tribute to his

memory, afford but one additional instance of the want of liber-
ality and enterprise which is a too common characteristic of the
publishers of our generation. His published works are, indeed,
confined to a spirited and elegant version of the *Argonautica* of
Valerius Flaccus, a volume of *Discourser upon the Several Event
in the Life of Joshua,* delivered in his Cathedral, and a number of
the charges which he pronounced at various visitations, to the
clergy of his Archdeaconry. These are distinguished by etc., etc.
The urbanity and hospitality of the subject of these lines will not
readily be forgotten by those who enjoyed his acquaintance. His
interest in the venerable and awful pile under whose hoary vault
he was so punctual an attendant, and particularly in the musical
portion of its rites, might be termed filial, and formed a strong
and delightful contrast to the polite indifference displayed by too
many of our Cathedral dignitaries at the present time."

The final paragraph, after informing us that Dr Haynes died a bachelor,
says:

"It might have been augured that an existence so placid and
benevolent would have been terminated in a ripe old age by a
dissolution equally gradual and calm. But how unsearchable are
the workings of Providence! The peaceful and retired seclusion
amid which the honoured evening of Dr Haynes's life was mel-
lowing to its close was destined to be disturbed, nay, shattered,
by a tragedy as appalling as it was unexpected. The morning of
the 26th of February —"

But perhaps I shall do better to keep back the remainder of the
narrative until I have told the circumstances which led up to it. These, as
far as they are now accessible, I have derived from another source.

I had read the obituary notice which I have been quoting, quite by
chance, along with a great many others of the same period. It had excited
some little speculation in my mind, but, beyond thinking that, if I ever
had an opportunity of examining the local records of the period indicated, I would try to remember Dr Haynes, I made no effort to pursue his
case.

Quite lately I was cataloguing the manuscripts in the library of the
college to which he belonged. I had reached the end of the numbered
volumes on the shelves, and I proceeded to ask the librarian whether there
were any more books which he thought I ought to include in my description. "I don't think there are," he said, "but we had better come and look
at the manuscript class and make sure. Have you time to do that now?" I

had time. We went to the library, checked off the manuscripts, and, at the end of our survey, arrived at a shelf of which I had seen nothing. Its contents consisted for the most part of sermons, bundles of fragmentary papers, college exercises, *Cyrus*, an epic poem in several cantos, the product of a country clergyman's leisure, mathematical tracts by a deceased professor, and other similar material of a kind with which I am only too familiar. I took brief notes of these. Lastly, there was a tin box, which was pulled out and dusted. Its label, much faded, was thus inscribed: "Papers of the Ven. Archdeacon Haynes. Bequeathed in 1834 by his sister, Miss Letitia Haynes."

I knew at once that the name was one which I had somewhere encountered, and could very soon locate it. "That must be the Archdeacon Haynes who came to a very odd end at Barchester. I've read his obituary in the *Gentleman's Magazine*. May I take the box home? Do you know if there is anything interesting in it?"

The librarian was very willing that I should take the box and examine it at leisure. "I never looked inside it myself," he said, "but I've always been meaning to. I am pretty sure that is the box which our old Master once said ought never to have been accepted by the college. He said that to Martin years ago; and he said also that as long as he had control over the library it should never he opened. Martin told me about it, and said that he wanted terribly to know what was in it; but the Master was librarian, and always kept the box in the lodge, so there was no getting at it in his time, and when he died it was taken away by mistake by his heirs, and only returned a few years ago. I can't think why I haven't opened it; but, as I have to go away from Cambridge this afternoon, you had better have first go at it. I think I can trust you not to publish anything undesirable in our catalogue."

I took the box home and examined its contents, and thereafter consulted the librarian as to what should he done about publication, and, since I have his leave to make a story out of it, provided I disguise the identity of the people concerned, I will try what can be done.

The materials are, of course, mainly journals and letters. How much I shall quote and how much epitomize must be determined by considerations of space. The proper understanding of the situation has necessitated a little—not very arduous—research, which has been greatly facilitated by the excellent illustrations and text of the Barchester volume in Bell's *Cathedral Series*.

When you enter the choir of Barchester Cathedral now, you pass through a screen of metal and coloured marbles, designed by Sir Gilbert Scott, and find yourself in what I must call a very bare and odiously furnished place. The stalls are modern, without canopies. The places of the dignitaries and the names of the prebends have fortunately been allowed to survive, and are inscribed on small brass plates affixed to the stalls. The organ is in the triforium, and what is seen of the case is Gothic. The reredos and its surroundings are like every other.

Careful engravings of a hundred years ago show a very different state of things. The organ is on a massive classical screen. The stalls are also classical and very massive. There is a baldacchino of wood over the altar, with urns upon its corners. Farther east is a solid altar screen, classical in design, of wood, with a pediment, in which is a triangle surrounded by rays, enclosing certain Hebrew letters in gold. Cherubs contemplate these. There is a pulpit with a great sounding-board at the eastern end of the stalls on the north side, and there is a black and white marble pavement. Two ladies and a gentleman are admiring the general effect. From other sources I gather that the archdeacon's stall then, as now, was next to the bishop's throne at the south-eastern end of the stalls. His house almost faces the west front of the church, and is a fine red-brick building of William the Third's time.

Here Dr Haynes, already a mature man, took op his abode with his sister in the year 1810. The dignity had long been the object of his wishes, but his predecessor refused to depart until he had attained the age of ninety-two. About a week after he had held a modest festival in celebration of that ninety-second birthday, there came a morning, late in the year, when Dr Haynes, hurrying cheerfully into his breakfast-room, rubbing his hands and humming a tune, was greeted, and checked in his genial flow of spirits, by the sight of his sister, seated, indeed, in her usual place behind the tea-urn, but bowed forward and sobbing unrestrainedly into her handkerchief. "What—what is the matter? What bad news?" he began. "Oh, Johnny, you've not heard? The poor dear archdeacon!" "The archdeacon, yes? What is it—ill, is he?" "No, no; they found him on the staircase this morning; it is so shocking." "Is it possible! Dear, dear, poor Pulteney! Had there been any seizure?" "They don't think so, and that is almost the worst thing about it. It seems to have been all the fault of that stupid maid of theirs, Jane." Dr Haynes paused. "I don't quite understand, Letitia. How was the maid at fault?" "Why, as far as I can make out, there was a stair-rod missing, and she never mentioned it, and the poor archdeacon set his foot quite on the edge of the step—you know how slippery that oak is—and it seems he must have fallen almost the whole flight and broken his neck. It is so sad for poor Miss Pulteney. Of course, they will get rid of the girl at once. I never liked her." Miss Haynes's grief resumed its sway, but eventually relaxed so far as to permit of her taking some breakfast. Not so her brother, who, after standing in silence before the window for some minutes, left the room, and did not appear again that morning.

I need only add that the careless maid-servant was dismissed forthwith, but that the missing stair-rod was very shortly afterwards found *under* the stair-carpet—an additional proof, if any were needed, of extreme stupidity and carelessness on her part.

For a good many years Dr Haynes had been marked out by his ability, which seems to have been really considerable, as the likely successor of Archdeacon Pulteney, and no disappointment was in store for him. He was duly installed, and entered with zeal upon the discharge of those functions which are appropriate to one in his position. A considerable space in his journals is occupied with exclamations upon the confusion in which Archdeacon Pulteney had left the business of his office and the documents appertaining to it. Dues upon Wringham and Barnswood have been uncollected for something like twelve years, and are largely irrecoverable; no visitation has been held for seven years; four chancels are almost past mending. The persons deputized by the archdeacon have been nearly as incapable as himself. It was almost a matter for thankfulness that this state of things had not been permitted to continue, and a letter from a friend confirms this view. "o katecwn," it says (in rather cruel allusion to the Second Epistle to the Thessalonians), "is removed at last. My poor friend! Upon what a scene of confusion will you be entering! I give you my word that, on the last occasion of my crossing his threshold, there was no single paper that he could lay hands upon, no syllable of mine that he could hear, and no fact in connection with my business that he could remember. But now, thanks to a negligent maid and a loose stair-carpet, there is some prospect that necessary business will be transacted without a complete loss alike of voice and temper." This letter was tucked into a pocket in the cover of one of the diaries.

There can be no doubt of the new archdeacon's zeal and enthusiasm. "Give me but time to reduce to some semblance of order the innumerable errors and complications with which I am confronted, and I shall gladly and sincerely join with the aged Israelite in the canticle which too many, I fear, pronounce but with their lips." This reflection I find, not in a diary, but a letter; the doctor's friends seem to have returned his correspondence to his surviving sister. He does not confine himself, however, to reflections. His investigation of the rights and duties of his office are very searching and business-like, and there is a calculation in one place that a period of three years will just suffice to set the business of the Archdeaconry upon a proper footing. The estimate appears to have been an exact one. For just three years he is occupied in reforms; but I look in vain at the end of that time for the promised *Nunc dimittis*. He has now found a new sphere of activity. Hitherto his duties have precluded him from more than an occasional attendance at the Cathedral services. Now he begins to take an interest in the fabric and the music. Upon his struggles with the organist, an old gentleman who had been in office since 1786, I have no time to dwell; they were not attended with any marked success.

More to the purpose is his sudden growth of enthusiasm for the Cathedral itself and its furniture. There is a draft of a letter to Sylvanus Urban (which I do not think was ever sent) describing the stalls in the choir. As I have said, these were of fairly late date—of about the year 1700, in fact.

"The archdeacon's stall, situated at the south-east end, west of the episcopal throne (now so worthily occupied by the truly excellent prelate who adorns the See of Barchester), is distinguished by some curious ornamentation In addition to the arms of Dean West, by whose efforts the whole of the internal furniture of the choir was completed, the prayer-desk is terminated at the eastern extremity by three small but remarkable statuettes in the grotesque manner. One is an exquisitely modelled figure of a cat, whose crouching posture suggests with admirable spirit the suppleness, vigilance, and craft of the redoubted adversary of the genus Mus. Opposite to this is a figure seated upon a throne and invested with the attributes of royalty; but it is no earthly monarch whom the carver has sought to portray. His feet are studiously concealed by the long robe in which he is draped: but neither the crown nor the cap which he wears suffice to hide the prick-ears and curving horns which betray his Tartarean origin; and the hand which rests upon his knee is armed with talons of horrifying length and sharpness. Between these two figures stands a shape muffled in a long mantle. This might at first sight be mistaken for a monk or "friar of orders grey," for the head is cowled and a knotted cord depends from somewhere about the waist. A slight inspection, however, will lead to a very different conclusion. The knotted cord is quickly seen to be a halter, held by a hand all but concealed within the draperies; while the sunken features and, horrid to relate, the rent flesh upon the cheek-bones, proclaim the King of Terrors. These figures are evidently the production of no unskilled chisel; and should it chance that any of your correspondents are able to throw light upon their origin and significance, my obligations to your valuable miscellany will be largely increased."

There is more description in the paper, and, seeing that the woodwork in question has now disappeared, it has a considerable interest. A paragraph at the end is worth quoting:

"Some late researches among the Chapter accounts have shown me that the carving of the stalls was not, as was very usually reported, the work of Dutch artists, but was executed by a native of this city or district named Austin. The timber was procured from an oak copse in the vicinity, the property of the Dean and Chapter, known as Holywood. Upon a recent visit to the parish within whose boundaries it is situated, I learned from the aged and truly respectable incumbent that traditions still lingered amongst the inhabitants of the great size and age of the oaks employed to furnish the materials of the stately structure which has been, however imperfectly, described in the above lines. Of one in particular, which stood near the centre of the grove, it is remembered that it was known as the Hanging Oak. The propriety of that title is confirmed by the fact that a quantity of human bones was found in the soil about its roots, and that at certain times of the year it was the custom for those who wished to secure a successful issue to their affairs, whether of love or the ordinary business of life, to suspend from its boughs small images or puppets rudely fashioned of straw, twigs, or the like rustic materials."

So much for the archdeacon's archaeological investigations. To return to his career as it is to be gathered from his diaries. Those of his first three years of hard and careful work show him throughout in high spirits, and, doubtless, during this time, that reputation for hospitality and urbanity which is mentioned in his obituary notice was well deserved. After that, as time goes on, I see a shadow coming over him—destined to develop into utter blackness—which I cannot but think must have been reflected in his outward demeanour. He commits a good deal of his fears and troubles to his diary; there was no other outlet for them, He was unmarried, and his sister was not always with him. But I am much mistaken if he has told all that he might have told. A series of extracts shall be given:

*Aug.*30, 1816—The days begin to draw in more perceptibly than ever. Now that the Archdeaconry papers are reduced to order, I must find some further employment for the evening hours of autumn and winter. It is a great blow that Letitia's health will not allow her to stay through these months. Why not go on with my *Defence of Episcopacy*? It may be useful.

Sept. 15—Letitia has left me for Brighton.

*Oct.*11—Candles lit in the choir for the first time at evening prayers. It came as a shock: I find that I absolutely shrink from the dark season.

*Nov.*17—Much struck by the character of the carving on my desk: I do not know that I had ever carefully noticed it before.

My attention was called to it by an accident. During the Magnificat I was, I regret to say, almost overcome with sleep. My hand was resting on the back of the carved figure of a cat which is the nearest to me of the three figures on the end of my stall. I was not aware of this, for I was not looking in that direction, until I was startled by what seemed a softness, a feeling as of rather rough and coarse fur, and a sudden movement, as if the creature were twisting round its head to bite me. I regained complete consciousness in an instant, and I have some idea that I must have uttered a suppressed exclamation, for I noticed that Mr. Treasurer turned his head quickly in my direction. The impression of the unpleasant feeling was so strong that I found myself rubbing my hand upon my surplice. This accident led me to examine the figures after prayers more carefully than I had done before, and I realized for the first time with what skill they are executed.

Dec. 6—I do indeed miss Letitia's company. The evenings, after I have worked as long as I can at my Defence, are very trying. The house is too large for a lonely man, and visitors of any kind are too rare. I get an uncomfortable impression when going to my room that there is company of some kind. The fact is (I may as well formulate it to myself) that I hear voices. This, I am well aware, is a common symptom of incipient decay of the brain—and I believe that I should be less disquieted than I am if I had any suspicion that this was the cause. I have none—none whatever, nor is there anything in my family history to give colour to such an idea. Work, diligent work, and a punctual attention to the duties which fall to me is my best remedy, and I have little doubt that it will prove efficacious.

Jan. 1—my trouble is, I must confess it, increasing upon me. Last night, upon my return after midnight from the Deanery, I lit my candle to go upstairs. I was nearly at the top when something whispered tome, "Let me wish you a happy New Year." I could not be mistaken: it spoke distinctly and with a peculiar emphasis. Had I dropped my candle, as I all but did, I tremble to think what the consequences must have been. As it was, I managed to get up the last flight, and was quickly in my room with the door locked, and experienced no other disturbance.

Jan. 15—I had occasion to come downstairs last night to my workroom for my watch, which I had inadvertently left on my table when I went up to bed. I think I was at the top of the last flight when I had a sudden impression of a sharp whisper in my ear *"Take care."* I clutched the balusters and naturally looked round at once. Of course, there was nothing. After a moment I went on—it was no good turning hack—but I had as nearly as possible fallen: a cat—a large one by the feel of it—slipped between my feet, but again, of course, I saw nothing. It may have been the kitchen cat, but I do not think it was.

Feb. 27—A curious thing last night, which I should like to forget. Perhaps if I put it down here I may see it in its true proportion. I worked in the library from about 9 to 10. The hall and staircase seemed to be unusually full of what I can only call movement without sound: by this I mean that there seemed to be continuous going and coming, and that whenever I ceased writing to listen, or looked out into the hall, the stillness was absolutely unbroken. Nor, in going to my room at an earlier hour than usual—about half-past ten—was I conscious of anything that I could call a noise. It so happened that I had told John to come to my room for the letter to the bishop which I wished to have delivered early in the morning at the Palace. He was to sit up, therefore, and come for it when he heard me retire. This I had for the moment forgotten, though I had remembered to carry the letter with me to my room. But when, as I was winding up my watch, I heard a light tap at the door, and a low voice saying, "May I come in?" (which I most undoubtedly did hear), I recollected the fact, and took up the letter from my dressing-table, saying, "Certainly: come in." No one, however, answered my summons, and it was now that, as I strongly suspect, I committed an error: for I opened the door and held the letter out. There was certainly no one at that moment in the passage, but, in the instant of my standing there, the door at the end opened and John appeared carrying a candle. I asked him whether he had come to the door earlier; but am satisfied that he had not. I do not like the situation; but although my senses were very much on the alert, and though it was some time before I could sleep, I must allow that I perceived nothing further of an untoward character.

With the return of spring, when his sister came to live with him for some months, Dr Haynes's entries become more cheerful, and, indeed, no symptom of depression is discernible until the early part of September, when he was again left alone. And now, indeed, there is evidence that he was incommoded again, and that more pressingly. To this matter I will return in a moment, but I digress to put in a document which, rightly or wrongly, I believe to have a bearing on the thread of the story.

The account-books of Dr Haynes, preserved along with his other papers, show, from a date but little later than that of his institution as archdeacon, a quarterly payment of 25 to J.L. Nothing could have been made of this, had it stood by itself. But I connect with it a very dirty and ill-written letter, which, like another that I have quoted, was in a pocket in the cover of a diary. Of date or postmark there is no vestige, and the decipherment was not easy. It appears to run:

Dr Sr.

I have bin expetin to her off you theis last wicks, and not Haveing done so must supose you have not got mine witch was saying how me and my man had met in with bad times this season all seems to go cross with us on the farm and which way to look for the rent we have no knowledge of it this been the sad case with us if you would have the great [liberality *probably, but the exact spelling defies reproduction*] to send fourty pounds otherwise steps will have to he took which I should not wish. Has you was the Means of me losing my place with Dr Pulteney I think it is only just what I am asking and you know best what I could say if I was Put to it but I do not wish anything of that unpleasant Nature being one that always wish to have everything Pleasant about me.

Your obedt Servt,
Jane Lee

About the time at which I suppose this letter to have been written there is, in fact, a payment of 40 to J.L.

We return to the diary:

Oct.22—At evening prayers, during the Psalms, I had that same experience which I recollect from last year. I was resting my hand on one of the carved figures, as before (I usually avoid that of the cat now), and—I was going to have said—a change came over it, but that seems attributing too much importance to what must after all, be due to some physical affection in myself; at any rate, the wood seemed to become chilly and soft as if made of wet linen. I can assign the moment at which I became sensible of this. The choir were singing the words (*Set thou an ungodly man to be ruler over him and) let Satan stand at his right hand.*

The whispering in my house was more persistent tonight. I seemed not to be rid of it in my room. I have not noticed this before. A nervous man, which I am not, and hope I am not becoming, would have been much annoyed, if not alarmed, by it. The cat was on the stairs tonight. I think it sits there always. There *is* no kitchen cat.

Nov. 5—Here again I must note a matter I do not understand. I am much troubled in sleep. No definite image presented itself, but I was pursued by the very vivid impression that wet lips were whispering into my ear with great rapidity and emphasis for some time together. After this, I suppose, I fell asleep, but was awakened with a start by a feeling as if a hand were laid on my shoulder. To my intense alarm I found myself standing at the top of the lowest flight of the first staircase. The moon was shining brightly enough through the large window to let me see that there was a large cat on the second or third step. I can make no comment. I crept up to bed again, I do not know how. Yea, mine is a heavy burden, [Then follows a line or two which has been scratched out. I fancy I read something like "acted for the best".]

Not long after this it is evident to me that the archdeacon's firmness began to give way under the pressure of these phenomena. I omit as unnecessarily painful and distressing the ejaculations and prayers which, in the months of December and January, appear for the first time and become increasingly frequent. Throughout this time, however, he is obstinate in clinging to his post. Why he did not plead ill-health and take refuge at Bath or Brighton I cannot tell; my impression is that it would have done him no good; that he was a man who, if he had confessed himself beaten by the annoyances, would have succumbed at once, and that he was conscious of this. He did seek to palliate them by inviting visitors to his house. The result he has noted in this fashion:

> *Jan.* 7—I have prevailed on my cousin Allen to give me a few days, and he is to occupy the chamber next to mine.
> *Jan.*11—A still night. Allen slept well, but complained of the wind. My own experiences were as before: still whispering and whispering: what is it that he wants to say?
> *Jan.* 9—Allen thinks this a very noisy house. He thinks, too, that my cat is an unusually large and fine specimen, but very wild.
> *Jan.* 10—Allen and I in the library until 11. He left me twice to see what the maids were doing in the hall: returning the second time he told me he had seen one of them passing through the door at the end of the passage, and said if his wife were here she would soon get them into better order. I asked him what coloured dress the maid wore; he said grey or white. I supposed it would be so.
> *Jan.*11—Allen left me today. I must be firm.

These words, *I must be firm*, occur again and again on subsequent days; sometimes they are the only entry. In these cases they are in an unusually large hand, and dig into the paper in a way which must have broken the pen that wrote them.

Apparently the archdeacon's friends did not remark any change in his behaviour, and this gives me a high idea of his courage and determination. The diary tells us nothing more than I have indicated of the last days of his life. The end of it all must be told in the polished language of the obituary notice:

> The morning of the 26th of February was cold and tempestuous. At an early hour the servants had occasion to go into the front hall of the residence occupied by the lamented subject of these lines. What was their horror upon observing the form of their beloved and respected master lying upon the landing of the principal staircase in an attitude which inspired the gravest fears. Assistance was procured, and an universal consternation was experienced upon the discovery that he had been the object of a brutal and a murderous attack. The vertebral column was fractured in more than one place. This might have been the result of a fall: it appeared that the stair-carpet was loosened at one point. But, in addition to this, there were injuries inflicted upon the eyes, nose and month, as if by the agency of some savage animal, which, dreadful to relate, rendered those features unrecognizable. The vital spark was, it is needless to add, completely extinct, and had been so, upon the testimony of respectable medical authorities, for several hours. The author or authors of this mysterious outrage are alike buried in mystery, and the most active conjecture has hitherto failed to suggest a solution of the melancholy problem afforded by this appalling occurrence.

The writer goes on to reflect upon the probability that the writings of Mr. Shelley, Lord Byron, and M. Voltaire may have been instrumental in bringing about the disaster, and concludes by hoping, somewhat vaguely, that this event may "operate as an example to the rising generation"; but this portion of his remarks need not be quoted in full.

I had already formed the conclusion that Dr Haynes was responsible for the death of Dr Pulteney. But the incident connected with the carved figure of death upon the archdeacon's stall was a very perplexing feature. The conjecture that it had been cut out of the wood of the Hanging Oak was not difficult, but seemed impossible to substantiate. However, I paid a visit to Barchester, partly with the view of finding out whether there were any relics of the woodwork to be heard of. I was introduced by one of the canons to the curator of the local musenm, who was, my friend said, more likely to be able to give me information on the point than anyone else. I told this gentlernan of the description of certain carved figures and arms formerly on the stalls, and asked whether any had survived. He was able to show me the arms of Dean West and some other fragments. These, he said, had been got from an old resident, who had also once owned a figure—perhaps one of those which I was inquiring for. There was a very odd thing about that figure, he said. "The old man who had it told me that he picked it up in a woodyard, whence he had obtained the still extant pieces, and had taken it home for his children. On the way home he was fiddling about with it and it came in two in his hands, and a bit of paper dropped out. This he picked up and, just noticing that there was writing on it, put it into his pocket, and subsequently into a vase on his mantelpiece. I was at his house not very long ago, and happened to pick up the vase and turn it over to see whether there were any marks on it, and the paper tell into my hand. The old man, on my handing it to him, told me the story I have told you, and said I might keep the paper. It was crumpled and rather torn, so I have mounted it on a card, which I have here. If you can tell me what it means I shall be very glad, and also, I may say, a good deal surprised."

He gave me the card. The paper was quite legibly inscribed in an old hand, and this is what was on it:

When I grew in the Wood
I was water'd wth Blood
Now in the Church I stand
Who that touches me with his Hand
If a Bloody hand he bear
I councell him to be ware
Lest he be fetcht away
Whether by night or day,
But chiefly when the wind blows high
In a night of February.
This I drempt, 26 Febr. Ao 1699. John Austin.

"I suppose it is a charm or a spell: wouldn't you call it something of that kind?" said the curator.

"Yes," I said, "I suppose one might. What became of the figure in which it was concealed?"

"Oh, I forgot," said he. "The old man told me it was so ugly and frightened his children so much that he burnt it."

But a lady has written me an earnest letter saying that fairy tales ought not to be taught to children even if they are true. She says that it is cruel to tell children fairy tales, because it frightens them. You might just as well say that it is cruel to give girls sentimental novels because it makes them cry. All this kind of talk is based on that complete forgetting of what a child is like which has been the firm foundation of so many educational schemes. If you keep bogies and goblins away from children they would make them up for themselves. One small child in the dark can invent more hells than Swedenborg. One small child can imagine monsters too big and black to get into any picture, and give them names too unearthly and cacophonous to have occurred in the cries of any lunatic. The child, to begin with, commonly likes horrors, and he continues to indulge in them even when he does not like them. There is just as much difficulty in saying exactly where pure pain begins in his case, as there is in ours when we walk of our own free will into the torture-chamber of a great tragedy. The fear does not come from fairy tales; the fear comes from the universe of the soul.

—G. K. Chesterton, "The Red Angel."

THE TREAſURE OF ABBOT THOMAſ

M. R. James

I

Verum usque in praesentem diem multa garriunt inter se Canonici de abscondito quodam istius Abbatis Thomae thesauro, quem saepe, quanquam adhuc incassum, quaesiverunt Steinfeld-enses. Ipsum enim Thomam adhuc florida in aetate existentem ingentem auri massam circa monasterium defodisse perhibent; de quo multoties interrogatus ubi esset, cum risu respondere solitus erat: "Job, Johannes, et Zacharias vel vobis vel posteris indicabunt"; idemque aliquando adiicere se inventuris minime invisurum. Inter alia huius Abbatis opera, hoc memoria praecipue dignum iudico quod fenestram magnam in orientali parte alae australis in ecclesia sua imaginibus optime in vitro depictis impleverit: id quod et ipsius effigies et insignia ibidem posita demonstrant. Domum quoque Abbatialem fere totam restauravit: puteo in atrio ipsius effosso et lapidibus marmoreis pulchre caelatis exornato. Decessit autem, morte aliquantulum subitanea perculsus, aetatis suae anno lxxiido, incarnationis vero Dominicae mdxxix°.

"I suppose I shall have to translate this," said the antiquary to himself, as he finished copying the above lines from that rather rare and exceedingly diffuse book, the *Sertum Steinfeldense Norbertinum.*[1] "Well,

[1] An account of the Premonstratensian Abbey of Steinfeld, in the Eiffel, with lives of the Abbots, published at Cologne in 1712 by Christian Albert Erhard, a resident in the district. The epithet *Norbertinum* is due to the fact that St. Norbert was founder of the Premonstratensian Order.

315

it may as well be done first as last," and accordingly the following rendering was very quickly produced:

> Up to the present day there is much gossip among the Can-
> ons about a certain hidden treasure of this Abbot Thomas, for
> which those of Steinfeld have often made search, though hith-
> erto in vain. The story is that Thomas, while yet in the vigour of
> life, concealed a very large quantity of gold somewhere in the
> monastery. He was often asked where it was, and always answered,
> with a laugh: "Job, John, and Zechariah will tell either you or
> your successors." He sometimes added that he should feel no
> grudge against those who might find it. Among other works car-
> ried out by this Abbot I may specially mention his filling the
> great window at the east end of the south aisle of the church with
> figures admirably painted on glass, as his effigy and arms in the
> window attest. He also restored almost the whole of the Abbot's
> lodging, and dug a well in the court of it, which he adorned with
> beautiful carvings in marble. He died rather suddenly in the
> seventy-second year of his age, AD 1529.

The object which the antiquary had before him at the moment was
that of tracing the whereabouts of the painted windows of the Abbey
Church of Steinfeld. Shortly after the Revolution, a very large quantity of
painted glass made its way from the dissolved abbeys of Germany and
Belgium to this country, and may now be seen adorning various of our
parish churches, cathedrals, and private chapels. Steinfeld Abbey was
among the most considerable of these involuntary contributors to our
artistic possessions (I am quoting the somewhat ponderous preamble of
the book which the antiquary wrote), and the greater part of the glass
from that institution can be identified without much difficulty by the help,
either of the numerous inscriptions in which the place is mentioned, or
of the subjects of the windows, in which several well-defined cycles or
narratives were represented.

The passage with which I began my story had set the antiquary on
the track of another identification. In a private chapel—no matter where—
he had seen three large figures, each occupying a whole light in a window, and evidently the work of one artist. Their style made it plain that
the artist had been a German of the sixteenth century; but hitherto the
more exact localizing of them had been a puzzle. They represented—will
you be surprised to hear it?—*Job Patriarcha, Johannes Evangelista,
Zacharias Propheta*, and each of them held a book or scroll, inscribed
with a sentence from his writings. These, as a matter of course, the antiquary had noted, and had been struck by the curious way in which they

differed from any text of the Vulgate that he had been able to examine. Thus the scroll in Job's hand was inscribed: "*Auro est locus in quo absconditur*" (for "conflatur");[2] on the book of John was: "Habent in vestimentis suis scripturam quam nemo novit"[3] (for "*in vestimento scriptum*", the following words being taken from another verse); and Zacharias had: "*Super lapidem unum septem oculi sunt*"[4] (which alone of the three presents an unaltered text).

A sad perplexity it had been to our investigator to think why these three personages should have been placed together in one window. There was no bond of connection between them, either historic, symbolic, or doctrinal, and he could only suppose that they must have formed part of a very large series of Prophets and Apostles, which might have filled, say, all the clerestory windows of some capacious church. But the passage from the *Sertum* had altered the situation by showing that the names of the actual personages represented in the glass now in Lord D—'s chapel had been constantly on the lips of Abbot Thomas von Eschenhausen of Steinfeld, and that this Abbot had put up a painted window, probably about the year 1520, in the south aisle of his abbey church. It was no very wild conjecture that the three figures might have formed part of Abbot Thomas's offering; it was one which, moreover, could probably be confirmed or set aside by another careful examination of the glass. And, as Mr. Somerton was a man of leisure, he set out on pilgrimage to the private chapel with very little delay. His conjecture was confirmed to the full. Not only did the style and technique of the glass suit perfectly with the date and place required, but in another window of the chapel he found some glass, known to have been bought along with the figures, which contained the arms of Abbot Thomas von Eschenhausen.

At intervals during his researches Mr. Somerton had been haunted by the recollection of the gossip about the hidden treasure, and, as he thought the matter over, it became more and more obvious to him that if the Abbot meant anything by the enigmatical answer which he gave to his questioners, he must have meant that the secret was to be found somewhere in the window he had placed in the abbey church. It was undeniable, furthermore, that the first of the curiously-selected texts on the scrolls in the window might be taken to have a reference to hidden treasure. Every feature, therefore, or mark which could possibly assist in elucidating the riddle which, he felt sure, the Abbot had set to posterity he noted with scrupulous care, and, returning to his Berkshire manor-house,

[2] There is a place for gold where it is hidden.
[3] They have on their raiment a writing which no man knoweth.
[4] Upon one stone are seven eyes.

consumed many a pint of the midnight oil over his tracings and sketches. After two or three weeks, a day came when Mr. Somerton announced to his man that he must pack his own and his master's things for a short journey abroad, whither for the moment we will not follow him.

II

Mr. Gregory, the Rector of Parsbury, had strolled out before break-fast, it being a fine autumn morning, as far as the gate of his carriage-drive, with intent to meet the postman and sniff the cool air. Nor was he disappointed of either purpose. Before he had had time to answer more than ten or eleven of the miscellaneous questions propounded to him in the lightness of their hearts by his young offspring, who had accom-panied him, the postman was seen approaching; and among the morning's budget was one letter bearing a foreign postmark and stamp (which became at once the objects of an eager competition among the youthful Gregorys), and was addressed in an uneducated, but plainly an English hand.

When the Rector opened it, and turned to the signature, he realized that it came from the confidential valet of his friend and squire, Mr. Somerton. Thus it ran:

> Honourd Sir,
> Has I am in a great anxeity about Master I write at is Wish to Beg you Sir if you could be so good as Step over. Master Has add a Nastey Shock and keeps His Bedd. I never Have known Him like this but No wonder and Nothing will serve but you Sir. Master says would I mintion the Short Way Here is Drive to Cobblince and take a Trap. Hopeing I Have maid all Plain, but am much Confused in Myself what with Anxiatey and Weakfulness at Night. If I might be so Bold Sir it will be a Pleasure to see a Honnest Brish Face among all These Forig ones. I am Sir
> Your obedt Servt
> William Brown
>
> P.S.—The Villiage for Town I will not Turm It is name Steenfeld.

The reader must be left to picture to himself in detail the surprise, confusion, and hurry of preparation into which the receipt of such a letter would be likely to plunge a quiet Berkshire parsonage in the year of grace 1859. It is enough for me to say that a train to town was caught in the course of the day, and that Mr. Gregory was able to secure a cabin in the Antwerp boat and a place in the Coblentz train. Nor was it difficult to manage the transit from that centre to Steinfeld.

I labour under a grave disadvantage as narrator of this story in that I have never visited Steinfeld myself, and that neither of the principal actors in the episode (from whom I derive my information) was able to give me anything but a vague and rather dismal idea of its appearance. I gather that it is a small place, with a large church despoiled of its ancient fittings; a number of rather ruinous great buildings, mostly of the seventeenth century, surround this church; for the abbey, in common with most of those on the Continent, was rebuilt in a luxurious fashion by its inhabitants at that period. It has not seemed to me worth while to lavish money on a visit to the place, for though it is probably far more attractive than either Mr. Somerton or Mr. Gregory thought it, there is evidently little, if anything, of first-rate interest to be seen—except, perhaps, one thing, which I should not care to see.

The inn where the English gentleman and his servant were lodged is, or was, the only "possible" one in the village. Mr. Gregory was taken to it at once by his driver, and found Mr. Brown waiting at the door. Mr. Brown, a model when in his Berkshire home of the impassive whiskered race who are known as confidential valets, was now egregiously out of his element, in a light tweed suit, anxious, almost irritable, and plainly anything but master of the situation. His relief at the sight of the "honest British face" of his Rector was unmeasured, but words to describe it were denied him. He could only say:

"Well, I ham pleased, I'm sure, sir, to see you. And so I'm sure, sir, will master."

"How is your master, Brown?" Mr. Gregory eagerly put in.

"I think he's better, sir, thank you; but he's had a dreadful time of it. I 'ope he's gettin' some sleep now, but—"

"What has been the matter—I couldn't make out from your letter? Was it an accident of any kind?"

"Well, sir, I 'ardly know whether I'd better speak about it. Master was very partickler he should be the one to tell you. But there's no bones broke—that's one thing I'm sure we ought to be thankful—"

"What does the doctor say?" asked Mr. Gregory.

They were by this time outside Mr. Somerton's bedroom door, and speaking in low tones. Mr. Gregory, who happened to be in front, was feeling for the handle, and chanced to run his fingers over the panels. Before Brown could answer, there was a terrible cry from within the room.

"In God's name, who is that?" were the first words they heard. "Brown, is it?"

"Yes, sir—me, sir, and Mr. Gregory," Brown hastened to answer, and there was an audible groan of relief in reply.

They entered the room, which was darkened against the afternoon sun, and Mr. Gregory saw, with a shock of pity, how drawn, how damp with drops of fear, was the usually calm face of his friend, who, sitting up in the curtained bed, stretched out a shaking hand to welcome him.

"Better for seeing you, my dear Gregory," was the reply to the Rector's first question, and it was palpably true.

After five minutes of conversation Mr. Somerton was more his own man, Brown afterwards reported, than he had been for days. He was able to eat a more than respectable dinner, and talked confidently of being fit to stand a journey to Coblentz within twenty-four hours.

"But there's one thing," he said, with a return of agitation which Mr. Gregory did not like to see, "which I must beg you to do for me, my dear Gregory. Don't," he went on, laying his hand on Gregory's to forestall any interruption— "don't ask me what it is, or why I want it done. I'm not up to explaining it yet; it would throw me back—undo all the good you have done me by coming. The only word I will say about it is that you run no risk whatever by doing it, and that Brown can and will show you tomorrow what it is. It's merely to put back—to keep—something—No; I can't speak of it yet. Do you mind calling Brown?"

"Well, Somerton," said Mr. Gregory, as he crossed the room to the door, "I won't ask for any explanations till you see fit to give them. And if this bit of business is as easy as you represent it to be, I will very gladly undertake it for you the first thing in the morning."

"Ah, I was sure you would, my dear Gregory; I was certain I could rely on you. I shall owe you more thanks than I can tell. Now, here is Brown. Brown, one word with you."

"Shall I go?" interjected Mr. Gregory.

"Not at all. Dear me, no. Brown, the first thing tomorrow morning— (you don't mind early hours, I know, Gregory) you must take the Rector to—there, you know" (a nod from Brown, who looked grave and anxious), "and he and you will put that back. You needn't be in the least alarmed; it's *perfectly* safe in the daytime. You know what I mean. It lies on the step, you know, where—where we put it." (Brown swallowed dryly once or twice, and, failing to speak, bowed.) "And—yes, that's all. Only this one other word, my dear Gregory. If you can manage to keep from questioning Brown about this matter, I shall be still more bound to you. Tomorrow evening, at latest, if all goes well, I shall be able, I believe, to tell you the whole story from start to finish. And now I'll wish you good night. Brown will be with me—he sleeps here—and if I were you, I should lock my door. Yes, be particular to do that. They—they like it, the people here, and it's better. Good night, good night."

They parted upon this, and if Mr. Gregory woke once or twice in the small hours and fancied he heard a fumbling about the lower part of his locked door, it was, perhaps, no more than what a quiet man, suddenly plunged into a strange bed and the heart of a mystery, might reasonably expect. Certainly he thought, to the end of his days, that he had heard such a sound twice or three times between midnight and dawn.

He was up with the sun, and out in company with Brown soon after. Perplexing as was the service he had been asked to perform for Mr. Somerton, it was not a difficult or an alarming one, and within half an hour from his leaving the inn it was over. What it was I shall not as yet divulge.

Later in the morning Mr. Somerton, now almost himself again, was able to make a start from Steinfeld; and that same evening, whether at Coblentz or at some intermediate stage on the journey I am not certain, he settled down to the promised explanation. Brown was present, but how much of the matter was ever really made plain to his comprehension he would never say, and I am unable to conjecture.

III

This was Mr. Somerton's story:

"You know roughly, both of you, that this expedition of mine was undertaken with the object of tracing something in connection with some old painted glass in Lord D—'s private chapel. Well, the starting-point of the whole matter lies in this passage from an old printed book, to which I will ask your attention."

And at this point Mr. Somerton went carefully over some ground with which we are already familiar.

"On my second visit to the chapel," he went on, "my purpose was to take every note I could of figures, lettering, diamond-scratchings on the glass, and even apparently accidental markings. The first point which I tackled was that of the inscribed scrolls. I could not doubt that the first of these, that of Job—'There is a place for the gold where it is hidden'— with its intentional alteration, must refer to the treasure; so I applied myself with some confidence to the next, that of St John—'They have on their vestures a writing which no man knoweth.' The natural question will have occurred to you: Was there an inscription on the robes of the figures? I could see none; each of the three had a broad black border to his mantle, which made a conspicuous and rather ugly feature in the window. I was nonplussed, I will own, and but for a curious bit of luck I think I should have left the search where the Canons of Steinfeld had left it before me. But it so happened that there was a good deal of dust on the surface of the glass, and Lord D—, happening to come in, noticed my blackened hands, and kindly insisted on sending for a Turk's-head broom to clean down the window. There must, I suppose, have been a rough piece in the broom; anyhow, as it passed over the border of one of the mantles, I noticed that it left a long scratch, and that some yellow stain instantly showed up. I asked the man to stop his work for a moment, and ran up the ladder to examine the place. The yellow stain was there, sure enough, and what had come away was a thick black pigment, which had evidently been laid on with the brush after the glass had been burnt, and could therefore be easily scraped off without doing any harm. I scraped, accordingly, and you will hardly believe—no, I do you an injustice; you will have guessed already—that I found under this black pigment two or three clearly-formed capital letters in yellow stain on a clear ground. Of course, I could hardly contain my delight.

"I told Lord D— that I had detected an inscription which I thought might be very interesting, and begged to be allowed to uncover the whole of it. He made no difficulty about it whatever, told me to do exactly as I pleased, and then, having an engagement, was obliged—rather to my relief, I must say—to leave me. I set to work at once, and found the task a fairly easy one. The pigment, disintegrated, of course, by time, came off almost at a touch, and I don't think that it took me a couple of hours, all told, to clean the whole of the black borders in all three lights. Each of the figures had, as the inscription said, 'a writing on their vestures which nobody knew.'

"This discovery, of course, made it absolutely certain to my mind that I was on the right track. And, now, what was the inscription? While I was cleaning the glass I almost took pains not to read the lettering, saving up the treat until I had got the whole thing clear. And when that was done, my dear Gregory, I assure you I could almost have cried from sheer disappointment. What I read was only the most hopeless jumble of letters that was ever shaken up in a hat. Here it is:

Job.	DREVICIOPEDMOOMSMVIVLISLCAVIBASBATAOVT
St John.	RDIIEAMRLESIPVSPODSEEIRSETTAAESGIAVVNR
Zechariah.	FTEEAILNQDPVAIVMTLEEATTOHIOONVMCAAT.H.Q.E

"Blank as I felt and must have looked for the first few minutes, my disappointment didn't last long. I realized almost at once that I was dealing with a cipher or cryptogram; and I reflected that it was likely to be of a pretty simple kind, considering its early date. So I copied the letters with the most anxious care. Another little point, I may tell you, turned up in the process which confirmed my belief in the cipher. After copying the letters on Job's robe I counted them, to make sure that I had them right. There were thirty-eight; and, just as I finished going through them, my eye fell on a scratching made with a sharp point on the edge of the border. It was simply the number xxxviii in Roman numerals. To cut the matter short, there was a similar note, as I may call it, in each of the other lights; and that made it plain to me that the glass-painter had had very strict orders from Abbot Thomas about the inscription, and had taken pains to get it correct.

"Well, after that discovery you may imagine how minutely I went over the whole surface of the glass in search of further light. Of course, I did not neglect the inscription on the scroll of Zechariah—'Upon one stone are seven eyes,' but I very quickly concluded that this must refer to some mark on a stone which could only be found in situ, where the treasure was concealed. To be short, I made all possible notes and sketches and tracings, and then came back to Parsbury to work out the cipher at leisure. Oh, the agonies I went through! I thought myself very clever at first, for I made sure that the key would be found in some of the old books on secret writing. The *Steganographia* of Joachim Trithemius, who was an earlier contemporary of Abbot Thomas, seemed particularly promising; so I got that, and Selenius's *Cryptographia* and Bacon's *de Augmentis Scientiarum*, and some more. But I could hit upon nothing. Then I tried the principle of the 'most frequent letter,' taking first Latin and then German as a basis. That didn't help, either; whether it ought to have done so, I am not clear. And then I came back to the window itself, and read over my notes, hoping almost against hope that the Abbot might himself have somewhat supplied the key I wanted. I could make nothing out of the colour or pattern of the robes. There were no landscape backgrounds with subsidiary objects; there was nothing in the canopies. The only resource possible seemed to be in the attitudes of the figures. 'Job,' I read: 'scroll in left hand, forefinger of right hand extended upwards. John: holds inscribed book in left hand; with right hand blesses, with two fingers. Zechariah: scroll in left hand; right hand extended upwards, as Job, but with three fingers pointing up.' In other words, I reflected, Job has *one* finger extended, John has *two*, Zechariah has *three*. May not there be a numeral key concealed in that? My dear Gregory," said Mr. Somerton, laying his hand on his friend's knee, "that was the key. I didn't get it to fit at first, but after two or three trials I saw what was meant. After the first letter of the inscription you skip *one* letter, after the next you skip *two*, and after that skip *three*. Now look at the result I got. I've underlined the letters which form words:

DREVICIOPEDMOOMSMVIVLISLCAVIBASBATAOVT

RDIIEAMRLESIPVSPODSEEIRSETTAAESGIAVNNR

FTEEAILNQDPVAIVMTLEEATTOHIOONVMCAAT.H.Q.E.

"Do you see it? *Decem millia auri reposita sunt in puteo in at...* (Ten thousand [pieces] of gold are laid up in a well in...), followed by an incomplete word beginning at. So far so good. I tried the same plan with the remaining letters; but it wouldn't work, and I fancied that perhaps the placing of dots after the three last letters might indicate some difference of procedure. Then I thought to myself, 'Wasn't there some allusion to a well in the account of Abbot Thomas in that book the *Sertum*?' Yes, there was: he built a *puteus in atrio* (a well in the court). There, of course, was my word *atrio*. The next step was to copy out the remaining letters of the inscription, omitting those I had already used. That gave what you will see on this slip:

RVIIOPDOOSMVVISCAVBSBTAOTDIEAMLSIVSPDEERS
ETAEGIANRFEEALQDVAIMLEATTHOOVMCA.H.Q.E.

"Now, I knew what the first three letters I wanted were namely, *rio*—to complete the word *atrio*; and, as you will see, these are all to be found in the first five letters. I was a little confused at first by the occurrence of two i's, but very soon I saw that every alternate letter must be taken in the remainder of the inscription. You can work it out for yourself; the result, continuing where the first 'round' left off, is this: —*rio domus abbatialis de Steinfeld a me, Thoma, qui posui custodem super ea. Gare à qui la touche.*

"So the whole secret was out:

"Ten thousand pieces of gold are laid up in the well in the court of the Abbot's house of Steinfeld by me, Thomas, who have set a guardian over them. *Gare à qui la touche.*

"The last words, I ought to say, are a device which Abbot Thomas had adopted. I found it with his arms in another piece of glass at Lord D—'s, and he drafted it bodily into his cipher, though it doesn't quite fit in point of grammar.

"Well, what would any human being have been tempted to do, my dear Gregory, in my place? Could he have helped setting off, as I did, to Steinfeld, and tracing the secret literally to the fountain-head? I don't believe he could. Anyhow, I couldn't, and, as I needn't tell you, I found myself at Steinfeld as soon as the resources of civilization could put me there, and installed myself in the inn you saw. I must tell you that I was not altogether free from forebodings—on one hand of disappointment, on the other of danger. There was always the possibility that Abbot Thomas's well might have been wholly obliterated, or else that someone, ignorant of cryptograms, and guided only by luck, might have stumbled on the treasure before me. And then"—there was a very perceptible shaking of the voice here—"I was not entirely easy, I need not mind confessing, as to the meaning of the words about the guardian of the treasure. But, if you don't mind, I'll say no more about that until—until it becomes necessary.

"At the first possible opportunity Brown and I began exploring the place. I had naturally represented myself as being interested in the re-mains of the abbey, and we could not avoid paying a visit to the church, impatient as I was to be elsewhere. Still, it did interest me to see the windows where the glass had been, and especially that at the east end of the south aisle. In the tracery lights of that I was startled to see some fragments and coats-of-arms remaining—Abbot Thomas's shield was there, and a small figure with a scroll inscribed *Oculos habent, et non videbunt* (They have eyes, and shall not see), which, I take it, was a hit of the Abbot at his Canons.

"But, of course, the principal object was to find the Abbot's house. There is no prescribed place for this, so far as I know, in the plan of a monastery; you can't predict of it, as you can of the chapter-house, that it will be on the eastern side of the cloister, or, as of the dormitory, that it will communicate with a transept of the church. I felt that if I asked many questions I might awaken lingering memories of the treasure, and I thought it best to try first to discover it for myself. It was not a very long or difficult search. That three-sided court south-east of the church, with deserted piles of building round it, and grass-grown pavement, which you saw this morning, was the place. And glad enough I was to see that it was put to no use, and was neither very far from our inn nor overlooked by any inhabited building; there were only orchards and paddocks on the slopes east of the church. I can tell you that fine stone glowed wonder-fully in the rather watery yellow sunset that we had on the Tuesday after-noon.

"Next, what about the well? There was not much doubt about that, as you can testify. It is really a very remarkable thing. That curb is, I think, of Italian marble, and the carving I thought must be Italian also. There were reliefs, you will perhaps remember, of Eliezer and Rebekah, and of Jacob opening the well for Rachel, and similar subjects; but, by way of disarming suspicion, I suppose, the Abbot had carefully abstained from any of his cynical and allusive inscriptions.

"I examined the whole structure with the keenest interest, of course—a square well-head with an opening in one side; an arch over it, with a wheel for the rope to pass over, evidently in very good condition still, for it had been used within sixty years, or perhaps even later, though not quite recently. Then there was the question of depth and access to the interior. I suppose the depth was about sixty to seventy feet; and as to

the other point, it really seemed as if the Abbot had wished to lead search-
ers up to the very door of his treasure-house, for, as you tested for yourself, there were big blocks of stone bonded into the masonry, and leading
down in a regular staircase round and round the inside of the well.

"It seemed almost too good to be true. I wondered if there was a trap—
if the stones were so contrived as to tip over when a weight was placed on
them; but I tried a good many with my own weight and with my stick,
and all seemed, and actually were, perfectly firm. Of course, I resolved
that Brown and I would make an experiment that very night.

"I was well prepared. Knowing the sort of place I should have to
explore, I had brought a sufficiency of good rope and bands of webbing
to surround my body, and crossbars to hold to, as well as lanterns and
candles and crowbars, all of which would go into a single carpet-bag and
excite no suspicion. I satisfied myself that my rope would be long enough,
and that the wheel for the bucket was in good working order, and then
we went home to dinner.

"I had a little cautious conversation with the landlord, and made out
that he would not be overmuch surprised if I went out for a stroll with
my man about nine o'clock, to make (Heaven forgive me!) a sketch of the
abbey by moonlight. I asked no questions about the well, and am not
likely to do so now. I fancy I know as much about it as anyone in Steinfeld:
at least"—with a strong shudder—"I don't want to know any more.

"Now we come to the crisis, and, though I hate to think of it, I feel
sure, Gregory, that it will be better for me in all ways to recall it just
as it happened. We started, Brown and I, at about nine with our bag, and
attracted no attention; for we managed to slip out at the hinder end of
the inn-yard into an alley which brought us quite to the edge of the
village. In five minutes we were at the well, and for some little time we
sat on the edge of the well-head to make sure that no one was stirring or
spying on us. All we heard was some horses cropping grass out of sight
farther down the eastern slope. We were perfectly unobserved, and had
plenty of light from the gorgeous full moon to allow us to get the rope
properly fitted over the wheel. Then I secured the band round my body
beneath the arms. We attached the end of the rope very securely to a ring
in the stonework. Brown took the lighted lantern and followed me; I had
a crowbar. And so we began to descend cautiously, feeling every step
before we set foot on it, and scanning the walls in search of any marked
stone.

"Half aloud I counted the steps as we went down, and we got as far as
the thirty-eighth before I noted anything at all irregular in the surface of
the masonry. Even here there was no mark, and I began to feel very blank,
and to wonder if the Abbot's cryptogram could possibly be an elaborate
hoax. At the forty-ninth step the staircase ceased. It was with a very

sinking heart that I began retracing my steps, and when I was back on the thirty-eighth—Brown, with the lantern, being a step or two above me— I scrutinized the little bit of irregularity in the stonework with all my might; but there was no vestige of a mark.

"Then it struck me that the texture of the surface looked just a little smoother than the rest, or, at least, in some way different. It might possibly be cement and not stone. I gave it a good blow with my iron bar. There was a decidedly hollow sound, though that might be the result of our being in a well. But there was more. A great flake of cement dropped on to my feet, and I saw marks on the stone underneath. I had tracked the Abbot down, my dear Gregory; even now I think of it with a certain pride. It took but a very few more taps to clear the whole of the cement away, and I saw a slab of stone about two feet square, upon which was engraven a cross. Disappointment again, but only for a moment. It was you, Brown, who reassured me by a casual remark. You said, if I remember right:

"'It's a funny cross; looks like a lot of eyes.'

"I snatched the lantern out of your hand, and saw with inexpressible pleasure that the cross was composed of seven eyes, four in a vertical line, three horizontal. The last of the scrolls in the window was explained in the way I had anticipated. Here was my 'stone with the seven eyes.' So far the Abbot's data had been exact, and, as I thought of this, the anxiety about the 'guardian' returned upon me with increased force. Still, I wasn't going to retreat now.

"Without giving myself time to think, I knocked away the cement all round the marked stone, and then gave it a prise on the right side with my crowbar. It moved at once, and I saw that it was but a thin light slab, such as I could easily lift out myself, and that it stopped the entrance to a cavity. I did lift it out unbroken, and set it on the step, for it might be very important to us to be able to replace it. Then I waited for several minutes on the step just above. I don't know why, but I think to see if any dreadful thing would rush out. Nothing happened. Next I lit a candle, and very cautiously I placed it inside the cavity, with some idea of seeing whether there were foul air, and of getting a glimpse of what was inside. There was some foulness of air which nearly extinguished the flame, but in no long time it burned quite steadily. The hole went some little way back, and also on the right and left of the entrance, and I could see some rounded light-coloured objects within which might be bags. There was no use in waiting. I faced the cavity, and looked in. There was nothing immediately in the front of the hole. I put my arm in and felt to the right, very gingerly...

"Just give me a glass of cognac, Brown. I'll go on in a moment, Gregory...

"Well, I felt to the right, and my fingers touched something curved, that felt—yes—more or less like leather; dampish it was, and evidently part of a heavy, full thing. There was nothing, I must say, to alarm one. I grew bolder, and putting both hands in as well as I could, I pulled it to me, and it came. It was heavy, but moved more easily than I expected. As I pulled it towards the entrance, my left elbow knocked over and extinguished the candle. I got the thing fairly in front of the mouth and began drawing it out. Just then Brown gave a sharp ejaculation and ran quickly up the steps with the lantern. He will tell you why in a moment. Startled as I was, I looked round after him, and saw him stand for a minute at the top and then walk away a few yards. Then I heard him call softly, 'All right, sir,' and went on pulling out the great bag, in complete darkness. It hung for an instant on the edge of the hole, then slipped forward on to my chest, and *put its arms round my neck*.

"My dear Gregory, I am telling you the exact truth. I believe I am now acquainted with the extremity of terror and repulsion which a man can endure without losing his mind. I can only just manage to tell you now the bare outline of the experience. I was conscious of a most horrible smell of mould, and of a cold kind of face pressed against my own, and moving slowly over it, and of several—I don't know how many—legs or arms or tentacles or something clinging to my body. I screamed out, Brown says, like a beast, and fell away backward from the step on which I stood, and the creature slipped downwards, I suppose, on to that same step. Providentially the band round me held firm. Brown did not lose his head, and was strong enough to pull me up to the top and get me over the edge quite promptly. How he managed it exactly I don't know, and I think he would find it hard to tell you. I believe he contrived to hide our implements in the deserted building near by, and with very great difficulty he got me back to the inn. I was in no state to make explanations, and Brown knows no German; but next morning I told the people some tale of having had a bad fall in the abbey ruins, which, I suppose, they believed. And now, before I go further, I should just like you to hear what Brown's experiences during those few minutes were. Tell the Rector, Brown, what you told me."

"Well, sir," said Brown, speaking low and nervously, "it was just this way. Master was busy down in front of the 'ole, and I was 'olding the lantern and looking on, when I 'eard somethink drop in the water from the top, as I thought. So I looked up, and I see someone's 'ead lookin' over at us. I s'pose I must ha' said somethink, and I 'eld the light up and run up the steps, and my light shone right on the face. That was a bad un, sir, if ever I see one! A holdish man, and the face very much fell in, and larfin, as I thought. And I got up the steps as quick pretty nigh as I'm tellin' you, and when I was out on the ground there warn't a sign of any person. There 'adn't been the time for anyone to get away, let alone a hold chap, and I made sure he warn't crouching down by the well, nor nothink. Next thing I hear master cry out somethink 'orrible, and hall I see was him hanging out by the rope, and, as master says, 'owever I got him up I couldn't tell you."

"You hear that, Gregory?" said Mr. Somerton. "Now, does any explanation of that incident strike you?"

"The whole thing is so ghastly and abnormal that I must own it puts me quite off my balance; but the thought did occur to me that possibly the—well, the person who set the trap might have come to see the success of his plan."

"Just so, Gregory, just so. I can think of nothing else so—likely, I should say, if such a word had a place anywhere in my story. I think it must have been the Abbot... Well, I haven't much more to tell you. I spent a miserable night, Brown sitting up with me. Next day I was no better; unable to get up; no doctor to be had; and, if one had been available, I doubt if he could have done much for me. I made Brown write off to you, and spent a second terrible night. And, Gregory, of this I am sure, and I think it affected me more than the first shock, for it lasted longer: there was someone or something on the watch outside my door the whole night. I almost fancy there were two. It wasn't only the faint noises I heard from time to time all through the dark hours, but there was the smell—the hideous smell of mould. Every rag I had had on me on that first evening I had stripped off and made Brown take it away. I believe he stuffed the things into the stove in his room; and yet the smell was there, as intense as it had been in the well; and, what is more, it came from outside the door. But with the first glimmer of dawn it faded out, and the sounds ceased, too; and that convinced me that the thing or things were creatures of darkness, and could not stand the daylight; and so I was sure that if anyone could put back the stone, it or they would be powerless until someone else took it away again. I had to wait until you came to get that done. Of course, I couldn't send Brown to do it by himself, and still less could I tell anyone who belonged to the place.

"Well, there is my story; and if you don't believe it, I can't help it. But I think you do."

"Indeed," said Mr. Gregory, "I can find no alternative. I must believe it! I saw the well and the stone myself, and had a glimpse, I thought, of the bags or something else in the hole. And, to be plain with you, Somerton, I believe my door was watched last night, too."

"I dare say it was, Gregory; but, thank goodness, that is over. Have you, by the way, anything to tell about your visit to that dreadful place?"

"Very little," was the answer. "Brown and I managed easily enough to get the slab into its place, and he fixed it very firmly with the irons and wedges you had desired him to get, and we contrived to smear the surface with mud so that it looks just like the rest of the wall. One thing I did notice in the carving on the well-head, which I think must have escaped you. It was a horrid, grotesque shape perhaps more like a toad than anything else, and there was a label by it inscribed with the two words, '*Depositum custodi*.'" [5]

[5] Keep that which is committed to thee.

THE UNCOMMON PRAYER-BOOK

M. R. James

Mr. Davidson was spending the first week in January alone in a country town. A combination of circumstances had driven him to that drastic
course: his nearest relations were enjoying winter sports abroad, and the
friends who had been kindly anxious to replace them had an infectious
complaint in the house. Doubtless he might have found someone else to
take pity on him; "but," he reflected, "most of them have made up their
parties, and after all it is only for three or four days at most that I have to
fend for myself, and it win be just as well if I can get a move on with my
introduction to the Leventhorp Papers. I might use the time by going
down as near as I can to Gaulsford and making acquaintance with the
neighbourhood. I ought to see the remains of the Leventhorp house, and
the tombs in the church."

The first day after his arrival at the Swan Hotel at Longbridge was so
stormy that he got no farther than the tobacconist's. The next, comparatively bright, he used for his visit to Gaulsford, which interested him more
than a little, but had no ulterior consequences. The third, which was
really a pearl of a day for early January, was too fine to be spent indoors.
He gathered from the landlord that a favourite practice of visitors in the
summer was to take a morning train to a couple of stations westward and
walk back down the valley of the Tent, through Stanford St. Thomas and
Stanford Magdalene, both of which were accounted highly picturesque
villages. He closed with this plan, and we now find him seated in a third-
class carriage at 9-45 a.m., on his way to Kingsbourne Junction, and studying the map of the district.

One old man was his only fellow-traveller, a piping old man, who
seemed inclined for conversation. So Mr. Davidson, after going through
the necessary versicles and responses about the weather, inquired whether
he was going far.

"No, sir, not far, not this morning, sir," said the old man. "I ain't only goin' so far as what they call Kingsbourne Junction. There isn't but two stations betwixt here and there. Yes, they calls it Kingsbourne Junction."

"I'm going there, too," said Mr. Davidson.

"Oh indeed, sir! do you know that part?"

"No, I'm only going for the sake of taking a walk back to Longbridge, and seeing a bit of the country."

"Oh indeed, sir! Well, 'tis a beautiful day for a gentleman as enjoys a bit of a walk."

"Yes, to be sure. Have you got far to go when you get to Kingsbourne?"

"No, sir, I ain't got far to go, once I get to Kingsbourne junction. I'm agoin' to see my daughter, sir. She live at Brockstone. That's about two mile across the fields from what they call Kingsbourne Junction, that is. You've got that marked down on your map, I expect, sir."

"I expect I have. Let me see, Brockstone, did you say? Here's Kingsbourne, yes; and which way is Brockstone—toward the Stanfords? All, I see it: Brockstone Court, in a park. I don't see the village, though."

"No, sir, you wouldn't see no village of Brockstone. There ain't only the Court and the chapel at Brockstone."

"Chapel? Oh yes, that's marked here too. The chapel; close by the Court, it seems to be. Does it belong to the Court?"

"Yes, sir, that's close up to the Court, only a step. Yes, that belong to the Court. My daughter, you see, sir, she's the keeper's wife now, and she live at the Court and look after things now the family's away."

"No one living there now, then?"

"No, sir, not for a number of years. The old gentleman he lived there when I was a lad, and the lady she lived on after him to very near upon ninety years of age. And then she died, and them that have it now, they've got this other place, in Warwickshire I believe it is, and they don't do nothin' about lettin' the Court out; but Colonel Wildman he have the shooting, and young Mr. Clark, he's the agent, he come over once in so many weeks to see to things, and my daughter's husband he's the keeper."

"And who uses the chapel? just the people round about, suppose."

"Oh no, no one don't use the chapel. Why, there ain't no one to go. All the people about, they go to Stanford St. Thomas Church; but my son-in-law he go to Kingsbourne Church now, because the gentleman at Stanford he have this Gregory singin', and my son-in-law he don't like that; he say he can hear the old donkey brayin' any day of the week, and he like something a little cheerful on the Sunday." The old man drew his hand across his mouth and laughed. "That's what my son-in-law say: he say he can hear the old donkey [etc., *da capo*]."

Mr. Davidson also laughed as honestly as he could, thinking meanwhile that Brockstone Court and chapel would probably be worth including in his walk, for the map showed that from Brockstone he could strike the Tent Valley quite as easily as by following the main Kingsbourne-Longbridge road. So, when the mirth excited by the remembrance of the son-in-law's *bon mot* had died down he returned to the charge, and ascertained that both the Court and the chapel were of the class known as "old-fashioned places," and that the old man would be very willing to take him thither, and his daughter would be happy to show him whatever she could.

"But that ain't a lot, sir, not as if the family was livin' there; all the lookin'-glasses is covered up, and the painting' and the curtains and carpets folded away: not but what I dare say she could show you a pair just to look at, because she go over them to see as the morth shouldn't get into 'em."

"I shan't mind about that, thank you: if she can show me the inside of the chapel, that's what I'd like best to see."

"Oh, she can show you that right enough, sir. She have the key of the door, you see, and most weeks she go in and dust about. That's a nice chapel, that is. My son-in-law he say he'll be bound they didn't have none of this Gregory singin' there. Dear! I can't help but smile when I think of him sayin' that about th' old donkey. "I can hear him bray," he say, "any day of the week"; and so he can, sir, that's true, anyway."

The walk across the fields from Kingsbourne to Brockstone was very pleasant. It lay for the most part on the top of the country, and commanded wide views over a succession of ridges, plough and pasture, or covered with dark-blue woods—all ending, more or less abruptly, on the right, in headlands that overlooked the wide valley of a great western river. The last field they crossed was bounded by a close copse, and no sooner were they in it than the path turned downwards very sharply, and it became evident that Brockstone was neatly fitted into a sudden and very narrow valley. It was not long before they had glimpses of groups of smokeless stone chimneys, and stone-tiled roofs, close beneath their feet; and not many minutes after that, they were wiping their shoes at the back door of Brockstone Court, while the keeper's dogs barked very loudly in unseen places, and Mrs. Porter in quick succession screamed at them to be quiet, greeted her father, and begged both her visitors to step in.

It was not to be expected that Mr. Davidson should escape being taken through the principal rooms of the Court, in spite of the fact that the house was entirely out of commission. Pictures, carpets, curtains, furniture, were all covered up or put away, as old Mr. Avery had said, and the admiration which our friend was very ready to bestow had to be lavished on the proportions of the rooms, and on the one painted ceiling, upon which an artist who had fled from London in the Plague-year had depicted the Triumph of Loyalty and Defeat of Sedition. In this Mr. Davidson could show an unfeigned interest. The portraits of Cromwell, Ireton, Bradshaw, Peters, and the rest, writhing in carefully-devised torments, were evidently the part of the design to which most pains had been devoted.

"That were the old Lady Sadleir had that paintin' done, same as the one what put up the chapel. They say she were the first that went up to London to dance on Oliver Cromwell's grave." So said Mr. Avery, and continued musingly: "Well, I suppose she got some satisfaction to 'er mind, but I don't know as I should want to pay the fare to London and back just for that, and my son-in-law he say the same: he say he don't know as he should have cared to pay all that money only for that. I was tellin' the gentleman as we come along in the train, Mary, what your 'Arry says about this Gregory singin' down at Stanford here. We 'ad a bit of a laugh over that, sir, didn't us?"

"Yes, to be sure we did; ha! ha!" Once again Mr. Davidson strove to do justice to the pleasantry of the keeper. "But," he said, "if Mrs. Porter can show me the chapel, I think it should be now, for the days aren't long, and I want to get back to Longbridge before it falls quite dark."

Even if Brockstone Court has not been illustrated in Rural Life (and I think it has not) I do not propose to point out its excellences here; but of the chapel a word must be said. It stands about a hundred yards from the house, and has its own little graveyard and trees about it. It is a stone building about seventy feet long, and in the gothic style, as that style was understood in the middle of the seventeenth century. On the whole it resembles some of the Oxford college chapels as much as anything, save that it has a distinct chancel, like a parish church, and a fanciful domed bell-turret at the south-west angle.

When the west door was thrown open, Mr. Davidson could not repress an exclamation of pleased surprise at the completeness and richness of the interior. Screen-work, pulpit, seating, and glass—all were of the same period; and as he advanced into the nave and sighted the organ-case with its gold embossed pipes in the western gallery, his cup of satisfaction was filled. The glass in the nave windows was chiefly armorial; in the chancel were figure-subjects, of the kind that may be seen at Abbey Dore, of Lord Scudamore's work. But this is not an archaeological Review.

While Mr. Davidson was still busy examining the remains of the organ (attributed to one of the Dallams, I believe) old Mr. Avery had stumped up into the chancel and was lifting the dust-cloths from the blue velvet cushions of the stall-desks—evidently it was here that the family sat. Mr. Davidson heard him say in a rather hushed tone of surprise, "Why, Mary, here's all the books open agin!"

The reply was in a voice that sounded peevish rather than surprised. "Tt-tt-tt, well, there, I never!"

Mrs. Porter went over to where her father was standing, and they continued talking in a lower key. Mr. Davidson saw plainly that something not quite in the common run was under discussion: so he came down the gallery stairs and joined them. There was no sign of disorder in the chancel any more than in the rest of the chapel, which was beautifully clean, but the eight folio Prayer-Books on the cushions of the stall-desks were indubitably open.

Mrs. Porter was inclined to be fretful over it. "Whoever can it be as does it?" she said, "for there's no key but mine, nor yet door but the one we come in by, and the winders is barred, every one of 'em: I don't like it, father, that I don't."

"What is it, Mrs. Porter? Anything wrong?" said Mr. Davidson.

"No, sir, nothing reely wrong, only these books. Every time pretty near that I come in to do up the place, I shuts 'em and spreads the cloths over 'em to keep off the dust, ever since Mr. Clark spoke about it when I first come; and yet there they are again, and always the same page—and as I says, whoever it can be as does it with the door and winders shut; and as I says, it makes anyone feel queer comin' in here alone as I 'ave to do, not as I'm given that way myself, not to be frightened easy, I mean to say; and there's not a rat in the place—not as no rat wouldn't trouble to do a thing like that, do you think, sir?"

"Hardly, I should say; but it sounds very queer. Are they always open at the same place, did you say?"

"Always the same place, sir, one of the psalms it is, and I didn't particular notice it the first time or two, till I see a little red line of printing, and it's always caught my eye since."

Mr. Davidson walked along the stalls and looked at the open books. Sure enough, they all stood at the same page: Psalm cix, and at the head of it, just between the number and the *Deus laudem*, was a rubric, "For the 25th day of April." Without pretending to minute knowledge of the history of the Book of Common Prayer, he knew enough to be sure that this was a very odd and wholly unauthorized addition to its text; and though he remembered that April 25 is St. Mark's Day, he could not imagine what appropriateness this very savage psalm could have to that festival. With slight misgivings, he ventured to turn over the leaves to examine the title-page, and knowing the need for particular accuracy in these matters, he devoted some ten minutes to making a line-for-line transcript of it. The date was 1653; the printer called himself Anthony Cadman. He turned to the list of Proper Psalms for certain days: yes, added to it was that same inexplicable entry: *For the 25th day of April: the 109th Psalm*. An expert would no doubt have thought of many other points to inquire into, but this antiquary, as I have said, was no expert. He took stock, however, of the binding, a handsome one of tooled blue leather, bearing the arms that figured in several of the nave windows in various combinations.

"How often," he said at last to Mrs. Porter, "have you found these books lying open like this?"

"Reely I couldn't say, sir, but it's a great many times now. Do you recollect, father, me telling you about it the first time I noticed it?"

"That I do, my dear: you was in a rare taking, and I don't so much wonder at it; that was five year ago I was paying you a visit at Michaelmas time, and you come in at tea-time, and says you, 'Father, there's the books layin' open under the cloths agin'; and I didn't know what my daughter was speakin' about, you see, sir, and I says, 'Books?' just like that, I says; and then it all came out. But as Harry says,—that's my son-in-law, sir,—'whoever it can be,' he says, 'as does it, because there ain't only the one door, and we keeps the key locked up,' he says, 'and the winders is barred, every one on 'em. Well,' he says, 'I lay once I could catch 'em at it they wouldn't do it a second time,' he says. And no more they wouldn't, I don't believe, sir. Well that was five year ago, and it's been happenin' constant ever since by your account, my dear. Young Mr. Clark he don't seem to think much to it, but then he don't live here, you see, and 'tisn't his business to come and clean up here of a dark afternoon, is it?"

"I suppose you never notice anything else odd when you are at work here, Mrs. Porter?" said Mr. Davidson.

"No, sir, I do not," said Mrs. Porter, "and it's a funny thing to me I don't, with the feeling I have as there's someone settin' here—no, it's the other side, just within the screen—and lookin' at me all the time I'm dustin' in the gallery and pews. But I never yet see nothin' worse than myself, as the sayin' goes, and I kindly hope I never may."

In the conversation that followed (there was not much of it) nothing was added to the statement of the case. Having parted on good terms with Mr. Avery and his daughter, Mr. Davidson addressed himself to his eight-mile walk. The little valley of Brockstone soon led him down into the broader one of the Tent, and on to Stanford St. Thomas, where he found refreshment.

We need not accompany him all the way to Longbridge. But as he was changing his socks before dinner, he suddenly paused and said half-aloud, "By Jove, that is a rum thing!" It had not occurred to him before how strange it was that any edition of the Prayer-Book should have been issued in 1653, seven years before the Restoration, five years before Cromwell's death, and when the use of the book, let alone the printing of it, was penal. He must have been a bold man who put his name and a date on that title-page. Only, Mr. Davidson reflected, it probably was not his name at all, for the ways of printers in difficult times were devious.

As he was in the front hall of the Swan that evening, making some investigations about trains, a small motor stopped in front of the door, and out of it came a small man in a fur coat, who stood on the steps and gave directions in a rather yapping foreign accent to his chauffeur. When he came into the hotel, he was seen to be black-haired and pale-faced, with a little pointed beard, and gold pince-nez; altogether, very neatly turned out.

He went to his room, and Mr. Davidson saw no more of him till dinner-time. As they were the only two dining that night, it was not difficult for the newcomer to find an excuse for falling into talk; he was evidently wishing to make out what brought Mr. Davidson into that neighbourhood at that season.

"Can you tell me how far it is from here to Arlingworth?" was one of his early questions, and it was one which threw some light on his own plans, for Mr. Davidson recollected having seen at the station an adver-tisement of, a sale at, Arlingworth Hall, comprising old furniture pic-tures, and books. This, then, was a London dealer.

"No," he said, "I've never been there. I believe it lies out by Kingsbourne—it can't be less than twelve miles. I see there's a sale there shortly."

The other looked at him inquisitively, and he laughed. "No," he said, as if answering a question, "you needn't be afraid of my competing; I'm leaving this place tomorrow."

This cleared the air, and the dealer, whose name was Homberger, admitted that he was interested in books, and thought there might be in these old country-house libraries something to repay a journey. "For," said he, "we English have always this marvellous talent for accumulating rarities in the most unexpected places, ain't it?"

And in the course of the evening he was most interesting on the sub-ject of finds made by himself and others. "I shall take the occasion after this sale to look round the district a bit: perhaps you could inform me of some likely spots, Mr. Davidson?" But Davidson, though he had seen some tempting locked-up bookcases at Brockstone Court, kept his counsel. He did not really like Mr. Homberger.

Next day, as he sat in the train, a little ray of light came to illuminate one of yesterday's puzzles. He happened to take out an almanac-diary that he had bought for the new year, and it occurred to him to look at the remarkable events for April 25. There it was: "St Mark. Oliver Cromwell born, 1599."

That, coupled with the painted ceiling, seemed to explain a good deal. The figure of old Lady Sadleir became more substantial to his imagina-tion, as of one in whom love for Church and King had gradually given place to intense hate of the power that had silenced the one and slaughtered the other. What curious evil service was that which she and a few like her had been wont to celebrate year by year in that remote valley? and how in the world had she managed to elude authority? And again, did not this persistent opening of the books agree oddly with the other traits of her portrait known to him?

It would be interesting for anyone who chanced to be near Brockstone on the twenty-fifth of April to look in at the chapel and see if anything exceptional happened. When he came to think of it, there seemed to be no reason why he should not be that person himself: he, and if possible, some congenial friend. He resolved that so it should be.

Knowing that he knew really nothing about the printing of Prayer-Books, he realized that he must make it his business to get the best light on the matter without divulging his reasons. I may say at once that his search was entirely fruitless. One writer of the early part of the nineteenth century, a writer of rather windy and rhapsodical chat about books, professed to have heard of a special anti-Cromwellian issue of the Prayer-Book in the very midst of the Commonwealth period. But he did not claim to have seen a copy, and no one had believed him. Looking into this matter, Mr. Davidson found that the statement was based on letters from a correspondent who had lived near Longbridge: so he was inclined to think that the Brockstone Prayer-Books were at the bottom of it, and had excited a momentary interest.

Months went on, and St. Mark's Day came near. Nothing interfered with Mr. Davidson's plans of visiting Brockstone, or with those of the friend whom he had persuaded to go with him, and to whom alone he had confided the puzzle. The same 9.45 train which had taken him in January took them now to Kingsbourne; the same field-path led them to Brockstone. But today they stopped more than once to pick a cowslip; the distant woods and ploughed uplands were of another colour, and in the copse there was, as Mrs. Porter said, "a regular charm of birds; why you couldn't hardly collect your mind sometimes with it."

She recognized Mr. Davidson at once and was very ready to do the honours of the chapel. The new visitor, Mr. Witham, was as much struck by the completeness of it as Mr. Davidson had been. "There can't be such another in England," he said.

"Books open again, Mrs. Porter?" said Davidson, as they walked up to the chancel.

"Dear, yes, I expect so, sir," said Mrs. Porter, as she drew off the cloths. "Well, there!" she exclaimed the next moment, "if they ain't shut! That's the first time ever I've found 'em so. But it's not for want of care on my part, I do assure you, gentlemen, if they wasn't, for I felt the cloths the last thing before I shut up last week, when the gentleman had done photografting the heast winder, and every one was shut, and where there was ribbons left I tied 'em. Now I think of it, I don't remember ever to 'ave done that before, and per'aps, whoever it is it just made the difference to 'em. Well, it only shows, don't it? If at first you don't succeed, try, try, try again."

Meanwhile the two men had been examining the books, and now Davidson spoke.

"I'm sorry to say I'm afraid there's something wrong here, Mrs. Porter. These are not the same books."

It would make too long a business to detail all Mrs. Porter's outcries, and the questionings that followed. The upshot was this. Early in January the gentleman had come to see over the chapel and thought a great deal of it and said he must come back in the spring weather and take some photografts. And only a week ago he had drove up in his motoring car, and a very 'eavy box with the slides in it, and she had locked him in because he said something about a long explosion, and she was afraid of some damage happening; and he says, no, not explosion, but it appeared the lantern what they take the slides with worked very slow, and so he was in there the best part of an hour and she come and let him out, and he drove off with his box and all and gave her his visiting-card, and oh, dear, dear, to think of such a thing! he must have changed the books and took the old ones away with him in his box.

"What sort of man was he?"

"Oh, dear, he was a small-made gentleman, if you can call him so after the way he've behaved, with black hair, that is if it was hair, and gold eye-glasses, if they was gold: reely, one don't know what to believe. Sometimes I doubt he weren't a reel Englishman at all, and yet he seemed to know the language, and had the name on his visiting-card like anybody else might."

"Just so; might we see the card? Yes: T. W. Henderson, and an address somewhere near Bristol. Well, Mrs. Porter, it's quite plain this Mr. Henderson, as he calls himself, has walked off with your eight Prayer-Books and put eight others about the same size in place of them. Now listen to me. I suppose you must tell your husband about this, but neither you nor he must say one word about it to anyone else. If you'll give me the address of the agent—Mr. Clark, isn't it? —I will write to him and tell him exactly what has happened, and that it really is no fault of yours. But, you understand, we must keep it very quiet: and why? Because this man who has stolen the books will of course try to sell them one at a time—for I may tell you they are worth a good deal of money— and the only way we can bring it home to him is by keeping a sharp look out and saying nothing."

By dint of repeating the same advice in various forms they succeeded in impressing Mrs. Porter with the real need for silence, and were forced to make a concession only in the case of Mr. Avery, who was expected on a visit shortly: "But you may be safe with father, sir," said Mrs. Porter. "Father ain't a talkin' man."

It was not quite Mr. Davidson's experience of him; still, there were no neighbours at Brockstone, and even Mr. Avery must be aware that gossip with anybody on such a subject would be likely to end in the Porters having to look out for another situation.

A last question was whether Mr. Henderson, so-called, had anyone with him.

"No, sir, not when he come he hadn't: he was working his own motoring car himself, and what luggage he had, let me see: there was his lantern and this box of slides inside the carriage, which I helped him into the chapel and out of it myself with it, if only I'd knowed! And as he drove away under the big yew tree by the monument I see the long white bundle laying on the top of the coach, what I didn't notice when he drove up. But he set in front, sit, and only the boxes inside behind him. And do you reely think, sir, as his name weren't Henderson at all? Oh dear me, what a dreadful thing! Why fancy what trouble it might bring to a innocent person that might never have set foot in the place but for that!"

They left Mrs. Porter in tears. On the way home there was much discussion as to the best means of keeping watch upon possible sales. What Henderson-Homberger (for there could be no real doubt of the identity) had done was, obviously, to bring down the requisite number of folio Prayer-Books—disused copies from college chapels and the like, brought ostensibly for the sake of the bindings, which were superficially like enough to the old ones—and to substitute them at his leisure for the genuine articles. A week had now passed without any public notice being taken of the theft. He would take a little time himself to find out about the rarity of the books, and would ultimately, no doubt, "place" them cautiously. Between them, Davidson and Witham were in a position to know a good deal of what was passing in the book-world, and they could map out the ground pretty completely. A weak point with them at the moment was that neither of them knew under what other name or names Henderson-Homberger carried on business. But there are ways of solving these problems.

And yet all this planning proved unnecessary.

We are transported to a London office on this same 25th of April. We find there, within closed doors, late in the day, two police inspectors, a commissionaire, and a youthful clerk. The two latter, both rather pale and agitated in appearance, are sitting on chairs and being questioned

"How long do you say you've been in this Mr. Poschwitz's employment? Six months? And what was his business? Attended sales in various parts and brought home parcels of books. Did he keep a shop anywhere? No? Disposed of 'em here and there, and sometimes to private collectors. Right. Now then, when did he go out last? Rather better than a week ago. Tell you where he was going? No? Said he was going to start next day from his private residence, and shouldn't be at the office—that's here, eh?—before two days: you was to attend as usual. Where is his private residence? Oh, that's the address, Norwood way; I see. Any family? Not in this country? Now, then, what account do you give of what's happened since he came back? Came back on the Tuesday, did he? and this is the Saturday. Bring any books? One package: where is it? In the safe: you got the key? No, to be sure, it's open, of course. How did he seem when he got back—cheerful? Well, but how do you mean curious? Thought he might be in for an illness: he said that, did he? Odd smell got in his nose, couldn't get rid of it: told you to let him know who wanted to see him before you let 'em in? That wasn't usual with him? Much the same all Wednesday, Thursday, Friday. Out a good deal; said he was going to the British Museum. Often went there to make inquiries in the way of his business. Walked up and down a lot in the office when he was in? Anyone call in on those days? Mostly when he was out. Anyone find him in? Oh, Mr. Collinson? Who's Mr. Collinson? An old customer: know his address? All right, give it us afterwards. Well, now, what about this morning? You left Mr. Poschwitz's here at twelve and went home. Anybody see you? Commissionaire, you did? Remained at home till summoned here. Very well.

"Now commissionaire; we have your name—Watkins, eh? Very well, make your statement: don't go too quick, so as we can get it down."

"I was on duty 'ere later than usual, Mr. Potwitch 'aving asked me to remain on, and ordered his lunching to be sent in, which come as ordered. I was in the lobby from eleven-thirty on, and see Mr. Bligh [the clerk] leave at about twelve. After that no one come in at all except Mr. Potwitch's lunching come at one o'clock and the man left in five minutes' time. Towards the afternoon I became tired of waitin' and I come up-stairs to this first floor. The outer door what lead to the orfice stood open, and I come up to the plate-glass door here. Mr. Potwitch he was standing behind the table smoking a cigar, and he laid it down on the mantelpiece and felt in his trouser pockets and took out a key and went across to the safe. And I knocked on the glass, thinkin' to see if he wanted me to come and take away his tray, but he didn't take no notice, bein' engaged with the safe door. Then he got it open and stooped down and seemed to be lifting up a package off of the floor of the safe. And then, sir, I see what looked to be like a great roll of old shabby white flannel about four to five feet high fall for'ards out of the inside of the safe right against Mr. Potwitch's shoulder as he was stooping over: and Mr. Potwitch be raised

himself up as it were, resting his hands on the package, and give a exclamation. And I can't hardly expect you should take what I says, but as true
as I stand here I see this roll had a kind of a face in the upper end of it,
sir. You can't be more surprised than what I was, I can assure *you*, and
I've seen a lot in me time... Yes, I can describe it if you wish it, sir: it was
very much the same as this wall here in colour [the wall had an earth-
coloured distemper] and it had a bit of a band tied round underneath,
and the eyes, well they was dry-like, and much as if there was two big
spiders' bodies in the holes... Hair? no, I don't know as there was much
hair to be seen: the flannel-stuff was over the top of the 'ead... I'm very
sure it warn't what it should have been... No, I only see it in a flash, but I
took it in like a photograft—wish I hadn't... Yest, sir, it fell right over on
to Mr. Potwitch's shoulder, and this face hid in his neck—yes, sir, about
where the injury was—more like a ferret goin' for a rabbit than anythink
else, and he rolled over, and of course I tried to get in at the door, but as
you know, sir, it were locked on the inside, and all I could do, I rung up
everyone, and the surgeon come, and the police and you gentlemen, and
you know as much as what I do. If you won't be requirin' me any more
today I'd be glad to be gettin' off home: it's shook me up more than I
thought for."

"Well," said one of the inspectors, when they were left alone, and
"Well?" said the other inspector: and, after a pause, "What's the surgeon's
report again? You've got it there. Yes. Effect on the blood like the worst
kind of snake-bite: death almost instantaneous. I'm glad of that for his
sake; he was a nasty sight. No case for detaining this man Watkins, anyway; we know all about him. And what about this safe, now? We'd better
go over it again, and, by the way, we haven't opened that package he was
busy with when he died."

"Well, handle it careful," said the other. "There might be this snake
in it, for what you know. Get a light into the corners of the place, too.
Well: there's room for a shortish person to stand up in; but what about
ventilation?"

"Perhaps," said the other slowly, as he explored the safe with an electric torch, "perhaps they didn't require much of that. My word! it strikes
warm coming out of that place! like a vault, it is. But here, what's this
bank-like of dust all spread out into the room? That must have come there
since the door was opened; it would sweep it all away if you moved it—
see? Now what do you make of that?"

"Make of it? About as much as I make of anything else in this case.
One of London's mysteries this is going to be, by what I can see, and I
don't believe a photographer's box full of large-size old fashioned Prayer-
Books is going to take us much further. For that's just what your package
is."

It was a natural but hasty utterance. The preceding narrative shows that there was in fact plenty of material for constructing a case, and when once Messrs. Davidson and Witham had brought their end to Scotland Yard, the join-up was soon made, and the circle completed.

To the relief of Mrs. Porter, the owners of Brockstone decided not to replace the books in the chapel: they repose, I believe, in a safe-deposit in town. The police have their own methods of keeping certain matters out of the newspapers: otherwise it can hardly be supposed that Watkins's evidence about Mr. Poschwitz's death could have failed to furnish a good many headlines of a startling character to the press.

And when the servant of the man of God rose early, and went out, behold, an army surrounded the city with horses and chariots. And his servant asked him, "Oh, my master! what shall we do?"

And he answered, "Fear not: for they that be with us are more than they that be with them."

And Elisha prayed, and said, "Lord, I pray thee, open his eyes, that he may see." Then the Lord opened the eyes of the servant; and he saw: and, behold, the hill was full of horses and chariots of fire around Elisha.

II Kings 6: 15-17

THE BOWMEN

Arthur Machen (1863-1947)

It was during the Retreat of the Eighty Thousand, and the authority of the Censorship is sufficient excuse for not being more explicit. But it was on the most awful day of that awful time, on the day when ruin and disaster came so near that their shadow fell over London far away; and, without any certain news, the hearts of men failed within them and grew faint; as if the agony of the army in the battlefield had entered into their souls.

On this dreadful day, then, when three hundred thousand men in arms with all their artillery swelled like a flood against the little English company, there was one point above all other points in our battle line that was for a time in awful danger, not merely of defeat, but of utter annihilation. With the permission of the Censorship and of the military expert, this corner may, perhaps, be described as a salient, and if this angle were crushed and broken, then the English force as a whole would be shattered, the Allied left would be turned, and Sedan would inevitably follow.

All the morning the German guns had thundered and shrieked against this corner, and against the thousand or so of men who held it. The men joked at the shells, and found funny names for them, and had bets about them, and greeted them with scraps of music-hall songs. But the shells came on and burst, and tore good Englishmen limb from limb, and tore brother from brother, and as the heat of the day increased so did the fury of that terrific cannonade. There was no help, it seemed. The English artillery was good, but there was not nearly enough of it; it was being steadily battered into scrap iron.

There comes a moment in a storm at sea when people say to one another, "It is at its worst; it can blow no harder," and then there is a blast ten times more fierce than any before it. So it was in these British trenches.

345

There were no stouter hearts in the whole world than the hearts of these men; but even they were appalled as this seven-times-heated hell of the German cannonade fell upon them and overwhelmed them and destroyed them. And at this very moment they saw from their trenches that a tremendous host was moving against their lines. Five hundred of the thousand remained, and as far as they could see the German infantry was pressing on against them, column upon column, a grey world of men, ten thousand of them, as it appeared afterwards.

There was no hope at all. They shook hands, some of them. One man improvised a new version of the battlesong, "Good-bye, good-bye to Tipperary," ending with "And we shan't get there." And they all went on firing steadily. The officers pointed out that such an opportunity for high-class, fancy shooting might never occur again; the Germans dropped line after line; the Tipperary humorist asked, "What price Sidney Street?" And the few machine guns did their best. But everybody knew it was of no use. The dead grey bodies lay in companies and battalions, as others came on and on and on, and they swarmed and stirred and advanced from beyond and beyond.

"World without end. Amen," said one of the British soldiers with some irrelevance as he took aim and fired. And then he remembered—he says he cannot think why or wherefore—a queer vegetarian restaurant in London where he had once or twice eaten eccentric dishes of cutlets made of lentils and nuts that pretended to be steak. On all the plates in this restaurant there was printed a figure of St. George in blue, with the motto, *Adsit Anglis Sanctus Geogius*—May St. George be a present help to the English. This soldier happened to know Latin and other useless things, and now, as he fired at his man in the grey advancing mass—300 yards away—he uttered the pious vegetarian motto. He went on firing to the end, and at last Bill on his right had to clout him cheerfully over the head to make him stop, pointing out as he did so that the King's ammunition cost money and was not lightly to be wasted in drilling funny patterns into dead Germans.

For as the Latin scholar uttered his invocation he felt something between a shudder and an electric shock pass through his body. The roar of the battle died down in his ears to a gentle murmur; instead of it, he says, he heard a great voice and a shout louder than a thunder-peal crying, "Array, array, array!"

His heart grew hot as a burning coal, it grew cold as ice within him, as it seemed to him that a tumult of voices answered to his summons. He heard, or seemed to hear, thousands shouting: "St. George! St. George!"

"Ha! messire; ha! sweet Saint, grant us good deliverance!"

"St. George for merry England!"

"Harow! Harow! Monseigneur St. George, succour us."

"Ha! St. George! Ha! St. George! a long bow and a strong bow."

"Heaven's Knight, aid us!"

And as the soldier heard these voices he saw before him, beyond the trench, a long line of shapes, with a shining about them. They were like men who drew the bow, and with another shout their cloud of arrows flew singing and tingling through the air towards the German hosts.

The other men in the trench were firing all the while. They had no hope; but they aimed just as if they had been shooting at Bisley. Suddenly one of them lifted up his voice in the plainest English, "Gawd help us!" he bellowed to the man next to him, "but we're blooming marvels! Look at those grey... gentlemen, look at them! D'ye see them? They're not going down in dozens, nor in 'undreds; it's thousands, it is. Look! look! there's a regiment gone while I'm talking to ye."

"Shut it!" the other soldier bellowed, taking aim, "what are ye gassing about!"

But he gulped with astonishment even as he spoke, for, indeed, the grey men were falling by the thousands. The English could hear the guttural scream of the German officers, the crackle of their revolvers as they shot the reluctant; and still line after line crashed to the earth.

All the while the Latin-bred soldier heard the cry: "Harow! Harow! Monseigneur, dear saint, quick to our aid! St. George help us!"

"High Chevalier, defend us!"

The singing arrows fled so swift and thick that they darkened the air; the heathen horde melted from before them.

"More machine guns!" Bill yelled to Tom.

"Don't hear them," Tom yelled back. "But, thank God, anyway; they've got it in the neck."

In fact, there were ten thousand dead German soldiers left before that salient of the English army, and consequently there was no Sedan. In Germany, a country ruled by scientific principles, the Great General Staff decided that the contemptible English must have employed shells containing an unknown gas of a poisonous nature, as no wounds were discernible on the bodies of the dead German soldiers. But the man who knew what nuts tasted like when they called themselves steak knew also that St. George had brought his Agincourt Bowmen to help the English.

Again I lifted up my eyes, and looked, and behold, there came four chariots out from between two mountains; and the mountains were mountains of bronze.

The first chariot had red horses; and the second chariot had black horses;

And the third chariot had white horses; and the fourth chariot had dappled horses—all of them powerful.

And I asked the angel who was speaking to me, "What are these, my lord?"

And the angel answered me, "These are the four spirits of the heavens, going out from standing before the Lord of the whole earth."

Zecharaiah 6: 1-5

THE SOLDIERS' REST

Arthur Machen

The soldier with the ugly wound in the head opened his eyes at last, and looked about him with an air of pleasant satisfaction.

He still felt drowsy and dazed with some fierce experience through which he had passed, but so far he could not recollect much about it. But—an agreeable glow began to steal about his heart—such a glow as comes to people who have been in a tight place and have come through it better than they had expected. In its mildest form this set of emotions may be observed in passengers who have crossed the Channel on a windy day without being sick. They triumph a little internally, and are suffused with vague, kindly feelings.

The wounded soldier was somewhat of this disposition as he opened his eyes, pulled himself together, and looked about him. He felt a sense of delicious ease and repose in bones that had been racked and weary, and deep in the heart that had so lately been tormented there was an assurance of comfort—of the battle won. The thundering, roaring waves were passed; he had entered into the haven of calm waters. After fatigues and terrors that as yet he could not recollect he seemed now to be resting in the easiest of all easy chairs in a dim, low room.

In the hearth there was a glint of fire and a blue, sweet-scented puff of wood smoke; a great black oak beam roughly hewn crossed the ceiling. Through the leaded panes of the windows he saw a rich glow of sunlight, green lawns, and against the deepest and most radiant of all blue skies the wonderful far-lifted towers of a vast, Gothic cathedral—mystic, rich with imagery.

"Good Lord!" he murmured to himself. "I didn't know they had such places in France. It's just like Wells. And it might be the other day when I was going past the Swan, just as it might be past that window, and asked the ostler what time it was, and he says, 'What time? Why, summer-time';

and there outside it looks like summer that would last for ever. If this was an inn they ought to call it *The Soldiers' Rest*."

He dozed off again, and when he opened his eyes once more a kindly looking man in some sort of black robe was standing by him.

"It's all right now, isn't it?" he said, speaking in good English.

"Yes, thank you, sir, as right as can be. I hope to be back again soon."

"Well well; but how did you come here? Where did you get that?" He pointed to the wound on the soldier's forehead.

The soldier put his hand: up to his brow and looked dazed and puzzled.

"Well, sir," he said at last, "it was like this, to begin at the beginning. You know how we came over in August, and there we were in the thick of it, as you might say, in a day or two. An awful time it was, and I don't know how I got through it alive. My best friend was killed dead beside me as we lay in the trenches. By Cambrai, I think it was.

"Then things got a little quieter for a bit, and I was quartered in a village for the best part of a week. She was a very nice lady where I was, and she treated me proper with the best of everything. Her husband he was fighting; but she had the nicest little boy I ever knew, a little fellow of five, or six it might be, and we got on splendid. The amount of their lingo that kid taught me—'We, we' and 'Bong swot' and 'Commong voo potty we' and all—and I taught him English. You should have heard that nipper say "Arf a mo', old un!' It was a treat.

"Then one day we got surprised. There was about a dozen of us in the village, and two or three hundred Germans came down on us early one morning. They got us; no help for 'it. Before we could shoot.

"Well there we were. They tied our hands behind our backs, and smacked our faces and kicked us a bit, and we were lined up opposite the house where I'd been staying.

"And then that poor little chap broke away from his mother, and he run out and saw one of the Boshes, as we call them, fetch me one over the jaw with his clenched fist. Oh dear! oh dear! he might have done it a dozen times if only that little child hadn't seen him.

"He had a poor bit of a toy I'd bought him at the village shop; a toy gun it was. And out he came running, as I say, Crying out something in French like 'Bad man! bad man! don't hurt my Anglish or I shoot you'; and he pointed that gun at the German soldier. The German, he took his bayonet, and he drove it right through the poor little chap's throat."

The soldier's face worked and twitched and twisted itself into a sort of grin, and he sat grinding his teeth and staring at the man in the black robe. He was silent for a little. And then he found his voice, and the oaths rolled terrible, thundering from him, as he cursed that murderous wretch, and bade him go down and burn for ever in hell. And the tears were raining down his face, and they choked him at last.

"I beg your pardon, sir, I'm sure," he said, "especially you being a minister of some kind, I suppose; but I can't help it, he was such a dear little man."

The man in black murmured something to himself: "*Pretiosa in conspectu Domini mors innocentium ejus*"—Dear in the sight of the Lord is the death of His innocents. Then he put a hand very gently on the soldier's shoulder.

"Never mind," said he; "I've seen some service in my time, myself. But what about that wound?"

"Oh, that; that's nothing. But I'll tell you how I got it. It was just like this. The Germans had us fair, as I tell you, and they shut us up in a barn in the village; just flung us on the ground and left us to starve seemingly. They barred up the big door of the barn, and put a sentry there, and thought we were all right.

"There were sort of slits like very narrow windows in one of the walls, and on the second day it was, I was looking out of these slits down the street, and I could see those German devils were up to mischief. They were planting their machine-guns everywhere handy where an ordinary man coming up the street would never see them, but I see them, and I see the infantry lining up behind the garden walls. Then I had a sort of a notion of what was coming; and presently, sure enough, I could hear some of our chaps singing 'Hullo, hullo, hullo!' in the distance; and I says to myself, 'Not this time.'

"So I looked about me, and I found a hole under the wall; a kind of a drain I should think it was, and I found I could just squeeze through. And I got out and crept, round, and away I goes running down the street, yelling for all I was worth, just as our chaps were getting round the corner at the bottom. 'Bang, bang!' went the guns, behind me and in front of me, and on each side of me, and then—bash! something hit me on the head and over I went; and I don't remember anything more till I woke up here just now."

The soldier lay back in his chair and closed his eyes for a moment. When he opened them he saw that there were other people in the room besides the minister in the black robes. One was a man in a big black cloak. He had a grim old face and a great beaky nose. He shook the soldier by the hand.

"By God! sir," he said, "you're a credit to the British Army; you're a damned fine soldier and a good man, and, by God! I'm proud to shake hands with you."

And then someone came out of the shadow, someone in queer clothes such as the soldier had seen worn by the heralds when he had been on duty at the opening of Parliament by the King.

"Now, by *Corpus Domini*," this man said, "of all knights ye be noblest and gentlest, and ye be of fairest report, and now ye be a brother of the noblest brotherhood that ever was since this world's beginning, since ye have yielded dear life for your friends' sake."

The soldier did not understand what the man was saying to him. There were others, too, in strange dresses, who came and spoke to him. Some spoke in what sounded like French. He could not make it out; but he knew that they all spoke kindly and praised him.

"What does it all mean?" he said to the minister. "What are they talking about? They don't think I'd let down my pals?"

"Drink this," said the minister, and he handed the soldier a great silver cup, brimming with wine.

The soldier took a deep draught, and in that moment all his sorrows passed from him.

"What is it?" he asked?

"*Vin nouveau du Royaume*," said the minister. "New Wine of the Kingdom, you call it." And then he bent down and murmured in the soldier's ear.

"What," said the wounded man, "the place they used to tell us about in Sunday school? With such drink and such joy—"

His voice was hushed. For as he looked at the minister the fashion of his vesture was changed. The black robe seemed to melt away from him. He was all in armour, if armour be made of starlight, of the rose of dawn, and of sunset fires; and he lifted up a great sword of flame.

Full in the midst, his Cross of Red
Triumphant Michael brandished,
    And trampled the Apostate's pride.

BEJIDE THE BEE-HIVEJ

Arthur Thomas Quiller-Couch (1863-1944)

On the outskirts of the village of Gantick stand two small semi-detached cottages, coloured with the same pale yellow wash, their front gardens descending to the high-road in parallel lines, their back gardens (which are somewhat longer) climbing to a little wood of secular elms, traditionally asserted to be the remnant of a mighty forest. The party hedge is heightened by a thick screen of white-thorn on which the buds were just showing pink when I took up my lodging in the left-hand cottage (the 10th of May by my diary); and at the end of it are two small arbours, set back to back, their dilapidated sides and roofs bound together by clematis.

The night of my arrival, my landlady asked me to make the least possible noise in unpacking my portmanteau, because there was trouble next door, and the partitions were thin. Our neighbour's wife was down with inflammation, she explained—inflammation of the lungs, as I learnt by a question or two. It was a bad case. She was a wisht, ailing soul to begin with. Also the owls in the wood above had been hooting loudly, for nights past: and yesterday a hedge-sparrow lit on the sill of the sick-room window, two sure tokens of approaching death. The sick woman was being nursed by her elder sister, who had lived in the house for two years, and practically taken charge of it. "Better the man had married *she*," my landlady added, somewhat unfeelingly.

I saw the man in his garden early next morning: a tall fellow, hardly yet on the wrong side of thirty, dressed in loose-fitting tweed coat and corduroys. A row of bee-hives stood along his side of the party wall, and he had taken the farthest one, which was empty, off its stand, and was rubbing it on the inside with a handful of elder-flower buds, by way of preparation for a new swarm. Even from my bed-room window I remarked, as he turned his head occasionally, that he was singularly

353

handsome. His movements were those of a lazy man in a hurry, though there seemed no reason for hurry in his task. But when it was done, and the hive replaced, his behaviour began to be so eccentric that I paused in the midst of my shaving, to watch.

He passed slowly down the line of bee-hives, halting beside each in turn, and bending his head down close to the orifice with the exact action of a man whispering a secret into another's ear. I believe he kept this attitude for a couple of minutes beside each hive—there were eight, besides the empty one. At the end of the row he lifted his head, straightened his shoulders, and cast a glance up at my window, where I kept well out of sight. A minute after, he entered his house by the back door, and did not reappear.

At breakfast I asked my landlady if our neighbour were wrong in his head at all. She looked astonished, and answered, "No: he was a do-nothing fellow—unless you counted it hard work to drive a carrier's van thrice a week into Tregarrick, and home the same night. But he kept very steady, and had a name for good nature."

Next day the man was in his garden at the same hour, and repeated the performance. Throughout the following night I was kept awake by a series of monotonous groans that reached me through the partition, and the murmur of voices speaking at intervals. It was horrible to lie within a few inches of the sick woman's head, to listen to her agony and be unable to help, unable even to see. Towards six in the morning, in bright daylight, I dropped off to sleep at last.

Two hours later the sound of voices came in at the open window and awoke me. I looked out into my neighbour's garden. He was standing, half-way up the path, in the sunshine, and engaged in a suppressed but furious altercation with a thin woman, somewhat above middle height. Both wore thick green veils over their faces and thick gloves on their hands. The woman carried a rusty tea-tray.

The man stood against her, motioning her back towards the house. I caught a sentence—"It'll be the death of her;" and the woman glanced back over her shoulder towards the window of the sick-room. She seemed about to reply, but shrugged her shoulders instead and went back into the house, carrying her tray. The man turned on his heel, walked hurriedly up the garden, and scrambled over its hedge into the wood. His veil and thick gloves were explained a couple of hours later, when I looked into the garden again and saw him hiving a swarm of bees that he had captured, the first of the season.

That same afternoon, about four o'clock, I observed that every window in the next house stood wide open. My landlady was out in the garden, "picking in" her week's washing from the thorn hedge where it had been suspended to dry; and I called her attention to this new freak of our neighbours.

"Ah, then, the poor soul must be nigh to her end," said she. "That's done to give her an easy death."

The woman died at half-past seven. And next morning her husband hung a scrap of black crape to each of the bee-hives.

She was buried on Sunday afternoon. From behind the drawn blinds of my sitting-room window I saw the funeral leave the house and move down the front garden to the high-road—the heads of the mourners, each with a white handkerchief pressed to its nose, appearing above the wall like the top of a procession in some Assyrian sculpture. The husband wore a ridiculously tall hat, and a hat-band with long tails. The whole affair had the appearance of an hysterical outrage on the afternoon sunshine. At the foot of the garden they struck up a "burying tune," and passed down the road, shouting it with all their lungs.

I caught up a book and rushed out into the back garden for fresh air. Even out of doors it was insufferably hot, and soon I flung myself down on the bench within the arbour and set myself to read. A plank behind me had started, and after a while the edge of it began to gall my shoulders as I leant back. I tried once or twice to push it into its place, without success, and then, in a moment of irritation, gave it a tug. It came away in my hand, and something rolled out on the bench before me, and broke in two.

I picked it up. It was a lump of dough, rudely moulded to the shape of a woman, with a rusty brass-headed nail stuck through the breast. Around the body was tied a lock of fine light-brown hair—a woman's, by its length.

After a careful examination, I untied the lock of hair, put the doll back in its place behind the plank, and returned to the house: for I had a question or two to put to my landlady.

"Was the dead woman at all like her elder sister?" I asked. "Was she black-haired, for instance?"

"No," answered my landlady; "she was shorter and much fairer. You might almost call her a light-haired woman."

I hoped she would pardon me for changing the subject abruptly and asking an apparently ridiculous question, but would she call a man mad if she found him whispering secrets into a bee-hive?

My landlady promptly replied that, on the contrary, she would think him extremely sensible; for that, unless bees were told of all that was happening in the household to which they belonged, they might consider themselves neglected, and leave the place in wrath. She asserted this to be a notorious fact.

"I have one more question," I said. "Suppose that you found in your garden a lock of hair—a lock such as this, for instance—what would you do with it?"

She looked at it, and caught her breath sharply.

"I'm no meddler," she said at last; "I should burn it."

"Why?"

"Because if 'twas left about, the birds might use it for their nests, and weave it in so tight that the owner couldn't rise on Judgment day"

So I burnt the lock of hair in her presence; because I wanted its owner to rise on Judgment day and state a case which, after all, was no affair of mine.

OCEANUS

Arthur Thomas Quiller-Couch

I

My Dear Violet,—So you "gather from the tone of two or three recent letters that my spirit is creeping back to light and warmth again"? Well, after a fashion you are right. I shall never laugh again as I used to laugh before Harry's death. The taste has gone out of that carelessness, and I turn even from the remembrance of it. But I can be cheerful, with a cheerfulness which has found the centre of gravity. I am myself again, as people say. After months of agitation in what seemed to be chaos the lost atom has dropped back to its place in the scheme of things, and even aspires (poor mite!) to do its infinitesimal business intelligently. So might a mote in a sunbeam feel itself at one with God!

But when you assume that my recovery has been a gradual process, you are wrong. You will think me more than ever deranged; but I assure you that it has been brought about, not by long strivings, but suddenly— without preparation of mine—*and by the immediate hand of our dead brother.*

Yes; you shall have the whole tale. The first effect of the news of Harry's death in October last was simply to stun me. You may remember how once, years ago when we were children, we rode home together across the old Racecourse after a long day's skating, our skates swinging at our saddle-bows; how Harry challenged us to a gallop; and how, midway, the roan mare slipped down neck over crop on the frozen turf and hurled me clean against the face of a stone dyke. I had been thrown from horseback more than once before, but somehow had always found the earth fairly elastic. So I had griefs before Harry died and took some rebound of hope from each: but that cast repeated in a worse degree the old shock—the springless brutal jar—of the stone dyke. With him the sun went out of my sky.

357

I understand that this torpor is quite common with men and women suddenly bereaved. I believe that a whole week passed before my brain recovered any really vital motion; and then such feeble thought as I could exert was wholly occupied with the desperate stupidity of the whole affair. If God were indeed shaping the world to any end, if any design of His underlay the activities of men, what insensate waste to quench such a heart and brain as Harry's!—to nip, as it seemed out of mere blundering wantonness, a bud which had begun to open so generously: to sacrifice that youth and strength, that comeliness, that enthusiasm, and all for nothing! Had some campaign claimed him, had he been spent to gain a citadel or defend a flag, I had understood. But that he should be killed on a friendly mission; attacked in ignorance by those East Coast savages while bearing gifts to their king; deserted by the porters whose comfort (on their own confession) he had studied throughout the march; left to die, to be tortured, mutilated—and all for no possible good: these things I could not understand. At the end he might have escaped; but as he caught hold of his saddle by the band between the holsters, it parted: it was not leather, but faced paper, the job of some cheating contractor. I thought of this, too. And Harry had been through Chitral!

But though a man may hate, he cannot easily despise God for long. "He is great—but wasteful," said the American. We are the dust on His great hands, and fly as He claps them carelessly in the pauses of His work. Yet this theory would not do at all: for the unlucky particles are not dust, not refuse, but exquisite and exquisitely fashioned, designed to *live*, and to every small function of life adapted with the minutest care. There were nights indeed when, walking along the shore where we had walked together on the night before Harry left England and looking from the dark waters which divided me from his grave up to the nightly moon and to the stars around her, I could well believe God wasteful of little things. Sirius flashing low, Orion's belt with the great nebula swinging like a pendant of diamonds; the ruby stars, Betelgueux and Aldebaran—my eyes went up beyond these to Perseus shepherding the Kids westward along the Milky way. From the right Andromeda flashed signals to him: and above sat Cassiopeia, her mother, resting her jewelled wrists on the arms of her throne. Low in the east Jupiter trailed his satellites in the old moon's path. As they all moved, silent, looking down on me out of the hollow spaces of the night, I could believe no splendid waste too costly for their perfection: and the Artificer who hung them there after millions of years of patient effort, if more intelligible than a God who produced them suddenly at will, certainly not less divine. But walking the same shore by daylight I recognised that the shells, the mosses, the flowers I trampled on, were, each in its way, as perfect as those great stars: that on these—and on Harry—as surely as on the stars—God had spent, if not infinite pains, then at least so superlative a wisdom that to conceive of them as wastage was to deny the mind which called them forth.

There they were: and that He who had skill to create them could blunder in using them was simply incredible.

But this led to worse: for having to admit the infallible design, I now began to admire it as an exquisite scheme of evil, and to accuse God of employing supreme knowledge and skill to gratify a royal lust of cruelty. For a month and more this horrible theory justified itself in all innocent daily sights. Throughout my country walks I "saw blood." I heard the rabbit run squeaking before the weasel; I watched the butcher crow working steadily down the hedge. If I turned seaward I looked beneath the blue and saw the dog-fish gnawing on the whiting. If I walked in the garden I surprised the thrush dragging worms from the turf, the cat slinking on the nest, the spider squatting in ambush. Behind the rosy face of every well-nourished child I saw a lamb gazing up at the butcher's knife. My dear Violet, that was a hideous time!

And just then by chance a book fell into my hands—Lamartine's *Chute d'un Ange*. Do you know the Seventh and Tenth Visions of that poem, which describe the favourite amusements of the Men-gods? Before the Deluge, beyond the rude tents of the nomad shepherds, there rose city upon city of palaces built of jasper and porphyry, splendid and utterly corrupt; inhabited by men who called themselves gods and explored the subtleties of all sciences to minister to their vicious pleasures.

At ease on soft couches, in hanging gardens set with fountains, these beings feasted with every refinement of cruelty. Kneeling slaves were their living tables; while for their food—

> *Tous les oiseaux de l'air, tous les poissons de l'onde,*
> Tout ce qui vole ou nage ou rampe dans le monde,
> Mourant pour leur plaisir des plus cruels trepas
> *De sanglantes savours composent leurs repas. . . .*

In these lines I believed that I discerned the very God of the universe, the God whom men worship—

> *Dans les infames jeux de leur divin loisir*
> Le supplice de l'homme est leur premier plaisir.
> Pour que leur oeil feroce a l'envi s'en repaisse
> Des bourreaux devant eux en immolent sans cesse.
> Tantot ils font lutter, dans des combats affreux,
> L'homme contre la brute et les hommes entre eux,
> *Aux longs ruisseaux de sang qui coulent de la veine,*
> *Aux palpitations des membres sur l'arene,*

Se levant a demi de leurs lits de repos
Des frissons de plaisir fremissent sur leurs peaux.
Le cri de la torture est leur douce harmonie,
Et leur oeil dans son oeil boit sa lente agonie.

I charged the Supreme Power with a cruelty deliberate, ruthless, serene. Nero the tyrant once commanded a representation in grim earnest of the Flight of Icarus; and the unhappy boy who took the part, at his first attempt to fly, fell headlong beside the Emperor's couch and spattered him with blood and brains. For the Emperor, says Suetonius, *perraro praesidere, ceterum accubans, parvis primum foraminibus, deinde toto podio adaperto, spectare consuerat.* So I believed that on the stage of this world men agonised for the delight of one cruel intelligence which watched from behind the curtain of a private box.

II

In this unhappy condition of mind, then, I was lying in my library chair here at Sevenhays, at two o'clock on the morning of January 4th. I had just finished another reading of the Tenth Vision and had tossed my book into the lap of an armchair opposite. Fire and lamp were burning brightly. The night outside was still and soundless, with a touch of frost.

I lay there, retracing in thought the circumstances of Harry's last parting from me, and repeating to myself a scrap here and there from the three letters he wrote on his way—the last of them, full of high spirits, received a full three weeks after the telegram which announced his death. There was a passage in this last letter describing a wonderful ride he had taken alone and by moonlight on the desert; a ride (he protested) which wanted nothing of perfect happiness but me, his friend, riding beside him to share his wonder. There was a sentence which I could not recall precisely, and I left my chair and was crossing the room towards the drawer in the writing-table where I kept his letters, when I heard a trampling of hoofs on the gravel outside, and then my Christian name called—with distinctness, but not at all loudly.

I went to the window, which was unshuttered; drew up the blind and flung up the sash. The moon, in its third quarter and about an hour short of its meridian, shone over the deodars upon the white gravel. And there, before the front door, sat Harry on his sorrel mare Vivandiere, holding my own Grey Sultan ready bridled and saddled. He was dressed in his old khaki riding suit, and his face, as he sat askew in his saddle and looked up towards my window, wore its habitual and happy smile.

Now, call this and what follows a dream, vision, hallucination, what you will; but understand, please, that from the first moment, so far as I considered the matter at all, I had never the least illusion that this was Harry in flesh and blood. I knew quite well all the while that Harry was dead and his body in his grave. But, soul or phantom— whatever relation to Harry this might bear—it had come to me, and the great joy of that was enough for the time. There let us leave the question. I closed the window, went upstairs to my dressing-room, drew on my riding-boots and overcoat, found cap, gloves, and riding-crop, and descended to the porch.

Harry, as I shall call him, was still waiting there on the off side of Grey Sultan, the farther side from the door. There could be no doubt, at any rate, that the grey was real horseflesh and blood, though he seemed unusually quiet after two days in stall. Harry freed him as I mounted, and we set off together at a walk, which we kept as far as the gate.

Outside we took the westward road, and our horses broke into a trot. As yet we had not exchanged a word; but now he asked a question or two about his people and his friends; kindly, yet most casually, as one might who returns after a week's holidaying. I answered as well as I could, with trivial news of their health. His mother had borne the winter better than usual—to be sure, there had been as yet no cold weather to speak of; but she and Ethel intended, I believed, to start for the south of France early in February. He inquired about you. His comments were such as a man makes on hearing just what he expects to hear, or knows beforehand. And for some time it seemed to be tacitly taken for granted between us that I should ask him no questions.

"As for me—" I began, after a while.

He checked the mare's pace a little. "I know," he said, looking straight ahead between her ears; then, after a pause, "it has been a bad time for you, You are in a bad way altogether. That is why I came."

"But it was for *you!*" I blurted out. "Harry, if only I had known why *you* were taken—and what it was to *you!*"

He turned his face to me with the old confident comforting smile.

"Don't you trouble about *that*. *That's* nothing to make a fuss about. Death?" he went on musing—our horses had fallen to a walk again—"It looks you in the face a moment: you put out your hands: you touch—and so it is gone. My dear boy, it isn't for us that you need worry."

"For whom, then?"

"Come," said he, and he shook Vivandiere into a canter.

III

I cannot remember precisely at what point in our ride the country had ceased to be familiar. But by-and-by we were climbing the lower slopes of a great down which bore no resemblance to the pastoral country around Sevenhays. We had left the beaten road for short turf—apparently of a copper-brown hue, but this may have been the effect of the moonlight. The ground rose steadily, but with an easy inclination, and we climbed with the wind at our backs; climbed, as it seemed, for an hour, or maybe two, at a footpace, keeping silence. The happiness of having Harry beside me took away all desire for speech.

This at least was my state of mind as we mounted the long lower slopes of the down. But in time the air, hitherto so exhilarating, began to oppress my lungs, and the tranquil happiness to give way to a vague discomfort and apprehension.

"What is this noise of water running?"

I reined up Grey Sultan as I put the question. At the same moment it occurred to me that this sound of water, distant and continuous, had been running in my ear for a long while.

Harry, too, came to a halt. With a sweep of the arm that embraced the dim landscape around and ahead, he quoted softly—

> *en detithei potamoio mega spenos Okeanoio*
> *antyga par pymaten sakeos pyka poietoio . . . .*

and was silent again.

I recalled at once and distinctly the hot summer morning ten years back, when we had prepared that passage of the Eighteenth Book together in our study at Clifton; I at the table, Harry lolling in the cane-seated armchair with the Liddell and Scott open on his knees; outside, the sunny close and the fresh green of the lime-trees.

Now that I looked more attentively the bare down, on which we climbed like flies, did indeed resemble a vast round shield, about the rim of which this unseen water echoed. And the resemblance grew more startling when, a mile or so farther on our way, as the grey dawn overtook us, Harry pointed upwards and ahead to a small boss or excrescence now lifting itself above the long curve of the horizon.

At first I took it for a hummock or tumulus. Then, as the day whitened about us, I saw it to be a building—a tall, circular barrack not unlike the Colosseum. A question shaped itself on my lips, but something in Harry's manner forbade it. His gaze was bent steadily forward, and I kept my wonder to myself, and also the oppression of spirit which had now grown to something like physical torture.

When first the great barrack broke into sight we must have been at least two miles distant. I kept my eyes fastened on it as we approached, and little by little made out the details of its architecture. From base to summit—which appeared to be roofless—six courses of many hundred arches ran around the building, one above the other; and between each pair a course, as it seemed, of plain worked stone, though I afterwards found it to be sculptured in low relief. The arches were cut in deep relief and backed with undressed stone. The lowest course of all, however, was quite plain, having neither arches nor frieze; but at intervals corresponding to the eight major points of the compass—so far as I who saw but one side of it could judge—pairs of gigantic stone figures supported archways pierced in the wall; or sluices, rather, since from every archway but one a full stream of water issued and poured down the sides of the hill. The one dry archway was that which faced us with open gate, and towards which Harry led the way; for oppression and terror now weighted my hand as with lead upon Grey Sultan's rein.

Harry, however, rode forward resolutely, dismounted almost in the very shadow of the great arch, and waited, smoothing his mare's neck. But for the invitation in his eyes, which were solemn, yet without a trace of fear, I had never dared that last hundred yards. For above the rush of waters I heard now a confused sound within the building—the thud and clanking of heavy machinery, and at intervals a human groan; and looking up I saw that the long friezes in bas-relief represented men and women tortured and torturing with all conceivable variety of method and circumstance—flayed, racked, burned, torn asunder, loaded with weights, pinched with hot irons, and so on without end. And it added to the horror of these sculptures that while the limbs and even the dress of each figure were carved with elaborate care and nicety of detail, the faces of all—of those who applied the torture and of those who looked on, as well as of the sufferers themselves—were left absolutely blank. On the same plan the two Titans beside the great archway had no faces. The sculptor had traced the muscles of each belly in a constriction of anguish, and had suggested this anguish again in moulding the neck, even in disposing the hair of the head; but the neck supported, and the locks fell around, a space of smooth stone without a feature.

Harry allowed me no time to feed on these horrors. Signing to me to dismount and leave Grey Sultan at the entrance, he led me through the long archway or tunnel. At the end we paused again, he watching, while I drew difficult breath. ...

I saw a vast amphitheatre of granite, curving away on either hand and reaching up, tier on tier, till the tiers melted in the grey sky overhead. The lowest tier stood twenty feet above my head; yet curved with so lordly a perspective that on the far side of the arena, as I looked across, it seemed almost level with the ground; while the human figures about the great archway yonder were diminished to the size of ants about a hole... For there were human figures busy in the arena, though not a soul sat in any of the granite tiers above. A million eyes had been less awful than those empty benches staring down in the cold dawn; bench after bench repeating the horror of the featureless carvings by the entrance-gate—repeating it in series without end, and unbroken, save at one point midway along the semicircle on my right, where the imperial seat stood out, crowned like a catafalque with plumes of purple horse-hair, and screened close with heavy purple hangings. I saw these curtains shake once or twice in the morning wind.

The floor of this amphitheatre I have spoken of as an arena; but as a matter of fact it was laid with riveted sheets of copper that recalled the dead men's shelves in the Paris *morgue*. The centre had been raised some few feet higher than the circumference, or possibly the whole floor took its shape from the rounded hill of which it was the apex; and from an open sluice immediately beneath the imperial throne a flood of water gushed with a force that carried it straight to this raised centre, over which it ran and rippled, and so drained back into the scuppers at the circum-ference. Before reaching the centre it broke and swirled around a row of what appeared to be tall iron boxes or cages, set directly in face of the throne. But for these ugly boxes the whole floor was empty. To and from these the little human figures were hurrying, and from these too proceeded the thuds and panting and the frequent groans that I had heard outside.

While I stood and gazed, Harry stepped forward into the arena. "This also?" I whispered.

He nodded, and led the way over the copper floor, where the water ran high as our ankles and again was drained off, until little dry spaces grew like maps upon the surface, and in ten seconds were flooded again. He led me straight to the cages, and I saw that while the roof and three sides of these were of sheet iron, the fourth side, which faced the throne, lay open. And I saw—in the first cage, a man scourged with rods; in the second, a body twisted on the rack; in the third, a woman with a starving babe, and a fellow that held food to them and withdrew it quickly (the torturers wore masks on their faces, and whenever blood flowed some threw handfuls of sawdust, and blood and sawdust together were carried off by the running water); in the fourth cage, a man tied, naked and help-less, whom a masked torturer pelted with discs of gold, heavy and keen-edged; in the fifth a brasier with irons heating, and a girl's body crouched in a corner—

"I will see no more!" I cried, and turned towards the great purple canopy. High over it the sun broke yellow on the climbing tiers of seats. "Harry! someone is watching behind those curtains! Is it—*He*?"

Harry bent his head.

"But this is all that I believed! This is Nero, and ten times worse than Nero! Why did you bring me here?" I flung out my hand towards the purple throne, and finding myself close to a fellow who scattered saw-dust with both hands, made a spring to tear his mask away. But Harry stretched out an arm.

"That will not help you," he said. "The man has no face."

"No face!"

"He once had a face, but it has perished. His was the face of these sufferers. Look at them."

I looked from cage to cage, and now saw that indeed all these suffer-ers—men and women—had but one face: the same wrung brow, the same wistful eyes, the same lips bitten in anguish. I knew the face. *We all know it.*

"His own Son! O devil rather than God!" I fell on my knees in the gushing water and covered my eyes.

"Stand up, listen and look!" said Harry's voice.

"What can I see? He hides behind that curtain."

"And the curtain?"

"It shakes continually."

"*That is with His sobs.* Listen! What of the water?"

"It runs from the throne and about the floor. It washes off the blood."

"That water is His tears. It flows hence down the hill, and washes all the shores of earth."

Then as I stood silent, conning the eddies at my feet, for the first time Harry took my hand.

"Learn this," he said. "There is no suffering in the world but ulti-mately comes to be endured by God."

Saying this, he drew me from the spot; gently, very gently led me away; but spoke again as we were about to pass into the shadow of the arch—

"Look once back: for a moment only."

I looked. The curtains of the imperial seat were still drawn close, but in a flash I saw the tiers beside it, and around, and away up to the sunlit crown of the amphitheatre, thronged with forms in white raiment. And all these forms leaned forward and bowed their faces on their arms and wept.

So we passed out beneath the archway. Grey Sultan stood outside, and as I mounted him the gate clashed behind. . . .

IV

I turned as it clashed. And the gate was just the lodge-gate of Sevenhays. And Grey Sultan was trampling the gravel of our own drive.

The morning sun slanted over the laurels on my right, and while I wondered, the stable clock struck eight.

The rest I leave to you; nor shall try to explain. I only know that, vision or no vision, my soul from that hour has gained a calm it never knew before. The sufferings of my fellows still afflict me; but always, if I stand still and listen, in my own room, or in a crowded street, or in a waste spot among the moors, I can hear those waters moving round the world—moving on their "priest-like task"—those lustral divine tears which are Oceanus.

THE SEVENTH MAN

Arthur Thomas Quiller-Couch

In a one-roomed hut, high within the Arctic Circle, and only a little
south of the eightieth parallel, six men were sitting—much as they had
sat, evening after evening, for months. They had a clock, and by it they
divided the hours into day and night. As a matter of fact, it was always
night. But the clock said half-past eight, and they called the time evening.

The hut was built of logs, with an inner skin of rough match-boarding,
daubed with pitch. It measured seventeen feet by fourteen; but opposite
the door four bunks—two above and two below—took a yard off the length,
and this made the interior exactly square. Each of these bunks had two
doors, with brass latches on the inner side; so that the owner, if he chose,
could shut himself up and go to sleep in a sort of cupboard. But as a rule,
he closed one of them only—that by his feet. The other swung back, with
its brass latch showing. The men kept these latches in a high state of
polish.

Across the angle of the wall, to the left of the door, and behind it
when it opened, three hammocks were slung, one above another. No one
slept in the uppermost.

But the feature of the hut was its fireplace; and this was merely a
square hearth-stone, raised slightly above the floor, in the middle of the
room. Upon it, and upon a growing mountain of soft grey ash, the fire
burned always. It had no chimney, and so the men lost none of its warmth.
The smoke ascended steadily and spread itself under the blackened beams
and roof-boards in dense blue layers. But about eighteen inches beneath
the spring of the roof there ran a line of small trap-doors with sliding
panels, to admit the cold air, and below these the room was almost clear
of smoke. A newcomer's eyes might have smarted, but these men stitched
their clothes and read in comfort. To keep the up-draught steady they
had plugged every chink and crevice in the match-boarding below the

367

trap-doors with moss, and payed the seams with pitch. The fire they fed from a stack of drift and wreck wood piled to the right of the door, and fuel for the fetching strewed the frozen beach outside—whole trees notched into lengths by lumberers' axes and washed thither from they knew not what continent. But the wreck-wood came from their own ship, the *J. R. MacNeill*, which had brought them from Dundee.

They were Alexander Williamson, of Dundee, better known as The Gaffer; David Faed, also of Dundee; George Lashman, of Cardiff; Long Ede, of Hayle, in Cornwall; Charles Silchester, otherwise The Snipe, of Ratcliff Highway or thereabouts; and Daniel Cooney, shipped at Tromso six weeks before the wreck, an Irish-American by birth and of no known address.

The Gaffer reclined in his bunk, reading by the light of a smoky and evil-smelling lamp. He had been mate of the *J. R. MacNeill*, and was now captain as well as patriarch of the party. He possessed three books—the Bible, Milton's "Paradise Lost," and an odd volume of "The Turkish Spy." Just now he was reading "The Turkish Spy." The lamplight glinted on the rim of his spectacles and on the silvery hairs in his beard, the slack of which he had tucked under the edge of his blanket. His lips moved as he read, and now and then he broke off to glance mildly at Faed and the Snipe, who were busy beside the fire with a greasy pack of cards; or to listen to the peevish grumbling of Lashman in the bunk below him. Lashman had taken to his bed six weeks before with scurvy, and complained incessantly; and though they hardly knew it, these complaints were wearing his comrades' nerves to fiddle-strings—doing the mischief that cold and bitter hard work and the cruel loneliness had hitherto failed to do. Long Ede lay stretched by the fire in a bundle of skins, reading in his only book, the Bible, open now at the Song of Solomon. Cooney had finished patching a pair of trousers, and rolled himself in his hammock, whence he stared at the roof and the moonlight streaming up there through the little trap-doors and chivying the layers of smoke. Whenever Lashman broke out into fresh quaverings of self-pity, Cooney's hands opened and shut again, till the nails dug hard into the palm. He groaned at length, exasperated beyond endurance.

"Oh, stow it, George! Hang it all, man!..."

He checked himself, sharp and short: repentant, and rebuked by the silence of the others. They were good seamen all, and tender dealing with a sick shipmate was part of their code.

Lashman's voice, more querulous than ever, cut into the silence like a knife—

"That's it. You've thought it for weeks, and now you say it. I've knowed it all along. I'm just an encumbrance, and the sooner you're shut of me the better, says you. You needn't to fret. I'll be soon out of it; out of it— out there, alongside of Bill—"

"Easy there, matey." The Snipe glanced over his shoulder and laid his cards face downward. "Here, let me give the bed a shake up. It'll ease yer."

"It'll make me quiet, you mean. Plucky deal you care about easin' me, any of yer!"

"Get out with yer nonsense! Dan didn' mean it." The Snipe slipped an arm under the invalid's head and rearranged the pillow of skins and gunny-bags.

"He didn't, didn't he? Let him say it then..."

The Gaffer read on, his lips moving silently. Heaven knows how he had acquired this strayed and stained and filthy little demi-octavo with the arms of Saumarez on its book-plate—"The Sixth Volume of Letters writ by a Turkish Spy, who liv'd Five-and-Forty Years Undiscovered at Paris: Giving an Impartial Account to the *Divan* at *Constantinople* of the most remarkable Transactions of Europe, And discovering several *Intrigues* and *Secrets* of the *Christian* Courts (especially of that of *France*)," etc., etc. "Written originally in *Arabick*. Translated into *Italian*, and from thence into *English* by the Translator of the First Volume. The Eleventh Edition. London: Printed for G. Strahan, S. Ballard"—and a score of booksellers—"MDCCXLI." Heavens knows why he read it; since he understood about one-half, and admired less than one-tenth. The Oriental reflections struck him as mainly blasphemous. But the Gaffer's religious belief marked down nine-tenths of mankind for perdition: which perhaps made him tolerant. At any rate, he read on gravely between the puffs of his short clay—

"On the 19th of this Moon, the King and the whole Court were present at a Ballet, representing the grandeur of the *French* monarchy. About the Middle of the Entertainment, there was an Antique Dance performed by twelve Masqueraders, in the suppos'd form of *Daemons*. But before they had advanc'd far in their Dance, they found an Interloper amongst 'em, who by encreasing the Number to thirteen, put them quite out of their Measure: For they practise every Step and Motion beforehand, till they are perfect. Being abash'd therefore at the unavoidable Blunders the thirteenth Antique made them commit, they stood still like Fools, gazing at one another: None daring to unmask, or speak a Word; for that would have put all the Spectators into a Disorder and Confusion. *Cardinal Mazarmi* (who was the chief Contriver of these Entertainments, to divert the King from more serious Thoughts) stood close by the young Monarch, with the Scheme of the Ballet in his Hand. Knowing therefore that this Dance was to consist but of twelve Antiques, and taking notice that there were actually thirteen, he at first imputed it to some Mistake. But, afterwards when he perceived the Confusion of the Dancers, he made a more narrow Enquiry into the Cause of this Disorder. To be brief, they convinced the *Cardinal* that it could be no Error of theirs, by a kind of Demonstration, in that they had but twelve Antique Dresses of that sort, which were made on purpose for this particular Ballet. That which made it seem the greater Mystery was, that when they came behind the Scenes to uncase, and examine the Matter, they found but twelve Antiques, whereas on the Stage there were thirteen..."

"Let him say it. Let him say he didn't mean it, the rotten Irishman!"

Cooney flung a leg wearily over the side of his hammock, jerked himself out, and shuffled across to the sick man's berth.

"Av coorse I didn' mane it. It just took me, ye see, lyin' up yondher and huggin' me thoughts in this—wilderness. I swear to ye, George: and ye'll just wet your throat to show there's no bad blood, and that ye belave me." He took up a pannikin from the floor beside the bunk, pulled a hot iron from the fire, and stirred the frozen drink. The invalid turned his shoulder pettishly. "I didn't mane it," Cooney repeated. He set down the pannikin, and shuffled wearily back to his hammock.

The Gaffer blew a long cloud and stared at the fire; at the smoke mounting and the grey ash dropping; at David Faed dealing the cards and licking his thumb between each. Long Ede shifted from one cramped elbow to another and pushed his Bible nearer the blaze, murmuring, "Take us the foxes, the little foxes, that spoil our vines."

"Full hand," the Snipe announced.

"Ay." David Faed rolled the quid in his cheek. The cards were so thumbed and tattered that by the backs of them each player guessed pretty shrewdly what the other held. Yet they went on playing night after night; the Snipe shrilly blessing or cursing his luck, the Scotsman phlegmatic as a bolster.

"Play away, man. What ails ye?" he asked.

The Snipe had dropped both hands to his thighs and sat up, stiff and listening.

"Whist! Outside the door...."

All listened. "I hear nothing," said David, after ten seconds.

"Hush, man—listen! There, again..."

They heard now. Cooney slipped down from his hammock, stole to the door and listened, crouching, with his ear close to the jamb. The sound resembled breathing—or so he thought for a moment. Then it seemed rather as if some creature were softly feeling about the door—fumbling its coating of ice and frozen snow.

Cooney listened. They all listened. Usually, as soon as they stirred from the scorching circle of the fire, their breath came from them in clouds. It trickled from them now in thin wisps of vapour. They could almost hear the soft grey ash dropping on the hearth.

A log spluttered. Then the invalid's voice clattered in—

"It's the bears—the bears! They've come after Bill, and next it'll be my turn. I warned you—I told you he wasn't deep enough. O Lord, have mercy... mercy...!" He pattered off into a prayer, his voice and teeth chattering.

"Hush!" commanded the Gaffer gently; and Lashman choked on a sob.

"It ain't bears," Cooney reported, still with his ear to the door. "Leastways... we've had bears before. The foxes, maybe... let me listen."

Long Ede murmured: "Take us the foxes, the little foxes..."

"I believe you're right," the Gaffer announced cheerfully. "A bear would sniff louder—though there's no telling. The snow was falling an hour back, and I dessay 'tis pretty thick outside. If 'tis a bear, we don't want him fooling on the roof, and I misdoubt the drift by the north corner is pretty tall by this time. Is he there still?"

"I felt something then... through the chink, here... like a warm breath. It's gone now. Come here, Snipe, and listen."

"'Breath,' eh? Did it *smell* like bear?"

"I don't know... I didn't smell nothing, to notice. Here, put your head down, close."

The Snipe bent his head. And at that moment the door shook gently. All stared; and saw the latch move up, up... and falteringly descend on the staple. They heard the click of it.

The door was secured within by two stout bars. Against these there had been no pressure. The men waited in a silence that ached. But the latch was not lifted again.

The Snipe, kneeling, looked up at Cooney. Cooney shivered and looked at David Faed. Long Ede, with his back to the fire, softly shook his feet free of the rugs. His eyes searched for the Gaffer's face. But the old man had drawn back into the gloom of his bunk, and the lamplight shone only on a grey fringe of beard. He saw Long Ede's look, though, and answered it quietly as ever.

"Take a brace of guns aloft, and fetch us a look round. Wait, if there's a chance of a shot. The trap works. I tried it this afternoon with the small chisel."

Long Ede lit his pipe tied down the ear-pieces of his cap, lifted a light ladder off its staples, and set it against a roof-beam: then, with the guns under his arm, quietly mounted. His head and shoulders wavered and grew vague to sight in the smoke-wreaths. "Heard anything more?" he asked. "Nothing since," answered the Snipe. With his shoulder Long Ede pushed up the trap. They saw his head framed in a panel of moonlight, with one frosty star above it. He was wriggling through. "Pitch him up a sleeping-bag, somebody," the Gaffer ordered, and Cooney ran with one. "Thank 'ee, mate," said Long Ede, and closed the trap.

They heard his feet stealthily crunching the frozen stuff across the roof. He was working towards the eaves over-lapping the door. Their breath tightened. They waited for the explosion of his gun. None came. The crunching began again: it was heard down by the very edge of the eaves. It mounted to the blunt ridge overhead; then it ceased.

"He will not have seen aught," David Faed muttered.

"Listen, you. Listen by the door again." They talked in whispers. Nothing; there was nothing to be heard. They crept back to the fire, and stood there warming themselves, keeping their eyes on the latch. It did not move. After a while Cooney slipped off to his hammock; Faed to his bunk, alongside Lashman's. The Gaffer had picked up his book again. The Snipe laid a couple of logs on the blaze, and remained beside it, cowering, with his arms stretched out as if to embrace it. His shapeless shadow wavered up and down on the bunks behind him; and, across the fire, he still stared at the latch.

Suddenly the sick man's voice quavered out—

"It's not him they want—it's Bill! They're after Bill, out there! That was Bill trying to get in.... Why didn't yer open? It was Bill, I tell yer!"

At the first word the Snipe had wheeled right-about-face, and stood now, pointing, and shaking like a man with ague.

"Matey... for the love of God..."

"I won't hush. There's something wrong here to-night. I can't sleep. It's Bill, I tell yer. See his poor hammock up there shaking...."

Cooney tumbled out with an oath and a thud. "Hush it, you white-livered swine! Hush it, or by—" His hand went behind him to his knife-sheath.

"Dan Cooney"—the Gaffer closed his book and leaned out—"go back to your bed."

"I won't, Sir. Not unless—"

"Go back."

"Flesh and blood—"

"Go back." And for the third time that night Cooney went back.

The Gaffer leaned a little farther over the ledge, and addressed the sick man.

"George, I went to Bill's grave not six hours agone. The snow on it wasn't even disturbed. Neither beast nor man, but only God, can break up the hard earth he lies under. I tell you that, and you may lay to it. Now go to sleep."

Long Ede crouched on the frozen ridge of the hut, with his feet in the sleeping-bag, his knees drawn up, and the two guns laid across them. The creature, whatever its name, that had tried the door, was nowhere to be seen; but he decided to wait a few minutes on the chance of a shot; that is, until the cold should drive him below. For the moment the clear tingling air was doing him good. The truth was Long Ede had begun to be afraid of himself, and the way his mind had been running for the last forty-eight hours upon green fields and visions of spring. As he put it to himself, something inside his head was melting. Biblical texts chattered within him like running brooks, and as they fleeted he could almost smell the blown meadow-scent. "Take us the foxes, the little foxes... for our vines have tender grapes... A fountain of gardens, a well of living waters, and streams from Lebanon... Awake, O north wind, and come, thou south... blow upon my garden, that the spices thereof may flow out..." He was light-headed, and he knew it. He must hold out. They were all going mad; were, in fact, three parts crazed already, all except the Gaffer. And the Gaffer relied on him as his right-hand man. One glimpse of the returning sun—one glimpse only—might save them yet.

He gazed out over the frozen hills, and northward across the ice-pack. A few streaks of pale violet—the ghost of the Aurora—fronted the moon. He could see for miles. Bear or fox, no living creature was in sight. But who could tell what might be hiding behind any one of a thousand hummocks? He listened. He heard the slow grinding of the ice-pack off the beach: only that. "Take us the foxes, the little foxes..."

This would never do. He must climb down and walk briskly, or return to the hut. Maybe there was a bear, after all, behind one of the hummocks, and a shot, or the chance of one, would scatter his head clear of these tom-fooling notions. He would have a search round.

What was that, moving... on a hummock, not five hundred yards away? He leaned forward to gaze.

Nothing now: but he had seen something. He lowered himself to the eaves by the north corner, and from the eaves to the drift piled there. The drift was frozen solid, but for a treacherous crust of fresh snow. His foot slipped upon this, and down he slid of a heap.

Luckily he had been careful to sling the guns tightly at his back. He picked himself up, and unstrapping one, took a step into the bright moon-light to examine the nipples; took two steps: and stood stock-still.

There, before him, on the frozen coat of snow, was a footprint. No: two, three, four—many footprints: prints of a naked human foot: right foot, left foot, both naked, and blood in each print—a little smear.

It had come, then. He was mad for certain. He saw them: he put his fingers in them; touched the frozen blood. The snow before the door was trodden thick with them—some going, some returning.

"The latch... lifted..." Suddenly he recalled the figure he had seen moving upon the hummock, and with a groan he set his face northward and gave chase. Oh, he was mad for certain! He ran like a madman—floundering, slipping, plunging in his clumsy moccasins. "Take us the foxes, the little foxes... My beloved put in his hand by the hole of the door, and my bowels were moved for him... I charge you, O daughters of Jerusalem... I charge you... I charge you..."

He ran thus for three hundred yards maybe, and then stopped as suddenly as he had started.

His mates—they must not see these footprints, or they would go mad too: mad as he. No, he must cover them up, all within sight of the hut. And to-morrow he would come alone, and cover those farther afield. Slowly he retraced his steps. The footprints—those which pointed towards the hut and those which pointed away from it—lay close together; and he knelt before each, breaking fresh snow over the hollows and carefully hiding the blood. And now a great happiness filled his heart; interrupted once or twice as he worked by a feeling that someone was following and watching him. Once he turned northwards and gazed, making a telescope of his hands. He saw nothing, and fell again to his long task.

Within the hut the sick man cried softly to himself. Faed, the Snipe, and Cooney slept uneasily, and muttered in their dreams. The Gaffer lay awake, thinking. After Bill, George Lashman; and after George?... Who next? And who would be the last—the unburied one? The men were weakening fast; their wits and courage coming down at the end with a rush. Faed and Long Ede were the only two to be depended on for a day. The Gaffer liked Long Ede, who was a religious man. Indeed he had a growing suspicion that Long Ede, in spite of some amiable laxities of belief, was numbered among the Elect: or might be, if interceded for. The Gaffer began to intercede for him silently; but experience had taught him that such "wrestlings," to be effective, must be noisy, and he dropped off to sleep with a sense of failure...

The Snipe stretched himself, yawned, and awoke. It was seven in the morning: time to prepare a cup of tea. He tossed an armful of logs on the fire, and the noise awoke the Gaffer, who at once inquired for Long Ede. He had not returned. "Go you up to the roof. The lad must be frozen." The Snipe climbed the ladder, pushed open the trap, and came back, reporting that Long Ede was nowhere to be seen. The old man slipped a jumper over his suits of clothing—already three deep—reached for a gun, and moved to the door. "Take a cup of something warm to fortify," the Snipe advised. "The kettle won't be five minutes boiling." But the Gaffer pushed up the heavy bolts and dragged the door open.

"What in the!... Here, bear a hand, lads!"

Long Ede lay prone before the threshold, his out-stretched hands almost touching it, his moccasins already covered out of sight by the powdery snow which ran and trickled incessantly—trickled between his long, dishevelled locks, and over the back of his gloves, and ran in a thin stream past the Gaffer's feet.

They carried him in and laid him on a heap of skins by the fire. They forced rum between his clenched teeth and beat his hands and feet, and kneaded and rubbed him. A sigh fluttered on his lips: something between a sigh and a smile, half seen, half heard. His eyes opened, and his comrades saw that it was really a smile.

"Wot cheer, mate?" It was the Snipe who asked.

"I—I seen..." The voice broke off, but he was smiling still.

What had he seen? Not the sun, surely! By the Gaffer's reckoning the sun would not be due for a week or two yet: how many weeks he could not say precisely, and sometimes he was glad enough that he did not know.

They forced him to drink a couple of spoonfuls of rum, and wrapped him up warmly. Each man contributed some of his own bedding. Then the Gaffer called to morning prayers, and the three sound men dropped on their knees with him. Now, whether by reason of their joy at Long Ede's recovery, or because the old man was in splendid voice, they felt their hearts uplifted that morning with a cheerfulness they had not known for months. Long Ede lay and listened dreamily while the passion of the Gaffer's thanksgiving shook the hut. His gaze wandered over their bowed forms—"The Gaffer, David Faed, Dan Cooney, the Snipe, and—and George Lashman in his bunk, of course—and me." But, then, *who was the seventh?* He began to count. "There's myself—Lashman, in his bunk—David Faed, the Gaffer, the Snipe, Dan Cooney... One, two, three, four—well, but that made *seven*. Then who was the seventh? Was it George who had crawled out of bed and was kneeling there? Decidedly there were five kneeling. No: there was George, plain enough, in his berth, and not able to move. Then who was the stranger? Wrong again: there was no stranger. He knew all these men—they were his mates. Was it—Bill? No, Bill was dead and buried: none of these was Bill, or like Bill. Try again—One, two, three, four, five—and us two sick men, seven. The Gaffer, David Faed, Dan Cooney—have I counted Dan twice? No, that's Dan, yonder to the right, and only one of him. Five men kneeling, and two on their backs: that makes seven every time. Dear God—suppose—"

The Gaffer ceased, and in the act of rising from his knees, caught sight of Long Ede's face. While the others fetched their breakfast-cans, he stepped over, and bent and whispered—

"Tell me. Ye've seen what?"

"Seen?" Long Ede echoed.

"Ay, seen what? Speak low—was it the sun?"

"The s—" But this time the echo died on his lips, and his face grew full of awe uncomprehending. It frightened the Gaffer.

"Ye'll be the better of a snatch of sleep," said he; and was turning to go, when Long Ede stirred a hand under the edge of his rugs.

"Seven... count..." he whispered.

"Lord have mercy upon us!" the Gaffer muttered to his beard as he moved away. "Long Ede; gone crazed!"

And yet, though an hour or two ago this had been the worst that could befall, the Gaffer felt unusually cheerful. As for the others, they were like different men, all that day and through the three days that followed. Even Lashman ceased to complain, and, unless their eyes played them a trick, had taken a turn for the better. "I declare, if I don't feel like pitching to sing!" the Snipe announced on the second evening, as much to his own wonder as to theirs. "Then why in thunder don't you strike up?" answered Dan Cooney, and fetched his concertina. The Snipe struck up, then and there—"Villikins and his Dinah"! What is more, the Gaffer looked up from his "Paradise Lost," and joined in the chorus.

By the end of the second day, Long Ede was up and active again. He went about with a dazed look in his eyes. He was counting, counting to himself, always counting. The Gaffer watched him furtively.

Since his recovery, though his lips moved frequently, Long Ede had scarcely uttered a word. But towards noon on the fourth day he said an extraordinary thing.

"There's that sleeping-bag I took with me the other night. I wonder if 'tis on the roof still. It will be froze pretty stiff by this. You might nip up and see, Snipe, and"—he paused—"if you find it, stow it up yonder on Bill's hammock."

The Gaffer opened his mouth, but shut it again without speaking. The Snipe went up the ladder.

A minute passed; and then they heard a cry from the roof—a cry that fetched them all trembling, choking, weeping, cheering, to the foot of the ladder.

"Boys! boys!—the Sun!"

Months later—it was June, and even George Lashman had recovered his strength—the Snipe came running with news of the whaling fleet. And on the beach, as they watched the vessels come to anchor, Long Ede told the Gaffer his story. "It was a hall—a hallu—what d'ye call it, I reckon. I was crazed, eh?" The Gaffer's eyes wandered from a brambling hopping about the lichen-covered boulders, and away to the sea-fowl wheeling above the ships: and then came into his mind a tale he had read once in "The Turkish Spy." "I wouldn't say just that," he answered slowly.

"Anyway," said Long Ede, "I believe the Lord sent a miracle to us to save us all."

"I wouldn't say just that, either," the Gaffer objected. "I doubt it was meant just for you and me, and the rest were presairved, as you might say incidentally."

Some thinkers would feel sorely hampered if at liberty to use no forms but such as existed in nature, or to invent nothing save in accordance with the laws of the world of the senses; but it must not therefore be imagined that they desire escape from the region of law. Nothing lawless can show the least reason why it should exist, or could at best have more than an appearance of life.

The natural world has its laws, and no man must interfere with them in the way of presentment any more than in the way of use; but they themselves may suggest laws of other kinds, and man may, if he pleases, invent a little world of his own, with its own laws; for there is that in him which delights in calling up new forms—which is the nearest, perhaps, he can come to creation. When such forms are new embodiments of old truths, we call them products of the Imagination; when they are mere inventions, however lovely, I should call them the work of the Fancy: in either case, Law has been diligently at work.

—George MacDonald, "The Fantastic Imagination."

A GENTLE GHOST

Mary E. Wilkins (1852-1930)

Out in front of the cemetery stood a white horse and a covered wagon. The horse was not tied, but she stood quite still, her four feet widely and ponderously planted, her meek white head hanging. Shadows of leaves danced on her back. There were many trees about the cemetery, and the foliage was unusually luxuriant for May. The four women who had come in the covered wagon remarked it. "I never saw the trees so forward as they are this year, seems to me," said one, gazing up at some magnificent gold-green branches over her head.

"I was sayin' so to Mary this mornin'," rejoined another. "They're uncommon forward, I think."

They loitered along the narrow lanes between the lots: four homely, middle-aged women, with decorous and subdued enjoyment in their worn faces. They read with peaceful curiosity and interest the inscriptions on the stones; they turned aside to look at the tender, newly blossomed spring bushes—the flowering almonds and the bridal wreaths. Once in a while they came to a new stone, which they immediately surrounded with eager criticism. There was a solemn hush when they reached a lot where some relatives of one of the party were buried. She put a bunch of flowers on a grave, then she stood looking at it with red eyes. The others grouped themselves deferentially aloof.

They did not meet any one in the cemetery until just before they left. When they had reached the rear and oldest portion of the yard, and were thinking of retracing their steps, they became suddenly aware of a child sitting in a lot at their right. The lot held seven old, leaning stones, dark and mossy, their inscriptions dimly traceable. The child sat close to one, and she looked up at the staring knot of women with a kind of innocent keenness, like a baby. Her face was small and fair and pinched. The women stood eying her.

379

"What's your name, little girl?" asked one. She had a bright flower in her bonnet and a smart lift to her chin, and seemed the natural spokeswoman of the party. Her name was Holmes. The child turned her head sideways and murmured something.

"What? We can't hear. Speak up; don't be afraid! What's your name?" The woman nodded the bright flower over her, and spoke with sharp pleasantness.

"Nancy Wren," said the child, with a timid catch of her breath.

"Wren?"

The child nodded. She kept her little pink, curving mouth parted.

"It's nobody I know," remarked the questioner, reflectively. "I guess she comes from—over there." She made a significant motion of her head towards the right. "Where do you live, Nancy?" she asked.

The child also motioned towards the right.

"I thought so," said the woman. "How old are you?"

"Ten."

The women exchanged glances. "Are you sure you're tellin' the truth?"

The child nodded.

"I never saw a girl so small for her age if she is," said one woman to another.

"Yes," said Mrs. Holmes, looking at her critically; "she is dreadful small. She's considerable smaller than my Mary was. Is there any of your folks buried in this lot?" said she, fairly hovering with affability and determined graciousness.

The child's upturned face suddenly kindled. She began speaking with a soft volubility that was an odd contrast to her previous hesitation.

"That's mother," said she, pointing to one of the stones, "an' that's father, an' there's John, an' Marg'ret, an' Mary, an' Susan, an' the baby, and here's—Jane."

The women stared at her in amazement. "Was it your—" began Mrs. Holmes; but another woman stepped forward, stoutly impetuous.

"Land! it's the Blake lot!" said she. "This child can't be any relation to 'em. You hadn't ought to talk so, Nancy."

"It's so," said the child, shyly persistent. She evidently hardly grasped the force of the woman's remark.

They eyed her with increased bewilderment. "It can't be," said the woman to the others. "Every one of them Blakes died years ago."

"I've seen Jane," volunteered the child, with a candid smile in their faces.

Then the stout woman sank down on her knees beside Jane's stone, and peered hard at it.

"She died forty year ago this May," said she, with a gasp. "I used to know her when I was a child. She was ten years old when she died. You ain't ever seen her. You hadn't ought to tell such stories."

"I ain't seen her for a long time," said the little girl.

"What made you say you'd seen her at all?" said Mrs. Holmes, sharply, thinking this was capitulation.

"I did use to see her a long time ago, an' she used to wear a white dress, an' a wreath on her head. She used to come here an' play with me."

The women looked at each other with pale, shocked faces; one nervous; one shivered. "She ain't quite right," she whispered. "Let's go." The women began filing away. Mrs. Holmes, who came last, stood about for a parting word to the child.

"You can't have seen her," said she, severely, "an' you are a wicked girl to tell such stories. You mustn't do it again, remember."

Nancy stood with her hand on Jane's stone, looking at her. "She did," she repeated, with mild obstinacy.

"There's somethin' wrong about her, I guess," whispered Mrs. Holmes, rustling on after the others.

"I see she looked kind of queer the minute I set eyes on her," said the nervous woman.

When the four reached the front of the cemetery they sat down to rest for a few minutes. It was warm, and they had still quite a walk, nearly the whole width of the yard, to the other front corner where the horse and wagon were.

They sat down in a row on a bank; the stout woman wiped her face; Mrs. Holmes straightened her bonnet. Directly opposite across the street stood two houses, so close to each other that their walls almost touched. One was a large square building, glossily white, with green blinds; the other was low, with a facing of whitewashed stone-work reaching to its lower windows, which somehow gave it a disgraced and menial air; there were, moreover, no blinds.

At the side of the low building stretched a wide ploughed field, where several halting old figures were moving about planting. There was none of the brave hope of the sower about them. Even across the road one could see the feeble stiffness of their attitudes, the half-palsied fling of their arms.

"I declare I shouldn't think them old men over there would ever get that field planted," said Mrs. Holmes, energetically watchful. In the front door of the square white house sat a girl with bright hair. The yard was full of green light from two tall maple-trees, and the girl's hair made a brilliant spot of color in the midst of it.

"That's Flora Dunn over there on the door-step, ain't it?" said the stout woman.

"Yes. I should think you could tell her by her red hair."

"I knew it. I should have thought Mr. Dunn would have hated to have had their house so near the poor-house. I declare I should!"

"Oh, he wouldn't mind," said Mrs. Holmes; "he's as easy as old Tilly. It wouldn't have troubled him any if they'd set it right in his front yard. But I guess she minded some. I heard she did. John said there wa'n't any need of it. The town wouldn't have set it so near, if Mr. Dunn had set his foot down he wouldn't have it there. I s'pose they wanted to keep that big field on the side clear; but they would have moved it along a little if he'd made a fuss. I tell you what 'tis, I've 'bout made up my mind—I dun know as it's Scripture, but I can't help it—if folks don't make a fuss they won't get their rights in this world. If you jest lay still an' don't rise up, you're goin' to get stepped on. If people like to be, they can; I don't."

"I should have thought he'd have hated to have the poor-house quite so close," murmured the stout woman.

Suddenly Mrs. Holmes leaned forward and poked her head among the other three. She sat on the end of the row. "Say," said she, in a mysterious whisper, "I want to know if you've heard the stories 'bout the Dunn house?"

"No; what?" chorused the other women, eagerly. They bent over towards her till the four faces were in a knot.

"Well," said Mrs. Holmes, cautiously, with a glance at the bright-headed girl across the way—"I heard it pretty straight—they say the house is haunted."

The stout woman sniffed and straightened herself. "Haunted!" repeated she.

"They say that ever since Jenny died there's been queer noises 'round the house that they can't account for. You see that front chamber over there, the one next to the poor-house; well, that's the room, they say."

The women all turned and looked at the chamber windows, where some ruffled white curtains were fluttering.

"That's the chamber where Jenny used to sleep, you know," Mrs. Holmes went on; "an' she died there. Well, they said that before Jenny died, Flora had always slept there with her, but she felt kind of bad about goin' back there, so she thought she'd take another room. Well, there was the awfulest moanin' an' takin' on up in Jenny's room, when she did, that Flora went back there to sleep."

"I shouldn't thought she could," whispered the nervous woman, who was quite pale.

"The moanin' stopped jest as soon as she got in there with a light. You see Jenny was always terrible timid an' afraid to sleep alone, an' had a lamp burnin' all night, an' it seemed to them jest as if it really was her, I s'pose."

"I don't believe one word of it," said the stout woman, getting up. "It makes me all out of patience to hear people talk such stuff, jest because the Dunns happen to live opposite a graveyard."

"I told it jest as I heard it," said Mrs. Holmes, stiffly.

"Oh, I ain't blamin' you; it's the folks that start such stories that I ain't got any patience with. Think of that dear, pretty little sixteen-year-old girl hauntin' a house!"

"Well, I've told it jest as I heard it," repeated Mrs. Holmes, still in a tone of slight umbrage. "I don't ever take much stock in such things myself."

The four women strolled along to the covered wagon and climbed in. "I declare," said the stout woman, conciliatingly, "I dun know when I've had such an outin'. I feel as if it had done me good. I've been wantin' to come down to the cemetery for a long time, but it's most more'n I want to walk. I feel real obliged to you, Mis' Holmes."

The others climbed in. Mrs. Holmes disclaimed all obligations gracefully, established herself on the front seat, and shook the reins over the white horse. Then the party jogged along the road to the village, past outlying farmhouses and rich green meadows, all freckled gold with dandelions. Dandelions were in their height; the buttercups had not yet come.

Flora Dunn, the girl on the door-step, glanced up when they started down the street; then she turned her eyes on her work; she was sewing with nervous haste.

"Who were those folks, did you see, Flora?" called her mother, out of the sitting-room.

"I didn't notice," replied Flora, absently.

Just then the girl whom the women had met came lingeringly out of the cemetery and crossed the street.

"There's that poor little Wren girl," remarked the voice in the sitting-room.

"Yes," assented Flora. After a while she got up and entered the house. Her mother looked anxiously at her when she came into the room.

"I'm all out of patience with you, Flora," said she. "You're jest as white as a sheet. You'll make yourself sick. You're actin' dreadful foolish."

Flora sank into a chair and sat staring straight ahead with a strained, pitiful gaze. "I can't help it; I can't do any different," said she. "I shouldn't think you'd scold me, mother."

"Scold you; I ain't scoldin' you, child; but there ain't any sense in your doin' so. You'll make yourself sick, an' you're all I've got left. I can't have anything happen to you, Flora." Suddenly Mrs. Dunn burst out in a low wail, hiding her face in her hands.

"I don't see as you're much better yourself, mother," said Flora, heavily.

"I don't know as I am," sobbed her mother; "but I've got you to worry about besides—everything else. Oh, dear! oh, dear, dear!"

"I don't see any need of your worrying about me." Flora did not cry, but her face seemed to darken visibly with a gathering melancholy like a cloud. Her hair was beautiful, and she had a charming delicacy of complexion; but she was not handsome, her features were too sharp, her expression too intense and nervous. Her mother looked like her as to the expression; the features were widely different. It was as if both had passed through one corroding element which had given them the similarity of scars. Certainly a stranger would at once have noticed the strong resemblance between Mrs. Dunn's large, heavy-featured face and her daughter's thin, delicately outlined one—a resemblance which three months ago had not been perceptible.

"I see, if you don't," returned the mother. "I ain't blind."

"I don't see what you are blaming me for."

"I ain't blamin' you, but it seems to me that you might jest as well let me go up there an' sleep as you."

Suddenly the girl also broke out into a wild cry. "I ain't going to leave her. Poor little Jenny! poor little Jenny! You needn't try to make me, mother; I won't!"

"Flora, don't!"

"I won't! I won't! I won't! Poor little Jenny! Oh, dear! oh, dear!"

"What if it is so? What if it is—her? Ain't she got me as well as you? Can't her mother go to her?"

"I won't leave her. I won't! I won't!"

Suddenly Mrs. Dunn's calmness seemed to come uppermost, raised in the scale by the weighty impetus of the other's distress. "Flora," said she, with mournful solemnity, "you mustn't do so; it's wrong. You mustn't wear yourself all out over something that maybe you'll find out wasn't so some time or other."

"Mother, don't you think it is—don't you?"

"I don't know what to think, Flora." Just then a door shut somewhere in the back part of the house. "There's father," said Mrs. Dunn, getting up; "an' the fire ain't made."

Flora rose also, and went about helping her mother to get supper. Both suddenly settled into a rigidity of composure; their eyes were red, but their lips were steady. There was a resolute vein in their characters; they managed themselves with wrenches, and could be hard even with their grief. They got tea ready for Mr. Dunn and his two hired men; then cleared it away, and sat down in the front room with their needlework. Mr. Dunn, a kindly, dull old man, was in there too, over his newspaper. Mrs. Dunn and Flora sewed intently, never taking their eyes from their work. Out in the next room stood a tall clock, which ticked loudly; just before it struck the hours it made always a curious grating noise. When it announced in this way the striking of nine, Mrs. Dunn and Flora exchanged glances; the girl was pale, and her eyes looked larger. She began folding up her work. Suddenly a low moaning cry sounded through the house, seemingly from the room overhead. "There it is!" shrieked Flora. She caught up a lamp and ran. Mrs. Dunn was following, when her husband, sitting near the door, caught hold of her dress with a bewildered air; he had been dozing. "What's the matter?" said he, vaguely.

"Don't you hear it? Didn't you hear it, father?"

The old man let go of her dress suddenly. "I didn't hear nothin'," said he. "Hark!"

But the cry, in fact, had ceased. Flora could be heard moving about in the room overhead, and that was all. In a moment Mrs. Dunn ran up-stairs after her. The old man sat staring. "It's all dum foolishness," he muttered, under his breath. Presently he fell to dozing again, and his vacantly smiling face lopped forward. Mr. Dunn, slow-brained, patient, and unimaginative, had had his evening naps interrupted after this manner for the last three months, and there was as yet no cessation of his bewilderment. He dealt with the simple, broad lights of life; the shadows were beyond his speculation. For his consciousness his daughter Jenny had died and gone to heaven; he was not capable of listening for her ghostly moans in her little chamber overhead, much less of hearing them with any credulity.

When his wife came down-stairs finally she looked at him, sleeping there, with a bitter feeling. She felt as if set about by an icy wind of loneliness. Her daughter, who was after her own kind, was all the one to whom she could look for sympathy and understanding in this subtle perplexity which had come upon her. And she would rather have dispensed with that sympathy, and heard alone those piteous, uncanny cries, for she was wild with anxiety about Flora. The girl had never been very strong. She looked at her distressfully when she came down the next morning.

"Did you sleep any last night?" said she.

"Some," answered Flora.

Soon after breakfast they noticed the little Wren girl stealing across the road to the cemetery again. "She goes over there all the time," remarked Mrs. Dunn. "I b'lieve she runs away. See her look behind her."

"Yes," said Flora, apathetically.

It was nearly noon when they heard a voice from the next house calling, "Nancy! Nancy! Nancy Wren!" The voice was loud and imperious, but slow and evenly modulated. It indicated well its owner. A woman who could regulate her own angry voice could regulate other people. Mrs. Dunn and Flora heard it understandingly.

"That poor little thing will catch it when she gets home," said Mrs. Dunn.

"Nancy! Nancy! Nancy Wren!" called the voice again.

"I pity the child if Mrs. Gregg has to go after her. Mebbe she's fell asleep over there. Flora, why don't you run over there an' get her?"

The voice rang out again. Flora got her hat and stole across the street a little below the house, so the calling woman should not see her. When she got into the cemetery she called in her turn, letting out her thin sweet voice cautiously. Finally she came directly upon the child. She was in the Blake lot, her little slender body, in its dingy cotton dress, curled up on the ground close to one of the graves. No one but Nature tended those old graves now, and she seemed to be lapsing them gently back to her own lines, at her own will. Of the garden shrubs which had been planted about them not one was left but an old low-spraying white rose-bush, which had just gotten its new leaves. The Blake lot was at the very rear of the yard, where it verged upon a light wood, which was silently stealing its way over its own proper boundaries. At the back of the lot stood a thicket of little thin trees, with silvery twinkling leaves. The ground was quite blue with houstonias.

The child raised her little fair head and stared at Flora, as if just awakened from sleep. She held her little pink mouth open, her innocent blue eyes had a surprised look, as if she were suddenly gazing upon a new scene.

"Where's she gone?" asked she, in her sweet, feeble pipe.

"Where's who gone?"

"Jane."

"I don't know what you mean. Come, Nancy, you must go home now."

"Didn't you see her?"

"I didn't see anybody," answered Flora, impatiently. "Come!"

"She was right here."

"What do you mean?"

"Jane was standin' right here. An' she had her white dress on, an' her wreath."

Flora shivered, and looked around her fearfully. The fancy of the child was overlapping her own nature. "There wasn't a soul here. You've been dreaming, child. Come!"

"No, I wasn't. I've seen them blue flowers an' the leaves winkin' all the time. Jane stood right there." The child pointed with her tiny finger to a spot at her side. "She hadn't come for a long time before," she added. "She's stayed down there." She pointed at the grave nearest her.

"You mustn't talk so," said Flora, with tremulous severity. "You must get right up and come home. Mrs. Gregg has been calling you and calling you. She won't like it."

Nancy turned quite pale around her little mouth, and sprang to her feet. "Is Mis' Gregg comin'?"

"She will come if you don't hurry."

The child said not another word. She flew along ahead through the narrow paths, and was in the almshouse door before Flora crossed the street.

"She's terrible afraid of Mrs. Gregg," she told her mother when she got home. Nancy had disturbed her own brooding a little, and she spoke more like herself.

"Poor little thing! I pity her," said Mrs. Dunn. Mrs. Dunn did not like Mrs. Gregg.

Flora rarely told a story until she had ruminated awhile over it herself. It was afternoon, and the two were in the front room at their sewing, before she told her mother about "Jane."

"Of course she must have been dreaming," Flora said.

"She must have been," rejoined her mother.

But the two looked at each other, and their eyes said more than their tongues. Here was a new marvel, new evidence of a kind which they had heretofore scented at, these two rigidly walking New England souls; yet walking, after all, upon narrow paths through dark meadows of mysticism. If they never lost their footing, the steaming damp of the meadows might come in their faces.

This fancy, delusion, superstition, whichever one might name it, of theirs had lasted now three months—ever since young Jenny Dunn had died. There was apparently no reason why it should not last much longer, if delusion it were; the temperaments of these two women, naturally nervous and imaginative, overwrought now by long care and sorrow, would perpetuate it.

If it were not delusion, pray what exorcism, what spell of book and bell, could lay the ghost of a little timid child who was afraid alone in the dark?

The days went on, and Flora still hurried up to her chamber at the stroke of nine. If she were a moment late, sometimes if she were not, that pitiful low wail sounded through the house.

The strange story spread gradually through the village. Mrs. Dunn and Flora were silent about it, but Gossip is herself of a ghostly nature, and minds not keys nor bars.

There was quite an excitement over it. People affected with morbid curiosity and sympathy came to the house. One afternoon the minister came and offered a prayer. Mrs. Dunn and Flora received them all with a certain reticence; they did not concur in their wishes to remain and hear the mysterious noises for themselves. People called them "dreadful close." They got more satisfaction out of Mr. Dunn, who was perfectly ready to impart all the information in his power and his own theories in the matter.

"I never heard a thing but once," said he, "an' then it sounded more like a cat to me than anything. I guess mother and Flora air kinder nervous."

The spring was waxing late when Flora went up-stairs one night with the oil low in her lamp. She had neglected filling it that day. She did not notice it until she was undressed; then she thought to herself that she must blow it out. She always kept a lamp burning all night, as she had in timid little Jenny's day. Flora herself was timid now.

So she blew the light out. She had barely laid her head upon the pillow when the low moaning wail sounded through the room. Flora sat up in bed and listened, her hands clinched. The moan gathered strength and volume; little broken words and sentences, the piteous ejaculations of terror and distress, began to shape themselves out of it.

Flora sprang out of bed, and stumbled towards her west window—the one on the almshouse side. She leaned her head out, listening a moment. Then she called her mother with wild vehemence. But her mother was already at the door with a lamp. When she entered, the moans ceased.

"Mother," shrieked Flora, "it ain't Jenny. It's somebody over there—at the poor-house. Put the lamp out in the entry, and come back here and listen."

Mrs. Dunn set out the lamp and came back, closing the door. It was a few minutes first, but presently the cries recommenced.

"I'm goin' right over there," said Mrs. Dunn. "I'm goin' to dress myself an' go over there. I'm goin' to have this affair sifted now."

"I'm going too," said Flora.

It was only half-past nine when the two stole into the almshouse yard. The light was not out in the room on the ground-floor, which the overseer's family used for a sitting-room. When they entered, the overseer was there asleep in his chair, his wife sewing at the table, and an old woman in a pink cotton dress, apparently doing nothing. They all started, and stared at the intruders.

"Good-evenin'," said Mrs. Dunn, trying to speak composedly. "We thought we'd come in; we got kind of started. Oh, there 'tis now! What is it, Mis' Gregg?"

In fact, at that moment, the wail, louder and more distinct, was heard.

"Why, it's Nancy," replied Mrs. Gregg, with dignified surprise. She was a large woman, with a masterly placidity about her. "I heard her a few minutes ago," she went on; "an' I was goin' up there to see to her if she hadn't stopped."

Mr. Gregg, a heavy, saturnine old man, with a broad bristling face, sat staring stupidly. The old woman in pink calico surveyed them all with an impersonal grin.

"Nancy!" repeated Mrs. Dunn, looking at Mrs. Gregg. She had not fancied this woman very much, and the two had not fraternized, although they were such near neighbors. Indeed, Mrs. Gregg was not of a sociable nature, and associated very little with anything but her own duties.

"Yes; Nancy Wren," she said, with gathering amazement. "She cries out this way 'most every night. She's ten years old, but she's as afraid of the dark as a baby. She's a queer child. I guess mebbe she's nervous. I don't know but she's got notions into her head, stayin' over in the grave-yard so much. She runs away over there every chance she can get, an' she goes over a queer rigmarole about playin' with Jane, and her bein' dressed in white an' a wreath. I found out she meant Jane Blake, that's buried in the Blake lot. I knew there wa'n't any children round here, an' I thought I'd look into it. You know it says 'Our Father,' an' 'Our Mother,' on the old folks' stones. An' there she was, callin' them father an' mother. You'd thought they was right there. I've got 'most out o' patience with the child. I don't know nothin' about such kind of folks." The wail continued. "I'll go right up there," said Mrs. Gregg, determinately, taking a lamp.

Mrs. Dunn and Flora followed. When they entered the chamber to which she led them they saw little Nancy sitting up in bed, her face pale and convulsed, her blue eyes streaming with tears, her little pink mouth quivering.

"Nancy—" began Mrs. Gregg, in a weighty tone. But Mrs. Dunn sprang forward and threw her arms around the child.

"You got frightened, didn't you?" whispered she; and Nancy clung to her as if for life.

A great wave of joyful tenderness rolled up in the heart of the be-reaved woman. It was not, after all, the lonely and fearfully wandering little spirit of her dear Jenny; she was peaceful and blessed, beyond all her girlish tumults and terrors; but it was this little living girl. She saw it all plainly now. Afterwards it seemed to her that any one but a woman with her nerves strained, and her imagination unhealthily keen through watching and sorrow, would have seen it before.

She held Nancy tight, and soothed her. She felt almost as if she held her own Jenny. "I guess I'll take her home with me, if you don't care," she said to Mrs. Gregg.

"Why, I don't know as I've got any objections, if you want to," answered Mrs. Gregg, with cold stateliness. "Nancy Wren has had every-thing done for her that I was able to do," she added, when Mrs. Dunn had wrapped up the child, and they were all on the stairs. "I ain't coaxed an' cuddled her, because it ain't my way. I never did with my own children."

"Oh, I know you've done all you could," said Mrs. Dunn, with ab-stracted apology. " I jest thought I'd like to take her home to-night. Don't you think I'm blamin' you, Mis' Gregg." She bent down and kissed the little tearful face on her shoulder: she was carrying Nancy like a baby. Flora had hold of one of her little dangling hands.

"You shall go right up-stairs an' sleep with Flora," Mrs. Dunn whis-pered in the child's ear, when they were going across the yard; "an' you shall have the lamp burnin' all night, an' I'll give you a piece of cake before you go."

It was the custom of the Dunns to visit the cemetery and carry flowers to Jenny's grave every Sunday afternoon. Next Sunday little Nancy went with them. She followed happily along, and did not seem to think of the Blake lot. That pitiful fancy, if fancy it were, which had peopled her empty childish world with ghostly kindred, which had led into it an angel playmate in white robe and crown, might lie at rest now. There was no more need for it. She had found her place in a nest of living hearts, and she was getting her natural food of human love.

They had dressed Nancy in one of the little white frocks which Jenny had worn in her childhood, and her hat was trimmed with some ribbon and rose-buds which had adorned one of the dead young girl's years before.

It was a beautiful Sunday. After they left the cemetery they strolled a little way down the road. The road lay between deep green meadows and cottage yards. It was not quite time for the roses, and the lilacs were turning gray. The buttercups in the meadows had blossomed out, but the dandelions had lost their yellow crowns, and their filmy skulls appeared. They stood like ghosts among crowds of golden buttercups; but none of the family thought of that; their ghosts were laid in peace.

THE SHADOWS ON THE WALL

Mary Wilkins

"Henry had words with Edward in the study the night before Edward died," said Caroline Glynn.

She was elderly, tall, and harshly thin, with a hard colourlessness of face. She spoke not with acrimony, but with grave severity. Rebecca Ann Glynn, younger, stouter and rosy of face between her crinkling puffs of gray hair, gasped, by way of assent. She sat in a wide flounce of black silk in the corner of the sofa, and rolled terrified eyes from her sister Caroline to her sister Mrs. Stephen Brigham, who had been Emma Glynn, the one beauty of the family. She was beautiful still, with a large, splendid, full-blown beauty; she filled a great rocking-chair with her superb bulk of femininity, and swayed gently back and forth, her black silks whispering and her black frills fluttering. Even the shock of death (for her brother Edward lay dead in the house,) could not disturb her outward serenity of demeanour. She was grieved over the loss of her brother: he had been the youngest, and she had been fond of him, but never had Emma Brigham lost sight of her own importance amidst the waters of tribulation. She was always awake to the consciousness of her own stability in the midst of vicissitudes and the splendour of her permanent bearing.

But even her expression of masterly placidity changed before her sister Caroline's announcement and her sister Rebecca Ann's gasp of terror and distress in response.

"I think Henry might have controlled his temper, when poor Edward was so near his end," said she with an asperity which disturbed slightly the roseate curves of her beautiful mouth.

"Of course he did not *know*," murmured Rebecca Ann in a faint tone strangely out of keeping with her appearance.

One involuntarily looked again to be sure that such a feeble pipe came from that full-swelling chest.

"Of course he did not know it," said Caroline quickly. She turned on her sister with a strange sharp look of suspicion. "How could he have known it?" said she. Then she shrank as if from the other's possible answer. "Of course you and I both know he could not," said she conclusively, but her pale face was paler than it had been before.

Rebecca gasped again. The married sister, Mrs. Emma Brigham, was now sitting up straight in her chair; she had ceased rocking, and was eyeing them both intently with a sudden accentuation of family likeness in her face. Given one common intensity of emotion and similar lines showed forth, and the three sisters of one race were evident.

"What do you mean?" said she impartially to them both. Then she, too, seemed to shrink before a possible answer. She even laughed an evasive sort of laugh. "I guess you don't mean anything," said she, but her face wore still the expression of shrinking horror.

"Nobody means anything," said Caroline firmly. She rose and crossed the room toward the door with grim decisiveness.

"Where are you going?" asked Mrs. Brigham.

"I have something to see to," replied Caroline, and the others at once knew by her tone that she had some solemn and sad duty to perform in the chamber of death.

"Oh," said Mrs. Brigham.

After the door had closed behind Caroline, she turned to Rebecca.

"Did Henry have many words with him?" she asked.

"They were talking very loud," replied Rebecca evasively, yet with an answering gleam of ready response to the other's curiosity in the quick lift of her soft blue eyes.

Mrs. Brigham looked at her. She had not resumed rocking. She still sat up straight with a slight knitting of intensity on her fair forehead, between the pretty rippling curves of her auburn hair.

"Did you—hear anything?" she asked in a low voice with a glance toward the door.

"I was just across the hall in the south parlour, and that door was open and this door ajar," replied Rebecca with a slight flush.

"Then you must have—"

"I couldn't help it."

"Everything?"

"Most of it."

"What was it?"

"The old story."

"I suppose Henry was mad, as he always was, because Edward was living on here for nothing, when he had wasted all the money father left him."

Rebecca nodded with a fearful glance at the door.

When Emma spoke again her voice was still more hushed. "I know how he felt," said she. "He had always been so prudent himself, and worked hard at his profession, and there Edward had never done anything but spend, and it must have looked to him as if Edward was living at his expense, but he wasn't."

"No, he wasn't."

"It was the way father left the property—that all the children should have a home here—and he left money enough to buy the food and all if we had all come home."

"Yes."

"And Edward had a right here according to the terms of father's will, and Henry ought to have remembered it."

"Yes, he ought."

"Did he say hard things?"

"Pretty hard from what I heard."

"What?"

"I heard him tell Edward that he had no business here at all, and he thought he had better go away."

"What did Edward say?"

"That he would stay here as long as he lived and afterward, too, if he was a mind to, and he would like to see Henry get him out; and then—"

"What?"

"Then he laughed."

"What did Henry say."

"I didn't hear him say anything, but—"

"But what?"

"I saw him when he came out of this room."

"He looked mad?"

"You've seen him when he looked so."

Emma nodded; the expression of horror on her face had deepened.

"Do you remember that time he killed the cat because she had scratched him?"

"Yes. Don't!"

Then Caroline reentered the room. She went up to the stove in which a wood fire was burning—it was a cold, gloomy day of fall—and she warmed her hands, which were reddened from recent washing in cold water.

Mrs. Brigham looked at her and hesitated. She glanced at the door, which was still ajar, as it did not easily shut, being still swollen with the damp weather of the summer. She rose and pushed it together with a sharp thud which jarred the house. Rebecca started painfully with a half exclamation. Caroline looked at her disapprovingly.

"It is time you controlled your nerves, Rebecca," said she.

"I can't help it," replied Rebecca with almost a wail. "I am nervous. There's enough to make me so, the Lord knows."

"What do you mean by that?" asked Caroline with her old air of sharp suspicion, and something between challenge and dread of its being met.

Rebecca shrank.

"Nothing," said she.

"Then I wouldn't keep speaking in such a fashion."

Emma, returning from the closed door, said imperiously that it ought to be fixed, it shut so hard.

"It will shrink enough after we have had the fire a few days," replied Caroline. "If anything is done to it it will be too small; there will be a crack at the sill."

"I think Henry ought to be ashamed of himself for talking as he did to Edward," said Mrs. Brigham abruptly, but in an almost inaudible voice.

"Hush!" said Caroline, with a glance of actual fear at the closed door.

"Nobody can hear with the door shut."

"He must have heard it shut, and—"

"Well, I can say what I want to before he comes down, and I am not afraid of him."

"I don't know who is afraid of him! What reason is there for anybody to be afraid of Henry?" demanded Caroline.

Mrs. Brigham trembled before her sister's look. Rebecca gasped again. "There isn't any reason, of course. Why should there be?"

"I wouldn't speak so, then. Somebody might overhear you and think it was queer. Miranda Joy is in the south parlour sewing, you know."

"I thought she went upstairs to stitch on the machine."

"She did, but she has come down again."

"Well, she can't hear."

"I say again I think Henry ought to be ashamed of himself. I shouldn't think he'd ever get over it, having words with poor Edward the very night before he died. Edward was enough sight better disposition than Henry, with all his faults. I always thought a great deal of poor Edward, myself."

Mrs. Brigham passed a large fluff of handkerchief across her eyes; Rebecca sobbed outright.

"Rebecca," said Caroline admonishingly, keeping her mouth stiff and swallowing determinately.

"I never heard him speak a cross word, unless he spoke cross to Henry that last night. I don't know, but he did from what Rebecca overheard," said Emma.

"Not so much cross as sort of soft, and sweet, and aggravating," sniffled Rebecca.

"He never raised his voice," said Caroline; "but he had his way."

"He had a right to in this case."

"Yes, he did."

"He had as much of a right here as Henry," sobbed Rebecca, "and now he's gone, and he will never be in this home that poor father left him and the rest of us again."

"What do you really think ailed Edward?" asked Emma in hardly more than a whisper. She did not look at her sister.

Caroline sat down in a nearby armchair, and clutched the arms convulsively until her thin knuckles whitened.

"I told you," said she.

Rebecca held her handkerchief over her mouth, and looked at them above it with terrified, streaming eyes.

"I know you said that he had terrible pains in his stomach, and had spasms, but what do you think made him have them?"

"Henry called it gastric trouble. You know Edward has always had dyspepsia."

Mrs. Brigham hesitated a moment. "Was there any talk of an—examination?" said she.

Then Caroline turned on her fiercely.

"No," said she in a terrible voice. "No."

The three sisters' souls seemed to meet on one common ground of terrified understanding though their eyes. The old-fashioned latch of the door was heard to rattle, and a push from without made the door shake ineffectually. "It's Henry," Rebecca sighed rather than whispered. Mrs. Brigham settled herself after a noiseless rush across the floor into her rocking-chair again, and was swaying back and forth with her head comfortably leaning back, when the door at last yielded and Henry Glynn entered. He cast a covertly sharp, comprehensive glance at Mrs. Brigham with her elaborate calm; at Rebecca quietly huddled in the corner of the sofa with her handkerchief to her face and only one small reddened ear as attentive as a dog's uncovered and revealing her alertness for his presence; at Caroline sitting with a strained composure in her armchair by the stove. She met his eyes quite firmly with a look of inscrutable fear, and defiance of the fear and of him.

Henry Glynn looked more like this sister than the others. Both had the same hard delicacy of form and feature, both were tall and almost emaciated, both had a sparse growth of gray blond hair far back from high intellectual foreheads, both had an almost noble aquilinity of feature. They confronted each other with the pitiless immovability of two statues in whose marble lineaments emotions were fixed for all eternity.

Then Henry Glynn smiled and the smile transformed his face. He looked suddenly years younger, and an almost boyish recklessness and irresolution appeared in his face. He flung himself into a chair with a gesture which was bewildering from its incongruity with his general appearance. He leaned his head back, flung one leg over the other, and looked laughingly at Mrs. Brigham.

"I declare, Emma, you grow younger every year," he said.

She flushed a little, and her placid mouth widened at the corners. She was susceptible to praise.

"Our thoughts to-day ought to belong to the one of us who will *never* grow older," said Caroline in a hard voice.

Henry looked at her, still smiling. "Of course, we none of us forget that," said he, in a deep, gentle voice, "but we have to speak to the living, Caroline, and I have not seen Emma for a long time, and the living are as dear as the dead."

"Not to me," said Caroline.

She rose, and went abruptly out of the room again. Rebecca also rose and hurried after her, sobbing loudly.

Henry looked slowly after them.

"Caroline is completely unstrung," said he. Mrs. Brigham rocked. A confidence in him inspired by his manner was stealing over her. Out of that confidence she spoke quite easily and naturally.

"His death was very sudden," said she.

Henry's eyelids quivered slightly but his gaze was unswerving.

"Yes," said he; "it was very sudden. He was sick only a few hours."

"What did you call it?"

"Gastric."

"You did not think of an examination?"

"There was no need. I am perfectly certain as to the cause of his death."

Suddenly Mrs. Brigham felt a creep as of some live horror over her very soul. Her flesh prickled with cold, before an inflection of his voice. She rose, tottering on weak knees.

"Where are you going?" asked Henry in a strange, breathless voice.

Mrs. Brigham said something incoherent about some sewing which she had to do, some black for the funeral, and was out of the room. She went up to the front chamber which she occupied. Caroline was there. She went close to her and took her hands, and the two sisters looked at each other.

"Don't speak, don't, I won't have it!" said Caroline finally in an awful whisper.

"I won't," replied Emma.

That afternoon the three sisters were in the study, the large front room on the ground floor across the hall from the south parlour, when the dusk deepened.

Mrs. Brigham was hemming some black material. She sat close to the west window for the waning light. At last she laid her work on her lap.

"It's no use, I cannot see to sew another stitch until we have a light," said she.

Caroline, who was writing some letters at the table, turned to Rebecca, in her usual place on the sofa.

"Rebecca, you had better get a lamp," she said.

Rebecca started up; even in the dusk her face showed her agitation.

"It doesn't seem to me that we need a lamp quite yet," she said in a piteous, pleading voice like a child's.

"Yes, we do," returned Mrs. Brigham peremptorily. "We must have a light. I must finish this to-night or I can't go to the funeral, and I can't see to sew another stitch."

"Caroline can see to write letters, and she is farther from the window than you are," said Rebecca.

"Are you trying to save kerosene or are you lazy, Rebecca Glynn?" cried Mrs. Brigham. "I can go and get the light myself, but I have this work all in my lap."

Caroline's pen stopped scratching.

"Rebecca, we must have the light," said she.

"Had we better have it in here?" asked Rebecca weakly.

"Of course! Why not?" cried Caroline sternly.

"I am sure I don't want to take my sewing into the other room, when it is all cleaned up for to-morrow," said Mrs. Brigham.

"Why, I never heard such a to-do about lighting a lamp."

Rebecca rose and left the room. Presently she entered with a lamp— a large one with a white porcelain shade. She set it on a table, an old-fashioned card-table which was placed against the opposite wall from the window. That wall was clear of bookcases and books, which were only on three sides of the room. That opposite wall was taken up with three doors, the one small space being occupied by the table. Above the table on the old-fashioned paper, of a white satin gloss, traversed by an indeterminate green scroll, hung quite high a small gilt and black-framed ivory miniature taken in her girlhood of the mother of the family. When the lamp was set on the table beneath it, the tiny pretty face painted on the ivory seemed to gleam out with a look of intelligence.

"What have you put that lamp over there for?" asked Mrs. Brigham, with more of impatience than her voice usually revealed. "Why didn't you set it in the hall and have done with it. Neither Caroline nor I can see if it is on that table."

"I thought perhaps you would move," replied Rebecca hoarsely.

"If I do move, we can't both sit at that table. Caroline has her paper all spread around. Why don't you set the lamp on the study table in the middle of the room, then we can both see?"

Rebecca hesitated. Her face was very pale. She looked with an appeal that was fairly agonizing at her sister Caroline.

"Why don't you put the lamp on this table, as she says?" asked Caroline, almost fiercely. "Why do you act so, Rebecca?"

"I should think you *would* ask her that," said Mrs. Brigham. "She doesn't act like herself at all."

Rebecca took the lamp and set it on the table in the middle of the room without another word. Then she turned her back upon it quickly and seated herself on the sofa, and placed a hand over her eyes as if to shade them, and remained so.

"Does the light hurt your eyes, and is that the reason why you didn't want the lamp?" asked Mrs. Brigham kindly.

"I always like to sit in the dark," replied Rebecca chokingly. Then she snatched her handkerchief hastily from her pocket and began to weep. Caroline continued to write, Mrs. Brigham to sew.

Suddenly Mrs. Brigham as she sewed glanced at the opposite wall. The glance became a steady stare. She looked intently, her work suspended in her hands. Then she looked away again and took a few more stitches, then she looked again, and again turned to her task. At last she laid her work in her lap and stared concentratedly. She looked from the wall around the room, taking note of the various objects; she looked at the wall long and intently. Then she turned to her sisters.

"What *is* that?" said she.

"What?" asked Caroline harshly; her pen scratched loudly across the paper.

Rebecca gave one of her convulsive gasps.

"That strange shadow on the wall," replied Mrs. Brigham.

Rebecca sat with her face hidden: Caroline dipped her pen in the inkstand.

"Why don't you turn around and look?" asked Mrs. Brigham in a wondering and somewhat aggrieved way.

"I am in a hurry to finish this letter, if Mrs. Wilson Ebbit is going to get word in time to come to the funeral," replied Caroline shortly.

Mrs. Brigham rose, her work slipping to the floor, and she began walking around the room, moving various articles of furniture, with her eyes on the shadow.

Then suddenly she shrieked out:

"Look at this awful shadow! What is it? Caroline, look, look! Rebecca, look! *What is it?*"

All Mrs. Brigham's triumphant placidity was gone. Her handsome face was livid with horror. She stood stiffly pointing at the shadow.

"Look!" said she, pointing her finger at it. "Look! What is it?"

Then Rebecca burst out in a wild wail after a shuddering glance at the wall:

"Oh, Caroline, there it is again! There it is again!"

"Caroline Glynn, you look!" said Mrs. Brigham. "Look! What is that dreadful shadow?"

Caroline rose, turned, and stood confronting the wall.

"How should I know?" she said.

"It has been there every night since he died," cried Rebecca.

"Every night?"

"Yes. He died Thursday and this is Saturday; that makes three nights," said Caroline rigidly. She stood as if holding herself calm with a vise of concentrated will.

"It—it looks like—like—" stammered Mrs. Brigham in a tone of intense horror.

"I know what it looks like well enough," said Caroline. "I've got eyes in my head."

"It looks like Edward," burst out Rebecca in a sort of frenzy of fear. "Only—"

"Yes, it does," assented Mrs. Brigham, whose horror-stricken tone matched her sister's, "only—Oh, it is awful! What is it, Caroline?"

"I ask you again, how should I know?" replied Caroline. "I see it there like you. How should I know any more than you?"

"It *must* be something in the room," said Mrs. Brigham, staring wildly around.

"We moved everything in the room the first night it came," said Rebecca; "it is not anything in the room."

Caroline turned upon her with a sort of fury. "Of course it is something in the room," said she. "How you act! What do you mean by talking so? Of course it is something in the room."

"Of course, it is," agreed Mrs. Brigham, looking at Caroline suspiciously. "Of course it must be. It is only a coincidence. It just happens so. Perhaps it is that fold of the window curtain that makes it. It must be something in the room."

"It is not anything in the room," repeated Rebecca with obstinate horror.

The door opened suddenly and Henry Glynn entered. He began to speak, then his eyes followed the direction of the others'. He stood stock still staring at the shadow on the wall. It was life size and stretched across the white parallelogram of a door, half across the wall space on which the picture hung.

"What is that?" he demanded in a strange voice.

"It must be due to something in the room," Mrs. Brigham said faintly.

"It is not due to anything in the room," said Rebecca again with the shrill insistency of terror.

"How you act, Rebecca Glynn," said Caroline.

Henry Glynn stood and stared a moment longer. His face showed a gamut of emotions—horror, conviction, then furious incredulity. Suddenly he began hastening hither and thither about the room. He moved the furniture with fierce jerks, turning ever to see the effect upon the shadow on the wall. Not a line of its terrible outlines wavered.

"It must be something in the room!" he declared in a voice which seemed to snap like a lash.

His face changed. The inmost secrecy of his nature seemed evident until one almost lost sight of his lineaments. Rebecca stood close to her sofa, regarding him with woeful, fascinated eyes. Mrs. Brigham clutched Caroline's hand. They both stood in a corner out of his way. For a few moments he raged about the room like a caged wild animal. He moved every piece of furniture; when the moving of a piece did not affect the shadow, he flung it to the floor, the sisters watching.

Then suddenly he desisted. He laughed and began straightening the furniture which he had flung down.

"What an absurdity," he said easily. "Such a to-do about a shadow."

"That's so," assented Mrs. Brigham, in a scared voice which she tried to make natural. As she spoke she lifted a chair near her.

"I think you have broken the chair that Edward was so fond of," said Caroline.

Terror and wrath were struggling for expression on her face. Her mouth was set, her eyes shrinking. Henry lifted the chair with a show of anxiety.

"Just as good as ever," he said pleasantly. He laughed again, looking at his sisters. "Did I scare you?" he said. "I should think you might be used to me by this time. You know my way of wanting to leap to the bottom of a mystery, and that shadow does look—queer, like—and I thought if there was any way of accounting for it I would like to without any delay."

"You don't seem to have succeeded," remarked Caroline dryly, with a slight glance at the wall.

Henry's eyes followed hers and he quivered perceptibly.

"Oh, there is no accounting for shadows," he said, and he laughed again. "A man is a fool to try to account for shadows."

Then the supper bell rang, and they all left the room, but Henry kept his back to the wall, as did, indeed, the others.

Mrs. Brigham pressed close to Caroline as she crossed the hall. "He looked like a demon!" she breathed in her ear.

Henry led the way with an alert motion like a boy; Rebecca brought up the rear; she could scarcely walk, her knees trembled so.

"I can't sit in that room again this evening," she whispered to Caroline after supper.

"Very well, we will sit in the south room," replied Caroline. "I think we will sit in the south parlour," she said aloud; "it isn't as damp as the study, and I have a cold."

So they all sat in the south room with their sewing. Henry read the newspaper, his chair drawn close to the lamp on the table. About nine o'clock he rose abruptly and crossed the hall to the study. The three sisters looked at one another. Mrs. Brigham rose, folded her rustling skirts compactly around her, and began tiptoeing toward the door.

"What are you going to do?" inquired Rebecca agitatedly.

"I am going to see what he is about," replied Mrs. Brigham cautiously.

She pointed as she spoke to the study door across the hall; it was ajar. Henry had striven to pull it together behind him, but it had somehow swollen beyond the limit with curious speed. It was still ajar and a streak of light showed from top to bottom. The hall lamp was not lit.

"You had better stay where you are," said Caroline with guarded sharpness.

"I am going to see," repeated Mrs. Brigham firmly.

Then she folded her skirts so tightly that her bulk with its swelling curves was revealed in a black silk sheath, and she went with a slow toddle across the hall to the study door. She stood there, her eye at the crack.

In the south room Rebecca stopped sewing and sat watching with dilated eyes. Caroline sewed steadily. What Mrs. Brigham, standing at the crack in the study door, saw was this:

Henry Glynn, evidently reasoning that the source of the strange shadow must be between the table on which the lamp stood and the wall, was making systematic passes and thrusts all over and through the intervening space with an old sword which had belonged to his father. Not an inch was left unpierced. He seemed to have divided the space into mathematical sections. He brandished the sword with a sort of cold fury and calculation; the blade gave out flashes of light, the shadow remained unmoved. Mrs. Brigham, watching, felt herself cold with horror.

Finally Henry ceased and stood with the sword in hand and raised as if to strike, surveying the shadow on the wall threateningly. Mrs. Brigham toddled back across the hall and shut the south room door behind her before she related what she had seen.

"He looked like a demon!" she said again. "Have you got any of that old wine in the house, Caroline? I don't feel as if I could stand much more."

Indeed, she looked overcome. Her handsome placid face was worn and strained and pale.

"Yes, there's plenty," said Caroline; "you can have some when you go to bed."

"I think we had all better take some," said Mrs. Brigham. "Oh, my God, Caroline, what—"

"Don't ask and don't speak," said Caroline.

"No, I am not going to," replied Mrs. Brigham; "but—"

Rebecca moaned aloud.

"What are you doing that for?" asked Caroline harshly.

"Poor Edward," returned Rebecca.

"That is all you have to groan for," said Caroline. "There is nothing else."

"I am going to bed," said Mrs. Brigham. "I sha'n't be able to be at the funeral if I don't."

Soon the three sisters went to their chambers and the south parlour was deserted. Caroline called to Henry in the study to put out the light before he came upstairs. They had been gone about an hour when he came into the room bringing the lamp which had stood in the study. He set it on the table and waited a few minutes, pacing up and down. His face was terrible, his fair complexion showed livid; his blue eyes seemed dark blanks of awful reflections.

Then he took the lamp up and returned to the library. He set the lamp on the centre table, and the shadow sprang out on the wall. Again he studied the furniture and moved it about, but deliberately, with none of his former frenzy. Nothing affected the shadow. Then he returned to the south room with the lamp and again waited. Again he returned to the study and placed the lamp on the table, and the shadow sprang out upon the wall. It was midnight before he went upstairs. Mrs. Brigham and the other sisters, who could not sleep, heard him.

The next day was the funeral. That evening the family sat in the south room. Some relatives were with them. Nobody entered the study until Henry carried a lamp in there after the others had retired for the night. He saw again the shadow on the wall leap to an awful life before the light.

The next morning at breakfast Henry Glynn announced that he had to go to the city for three days. The sisters looked at him with surprise. He very seldom left home, and just now his practice had been neglected on account of Edward's death. He was a physician.

"How can you leave your patients now?" asked Mrs. Brigham wonderingly.

"I don't know how to, but there is no other way," replied Henry easily. "I have had a telegram from Doctor Mitford."

"Consultation?" inquired Mrs. Brigham.

"I have business," replied Henry.

Doctor Mitford was an old classmate of his who lived in a neighbouring city and who occasionally called upon him in the case of a consultation.

After he had gone Mrs. Brigham said to Caroline that after all Henry had not said that he was going to consult with Doctor Mitford, and she thought it very strange.

"Everything is very strange," said Rebecca with a shudder.

"What do you mean?" inquired Caroline sharply.

"Nothing," replied Rebecca.

Nobody entered the library that day, nor the next, nor the next. The third day Henry was expected home, but he did not arrive and the last train from the city had come.

"I call it pretty queer work," said Mrs. Brigham. "The idea of a doctor leaving his patients for three days anyhow, at such a time as this, and I know he has some very sick ones; he said so. And the idea of a consultation lasting three days! There is no sense in it, and *now* he has not come. I don't understand it, for my part."

"I don't either," said Rebecca.

They were all in the south parlour. There was no light in the study opposite, and the door was ajar.

Presently Mrs. Brigham rose—she could not have told why; something seemed to impel her, some will outside her own. She went out of the room, again wrapping her rustling skirts around that she might pass noiselessly, and began pushing at the swollen door of the study.

"She has not got any lamp," said Rebecca in a shaking voice.

Caroline, who was writing letters, rose again, took a lamp (there were two in the room) and followed her sister. Rebecca had risen, but she stood trembling, not venturing to follow.

The doorbell rang, but the others did not hear it; it was on the south door on the other side of the house from the study. Rebecca, after hesitating until the bell rang the second time, went to the door; she remembered that the servant was out.

Caroline and her sister Emma entered the study. Caroline set the lamp on the table. They looked at the wall. "Oh, my God," gasped Mrs. Brigham, "there are—there are *two*—shadows." The sisters stood clutching each other, staring at the awful things on the wall. Then Rebecca came in, staggering, with a telegram in her hand. "Here is—a telegram," she gasped. "Henry is—dead."

For the end of imagination is *harmony*. A right imagination, being the reflex of the creation, will fall in with the divine
order of things as the highest form of its own operation; "will
tune its instrument here at the door" to the divine harmonies
within; will be content alone with growth towards the divine
idea, which includes all that is beautiful in the imperfect imagi-
nations of men; will know that every deviation from that
growth is downward; and will therefore send the man forth
from its loftiest representations to do the commonest duty
of the most wearisome calling in a hearty and hopeful spirit.
This is the work of the right imagination; and towards this
work every imagination, in proportion to the rightness that is
in it, will tend. The reveries even of the wise man will make him
stronger for his work; his dreaming as well as his thinking
will render him sorry for past failure, and hopeful of future
success.

—George MacDonald, "The Imagination:
Its Functions and Its Culture."

THE SOUTHWEST CHAMBER

Mary Wilkins

"That school-teacher from Acton is coming to-day," said the elder Miss Gill, Sophia.

"So she is," assented the younger Miss Gill, Amanda.

"I have decided to put her in the southwest chamber," said Sophia.

Amanda looked at her sister with an expression of mingled doubt and terror. "You don't suppose she would—" she began hesitatingly.

"Would what?" demanded Sophia, sharply. She was more incisive than her sister. Both were below the medium height, and stout, but Sophia was firm where Amanda was flabby. Amanda wore a baggy old muslin (it was a hot day), and Sophia was uncompromisingly hooked up in a starched and boned cambric over her high shelving figure.

"I didn't know but she would object to sleeping in that room, as long as Aunt Harriet died there such a little time ago," faltered Amanda.

"Well!" said Sophia, "of all the silly notions! If you are going to pick out rooms in this house where nobody has died, for the boarders, you'll have your hands full. Grandfather Ackley had seven children; four of them died here to my certain knowledge, besides grandfather and grandmother. I think Great-grandmother Ackley, grandfather's mother, died here, too; she must have; and Great-grandfather Ackley, and grandfather's unmarried sister, Great-aunt Fanny Ackley. I don't believe there's a room nor a bed in this house that somebody hasn't passed away in."

"Well, I suppose I am silly to think of it, and she had better go in there," said Amanda.

"I know she had. The northeast room is small and hot, and she's stout and likely to feel the heat, and she's saved money and is able to board out summers, and maybe she'll come here another year if she's well accommodated," said Sophia. "Now I guess you'd better go in there and see if

405

any dust has settled on anything since it was cleaned, and open the west windows and let the sun in, while I see to that cake."

Amanda went to her task in the southwest chamber while her sister stepped heavily down the back stairs on her way to the kitchen.

"It seems to me you had better open the bed while you air and dust, then make it up again," she called back.

"Yes, sister," Amanda answered, shudderingly.

Nobody knew how this elderly woman with the untrammeled imagination of a child dreaded to enter the southwest chamber, and yet she could not have told why she had the dread. She had entered and occupied rooms which had been once tenanted by persons now dead. The room which had been hers in the little house in which she and her sister had lived before coming here had been her dead mother's. She had never reflected upon the fact with anything but loving awe and reverence. There had never been any fear. But this was different. She entered and her heart beat thickly in her ears. Her hands were cold. The room was a very large one. The four windows, two facing south, two west, were closed, the blinds also. The room was in a film of green gloom. The furniture loomed out vaguely. The gilt frame of a blurred old engraving on the wall caught a little light. The white counterpane on the bed showed like a blank page.

Amanda crossed the room, opened with a straining motion of her thin back and shoulders one of the west windows, and threw back the blind. Then the room revealed itself an apartment full of an aged and worn but no less valid state. Pieces of old mahogany swelled forth; a peacock-patterned chintz draped the bedstead. This chintz also covered a great easy chair which had been the favourite seat of the former occupant of the room. The closet door stood ajar. Amanda noticed that with wonder. There was a glimpse of purple drapery floating from a peg inside the closet. Amanda went across and took down the garment hanging there. She wondered how her sister had happened to leave it when she cleaned the room. It was an old loose gown which had belonged to her aunt. She took it down, shuddering, and closed the closet door after a fearful glance into its dark depths. It was a long closet with a strong odour of lovage. The Aunt Harriet had had a habit of eating lovage and had carried it constantly in her pocket. There was very likely some of the pleasant root in the pocket of the musty purple gown which Amanda threw over the easy chair.

Amanda perceived the odour with a start as if before an actual presence. Odour seems in a sense a vital part of a personality. It can survive the flesh to which it has clung like a persistent shadow, seeming to have in itself something of the substance of that to which it pertained. Amanda was always conscious of this fragrance of lovage as she tidied the room. She dusted the heavy mahogany pieces punctiliously after she had opened the bed as her sister had directed. She spread fresh towels over the wash-stand and the bureau; she made the bed. Then she thought to take the purple gown from the easy chair and carry it to the garret and put it in the trunk with the other articles of the dead woman's wardrobe which had been packed away there; *but the purple gown was not on the chair!*

Amanda Gill was not a woman of strong convictions even as to her own actions. She directly thought that possibly she had been mistaken and had not removed it from the closet. She glanced at the closet door and saw with surprise that it was open, and she had thought she had closed it, but she instantly was not sure of that. So she entered the closet and looked for the purple gown. *It was not there!*

Amanda Gill went feebly out of the closet and looked at the easy chair again. The purple gown was not there! She looked wildly around the room. She went down on her trembling knees and peered under the bed, she opened the bureau drawers, she looked again in the closet. Then she stood in the middle of the floor and fairly wrung her hands.

"What does it mean?" she said in a shocked whisper.

She had certainly seen that loose purple gown of her dead Aunt Harriet's.

There is a limit at which self-refutation must stop in any sane person. Amanda Gill had reached it. She knew that she had seen that purple gown in that closet; she knew that she had removed it and put it on the easy chair. She also knew that she had not taken it out of the room. She felt a curious sense of being inverted mentally. It was as if all her traditions and laws of life were on their heads. Never in her simple record had any garment not remained where she had placed it unless removed by some palpable human agency.

Then the thought occurred to her that possibly her sister Sophia might have entered the room unobserved while her back was turned and removed the dress. A sensation of relief came over her. Her blood seemed to flow back into its usual channels; the tension of her nerves relaxed.

"How silly I am," she said aloud.

She hurried out and downstairs into the kitchen where Sophia was making cake, stirring with splendid circular sweeps of a wooden spoon a creamy yellow mass. She looked up as her sister entered.

"Have you got it done?" said she.

"Yes," replied Amanda. Then she hesitated. A sudden terror overcame her. It did not seem as if it were at all probable that Sophia had left that foamy cake mixture a second to go to Aunt Harriet's chamber and remove that purple gown.

"Well," said Sophia, "if you have got that done I wish you would take hold and string those beans. The first thing we know there won't be time to boil them for dinner."

Amanda moved toward the pan of beans on the table, then she looked at her sister.

"Did you come up in Aunt Harriet's room while I was there?" she asked weakly.

She knew while she asked what the answer would be.

"Up in Aunt Harriet's room? Of course I didn't. I couldn't leave this cake without having it fall. You know that well enough. Why?"

"Nothing," replied Amanda.

Suddenly she realized that she could not tell her sister what had happened, for before the utter absurdity of the whole thing her belief in her own reason quailed. She knew what Sophia would say if she told her. She could hear her.

"Amanda Gill, have you gone stark staring mad?"

She resolved that she would never tell Sophia. She dropped into a chair and begun shelling the beans with nerveless fingers. Sophia looked at her curiously.

"Amanda Gill, what on earth ails you?" she asked.

"Nothing," replied Amanda. She bent her head very low over the green pods.

"Yes, there is, too! You are as white as a sheet, and your hands are shaking so you can hardly string those beans. I did think you had more sense, Amanda Gill."

"I don't know what you mean, Sophia."

"Yes, you do know what I mean, too; you needn't pretend you don't. Why did you ask me if I had been in that room, and why do you act so queer?"

Amanda hesitated. She had been trained to truth. Then she lied.

"I wondered if you'd noticed how it had leaked in on the paper over by the bureau, that last rain," said she.

"What makes you look so pale then?"

"I don't know. I guess the heat sort of overcame me."

"I shouldn't think it could have been very hot in that room when it had been shut up so long," said Sophia.

She was evidently not satisfied, but then the grocer came to the door and the matter dropped.

For the next hour the two women were very busy. They kept no servant. When they had come into possession of this fine old place by the death of their aunt it had seemed a doubtful blessing. There was not a cent with which to pay for repairs and taxes and insurance, except the twelve hundred dollars which they had obtained from the sale of the little house in which they had been born and lived all their lives. There had been a division in the old Ackley family years before. One of the daughters had married against her mother's wish and had been disinherited.

She had married a poor man by the name of Gill, and shared his humble lot in sight of her former home and her sister and mother living in prosperity, until she had borne three daughters; then she died, worn out with overwork and worry.

The mother and the elder sister had been pitiless to the last. Neither had ever spoken to her since she left her home the night of her marriage. They were hard women.

The three daughters of the disinherited sister had lived quiet and poor, but not actually needy lives. Jane, the middle daughter, had married, and died in less than a year. Amanda and Sophia had taken the girl baby she left when the father married again. Sophia had taught a primary school for many years; she had saved enough to buy the little house in which they lived. Amanda had crocheted lace, and embroidered flannel, and made tidies and pincushions, and had earned enough for her clothes and the child's, little Flora Scott.

Their father, William Gill, had died before they were thirty, and now in their late middle life had come the death of the aunt to whom they had never spoken, although they had often seen her, who had lived in solitary state in the old Ackley mansion until she was more than eighty. There had been no will, and they were the only heirs with the exception of young Flora Scott, the daughter of the dead sister.

Sophia and Amanda thought directly of Flora when they knew of the inheritance.

"It will be a splendid thing for her; she will have enough to live on when we are gone," Sophia said.

She had promptly decided what was to be done. The small house was to be sold, and they were to move into the old Ackley house and take boarders to pay for its keeping. She scouted the idea of selling it. She had an enormous family pride. She had always held her head high when she had walked past that fine old mansion, the cradle of her race, which she was forbidden to enter. She was unmoved when the lawyer who was advising her disclosed to her the fact that Harriet Ackley had used every cent of the Ackley money.

"I realize that we have to work," said she, "but my sister and I have determined to keep the place."

That was the end of the discussion. Sophia and Amanda Gill had been living in the old Ackley house a fortnight, and they had three boarders: an elderly widow with a comfortable income, a young congregationalist clergyman, and the middle-aged single woman who had charge of the village library. Now the school-teacher from Acton, Miss Louisa Stark, was expected for the summer, and would make four.

Sophia considered that they were comfortably provided for. Her wants and her sister's were very few, and even the niece, although a young girl, had small expenses, since her wardrobe was supplied for years to come from that of the deceased aunt. There were stored away in the garret of the Ackley house enough voluminous black silks and satins and bombazines to keep her clad in somber richness for years to come.

Flora was a very gentle girl, with large, serious blue eyes, a seldom-smiling, pretty mouth, and smooth flaxen hair. She was delicate and very young—sixteen on her next birthday.

She came home soon now with her parcels of sugar and tea from the grocer's. She entered the kitchen gravely and deposited them on the table by which her Aunt Amanda was seated stringing beans. Flora wore an obsolete turban-shaped hat of black straw which had belonged to the dead aunt; it set high like a crown, revealing her forehead. Her dress was an ancient purple-and-white print, too long and too large except over the chest, where it held her like a straight waistcoat.

"You had better take off your hat, Flora," said Sophia. She turned suddenly to Amanda. "Did you fill the water-pitcher in that chamber for the schoolteacher?" she asked severely. She was quite sure that Amanda had not filled the water-pitcher.

Amanda blushed and started guiltily. "I declare, I don't believe I did," said she.

"I didn't think you had," said her sister with sarcastic emphasis.

"Flora, you go up to the room that was your Great-aunt Harriet's, and take the water-pitcher off the wash-stand and fill it with water. Be real careful, and don't break the pitcher, and don't spill the water."

"In *that* chamber?" asked Flora. She spoke very quietly, but her face changed a little.

"Yes, in that chamber," returned her Aunt Sophia sharply. "Go right along."

Flora went, and her light footstep was heard on the stairs. Very soon she returned with the blue-and-white water-pitcher and filled it carefully at the kitchen sink.

"Now be careful and not spill it," said Sophia as she went out of the room carrying it gingerly.

Amanda gave a timidly curious glance at her; she wondered if she had seen the purple gown.

Then she started, for the village stagecoach was seen driving around to the front of the house. The house stood on a corner.

"Here, Amanda, you look better than I do; you go and meet her," said Sophia. "I'll just put the cake in the pan and get it in the oven and I'll come. Show her right up to her room."

Amanda removed her apron hastily and obeyed. Sophia hurried with her cake, pouring it into the baking-tins. She had just put it in the oven, when the door opened and Flora entered carrying the blue water-pitcher.

"What are you bringing down that pitcher again for?" asked Sophia.

"She wants some water, and Aunt Amanda sent me," replied Flora.

Her pretty pale face had a bewildered expression.

"For the land sake, she hasn't used all that great pitcherful of water so quick?"

"There wasn't any water in it," replied Flora.

Her high, childish forehead was contracted slightly with a puzzled frown as she looked at her aunt.

"Wasn't any water in it?"

"No, ma'am."

"Didn't I see you filling the pitcher with water not ten minutes ago, I want to know?"

"Yes, ma'am."

"What did you do with that water?"

"Nothing."

"Did you carry that pitcherful of water up to that room and set it on the washstand?"

"Yes, ma'am."

"Didn't you spill it?"

"No, ma'am."

"Now, Flora Scott, I want the truth! Did you fill that pitcher with water and carry it up there, and wasn't there any there when she came to use it?"

"Yes, ma'am."

"Let me see that pitcher." Sophia examined the pitcher. It was not only perfectly dry from top to bottom, but even a little dusty. She turned severely on the young girl. "That shows," said she, "you did not fill the pitcher at all. You let the water run at the side because you didn't want to carry it upstairs. I am ashamed of you. It's bad enough to be so lazy, but when it comes to not telling the truth—"

The young girl's face broke up suddenly into piteous confusion, and her blue eyes became filmy with tears.

"I did fill the pitcher, honest," she faltered, "I did, Aunt Sophia. You ask Aunt Amanda."

"I'll ask nobody. This pitcher is proof enough. Water don't go off and leave the pitcher dusty on the inside if it was put in ten minutes ago. Now you fill that pitcher full quick, and you carry it upstairs, and if you spill a drop there'll be something besides talk."

Flora filled the pitcher, with the tears falling over her cheeks. She sniveled softly as she went out, balancing it carefully against her slender hip. Sophia followed her.

"Stop crying," said she sharply; "you ought to be ashamed of yourself. What do you suppose Miss Louisa Stark will think. No water in her pitcher in the first place, and then you come back crying as if you didn't want to get it."

In spite of herself, Sophia's voice was soothing. She was very fond of the girl. She followed her up the stairs to the chamber where Miss Louisa Stark was waiting for the water to remove the soil of travel. She had removed her bonnet, and its tuft of red geraniums lightened the obscurity of the mahogany dresser. She had placed her little beaded cape carefully on the bed. She was replying to a tremulous remark of Amanda's, who was nearly fainting from the new mystery of the water-pitcher, that it was warm and she suffered a good deal in warm weather.

Louisa Stark was stout and solidly built. She was much larger than either of the Gill sisters. She was a masterly woman inured to command from years of school-teaching. She carried her swelling bulk with majesty; even her face, moist and red with the heat, lost nothing of its dignity of expression.

She was standing in the middle of the floor with an air which gave the effect of her standing upon an elevation. She turned when Sophia and Flora, carrying the water-pitcher, entered.

"This is my sister Sophia," said Amanda tremulously.

Sophia advanced, shook hands with Miss Louisa Stark and bade her welcome and hoped she would like her room. Then she moved toward the closet. "There is a nice large closet in this room—the best closet in the house. You might have your trunk—" she said, then she stopped short.

The closet door was ajar, and a purple garment seemed suddenly to swing into view as if impelled by some wind.

"Why, here is something left in this closet," Sophia said in a mortified tone. "I thought all those things had been taken away."

She pulled down the garment with a jerk, and as she did so Amanda passed her in a weak rush for the door.

"I am afraid your sister is not well," said the school-teacher from Acton. "She looked very pale when you took that dress down. I noticed it at once. Hadn't you better go and see what the matter is? She may be going to faint."

"She is not subject to fainting spells," replied Sophia, but she followed Amanda.

She found her in the room which they occupied together, lying on the bed, very pale and gasping. She leaned over her.

"Amanda, what is the matter; don't you feel well?" she asked.

"I feel a little faint."

Sophia got a camphor bottle and began rubbing her sister's forehead. "Do you feel better?" she said.

Amanda nodded.

"I guess it was that green apple pie you ate this noon," said Sophia. "I declare, what did I do with that dress of Aunt Harriet's? I guess if you feel better I'll just run and get it and take it up garret. I'll stop in here again when I come down. You'd better lay still. Flora can bring you up a cup of tea. I wouldn't try to eat any supper."

Sophia's tone as she left the room was full of loving concern. Presently she returned; she looked disturbed, but angrily so. There was not the slightest hint of any fear in her expression.

"I want to know," said she, looking sharply and quickly around, "if I brought that purple dress in here, after all?"

"I didn't see you," replied Amanda.

"I must have. It isn't in that chamber, nor the closet. You aren't lying on it, are you?"

"I lay down before you came in," replied Amanda.

"So you did. Well, I'll go and look again."

Presently Amanda heard her sister's heavy step on the garret stairs. Then she returned with a queer defiant expression on her face.

"I carried it up garret, after all, and put it in the trunk," said, she. "I declare, I forgot it. I suppose your being faint sort of put it out of my head. There it was, folded up just as nice, right where I put it."

Sophia's mouth was set; her eyes upon her sister's scared, agitated face were full of hard challenge.

"Yes," murmured Amanda.

"I must go right down and see to that cake," said Sophia, going out of the room. "If you don't feel well, you pound on the floor with the umbrella."

Amanda looked after her. She knew that Sophia had not put that purple dress of her dead Aunt Harriet in the trunk in the garret.

Meantime Miss Louisa Stark was settling herself in the southwest chamber. She unpacked her trunk and hung her dresses carefully in the closet. She filled the bureau drawers with nicely folded linen and small articles of dress. She was a very punctilious woman. She put on a black India silk dress with purple flowers. She combed her grayish-blond hair in smooth ridges back from her broad forehead. She pinned her lace at her throat with a brooch, very handsome, although somewhat obsolete—a bunch of pearl grapes on black onyx, set in gold filagree. She had purchased it several years ago with a considerable portion of the stipend from her spring term of school-teaching.

As she surveyed herself in the little swing mirror surmounting the old-fashioned mahogany bureau she suddenly bent forward and looked closely at the brooch. It seemed to her that something was wrong with it. As she looked she became sure. Instead of the familiar bunch of pearl grapes on the black onyx, she saw a knot of blonde and black hair under glass surrounded by a border of twisted gold. She felt a thrill of horror, though she could not tell why. She unpinned the brooch, and it was her own familiar one, the pearl grapes and the onyx. "How very foolish I am," she thought. She thrust the pin in the laces at her throat and again looked at herself in the glass, and there it was again—the knot of blond and black hair and the twisted gold.

Louisa Stark looked at her own large, firm face above the brooch and it was full of terror and dismay which were new to it. She straightway began to wonder if there could be anything wrong with her mind. She remembered that an aunt of her mother's had been insane. A sort of fury with herself possessed her. She stared at the brooch in the glass with eyes at once angry and terrified. Then she removed it again and there was her own old brooch. Finally she thrust the gold pin through the lace again, fastened it and turning a defiant back on the glass, went down to supper.

At the supper table she met the other boarders—the elderly widow, the young clergyman and the middle-aged librarian. She viewed the elderly widow with reserve, the clergyman with respect, the middle-aged librarian with suspicion. The latter wore a very youthful shirt-waist, and her hair in a girlish fashion which the school-teacher, who twisted hers severely from the straining roots at the nape of her neck to the small, smooth coil at the top, condemned as straining after effects no longer hers by right.

The librarian, who had a quick acridness of manner, addressed her, asking what room she had, and asked the second time in spite of the school-teacher's evident reluctance to hear her. She even, since she sat next to her, nudged her familiarly in her rigid black silk side.

"What room are you in, Miss Stark?" said she.

"I am at a loss how to designate the room," replied Miss Stark stiffly.

"Is it the big southwest room?"

"It evidently faces in that direction," said Miss Stark.

The librarian, whose name was Eliza Lippincott, turned abruptly to Miss Amanda Gill, over whose delicate face a curious colour compounded of flush and pallour was stealing.

"What room did your aunt die in, Miss Amanda?" asked she abruptly.

Amanda cast a terrified glance at her sister, who was serving a second plate of pudding for the minister.

"That room," she replied feebly.

"That's what I thought," said the librarian with a certain triumph. "I calculated that must be the room she died in, for it's the best room in the house, and you haven't put anybody in it before. Somehow the room that anybody has died in lately is generally the last room that anybody is put in. I suppose *you* are so strong-minded you don't object to sleeping in a room where anybody died a few weeks ago?" she inquired of Louisa Stark with sharp eyes on her face.

"No, I do not," replied Miss stark with emphasis.

"Nor in the same bed?" persisted Eliza Lippincott with a kittenish reflection.

The young minister looked up from his pudding. He was very spiritual, but he had had poor pickings in his previous boarding place, and he could not help a certain abstract enjoyment over Miss Gill's cooking.

"You would certainly not be afraid, Miss Lippincott?" he remarked, with his gentle, almost caressing inflection of tone. "You do not for a minute believe that a higher power would allow any manifestation on the part of a disembodied spirit—who we trust is in her heavenly home—to harm one of His servants?"

"Oh, Mr. Dunn, of course not," replied Eliza Lippincott with a blush. "Of course not. I never meant to imply—"

"I could not believe you did," said the minister gently. He was very young, but he already had a wrinkle of permanent anxiety between his eyes and a smile of permanent ingratiation on his lips. The lines of the smile were as deeply marked as the wrinkle.

"Of course dear Miss Harriet Gill was a professing Christian," remarked the widow, "and I don't suppose a professing Christian would come back and scare folks if she could. I wouldn't be a mite afraid to sleep in that room; I'd rather have it than the one I've got. If I was afraid to sleep in a room where a good woman died, I wouldn't tell of it. If I saw things or heard things I'd think the fault must be with my own guilty conscience." Then she turned to Miss Stark. "Any time you feel timid in that room I'm ready and willing to change with you," said she.

"Thank you; I have no desire to change. I am perfectly satisfied with my room," replied Miss Stark with freezing dignity, which was thrown away upon the widow.

"Well," said she, "any time, if you should feel timid, you know what to do. I've got a real nice room; it faces east and gets the morning sun, but it isn't so nice as yours, according to my way of thinking. I'd rather take my chances any day in a room anybody had died in than in one that was hot in summer. I'm more afraid of a sunstroke than of spooks, for my part."

Miss Sophia Gill, who had not spoken one word, but whose mouth had become more and more rigidly compressed, suddenly rose from the table, forcing the minister to leave a little pudding, at which he glanced regretfully.

Miss Louisa Stark did not sit down in the parlour with the other boarders. She went straight to her room. She felt tired after her journey, and meditated a loose wrapper and writing a few letters quietly before she went to bed. Then, too, she was conscious of a feeling that if she delayed, the going there at all might assume more terrifying proportions. She was full of defiance against herself and her own lurking weakness.

So she went resolutely and entered the southwest chamber. There was through the room a soft twilight. She could dimly discern everything, the white satin scroll-work on the wall paper and the white counterpane on the bed being most evident. Consequently both arrested her attention first. She saw against the wall-paper directly facing the door the waist of her best black satin dress hung over a picture.

"That is very strange," she said to herself, and again a thrill of vague horror came over her.

She knew, or thought she knew, that she had put that black satin dress waist away nicely folded between towels in her trunk. She was very choice of her black satin dress.

She took down the black waist and laid it on the bed preparatory to folding it, but when she attempted to do so she discovered that the two sleeves were firmly sewed together. Louisa Stark stared at the sewed sleeves. "What does this mean?" she asked herself. She examined the sewing carefully; the stitches were small, and even, and firm, of black silk.

She looked around the room. On the stand beside the bed was something which she had not noticed before: a little old-fashioned work-box with a picture of a little boy in a pinafore on the top. Beside this work-box lay, as if just laid down by the user, a spool of black silk, a pair of scissors, and a large steel thimble with a hole in the top, after an old style. Louisa stared at these, then at the sleeves of her dress. She moved toward the door. For a moment she thought that this was something legitimate about which she might demand information; then she became doubtful. Suppose that work-box had been there all the time; suppose she had forgotten; suppose she herself had done this absurd thing, or suppose that she had not, what was to hinder the others from thinking so; what was to hinder a doubt being cast upon her own memory and reasoning powers?

Louisa Stark had been on the verge of a nervous breakdown in spite of her iron constitution and her great will power. No woman can teach school for forty years with absolute impunity. She was more credulous as to her own possible failings than she had ever been in her whole life. She was cold with horror and terror, and yet not so much horror and terror of the supernatural as of her own self. The weakness of belief in the supernatural was nearly impossible for this strong nature. She could more easily believe in her own failing powers.

"I don't know but I'm going to be like Aunt Marcia," she said to herself, and her fat face took on a long rigidity of fear.

She started toward the mirror to unfasten her dress, then she remembered the strange circumstance of the brooch and stopped short. Then she straightened herself defiantly and marched up to the bureau and looked in the glass. She saw reflected therein, fastening the lace at her throat, the old-fashioned thing of a large oval, a knot of fair and black hair under glass, set in a rim of twisted gold. She unfastened it with trembling fingers and looked at it. It was her own brooch, the cluster of pearl grapes on black onyx. Louisa Stark placed the trinket in its little box on the nest of pink cotton and put it away in the bureau drawer. Only death could disturb her habit of order.

Her fingers were so cold they felt fairly numb as she unfastened her dress; she staggered when she slipped it over her head. She went to the closet to hang it up and recoiled. A strong smell of lovage came in her nostrils; a purple gown near the door swung softly against her face as if impelled by some wind from within. All the pegs were filled with garments not her own, mostly of somber black, but there were some strange-patterned silk things and satins.

Suddenly Louisa Stark recovered her nerve. This, she told herself, was something distinctly tangible. Somebody had been taking liberties with her wardrobe. Somebody had been hanging some one else's clothes in her closet. She hastily slipped on her dress again and marched straight down to the parlour. The people were seated there; the widow and the minister were playing backgammon. The librarian was watching them. Miss Amanda Gill was mending beside the large lamp on the centre table. They all looked up with amazement as Louisa Stark entered. There was something strange in her expression. She noticed none of them except Amanda.

"Where is your sister?" she asked peremptorily of her.

"She's in the kitchen mixing up bread," Amanda quavered; "is there anything—" But the school-teacher was gone.

She found Sophia Gill standing by the kitchen table kneading dough with dignity. The young girl Flora was bringing some flour from the pantry. She stopped and stared at Miss Stark, and her pretty, delicate young face took on an expression of alarm.

Miss Stark opened at once upon the subject in her mind.

"Miss Gill," said she, with her utmost school-teacher manner, "I wish to inquire why you have had my own clothes removed from the closet in my room and others substituted?"

Sophia Gill stood with her hands fast in the dough, regarding her. Her own face paled slowly and reluctantly, her mouth stiffened.

"What? I don't quite understand what you mean, Miss Stark," said she.

"My clothes are not in the closet in my room and it is full of things which do not belong to me," said Louisa Stark.

"Bring me that flour," said Sophia sharply to the young girl, who obeyed, casting timid, startled glances at Miss Stark as she passed her. Sophia Gill began rubbing her hands clear of the dough. "I am sure I know nothing about it," she said with a certain tempered asperity. "Do you know anything about it, Flora?"

"Oh, no, I don't know anything about it, Aunt Sophia," answered the young girl, fluttering.

Then Sophia turned to Miss Stark. "I'll go upstairs with you, Miss Stark," said she, "and see what the trouble is. There must be some mistake." She spoke stiffly with constrained civility.

"Very well," said Miss Stark with dignity. Then she and Miss Sophia went upstairs. Flora stood staring after them.

Sophia and Louisa Stark went up to the southwest chamber. The closet door was shut. Sophia threw it open, then she looked at Miss Stark. On the pegs hung the schoolteacher's own garments in ordinary array.

"I can't see that there is anything wrong," remarked Sophia grimly.

Miss Stark strove to speak but she could not. She sank down on the nearest chair. She did not even attempt to defend herself. She saw her own clothes in the closet. She knew there had been no time for any human being to remove those which she thought she had seen and put hers in their places. She knew it was impossible. Again the awful horror of herself overwhelmed her.

"You must have been mistaken," she heard Sophia say.

She muttered something, she scarcely knew what. Sophia then went out of the room. Presently she undressed and went to bed. In the morning she did not go down to breakfast, and when Sophia came to inquire, requested that the stage be ordered for the noon train. She said that she was sorry, but was ill, and feared lest she might be worse, and she felt that she must return home at once. She looked ill, and could not take even the toast and tea which Sophia had prepared for her. Sophia felt a certain pity for her, but it was largely mixed with indignation. She felt that she knew the true reason for the school-teacher's illness and sudden departure, and it incensed her.

"If folks are going to act like fools we shall never be able to keep this house," she said to Amanda after Miss Stark had gone; and Amanda knew what she meant.

Directly the widow, Mrs. Elvira Simmons, knew that the school-teacher had gone and the southwest room was vacant, she begged to have it in exchange for her own. Sophia hesitated a moment; she eyed the widow sharply. There was something about the large, roseate face worn in firm lines of humour and decision which reassured her.

"I have no objection, Mrs. Simmons," said she, "if—"

"If what?" asked the widow.

"If you have common sense enough not to keep fussing because the room happens to be the one my aunt died in," said Sophia bluntly.

"Fiddlesticks!" said the widow, Mrs. Elvira Simmons.

That very afternoon she moved into the southwest chamber. The young girl Flora assisted her, though much against her will.

"Now I want you to carry Mrs. Simmons' dresses into the closet in that room and hang them up nicely, and see that she has everything she wants," said Sophia Gill. "And you can change the bed and put on fresh sheets. What are you looking at me that way for?"

"Oh, Aunt Sophia, can't I do something else?"

"What do you want to do something else for?"

"I am afraid."

"Afraid of what? I should think you'd hang your head. No; you go right in there and do what I tell you."

Pretty soon Flora came running into the sitting-room where Sophia was, as pale as death, and in her hand she held a queer, old-fashioned frilled nightcap.

"What's that?" demanded Sophia.

"I found it under the pillow."

"What pillow?"

"In the southwest room."

Sophia took it and looked at it sternly.

"It's Great-aunt Harriet's," said Flora faintly.

"You run down street and do that errand at the grocer's for me and I'll see that room," said Sophia with dignity. She carried the nightcap away and put it in the trunk in the garret where she had supposed it stored with the rest of the dead woman's belongings. Then she went into the southwest chamber and made the bed and assisted Mrs. Simmons to move, and there was no further incident.

The widow was openly triumphant over her new room. She talked a deal about it at the dinner-table.

"It is the best room in the house, and I expect you all to be envious of me," said she.

"And you are sure you don't feel afraid of ghosts?" said the librarian.

"Ghosts!" repeated the widow with scorn. "If a ghost comes I'll send her over to you. You are just across the hall from the southwest room."

"You needn't," returned Eliza Lippincott with a shudder. "I wouldn't sleep in that room, after—" she checked herself with an eye on the minister.

"After what?" asked the widow.

"Nothing," replied Eliza Lippincott in an embarrassed fashion.

"I trust Miss Lippincott has too good sense and too great faith to believe in anything of that sort," said the minister.

"I trust so, too," replied Eliza hurriedly.

"You did see or hear something—now what was it, I want to know?" said the widow that evening when they were alone in the parlour. The minister had gone to make a call.

Eliza hesitated.

"What was it?" insisted the widow.

"Well," said Eliza hesitatingly, "if you'll promise not to tell."

"Yes, I promise; what was it?"

"Well, one day last week, just before the school-teacher came, I went in that room to see if there were any clouds. I wanted to wear my gray dress, and I was afraid it was going to rain, so I wanted to look at the sky at all points, so I went in there, and—"

"And what?"

"Well, you know that chintz over the bed, and the valance, and the easy chair; what pattern should you say it was?"

"Why, peacocks on a blue ground. Good land, I shouldn't think any one who had ever seen that would forget it."

"Peacocks on a blue ground, you are sure?"

"Of course I am. Why?"

"Only when I went in there that afternoon it was not peacocks on a blue ground; it was great red roses on a yellow ground."

"Why, what do you mean?"

"What I say."

"Did Miss Sophia have it changed?"

"No. I went in there again an hour later and the peacocks were there."

"You didn't see straight the first time."

"I expected you would say that."

"The peacocks are there now; I saw them just now."

"Yes, I suppose so; I suppose they flew back."

"But they couldn't."

"Looks as if they did."

"Why, how could such a thing be? It couldn't be."

"Well, all I know is those peacocks were gone for an hour that afternoon and the red roses on the yellow ground were there instead."

The widow stared at her a moment, then she began to laugh rather hysterically.

"Well," said she, "I guess I sha'n't give up my nice room for any such tomfoolery as that. I guess I would just as soon have red roses on a yellow ground as peacocks on a blue; but there's no use talking, you couldn't have seen straight. How could such a thing have happened?"

"I don't know," said Eliza Lippincott; "but I know I wouldn't sleep in that room if you'd give me a thousand dollars."

"Well, I would," said the widow, "and I'm going to."

When Mrs. Simmons went to the southwest chamber that night she cast a glance at the bed-hanging and the easy chair. There were the peacocks on the blue ground. She gave a contemptuous thought to Eliza Lippincott.

"I don't believe but she's getting nervous," she thought. "I wonder if any of her family have been out at all."

But just before Mrs. Simmons was ready to get into bed she looked again at the hangings and the easy chair, and there were the red roses on the yellow ground instead of the peacocks on the blue. She looked long and sharply. Then she shut her eyes, and then opened them and looked. She still saw the red roses. Then she crossed the room, turned her back to the bed, and looked out at the night from the south window. It was clear and the full moon was shining. She watched it a moment sailing over the dark blue in its nimbus of gold. Then she looked around at the bed hangings. She still saw the red roses on the yellow ground.

Mrs. Simmons was struck in her most vulnerable point. This apparent contradiction of the reasonable as manifested in such a commonplace thing as chintz of a bed-hanging affected this ordinarily unimaginative woman as no ghostly appearance could have done. Those red roses on the yellow ground were to her much more ghostly than any strange figure clad in the white robes of the grave entering the room.

She took a step toward the door, then she turned with a resolute air. "As for going downstairs and owning up I'm scared and having that Lippincott girl crowing over me, I won't for any red roses instead of peacocks. I guess they can't hurt me, and as long as we've both of us seen 'em I guess we can't both be getting loony," she said.

Mrs. Elvira Simmons blew out her light and got into bed and lay staring out between the chintz hangings at the moonlit room. She said her prayers in bed always as being more comfortable, and presumably just as acceptable in the case of a faithful servant with a stout habit of body. Then after a little she fell asleep; she was of too practical a nature to be kept long awake by anything which had no power of actual bodily effect upon her. No stress of the spirit had ever disturbed her slumbers. So she slumbered between the red roses, or the peacocks, she did not know which.

But she was awakened about midnight by a strange sensation in her throat. She had dreamed that some one with long white fingers was strangling her, and she saw bending over her the face of an old woman in a white cap. When she waked there was no old woman, the room was almost as light as day in the full moonlight, and looked very peaceful; but the strangling sensation at her throat continued, and besides that, her face and ears felt muffled. She put up her hand and felt that her head was covered with a ruffled nightcap tied under her chin so tightly that it was exceedingly uncomfortable. A great qualm of horror shot over her. She tore the thing off frantically and flung it from her with a convulsive effort as if it had been a spider. She gave, as she did so, a quick, short scream of terror. She sprang out of bed and was going toward the door, when she stopped.

It had suddenly occurred to her that Eliza Lippincott might have entered the room and tied on the cap while she was asleep. She had not locked her door. She looked in the closet, under the bed; there was no one there. Then she tried to open the door, but to her astonishment found that it was locked—bolted on the inside. "I must have locked it, after all," she reflected with wonder, for she never locked her door. Then she could scarcely conceal from herself that there was something out of the usual about it all. Certainly no one could have entered the room and departed locking the door on the inside. She could not control the long shiver of horror that crept over her, but she was still resolute. She resolved that she would throw the cap out of the window. "I'll see if I have tricks like that played on me, I don't care who does it," said she quite aloud. She was still unable to believe wholly in the supernatural. The idea of some human agency was still in her mind, filling her with anger.

She went toward the spot where she had thrown the cap—she had stepped over it on her way to the door—but it was not there. She searched the whole room, lighting her lamp, but she could not find the cap. Finally she gave it up. She extinguished her lamp and went back to bed. She fell asleep again, to be again awakened in the same fashion. That time she tore off the cap as before, but she did not fling it on the floor as before. Instead she held to it with a fierce grip. Her blood was up.

Holding fast to the white flimsy thing, she sprang out of bed, ran to the window which was open, slipped the screen, and flung it out; but a sudden gust of wind, though the night was calm, arose and it floated back in her face. She brushed it aside like a cobweb and she clutched at it. She was actually furious. It eluded her clutching fingers. Then she did not see it at all. She examined the floor, she lighted her lamp again and searched, but there was no sign of it.

Mrs. Simmons was then in such a rage that all terror had disappeared for the time. She did not know with what she was angry, but she had a sense of some mocking presence which was silently proving too strong against her weakness, and she was aroused to the utmost power of resistance. To be baffled like this and resisted by something which was as nothing to her straining senses filled her with intensest resentment.

Finally she got back into bed again; she did not go to sleep. She felt strangely drowsy, but she fought against it. She was wide awake, staring at the moonlight, when she suddenly felt the soft white strings of the thing tighten around her throat and realized that her enemy was again upon her. She seized the strings, untied them, twitched off the cap, ran with it to the table where her scissors lay and furiously cut it into small bits. She cut and tore, feeling an insane fury of gratification.

"There!" said she quite aloud. "I guess I sha'n't have any more trouble with this old cap."

She tossed the bits of muslin into a basket and went back to bed. Almost immediately she felt the soft strings tighten around her throat. Then at last she yielded, vanquished. This new refutal of all laws of reason by which she had learned, as it were, to spell her theory of life, was too much for her equilibrium. She pulled off the clinging strings feebly, drew the thing from her head, slid weakly out of bed, caught up her wrapper and hastened out of the room. She went noiselessly along the hall to her own old room: she entered, got into her familiar bed, and lay there the rest of the night shuddering and listening, and if she dozed, waking with a start at the feeling of the pressure upon her throat to find that it was not there, yet still to be unable to shake off entirely the horror.

When daylight came she crept back to the southwest chamber and hurriedly got some clothes in which to dress herself. It took all her resolution to enter the room, but nothing unusual happened while she was there. She hastened back to her old chamber, dressed herself and went down to breakfast with an imperturbable face. Her colour had not faded. When asked by Eliza Lippincott how she had slept, she replied with an appearance of calmness which was bewildering that she had not slept very well. She never did sleep very well in a new bed, and she thought she would go back to her old room.

Eliza Lippincott was not deceived, however, neither were the Gill sisters, nor the young girl, Flora. Eliza Lippineott spoke out bluntly.

"You needn't talk to me about sleeping well," said she. "I know something queer happened in that room last night by the way you act."

They all looked at Mrs. Simmons, inquiringly—the librarian with malicious curiosity and triumph, the minister with sad incredulity, Sophia Gill with fear and indignation, Amanda and the young girl with unmixed terror. The widow bore herself with dignity.

"I saw nothing nor heard nothing which I trust could not have been accounted for in some rational manner," said she.

"What was it?" persisted Eliza Lippincott.

"I do not wish to discuss the matter any further," replied Mrs. Simmons shortly. Then she passed her plate for more creamed potato. She felt that she would die before she confessed to the ghastly absurdity of that nightcap, or to having been disturbed by the flight of peacocks off a blue field of chintz after she had scoffed at the possibility of such a thing. She left the whole matter so vague that in a fashion she came off the mistress of the situation. She at all events impressed everybody by her coolness in the face of no one knew what nightly terror.

After breakfast, with the assistance of Amanda and Flora, she moved back into her old room. Scarcely a word was spoken during the process of moving, but they all worked with trembling haste and looked guilty when they met one another's eyes, as if conscious of betraying a common fear.

That afternoon the young minister, John Dunn, went to Sophia Gill and requested permission to occupy the southwest chamber that night.

"I don't ask to have my effects moved there," said he, "for I could scarcely afford a room so much superior to the one I now occupy, but I would like, if you please, to sleep there to-night for the purpose of refuting in my own person any unfortunate superstition which may have obtained root here."

Sophia Gill thanked the minister gratefully and eagerly accepted his offer.

"How anybody with common sense can believe for a minute in any such nonsense passes my comprehension," said she.

"It certainly passes mine how anybody with Christian faith can believe in ghosts," said the minister gently, and Sophia Gill felt a certain feminine contentment in hearing him. The minister was a child to her; she regarded him with no tincture of sentiment, and yet she loved to hear two other women covertly condemned by him and she herself thereby exalted.

That night about twelve o'clock the Reverend John Dunn essayed to go to his nightly slumber in the southwest chamber. He had been sitting up until that hour preparing his sermon.

He traversed the hall with a little night-lamp in his hand, opened the door of the southwest chamber, and essayed to enter. He might as well have essayed to enter the solid side of a house. He could not believe his senses. The door was certainly open; he could look into the room full of soft lights and shadows under the moonlight which streamed into the windows. He could see the bed in which he had expected to pass the night, but he could not enter. Whenever he strove to do so he had a curious sensation as if he were trying to press against an invisible person who met him with a force of opposition impossible to overcome. The minister was not an athletic man, yet he had considerable strength. He squared his elbows, set his mouth hard, and strove to push his way through into the room. The opposition which he met was as sternly and mutely terrible as the rocky fastness of a mountain in his way.

For a half hour John Dunn, doubting, raging, overwhelmed with spiritual agony as to the state of his own soul rather than fear, strove to enter that southwest chamber. He was simply powerless against this uncanny obstacle. Finally a great horror as of evil itself came over him. He was a nervous man and very young. He fairly fled to his own chamber and locked himself in like a terror-stricken girl.

The next morning he went to Miss Gill and told her frankly what had happened, and begged her to say nothing about it lest he should have injured the cause by the betrayal of such weakness, for he actually had come to believe that there was something wrong with the room.

"What it is I know not, Miss Sophia," said he, "but I firmly believe, against my will, that there is in that room some accursed evil power at work, of which modern faith and modern science know nothing."

Miss Sophia Gill listened with grimly lowering face. She had an inborn respect for the clergy, but she was bound to hold that southwest chamber in the dearly beloved old house of her fathers free of blame.

"I think I will sleep in that room myself to-night," she said, when the minister had finished.

He looked at her in doubt and dismay.

"I have great admiration for your faith and courage, Miss Sophia," he said, "but are you wise?"

"I am fully resolved to sleep in that room to-night," said she conclusively. There were occasions when Miss Sophia Gill could put on a manner of majesty, and she did now.

It was ten o'clock that night when Sophia Gill entered the southwest chamber. She had told her sister what she intended doing and had been proof against her tearful entreaties. Amanda was charged not to tell the young girl, Flora.

"There is no use in frightening that child over nothing," said Sophia.

Sophia, when she entered the southwest chamber, set the lamp which she carried on the bureau, and began moving about the rooms pulling down the curtains, taking off the nice white counterpane of the bed, and preparing generally for the night.

As she did so, moving with great coolness and deliberation, she became conscious that she was thinking some thoughts that were foreign to her. She began remembering what she could not have remembered, since she was not then born: the trouble over her mother's marriage, the bitter opposition, the shutting the door upon her, the ostracizing her from heart and home. She became aware of a most singular sensation as of bitter resentment herself, and not against the mother and sister who had so treated her own mother, but against her own mother, and then she became aware of a like bitterness extended to her own self. She felt malignant toward her mother as a young girl whom she remembered, though she could not have remembered, and she felt malignant toward her own self, and her sister Amanda, and Flora. Evil suggestions surged in her brain—suggestions which turned her heart to stone and which still fascinated her. And all the time by a sort of double consciousness she knew that what she thought was strange and not due to her own volition. She knew that she was thinking the thoughts of some other person, and she knew who. She felt herself possessed.

But there was tremendous strength in the woman's nature. She had inherited strength for good and righteous self-assertion, from the evil strength of her ancestors. They had turned their own weapons against themselves. She made an effort which seemed almost mortal, but was conscious that the hideous thing was gone from her. She thought her own thoughts. Then she scouted to herself the idea of anything supernatural about the terrific experience. "I am imagining everything," she told herself. She went on with her preparations; she went to the bureau to take down her hair. She looked in the glass and saw, instead of her softly parted waves of hair, harsh lines of iron-gray under the black borders of an old-fashioned head-dress. She saw instead of her smooth, broad forehead, a high one wrinkled with the intensest concentration of selfish reflections of a long life; she saw instead of her steady blue eyes, black ones with depths of malignant reserve, behind a broad meaning of ill will; she saw instead of her firm, benevolent mouth one with a hard, thin line, a network of melancholic wrinkles. She saw instead of her own face, middle-aged and good to see, the expression of a life of honesty and good will to others and patience under trials, the face of a very old woman scowling forever with unceasing hatred and misery at herself and all others, at life, and death, at that which had been and that which was to come. She saw instead of her own face in the glass, the face of her dead Aunt Harriet, topping her own shoulders in her own well-known dress!

Sophia Gill left the room. She went into the one which she shared with her sister Amanda. Amanda looked up and saw her standing there. She had set the lamp on a table, and she stood holding a handkerchief over her face. Amanda looked at her with terror.

"What is it? What is it, Sophia?" she gasped.

Sophia still stood with the handkerchief pressed to her face.

"Oh, Sophia, let me call somebody. Is your face hurt? Sophia, what is the matter with your face?" fairly shrieked Amanda.

Suddenly Sophia took the handkerchief from her face.

"Look at me, Amanda Gill," she said in an awful voice.

Amanda looked, shrinking.

"What is it? Oh, what is it? You don't look hurt. What is it, Sophia?"

"What do you see?"

"Why, I see you."

"Me?"

"Yes, you. What did you think I would see?"

Sophia Gill looked at her sister. "Never as long as I live will I tell you what I thought you would see, and you must never ask me," said she.

"Well, I never will, Sophia," replied Amanda, half weeping with terror.

"You won't try to sleep in that room again, Sophia?"

"No," said Sophia; "and I am going to sell this house."

For by him were all things created: all things in heaven and on the earth, the visible and the invisible, whether thrones, or dominions, or principalities, or powers: all things were created by him and for him.

Colossians 1: 16

For our conflict is not against flesh and blood, but against principalities, against powers, against the rulers of this dark world, against spiritual forces of evil in the heavenlies.

Ephesians 6: 12

THE SHADOWS

Henry S. Whitehead (1882-1932)

I did not begin to see the shadows until I had lived in Old Morris'
house for more than a week. Old Morris, dead and gone these many years,
had been the scion of a still earlier Irish settler in Santa Cruz, of a family
which had come into the island when the Danes, failing to colonize its
rich acres, had opened it, in the middle of the Eighteenth Century, to
colonists; and younger sons of Irish, Scottish, and English gentry had
taken up sugar estates and commenced that baronial life which lasted
for a century and which declined after the abolition of slavery and the
German bounty on beet sugar had started the long process of West
Indian commercial decadence. Mr. Morris' youth had been spent in the
French islands.

The shadows were at first so vague that I attributed them wholly to
the slight weakness which began to affect my eyes in early childhood,
and which, while never materially interfering with the enjoyment of life
in general, had necessitated the use of glasses when I used my eyes to
read or write. My first experience of them was about one o'clock in the
morning. I had been at a "Gentlemen's Party" at Hacker's house, "Emerald," as some poetic-minded ancestor of Hacker's had named the family
estate three miles out of Christiansted, the northerly town, built on the
site of the ancient abandoned French town of Bassin.

I had come home from the party and was undressing in my bedroom,
which is one of two rooms on the westerly side of the house which stands
at the edge of the old "Sunday Market." These two bedrooms open on the
marketplace, and I had chosen them, rather than the more airy rooms on
the other side, because of the space outside. I like to look out on trees in
the early mornings, whenever possible, and the ancient market-place is
overshadowed with the foliage of hundred-year-old mahogany trees, and
a few gnarled "otaheites" and Chinese-bean trees.

429

I had nearly finished undressing, had noted that my servant had let down and properly fastened the mosquito netting, and had stepped into the other bedroom to open the jalousies so that I might get as much of the night-breeze as possible circulating through the house. I was coming back through the doorway between the two bedrooms, and taking off my dressing gown, at the moment, when the first faint perception of what I have called "the shadows" made itself apparent. It was very dark, just after switching off the electric light in that front bedroom. I had, in fact, to feel for the doorway. In this I experienced some difficulty, and my eyes had not fully adjusted themselves to the thin starlight seeping in through the slanted jalousies of my own room when I passed through the doorway and groped my way toward the great mahogany four-poster in which I was about to lie down for my belated rest.

I saw the nearest post looming before me, closer than I had expected. Putting out my hand, I grasped—nothing. I winked in some surprise, and peered through the slightly increasing light, as my eyes adjusted themselves to the sudden change. Yes, surely,—there was the corner of the bedstead just in front of my face! By now my eyes were sufficiently attuned to the amount of light from outside to see a little plainer. I was puzzled. The bed was not where I had supposed it to be. What could have happened? That the servants should have moved my bed without orders to do so was incredible. Besides, I had undressed, in full electric light in that room, not more than a few minutes ago, and then the bed was standing exactly where it had been since I had had it moved into that room a week before. I kicked, gently, before me with a slippered foot, against the place where that bedpost appeared to be standing—and my foot met no resistance.

I stepped over to the light in my own room, and snapped the button. In the sudden glare, everything readjusted itself to normal. There stood my bed, and here in their accustomed places about the room were ranged the chairs, the polished wardrobe (we do not use cupboards in the West India Islands), the mahogany dressing table,—even my clothes which I had hung over a chair where Albertina my servant would find them in the morning and put them (they were of white drill) into the soiled-clothes bag in the morning.

I shook my head. Light and shadow in these islands seem, somehow, different from what they are like at home in the United States! The tricks they play are different tricks, somehow.

I snapped off the light again, and in the ensuing dead blackness, I crawled in under the loose edge of the mosquito netting, tucked it along under the edge of the mattress on that side, adjusted my pillows and the sheets, and settled myself for a good sleep. Even to a moderate man, these gentlemen's parties are rather wearing sometimes. They invariably last too long. I closed my eyes and was asleep before I could have put these last ideas into words.

In the morning the recollection of the experience with the bed-being-in-the-wrong-place was gone. I jumped out of bed and into my shower bath at half-past six, for I had promised O'Brien, captain of the U. S. Marines, to go out with him to the rifle range at La Grande Princesse that morning and look over the butts with him. I like O'Brien, and I am not uninterested in the efficiency of Uncle Sam's Marines, but my chief objective was to watch the pelicans. Out there on the glorious beach of Estate Grande Princesse ("Big Princess" as the Black People call it), a colony of pelicans make their home, and it is a never-ending source of amusement to me to watch them fish. A Caribbean pelican is probably the most graceful flier we have in these latitudes,—barring not even the hurricane bird, that describer of noble arcs and parabolas,—and the most insanely, absurdly awkward creature on land that Providence has cared in a light-hearted moment to create!

I expressed my interest in Captain O'Brien's latest improvements, and while he was talking shop to one of his lieutenants and half a dozen enlisted men he has camped out there, I slipped down to the beach to watch the pelicans fish. Three or four of them were describing curves and turns of indescribable complexity and perfect grace over the green water of the reef-enclosed white beach. Ever and again one would stop short in the air, fold himself up like a jackknife, turn head downward, his great pouched bill extended like the head of a cruel spear, and drop like a plummet into the water, emerging an instant later with the pouch distended with a fish.

I stayed a trifle too long,—for my eyes. Driving back I observed that I had picked up several sun-spots, and when I arrived home I polished a set of yellowish sun-spectacles I keep for such emergencies and put them on.

The east side of the house had been shaded against the pouring morning sunlight, and in this double shade I looked to see my eyes clear up. The sun-spots persisted, however, in that annoying, recurrent way they have,—almost disappearing and then returning in undiminished kaleidoscopic grotesqueness,—those strange blocks and parcels of pure color changing as one winks from indigo to brown and from brown to orange and then to a blinding turquoise-blue, according to some eery natural law of physics, within the fluids of the eye itself.

The sun-spots were so persistent that morning that I decided to keep my eyes closed for some considerable time and see if that would allow them to run their course and wear themselves out. Blue and mauve grotesques of the vague, general shape of diving pelicans swam and jumped inside my eyes. It was very annoying. I called to Albertina.

"Albertina," said I, when she had come to the door, "please go into my bedroom and close all the jalousies tight. Keep out all the light you can, please."

"Ahl roight, sir," replied the obedient Albertina, and I heard her slapping the jalousie-blinds together with sharp little clicks.

"De jalousie ahl close, sir," reported Albertina. I thanked her, and proceeded with half-shut eyes into the bedroom, which, not yet invaded with afternoon's sunlight and closely shuttered, offered an appearance of deep twilight. I lay, face down, across the bed, a pillow under my face, and my eyes buried in darkness.

Very gradually, the diving pelican faded out, to a cube, to a dim, recurrent blur, to nothingness. I raised my head and rolled over on my side, placing the pillow back where it belonged. And as I opened my eyes on the dim room, there stood, in faint, shadowy outline, in the opposite corner of the room, away from the outside wall on the market-place side, the huge, Danish bedstead I had vaguely noted the night before, or rather, early that morning.

It was the most curious sensation, looking at that bed in the dimness of the room. I was reminded of those fourth-dimensional tales which are so popular nowadays, for the bed impinged, spatially, on my large bureau, and the curious thing was that I could see the bureau at the same time! I rubbed my eyes, a little unwisely, but not enough to bring back the pelican sun-spots into them, for I remembered and desisted pretty promptly. I looked, fixedly, at the great bed, and it blurred and dimmed and faded out of my vision.

Again, I was greatly puzzled, and I went over to where it seemed to stand and walked through it,—it being no longer visible to my now restored vision, free of the effects of the sun-spots,—and then I went out into the "hall"—a West Indian drawing room is called "the hall"—and sat down to think over this strange phenomenon. I could not account for it. If it had been poor Prentice, now! Prentice attended all the "gentlemen's parties" to which he was invited with a kind of religious regularity, and had to be helped into his car with a similar regularity, a regularity which was verging on the monotonous nowadays, as the invitations became more and more strained. No,—in my case it was, if there was anything certain about it, assuredly not the effects of strong liquors, for barring an occasional sociable swizzel I retained here in my West Indian residence my American convictions that moderation in such matters was a reasonable virtue. I reasoned out the matter of the phantom bedstead,—for so I was already thinking of it,—as far as I was able. That it was a phantom of defective eyesight I had no reasonable doubt. I had had my eyes examined in New York three months before, and the oculist had pleased me greatly by assuring me that there were no visible indications of deterioration. In fact, Dr. Jusserand had said at that time that my eyes were stronger, sounder, than when he had made his last examination six months before.

Perhaps this conviction,—that the appearance was due to my own physical shortcoming—accounts for the fact that I was not (what shall I say?) *disturbed*, by what I saw, or thought I saw. Confront the most thoroughgoing materialist with a ghost, and he will act precisely like anyone else; like any normal human being who believes in the material world as the outward and visible sign of something which animates it. All normal human beings, it seems to me, are sacramentalists!

I was, for this reason, able to thing clearly about the phenomenon. My mind was not clouded and bemused with fear, and its known physiological effects. I can, quite easily, record what I "saw" in the course of the next few days. The bed was clearer to my vision and apprehension than it had been. It seemed to have grown in visibility; in a kind of substantialness, if there is such a word! It appeared more *material* than it had before, less shadowy.

I looked about the room and saw other furniture: a huge, old-fashioned mahogany bureau with men's heads carved on the knuckles of the front legs, Danish fashion. There is precisely such carving on pieces in the museum in Copenhagen, they tell me, those who have seen my drawing of it. I was actually able to do that, and had completed a kind of plan-picture of the room, putting in all the shadow-furniture, and leaving my own, actual furniture out. Thank the God in whom I devoutly believe,—and know to be more powerful than the Powers of Evil,—I was able to finish that rather elaborate drawing before... Well, I must not "run ahead of my story."

That night when I was ready to retire, and had once more opened up the jalousies of the front bedroom, and had switched off the light, I looked, naturally enough under the circumstances, for the outlines of that ghostly furniture. They were much clearer now. I studied them with a certain sense of almost "scientific" detachment. It was, even then, apparent to me that no weakness of the strange complexity which is the human eye could reasonably account for the presence of a well-defined set of mahogany furniture in a room already furnished with real furniture. But I was by now sufficiently accustomed to it to be able to examine it all without that always-disturbing element of fear,—strangeness. I looked at the bedstead and the "roll-back" chairs, and the great bureau, and a ghostly, huge, and quaintly carved wardrobe, studying their outlines, noting their relative positions. It was on that occasion that it occurred to me that it would be of interest to make some kind of drawing of them. I looked the harder after that, fixing the details and the relations of them all in my mind, and then I went into the hall and got some paper and a pencil and set to work.

It was hard work, this of reproducing something which I was well aware was some kind of an "apparition," especially after looking at the furniture in the dark bedroom, switching on the light in another room and then trying to reproduce. I could not, of course, make a direct comparison. I mean it was impossible to look at my drawing and then look at the furniture. There was always a necessary interval between the two processes. I persisted through several evenings, and even for a couple of evenings fell into the custom of going into my bedroom in the evening's darkness, looking at what was there, and then attempting to reproduce it. After five or six days, I had a fair plan, in considerable detail, of the arrangement of this strange furniture in my bedroom,—a plan or drawing which would be recognizable if there were anyone now alive who remembered such an arrangement of such furniture. It will be apparent that a story had been growing up in my mind, or, at least, that I had come to some kind of conviction that what I "saw" was a reproduction of something that had once existed in that same detail and that precise order!

On the seventh night, there came an interruption.

I had, by that time, finished my work, pretty well. I had drawn the room as it would have looked with that furniture in it, and had gone over the whole with India ink, very carefully. As a drawing, the thing was finished, so far as my indifferent skill as a draftsman would permit.

That seventh evening, I was looking over the appearance of the room, such qualms as the eeriness of the situation might have otherwise produced reduced to next-to-nothing partly by my interest, in part by having become accustomed to it all. I was making, this evening, as careful a comparison as possible between my remembered work on paper and the detailed appearance of the room. By now, the furniture stood out clearly, in a kind of light of its own which I can roughly compare only to "phosphorescence." It was not, quite, that. But that will serve, lame as it is, and trite perhaps, to indicate what I mean. I suppose the appearance of the room was something like what a cat "sees" when she arches her back,—as Algernon Blackwood has pointed out, in *John Silence*,—and rubs against the imaginary legs of some personage entirely invisible to the man in the armchair who idly wonders what has taken possession of his house-pet.

I was, as I say, studying the detail. I could not find that I had left out anything salient. The detail was, too, quite clear now. There were no blurred outlines as there had been on the first few nights. My own, material furniture had, so to speak, sunk back into invisibility, which was sensible enough, seeing that I had put the room in as nearly perfect darkness as I could, and there was no moon to interfere, those nights.

I had run my eyes all around it, up and down the twisted legs of the great bureau, along the carved ornamentation of the top of the wardrobe, along the lines of the chairs, and had come back to the bed. It was at this point of my checking-up that I got what I must describe as the first "shock" of the entire experience.

Something moved, beside the bed.

I peered, carefully, straining my eyes to catch what it might be. It had been something bulky, a slow-moving object, on the far side of the bed, blurred, somewhat, just as the original outlines had been blurred in the beginning of my week's experience. The now strong and clear outlines of the bed, and what I might describe as its ethereal substance, stood between me and it. Besides, the vision of the slow-moving mass was further obscured by a ghostly mosquito-net, which had been one of the last of the details to come into the scope of my strange night-vision.

Those folds of the mosquito-netting moved,—waved, before my eyes.

Someone, it might almost be imagined, was getting into that bed!

I sat, petrified. This was a bit too much for me. I could feel the little chills run up and down my spine. My scalp prickled. I put my hands on my knees, and pressed hard. I drew several deep breaths. "All-overish" is an old New England expression, once much used by spinsters, I believe, resident in that intellectual section of the United States. Whatever the precise connotation of the term, that was the way I felt. I could feel the reactive sensation, I mean, of that particular portion of the whole experience, in every part of my being,—body, mind, and soul! It was,—paralyzing. I reached up a hand that was trembling violently,—I could barely control it, and the fingers, when they touched the hard-rubber button, felt numb,—and switched on the bedroom light, and spent the next ten minutes recovering.

That night, when I came to retire, I dreaded,—actually dreaded,—what might come to my vision when I snapped off the light. This, however, I managed to reason out with myself. I used several arguments—nothing had so far occurred to annoy or injure me; if this were to be a cumulative experience, if something were to be "revealed" to me by this deliberate process of slow materialization which had been progressing for the last week or so, then it might as well be for some good and useful purpose. I might be, in a sense, the agent of Providence! If it were otherwise; if it were the evil work of some discarnate spirit, or something of the sort, well, every Sunday since my childhood, in church, I had recited the Creed, and so admitted, along with the clergy and the rest of the congregation, that God our Father had created all things,—visible *and invisible!* If it were this part of His creation at work, for *any* purpose, then He was stronger than they. I said a brief prayer before turning off that light, and put my trust in Him. It may appear to some a bit old-fashioned,—even Victorian! But He does not change along with the current fashions of human thought about Him, and this "human thought," and "the modern mind," and all the rest of it, does not mean the vast, the overwhelming majority of people. It involves only a few dozen prideful "intellectuals" at best, or worst! I switched off the light, and, already clearer, I saw what must have been Old Morris, getting into bed.

I had interviewed old Mr. Bonesteel, the chief government surveyor, a gentleman of parts and much experience, a West Indian born on this island. Mr. Bonesteel, in response to my guarded enquiries,—for I had, of course, already suspected Old Morris; was not my house still called his?—had stated that he remembered Old Morris well, in his own remote youth. His description of that personage and this apparition tallied. This, undoubtedly, was Old Morris. That it was *someone*, was apparent. I felt, somehow, rather relieved to realize that it was he. I knew something about him, you see. Mr. Bonesteel had given me a good description and many anecdotes, quite freely, and as though he enjoyed being called on for information about one of the old-timers like Morris. He had been more reticent, guarded, in fact, when I pressed him for details of Morris' end. That there had been some obscurity,—intentional or otherwise, I could never ascertain,—about the old man, I had already known. Such casual enquiries as I had made on other occasions through natural interest in the person whose name still clung to my house sixty years or more since be had lived in it, had never got me anywhere. I had only gathered what Mr. Bonesteel's more ample account corroborated: that Morris had been eccentric, in some ways, amusingly so. That he had been extraordinarily well-to-do. That he gave occasional large parties, which, contrary to the custom of the hospitable island of St. Croix, were always required to come to a conclusion well before midnight. Why, there was a story of Old Morris almost literally getting rid of a few reluctant guests, by one device or another, from these parties, a circumstance on which hinged several of the amusing anecdotes of that eccentric person!

Old Morris, as I knew, had not always lived on St. Croix. His youth had been spent in Martinique, in the then smaller and less important town of Fort-de-France. That, of course, was many years before the terrific calamity of the destruction of St. Pierre had taken place, by the eruption of Mt. Pelée. Old Morris, coming to St. Croix in young middle age,—forty-five or there-abouts,—had already been accounted a rich man. He had been engaged in no business. He was not a planter, not a store-keeper, had no profession. Where he produced his affluence was one of the local mysteries. His age, it seemed, was the other.

"I suppose," Mr. Bonesteel had said, "that Morris was nearer a hundred than ninety, when he,—ah,—died. I was a child of about eight at that time. I shall be seventy next August-month. That, you see, would be about sixty-two years ago, about 1861, or about the time your Civil War was begin-ning. Now my father has told me,—he died when I was nineteen,—that

Old Morris looked exactly the same when he was a boy! Extraordinary. The Black People used to say—" Mr. Bonesteel fell silent, and his eyes had an old man's dim, far-away look.

"The Black People have some very strange beliefs, Mr. Bonesteel," said I, attempting to prompt him. "A good many of them I have heard about myself, and they interest me very much. What particular—"

Mr. Bonesteel turned his mild, blue eyes upon me, reflectively.

"You must drop in at my house one of these days, Mr. Stewart," said he, mildly. "I have some rare old rum that I'd be glad to have you sample, sir! There's not much of it on the island these days, since Uncle Sam turned his prohibition laws loose on us in 1922."

"Thank you very much indeed, Mr. Bonesteel," I replied. "I shall take the first occasion to do so, sir; not that I care especially for 'old rum' except a spoonful in a cup of tea, or in pudding sauce, perhaps; but the pleasure of your company, sir, is always an inducement."

Mr. Bonesteel bowed to me gravely, and I returned his bow from where I sat in his airy office in Government House.

"Would you object to mentioning what that 'belief' was, sir?"

A slightly pained expression replaced my old friend's look of hospitality.

"All that is a lot of foolishness!" said he, with something like asperity. He looked at me, contemplatively.

"Not that I believe in such things, you must understand. Still, a man sees a good many things in these islands, in a lifetime, you know! Well, the Black People—" Mr. Bonesteel looked apprehensively about him, as though reluctant to have one of his clerks overhear what he was about to say, and leaned toward me from his chair, lowering is voice to a whisper.

"They said,—it was a remark here and a kind of hint there, you must understand; nothing definite,—that Morris had interfered, down there in Martinique, with some of their queer doings—offended the Zombi,— sometbing of the kind; that Morris had made some kind of conditions— oh, it was very vague, and probably all mixed up!—you know, whereby he was to have a long life and all the money he wanted, something like that,— and afterward ...

"Well, Mr. Stewart, you just ask somebody, sometime about Morris' death."

Not another word about Old Morris could I extract out of Mr. Bonesteel.

But of course he had me aroused. I tried Despard, who lives on the other end of the island, a man educated at the Sorbonne, and who knows, it is said, everything there is to know about the island and its affairs.

It was much the same with Mr. Despard, who is an entirely different kind of person; younger, for one thing, than my old friend the government surveyor.

Mr. Despard smiled, a kind of wry smile. "Old Morris!" said he, reflectively, and paused.

"Might I venture to ask—no offense, my dear sir!—why you wish to rake up such an old matter as Old Morris' death?"

I was a bit nonplussed, I confess. Mr. Despard had been perfectly courteous, as he always is, but, somehow, I had not expected such an intervention on his part.

"Why," said I, "I should find it hard to tell you, precisely, Mr. Despard. It is not that I am averse to being frank in the face of such an inquiry as yours, sir. I was not aware that there was anything important,—serious, as your tone implies,—about that matter. Put it down to mere curiosity if you will, and answer or not, as you wish, sir."

I was, perhaps, a little nettled at this unexpected, and, as it then seemed to me, finicky obstruction being placed in my way. What could there be in such a case for this formal reticence,—these verbal safeguards? If it were a "jumbee" story, there was no importance to it. If otherwise, well, I might be regarded by Despard as a person of reasonable discretion. Perhaps Despard was some relative of Old Morris, and there was something a bit off-color about his death. That, too, might account for Mr. Bonesteel's reticence.

"By the way," I enquired, noting Despard's reticence, "might I ask another question, Mr. Despard?"

"Certainly, Mr. Stewart."

"I do not wish to impress you as idly or unduly curious, but—are you and Mr. Bonesteel related in any way?"

"No, sir. We are not related in any way at all, sir."

"Thank you, Mr. Despard," said I, and, bowing to each other after the fashion set here by the Danes, we parted.

I had not learned a thing about Old Morris' death.

I went in to see Mrs. Heidenklang. Here, if anywhere, I should find out what was intriguing me.

Mrs. Heidenklang is an ancient Creole lady, relict of a prosperous storekeeper, who lives, surrounded by a certain state of her own, propped up in bed in an environment of a stupendous quantity of lacy things and gauzy ruffles. I did not intend to mention Old Morris to her, but only to get some information about the Zombi, if that should be possible.

I found the old lady, surrounded by her ruffles and lace things, in one of her good days. Her health has been precarious for twenty years!

It was not difficult to get her talking about the Zombi.

"Yes," said Mrs. Heidenklang, "it is extraordinary how the old beliefs and the old words cling in their minds! Why, Mr. Stewart, I was hearing about a trial in the police court a few days ago. One old Black woman had summoned another for abusive language. On the witness stand the complaining old woman said: 'She cahl me a wuthless ole Cartagene, sir!' Now, think of that! Carthage was destroyed 'way back in the days of Cato the Elder, you know, Mr. Stewart! The greatest town of all Africa. To be a Carthaginian meant to be a sea-robber,—a pirate; that is, a thief. One old woman on this island, more than two thousand years afterward, wishes to call another a thief, and the word 'Cartagene' is the word she naturally uses! I suppose that has persisted on the West Coast and throughout all those village dialects in Africa without a break, all these centuries! The Zombi of the French islands? Yes, Mr. Stewart. There are some extraordinary beliefs. Why, perhaps you've heard mention made of Old Morris, Mr. Stewart. He used to live in your house, you know?"

I held my breath. Here was a possible trove. I nodded my head. I did not dare to speak!

"Well, Old Morris, you see, lived most of his earlier days in Martinique, and, it is said, he had a somewhat adventurous life there, Mr. Stewart. Just what he did or how he got himself involved, seems never to have been made clear, but—in some way, Mr. Stewart, the Black People believe, Morris got himself involved with a very powerful 'Jumbee,' and that is where what I said about the persistence of ancient beliefs comes in. Look on that table there, among those photographs, Mr. Stewart. There! that's the place. I wish I were able to get up and assist you. These maids! Everything askew, I have no doubt! Do you observe a kind of fish-headed thing, about as big as the palm of your hand? Yes! that is it!"

I found the "fish-headed thing" and carried it over to Mrs. Heidenklang. She took it in her hand and looked at it. It lacked a nose, but otherwise it was intact, a strange, uncouth-looking little godling, made of anciently-polished volcanic stone, with huge, protruding eyes, small, humanlike ears, and what must have been a nose like a Tortola jackfish, or a black witch-bird, with its parrot beak.

"Now that," continued Mrs. Heidenklang, "is one of the very ancient household gods of the aborigines of Martinique, and you will observe the likeness in the idea to the *Lares* and *Penates* of your school-Latin days. Whether this is a *lar* or a *penate*, I can not tell," and the old lady paused to smile at her little joke, "but at any rate he is a representation of something very powerful,—a fish-god of the Caribs. There's something Egyptian about the idea, too, I've always suspected; and, Mr. Stewart, a Carib or an Arawak Indian, there were both in these islands, you know,— looked much like an ancient Egyptian; perhaps half like your Zuñi or Aztec Indians, and half Egyptian, would be a fair statement of his appearance. These fish-gods had men's bodies, you see, precisely like the hawk-headed and jackal-headed deities of ancient Egypt.

"It was one of those, the Black People say, with which Mr. Morris got himself mixed up,— 'Gahd knows' as they say—how! And, Mr. Stewart, they say, his death was terrible! The particulars I've never heard, but my father knew, and he was sick for several days, after seeing Mr. Morris' body. Extraordinary, isn't it? And when are you coming this way again, Mr. Stewart? Do drop in and call on an old lady."

I felt that I was progressing. The next time I saw Mr. Bonesteel, which was that very evening, I stopped him on the street and asked for a word with him.

"What was the date, or the approximate date, Mr. Bonesteel, of Mr. Morris' death? Could you recall that, sir?"

Mr. Bonesteel paused and considered.

"It was just before Christmas," said he. "I remember it not so much by Christmas as by the races, which always take place the day after Christmas. Morris had entered his sorrel mare Santurce, and, as he left no heirs, there was no one who 'owned' Santurce, and she had to be withdrawn from the races. It affected the betting very materially and a good many persons were annoyed about it, but there wasn't anything that could be done."

I thanked Mr. Bonesteel, and not without reason, for his answer had fitted into something that had been growing in my mind. Christmas was only eight days off. This drama of the furniture and Old Morris getting into bed, I had thought (and not unnaturally, it seems to me), might be a kind of re-enactment of the tragedy of his death. If I had the courage to watch, night after night, I might be relieved of the necessity of asking any questions. I might witness whatever had occurred, in some weird reproduction, engineered, God knows how!

For three nights now, I had seen the phenomenon of Old Morris getting into bed repeated, and each time it was clearer. I had sketched him into my drawing, a short, squat figure, rather stooped and fat, but possessed of a strange, gorillalike energy. His movements, as he walked toward the bed, seized the edge of the mosquito-netting and climbed in, were, somehow, full of *power*, which was the more apparent since these were ordinary motions. One could not help imagining that Old Morris would have been a tough customer to tackle, for all his alleged age!

This evening, at the hour when this phenomenon was accustomed to enact itself, that is, about eleven o'clock, I watched again. The scene was very much clearer, and I observed something I had not noticed before. Old Morris' *simulacrum* paused just before seizing the edge of the netting, raised its eyes, and began, with its right hand, a motion precisely like one who is about to sign himself with the cross. The motion was abruptly arrested, however, only the first of the four touches on the body being made.

I saw, too, something of the expression of the face that night, for the first time. At the moment of making the arrested sign, it was one of despairing horror. Immediately afterward, as this motion appeared to be abandoned for the abrupt clutching of the lower edge of the mosquito-net, it changed into a look of ferocious stubbornness, of almost savage self-confidence. I lost the facial expression as the appearance sank down upon the bed and pulled the ghostly bedclothes over itself.

Three nights later, when all this had become as greatly intensified as had the clearing-up process that had affected the furniture, I observed another motion, or what might be taken for the faint foreshadowing of another motion. This was not on the part of Old Morris. It made itself apparent as lightly and elusively as the swift flight of a moth across the reflection of a lamp, over near the bedroom door (the doors in my house are more than ten feet high, in fourteen-foot-high-walls), a mere flicker of something,—something entering the room. I looked, and peered at that corner, straining my eyes, but nothing could I see save what I might describe as an intensification of the black shadow in that corner near the door, vaguely formed like a slim human figure, though grossly out of all human proportion. The vague shadow looked purple against the black. It was about ten feet high, and otherwise as though cast by an incredibly tall, thin human being.

I made nothing of it then; and again, despite all this cumulative experience with the strange shadows of my bedroom, attributed this last phenomenon to my eyes. It was too vague to be at that time accounted otherwise than as a mere subjective effect.

But the night following, I watched for it at the proper moment in the sequence of Old Morris' movements as he got into bed, and this time it was distinctly clearer. The shadow, it was, of some monstrous shape, ten feet tall, long, angular, of vaguely human appearance, though even in its merely shadowed form, somehow cruelly, strangely inhuman! I can not describe the cold horror of its realization. The head-part was, relatively to the proportions of the body, short and broad, like a pump-kin head of a "man" made of sticks by boys, to frighten passersby on Hallowe'en.

The next evening I was out again to an entertainment at the residence of one of my hospitable friends, and arrived home after midnight. There stood the ghostly furniture, there on the bed was the form of the apparently sleeping Old Morris, and there in the corner stood the shadow, little changed from last night's appearance.

The next night would be pretty close to the date of Old Morris' death. It would be that night, or the next at latest, according to Mr. Bonesteel's statement. The next day I could not avoid the sensation of something impending!

I entered my room and turned off the light a little before eleven, seated myself, and waited.

The furniture tonight was, to my vision, absolutely indistinguishable from reality. This statement may sound somewhat strange, for it will be remembered that I was sitting in the dark. Approximating terms again, I may say, however, that the furniture was visible in a light of its own, a kind of "phosphorescence," which apparently emanated from it. Certainly there was no natural source of light. Perhaps I may express the matter thus: that light and darkness were *reversed* in the case of this ghostly bed, bureau, wardrobe, and chairs. When actual light was turned on, they disappeared. In darkness, which, of course, is the absence of physical light, they emerged. That is the nearest I can get to it. At any rate, to-night the furniture was entirely, perfectly, visible to me.

Old Morris came in at the usual time. I could see him with a clarity exactly comparable to what I have said about the furniture. He made his slight pause, his arrested motion of the right hand, and then, as usual, cast from him, according to his expression, the desire for that protective gesture, and reached a hard-looking, gnarled fist out to take hold of the mosquito-netting.

As he did so, a fearful thing leaped upon him, a thing out of the corner by the high doorway,—the dreadful, purplish shadow-thing. I had not been looking in that direction, and while I had not forgotten this newest of the strange items in this fantasmagoria which had been repeating itself before my eyes for many nights, I was wholly unprepared for its sudden appearance and malignant activity.

I have said the shadow was purplish against black. Now that it had taken form, as the furniture and Old Morris himself had taken form, I observed that this purplish coloration was actual. It was a glistening, humanlike, almost metallic-appearing thing, certainly ten feet high, completely covered with great, iridescent fish-scales, each perhaps four square inches in area, which shimmered as it leaped across the room. I saw it for only a matter of a second or two. I saw it clutch surely and with a deadly malignity, the hunched body of Old Morris, from behind, just, you will remember, as the old man was about to climb into his bed. The dreadful thing turned him about as a wasp turns a fly, in great, flail-like, glistening arms, and never, to the day of my death, do I ever expect to be free of the look on Old Morris' face,—a look of a lost soul who knows that there is no hope for him in this world or the next,—as the great, squat, rounded head, a head precisely like that of Mrs. Heidenklang's little fish-jumbee, descended, revealing to my horrified sight one glimpse of a huge, scythelike parrot-beak which it used, with a nodding motion of the ugly head, to plunge into its writhing victim's breast, with a tearing motion like the barracuda when it attacks and tears....

I fainted then, for that was the last of the fearful picture which I can remember.

I awakened a little after one o'clock, in a dark and empty room, peopled by no ghosts, and with my own, more commonplace, mahogany furniture thinly outlined in the faint light of the new moon which was shining cleanly in a starry sky. The fresh night-wind stirred the netting of my bed. I rose, shakily, and went and leaned out of the window, and lit and puffed rapidly at a cigarette, which perhaps did something to settle my jangling nerves.

The next morning, with a feeling of loathing which has gradually worn itself out in the course of the months which have now elapsed since my dreadful experience, I took up my drawing again, and added as well as I could the fearful scene I had witnessed. The completed picture was a horror, crude as is my work in this direction. I wanted to destroy it, but I did not, and I laid it away under some unused clothing in one of the large drawers of my bedroom wardrobe.

Three days later, just after Christmas, I observed Mr. Despard's car driving through the streets, the driver being alone. I stopped the boy and asked him where Mr. Despard was at the moment. The driver told me Mr. Despard was having breakfast,—the West Indian midday meal,—with Mr. Bonesteel at that gentleman's house on the Prince's Cross Street. I thanked him and went home. I took out the drawing, folded it, and placed it in the inside breast pocket of my coat, and started for Bonesteel's house.

I arrived fifteen minutes or so before the breakfast hour, and was pleasantly received by my old friend and his guest. Mr. Bonesteel pressed me to join them at breakfast, but I declined.

Mr. Bonesteel brought in a swizzel, compounded of his very old rum, and after partaking of this in ceremonious fashion, I engaged the attention of both gentlemen.

"Gentlemen," said I, "I trust that you will not regard me as too much of a bore, but I have, I believe, a legitimate reason for asking you if you will tell me the manner in which the gentleman known as Old Morris, who once occupied my house, met his death."

I stopped there, and immediately discovered that I had thrown my kind old host into a state of embarrassed confusion. Glancing at Mr. Despard, I saw at once that if I had not actually offended him, I had, by my question, at least put him "on his dignity." He was looking at me severely, rather, and I confess that for a moment I felt a bit like a schoolboy. Mr. Bonesteel caught something of this atmosphere, and looked helplessly at Despard. Both men shifted uneasily in their chairs; each waited for the other to speak.

Despard, at last, cleared his throat.

"You will excuse me, Mr. Stewart," said he, slowly, "but you have asked a question which for certain reasons, no one, aware of the circumstances, would desire to answer. The reasons are, briefly, that Mr. Morris, in

certain respects, was—what shall I say, not to do the matter an injustice?—well, perhaps I might say he was abnormal. I do not mean that he
was crazy. He was, though, eccentric. His end was such that stating it
would open up a considerable argument, one which agitated this island
for a long time after he was found dead. By a kind of general consent,
that matter is taboo on the island. That will explain to you why no one
wishes to answer your question. I am free to say that Mr. Bonesteel here,
in considerable distress, told me that you had asked it of him. You also
asked me about it not long ago. I can add only that the manner of Mr.
Morris' end was such that—" Mr. Despard hesitated, and looked down, a
frown on his brow, at his shoe, which he tapped nervously on the tiled
floor of the gallery where we were seated.

"Old Morris, Mr. Stewart," he resumed, after a moment's reflection,
in which, I imagined, he was carefully choosing his words, "was, to put it
plainly, murdered! There was much discussion over the identity of the
murderer, but the most of it, the unpleasant part of the discussion, was
rather whether he was killed by human agency or not! Perhaps you will
see now, sir, the difficulty of the matter. To admit that he was murdered
by an ordinary murderer is, to my mind, an impossibility. To assert that
some other agency, something abhuman, killed him, opens up the question of one's belief, one's credulity. 'Magic' and occult agencies are, as
you are aware, strongly entrenched in the minds of the ignorant people
of these islands. None of us cares to admit a similar belief. Does that
satisfy you, Mr. Stewart, and will you let the matter rest there, sir?"

I drew out the picture, and, without unfolding it, laid it across my
knees. I nodded to Mr. Despard, and, turning to our host, asked:

"As a child, Mr. Bonesteel, were you familiar with the arrangement
of Mr. Morris' bedroom?"

"Yes, sir," replied Mr. Bonesteel, and added: "Everybody was! Persons who had never been in the old man's house, crowded in when—" I
intercepted a kind of warning look passing from Despard to the speaker.
Mr. Bonesteel, looking much embarrassed, looked at me in that helpless
fashion I have already mentioned, and remarked that it was hot weather
these days!

"Then," said I, "perhaps you will recognize its arrangement and even
some of the details of its furnishing," and I unfolded the picture and
handed it to Mr. Bonesteel.

If I had anticipated its effect upon the old man, I would have been
more discreet, but I confess I was nettled by their attitude. By handing it
to Mr. Bonesteel (I could not give it to both of them at once) I did the
natural thing, for he was our host. The old man looked at what I had
handed him, and (this is the only way I can describe what happened)
became, suddenly, as though petrified. His eyes bulged out of his head,

his lower jaw dropped and hung open. The paper slipped from his nerveless grasp and fluttered and zigzagged to the floor, landing at Despard's feet. Despard stooped and picked it up, ostensibly to restore it to me, but in doing so, he glanced at it, and had his reaction. He leaped frantically to his feet, and positively goggled at the picture, then at me. Oh, I was having my little revenge for their reticence, right enough!

"My God!" shouted Despard. "My God, Mr. Stewart, where did you get such a thing?"

Mr. Bonesteel drew in a deep breath, the first, it seemed, for sixty seconds, and added his word.

"Oh my God!" muttered the old man, shakily. "Mr. Stewart, Mr. Stewart! what is it, what is it? where—"

"It is a Martinique fish-zombi, what is known to professional occult investigators like Elliott O'Donnell and William Hope Hodgson as an 'elemental'," I explained, calmly.

"It is a representation of how poor Mr. Morris actually met his death; until now, as I understand it, a purely conjectural matter. Christiansted is built on the ruins of French Bassin, you will remember," I added. "It is a very likely spot for an 'elemental'!"

"But, but," almost shouted Mr. Despard, "Mr. Stewart, where did you get this, its—"

"I made it," said I, quietly, folding up the picture and placing it back in my inside pocket.

"But how—?" this from both Despard and Bonesteel, speaking in unison.

"I saw it happen, you see," I replied, taking my hat, bowing formally to both gentlemen, and murmuring my regret at not being able to remain for breakfast, I departed.

And as I reached the bottom of Mr. Bonesteel's gallery steps and turned along the street in the direction of Old Morris' house, where I live, I could hear their voices speaking together:

"But how, how—?" This was Bonesteel.

"Why, why—?" And that was Despard.

In one of Stevenson's letters there is a characteristically humorous remark about the appalling impression produced on him in childhood by the beasts with many eyes in the Book of Revelations: "If that was heaven, what in the name of Davy Jones was hell like?" Now in sober truth there is a magnificent idea in these monsters of the Apocalypse. It is, I suppose, the idea that beings really more beautiful or more universal than we are might appear to us frightful and even confused. Especially they might seem to have senses at once more multiplex and more staring; an idea very imaginatively seized in the multitude of eyes. I like those monsters beneath the throne very much. It is when one of them goes wandering in deserts and finds a throne for himself that evil faiths begin, and there is (literally) the devil to pay—to pay in dancing girls or human sacrifice. As long as those misshapen elemental powers are around the throne, remember that the thing that they worship is the likeness of the appearance of a man.

That is, I fancy, the true doctrine on the subject of Tales of Terror and such things, which unless a man of letters do well and truly believe, without doubt he will end by blowing his brains out or by writing badly. Man, the central pillar of the world must be upright and straight; around him all the trees and beasts and elements and devils may crook and curl like smoke if they choose. All really imaginative literature is only the contrast between the weird curves of Nature and the straightness of the soul. Man may behold what ugliness he likes if he is sure that he will not worship it; but there are some so weak that they will worship a thing only because it is ugly. These must be chained to the beautiful. It is not always wrong even to go, like Dante, to the brink of the lowest promontory and look down at hell. It is when you look up at hell that a serious miscalculation has probably been made.

—G. K. Chesterton, "The Nightmare."

PASSING OF A GOD

Henry S. Whitehead

"You say that when Carswell came into your hospital over in Port au Prince his fingers looked as though they had been wound with string," said I, encouragingly.

"It is a very ugly story, that, Canevin," replied Doctor Pelletier, still reluctant, it appeared.

"You promised to tell me," I threw in.

"I know it, Canevin," admitted Doctor Pelletier of the U. S. Navy Medical Corps, now stationed here in the Virgin Islands. "But," he proceeded, "you couldn't use this story, anyhow. There are editorial *tabus*, aren't there? The thing is too—what shall I say?—too outrageous, too incredible."

"Yes," I admitted in turn, "there are *tabus*, plenty of them. Still, after hearing about those fingers, as though wound with string—why not give me the story, Pelletier; leave it to me whether or not I 'use' it. It's the story I want, mostly. I'm burning up for it!"

"I suppose it's your lookout," said my guest. "If you find it too gruesome for you, tell me and I'll quit."

I plucked up hope once more. I had been trying for this story, after getting little scraps of it which allured and intrigued me, for weeks.

"Start in," I ventured, soothingly, pushing the silver swizzel-jug after the humidor of cigarettes from which Pelletier was even now making a selection. Pelletier helped himself to the swizzel frowningly. Evidently he was torn between the desire to pour out the story of Arthur Carswell and some complication of feelings against doing so. I sat back in my wicker lounge-chair and waited.

Pelletier moved his large bulk about in his chair. Plainly now he was cogitating how to open the tale. He began, meditatively:

"I don't know as I ever heard public discussion of the malignant bodily growths except among medical people. Science knows little about them.

447

The fact of such diseases, though, is well known to everybody, through campaigns of prevention, the life insurance companies, appeals for funds—

"Well, Carswell's case, primarily, is one of those cases."

He paused and gazed into the glowing end of his cigarette.

"'Primarily?'" I threw in encouragingly.

"Yes. Speaking as a surgeon, that's where this thing begins, I suppose."

I kept still, waiting.

"Have you read Seabrook's book, *The Magic Island*, Canevin?" asked Pelletier suddenly.

"Yes," I answered. "What about it?"

"Then I suppose that from your own experience knocking around the West Indies and your study of it all, a good bit of that stuff of Seabrook's is familiar to you, isn't it? —the *vodu*, and the hill customs, and all the rest of it, especially over in Haiti—you could check up on a writer like Seabrook, couldn't you, more or less?"

"Yes," said I, "practically all of it was an old story to me—a very fine piece of work, however, the thing clicks all the way through—an honest and thorough piece of investigation."

"Anything in it new to you?"

"Yes—Seabrook's statement that there was an exchange of personalities between the sacrificial goat—at the 'baptism'—and the young Black girl, the chapter he calls: *Girl-Cry—Goat-Cry*. That, at least, was a new one on me, I admit."

"You will recall, if you read it carefully, that he attributed that phenomenon to his own personal 'slant' on the thing. Isn't that the case, Canevin?"

"Yes," I agreed, "I think that is the way he put it."

"Then," resumed Doctor Pelletier, "I take it that all that material of his—I notice that there have been a lot of story-writers using his terms lately!—is sufficiently familiar to you so that you have some clear idea of the Haitian-African demigods, like Ogoun Badagris, Damballa, and the others, taking up their residence for a short time in some devotee?"

"The idea is very well understood," said I. "Mr. Seabrook mentions it among a number of other local phenomena. It was an old negro who came up to him while he was eating, thrust his soiled hands into the dishes of food, surprised him considerably—then was surrounded by worshippers who took him to the nearest *houmfort* or *vodu*-house, let him sit on the altar, brought him food, hung all their jewelry on him, worshipped him for the time being; then, characteristically, quite utterly ignored the original old fellow after the 'possession' on the part of the 'deity' ceased and reduced him to an unimportant old pantaloon as he was before."

"That summarizes it exactly," agreed Doctor Pelletier. "That, Canevin, that kind of thing, I mean, is the real starting-place of this dreadful matter of Arthur Carswell."

"You mean—?" I barged out at Pelletier, vastly intrigued. I had had no idea that there was *vodu* mixed in with the case.

"I mean that Arthur Carswell's first intimation that there was anything pressingly wrong with him was just such a 'possession' as the one you have recounted."

"But—but," I protested, "I had supposed—I had every reason to believe, that it was a surgical matter! Why, you just objected to telling about it on the ground that—"

"Precisely," said Doctor Pelletier, calmly. "It was such a surgical case, but, as I say, it *began* in much the same way as the 'occupation' of that old negro's body by Ogoun Badagris or whichever one of their devilish deities that happened to be, just as, you say, is well known to fellows like yourself who go in for such things, and just as Seabrook recorded it."

"Well," said I, "You go ahead in your own way, Pelletier. I'll do my best to listen. Do you mind an occasional question?"

"Not in the least," said Doctor Pelletier considerately, shifted himself to a still more pronouncedly recumbent position in my Chinese rattan lounge-chair, lit a fresh cigarette, and proceeded:

"Carswell had worked up a considerable intimacy with the snake-worship of interior Haiti, all the sort of thing familiar to you; the sort of thing set out, probably for the first time in English at least, in Seabrook's book; all the gatherings, and the 'baptism,' and the sacrifices of the fowls and the bull, and the goats; the orgies of the worshippers, the boom and thrill of the *rata* drums—all that strange, incomprehensible, rather silly-surfaced, deadly-underneathed worship of 'the Snake' which the Dahomeyans brought with them to old Hispaniola, now Haiti and the Dominican Republic.

"He had been there, as you may have heard, for a number of years; went there in the first place because everybody thought he was a kind of failure at home; made a good living, too, in a way nobody but an original-minded fellow like him would have thought of—shot ducks on the Léogane marshes, dried them, and exported them to New York and San Francisco to the United States' two largest Chinatowns!

"For a 'failure,' too, Carswell was a particularly smart-looking chap, in the English sense of that word. He was one of those fellows who was always shaved, clean, freshly groomed, even under the rather adverse conditions of his living, there in Léogane by the salt marshes; and of his trade, which was to kill and dry ducks. A fellow can get pretty careless and let himself go at that sort of thing, away from 'home'; away, too, from such niceties as there are in a place like Port au Prince.

"He looked, in fact, like a fellow just off somebody's yacht the first time I saw him, there in the hospital in Port au Prince, and that, too, was right after a rather singular experience which would have unnerved or unsettled pretty nearly anybody.

"But not so old Carswell. No, indeed. I speak of him as 'Old Carswell,' Canevin. That, though, is a kind of affectionate term. He was somewhere about forty-five then; it was two years ago, you see, and, in addition to his being very spick and span, well groomed, you know, he looked surprisingly young, somehow. One of those faces which showed experience, but, along with the experience, a philosophy. The lines in his face were good lines, if you get what I mean—lines of humor and courage; no dissipation, no letdown kind of lines, nothing of slackness such as you would see in the face of even a comparatively young beachcomber. No, as he strode into my office, almost jauntily, there in the hospital, there was nothing, nothing whatever, about him, to suggest anything else but a prosperous fellow American, a professional chap, for choice, who might, as I say, have just come ashore from somebody's yacht.

"And yet—good God, Canevin, the story that came out—!"

Naval surgeon though he was, with service in Haiti, at sea, in Nicaragua, the China Station to his credit, Doctor Pelletier rose at this point, and, almost agitatedly, walked up and down my gallery. Then he sat down and lit a fresh cigarette.

"There is," he said, reflectively, and as though weighing his words carefully, "there is, Canevin, among various others, a somewhat 'wild' theory that somebody put forward several years ago, about the origin of malignant tumors. It never gained very much approval among the medical profession, but it has, at least, the merit of originality, and—it was new. Because of those facts, it had a certain amount of currency, and there are those, in and out of medicine, who still believe in it. It is that there are certain nuclei, certain masses, so to speak, of the bodily material which have persisted—not generally, you understand, but in certain cases—among certain persons, the kind who are 'susceptible' to this horrible disease, which, in the prenatal state, did not develop fully or normally—little places in the bodily structure, that is—if I make myself clear?—which remain undeveloped.

"Something, according to this hypothesis, something like a sudden jar, or a bruise, a kick, a blow with the fist, the result of a fall, or whatnot, causes traumatism—physical injury, that is, you know—to one of the focus-places, and the undeveloped little mass of material starts in to grow, and so displaces the normal tissue which surrounds it.

"One objection to the theory is that there are at least two varieties, well-known and recognized scientifically; the carcinoma, which is itself subdivided into two kinds, the hard and the soft carcinomas, and the sarcoma, which is a soft thing, like what is popularly understood by a 'tumor.' Of course they are all 'tumors,' particular kinds of tumors, malignant tumors. What lends a certain credibility to the theory I have just mentioned is the malignancy, the growing element. For, whatever the underlying reason, they grow, Canevin, as is well recognized, and this explanation I have been talking about gives a reason for the growth. The 'malignancy' is, really, that one of the things seems to have, as it were, its own life. All this, probably, you know?"

I nodded. I did not wish to interrupt. I could see that this side-issue on a scientific by-path must have something to do with the story of Carswell.

"Now," resumed Pelletier, "notice this fact, Canevin. Let me put it in the form of a question, like this: To what kind, or type, of *vodu* worshipper, does the 'possession' by one of their deities occur—from your own knowledge of such things, what would you say?"

"To the incomplete; the abnormal, to an *old* man, or woman," said I, slowly, reflecting, "or—to a child, or, perhaps, to an idiot. Idiots, ancient crones, backward children, 'town-fools' and the like, all over Europe, are supposed to be in some mysterious way *en rapport* with deity—or with Satan! It is an established peasant belief. Even among the Mahometans, the moron or idiot is 'the afflicted of God.' There is no other better established belief along such lines of thought."

"Precisely!" exclaimed Pelletier, "and, Canevin, go back once more to Seabrook's instance that we spoke about. What type of person was 'possessed'?"

"An old doddering man," said I, "one well gone in his dotage apparently."

"Right once more! Note now, two things. First, I will admit to you, Canevin, that that theory I have just been expounding never made much of a hit with me. It might be true, but—very few first-rate men in our profession thought much of it, and I followed that negative lead and didn't think much of it, or, indeed, much about it. I put it down to the vaporings of the theorist who first thought it out and published it, and let it go at that. Now, Canevin, *I am convinced that it is true!* The second thing, then: When Carswell came into my office in the hospital over there in Port au Prince, the first thing I noticed about him—I had never seen him before, you see—was a peculiar, almost an indescribable, discrepancy. It was between his general appearance of weather-worn cleanliness, general fitness, his 'smart' appearance in his clothes—all that, which fitted together about the clean-cut, open character of the fellow; and what I can only describe as a pursiness. He seemed in good condition, I mean to say, and yet—there was something, somehow, flabby somewhere in his makeup. I couldn't put my finger on it, but—it was there, a suggestion of something that detracted from the impression he gave as being an upstanding fellow, a good-fellow-to-have-beside-you-in-a-pinch—that kind of person.

"The second thing I noticed, it was just after he had taken a chair beside my desk, was his fingers, and thumbs. They were swollen, Canevin, looked sore, as though they had been wound with string. That was the first thing I thought of, being wound with string. He saw me looking at them, held them out to me abruptly, laid them side by side, his hands I mean, on my desk, and smiled at me.

"'I see you have noticed them, Doctor,' he remarked, almost jovially. 'That makes it a little easier for me to tell you what I'm here for. It's— well, you might put it down as a "symptom."'

"I looked at his fingers and thumbs; every one of them was affected in the same way; and ended up with putting a magnifying glass over them.

"They were all bruised and reddened, and here and there on several of them, the skin was abraded, broken, *circularly*—it was a most curious-looking set of digits. My new patient was addressing me again:

"'I'm not here to ask you riddles, Doctor,' he said, gravely, this time, 'but—would you care to make a guess at what did that to those fingers and thumbs of mine?'

"'Well,' I came back at him, 'without knowing what's happened, it looks as if you'd been trying to wear about a hundred rings, all at one time, and most of them didn't fit!'

"Carswell nodded his head at me. 'Score one for the medico,' said he, and laughed. 'Even numerically you're almost on the dot, sir. The precise number was one hundred and six!'

"I confess, I stared at him then. But he wasn't fooling. It was a cold, sober, serious fact that he was stating; only, he saw that it had a humorous side, and that intrigued him, as anything humorous always did, I found out after I got to know Carswell a lot better than I did then."

"You said you wouldn't mind a few questions, Pelletier," I interjected.

"Fire away," said Pelletier. "Do you see any light, so far?"

"I was naturally figuring along with you, as you told about it all," said I. "Do I infer correctly that Carswell, having lived there—how long, four or five years or so?—"

"Seven, to be exact," put in Pelletier.

"—that Carswell, being pretty familiar with the native doings, had mixed into things, got the confidence of his Black neighbors in and around Léogane, become somewhat 'adept,' had the run of the *houmforts*, so to speak—'votre bougie, M'sieu'—the fortune-telling at the festivals, and so forth, and—had been 'visited' by one of the Black deities? That, apparently, if I'm any judge of tendencies, is what your account seems to be leading up to. Those bruised fingers—the one hundred and six rings— good heavens, man, is it really possible?"

"Carswell told me all about that end of it, a little later—yes, that was, precisely, what happened, but—that surprizing, incredible as it seems, is only the small end of it all. You just wait—"

"Go ahead," said I, "I am all ears, I assure you!"

"Well, Carswell took his hands off the desk after I had looked at them through my magnifying glass, and then waved one of them at me in a kind of deprecating gesture.

"'I'll go into all that, if you're interested to hear about it, Doctor,' he assured me, 'but that isn't what I'm here about.' His face grow suddenly very grave. 'Have you plenty of time?' he asked. 'I don't want to let my case interfere with anything.'

"'Fire ahead,' says I, and he leaned forward in his chair.

"'Doctor,' says he, 'I don't know whether or not you ever heard of me before. My name's Carswell, and I live over Léogane way. I'm an American, like yourself, as you can probably see, and, even after seven years of it, out there, duck-hunting, mostly, with virtually no White-man's doings for a pretty long time, I haven't "gone native" or anything of the sort. I wouldn't want you to think I'm one of those wasters.' He looked up at me inquiringly for my estimate of him. He had been by himself a good deal; perhaps too much. I nodded at him. He looked me in the eye, squarely, and nodded back. 'I guess we understand each other,' he said. Then he went on.

"'Seven years ago, it was, I came down here. I've lived over there ever since. What few people know about me regard me as a kind of failure, I daresay. But—Doctor, there was a reason for that, a pretty definite reason. I won't go into it beyond your end of it—the medical end, I mean. I came down because of this.'

"He stood up then, and I saw what made that 'discrepancy' I spoke about, that 'flabbiness' which went so ill with the general cut of the man. He turned up the lower ends of his white drill jacket and put his hand a little to the left of the middle of his stomach. 'Just notice this,' he said, and stepped toward me.

"There, just over the left center of that area and extending up toward the spleen, on the left side, you know, there was a protuberance. Seen closely it was apparent that here was some sort of internal growth. It was that which had made him look flabby, stomachish.

"'This was diagnosed for me in New York,' Carswell explained, 'a little more than seven years ago. They told me it was inoperable then. After seven years, probably, I daresay it's worse, if anything. To put the thing in a nutshell, Doctor, I had to "let go" then. I got out of a promising business, broke off my engagement, came here. I won't expatiate on it all, but—it was pretty tough, Doctor, pretty tough. I've lasted all right, so far. It hasn't troubled me—until just lately. That's why I drove in this afternoon, to see you, to see if anything could be done.'

"'Has it been kicking up lately?' I asked him.

"'Yes,' said Carswell, simply. 'They said it would kill me, probably within a year or so, as it grew. It hasn't grown—much. I've lasted a little more than seven years, so far.'

"'Come in to the operating-room,' I invited him, 'and take your clothes off, and let's get a good look at it.'

"'Anything you say,' returned Carswell, and followed me back into the operating-room then and there.

"I had a good look at Carswell, first, superficially. That preliminary examination revealed a growth quite typical, the self-contained, not the 'fibrous' type, in the location I've already described, and about the size of an average man's head. It lay imbedded, fairly deep. It was what we call 'encapsulated.' That, of course, is what had kept Carswell alive.

"Then we put the X-rays on it, fore-and-aft, and sidewise. One of those things doesn't always respond very well to skiagraphic examination, to the X-ray, that is, but this one showed clearly enough. Inside it appeared a kind of dark, triangular mass, with the small end at the top. When Doctor Smithson and I had looked him over thoroughly, I asked Carswell whether or not he wanted to stay with us, to come into the hospital as a patient, for treatment.

"'I'm quite in your hands, Doctor,' be told me. 'I'll stay, or do whatever you want me to. But, first,' and for the first time he looked a trifle embarrassed, 'I think I'd better tell you the story that goes with my coming here! However, speaking plainly, do you think I have a chance?'

"'Well,' said I, 'speaking plainly, yes, there is a chance, maybe a "fifty-fifty" chance, maybe a little less. On the one hand, this thing has been let alone for seven years since original diagnosis. It's probably less operable than it was when you were in New York. On the other hand, we know a lot more, not about these things, Mr. Carswell, but about surgical technique, than they did seven years ago. On the whole, I'd advise you to stay and get ready for an operation, and, say about "forty-sixty" you'll go back to Léogane, or back to New York if you feel like it, several pounds lighter in weight and a new man. If it takes you, on the table, well, you've had a lot more time out there gunning for ducks in Léogane than those New York fellows allowed you.'

"'I'm with you,' said Carswell, and we assigned him a room, took his 'history,' and began to get him ready for his operation.

"We did the operation two days later, at ten-thirty in the morning, and in the meantime Carswell told me his 'story' about it.

"It seems that he had made quite a place for himself, there in Léogane, among the negroes and the ducks. In seven years a man like Carswell, with his mental and dispositional equipment, can go quite a long way, anywhere. He had managed to make quite a good thing out of his duck-drying industry, employed five or six 'hands' in his little wooden 'factory,' rebuilt a rather good house he had secured there for a song right after he had arrived, collected local antiques to add to the equipment he had brought along with him, made himself a real home of a peculiar, bachelor kind, and, above all, got in solid with the Black People all around him. Almost incidentally I gathered from him—he had no gift of narrative, and I had to question him a great deal—he had got onto, and into, the know in the *vodu* thing. There wasn't, as far as I could get it, any aspect of it all that he hadn't been in on, except, that is, *'la chevre sans cornes'*—the goat without horns, you know—the human sacrifice on great occasions. In fact, he strenuously denied that the *voduists* resorted to that; said it was a canard against them; that they never, really, did such things, never had, unless back in prehistoric times, in Guinea-Africa.

"But, there wasn't anything about it all that he hadn't at his very finger ends, and at first-hand, too. The man was a walking encyclopedia of the native beliefs, customs, and practises. He knew, too, every turn and twist of their speech. He hadn't, as he had said at first, 'gone native' in the slightest degree, and yet, without lowering his White Man's dignity by a trifle, he had got it all.

"That brings us to the specific happening, the 'story' which, he had said, went along with his reason for coming in to the hospital in Port au Prince, to us.

"It appears that his sarcoma had never, practically, troubled. Beyond noting a very gradual increase in its size from year to year, be said, he 'wouldn't know he had one.' In other words, characteristically, it never gave him any pain or direct annoyance beyond the sense of the wretched thing being there, and increasing on him, and always drawing him closer to that end of life which the New York doctors had warned him about.

"Then, it had happened only three days before he came to the hospital, he had gone suddenly unconscious one afternoon, as he was walking down his shell path to his gateway. The last thing he remembered then was being 'about four steps from the gate.' When he woke up, it was dark. He was seated in a big chair on his own front gallery, and the first thing he noticed was that his fingers and thumbs were sore and ached very painfully. The next thing was that there were flares burning all along the edge of the gallery, and down in the front yard, and along the road outside the paling fence that divided his property from the road, and in the light of these flares, there swarmed literally hundreds of negroes, gathered about him and mostly on their knees; lined along the gallery and on the grounds below it; prostrating themselves, chanting, putting earth and sand on their heads; and, when he leaned back in his chair, something hurt the back of his neck, and he found that he was being nearly choked with the necklaces, strings of beads, gold and silver coin-strings, and other kinds, that had been draped over his head. His fingers, and the thumbs as well, were covered with gold and silver rings, many of them jammed on so as to stop the circulation.

"From his knowledge of their beliefs, he recognized what had happened to him. He had, he figured, probably fainted, although such a thing was not at all common with him, going down the pathway to the yard gate, and the Blacks had supposed him to be 'possessed' as he had several times seen Black people, children, old men and women, morons, chiefly, similarly 'possessed.' He knew that, now that he was recovered from whatever had happened to him, the 'worship' ought to cease and if he simply sat quiet and took what was coming to him, they would, as soon as they realized he was 'himself' once more, leave him alone and he would get some relief from this uncomfortable set of surroundings; get rid of the necklaces and the rings; get a little privacy.

"But—the queer part of it all was that they didn't quit. No, the mob around the house and on the gallery increased rather than diminished, and at last he was put to it, from sheer discomfort—he said he came to the point where he felt he couldn't stand it all another instant—to speak up and ask the people to leave him in peace.

"They left him, he says, at that, right off the bat, immediately, without a protesting voice, but—and here was what started him on his major puzzlement—they didn't take off the necklaces and rings. No—they left the whole set of that metallic drapery which they had hung and thrust upon him right there, and, after he had been left alone, as he had requested, and had gone into his house, and lifted off the necklaces and worked the rings loose, the *next* thing that happened was that old Pa'p Josef, the local *papaloi*, together with three or four other neighboring *papalois*, witch-doctors from nearby villages, and followed by a very old man who was known to Carswell as the *hougan*, or head witch-doctor of the whole countryside thereabouts, came in to him in a kind of procession, and knelt down all around him on the floor of his living-room, and laid down gourds of cream and bottles of red rum and cooked chickens, and even a big china bowl of Tannia soup—a dish he abominated, said it always tasted like soapy water to him!—and then backed out leaving him to these comestibles.

"He said that this sort of attention persisted in his case, right through the three days that he remained in his house in Léogane, before he started out for the hospital; would, apparently, be still going on if he hadn't come in to Port au Prince to us.

"But—his coming in was not, in the least, because of this. It had puzzled him a great deal, for there was nothing like it in his experience, nor, so far as he could gather from their attitude, in the experience of the people about him, of the *papalois*, or even of the *hougan* himself. They acted, in other words, precisely as though the 'deity' supposed to have taken up his abode within him had remained there, although there seemed no precedent for such an occurrence, and, so far as he knew, he felt precisely just as he had felt right along, that is, fully awake, and, certainly, not in anything like an abnormal condition, and, very positively, not in anything like a fainting-fit!

"That is to say—he felt precisely the same as usual except that—he attributed it to the probability that he must have fallen on the around that time when he lost consciousness going down the pathway to the gate (he had been told that passersby had picked him up and carried him to the gallery where he had awakened, later, these Good Samaritans meanwhile recognizing that one of the 'deities' had indwelt him)—he felt the same except for recurrent, almost unbearable pains in the vicinity of his lower abdominal region.

"There was nothing surprising to him in this accession of the new painfulness. He had been warned that that would be the beginning of the end. It was in the rather faint hope that something might be done that he had come in to the hospital. It speaks volumes for the man's fortitude, for his strength of character, that he came in so cheerfully; acquiesced in what we suggested to him to do; remained with us, facing those comparatively slim chances with complete cheerfulness.

"For—we did not deceive Carswell—the chances were somewhat slim. 'Sixty-forty' I had said, but as I afterward made clear to him, the favorable chances, as gleaned from the mortality tables, were a good deal less than that.

"He went to the table in a state of mind quite unchanged from his accustomed cheerfulness. He shook hands good-bye with Doctor Smithson and me, 'in case,' and also with Doctor Jackson, who acted as anesthetist.

"Carswell took an enormous amount of ether to get him off. His consciousness persisted longer, perhaps, than that of any surgical patient I can remember. At last, however, Doctor Jackson intimated to me that I might begin, and, Doctor Smithson standing by with the retracting forceps, I made the first incision. It was my intention, after careful study of the X-ray plates, to open it up from in front, in an up-and-down direction, establish drainage directly, and, leaving the wound in the sound tissue in front of it open, to attempt to get it healed up after removing its contents. Such is the technique of the major portion of successful operations.

"It was a comparatively simple matter to expose the outer wall. This accomplished, and after a few words of consultation with my colleague, I very carefully opened it. We recalled that the X-ray had shown, as I mentioned, a triangular-shaped mass within. This apparent content we attributed to some obscure chemical coloration of the contents. I made my incisions with the greatest care and delicacy, of course. The critical part of the operation lay right at this point, and the greatest exactitude was indicated, of course.

"At last the outer coats of it were cut through, and retracted, and with renewed caution I made the incision through the inmost wall of tissue. To my surprise, and to Doctor Smithson's, the inside was comparatively dry. The gauze which the nurse attending had caused to follow the path of the knife, was hardly moistened. I ran my knife down below the original scope of the last incision, then upward from its upper extremity, greatly lengthening the incision as a whole, if you are following me.

"Then, reaching my gloved hand within this long up-and-down aperture, I felt about and at once discovered that I could get my fingers in around the inner containing wall quite easily. I reached and worked my fingers in farther and farther, finally getting both hands inside and at last feeling my fingers touch inside the posterior or rear wall. Rapidly, now, I ran the edges of my hands around inside, and, quite easily, lifted out the 'inside.' This, a mass weighing several pounds, of more or less solid material, was laid aside on the small table beside the operating-table, and, again pausing to consult with Doctor Smithson—the operation was going, you see, a lot better than either of us had dared to anticipate—and being encouraged by him to proceed to a radical step which we had not hoped to be able to take, I began the dissection from the surrounding, normal tissue, of the now collapsed walls. This, a long, difficult, and harassing job, was accomplished at the end of, perhaps, ten or twelve minutes of gruelling work, and the bag-like thing, now completely severed from the tissues in which it had been for so long imbedded, was placed also on the side table.

"Doctor Jackson reporting favorably on our patient's condition under the anesthetic, I now proceeded to dress the large aperture, and to close the body-wound. This was accomplished in a routine manner, and then, together, we bandaged Carswell, and he was taken back to his room to await awakening from the ether.

"Carswell disposed of, Doctor Jackson and Doctor Smithson left the operating-room and the nurse started in cleaning up after the operation; dropping the instruments into the boiler, and so on—a routine set of duties. As for me, I picked up the shell in a pair of forceps, turned it about under the strong electric operating-light, and laid it down again. It presented nothing of interest for a possible laboratory examination.

"Then I picked up the more or less solid contents which I had laid, very hastily, and without looking at it—you see, my actual removal of it had been done inside, in the dark for the most part and by the sense of feeling, with my hands, you will remember—I picked it up; I still had my operating-gloves on to prevent infection when looking over these specimens, and, still, not looking at it particularly, carried it out into the laboratory.

"Canevin"—Doctor Pelletier looked at me somberly through the very gradually fading light of late afternoon, the period just before the abrupt falling of our tropic dusk— "Canevin," he repeated, "honestly, I don't know how to tell you! Listen now, old man, do something for me, will you?"

"Why, yes—of course," said I, considerably mystified. "What is it you want me to do, Pelletier?"

"My car is out in front of the house. Come on home with me, up to my house, will you? Let's say I want to give you a cocktail! Anyhow, maybe you'll understand better when you are there, *I want to tell you the rest up at my house, not here.* Will you please come, Canevin?"

I looked at him closely. This seemed to me a very strange, an abrupt, request. Still, there was nothing whatever unreasonable about such a sudden whim on Pelletier's part.

"Why, yes, certainly I'll go with you, Pelletier, if you want me to."

"Come on, then," said Pelletier, and we started for his car.

The doctor drove himself, and after we had taken the first turn in the rather complicated route from my house to his, on the extreme airy top of Denmark Hill, he said, in a quiet voice:

"Put together, now, Canevin, certain points, if you please, in this story. Note, kindly, how the Black people over in Léogane acted, according to Carswell's story. Note, too, that theory I was telling you about; do you recollect it clearly?"

"Yes," said I, still more mystified.

"Just keep those two points in mind, then," added Doctor Pelletier, and devoted himself to navigating sharp turns and plodding up two steep roadways for the rest of the drive to his house.

We went in and found his houseboy laying the table for his dinner. Doctor Pelletier is unmarried, keeps a hospitable bachelor establishment. He ordered cocktails, and the houseboy departed on this errand. Then he led me into a kind of office, littered with medical and surgical paraphernalia. He lifted some papers off a chair, motioned me into it, and took another near by. "Listen, now!" he said, and held up a finger at me.

"I took that thing, as I mentioned, into the laboratory," said he. "I carried it in my hand, with my gloves still on, as aforesaid. I laid it down on a table and turned on a powerful light over it. It was only then that I took a good look at it. It weighed several pounds at least, was about the bulk and heft of a full-grown coconut, and about the same color as a hulled coconut, that is, a kind of medium brown. As I looked at it, I saw that it was, as the X-ray had indicated, vaguely triangular in shape. It lay over on one of its sides under that powerful light, and—Canevin, so help me God"—Doctor Pelletier leaned toward me, his face working, a great seriousness in his eyes—"it moved, Canevin," he murmured; "and, as I looked—the thing *breathed!* I was just plain dumfounded. A biological specimen like that—does not move, Canevin! I shook all over, suddenly. I felt my hair prickle on the roots of my scalp. I felt chills go down my spine. Then I remembered that here I was, after an operation, in my own biological laboratory. I came close to the thing and propped it up, on what might be called its logical base, if you see what I mean, so that it stood as nearly upright as its triangular conformation permitted.

"And then I saw that it had faint yellowish markings over the brown, and that what you might call its skin was moving, and—as I stared at the thing, Canevin—two things like little arms began to move, and the top of it gave a kind of convulsive shudder, and it opened straight at me, Canevin, a pair of eyes and looked me in the face.

"Those eyes—my God, Canevin, those eyes! They were eyes of something more than human, Canevin, something incredibly evil, something vastly old, sophisticated, cold, immune from anything except pure evil, the eyes of something that had been worshipped, Canevin, from ages and ages out of a past that went back before all known human calculation, eyes that showed all the deliberate, lurking wickedness that has ever been in the world. The eyes closed, Canevin, and the thing sank over onto its side, and heaved and shuddered convulsively.

"*It was sick, Canevin*; and now, emboldened, holding myself together, repeating over and over to myself that I had a case of the quavers, of post-operative 'nerves,' I forced myself to look closer, and as I did so I got from it a faint whiff of ether. Two tiny, ape-like nostrils, over a clamped-shut slit of a mouth, were exhaling and inhaling; drawing in the good, pure air, exhaling ether fumes. It popped into my head that Carswell had consumed a terrific amount of ether before he went under; we had commented on that, Doctor Jackson particularly. I put two and two together, Canevin, remembered we were in Haiti, where things are not like New York, or Boston, or Baltimore! Those negroes had believed that the 'deity' had not come out of Carswell, do you see? That was the thing that held the edge of my mind. The thing stirred uneasily, put out one of its 'arms,' groped about, stiffened.

"I reached for a near-by specimen-jar, Canevin, reasoning, almost blindly, that if this thing were susceptible to ether, it would be susceptible to—well, my gloves were still on my hands, and—now shuddering so that I could hardly move at all, I had to force every motion—I reached out and took hold of the thing—it felt like moist leather—and dropped it into the jar. Then I carried the carboy of preserving alcohol over to the table and poured it in till the ghastly thing was entirely covered, the alcohol near the top of the jar. It writhed once, then rolled over on its 'back,' and lay still, the mouth now open. Do you believe me, Canevin?"

"I have always said that I would believe anything, on proper evidence," said I, slowly, "and I would be the last to question a statement of yours, Pelletier. However, although I have, as you say, looked into some of these things perhaps more than most, it seems, well—"

Doctor Pelletier said nothing. Then he slowly got up out of his chair. He stepped over to a wall-cupboard and returned, a wide-mouthed specimen-jar in his hand. He laid the jar down before me, in silence.

I looked into it, through the slightly discolored alcohol with which the jar, tightly sealed with rubber-tape and sealing-wax, was filled nearly to the brim. There, on the jar's bottom, lay such a thing as Pelletier had described (a thing which, if it had been "seated," upright, would somewhat have resembled that representation of the happy little godling "Billiken" which was popular twenty years ago as a desk ornament), a thing suggesting the sinister, the unearthly, even in this desiccated form. I looked long at the thing.

"Excuse me for even seeming to hesitate, Pelletier," said I, reflectively.

"I can't say that I blame you," returned the genial doctor. "It is, by the way, the first and only time I have ever tried to tell the story to anybody."

"And Carswell?" I asked. "I've been intrigued with that good fellow and his difficulties. How did be come out of it all?"

"He made a magnificent recovery from the operation," said Pelletier, "and afterward, when he went back to Léogane, he told me that the negroes, while glad to see him quite usual, had quite lost interest in him as the throne of a 'divinity'."

"H'm," I remarked, "it would seem, that, to bear out—"

"Yes," said Pelletier, "I have always regarded that fact as absolutely conclusive. Indeed, how otherwise could one possibly account for—*this?*" He indicated the contents of the laboratory jar.

I nodded my head, in agreement with him. "I can only say that—if you won't feel insulted, Pelletier—that you are singularly open-minded, for a man of science! What, by the way, became of Carswell?"

The houseboy came in with a tray, and Pelletier and I drank to each other's good health.

"He came in to Port au Prince," replied Pelletier after he had done the honors. "He did not want to go back to the States, he said. The lady to whom he had been engaged had died a couple of years before; he felt that he would be out of touch with American business. The fact is—he had stayed out here too long, too continuously. But, he remains an 'authority' on Haitian native affairs, and is consulted by the High Commissioner. He knows, literally, more about Haiti than the Haitians themselves. I wish you might meet him; you'd have a lot in common."

"I'll hope to do that," said I, and rose to leave. The houseboy appeared at the door, smiling in my direction.

"The table is set for two, sar," said he.

Doctor Pelletier led the way into the dining-room, taking it for granted that I would remain and dine with him. We are informal in St. Thomas, about such matters. I telephoned home and sat down with him.

Pelletier suddenly laughed—he was half-way through his soup at the moment. I looked up inquiringly. He put down his soup spoon and looked across the table at me.

"It's a bit odd," he remarked, "when you stop to think of it! There's one thing Carswell doesn't know about Haiti and what happens there!"

"What's that?" I inquired.

"That—thing—in there," said Pelletier, indicating the office with his thumb in the way artists and surgeons do. "I thought he'd had troubles enough without *that* on his mind, too."

I nodded in agreement and resumed my soup. Pelletier has a cook in a thousand.

THE ∫HUT ROOM

Henry S. Whitehead

It was Sunday morning and I was coming out of All Saints' Church, Margaret Street, along with the other members of the hushed and reverent congregation, when, near the entrance doors, a hand fell lightly on my shoulder. Turning, I perceived that it was the Earl of Carruth. I nodded, without speaking, for there is that in the atmosphere of this great church, especially after one of its magnificent services and heart-searching sermons, which precludes anything like the hum of conversation which one meets with in many places of worship.

In these worldly and "scientific" days it is unusual to meet with a person of Lord Carruth's intellectual and scientific attainments who troubles very much about religion. As for me, Gerald Canevin, I have always been a church-going fellow.

Carruth accompanied me in silence through the entrance doors and out into Margaret Street. Then, linking his arm in mine, he guided me, still in silence, to where his Rolls-Royce car stood at the curb-stone.

"Have you any luncheon engagement, Mr. Canevin?" he inquired, when we were just beside the car, the footman holding the door open.

"None whatever," I replied.

"Then do me the pleasure of lunching with me," invited Carruth.

"I was planning on driving from church to your rooms," he explained, as soon as we were seated and the car whirling us noiselessly toward his town house in Mayfair. "A rather extraordinary matter has come up, and Sir John has asked me to look into it. Should you care to hear about it?"

"Delighted," I acquiesced, and settled myself to listen.

To my surprise, Lord Carruth began reciting a portion of the Nicene Creed, to which, sung very beautifully by All Saints' choir, we had recently been listening.

"Maker of Heaven and earth," quoted Carruth, musingly, "and of all things—visible and *invisible*." I started forward in my seat. He had given a peculiar emphasis to the last word, "invisible."

"A fact," I ejaculated, "constantly forgotten by the critics of religion! The Church has always recognized the existence of the invisible creation."

"Right, Mr. Canevin. And—this invisible creation; it doesn't mean merely angels!"

"No one who has lived in the West Indies can doubt that," I replied.

"Nor in India," countered Carruth. "The fact—that the Creed attributes to God the authorship of an invisible creation—is an interesting commentary on the much-quoted remark of Hamlet to Horatio: 'There are more things in Heaven and earth, Horatio, than are dreamed of in your philosophy.' Apparently, Horatio's philosophy, like that of the present day, took little account of the spiritual side of affairs; left out God *and what He had made*. Perhaps Horatio had recited the creed a thousand times, and never realized what that clause implies!"

"I have thought of it often, myself," said I. "And now—I am all curiosity—what, please, is the application?"

"It is an occurrence in one of the old coaching inns," began Carruth, "on the Brighton Road; a very curious matter. It appears that the proprietor—a gentleman, by the way, Mr. William Snow, purchased the inn for an investment just after the Armistice—has been having a rather unpleasant time of it. It has to do with shoes!"

"Shoes?" I inquired; "shoes!" It seemed, an abrupt transition from the Nicene Creed to shoes!

"Yes," replied Carruth, "and not only shoes but all sorts of leather affairs. In fact, the last and chief difficulty was about the disappearance of a commercial traveler's leather sample-case. But I perceive we are arriving home. We can continue the account at luncheon."

During lunch he gave me a rather full account, with details, of what had happened at "The Coach and Horses" Inn on the Brighton Road, an account which I will briefly summarize as follows:

Snow, the proprietor, had bought the old inn partly for business reasons, partly for sentimental. It had been a portion, up to about a century before, of his family's landed property. He had repaired and enlarged it, modernized it in some ways, and in general restored a much run-down institution, making "The Coach and Horses" into a paying investment. He had retained, so far as possible, the antique architectural features of the old coaching inn, and before very long had built up a motor clientele of large proportions by sound and careful management.

Everything, in fact, had prospered with the gentleman-innkeeper's affairs until there began, some four months back, a series of unaccountable disappearances. The objects which had, as it were, vanished into thin air, were all—and this seemed to me the most curious and bizarre feature of Carruth's recital—leather articles. Pair after pair of shoes or boots, left outside bedroom doors at night, would be gone the next morning. Naturally the "boots" was suspected of theft. But the "boots" had been able to prove his innocence easily enough. He was, it seemed, a rather intelligent broken-down jockey, of a keen wit. He had assured Mr. Snow of his surprise as well as of his innocence, and suggested that he take a week's holiday to visit his aged mother in Kent and that a substitute "boots," chosen by the proprietor, should take his place. Snow had acquiesced, and the disappearance of guests' footwear had continued, to the consternation of the substitute, a total stranger, obtained from a London agency.

That exonerated Billings, the jockey, who came back to his duties at the end of his holiday with his character as an honest servant intact. Moreover, the disappearances had not been confined to boots and shoes. Pocketbooks, leather luggage, bags, cigarette cases—all sorts of leather articles went the way of the earlier boots and shoes, and besides the expense and annoyance of replacing these, Mr. Snow began to be seriously concerned about the reputation of his house. An inn in which one's leather belongings are known to be unsafe would not be a very strong financial asset. The matter had come to a head through the disappearance of the commercial traveler's sample-case, as noted by Carruth in his first brief account of this mystery. The main difficulty in this affair was that the traveler had been a salesman of jewelry, and Snow had been confronted with a bill for several hundred pounds, which he had felt constrained to pay. After that he had laid the mysterious matter before Sir John Scott, head of Scotland Yard, and Scott had called in Carruth because he recognized in Snow's story certain elements which caused him to believe this was no case for mere criminal investigation.

After lunch Carruth ordered the car again, and, after stopping at my rooms for some additional clothing and the other necessities for an overnight visit, we started along the Brighton Road for the scene of the difficulty.

We arrived about four that Sunday afternoon, and immediately went into conference with the proprietor.

Mr. William Snow was a youngish, middle-aged gentleman, very well dressed, and obviously a person of intelligence and natural attainments. He gave us all the information possible, repeating, with many details, the matters which I have already summarized, while we listened in silence. When he had finished:

"I should like to ask some questions," said Carruth.

"I am prepared to answer anything you wish to enquire about," Mr. Snow assured us.

"Well, then, about the sentimental element in your purchase of the inn, Mr. Snow—tell us, if you please, what you may know of the more ancient history of this old hostelry. I have no doubt there is history connected with it, situated where it is. Undoubtedly, in the coaching days of the Four Georges, it must have been the scene of many notable gatherings."

"You are right, Lord Carruth. As you know, it was a portion of the property of my family. All the old registers are intact, and are at your disposal. It is an inn of very ancient foundation. It was, indeed, old in those days of the Four Georges, to whom you refer. The records go back well into the Sixteenth Century, in fact; and there was an inn here even before registers were kept. They are of comparatively modem origin, you know. Your ancient landlord kept, I imagine, only his 'reckoning'; he was not concerned with records; even licenses are comparatively modern, you know."

The registers were produced, a set of bulky, dry-smelling, calf-bound volumes. There were eight of them. Carruth and I looked at each other with a mutual shrug.

"I suggest," said I, after a slight pause, "that perhaps you, Mr. Snow, may already be familiar with the contents of these. I should imagine it might require a week or two of pretty steady application even to go through them cursorily."

Mr. William Snow smiled. "I was about to offer to mention the high points," said he. "I have made a careful study of these old volumes, and I can undoubtedly save you both a great deal of reading. The difficulty is— what shall I tell you? If only I knew what to put my finger upon—but I do not, you see!"

"Perhaps we can manage that," threw in Carruth, "but first, may we not have Billings in and question him?"

The former jockey, now the boots at "The Coach and Horses," was summoned and proved to be a wizened, copper-faced individual, with a keen eye and a deferential manner. Carruth invited him to a seat and he sat, gingerly, on the very edge of a chair while we talked with him. I will make no attempt to reproduce his accent, which is quite beyond me. His account was somewhat as follows, omitting the questions asked him both by Carruth and myself.

"At first it was only boots and shoes. Then other things began to go. The things always disappeared at night. Nothing ever disappeared before midnight, because I've sat up and watched many's the time. Yes, we tried everything: watching, even tying up leather things, traps! Yes, sir— steel traps, baited with a boot! Twice we did that. Both times the boot was gone in the morning, the trap not even sprung. No, Sir—no one possibly among the servants. Yet, an 'inside' job; it couldn't have been otherwise. From all over the house, yes. My old riding-boots—two pairs—gone completely; not a trace; right out of my room. That was when I was down in Kent as Mr. Snow's told you, gentlemen. The man who took my place slept in my room, left the door open one night—boots gone in the morning, right under his nose.

"Seen anything? Well, sir, in a manner, yes—in a manner, no! To be precise, no. I can't say that I ever saw anything, that is, anybody; no, nor any apparatus as you might say, in a manner of speaking—no hooks, no strings, nothing used to take hold of the things—but—" Here Billings hesitated, glanced at his employer, looked down at his feet, and his coppery face turned a shade redder.

"Gentlemen," said be, as though coming to a resolution, "I can only tell you the God's truth about it. You may think me barmy—shouldn't blame you if you did! But—I'm as much interested in this 'ere thing as Mr. Snow 'imself, barrin' that I 'aven't had to pay the score—make up the value of the things, I mean, as 'e 'as. I'll tell you—so 'elp me Gawd, gentlemen, it's a fact—I 'ave seen something, absurd as it'll seem to you. I've seen—"

Billings hesitated once more, dropped his eyes, looked distressed, glanced at all of us in the most shamefaced, deprecating manner imaginable, twiddled his hands together, looked, in short, as though he were about to own up to it that he was, after all, responsible for the mysterious disappearances; then finally said:

"I've seen things disappear—through the air! Now—it's hout! But it's a fact, gentlemen all—so 'elp me, it's the truth. Through the air, just as if someone were carrying them away—someone invisible I mean, in a manner of speaking—bloomin' pair of boots, swingin' along through the bloomin' air—enough to make a man say 'is prayers, for a fact!"

It took considerable assuring on the part of Carruth and myself to convince the man Billings that neither of us regarded him as demented, or, as he pithily expressed it, "barmy." We assured him, while our host sat looking at his servant with a slightly puzzled frown, that, on the contrary, we believed him implicitly, and furthermore that we regarded his statement as distinctly helpful. Mr. Snow, obviously convinced that something in his diminutive servitor's mental works was unhinged, almost demurred to our request that we go, forthwith, and examine the place in the hotel where Billings alleged his marvel to have occurred.

We were conducted up two flights of winding steps to the story which had, in the inn's older days, plainly been an attic. There, Billings indicated, was the scene of the disappearance of the "bloomin' boot, swingin' along—unaccompanied—through the bloomin' air."

It was a sunny corridor, lighted by the spring sunlight through several quaint, old-fashioned, muflioned windows. Billings showed us where he had sat, on a stool in the corridor, watching; indicated the location of the boots, outside a doorway of one of the less expensive guest-rooms; traced for us the route taken by the disappearing boots.

This route led us around a corner of the corridor, a corner which, the honest "boots" assured us, he had been "too frightened" to negotiate on the dark night of the alleged marvel.

But we went around it, and there, in a small, right-angled hallway, it became at once apparent to us that the boots on that occasion must have gone through one of two doorways, opposite each other at either side, or else vanished into thin air.

Mr. Snow, in answer to our remarks on this subject, threw open the door at the right. It led into a small, but sunny and very comfortable-looking bed-chamber, shining with honest cleanliness and decorated tastefully with chintz curtains with valances, and containing several articles of pleasant, antique furniture. This room, as the repository of air-traveling boots, seemed unpromising. We looked in in silence.

"And what is on the other side of this short corridor?" I enquired.

"The 'shut room,'" replied Mr. William Snow.

Carruth and I looked at each other.

"Explain, please," said Carruth.

"It is merely a room which has been kept shut, except for an occasional cleaning," replied our host, readily, "for more than a century. There was, as a matter of fact, a murder committed in it in the year 1818, and it was, thereafter, disused. When I purchased the inn, I kept it shut, partly, I daresay, for sentimental reasons; partly, perhaps, because it seemed to me a kind of asset for an ancient hostelry. It has been known as 'the shut room' for more than a hundred years. There was, otherwise, no reason why I should not have put the room in use. I am not in the least superstitious."

"When was the room last opened?" I enquired.

"It was cleaned about ten days ago, I believe," answered Mr. Snow.

"May we examine it?" asked Carruth.

"Certainly," agreed Snow, and forthwith sent Billings after the key.

"And may we hear the story—if you know the details—of the murder to which you referred?" Carruth asked.

"Certainly," said Snow, again. "But it is a long and rather complicated story. Perhaps it would do better during dinner."

In this decision we acquiesced, and, Billings returning with the key, Snow unlocked the door and we looked into "the shut room." It was quite empty, and the blinds were drawn down over the two windows. Carruth raised these, letting in a flood of sunlight. The room was utterly characterless to all appearance, but—I confess to a certain "sensitivity" in such matters—I "felt" something like a faint, ominous chill. It was not, as the word I have used suggests, anything like physical cold. It was, so to express it, mentally cold. I despair of expressing what I mean more clearly. We looked over the entire room, an easy task as there was absolutely nothing to attract the eye. Both windows were in the wall at our right hand as we entered, and, save for the entrance door through which we had just come, the other three walls were quite blank.

Carruth stepped half-way out through the doorway and looked at the width of the wall in which the door was set. It was, perhaps, ten inches thick. He came back into the room, measured with his glance the distance from window-wall to the blank wall opposite the windows, again stepped outside, into the passageway this time, and along it until he came to the place where the short passage turned into the longer corridor from which we had entered it. He turned to his right this time, I following him curiously, that is, in the direction opposite that from which we had walked along the corridor, and tapped lightly on the wall there.

"About the same thickness, what?" he enquired of Snow.

"I believe so," came the answer. "We can easily measure it."

"No, it will not be necessary, I think. We know that it is approximately the same." Carruth ceased speaking and we followed him back into the room once more. He walked straight across it, rapped on the wall opposite the doorway.

"And how thick is this wall?" he enquired.

It is impossible to say," replied Snow, looking slightly mystified. "You see, there are no rooms on that side, only the outer wall, and no window through which we could easily estimate the thickness. I suppose it is the same as the others, about ten inches I'd imagine."

Carruth nodded, and led the way out into the hallway once more. Snow looked enquiringly at Carruth, then at me.

"It may as well be locked again," offered Carruth, "but—I'd be grateful if you'd allow me to keep the key until tomorrow."

Snow handed him the key without comment, but a slight look of puzzlement was on his face as he did so. Carruth offered no comment, and I thought it wise to defer the question which was on my lips until later when we were alone. We started down the long corridor toward the staircase, Billings touching his forehead and stepping on ahead of us and disappearing rapidly down the stairs, doubtless to his interrupted duties in the scullery.

"It is time to think of which rooms you would prefer," suggested our pleasant-voiced host as we neared the stairs. "Suppose I show you some which are not occupied, and you may, of course, choose what suit you best."

"On this floor, if you please," said Carruth, positively.

"As you wish, of course," agreed Snow, "but, the better rooms are on the floor below. Would you not, perhaps, prefer—"

"Thank you no," answered Carruth. "We shall prefer to be up here if we may, and—if convenient—a large room with two beds."

"That can be managed very easily," agreed Snow. He stepped back a few paces along the corridor, and opened a door. A handsome, large room, very comfortably and well furnished, came to our view. Its excellence spoke well for the management of "The Coach and Horses." The "better" rooms must indeed be palatial if this were a fair sample of those somewhat less desirable.

"This will answer admirably," said Carruth, directing an eyebrow at me. I nodded hastily. I was eager to acquiesce in anything he might have in mind.

"Then we shall call it settled," remarked Snow. "I shall have your things brought up at once. Perhaps you would like to remain here now?"

"Thank you," said Carruth. "What time do we dine?"

"At seven, if you please, or later if you prefer. I am having a private room for the three of us."

"That will answer splendidly," agreed Carruth, and I added a word of agreement. Mr. Snow hurried off to attend to the sending up of our small luggage, and Carruth drew me at once into the room.

"I am a little more than anxious," he began, "to hear that tale of the murder. It is an extraordinary step forward—do you not agree with me?— that Billings' account of the disappearing boots—'through the air'—should fit so neatly and unexpectedly into their going around that corner of the Corridor where 'the shut room' is. It sets us forward, I imagine. What is your impression, Mr. Canevin?"

"I agree with you heartily," said I. "The only point on which I am not clear is the matter of the thickness of the walls. Is there anything in that?"

"If you will allow me, I'll defer that explanation until we have had the account of the murder at dinner," said Carruth, and, our things arriving at that moment, we set about preparing for dinner.

Dinner, in a small and beautifully furnished private room, did more, if anything more were needed, to convince me that Mr. William Snow's reputation as a successful modern innkeeper had been well earned. It was a thoroughly delightful meal in all respects, but that, in a general way, is really all that I remember about it because my attention was wholly occupied in taking in every detail of the strange story which our host unfolded to us beginning with the fish course—I think it was a fried sole— and which ended only when we were sipping the best coffee I had tasted since my arrival in England from our United States.

"In the year 1818," said Mr. Snow, "near the end of the long reign of King George III—the king, you will remember, Mr. Canevin, who gave you Americans your Fourth of July—this house was kept by one James Titmarsh. Titmarsh was a very old man. It was his boast that he had taken over the landlordship in the year that His Most Gracious Majesty, George III, had come to the throne, and that he would last as long as the king reigned! That was in the year 1760, and George III had been reigning for fifty-eight years. Old Titmarsh, you see, must have been somewhere in the neighborhood of eighty, himself.

"Titmarsh was something of a 'character.' For some years the actual management of the inn had devolved upon his nephew, Oliver Titmarsh, who was middle-aged, and none too respectable, though, apparently, an able taverner. Old Titmarsh if tradition is to be believed, had many a row with his deputy, but, being himself childless, he was more or less dependent upon Oliver, who consorted with low company for choice, and did not bear the best of reputations in the community. Old Titmarsh's chief bugbear, in connection with Oliver, was the latter's friendship with Simon Forrester. Forrester lacked only a bard to be immortal. But—there was no Cowper to his John Gilpin, so to speak. No writer of the period, nor, indeed, since, has chosen to set forth Forrester's exploits. Nevertheless, these were highly notable. Forrester was the very king-pin of the highwaymen, operating with extraordinary success and daring along the much-traveled Brighton Road.

"Probably Old Titmarsh was philosopher enough to ignore his nephew's associations and acts so long as he attended to the business of the inn. The difficulty, in connection with Forrester, was that Forrester, an extraordinarily bold fellow, whose long immunity from the gallows had caused him to believe himself possessed of a kind of charmed life, constantly resorted to 'The Coach and Horses,' which, partly because of its convenient location, and partly because of its good cheer, he made his house-of-call.

"During the evening of the first of June, in the year 1818, a Royal Courier paused at 'The Coach and Horses' for some refreshment and a fresh mount. This gentleman carried one of the old king's peremptory messages to the Prince of Wales, then sojourning at Brighton, and who, under his sobriquet of 'First Gentleman of Europe,' was addicted to a life which sadly irked his royal parent at Whitehall. It was an open secret that only Prince George's importance to the realm as heir apparent to the throne prevented some very drastic action being taken against him for his innumerable follies and extravagances, on the part of king and parliament. This you will recall, was two years before the old king died and 'The First Gentleman' came to the throne as George IV.

"The Royal Messenger, Sir William Greaves, arriving about nine in the evening after a hard ride, went into the coffee-room, to save the time which the engagement and preparation of a private room would involve, and when he paid his score, he showed a purse full of broad gold pieces. He did not know that Simon Forrester, sitting behind him over a great mug of mulled port, took careful note of this unconscious display of wealth in ready money. Sir William delayed no longer than necessary to eat a chop and drink a pot of 'Six Ale.' Then, his spurs clanking, he took his departure.

"He was barely out of the room before Forrester, his wits, perhaps, affected by the potations which he had been imbibing, called for his own mount, Black Bess, and rose, slightly stumbling to his feet, to speed the pot-boy on his way to the stables.

"'Ye'll not be harrying a Royal Messenger a-gad's sake, Simon,' protested his companion, who was no less a person than Oliver Titmarsh, seizing his crony by his ruffled sleeve of laced satin.

"'Unhand me!' thundered Forrester; then, boastfully, 'There's no power in England'll stay Sim Forrester when he chooses to take the road!'

"Somewhat unsteadily he strode to the door, and roared his commands to the stable-boy who was not leading Black Bess rapidly enough to suit his drunken humor. Once in the saddle, the fumes of the wine he had drunk seemed to evaporate. Without a word Simon Forrester set out, sitting his good mare like a statue, in the wake of Sir William Greaves toward Brighton.

"The coffee-room—as Oliver Titmarsh turned back into it from the doorway whither he had accompanied Forrester—seethed into an uproar. Freed from the dominating presence of the truculent ruffian who would as soon slit a man's throat as look him in the eye along the sights of his horse-pistol from behind the black mask, the numerous guests, silent before, had found their tongues. Oliver Titmarsh sought to drown out their clamor of protest, but before he could succeed, Old Titmarsh, attracted by the unwonted noise, had hobbled down the short flight of steps from his private cubbyhole and entered the room.

"It required only a moment despite Oliver's now frantic efforts to stem the tide of comment, before the old man had grasped the purport of what was toward. Oliver secured comparative silence, then urged his aged uncle to retire. The old man did so, muttering helplessly, internally cursing his age and feebleness which made it out of the question for him to regulate this scandal which had originated in his inn. A King's Messenger, then as now, was sacred in the eyes of all decent citizens. A King's Messenger—to be called on to 'stand and deliver' by the villainous Forrester! It was too much. Muttering and grumbling, the old man left the room, but, instead of going back to his easy-chair and his pipe and glass, he stepped out through the kitchens, and, without so much as a lantern to light his path, groped his way to the stables.

"A few minutes later the sound of horse's hoofs in the cobbled stable-yard brought a pause in the clamor which had once more broken out and now raged in the coffee-room. Listening, those in the coffee-room heard the animal trot out through the gate, and the diminishing sound of its galloping as it took the road toward Brighton. Oliver Titmarsh rushed to the door, but the horse and its rider were already out of sight. Then he ran up to his ancient uncle's room, only to find the crafty old man apparently dozing in his chair. He hastened to the stables. One of the grooms was gone, and the best saddle-horse. From the others, duly warned by Old Titmarsh, he could elicit nothing. He returned to the coffee-room in a towering rage and forthwith cleared it, driving his guests out before him in a protesting herd.

"Then he sat down, alone, a fresh bottle before him, to await developments.

"It was more than an hour later when he heard the distant beat of a galloping horse's hoofs through the quiet June night, and a few minutes later Simon Forrester rode into the stable-yard and cried out for an hostler for his Bess.

"He strode into the coffee-room a minute later, a smirk of satisfaction on his ugly, scarred face. Seeing his crony, Oliver, alone, he drew up a chair opposite him, removed his coat, hung it over the back of his chair, and placed over its back where the coat hung, the elaborate leather harness consisting of crossed straps and holsters which he always wore. From the holsters protruded the grips of 'Jem and Jack,' as Forrester had humorously named his twin horsepistols, huge weapons, splendidly kept, each of which threw an ounce ball. Then, drawing back the chair, he sprawled in it at his case, fixing on Oliver Titmarsh an evil grin and bellowing loudly for wine.

"'For,' he protested, 'my throat is full of the dust of the road, Oliver, and, lad, there's enough to settle the score, never doubt me!' and out upon the table he cast the bulging purse which Sir William Greaves had momentarily displayed when he paid his score an hour and half back.

"Oliver Titmarsh, horrified at this evidence that his crony had actually dared to molest a King's Messenger, glanced hastily and fearfully about him, but the room, empty and silent save for their own presence, held no prying inimical informer. He began to urge upon Forrester the desirability of retiring. It was approaching eleven o'clock, and while the coffee-room was, fortunately, empty, no one knew who might enter from the road or come down from one of the guest-rooms at any moment. He shoved the bulging purse, heavy with its broad gold-pieces, across the table to his crony, beseeching him to pocket it, but Forrester, drunk with the pride of his exploit, which was unique among the depredations of the road's gentry, boasted loudly and tossed off glass after glass of the heavy port wine a trembling pot-boy had fetched him.

"Then Oliver's entreaties were supplemented from an unexpected source. Old Titmarsh, entering through a door in the rear wall of the coffee-room, came silently and leaned over the back of the ruffian's chair, and added a persuasive voice to his nephew's entreaties.

"'Best go up to bed, now, Simon, my lad,' croaked the old man, wheedlingly, patting the bulky shoulders of the hulking ruffian with his palsied old hands.

"Forrester, surprised, turned his head and goggled at the graybeard. Then, with a great laugh, and tossing off a final bumper, he rose unsteadily to his feet, and thrust his arms into the sleeves of the fine coat which old Titmarsh, having detached from the back of the chair held out to him.

"'I'll go, I'll go, old Gaffer,' he kept repeating as he struggled into his coat, with mock jocularity, 'seeing you're so careful of me! Gad's hooks! I might as well! There be no more purses to rook this night, it seems!'

"And with this, pocketing the purse and taking over his arm the pistol-harness which the old man thrust at him, the villain lumbered up the stairs to his accustomed room.

"'Do thou go after him, Oliver,' urged the old man. 'I'll bide here and lock the doors. There'll likely be no further custom this night.'

"Oliver Titmarsh, sobered, perhaps, by his fears, followed Forrester up the stairs, and the old man, crouched in one of the chairs, waited and listened, his ancient ears cocked against a certain sound he was expecting to hear.

"It came within a quarter of an hour-the distant beat of the hoofs of horses, many horses. It was, indeed, as though a considerable company approached 'The Coach and Horses' along the Brighton Road. Old Titmarsh smiled to himself and crept toward the inn doorway. He laboriously opened the great oaken door and peered into the night. The sound of many hoofbeats was now clearer, plainer.

"Then, abruptly, the hoofbeats died on the calm June air. Old Titmarsh, somewhat puzzled, listened, tremblingly. Then he smiled in his beard once more. Strategy, this! Someone with a head on his shoulders was in command of that troop! They had stopped, at some distance, lest the hoofbeats should alarm their quarry.

"A few minutes later the old man heard the muffled sound of careful footfalls, and, within another minute, a King's Officer in his red coat had crept up beside him.

"'He's within,' whispered Old Titmarsh, 'and well gone by now in his damned drunkard's slumber. Summon the troopers, Sir. I'll lead ye to where the villain sleeps. He hath the purse of His Majesty's Messenger upon him. What need ye of better evidence?'

"'Nay,' replied the train-band captain in a similar whisper, 'that evidence, even, is not required. We have but now taken up the dead body of

Sir William Greaves beside the highroad, an ounce ball through his honest heart. 'Tis a case, this, of drawing and quartering, Titmarsh; thanks to your good offices in sending your boy for me.'

"The troopers gradually assembled. When eight had arrived, the captain, preceded by Old Titmarsh and followed in turn by his trusty eight, mounted the steps to where Forrester slept. It was, as you have guessed, the empty room you examined this afternoon, 'the shut room' of this house.

"At the foot of the upper stairs the captain addressed his men in a whisper: 'A desperate man, this, lads. 'Ware bullets! Yet—he must needs be taken alive, for the assizes, and much credit to them that take him. He hath been a pest of the road as well ye know these many years agone. Upon him, then, ere he rises from his drunken sleep! He hath partaken heavily. Pounce upon him ere he rises.'

"A mutter of acquiescence came from the troopers. They tightened their belts, and stepped alertly, silently, after their leader, preceded by their ancient guide carrying a pair of candles.

"Arrived at the door of the room the captain disposed his men and crying out 'in the King's name!' four of these stout fellows threw themselves against the door. It gave at once under that massed impact, and the men rushed into the room, dimly lighted by Old Titmarsh's candles.

"Forrester, his eyes blinking evilly in the candle-light, was half-way out of bed when they got into the room. He slept, he was accustomed to boast, 'with one eye open, drunk or sober!' Throwing off the coverlid, the highwayman leaped for the chair over the back of which hung his fine laced coat, the holsters uppermost. He plunged his hands into the holsters, and stood, for an instant, the very picture of baffled amazement.

"The holsters were empty!

"Then, as four stalwart troopers flung themselves upon him to bear him to the floor, there was heard Old Titmarsh's harsh, senile cackle:

"''Twas I that robbed ye, ye villain—took your pretty boys, your 'Jem' and your 'Jack' out the holsters whiles ye were strugglin' into your fine coat! Ye'll not abide in a decent house beyond this night, I'm thinking; and 'twas the old man who did for ye, murdering wretch that ye are!'

"A terrific struggle ensued. With or without his 'Pretty Boys' Simon Forrester was a thoroughly tough customer, versed in every sleight of hand-to-hand fighting. He bit and kicked; he elbowed and gouged. He succeeded in hurling one of the troopers bodily against the blank wall, and the man sank there and lay still, a motionless heap. After a terrific struggle with the other three who had cast themselves upon him, the remaining troopers and their captain standing aside because there was not room to get at him in the mêlée, he succeeded in getting the forefinger of one of the troopers, who had reached for a face-hold upon him, between his teeth, and bit through it at the joint.

"Frantic with rage and pain this trooper, disengaging himself, and before he could be stopped, seized a heavy oaken bench and, swinging it through the air, brought it down on Simon Forrester's skull. No human bones, even Forrester's, could sustain that murderous assault. The tough wood crunched through his skull, and thereafter he lay quiet. Simon Forrester would never be drawn and quartered, nor even hanged. Simon Forrester, ignobly, as he had lived, was dead; and it remained for the troopers only to carry out the body and for their captain to indite his report.

"Thereafter, the room was stripped and closed by Old Titmarsh himself, who lived on for two more years, making good his frequent boast that his reign over 'The Coach and Horses' would equal that of King George III over his realm. The old king died in 1820, and Old Titmarsh did not long survive him. Oliver, now a changed man, because of this occurrence, succeeded to the lease of the inn, and during his landlordship the room remained closed. It has been closed, out of use, ever since.

Mr. Snow brought his story, and his truly excellent dinner, to a close simultaneously. It was I who broke the little silence which followed his concluding words.

"I congratulate you, sir, upon the excellence of your narrative-gift. I hope that if I come to record this affair, as I have already done with respect to certain odd happenings which have come under my view, I shall be able as nearly as possible, to reproduce your words." I bowed to our host over my coffee cup.

"Excellent, excellent, indeed!" added Carruth, nodding and smiling pleasantly in Mr. Snow's direction. "And now—for the questions, if you don't mind. There are several which have occurred to me; doubtless also to Mr. Canevin."

Snow acquiesced affably. "Anything you care to ask, of course."

"Well, then," it was Carruth, to whom I had indicated precedence in the questioning, "tell us, if you please, Mr. Snow—you seem to have every particular at your very fingers' ends—the purse with the gold? That, I suppose, was confiscated by the train-band captain and eventually found its way back to Sir William Greaves' heirs. That is the high probability, but—do you happen to know as a matter of fact?"

"The purse went back to Lady Greaves."

"Ah! and Forrester's effects—I understand he used the room from time to time. Did he have anything, any personal property in it? If so, what became of it?"

"It was destroyed, burned. No one claimed his effects. Perhaps he had no relatives. Possibly no one dared to come forward. Everything in his possession was stolen, or, what is the same, the fruit of his thefts."

"And—the pistols, 'Jem and Jack?' Those names rather intrigued me! What disposition was made of them, if you happen to know? Old Titmarsh had them, of course, concealed somewhere; probably in that 'cubby-hole' of his which you mentioned."

"Ah," said Mr. Snow, rising, "there I can really give you some evidence. The pistols are in my office—in the Chubbs' safe, along with the holster-apparatus, the harness which Forrester wore under his laced coat. I will bring them in."

"Have you the connection, Mr. Canevin?" Lord Carruth enquired of me as soon as Snow had left the dining-room.

"Yes," said I, "the connection is clear enough; clear as a pikestaff, to use one of your time-honored British expressions, although I confess never to have seen a pikestaff in my life! But—apart from the fact that the holsters are made of leather; the well-known background of the unfulfilled desire persisting after death; and the obvious connection between the point of disappearance of those 'walking-boots' of Billings', with 'the shut room,' I must confess myself at a loss. The veriest tyro at this sort of thing would connect those points, I imagine. There it is, laid out for us, directly before our mental eyes, so to speak. But—what I fail to understand is not so much who takes them—that by a long stretch of the imagination might very well be the persistent 'shade', 'Ka,' 'projected embodiment' of Simon Forrester. No—what gets me is—*where does the carrier of boots and satchels and jewelers' sample-cases put them?* That room is utterly, absolutely, physically empty, and boots and shoes are material affairs, Lord Carruth."

Carruth nodded gravely. "You have put your finger on the main difficulty, Mr. Canevin. I am not at all sure that I can explain it, or even that we shall be able to solve the mystery after all. My experience in India does not help. But—there is one very vague case, right here in England, which may be a parallel one. I suspect, not to put too fine a point upon the matter, that the abstracted things may very well be behind that rearmost wall, the wall opposite the doorway in 'the shut room.'"

"But," I interjected, "that is impossible, is it not? The wall is material—brick and stone and plaster. It is not subject to the strange laws of personality. How—?"

The return of the gentleman-landlord of "The Coach and Horses" at this moment put an end to our conversation, but not to my wonder. I imagined that the "case" alluded to by my companion would be that of the tortured "ghost" of the jester which, with a revenge-motive, haunted a room in an ancient house and even managed to equip the room itself with some of its revengeful properties or motives. The case had been recorded by Mr. Hodgson, and later Carruth told me that this was the one he had in mind. This, it seemed to me, was a very different matter. However—

Mr. Snow laid the elaborate and beautifully made "harness" of leather straps out on the table beside the after-dinner coffee service. The grips of "Jem and Jack" peeped out of their holsters. The device was not unlike those used by our own American desperadoes, men like the famous Earp brothers and "Doc" Holliday whose "six-guns" were carried handily in slung holsters in front of the body. We examined these antique weapons, murderous-looking pistols of the "bulldog" type, built for business, and Carruth ascertained that neither "Jem" nor "Jack" was loaded.

"Is there anyone on that top floor?" enquired Carruth.

"No one save yourselves, excepting some of the servants, who are in the other end of the house," returned Snow.

"I am going to request you to let us take these pistols and the 'harness' with us upstairs when we retire," said Carruth, and again the obliging Snow agreed. "Everything I have is at your disposal, gentlemen," said he, "in the hope that you will be able to end this annoyance for me. It is too early in the season at present for the inn to have many guests. Do precisely as you wish, in all ways."

Shortly after nine o'clock, we took leave of our pleasant host, and carrying the "harness" and pistols divided between us, we mounted to our commodious bedchamber. A second bed had been moved into it, and the fire in the grate took off the slight chill of the spring evening. We began our preparations by carrying the high-powered electric torches we had obtained from Snow along the corridor and around the corner to "the shut room." We unlocked the door and ascertained that the two torches would be quite sufficient to work by. Then we closed but did not lock the door, and returned to our room.

Between us, we moved a solidly built oak table to a point diagonally across the corridor from our open bedroom door, and on this we placed the "harness" and pistols. Then, well provided with smoke-materials, we sat down to wait, seated in such positions that both of us could command the view of our trap. It was during the conversation which followed that Carruth informed me that the case to which he had alluded was the one recorded by the occult writer, Hodgson. It was familiar to both of us. I will not cite it. It may be read by anybody who has the curiosity to examine it in the collection entitled *Carnacki the Ghost-Finder* by William Hope Hodgson. In that account it is the floor of the "haunted" room which became adapted to the revenge-motive of the persistent "shade" of the malignant court jester, tortured to death many years before his "manifestation" by his fiendish lord and master.

We realized that, according to the man Billings' testimony, we need not be on the alert before midnight. Carruth therefore read from a small book which he had brought with him, and I busied myself in making the careful notes which I have consulted in recording Mr. Snow's narrative of Simon Forrester, while that narrative was fresh in my memory. It was a quarter before midnight when I had finished. I took a turn about the room to refresh my somewhat cramped muscles, and returned to my comfortable chair.

Midnight struck from the French clock on our mantelpiece, and Carruth and I both, at that signal, began to give our entire attention to the articles on the table in the hallway out there.

It occurred to me that this joint watching, as intently as the circumstances seemed to warrant to both of us, might prove very wearing, and I suggested that we watch alternately, for about fifteen minutes each. We did so, I taking the first turn. Nothing occurred—not a sound, not the smallest indication that there might be anything untoward going on out there in the corridor.

At twelve-fifteen, Carruth began to watch the table, and it was, I should imagine, about five minutes later that his hand fell lightly on my arm, pressing it and arousing me to the keenest attention. I looked intently at the things on the table. The "harness" was moving toward the left-hand edge of the table. We could both hear, now, the slight scraping sound made by the leather weighted by the twin pistols, and, even as we looked, the whole apparatus lifted itself—or so it appeared to us—from the supporting table, and began, as it were, to float through the air a distance of about four feet from the ground toward the turn which led to "the shut room."

We rose, simultaneously, for we had planned carefully on what we were to do, and followed. We were in time to see the articles "float" around the corner, and, increasing our pace—for we had been puzzled about how anything material, like the boots, could get through the locked door—watched, in the rather dim light of that short hallway, what would happen.

What happened was that the "harness" and pistols reached the door, and then the door opened. They went through, and the door shut behind them precisely as though someone, invisible to us, were carrying them. We heard distinctly the slight sound which a gently closed door makes as it came to, and there we were, standing outside in the hallway looking at each other. It is one thing to figure out, beforehand, the science of occult occurrences, even upon the basis of such experience as Carruth and I both possessed. It is, distinctly, another, to face the direct operation of something motivated by the Powers beyond the ordinary ken of humanity. I confess to certain "cold chills," and Carruth's face was very pale.

We switched on our electric torches as we had arranged to do, and Carruth, with a firm hand which I admired if I did not, precisely, envy, reached out and turned the knob of the door. We walked into "the shut room...."

Not all our joint experience had prepared us for what we saw. I could not forbear clutching Carruth's free arm, the one not engaged with the torch, as he stood beside me. And I testify that his arm was as still and firm as a rock. It steadied me to realize such fortitude, for the sight which was before us was enough to unnerve the most hardened investigator of the unearthly.

Directly in front of us, but facing the blank wall at the far end of the room, stood a half-materialized man. The gleam of my torch threw a faint shadow on the wall in front of him, the rays passing through him as though he were not there, and yet with a certain dimming. The shadow visibly increased in the few brief instants of our utter silence, and then we observed that the figure was struggling with something. Mechanically we concentrated both electric rays on the figure and then we saw clearly. A bulky man, with a bull-neck and close-cropped, iron-gray hair, wearing a fine satin coat and what were called, in their day, "small cloths," or tight-fitting knee-trousers with silk stockings and heavy, buckled shoes, was raising and fitting about his waist, over the coat, the "harness" with the pistols.

Abruptly, the materialization appearing to be now complete, he turned upon us, with an audible snarl and baleful, glaring little eyes like a pig's, deep set in a hideous, scarred face, and then he spoke—he spoke, and he had been dead for more than a century!

"Ah-h-h-h!" he snarled, evilly, "ye would come in upon me, eh, my fine gents—into this my chamber, eh! I'll teach ye manners..." and he ended this diatribe with a flood of the foulest language imaginable, stepping, with little, almost mincing, down-toed steps toward us all the time he poured out his filthy curses and revilings. I was completely at a loss what to do. I realized—these ideas went through my mind with the rapidity of thought—that the pistols were unloaded! I told myself that this was some weird hallucination—that the shade of no dead-and-gone desperado could harm us. Yet—it was a truly terrifying experience, be the man shade or true flesh and blood.

Then Carruth spoke to him, in quiet, persuasive tones.

"But—you have your pistols now, Simon Forrester. It was we who put them where you could find them, your pretty boys, 'Jem and Jack.' That was what you were trying to find, was it not? And now—you have them. There is nothing further for you to do—you have them, they are just under your hands where you can get at them whenever you wish."

At this the specter, or materialization of Simon Forrester, blinked at us, a cunning light in his evil little eyes, and dropped his hands with which he had but now been gesticulating violently on the grips of the pistols. He grinned, evilly, and spat in a strange fashion, over his shoulder.

"Ay," said he, more moderately now, "ay—I have 'em—Jemmy and Jack, my trusties, my pretty boys." He fondled the butts with his huge hands, hands that could have strangled an ox, and spat over his shoulder.

"There is no necessity for you to remain, then, is there?" said Carruth softly, persuasively.

The simulacrum of Simon Forrester frowned, looked a bit puzzled, then nodded its head several times.

"You can rest now—now that you have Jem and Jack," suggested Carruth, almost in a whisper, and as he spoke, Forrester turned away and stepped over to the blank wall at the far side of the room, opposite the doorway, and I could hear Carruth draw in his breath softly and feel the iron grip of his fingers on my arm. "Watch!" he whispered in my ear; "watch now."

The solid wall seemed to wave and buckle before Forrester, almost as though it were not a wall but a sheet of white cloth, held and waved by hands as cloth is waved in a theater to simulate waves. More and more cloth-like the wall became, and, as we gazed at this strange sight, the simulacrum of Simon Forrester seemed to become less opaque, to melt and blend in with the wavering wall, which gradually ceased to move, and then he was gone and the wall was as it had been before....

On Monday morning, at Carruth's urgent solicitation, Snow assembled a force of laborers, and we watched while they broke down the wall of "the shut room" opposite the doorway. At last, as Carruth had expected, a pick went through, and, the interested workmen, laboring with a will, broke through into a small, narrow, cell-like room the Plaster of which indicated that it had been walled up perhaps two centuries before, or even earlier—a "priest's hole" in all probability, of the early post-reformation period near the end of the Sixteenth Century.

Carruth stopped the work as soon as it was plain what was here, and turned out the workmen, who went protestingly. Then, with only our host working beside us, and the door of the room locked on the inside' we continued the job. At last the aperture was large enough, and Carruth went through. We heard an exclamation from him, and then he began to hand out articles through the rough hole in the masonry—leather articles—boots innumerable, ladies' reticules, hand-luggage, the missing jeweler's sample case with its contents intact—innumerable other articles, and, last of all, the "harness" with the pistols in the holsters.

Carruth explained the "jester case" to Snow, who shook his head over it. "It's quite beyond me, Lord Carruth," said he, "but, as you say this annoyance is at an end, I am quite satisfied; and—I'll take your advice and make sure by pulling down the whole room, breaking out the corridor walls, and joining it to the room across the way. I confess I can not make head or tail of your explanation—the unfulfilled wish, the 'sympathetic pervasion' of the room as you call it, the 'materialization,' and the strange fact that this business began only a short time ago. But— I'll do exactly what you have recommended, about the room, that is. The restoration of the jeweler's case will undoubtedly make it possible for me to get back the sum I paid Messrs. Hopkins and Barth of Liverpool when it disappeared in my house. Can you give any explanation of why the 'shade' of Forrester remained quiet for a century and more and only started up the other day, so to speak?"

"It is because the power to materialize came very slowly," answered Carruth, "coupled as it undoubtedly was with the gradual breaking down of the room's material resistance. It is very difficult to realize the extra-ordinary force of an unfulfilled wish, on the part of a forceful, brutal, wholly selfish personality like Forrester's. It is, really, what we must call spiritual power, even though the 'spirituality' was the reverse of what we commonly understand by that term. The wish and the force of Forrester's persistent desire, through the century, have been working steadily, and, as you have told us, the room has been out of use for more than a century. There were no common, everyday affairs to counteract that malign influence—no 'interruptions', if I make myself clear."

"Thank you," said Mr. Snow. "I do not clearly understand. These matters are outside my province. But—I am exceedingly grateful—to you both." Our host bowed courteously. "Anything that I can possibly do, in return—"

"There is nothing—nothing whatever," said Carruth quietly; "but, Mr. Snow, there is another problem on your hands which perhaps you will have some difficulty in solving, and concerning which, to our regret"—he looked gravely at me—"I fear neither Mr. Canevin with his experience, nor I with mine, will be able to assist you."

"And what, pray, is that?" asked Mr. Snow, turning slightly pale. He would, I perceive, be very well satisfied to have his problems behind him.

"The problem is," said Carruth, even more gravely I imagined, "it is— what disposal are you to make of fifty-eight pairs of assorted boots and shoes!"

And Snow's relieved laughter was the last of the impressions which I took with me as we rode back to London in Carruth's car, of "The Coach and Horses" inn on the Brighton Road.

BLACK TERROR

Henry S. Whitehead

I woke up in the great mahogany bed of my house in Christiansted with an acute sense of something horribly wrong, something frightful, tearing at my mind. I pulled myself together, shook my head to get the sleep out of my eyes, pulled aside the mosquito-netting. That was better! The strange sense of horror which had pursued me out of sleep was fading now.

I groped vaguely, back into the dream, or whatever it had been—it did not seem to have been a dream; it was something else. I could now, somehow, localize it. I found now that I was listening, painfully, to a sustained, aching sound, like a steam calliope fastened onto one high, piercing, raucous note. I knew it could not be a steam calliope. There had been no such thing on the Island of Santa Cruz since Columbus discovered it on his Second Voyage in 1493. I got up and into my slippers and muslin bathrobe, still puzzled.

Then abruptly the note ended, cut off clean like the ceasing of the drums when the Black people are having one of their *ratas* back of the town in the hills.

Then, and only then, I knew what it was that had disturbed me. It had been a woman, screaming.

I ran out to the semi-enclosed gallery which runs along the front of my house on the Copagnie Gade, the street of hard-pounded earth below, and looked down.

A group of early risen Blacks in nondescript garb was assembled down there, and the number was increasing every instant. Men, women, small Black children were gathered in a rapidly tightening knot directly in front of the house, their guttural mumbles of excitement forming a contrapuntal background to the solo of that sustained scream; for the woman, there in the center, was at it again now, with fresh breath, uttering her

483

blood-curdling, hopeless, screeching wail, a thing to make the listener wince.

Not one of the throng of Blacks touched the woman in their midst. I listened to their guttural Creole, trying to catch some clue to what this disturbance was about. I would catch a word of the broad *patois* here and there, but nothing my mind could lay hold upon. At last it came, the clue; in a childish, piping treble; the clear-cut word, *Jumbee.*

I had it now. The screaming woman believed, and the crowd about her believed, that some evil witchery was afoot. Some enemy had enlisted the services of the dreaded witch-doctor—the *papaloi*—and something fearful, some curse or charm, had been "put on" her or some one belonging to her family. All that the word "Jumbee" had told me clearly.

I watched now for whatever was going to happen. Meanwhile I wondered why a policeman did not come along and break up this public gathering. Of course the policeman, being a Black man himself, would be as much intrigued as any of the others, but he would do his duty nevertheless. "Put a Black to drive a Black!" The old adage was as true nowadays as in the remote days of West Indian slavery.

The woman, now convulsed, rocking backward and forward, seemed as though possessed. Her screams had now an undertone or cadence of pure horror. It was ghastly.

A policeman, at last! Two policemen, in fact, one of them Old Kraft, once a Danish top-sergeant of garrison troops. Kraft was nearly pure Caucasian, but, despite his touch of African, he would tolerate no nonsense. He advanced, waving his truncheon threateningly, barking hoarse reproaches, commands to disperse. The group of Black people began to melt away in the general direction of the Sunday Market, herded along by Sergeant Kraft's dark brown patrolman.

Now only Old Kraft and the Black woman who had screamed remained, facing each other in the street below. I saw the old man's face change out of its harsh, professional, man-handling frown to something distinctly more humane. He spoke to the woman in low tones. She answered him in mutters, not unwillingly, but as though to avoid being overheard.

I spoke from the gallery.

"What is it, Herr Kraft? Can I be of assistance?"

Old Kraft looked, recognized me, touched his cap.

"Stoopide-ness!" exploded Old Kraft, explanatorily. "The woo-man, she haf had—" Old Kraft paused and made a sudden, stiff, dramatic gesture and looked at me meaningly. His eyes said: "I could tell you all about it, but not from here."

"A chair on the gallery for the poor woman?" I suggested, nodding to him.

"Come!" said he to the woman, and she followed him obediently up the outside gallery steps while I walked across to unfasten the door at the gallery's end.

We placed the woman, who seemed dazed now and kept a hand on her head, in one of my chairs, where she rocked slowly back and forth whispering to herself, and Kraft and I went inside the house, where I led him through to the dining-room.

There, at the sideboard, I did the honors for my friend Sergeant Kraft of the Christiansted Police.

"The woman's screaming awakened me, half an hour early," I began, invitingly, as soon as the sergeant had been duly refreshed and had said his final "skoal," his eyes on mine in the Danish manner.

"Yah, yah," returned Kraft, nodding a wise old head. "She tell me de Obiman fix her right, dis time!"

This sounded promising. I waited for more.

"But joost what it iss, I can not tell at-all," continued Kraft, disappointingly, as though aware of the secretiveness which should animate a police sergeant.

"Will you have—another, Herr Kraft?" I suggested.

The sergeant obliged, ending the ceremony with another "skoal." This libation, as I had hoped, had the desired effect. I will spare Kraft's accent, which could be cut with a knife. What he told me was that this woman, Elizabeth Aagaard, living in a village estate-cabin near the Central Factory, a few miles outside of Christiansted, had a son, one Cornelis McBean. The young fellow was what is locally known as a "gallows-bird," in short a gambler, thief, and general bad-egg. He had been in the police court several times for petty offenses, and in jail in the Christiansfort more than once.

But, as Kraft expressed it, "it ain' de thievin' dat make de present difficoolty." No! it was that young Cornelis McBean had presumed beyond his station, and had committed the crime of falling in love with Estrella Collins, the daughter of a prosperous Black storekeeper in one of Christiansted's side streets. Old Collins, utterly disapproving, and his words to McBean having had no effect whatever upon that stubborn lover, had, in short, employed the services of a *papaloi* to get rid of McBean.

"But," I protested, "I know Old Collins. I understand, of course, how he might object to the attentions of such a young ne'er-do-well, but—a storekeeper like him, a comparatively rich man, to call in a *papaloi*—it seems—"

"Him Black!" replied Sergeant Kraft with a little, significant gesture which made everything plain.

"What," said I, after thinking a little, "what particular kind of *ouanga* has Collins had 'put on' him?"

The old sergeant gave me a quick glance at that word. It is a mean-ingful word. In Haiti it is very common. It means both talisman and amulet; something, that is, to attract, or something to repel, to defend the wearer. But here in Santa Cruz the magic of our Blacks is neither so clear-cut nor (as some imagine) quite so deadly as the magickings of the *papalois* and the *hougans* in Haiti's infested hills with their thousands of *vodu* altars to Ougoun Badagaris, to Damballa, to the Snake of far, dreadful Guinea. Over even so much as the manufacture of *ouangas* I may not linger. One can not. The details—

"It is, I think, a 'sweat-ouanga,'" whispered Old Kraft, and went a shade lighter than his accustomed sunburned ivory. "De wooman allege," he continued, "that the boy sicken an' die at noon-today. For that reason she is walk into de town early, because there is no help. She desire to bewail-like, dis trouble restin' 'pon her head."

Kraft had given me all the information he possessed. He rated a reward. I approached the sideboard a third time.

"You will excuse me again, Sergeant. It is a little early in the day for me. Still, 'a man can't walk on one leg!'"

The sergeant grinned at this Santa Crucian proverb which means that a final stirrup-cup is always justified, and remarked:

"He should walk goot—on three!" After this reference to the number of his early-morning refreshments, he accepted the last of these, boomed his "skoal," and became a police sergeant once more.

"Shall I take de wooman along, sir?" he inquired as we reached the gallery where Elizabeth Aagaard still rocked and moaned and whispered to herself in her trouble.

"Leave her here, please," I replied, "and I will see that Esmerelda finds her something to eat." The sergeant saluted and departed.

"Gahd bless yo', sar," murmured the poor soul. I left her there and went to the kitchen to drop a word in the sympathetic ear of my old cook. Then I started toward my belated shower-bath. It was nearly seven by now.

After breakfast I inquired for Elizabeth Aagaard. She had had food and had delivered herself at length upon her sorrows to Esmerelda and the other house-servants. Esmerelda's account established the belief that young McBean had been marked for death by one of the oldest and dead-liest devices known to primitive barbarism; one which, as all Caucasians who know of it will assure you, derives its sole efficacy from the psychol-ogy of fear, that fear of the occult which has stultified the African's mind through countless generations of warfare against the jungle and the domi-nance of his fetish-men and *vodu* priests.

As is well known to all students of African "magic," portions of the human body, such as hair, the clippings of nails, or even some garment

long worn in contact with the body, is regarded as having a magical connection with the body itself and a corresponding influence upon it. A
portion of the shirt which has been worn next the body and which has
absorbed perspiration is especially highly regarded as material for the
making of a protective charm or amulet, as well as for its opposite, planted
against a person for the purpose of doing him harm. Blood, etc., could be
included in this weird category.

In the case of young Cornelis McBean, this is what had been done.
The *papaloi* had managed to get hold of one of Cornelis's shirts. In this
he had dressed the recently buried body of an aged negro who had died a
few days before, of senility. This shirt, after it had been in the coffin for
three days and nights, had been cunningly put back for Cornelis to find
and wear again. It had been, supposedly, mislaid. Young McBean, finding it in his mother's cabin, *had worn it again.*

And, as if this, in itself enough to cause his death from sheer terror as
soon as he knew of it, was not sufficient, it had just come to the knowledge of the mother and son by the curious African method known as the
Grapevine Route, that a small *ouanga*, made up of some of Cornelis' nail-
parings, stubble of a week's beard collected from discarded lather after
shaving, various other portions of his exterior personality, had been
"fixed" by the Christiansted *papaloi*, and "buried against him."

This meant that unless the *ouanga* could be discovered and dug up
and burned, he would die at noon. As he had learned of the "burying" of
the *ouanga* only the evening before, and as the Island of Santa Cruz has
an area of more than eighty square miles, there was, perhaps, one chance
in some hundred trillion that he could find the *ouanga*, disinter it, and
render it harmless by burning. Taking into consideration that his ancestors for countless eons had given their full and firm belief to this method
of murder by mental process, it looked as though young Cornelis McBean,
ne'er-do-well, Black island gallow's-bird, aspiring admirer of a young
negress somewhat beyond his station in life according to African West
Indian caste systems, was doomed to pass out on the stroke of twelve
that day.

That, with an infinitude of detail, was the substance of the story of
Elizabeth Aagaard.

I sat and looked at her, quiet and humble now, no longer the screaming fury she had appeared to be at that morning's crack of dawn. And as
I looked at the poor soul, with the dumb, distressed, motherhood in her
dim eyes from which the unchecked tears ran down her coal-black face,
it came to me that I wanted to help; that this thing was outrageous; wicked
with a wickedness far surpassing the ordinary sinfulness of ordinary
people. I did not want to sit by, as it were, and allow the unknown McBean
to pass out at the behest of a paid rascal of a *papaloi* merely because

unctuous Old Collins had decided on that method for his exit from this life—a matter involving, perhaps fifteen dollars' fee to the witch-doctor; the collection and burial of some bits of offal somewhere on Santa Cruz.

I could imagine the young Black fellow, livid with a nameless fear, a complex of ancient, inherited, unreasonable dreads, shivering, cowering, sickened to his dim soul by what lay ahead of him, three hours away when twelve should strike from the Christiansfort clock in the old tower by the harbor; writhing helplessly in his mind before the approach of the ghastly doom which he had brought upon himself because he had happened to fall in love with brown Estrella Collins, whose sleek brown father carried a collection-plate every Sunday up and down the aisle of his place of worship!

There was an element of absurdity in it all, now that I was actually sitting here looking at McBean's mother. She had given up now, it appeared, was resigned to the fate of her only son. "Him Black!" Old Kraft had remarked.

That thought of the collection-plate in Old Collins' pudgy, storekeeper's hands, reminded me of something.

"What is your church, Elizabeth?" I inquired suddenly.

"Me English Choorch, sar—de boy also. Him make great *shandra-madan*, sar, him gamble an' perhaps a tief, but him one-time communicant, sar."

An inspiration came to me then. Perhaps I could prevail upon one of the English Church clergy to help. It was, when one came down to the brass tacks of the situation, a question of *belief*. A similar *ouanga*, "buried against" me, would have no effect whatever, because to me, such a means of getting rid of a person was merely the height of absurdity, like the charm-killing of the Polynesians by making them look at their reflection in a gourd of water and then shaking the gourd and so destroying the image! Perhaps, if Elizabeth and her son could be persuaded to do their parts.... I spoke long and earnestly to Elizabeth.

At the end of my speech, which had emphasized the superior power of Divinity when compared to even the most powerful of the African fetishes, even the dreaded snake himself, Elizabeth, her hopes somewhat aroused, I imagined, took her departure, and I jumped into my car and ran up the hill toward the English Church rectory.

Father Richardson, the pastor, himself a West Indian born, was at home. To him I explained the case. When I had ended—

"I am obliged to you, Mr. Canevin," said the clergyman. "If only they would realize—er—precisely what you told the woman; that Divinity is infinitely more powerful than their beliefs! I will accompany you, at once. It is, really, the release, perhaps, of a human soul. And they come to us clergy over such things as the theft of a couple of coconuts!"

Father Richardson left me, came back in two minutes with a black bag, and we started for Elizabeth Aagaard's village along a lovely shore road by the gleaming, placid, blue Caribbean.

The negro estate-village was surprisingly quiet when we arrived. The clergyman got out at Elizabeth's cabin, and I drove the car out of the way, off the road into rank guinea-grass. I saw Father Richardson, a commanding, tall figure, austere in his long, black cassock, striding in at the cabin door. I followed, and got inside just in time to witness a strange performance.

The Black boy, livid and seeming shrunken with terror, cowered under a thin blanket on a small iron bedstead. Over him towered the clergyman, and just as I came in, he stooped and with a small, sharp pocketknife cut something loose from the boy's neck and flung it contemptuously on the hard-earth floor of the cabin. It landed just at my feet and I looked at it curiously. It was a small black bag, of some kind of cotton material, with a tuft of black cock's feathers at its top which was bound around with many windings of bright red thread. The whole thing was about the size of an egg. I recognized it as a protective amulet.

His teeth chattering, the cold fear of death upon him, the Black boy protested in the guttural Creole. The clergyman answered him gravely.

"There can be no half-way measures, Cornelis. When a person asks God for His help, he must put away everything else." A mutter of assent came from the woman, who was arranging a small table with a candle in the corner of the cabin.

From his black bag Father Richardson now took a small bottle with a sprinkler arrangement at its top, and from this he cast a shower of drops upon the *ouanga* charm lying on the floor. Then he proceeded to sprinkle the whole cabin with this holy water, ending with Elizabeth, myself, and finally, the boy on the bed. As the water touched his face the boy winced visibly and shuddered; and suddenly it came over me that here was a strange matter; again, I daresay, a matter of belief. The change from the supposed protection of the charm which the priest had cut away from his neck and contemptuously tossed away, to the prescribed method of the Church must have been, somehow, and in some obscure mental fashion, a very striking one to the young fellow.

The bottle went back into the bag and now Father Richardson was speaking to the boy on the bed:

"God is intervening for you, my child, and—God's power is supreme over all things, visible *and invisible*. He holds all in the hollow of His hand. He will now put away your fear, and take this weight from your soul, *and you shall live*. You must now do your part, if you would be fortified by the Sacrament. You just purify your soul. Penance first. Then—"

The boy, now appreciably calmer, nodded his head, and the priest motioned me out, including the woman in his gesture. I opened the cabin door and stepped out, closely followed by Elizabeth Aagaard. I left her, twenty paces from her cabin, wringing her hands, her lips murmuring in prayer, while I went and sat in my car.

Ten minutes later the cabin door opened and the priest beckoned us within. The boy lay quiet now, and Father Richardson was engaged in repacking his black bag. He turned to me:

"Good-bye, and—thank you. It was very good of you to bring me."

"But—aren't you coming?"

"No"—this reflectively. "No—I must see him through." He glanced at his wrist-watch. "It is eleven-fifteen now. It was at noon you said—"

"I'm staying with you, then," said I, and sat down on a chair in the far corner of the little cabin room.

The priest stood by the bedside, looking down at the Black boy, his back to me. The woman was, apparently, praying earnestly to herself in another corner, out of the way. The priest stooped and took the limp hand and wrist in his large, firm white hands, and counted the pulse, glancing at his watch. Then he came and sat beside me.

"Half an hour!" he murmured.

The Black woman, Elizabeth, prayed without a sound in her corner on the hard, earth floor, where she knelt, rigidly. We sat, without conversation, for a long twenty minutes during which the sense of strain in the cabin became more and more apparent to me.

Abruptly the boy's mouth fell open. The priest sprang toward him, seized and chafed the dull-black hands. The boy's head turned on the pillow and his jaws came together again, his eyelids fluttering. Then a slight spasm, perceptible through the light covering, ran through him, and, breathing a few times deeply, he resumed his coma-like sleep. The priest now remained beside him. I counted off the minutes to noon. Nine—eight—seven—at least, three minutes before noon. When I had got that far I heard the priest's deep, monotonous voice reciting in a low tone. Listening, I caught his words here and there. He held the boy's hand while the words rolled out low and impressively.

"... to withstand and overcome all assaults of thine adversary ... unto thee ghostly strength ... and that he nowise prevail against thee." Then, dropping a note, to my surprise, the clerical voice of this most Anglican of clergymen began to declaim the words of an older liturgical language: *et effugiat atque discedat omnis phantasia et nequitia ... vel versutia diabolicae fraudis omnisque spiritus immundis adjuratis...."*

The words, gaining in volume with the priest's earnestness, rolled out now. I saw that we were on the very verge of noon, and, looking back to the bed from my glance at my watch, I saw convulsion after convulsion shake the thin body on the bed. Then the cabin itself began to tremble in a sudden wind that had sprung up from nowhere. The dry palm fronds lashed back and forth outside and the whistle of the wind blew under the crazily hung door. The muslin curtain of the small window suddenly billowed like a sail. Then, suddenly, the harsh voice of the Black boy.

"Damballa!" it said, clearly, and moaned.

Damballa is one of the Greater Mysteries of the *vodu* worship. I shuddered in spite of myself.

But now higher, more commanding, came the voice of Father Richardson, positively intoning now—great sentences of Power, formulas interposed, as he himself stood, interposed, between the feeble Black boy and the Powers of Evil which seemed to seek him out for their own fell ends. The priest seemed to stretch a mantle of mystic protection over the grovelling, writhing body.

The mother lay prone on the dirt floor, now, her arms stretched out crosslike—the last, most abject gesture of supplication of which humanity is physically capable. As I glanced down at her I saw, in the extreme corner of the little room, something oddly shaped projecting from a pile of discarded garments.

It was now exactly noon. As I looked carefully at my watch, the distant stroke of the Angelus came resoundingly from the heavy bell of St. John's Church. Father Richardson ceased his recitation, laid back the boys hand on the coverlid, and began the Angelus. I stood up at this, and, as he finished, I plucked his sleeve. The wind, curiously enough, was gone, utterly. Only the noon sun beat down suffocatingly on the iron roof of the frail cabin. Father Richardson looked at me inquiringly. I pointed to that corner, under the pile of clothes. He walked to the corner, stooped, and drew out a crude wooden image of a snake. He glanced accusingly at Elizabeth, who grovelled afresh.

"Take it up, Elizabeth," commanded Father Richardson, "break it in two, and throw it out of the doorway."

The woman crawled to the corner, lifted the thing, snapped it in two, and then, rising, her face gray with fear, opened the cabin door and threw out the pieces. We went back to the bedside, where the boy breathed quietly now. The priest shook him. He opened swimming eyes, eyes like a drunken man's. He goggled stupidly at us.

"You are alive—by the mercy of God," said the priest, severely. "Come now, get up! It is well past noon. Here! Mr. Canevin will show you his watch. You are not dead. Let this be a lesson to you to leave alone what God has put outside your knowledge."

The boy sat up, still stupidly, the thin blanket drawn about him, on the side of the bed.

"We may as well drive back now," said Father Richardson, picking up his black bag in a business-like manner.

As I turned my car to the right just outside the estate-village stone gateway, I glanced back toward the village. It swarmed with Blacks, all crowding about the cabin of Elizabeth Aagaard. Beside me, I heard the rather monotonous voice of Father Richardson. He seemed to be talking to himself; thinking aloud, perhaps.

"Creator of all things—visible *and invisible.*"

I drove slowly to avoid the ducks, fowls, pigs, children and burro-carts between the edge of town and the rectory.

"It was," said I, as I held his hand at parting, "an experience—that."

"Oh—that! Yes, yes, quite! I was thinking—you'll excuse me, Mr. Canevin—of my afternoon sick-calls. My curate isn't quite over that last attack of dengue fever. I have a full afternoon. Come in and have tea with us—any afternoon, about five."

I drove home slowly. A West Indian priest! That sudden wind—the little wooden snake—the abject fear in the eyes of the Black boy! All that had been merely in the day's work for Father Richardson, in those rather awkward, large, square hands, the hands which held the Sacrament every morning. Sometimes I would get up early and go to church myself on a weekday morning, along the soft roads through the pre-dawn dusk along with scores of soft-stepping, barefooted Blacks, plodding to church in the early dawn, going to get strength, power, to fight the age-long battle between God and Satan—the Snake—here where the sons of Ham tremble beneath the lingering fears of that primeval curse which came upon their ancestor because he dared to laugh at his father Noah.

ET IN SEMPITERNUM PEREANT

Charles Williams (1886-1945)

Lord Arglay came easily down the road. About him the spring was as gaudy as the restraint imposed by English geography ever lets it be. The last village lay a couple of miles behind him; as far in front, he had been told, was a main road on which he could meet a motor bus to carry him near his destination. A casual conversation in a club had revealed to him, some months before, that in a country house of England there were supposed to lie a few yet unpublished legal opinions of the Lord Chancellor Bacon. Lord Arglay, being no longer Chief Justice, and having finished and published his *History of Organic Law*, had conceived that the editing of these papers might provide a pleasant variation upon his present business of studying the more complex parts of the Christian Schoolmen. He had taken advantage of a week-end spent in the neigh-bourhood to arrange, by the good will of the owner, a visit of inspection; since, as the owner had remarked, with a bitterness due to his financial problems, "everything that is smoked isn't Bacon." Lord Arglay had smiled—it hurt him a little to think that he had smiled—and said, which was true enough, that Bacon himself would not have made a better joke.

It was a very deserted part of the country through which he was walk-ing. He had been careful to follow the directions given him, and in fact there were only two places where he could possibly have gone wrong, and at both of them Lord Arglay was certain he had not gone wrong. But he seemed to be taking a long time—a longer time than he had expected. He looked at his watch again, and noted with sharp disapproval of his own judgment that it was only six minutes since he had looked at it last. It had seemed more like sixteen. Lord Arglay frowned. He was usually a good walker, and on that morning he was not conscious of any unusual weariness. His host had offered to send him in a car, but he had declined. For a moment, as he put his watch back, he was almost sorry he had

493

declined. A car would have made short time of this road, and at present his legs seemed to be making rather long time of it. "Or," Lord Arglay said aloud, "making time rather long." He played a little, as he went on, with the fancy that every road in space had a corresponding measure in time; that it tended, merely of itself, to hasten or delay all those that drove or walked upon it. The nature of some roads, quite apart from their material effectiveness, might urge men to speed, and of others to delay. So that the intentions of all travellers were counterpointed continually by the media they used. The courts, he thought, might reasonably take that into consideration in case of offences against right speed, and a man who accelerated upon one road would be held to have acted under the improper influence of the way, whereas one who did the same on another would be known to have defied and conquered the way.

Lord Arglay just stopped himself looking at his watch again. It was impossible that it should be more than five minutes since he had last done so. He looked back to observe, if possible, how far he had since come. It was not possible; the road narrowed and curved too much. There was a cloud of trees high up behind him; it must have been half an hour ago that he passed through it, yet it was not merely still in sight, but the trees themselves were in sight. He could remark them as trees; he could almost, if he were a little careful, count them. He thought, with some irritation, that he must be getting old more quickly, and more unnoticeably, than he had supposed. He did not much mind about the quickness, but he did mind about the unnoticeableness. It had given him pleasure to watch the various changes which age tended to bring; to be as stealthy and as quick to observe those changes as they were to come upon him—the slower pace, the more meditative voice, the greater reluctance to decide, the inclination to fall back on habit, the desire for the familiar which is the first skirmishing approach of unfamiliar death. He neither welcomed nor grudged such changes; he only observed them with a perpetual interest in the curious nature of the creation. The fantasy of growing old, like the fantasy of growing up, was part of the ineffable sweetness, touched with horror, of existence, itself the lordliest fantasy of all. But now, as he stood looking back over and across the hidden curves of the road, he felt suddenly that time had outmarched and out-twisted him, that it was spreading along the countryside and doubling back on him, so that it troubled and deceived his judgment. In an unexpected and unusual spasm of irritation he put his hand to his watch again. He felt as if it were a quarter of an hour since he had looked at it; very well, making just allowance for his state of impatience, he would expect the actual time to be five minutes. He looked; it was only two.

Lord Arglay made a small mental effort, and almost immediately recognized the effort. He said to himself. "This is another mark of age. I am losing my sense of duration." He said also: "It is becoming an effort to recognize these changes." Age was certainly quickening its work in him. It approached him now doubly; not only his method of experience, but his awareness of experience was attacked. His knowledge of it comforted him—perhaps, he thought, for the last time. The knowledge would go. He would savour it then while he could. Still looking back at the trees, "It seems I'm decaying," Lord Arglay said aloud. "And that anyhow is one up against decay. Am I procrastinating? I am, and in the circumstances procrastination is a proper and pretty game. It is the thief of time, and quite right too! Why should time have it all its own way?"

He turned to the road again, and went on. It passed now between open fields; in all those fields he could see no one. It was pasture, but there were no beasts. There was about him a kind of void, in which he moved, hampered by this growing oppression of duration. Things lasted. He had exclaimed, in his time, against the too swift passage of the world. This was a new experience; it was lastingness—almost, he could have believed, everlastingness. The measure of it was but his breathing, and his breathing, as it grew slower and heavier, would become the measure of everlasting labour—the labour of Sisyphus, who pushed his own slow heart through each infinite moment, and relaxed but to let it beat back and so again begin. It was the first touch of something Arglay had never yet known, of simple and perfect despair.

At that moment he saw the house. The road before him curved sharply, and as he looked he wondered at the sweep of the curve; it seemed to make a full half-circle and so turn back in the direction that he had come. At the farthest point there lay before him, tangentially, another path. The sparse hedge was broken by an opening which was more than footpath and less than road. It was narrow, even when compared with the narrowing way by which he had come, yet hard and beaten as if by the passage of many feet. There had been innumerable travellers, and all solitary, all on foot. No cars or carts could have taken that path; if there had been burdens, they had been carried on the shoulders of their owners. It ran for no long distance, no more than in happier surroundings might have been a garden path from gate to door. There, at the end, was the door.

Arglay, at the time, took all this in but half-consciously. His attention was not on the door but on the chimney. The chimney, in the ordinary phrase, was smoking. It was smoking effectively and continuously. A narrow and dense pillar of dusk poured up from it, through which there glowed every now and then, a deeper undershade of crimson, as if some trapped genius almost thrust itself out of the moving prison that held it. The house itself was not much more than a cottage. There was a door, shut; on the left of it a window, also shut; above, two little attic windows, shut, and covered within by some sort of dark hanging, or perhaps made opaque by smoke that filled the room. There was no sign of life anywhere, and the smoke continued to mount to the lifeless sky. It seemed to Arglay curious that he had not noticed this grey pillar in his approach, that only now when he stood almost in the straight and narrow path leading to the house did it become visible, an exposition of tall darkness reserved to the solitary walkers upon that wearying road.

Lord Arglay was the last person in the world to look for responsibilities. He shunned them by a courteous habit; a responsibility had to present itself with a delicate emphasis before he acceded to it. But when any so impressed itself he was courteous in accepting as in declining; he sought friendship with necessity, and as young lovers call their love fatal, so he turned fatality of life into his love. It seemed to him, as he stood and gazed at the path, the shut door, the smoking chimney, that here perhaps was a responsibility being delicately emphatic. If everyone was out—if the cottage had been left for an hour-ought he to do something? Of course, they might be busy about it within; in which case a thrusting stranger would be inopportune. Another glow of crimson in the pillar of cloud decided him. He went up the path.

As he went he glanced at the little window, but it was blurred by dirt—he could not very well see whether the panes did or did not hide smoke within. When he was so near the threshold that the window had almost passed out of his vision, he thought he saw a face looking out of it—at the extreme edge, nearest the door—and he checked himself, and went back a step to look again. It had been only along the side of his glance that the face, if face it were, had appeared, a kind of sudden white scrawl against the blur, as if it were a mask hung by the window rather than any living person, or as if the glass of the window itself had looked sideways at him, and he had caught the look without understanding its cause. When he stepped back, he could see no face. Had there been a sun in the sky he would have attributed the apparition to a trick of the light, but in the sky over this smoking house there was no sun. It had shone brightly that morning when he started; it had paled and faded and finally been lost to him as he had passed along his road. There was neither sun nor peering face. He stepped back to the threshold, and knocked with his knuckles on the door.

There was no answer. He knocked again and again waited, and as he stood there he began to feel annoyed. The balance of Lord Arglay's mind had not been achieved without the creation of a considerable counter-energy to the violence of Lord Arglay's natural temper. There had been people whom he had once come very near hating, hating with a fury of selfish rage and detestation; for instance, his brother-in-law. His brother-in-law had not been a nice man; Lord Arglay, as he stood by the door and, for no earthly reason, remembered him, admitted it. He admitted, at the same moment, that no lack of niceness on that other's part could excuse any indulgence of vindictive hate on his own, nor could he think why, then and there, he wanted him, wanted to have him merely to hate. His brother-in-law was dead. Lord Arglay almost regretted it. Almost he desired to follow, to be with him, to provoke and torment him, to ...

Lord Arglay struck die door again. "There is," he said to himself, "entire clarity in the Omnipotence." It was his habit of devotion, his means of recalling himself into peace out of the angers, greeds, sloths and perversities that still too often possessed him. It operated; the temptation passed into the benediction of the Omnipotence and disappeared. But there was still no answer from within. Lord Arglay laid his hand on the latch. He swung the door, and, lifting his hat with his other hand, looked into the room-a room empty of smoke as of fire, and of all as of both.

Its size and appearance were those of a rather poor cottage, rather indeed a large brick hut than a cottage. It seemed much smaller within than without. There was a fireplace—at least, there was a place for a fire—on his left. Opposite the door, against the right-hand wall, there was a ramshackle flight of wooden steps, going up to the attics, and at its foot, swinging on a broken hinge, a door which gave a way presumably to a cellar. Vaguely, Arglay found himself surprised; he had not supposed that a dwelling of this sort would have a cellar. Indeed, from where he stood, he could not be certain. It might only be a cupboard. But, unwarrantably, it seemed more, a hinted unseen depth, as if the slow slight movement of the broken wooden door measured that labour of Sisyphus, as if the road ran past him and went coiling spirally into the darkness of the cellar. In the room there was no furniture, neither fragment of paper nor broken bit of wood; there was no sign of life, no flame in the grate nor drift of smoke in the air. It was completely and utterly void.

Lord Arglay looked at it. He went back a few steps and looked up again at the chimney. Undoubtedly the chimney was smoking. It was received into a pillar of smoke; there was no clear point where the dark chimney ended and the dark smoke began. House leaned to roof, roof to chimney, chimney to smoke, and smoke went up for ever and ever over those roads where men crawled infinitely through the smallest measurements of time. Arglay returned to the door, crossed the threshold, and stood in the room. Empty of flame, empty of flame's material, holding within its dank air the very opposite of flame, the chill of ancient years, the room lay round him. Lord Arglay contemplated it. "There's no smoke without fire," he said aloud. "Only apparently there is. Thus one lives and learns. Unless indeed this is the place where one lives without learning."

The phrase, leaving his lips, sounded oddly about the walls and in the comers of the room. He was suddenly revolted by his own chance words—"a place where one lives without learning," where no courtesy or integrity could any more be fined or clarified. The echo daunted him; he made a sharp movement, he took a step aside towards the stairs, and before the movement was complete, was aware of a change. The dank chill became a concentration of dank and deadly heat, pricking at him, entering his nostrils and his mouth. The fantasy of life without knowledge materialized, inimical, in the air, life without knowledge, corrupting life without knowledge, jungle and less than jungle, and though still the walls of the bleak chamber met his eyes, a shell of existence, it seemed that life, withdrawn from all those normal habits of which the useless memory was still drearily sustained by the thin phenomenal fabric, was collecting and corrupting in the atmosphere behind the door he had so rashly passed—outside the other door which swung crookedly at the head of the darker hole within.

He had recoiled from the heat, but not so as to escape it. He had even taken a step or two up the stairs, when he heard from without a soft approach. Light feet were coming up the beaten path to the house. Some other Good Samaritan, Arglay thought, who would be able to keep his twopence in his pocket. For certainly, whatever was the explanation of all this and wherever it lay, in the attics above or in the pit of the cellar below, responsibility was gone. Lord Arglay did not conceive that either he or anyone else need rush about the country in an anxious effort to preserve a house which no one wanted and no one used. Prematurely enjoying the discussion, he waited. Through the doorway someone came in.

It was, or seemed to be, a man, of ordinary height, wearing some kind of loose dark overcoat that flapped about him. His head was bare; so, astonishingly, were his legs and feet. At first, as he stood just inside the door, leaning greedily forward, his face was invisible, and for a moment Arglay hesitated to speak. Then the stranger lifted his face and Arglay uttered a sound. It was emaciated beyond imagination; it was astonishing, at the appalling degree of hunger revealed, that the man could walk or move at all, or even stand as he was now doing, and turn that dreadful skull from side to side. Arglay came down the steps of the stair in one jump; he cried out again, he ran forward, and as he did so the deep burning eyes in the turning face of bone met his full and halted him. They did not see him, or if they saw did not notice; they gazed at him and moved on. Once only in his life had Arglay seen eyes remotely like those; once, when he had pronounced the death-sentence upon a wretched man who had broken under the long strain of his trial and filled the court with shrieks. Madness had glared at Lord Arglay from that dock, but at least it had looked at him and seen him; these eyes did not. They sought something—food, life, or perhaps only a form and something to hate, and in that energy the stranger moved. He began to run round the room. The bones that were his legs and feet jerked up and down. The head turned from side to side. He ran circularly, round and again round, crossing and recrossing, looking up, down, around, and at last, right in the centre of the room, coming to a halt, where, as if some terrible pain of starvation gripped him, he bent and twisted downward until he squatted grotesquely on the floor. There, squatting and bending, he lowered his head and raised his arm, and as the fantastic black coat slipped back, Arglay saw a wrist, saw it marked with scars. He did not at first think what they were; only when the face and wrist of the figure swaying in its pain came together did he suddenly know. They were teeth-marks; they were bites; the mouth closed on the wrist and gnawed. Arglay cried out and sprang forward, catching the arm, trying to press it down, catching the other shoulder, trying to press it back. He achieved nothing. He held, he felt, he grasped; he could not control. The long limb remained raised, the fierce teeth gnawed. But as Arglay bent, he was aware once more of that effluvia of heat risen round him, and breaking out with the more violence when suddenly the man, if it were man, cast his arm away, and with a jerk of movement rose once more to his feet. His eyes, as the head went back, burned close into Arglay's, who, what with the heat, the eyes, and his sickness at the horror, shut his own against them, and was at the same moment thrown from his balance by the rising form, and sent staggering a step or two away, with upon his face the sensation of a light hot breath, so light that only in the utter stillness of time could it be felt, so hot that it might have been the inner fire from which the pillar of smoke poured outward to the world.

He recovered his balance; he opened his eyes; both motions brought him into a new comer of that world. The odd black coat the thing had worn had disappeared, as if it had been a covering imagined by a habit of mind. The thing itself, a wasted flicker of pallid movement, danced and gyrated in white flame before him. Arglay saw it still, but only now as a dreamer may hear, half-asleep and half-awake, the sound of dogs barking or the crackling of fire in his very room. For he opened his eyes not to such things, but to the thing that on the threshold of this place, some seconds earlier or some years, he had felt and been pleased to feel, to the reality of his hate. It came in a rush within him, a fountain of fire, and without and about him images of the man he hated swept in a thick cloud of burning smoke. The smoke burned his eyes and choked his mouth; he clutched at it, at images within it—at his greedy loves and greedy hates— at the cloud of the sin of his life, yearning to catch but one image and renew again the concentration for which he yearned. He could not. The smoke blinded and stifled him, yet more than stifling or blinding was the hunger for one true thing to lust or hate. He was starving in the smoke, and all the hut was full of smoke, for the hut and the world were smoke, pouring up round him, from him and all like him—a thing once wholly, and still a little, made visible to his corporeal eyes in forms which they recognized, but in itself of another nature. He swung and twisted and crouched. His limbs ached from long wrestling with the smoke, for as the journey to this place had prolonged itself infinitely, so now, though he had no thought of measurement, the clutch of his hands and the growing sickness that invaded him struck through him the sensation of the passage of years and the knowledge of the passage of moments. The fire sank within him, and the sickness grew, but the change could not bring him nearer to any end. The end here was not at the end, but in the beginning. There was no end to this smoke, to this fever and this chill, to crouching and rising and searching, unless the end was now. Now—now was the only possible other fact, chance, act. He cried out, defying infinity, "Now!"

Before his voice the smoke of his prison yielded, and yielded two ways at once. From where he stood he could see in one place an alteration in that perpetual grey, an alternate darkening and lightening as if two ways, of descent and ascent, met. There was, he remembered, a way in, therefore a path out; he had only to walk along it. But also there was a way still farther in, and he could walk along that. Two doors had swung, to his outer senses, in that small room. From every gate of hell there was a way to heaven, yes, and in every way to heaven there was a gate to deeper hell.

Yet for a moment he hesitated. There was no sign of the phenomenon by which he had discerned the passage of that other spirit. He desired—very strongly he desired—to be of use to it. He desired to offer himself to it, to make a ladder of himself, if that should be desired, by which it might perhaps mount from the nature of the lost, from the dereliction of all minds that refuse living and learning, postponement and irony, whose dwelling is necessarily in their undying and perishing selves. Slowly, unconsciously, he moved his head as if to seek his neighbour.

He saw, at first he felt, nothing. His eyes returned to that vibrating oblong of an imagined door, the heart of the smoke beating in the smoke. He looked at it; he remembered the way; he was on the point of movement, when the stinging heat struck him again, but this time from behind. It leapt through him; he was seized in it and loosed from it; its rush abandoned him. The torrent of its fiery passage struck the darkening hollow in the walls. At the instant that it struck, there came a small sound; there floated up a thin shrill pipe, too short to hear, too certain to miss, faint and quick as from some single insect in the hedgerow or the field, and yet more than single—a weak wail of multitudes of the lost. The shrill lament struck his ears, and he ran. He cried as he sprang: "Now is God:

now is glory in God," and as the dark door swung before him it was the threshold of the house that received his flying feet. As he passed, another form slipped by him, slinking hastily into the house, another of the hordes going so swiftly up that straight way, hard with everlasting time; each driven by his own hunger, and each alone. The vision, a face looking in as a face had looked out, was gone. Running still, but more lightly now, and with some communion of peace at heart, Arglay came into the curving road. The trees were all about him; the house was at their heart. He ran on through them; beyond, he saw, he reached, the spring day and the sun. At a little distance a motor bus, gaudy within and without, was coming down the road. The driver saw him. Lord Arglay instinctively made a sign, ran, mounted. As he sat down, breathless and shaken, "*E quindi uscimmo,*" his mind said, "*a riveder le stelle.*"

Coachwhip Publications
CoachwhipBooks.com

Classic Science Fiction and Fantaasy

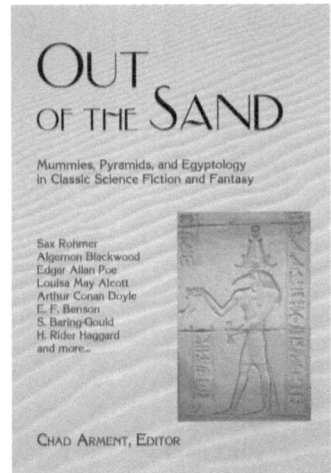

Coachwhip Publications
CoachwhipBooks.com

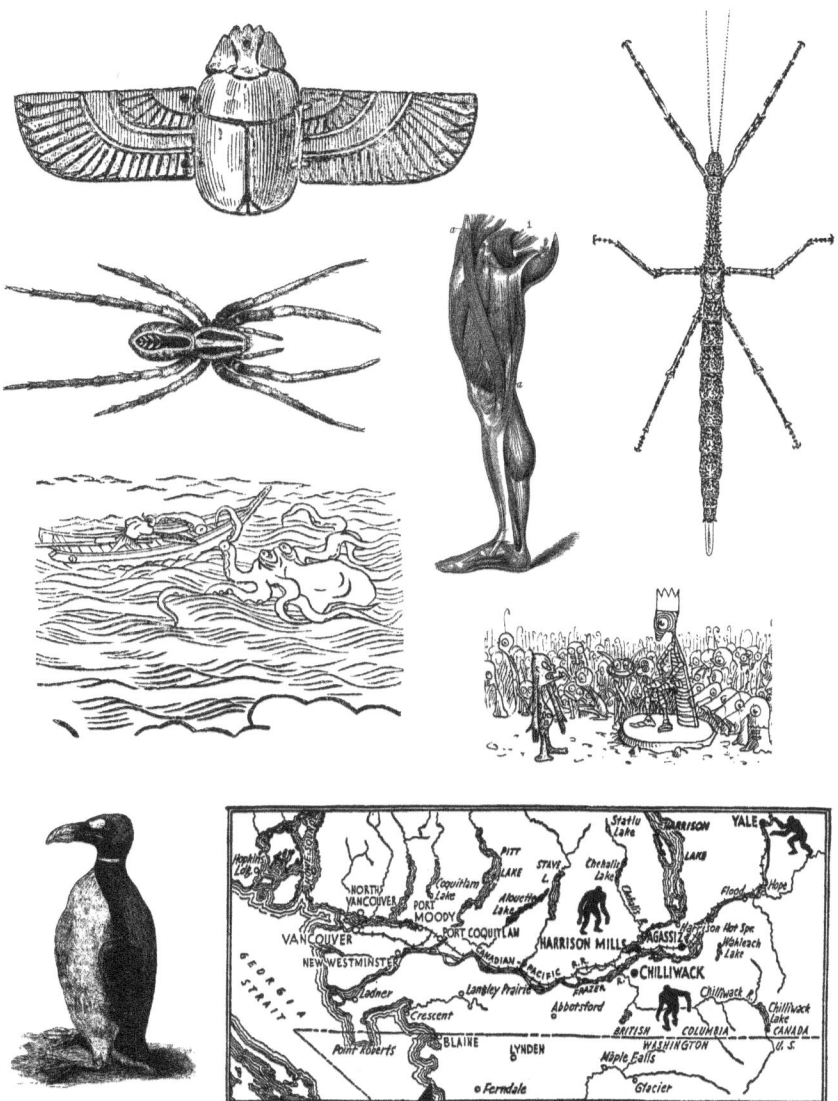